David Masson

The Collected Writings Of Thomas De Quincey - Vol. VI

The Collected Writings Of Thomas De Quincey - Vol. VI

David Masson

The Collected Writings Of Thomas De Quincey - Vol. VI

ISBN/EAN: 9783742857934

Manufactured in Europe, USA, Canada, Australia, Japa

Cover: Foto ©Andreas Hilbeck / pixelio.de

Manufactured and distributed by brebook publishing software
(www.brebook.com)

David Masson

The Collected Writings Of Thomas De Quincey - Vol. VI

THE
COLLECTED WRITINGS
OF
THOMAS
DE QUINCEY

DAVID MASSON

VOL. VI

LONDON

1897

CONTENTS OF VOL. VI

EDITOR'S PREFACE

IN the present volume and the next the reader comes to a class of De Quincey's writings differing from those which have occupied the preceding volumes, and belonging rather to the second of the three varieties into which he has himself suggested that his writings might be distributed. "Into the second class," he said (General Preface, Vol. I, p. 10), "I throw those papers which address themselves " purely to the understanding as an insulated faculty, " or do so primarily. Let me call them by the general " name of ESSAYS." To leave no doubt as to what he meant to include under the term so defined, the very papers he proceeded to mention as conspicuously representative examples of the class of his writings he had in view were three of his historical papers,—to wit, *Cicero* and *The Cæsars*, which form a large part of the contents of the present volume, and *The Essenes*, which lies over for the next. As the other papers in the same two volumes are all, more or less, of a similar nature, it is evident that these two volumes may offer themselves as containing exactly such writings of De Quincey as he himself thought entitled to the special name of "Essays." That name, however, as De Quincey really intended it, is of somewhat extensive signification. An "Essay," in his definition of it (which, however, may not be universally accepted), is a paper addressed purely or primarily to the understanding as an insulated faculty,—*i.e.* distinguished from other papers by containing a good deal of the speculative element. It does not merely give information by presenting in a compact shape all the existing.

B

knowledge on any subject; nor is its main object that of delight to the reader by dreams and pictures of the poetical kind; nor does it seek merely to rouse and stimulate the feelings for active exertion of some sort; but, without any of these aims, or while perhaps studying one or other of them to some extent, it has in view always the solution of some problem, the investigation of some question, so as to effect a modification or advance of the existing doctrine on the subject. How firmly De Quincey held by this notion of the distinctive characteristic of the "Essay," as compared with other kinds of writing, appears from the striking words in which, after referring to the three above-named essays as examples of his own efforts in this line, he claims the merit of fidelity to his principle, in intention at least, in all his other efforts of the same general character. "These speci-"mens," he says, meaning *Cicero*, *The Cæsars*, and *The Essenes*, " are sufficient for the purpose of informing the reader that " I do not write without a thoughtful consideration of my " subject, and also that to think reasonably upon any " question has never been allowed by me as a sufficient " ground for writing upon it, unless I believed myself able " to offer some considerable novelty." What a panic in the writing industry, what a dropping of pens, what a sup-pression of cartloads of intended matter for the press, if this principle of De Quincey's were made imperative,—viz. the principle (to state it in its fullest form) that all literature worthy of the name must, in some way or other, and to some extent or other, consist of the previously unknown, un-imagined, or uncommunicated! Meanwhile it is with Essay literature that we are immediately concerned. Now, although it was to three *historical* essays that De Quincey pointed as illustrations of his own practice in Essay-writing, that was a mere accident of the moment. He might have pointed to other papers of his, not expressly historical, or less obviously historical, which for that very reason would have perhaps better illustrated his notion of the charac-teristic distinction of an Essay,—viz. that it should exhibit the strictly speculative or ratiocinative mode of intellect at work in the investigation of some question or the solution of some problem. Such papers of his await us in future volumes,—*e.g.* in a volume which is to consist specially of what may be called his "Speculative and Theological Essays." Indeed, in all De Quincey's writings, even those papers of Autobiography, Literary Reminiscence, and Biography, which we have now left behind us, the strength of the speculative vein in his genius is remarkable, asserting itself often in digressions and interpolated discourses, sometimes even to the degree of obtrusiveness. What is required of us at present, however, is to attend to his instruction that the historical papers with which we are here dealing are to be regarded as typical "essays" of his, equally with other papers less ostensibly historical. And this is true. While the papers consist of matter of scholarship, erudition, tradition from the past, and so belong to Historical Literature, or, as Bacon called it, the Literature of Memory, all of them, or most of them, are pervaded by a distinctly speculative element, and some of them are among the most notable exhibitions of De Quincey's faculty in propounding subtle problems, questioning old doctrines, and starting paradoxes. Inasmuch, however, as they differ among themselves in respect of the *proportion* of the speculative ingredient to the descriptive and narrative substance, and some of them are more of the nature of mere compiled digests of information than others, the best name for them collectively may be that which we have chosen. Let the name HISTORICAL ESSAYS AND RESEARCHES be accepted, therefore, as sufficiently descriptive of the papers in this volume and the next.

The papers are arranged, as nearly as may be, in the chronological order of their subjects. In *Homer and the Homeridæ* and in *The Philosophy of Herodotus* we are back in the earliest ages of the world as known through Greek record and tradition. We are listening to De Quincey as he opens to us his budget of carefully acquired erudition, often most curious and out of the way, respecting the actualities that lie in those old mists, and extracts gleams of credibility and conceivability for us out of the vast opaque, chatting to us meanwhile of the errors and absurdities of previous scholars, especially those of the duller sort, in their attempts in the same business, and of his faith, if people would but trust him, in the results of his own superior inquisitiveness. In the brief paper called *The Theban Sphinx* we are still kept on Greek ground, though only for the purpose of obliging De Quincey by attending to his ingeniously fantastic re-interpretation of one particular Greek legend. The *Toilette of the Hebrew Lady* is an independent paper of mere digested or compiled information of the archæological kind, with little or nothing of speculative interfusion. Then, coming to the Romans in the days of their assured supremacy over the whole world, *i.e.* over the Mediterranean and its adjuncts, he launches out,—first in his *Cicero*, then in his series of papers called *The Cæsars* (from which the clever trifle called *Aelius Lamia* may be regarded as a detached splinter), and finally in his *Philosophy of Roman History*,—on the centuries-long current of that great theme. Nothing abashed by its greatness or its complexity, but as if with the fascination of a prepared scholarly familiarity with its whole extent, he asserts his right not merely to select passages of the old story for more impressive visual treatment than usual, but also to challenge former interpretations of the facts and intermingle new explanations and comments with the flow of the scenic procession. His most ambitious attempt of this kind is in his papers on *The Cæsars*. These, making as they do in their aggregate a little book by itself, present us with a panoramic view of the history of Imperial Rome, from the days of the " mightiest Julius" (estimated by De Quincey, one is glad to find, as he was by Shakespeare, and has been by every other fit modern authority, as the noblest of Roman men), on to the time of Diocletian, the split between the East and the West, and that organised division of the Cæsarship which was the prelude to the final disintegration. With all its defects and occasional cloudiness, it is perhaps the most vivid panoramic sketch of the Imperial History to be found in our language. It is certainly entitled, at all events, to De Quincey's claim for it, that it is far from being " a simple recapitulation or *résumé*," inasmuch as, though " it moves rapidly over the ground," it does so with an " exploring eye " wherever the darkness is deepest. Here, in fact, as in others of his historical essays, the objection of later scholars, reviewing what he has written, is likely to be that his " exploring eye " has sometimes been beguiled by a vagrant will-o'-the-wisp, or even a casual flicker of light within its own socket, and so that what he offers as "novelties" are sometimes mere mistakes.

Whatever may be the worth of this last objection with respect to the particular essays included in the present volume, it certainly hits on one peculiarity of De Quincey's character. Gentle and shy though he was personally, placid and polite to the uttermost in his demeanour within his own nook, he carried in him nevertheless an unusual fund of what may be called *opinionativeness*, which could be translated on occasion into *pugnacity*, or even a kind of *fierceness*, on behalf of any opinion of his which he specially valued and found specially resisted. Whether his passion for speculative novelty, even in his historical researches, did not sometimes lead him into violent paradoxes, and whether his readiness to propound these at any risk of subsequent confutation did not proceed from this excess in him of sheer *opinionativeness*, are questions which can hardly be answered without a specification of his paradoxes one by one, and a consideration in each case of the evidences for and against. That is beyond our duty here; and there will be a better opportunity for any approach to a hint on the subject in connexion with a historical paradox, reputed by some the most flagrant of all De Quincey's ventures of that kind, which will make its appearance in next volume. Meanwhile, for the Historical Essays and Researches which compose this volume one may claim, whatever may be the abatements on the ground indicated or on any other, the admiration due to rare intellectual power and fine literary management. The combination in them of ripe and curious erudition with speculative subtlety and sagacity, and of both with pictorial effect and general literary charm, is really remarkable. In the last particular the reader will not fail to note for himself how much of the charm depends on a constant lightsomeness, a recurring play of wit and humour, in the treatment of the gravest matters. It was De Quincey's determination that whatever he wrote in a magazine should be as interesting and amusing for magazine readers as the subject would permit; and he certainly succeeded in this where other writers would have

failed.   Hence, or rather perhaps from no such determination at all, but simply because, being De Quincey, he
could not write otherwise than as De Quincey, those whimsical extravagances of fancy and phrase, those detections of
fun in the midst of the antique and stately, those descents
into colloquialism and even into slang, in which some readers
find cause of offence.   All in all, however, and with this
last fault added to any others that may be in the reckoning,
where have we such historical magazine-writing nowadays,
matter and manner taken together, as in these Greek and
Roman Essays of De Quincey?

With the exception of the two slightest, they all appeared
in *Blackwood's Magazine* during the palmy days of De Quincey's .
contributorship to that periodical between 1828 and 1842.
Was it that the standard of scholarship in magazine-writing
generally was different in those days from what it has become since ; or was it that *Blackwood* in particular could make
its standard of scholarship exceptionally high because there
was a man in Edinburgh called De Quincey and Christopher
North knew his worth ?   D. M.

HOMER AND THE HOMERIDÆ[1]

PART I

HOMER, the general patriarch of Occidental Literature, reminds us oftentimes, and powerfully, of the river Nile. If
you, reader, should (as easily you may) be seated on the
banks of that river in the months of February or March
1858, you may count on two luxuries for a poetic eye : first,
on a lovely cloudless morning ; secondly, on a gorgeous
Flora.   For it has been remarked that nowhere out of
tropical regions is the vernal equipage of nature so rich, so
pompously variegated, in buds, and bells, and blossoms, as
precisely in this unhappy Egypt—"a house of bondage,"
undeniably, in all ages, to its own working population ; and
yet, as if to mock the misery it witnesses, the gayest of all
lands in its spontaneous Flora.   Now, supposing yourself to
be seated, together with a child or two, on some flowery
carpet of the Delta ; and supposing the Nile—" that ancient
river"—within sight ; happy infancy on the one side, the
everlasting pomp of waters on the other, and the thought
still intruding that on some quarter of your position, perhaps fifty miles out of sight, stand pointing to the heavens
the mysterious pyramids : these circumstances presupposed,
it is inevitable that your thoughts should wander upwards to
the dark fountains of origination.   The pyramids, why and
when did they arise ?   This infancy, so lovely and innocent,

[1] From *Blackwood's Magazine* for October, November, and December 1841 ; reprinted by De Quincey in 1857, with merely verbal
changes, in the sixth volume of his Collected Writings.—M.

whence does it come, whither does it go? This creative river, what are its ultimate well-heads? That last question was viewed by antiquity as charmed against solution. It was not permitted, they fancied, to dishonour the river Nile by stealing upon his solitude in a state of weakness and childhood—

"Nec licuit populis parvum te, Nile, videre."

"No license there was to the nations of earth for seeing thee, O Nile ! in a condition of infant imbecility."

So said Lucan. And in those days no image that the earth suggested could so powerfully express a mysterious secrecy as the coy fountains of the Nile. At length came Abyssinian Bruce ; and that superstition seemed to vanish. Yet no ! for now again the mystery has revolved upon us. You have drunk, you say, from the fountains of the Nile. Good ; but, my friend, from which fountains? "Which king, Bezonian ?" Understand that there is another branch of the Nile—another mighty arm, whose fountains lie in far other regions. The great letter Y, that Pythagorean marvel, is still covered with shades in one-half of its bifurcation. And the darkness which, from the eldest of days, has invested Father Nile with fabulous awe still broods over the most ancient of his fountains, defies our curious impertinence, and will not suffer us to behold the survivor of Memphis in his cradle, and of Thebes the hundred-gated other than in his grandeur as the benefactor of nations.

Such thoughts, a world of meditations pointing in the same direction, settle also upon Homer. Eight-and-twenty hundred years, according to the improved views of chronology, have men drunk from the waters of this earliest among known poets. Himself, under one of his denominations, the son of a river (Melesigenes), or the grandson of a river (Mæonides), he has been the parent of fertilising streams carried off derivatively into every land. Not the fountains of the Nile have been so diffusive, or so creative, as those of Homer—

"A quo, ceu fonte perenni,
Vatum Pierus ora rigantur aquis."

"From whom, as from a perennial fountain, the mouths of poets are refreshed with Pierian streams "

There is the same gaiety of atmosphere, the same "blue rejoicing sky," the same absence of the austere and the gloomy sublime, investing the Grecian Homer as invests the Nile of the Delta. And, again, if you would go upwards to the fountains of this ancient Nile, or of this ancient Homer, you would find the same mysterious repulsion. In both cases you find their fountains shyly retreating before you, and, like the sacred peaks of Ararat, where the framework of Noah's ark reposes, never less surmounted than when a man fancies himself within arm's reach of their central recesses.[1]

A great poet appearing in early ages, and a great river, bear something of the same relation to human civility and culture. In this view, with a peculiar sublimity, the Hindoos consider a mighty fertilising river, when bursting away with torrent rapture from its mountain cradle, and billowing onwards through two thousand miles of realms made rich by itself, as in some special sense "the Son of God." The word Burrampooter is said to bear that sublime interpretation. Hence arose the profound interest about the Nile: what cause could produce its annual swelling? Even as a phenomenon (had it led to nothing) *this* was awful, but much more so as a creative agency ; for it was felt that Egypt, which is

---

[1] Seven or eight Europeans—some Russian, some English—have not only taken possession of the topmost crag on Ararat by means of the broadest disk which their own persons offered, but have left flags flying to mark out for those below the exact station which they had reached. All to no purpose ! The bigoted Armenian still replied— "These are mere illusions worked by demons." This incredulity in the people of Armenia is the result of mere religious bigotry. But in a similar case, amongst people that ought to be more enlightened—yes, amongst educated Sicilians of high social standing—the same angry disbelief is the product of pure mortified vanity. About the time of Waterloo, Captain Smyth settled the height of Mount Etna finally at 10,874 feet ; this result was scientifically obtained, and not open to any reasonable doubts. Nine years later, Sir John Herschel, knowing nothing of this previous measurement, ascertained the height to be 10,872½ feet—a most remarkable coincidence ; and the more satisfactory as being obtained barometrically, whilst Captain Smyth's measurement had been trigonometrical. Many of the people in Catania, however, who had been in the habit for half-a-century of estimating the height at 13,000 feet, were so incensed at this degradation of their pretensions that even yet (thirty-three years later) they have not reconciled themselves to the mathematical truth.

but the valley ploughed out for itself by the Nile, had been the mere creation of the river annually depositing its rich layers of slime. Hence also arose the corresponding interest about Homer; for Greece and the Grecian Isles were in many moral respects as much the creation of Homer as Egypt of the Nile. And, if, on the one hand, it is unavoidable to assume some degree of civilisation before a Homer could exist, on the other it is certain that Homer, by the picture of unity which he held aloft to the Greeks in making them co-operate to a common enterprise against Asia, and also by the intellectual pleasure which he first engrafted upon the innumerable festivals of Hellas, did more than lawgivers to propagate this early civilisation, and to protect it against . those barbarising feuds or migrations which through some centuries menaced its existence.

Having, therefore, the same motive of curiosity,—having, in the indulgence of this curiosity, the same awe, connected, first, with secrecy, secondly, with remoteness, and, thirdly, with beneficent power, which turns our inquiries to the infant Nile,—let us pursue a parallel investigation with regard to the infant Homer. How was Homer possible ? how could such a poet as Homer, how could such a poem as the "Iliad," arise in days so illiterate ? Or rather, and first of all, *was* Homer possible ? If the "Iliad" could and did arise, not as a long series of separate phenomena, but as one solitary birth of revolutionary power, how was it preserved ? how passed onwards from generation to generation ? how propagated over Greece during centuries, when our modern facilities for copying on paper, and the general art of reading, were too certainly unknown ?

I presume every man of letters to be aware that since the time of the great German philologer Fred. Augustus Wolf[1] (for whose life and services to literature see Wilhelm Koerte's "Leben und Studien Friedr. Aug. Wolfs" : "Life and Studies of F. A. Wolf," 1833), a great shock has been given to the slumbering credulity of men on these Homeric subjects ; a galvanic resuscitation to the ancient scepticism on the mere possibility of an "Iliad," such as we now have it, issuing sound and complete, in the tenth or eleventh

<hr>

[1] F. A. Wolf, 1759-1824.—M.

century before Christ, from the brain of a blind man, who had not (*they say*) so much as chalk towards the scoring down of his thoughts. The doubts moved by Wolf in 1795 propagated a controversy in Germany which has subsisted down to the present time. This controversy concerns Homer himself, and his first-born child, the "Iliad"; for, as to the "Odyssey," sometimes reputed the child of his old age, and as to the minor poems, which never could have been ascribed to him by philosophic critics, these are universally given up, as having no more connexion with Homer personally than any other of the many epic and cyclical poems which arose during post-Homeric ages, in a spirit of imitation, more or less widely diverging from the primitive Homeric model.

Fred. Wolf raised the question soon after the time of the French Revolution. Afterwards he pursued it (1797) in his letters to Heyne. But it is remarkable that a man so powerful in scholarship, witnessing the universal fermentation he had caused, should not have responded to the general call _upon himself to come forward and close the dispute with a comprehensive valuation of all that had been said, and all that yet remained to be said, upon this difficult problem. Voss, the celebrated translator of Homer into German dactylic hexameters,[1] was naturally interested by a kind of personal stake in the controversy. He wrote to Wolf—warmly, perhaps, and in a tone almost of moral remonstrance—but without losing his temper, or forgetting the urbanity of a scholar. "I believe," said he in his later correspondence of the year 1796—"I believe in one 'Iliad,' in one 'Odyssey,' and in one Homer as the sole father of both. Grant that Homer could not write his own name—and so much I will concede that your acute arguments have almost demonstrated —still to my thinking *that* only enhances the glory of the poet. The unity of this poet [that there were not more authors of the 'Iliad' than one], and the unity of his works [that the 'Iliad' was not made up by welding into a fictitious unity many separate heroic ballads], are as yet to me unshaken ideas. But what then? I am no bigot in my creed, so as to close my ears against all hostile arguments. And these arguments, let me say plainly, you now owe to us all;

[1] J. H. Voss, 1751-1826 —M

arguments drawn from the *internal* structure of the Homeric poems.   You have wounded us, Mr. Wolf, in our affections ; Mr. Wolf, you have affronted us in our tenderest sensibilities. You *have*, Mr. Wolf.   But still we are just men ; ready to listen, willing to bear and to forbear.   Meantime the matter cannot rest here.   You owe it, Mr. Wolf, to the dignity of the subject, not to keep back those proofs which doubtless you possess ; proofs, observe, conclusive proofs.   For hitherto, permit me to say, you have merely played with the surface of the question.   True, even that play has led to some important results ; and for these no man is more grateful than myself.   But the main battle, Mr. Wolf, is still in arrear."

Mr. Wolf, however, hearkened not to such appeals.   He had called up spirits, by his evocation, more formidable than he looked for or could lay.   Perhaps, like the goddess Eris at the wedding feast, he had merely sought to amuse himself by throwing a ball of contention amongst the literati : a little mischief was all that he intended, and a little learned billingsgate all that he expected.   Things had taken a wider circuit.   Wolf's acuteness in raising objections to all the received opinions had fallen upon a kindly soil ; the public mind had reacted powerfully ; for the German mind is but too naturally disposed to scepticism ; and Mr. Wolf found himself at length in this dilemma : viz. that either, by writing a very inadequate sequel, he must forfeit the reputation he had acquired ; or else that he must prepare himself for a compass of research to which his spirits were not equal, and to which his studies had not latterly been directed.   A man of high celebrity may be willing to come forward in undress, and to throw out such casual thoughts as the occasion may prompt, provided he can preserve his *incognito* ; but, if he sees a vast public waiting to receive him with theatric honours, and a flourish of trumpets announcing his approach, reasonably he may shrink from facing expectations so highly raised ; and perhaps in this case he might truly plead an absolute impossibility of pursuing further the many questions arising, under such original sterility of materials, and after so elaborate a cultivation by other labourers.

Wolf, therefore, is not to be blamed for having declined,

in its mature stages, to patronise his own quarrel. *His own*
I call it, because he first pressed its strongest points ; because
he first kindled it into a public feud ; and because, by his
own revisal of the Homeric text, he gave to the world,
simultaneously with his doubts, the very strongest credentials
of his right to utter doubts. And the public, during the
interval of half-a-century which has succeeded to his first
opening of the case, have viewed the question as so exclusively
his that it is generally known under the name of the Wolfian
hypothesis. All this is so natural that it is almost fair :
that rebel who heads the mob of insurgents is rightly viewed
as the father of the insurrection, whether partially disowning
it or not. Yet still, in the rigour of justice, we must not
overlook the earlier conspirators. Not to speak here of more
ancient sceptics, it is certain that in modern times Bentley,
something more than one hundred and sixty years back, with
his usual divinity of eye, saw the opening for doubts.
Already in the year 1689, when he was a young man fresh
from college, Bentley gave utterance to several of those
particular scruples which a later generation called by the
too exclusive name of " *Wolfian.*" And, indeed, had he done
nothing more than call attention to the digamma, as applied
to the text of Homer, he could not have escaped feeling and
communicating these scruples. To a man who was one day
speaking of some supposed *hiatus* in the " Iliad," Bentley,
from whom courtesy flowed as naturally as " milk from a
male tiger," called out, " *Hiatus*, man ! *Hiatus* in your
throat ! There is no such thing in Homer." And, when
the other had timidly submitted to him such cases as μεγα
εἰπων or καλα ἐργα, or μελιηδεα οἰνον, Bentley showed him
that, unless where the final syllable of the prior word happened to be *in arsi* (as suppose in Πηληιαδεω Ἀχιληος),
universally the *hiatus* had not existed to the ears of Homer.
And why ? Because it was cured by the interposition of the
digamma : " Apud Homerum sæpe *videtur* hiatus esse, ubi
prisca littera digamma explebat intermedium spatium." [In
Homer there often *seems* to be a hiatus, where in fact that
ancient letter the digamma filled up the intermediate space.]
Thus μελιηδεα οἰνον in Homer's age was μελιηδεα Ϝοινον ;
from which Æolic form of οἰνος (the Greek word for *wine*) is

derived our modern word for *wine* in all the western and central languages of Christendom. F is V, and V is W, all the world over—whence, therefore, vin, wine, vino, wein, wun, and so on ; all originally depending upon that Æolic letter F, or digamma,—that is V, that is W,—which is so necessary to the metrical integrity of Homer. Now, when once a man of Bentley's sagacity had made that step—forcing him to perceive that here of old time had been people tampering with Homer's text (else how had the digamma dropped out of the place which once it must have occupied ?) —he could not but go a little further. If you see one or two of the indorsements on a bill misspelt, you begin to suspect a case of *general* forgery. When the text of Homer had once become frozen and settled, no man could take liberties with it at the risk of being tripped up himself on its glassy surface, and landed in a lugubrious sedentary posture, to the derision of all critics, compositors, pressmen, devils, and devilets. But, whilst the text was yet in a state of fusion, or lukewarm, or in the transitional state of cooling, every man who had a private purpose to serve might impress upon its plastic wax whatever alterations he pleased, whether by direct addition or by substitution, provided only he had skill to evade any ugly seam or cicatrice. It is true, he could run this adulterated Homer only on that particular road to which he happened to have access. But then, in after generations, when all the Homers were called in by authority for general collation, *his* would go up with the rest ; his forgery would be accepted for a various reading, and would thus have a fair chance of coming down to posterity —which word means, at this moment, the reader and myself. We are posterity. Yes, even we have been humbugged by this Pagan rascal ; and have doubtless drunk off much of his swipes, under the firm faith that we were drinking the pure fragrant wine (the μελιηδεα Ϝοινον) of Homer.

Bentley having thus warned the public, by one general *caveat*, that tricks upon travellers might be looked for on this road, was succeeded by Wood,[1] who, in his " Essay on the Genius of Homer," occasionally threw up rockets in the same direction. This essay first crept out in the year 1769,

---

[1] Robert Wood, 1716-1771.—M.

but only to the extent of seven copies ; and it was not until
the year 1775 [1] that a second edition diffused the new views
freely amongst the world.　The next memorable era for this
question occurred in 1788, during which year it was that
Villoisin [2] published his " Iliad " ; and, as part of its apparatus,
he printed the famous Venetian " Scholia," hitherto known
only to inspectors of MSS.　These " Scholia " gave strength
to the modern doubts, by showing that many of them were
but ancient doubts in a new form.　Still, as the worshipful
Scholiasts do not offer the pleasantest reading in the world,
most of them being rather drowsy or so—truly respectable
men, but somewhat apoplectic,—it could not be expected that
any explosion of sympathy should follow : the clouds
thickened ; but the man who was to draw forth the lightnings
from their surcharged volumes had not yet come forward.
In the meantime, Herder,[3] not so much by learning as by the
sagacity of his genius, threw out some pregnant hints of the
disputable points.　And finally, in 1795, Wolf marched
forth in complete mail, a sheaf of sceptical arrows rattling on
his harness, all of which he pointed and feathered, giving by his
learning, or by masculine sense, buoyancy to their flight, so
as to carry them into every corner of literary Europe.
Then began the " row "—then the steam was mounted which
has never since subsided—and then opened upon Germany a
career of scepticism which from the very first promised to be
contagious.　It was a mode of revolutionary disease, which
could not by its very nature confine itself to Homer.　The
religious reader has since had occasion to see, with pain, the
same principles of audacious scepticism applied to books and
questions more important ; but, as might be shown upon a
fitting occasion, with no reason whatever for serious anxiety
as to any popular effect.　Meantime, for those numerous
persons who do not read Latin or German with fluency, but
are familiar with French, the most comprehensive view of

---

[1] It is a proof, however, of the interest even at that time taken by
Germany in English literature, as well as of the interest taken in this
Homeric question, that one of the seven copies published in 1769 must
have found its way to some German scholar ; for already in 1773 a
German translation of Wood had been published at Frankfort.

[2] J. B. G. de Villoisin, 1750-1805.—M.

[3] Herder, 1744-1803.—M.

Wolf's arguments (as given in his Homeric "Prolegoména," or subsequently in his "Briefe an Heyne": "Letters to Heyne") is to be found in Franceson's "Essai sur la question Si Homére a connu l'usage de l'écriture: Berlin, 1818."

This French work on the question whether Homer were acquainted with the art of writing I mention as meeting the wants of those who simply wish to know how the feud began. But, as that represents only the early stages of the entire speculation, it will be more satisfactory for all who are seriously interested in Homer, and without partisanship seek to know the plain unvarnished truth—"Is Homer a hum, and the 'Iliad' a hoax?"—to consult the various papers on . this subject which have been contributed by Nitzsch to the great "Allgemeine Encyclopædie" ("Universal Encyclopædia") of modern Germany. Nitzsch's name is against him. It is intolerable to see such a thicket of consonants with but one little bit of a vowel amongst them; it is like the proportions between Falstaff's bread and his sack. However, after all, the man did not make his own name; and the name looks worse than it sounds; for it is but our own word *niche*, barbarously written. This man's essays are certainly the most full and representative pleadings which this extensive question has produced. On the other hand, they labour in excess with the prevailing vices of German speculation: viz., first, vague indeterminate conception; secondly, total want of power to methodise or combine the parts, and, indeed, generally, a barbarian inaptitude for composition. But, waiving our quarrel with Nitzsch and with Nitzsch's name, no work of his can be considered as generally accessible; his body is not in court, and, if it were, it talks German. So in his chair I shall seat myself; and now, with one advantage over him—viz. that I shall never leave the reader to muse for an hour over my meaning—I propose to state the outline of the controversy, to report the decisions upon the several issues sent down for trial upon this complex suit, and the apparent tendencies, so far as they are yet discoverable, towards that kind of general judgment which must be delivered by the Chancery of European criticism before this dispute will subside into repose.

The great sectional or subordinate points into which the Homeric controversy breaks up are these :—

1. *Homer*—that is, the poet as distinct from his works ; the poet apart from the poems.

2. The " *Iliad* " and the " *Odyssey* "—that is, the poems as distinct from their author ; the poems apart from the poet.

3. The *Rhapsodoi*, or poetic chanters of Greece ; these, and their predecessors or their contemporaries—the *Aoidoi*, the *Citharœdi*, the *Homeridai*.

4. *Lycurgus*.

5. *Solon*—and the Pisistratidæ.

6. The *Diasceuastæ ;* the Remodellers, or publishers of Recasts.

I hardly know at what point to take up this ravelled tissue ; but, by way of tracing the whole theme *ab ovo*, suppose, reader, we begin by stating the chronological bearings of the principal objects (things as well as persons) connected with the " Iliad."

Ilium, or Troy, was that city of Asia Minor whose memorable fortunes and catastrophe furnished the subject of the " Iliad." At what period of human history may we reasonably suppose this catastrophe to have occurred ? Never did a great man err so much as apparently Sir Isaac Newton, on this very question, in deducing the early chronology of Greece. The semi-fabulous section of Grecian annals he crowded into so narrow a space, and he depressed the whole into such close proximity to the regular opening of History (that is, to the Olympiads), that we are perfectly at a loss to imagine with what sort of men, events, and epochs Sir Isaac would have peopled that particular interval of a thousand years in Grecian chronology which corresponds to the Scriptural interval between the patriarch Abraham and Solomon the Jewish king. This interval commences with the year 2000 before Christ, and terminates with the year 1000 before Christ. But such is the fury of Sir Isaac for depressing all events not absolutely fabulous below this latter terminus that he has really left himself without counters to mark the progress of man, or to fill the cells of history, through a millennium of Grecian life. The whole thousand years, as respects Hellas, is a mere desert upon Sir Isaac's map of time. As one instance of Sir Isaac's modernising propensities, I never could sufficiently marvel at his supposing the map of the heavens, including those constellations which are derived from the Argonautic enterprise, to have been completed about the very time of that enterprise ; as if it were possible that a coarse clumsy hulk like the ship Argo, at which no possible Newcastle collier but would have sneezed, or that any of the men who navigated her, could take a consecrated place in men's imagination, or could obtain an everlasting memorial in the starry heavens, until time, by removing gross features, and by blending all the circumstances with the solemnities of vast distance, had reconciled the feelings to a sanctity which must have been shocking if applied to things local and familiar.

Far different from Sir Isaac's is the present chronological theory. Almost universally it is now agreed that the Siege of Troy occurred about 1300, or, at the lowest calculation, more than 1200 years before Christ. What, then, is the chronological relation of Homer to Troy ? Perhaps the most tenable theory on this relation is that which represents the period of his flourishing as having been from two to three centuries after Troy. By some it was imagined that Homer himself had been a Trojan, and therefore contemporary with the very heroes whom he exhibits. Others, like our Jacob Bryant,[1] have fancied that he was not merely coeval with those heroes, but actually was one of those heroes—viz. Ulysses ; and that the "Odyssey," therefore, rehearses the personal adventures, the voyages, the calamities of Homer himself. It is our old friend the poet, but with a new face ; he is now a soldier, a sailor, a king, and, in case of necessity, a very fair boxer, or "fistic artist," for the abatement of masterful beggars, "sorners," and other nuisances. But these wild fancies have found no success. All scholars have agreed in placing a deep gulf of years between Homer and that Ilium which he sang. Aristarchus fixes the era of Homer at 140 years after the Trojan war ; Philochorus at 180 years ; Apollodorus at 240 ; the Arundel Marbles at 302 ; and Herodotus, who places Homer about 400 years before his own time (which "*own time*" may be dated as

---

[1] Jacob Bryant, 1715-1804.—M.

about 450 B.C.), ought, therefore, to be interpreted as assuming 350 years at least between Homer and Troy. So that the earliest series of events connected from before and from behind with the Grecian bard may be thus arranged :—

Years before
 Christ.

1220—Trojan Expedition.

1000—Homer a young man, and contemporary with the building of the *first* Temple at Jerusalem.

820—Lycurgus brings into the Peloponnesus from the island of Crete (or else from Ionia—that is, not from any island, but from some place in the mainland of Asia Minor) the Homeric poems, hitherto unknown upon the Grecian continent.

Up to this epoch (the epoch of transplanting the "Iliad" from Greece insular and Greece colonial to Greece continental) the Homeric poems had been left to the custody of two schools or professional orders, interested in the text of these poems : *how* interested, or in what way their duties connected them with Homer, I will not at this point inquire. Suffice it, that these two separate orders of men *did* confessedly exist— one being elder, perhaps, than Homer himself, or even than Troy : viz. the *Aoidoi*, or Chanters, and *Citharœdi*, or Harpers. These, no doubt, had originally no more relation to Homer than to any other narrative poet ; their duty of musical recitation had brought them connected with Homer, as it would have done with any other popular poet ; and it was only the increasing current of Homer's predominance over all rival poets which gradually gave such a bias and inflection to these men's professional art as at length to suck them within the great Homeric tide. They became, but were not originally, a sort of Homeric choir and orchestra— a chapel of priests having a ministerial duty in the vast Homeric cathedral. Through them exclusively, or, if not, certainly through them chiefly, the two great objects were secured : first, that to each successive generation of men Homer was *published* with all the advantages of a musical accompaniment ; secondly, that for distant generations Homer was *preserved.* I do not thus beg the question as to the existence of alphabetic writing in the days of Homer ; on the contrary,

I go along with Nitzsch and others in opposing Wolf upon that point. I believe that a laborious and painful art of writing *did* exist; but with such disadvantages as to writing materials that Homer (I am satisfied) would have fared ill as regarded his chance of reaching the polished age of Pericles had he relied on written memorials, or upon any mode of publication less impassioned than the orchestral chanting of the *Rhapsodoi*.

The other order of men dedicated to some Homeric interest, whatever that might be, were those technically known as the *Homeridæ*. The functions of these men have never been satisfactorily ascertained, or so as to discriminate them broadly and firmly from the *Citharædi* and *Rhapsodoi*. But in two features it is evident that they differed essentially: first, that the *Homeridæ* constituted a more *local* and domestic college of Homeric ministers, confined originally to a single island, not diffused (as were the *Rhapsodoi*) over all Greece; secondly, that by their very name, which refers them back to Homer as a mere radiation from his life-breathing orb, this class of followers is barred from pretending in the Homeric equipage (like the *Citharædi*) to any independent existence, still less to any anterior existence. The musical reciters had been originally a general and neutral class of public ministers, gradually sequestered into the particular service of Homer; but the *Homeridæ* were, in some way or other, possibly by blood, or by fiction of love and veneration, Homer's direct personal representatives,—like the green-turbaned Seyuds of Islamism, who claim a relation of consanguinity to the Prophet himself.

Thus far, however, though there is evidence of two separate colleges or incorporations who charged themselves with the general custody, transmission, and *publication* of the Homeric poems, we hear of no care applied to the periodical *review* of the Homeric text; we hear of no man taking pains to qualify himself for that office by collecting copies from all quarters, or by applying the supreme political authority of his own peculiar commonwealth to the conservation and the authentication of the Homeric poems. The text of no book can become an object of anxiety until by numerous corruptions it has become an object of doubt. Lycurgus, it is true, the Spartan lawgiver, *did* apply his own authority, in a very early age, to the general purpose of importing and naturalising the "Iliad." But there his office terminated. Critical skill, applied to the investigation of an author's text, was a function of the human mind as much unknown in the Greece of Lycurgus as in the Germany of Tacitus, or in the Tongataboo of Captain Cook. And, of all places in Greece, such delicate reactions of the intellect upon its own creations were least likely to arise amongst the illiterate Dorian tribes of the Peloponnesus—wretches that hugged their own barbarising institutions as the very jewels of their birthright, and would most certainly have degenerated rapidly into African brutality had they not been held steady, hustled and forcibly shouldered into social progress, by the press of surrounding tribes, fortunately more intellectual than themselves.

Thus continued matters through about four centuries from Homer. And by that time we begin to feel anxious about the probable state of the Homeric text. Not that I suppose any *interregnum* in Homer's influence—not that I believe in any possible defect of links in that vast series of traditional transmitters; the integrity of that succession was guaranteed by its interwreathing itself with human pleasures, with religious ceremonies, with household and national festivals. It is not that Homer would have become apocryphal or obscure for *want* of public repetition; on the contrary, he would have suffered by too much repetition— too constant and too fervent a repetition would have been the main source of corruptions in the text. Sympathy in the audience must always have been a primary demand with the *Rhapsodoi;* and, to a perfect sympathy, it is one antecedent condition to be perfectly understood. Hence, when allusions were no longer intelligible or effectual, what result would be likely to follow? Too often it must happen that they would be dropped from the text; and, when any Homeric family or city had become extinct, the temptation would be powerful for substituting the names of others who could delight the chanter by fervid gratitude for such a vicarious distinction where it had been merited, or could reward him with gifts where it had not. But it is not necessary to go over the many causes in preparation, after a course of four centuries, for gradually sapping the integrity of Homer's text. Everybody will agree that it was at length high time to have some edition "by authority"; and that, had the "Iliad" and "Odyssey" received no freezing arrest in their licentious tendency towards a general interfusion of their substance, and an adulterating of their diction, with modern words and ideas, most certainly by the time of Alexander— *i.e.* about seven centuries from Homer—either poem would have existed only in fractions. The connecting parts between the several books would have dropped out; and all the ἀριστεῖαι, or episodes dedicated to the honour of a particular hero, might, with regard to names less hallowed in the imagination of Greece, or where no representatives of the house remained, have perished utterly. Considering the great functions of the Greek language subsequently in propagating Christianity, it was a real providential provision which caused the era of state editions to supersede the *ad libitum* text of the careless or the interested, and just at that precise period when the rapidly rising tide of Athenian refinement would else soon have swept away all the landmarks of primitive Greece, and when the altered character of the public reciters would have co-operated with the other difficulties of the case to make a true Homeric text irrecoverable. For the *Rhapsodoi* were in a regular course of degradation to the rank of mere mercenary artists, from that of sacred minstrels who connected the past with the present, and who *sang*—precisely because their burden of truth was too solemn for unimpassioned speech. This was the station they *had* occupied ; but it remains in evidence against them, that they were rapidly sinking under the changes of the times ; were open to bribes ; and, as one consequence (whilst partly it was one cause) of this degradation, that they had ceased to command the public respect. The very same changes, and through the very same steps, and under the very same agencies, have been since exhibited to Europe in the parallel history of our mediæval minstrels. The pig-headed Ritson,[1] in mad pursuit of that single idea (no matter what) which might vex Bishop Percy,[2] made it his business, in one essay,

---

[1] Joseph Ritson, 1752-1803.—M.

[2] Bishop Thomas Percy, 1728 - 1811. His famous *Reliques of English Poetry* appeared in 1765.—M.

to prove, out of the statutes at large, and out of local court records, that the minstrel, so far from being that honoured guest in the courts of princes whom the bishop had described, was in fact, by Act of Parliament, a rogue and a vagabond, standing in awe of the parish beadle, and liable to be kicked out of any hundred or tithing where he should be found trespassing. But what nonsense! All that Ritson said was virtually false, though plausibly half-true. The minstrel was, and he was not, all that the bishop and others had affirmed. The contradiction lay in the *time :* Percy and Ritson were speaking of different periods ; the bishop of the twelfth, thirteenth, and fourteenth centuries—the attorney [1] of the sixteenth and seventeenth. Now, the Grecian *Rhapsodoi* passed through corresponding stages of declension. Having ministered through many centuries to advancing civilisation, finally they themselves fell before a higher civilisation ; and the particular aspect of the new civilisation which proved fatal to *them* was the general diffusion of reading as an art of liberal education. In the age of Pericles every well-educated man could read ; and one result from his skill, as no doubt it had also been one amongst its exciting causes, was that he had a fine copy at home, beautifully adorned, of the " Iliad " and " Odyssey." Paper and vellum, for the last six centuries B.C. (that is, from the era of the Egyptian king Psammetichus), were much less scarce in Greece than during the ages immediately consecutive to Homer ; and this scarcity it was that had retarded manuscript literature, as subsequently it retarded the art of printing.

How providential, therefore—and, with the recollection of that great part played by Greece in propagating Christianity through the previous propagation of her own literature and language, what is there in such an interference unworthy of Providence ?—how providential, that precisely in that interval of one hundred and eleven years between the year 555 B.C., the *locus* of Pisistratus, and 444 B.C., the

---

[1] Ritson was the most litigious of attorneys ; the leader of all black-letter literature ; dreaded equally by Bishop Percy and Sir Walter Scott ; but constantly falling into error through pure mulish perverseness. Of Greek he knew nothing. In Latin he was self-taught, and consequently laid himself open to the scoffs of scholars better taught.

locus of Pericles, whilst as yet the traditional text of Homer was retrievable, though rapidly nearing to the time when it would be strangled with weeds, and whilst as yet the arts of reading and writing had not weakened the popular devotion to Homer by dividing it amongst multiplied books, just then, in that critical isthmus of transitional time, did two or three Athenians of rank—first Solon, next Pisistratus, and lastly (if Plato is right) Hipparchus—step forward to make a public, solemn, and *legally* operative review of the Homeric poems. They drew the old hulk into dock; laid bare its timbers; and stopped the further progress of decay. What more they did than this, and by what characteristic services each connected his name with a separate province in this memorable restoration of the "Iliad" and "Odyssey," I shall inquire further on.

One century after Pisistratus we come to Pericles; or, counting from the *locus* of each (555 B.C., and 444 B.C.), exactly one hundred and eleven years divide them. One century after Pericles we come to Alexander the Great; or, counting from the *locus* of each (444 B.C., and 333 B.C.), exactly one hundred and eleven years divide them. During this period of two hundred and twenty-two years Homer had rest. Nobody was tempted by any oblique interest to torment his text any more. And it is singular enough that this period of two hundred and twenty-two years, during which Homer reigned in the luxury of repose, having nothing to do but to let himself be read and admired, was precisely that ring-fence of years within which lies true Grecian history; for, if any man wishes to master the Grecian history, he needs not to ascend above Pisistratus, nor to come down below Alexander. Before Pisistratus all is mist and fable; after Alexander all is dependency and servitude. And remarkable it is that, soon after Alexander, and indirectly through changes caused by him, Homer was again drawn out for the pleasure of the tormentors. Among the dynasties founded by Alexander's lieutenants was one memorably devoted to literature. The Macedonian house of the Ptolemies, when seated on the throne of Egypt, had founded the very first public library and the first learned public. Alexander died in the year 320 B.C.; and already in the year

280 B.C. (that is, not more than forty years after) the learned Jews of Alexandria and Palestine had commenced, under the royal patronage, that translation of the Hebrew Scriptures into Greek which, from the supposed number of the translators—(viz. *septuaginta, seventy*)—has obtained the name of the "Septuagint." This was a service to posterity. But the earliest *Grecian* service to which this Alexandrian Library ministers was Homeric ; and it strikes us as singular when we contrast it with the known idolatry towards Homer of that royal soldier from whom the city itself, with all its novelties, drew its name and foundation. Had Alexander survived forty years longer, as very easily he might if he had insisted upon leaving his heel-taps at Babylon, how angry it would have made him that the very first trial of this new and powerful galvanic battery, involved in the institution of a public library, should be upon the body of the "Iliad" !

From 280 B.C. to 160 B.C. there was a constant succession of Homeric critics. The immense material found in the public library towards a direct history of Homer and his fortunes would alone have sufficed to evoke a school of critics. But there was, besides, another invitation to Homeric criticism, more oblique, and eventually more effective. The Alexandrian Library contained vast collections towards the study of the Greek language through all its dialects, and through all its chronological stages. This study led back by many avenues to Homer. A verse or a passage which hitherto had passed for genuine, and which otherwise, perhaps, yielded no internal argument for suspicion, was now found to be veined by some phrase, dialect, terminal form, or mode of using words, that might be too modern for Homer's age, or too far removed in space from Homer's Ionian country. We moderns, from our vast superiority to the Greeks themselves in Greek metrical science, have in this science found an extra resource laid open to us for detecting the spurious in Greek poetry ; and many are the condemned passages in our modern editions of Greek books against which no jealousy would ever have arisen amongst unmetrical scholars. Here, however, the Alexandrian critics, with all their slashing insolence, showed themselves sons of the feeble ; they groped about in twilight. But, even without that resource, they contrived to riddle Homer through and through with desperate gashes. In fact, after being "treated" and "handled" by three generations of critics, Homer came forth (just as we may suppose one of Lucan's legionary soldiers from the rencounter with the amphisbæna, the dipsas, and the water-snake of the African wilderness) one vast wound, one huge system of confluent ulcers. Often, in reviewing the labours of three particularly amongst these Alexandrian scorpions, I think of the Æsopian fable, in which an old man with two wives, one aged as befitted him, and the other young, submits his head alternately to what may be called the Alexandrian revision of each. The old lady goes to work first; and upon "moral principle" she indignantly extirpates all the black hairs which could ever have inspired him with the absurd fancy of being young and making love to a girl. Next comes the young critic: she is disgusted with age; and upon system eliminates (or, to speak with Aristarchus, "obelises") all the grey hairs. And thus, between the two ladies and their separate editions of the old gentleman, he, poor Homeric creature, comes forth as bald as the back of one's hand. Aristarchus might well boast that he had cured Homer of the dry-rot! he *has*, and by leaving hardly one whole spar of his ancient framework. Nor can I, with my poor share of penetration, comprehend what sort of abortion it is which Aristarchus would have us to accept and entertain in the room of our old original "Iliad" and "Odyssey." To cure a man radically of the toothache by knocking all his teeth down his throat seems a suspicious recommendation for "dental surgery." And, with respect to the Homer of Aristarchus, it is to be considered that, besides the lines, sentences, and long passages to which that Herod of critics affixed his *obelus* (†) or stiletto,[1] there were entire books which he found no use in obelising piecemeal; because it was not this line or that line into which he wished to thrust his dagger, but the whole rabble of lines—"tag, rag, and bobtail." Which reminds me of John Paul Richter, who suggests to some author anxiously revising the table of

---

[1] This *obelus*, or little spit, or in fact dagger, prefixed to a word, or verse, or paragraph, indicated that it might consider itself stabbed, and assassinated for ever.

his own errata, that, perhaps, on reflection, he might see cause to put his whole book into the list of *errata*, requesting of the reader kindly to erase the total work as one entire oversight and continuous blunder, from page one down to the word *finis*. In such cases, as Martial observes, no plurality of cancellings or erasures will answer the critic's purpose : but "*una* litura potest." One mighty bucket of ink thrown over the whole will execute the critical sentence; but, as to obelising, *that* is no better than snapping pocket-pistols in a sea-fight.

With the Alexandrian tormentors we may say that Homer's pre-Christian martyrdom came to an end. His post-Christian sufferings have been due chiefly to the Germans, who have renewed the warfare not only of Alexandrian critics, but of the ancient *Chorizontes*. These people I have not mentioned separately, because, in fact, nothing remains of their labours, and the general spirit of their warfare may be best understood from that of modern Germany. They acquired their name of *Chorizontes* (or separators) from their principle of breaking up the "Iliad" into multiform groups of little tadpole "Iliads"; as also of splitting the one old hazy but golden Homer, that looms upon us so venerably through a mist of centuries, into a vast reverberation of little silver Homers, that twinkled up and down the world, and lived where they found it convenient.

Now let us converge the separate points of this chronological deduction into one focus ; after which I will try to review, each for itself, the main questions which I have already numbered as making up the elements of the controversy.

Years before
Christian Era.

1220—Troy captured and burned after a ten years' siege.

1000—Solomon the king of Jewry, and Homer the Grecian poet, both young men "on the spree." In the thousandth year before Christ, without sound of chisel or hammer, the elder Temple was built in Jerusalem. In that same year, or thereabouts, rose silently, like an exhalation, the great Homeric temple of the "Iliad."

Years before
Christian Era.

800—Lycurgus the lawgiver imports the "Iliad" into Sparta;
and thus first transplants it from Greece insular
and Greece colonial into Greece continental.

555—Solon, the Athenian lawgiver, Pisistratus, the ruler
of Athens, and Hipparchus, his son, do something
as yet undetermined for the better ascertaining and
maintaining of the original Homeric text.

444—From the text thus settled must presumably have
been cited the numerous Homeric passages which
we find in Plato and other wits of this period,
the noontide of Greek literature—viz. the period
of Pericles ; and these passages generally coincide
with our present text, so that, upon the whole, we
have good reason to rely upon our present "Iliad"
as essentially the same with that which was used
and read in the family of Pisistratus.

333—This is the main year (at least it is the inaugurating
year) of Alexander's Persian expedition, and probably the year in which his tutor, Aristotle, published those notions about the tragic and epic
"*unities*" which have since had so remarkable
effect upon the arrangement of the "Iliad." In
particular, the notion of " episodes," or digressional
narratives, interwoven parenthetically with the
principal narrative, was entirely Aristotelian, and
was explained and regulated by him ; and under
that notion people submitted easily to interpolations in the text of the "Iliad" which would else
have betrayed themselves for what they are.

320—Alexander the Great dies.

280—The Alexandrian Library is applied to the searching
down   revision of Homer ; and a school of Alexandrian
to   critics (in which school, through three consecutive
160   generations, flourished, as its leaders, Zenodotus,
Aristophanes, and Aristarchus) dedicated themselves to Homer. They are usually called the
Alexandrian "*grammatici*" ; which word "*grammatici*," as I have explained some scores of times,

did not express so limited a notion as that of *grammarians*, but was the orthodox mode of indicating classically those whom the French call *littérateurs*, and we English less compactly call *men of letters.*

After the era of 160 B.C., by which time the Second (which is in effect the only great) Punic War had liberated Rome from her African rival, the Grecian or eastern states of the Mediterranean began rapidly to fall under Roman conquest. Henceforwards the text of Homer suffered no further disturbance or inquisition, until it reached that little wicked generation (ourselves and our immediate fathers) which I have the honour to address. Now, let us turn from the "Iliad" viewed in its chronological series of fortunes to the "Iliad" viewed in itself and its relations; *i.e.* in reference to its author, to its Grecian propagators, to its reformers or restorers, its re-casters or interpolators, and its critical explorers.

A.—HOMER.

About the year 1797 Messrs. Pitt and Harry Dundas laboured under the scandal of sometimes appearing drunk in the House of Commons ; and on one particular evening this impression was so strong against them that the morning papers of the following three days fired a salute of exactly one hundred-and-one epigrams on the occasion. One was this :—

> PITT.—I cannot see the Speaker, Hal—can *you ?*
> DUND.—Not see the Speaker ! D—m'e, I see two.

Thus it has happened to Homer. Some say, "There never was such a person as Homer."—"No such person as Homer ! On the contrary," say others, "there were scores." This latter hypothesis has much more to plead for itself than the other. Numerous Homers were postulated with some apparent reason, by way of accounting for the numerous Homeric poems, and numerous Homeric birthplaces. One man, it was felt, never could be equal to so many claims. Ten camel-loads of poems you may see ascribed to Homer in the "Bibliotheca Græca" of Fabricius ; and more states than

seven claimed the man.   These claims, it is true, would
generally have vanished if there had been the means of
critically probing them ; but still there was a *primâ facie*
case made out for believing in a plurality of Homers ; whilst,
on the other hand, for denying Homer there never was any
but a verbal reason.   The Polytheism of the case was
natural ; but the Atheism was monstrous.   Ilgen, in the preface to his edition of the Homeric Hymns, says, "Homeri
nomen, si recte video, derivandum est ex ὁμου et αρω."   And
so, because the name (like many names) can be made to yield
a fanciful emblematic meaning, Homer must be a myth.
But, in fact, Mr. Ilgen has made little advance towards a
settlement, if that was what he aimed at, with his ὁμου αρω.
What do the words mean ?   Αρω is to join, to fit, to adapt
—ὁμου is together, or in harmony.   But such a mere outline or schematism of an idea may be filled up under many
different constructions.   One critic, for instance, understands
it in the sense of dovetailing, or metaphorical cabinet-making,
as if it applied chiefly to the art of uniting words into
metrical combinations.   Another—viz. Mr. Ilgen himself—
takes it quite differently ; it describes not the poetical composition, or any labour whatever of the poet as a poet, but
the skill of the musical accompaniment and adaptations.
Homer means the man that put together, or fitted into concert,
the words and the music—the *libretto* of the opera and its
fine Mozartian accompaniment.   By accident the poet may
chance to be also the musical reciter of the poem ; and in
that character he may have an interest in this name of Ὀμηρος,
but not as a poet.   Ὀμηρειν and ὁμηρευειν, says Hesychius,
mean συμφωνειν (to harmonise in point of sound) ; the latter
of the two is used in this sense by Hesiod ; and more nicely,
says Mr. Ilgen, it means *accinere*, to sing an accompaniment
to another voice or to an instrument ; and it means also
succinere, to sing such an accompaniment in an under-key, or
to sing what we moderns call a second—*i.e.* an arrangement
of notes corresponding, but subordinated, to the other or leading part.   So says Ilgen in mixed Latin, German, and Greek.
Now, I also have my pocket theory.   I maintain that ὁμου
αρω is Greek for packing up.   And my view of the case is
this :—" Homer " was a sort of Delphic or prophetic name

given to the poet under a knowledge of that fate which awaited him in Crete, where, if he did not pack up any trunk that has yet been discovered, he was, however, himself packed up in the portmanteau of Lycurgus. Such, at least, is the colouring which the credulous Plutarch, nine hundred years after Lycurgus, gives to the story. "Man alive!" says a German, apostrophising this thoughtless Plutarch, how could Lycurgus make a shipment of Homer's poems in the shape of a parcel for importation, unless there were written copies in Crete at a time when nobody could write? Or, how, why, and for what intelligible purpose, could he have consigned this bale to a house in the Peloponnesus—viz. *Somebody & Co.* —when notoriously neither *Somebody* nor *Co.* could read? Homer, he thinks, could be imported at that period only in the shape of an orchestra, as a band of Homeric chanters. But, returning seriously to the name Ὅμηρος, I say that, were this name absolutely bursting with hieroglyphic life, *that* would be no proof that the man Homer, instead of writing a considerable number of octavo volumes, was (to use Mr. Ilgen's uncivil language) "an abstract idea." Decent people's children are not to be treated as "abstract ideas" because their names may chance to look allegoric. Bunyan's "Mr. Ready-to-sink" might seem suspicious in offering himself for a life-insurance; but Mr. Strong-i'-th'-arm, who would have been a desirable companion for such an exhausted gentleman, is no abstract idea at all; he is, to my personal knowledge, a broad-shouldered reality in a most celebrated street of London, liable to bills, duns, and other affections of our common humanity. Suppose, therefore, that Homer, in some one of his names, really *had* borne a designation glancing at a symbolical meaning, what of that? this should rather be looked upon as a reflex name, artificially constructed for expressing and reverberating his glory after it had gathered, than as any predestinating (and so far marvellous) name. Chrysostom, for instance, that eloquent father of early Christianity, had he been baptized by such a name as golden-mouthed (Chrysostomos), you would have suspected for one of Mr. Ilgen's "abstract ideas"; but, as it happens, we all know that he existed in the body, and that the appellation by which he is usually recognised was a name of honour conferred upon him by the public in commemoration of his eloquence. However, I will bring this point to a short issue, by drawing the reader's attention to the following case :—Any man who has looked into the body of Greek rhetoricians must know that, in that *hebdomas idearum*, or septenary system of rhetorical forms, which Hermogenes and many others illustrated, two of the seven (and the foremost two) were the qualities called *gorgotes* and *deinotes*. Now, turn to the list of early Greek rhetoricians or popular orators, and who stands first ? Chronologically, the *very* first is a certain Tisias, perhaps ; but he is a mere *nominis umbra*. The first who made himself known to the literature of Greece is *Gorgias* ; that Gorgias who visited Athens in the days of Socrates (see Athenæus for a rigorous examination of the date assigned to that visit by Plato) ; the same Gorgias from whose name Plato has derived a title for one of his dialogues. Again, amongst the early Greek orators, you will see *Deinarchus*. Gorgias and Deinarchus ! Who is there but would say, were it not that these men had flourished in the meridian light of Athenian literature—" Here we behold two ideal or symbolic orators typifying the qualities of *gorgotes* and *deinotes !* "—But a stronger case still is that of Demosthenes. Were this great orator not (by comparison with Homer) a modern person, under the full blaze of history, and coeval with Alexander the Great, 333 years B.C., who is there that would not pronounce him a mere allegoric man, upon reflecting that the name was composed of these two elements—*Demos*, the " people " in its most democratic expression, and *sthenos*, " strength " ? this last word having been notoriously used by Homer (*mega sthenos Okeanoio*) to express that sort of power which makes itself known by thundering sound, " the thundering strength of the people ! " or, " *the people's fulminating might !* "[1]—who would believe that the most potent of Greek orators had actually brought with him into his cradle this ominous and magnificent name, this natural patent of precedency to the Athenian hustings ?

---

[1] Which (to borrow Milton's grand words from " Paradise Regained ")

> " Thundered over Greece
> To Macedon and Artaxerxes' throne."

It startles us to find lurking in any man's name a prophecy of his after career ; as, for instance, to find a Latin legend— "*And his glory shall be from the Nile*" (*Est honor à Nilo*) concealing itself in the name *Horatio Nelson*.[1] But *there* the prophecy lies hidden, and cannot be extracted without a painful corkscrew process of anagram. Whereas, in *Demosthenes*, the handwriting is plain to every child : it seems witchcraft —and a man is himself alarmed at his own predestinating name. Yet, for all that, with Mr. Ilgen's permission, Demosthenes was not an "abstract idea." Consequently, had Homer brought his name in his waistcoat-pocket to the composition of the "Iliad," he would still not have been half as mythical in appearance as several well-authenticated men, decent people's sons, who have kicked up an undeniable dust on the Athenian hustings. Besides, the word *Homer* has other significant or symbolising senses. It means a hostage, it means a blind man, as much as a cabinet-maker, or even as a packer of trunks. Many of these "significant names" either express accidents of birth commonly recurring—such as *Benoni*, "the child of sorrow," a name frequently given by young women in Westmoreland to any child born under circumstances of desertion, sudden death, &c., on the part of the father—or express those qualities which are always presumable in woman by the courtesy of the human race. Honour, Prudence, Patience, &c., are common female names : or, if they imply anything special, any peculiar determination of general qualities that never could have been foreseen, in that case they must be referred to an admiring posterity—that *senior* posterity which was such for Homer, but for us has long ago become a worshipful ancestry.

From the name it is a natural step to the country. All the world knows, by means of a satirical couplet, that

> "Seven cities claimed the mighty Homer dead,
>   Through which that Homer, living, begged his bread."

What were the names of those seven cities (and islands) I can

---

[1] A still more startling (because more complex) anagram is found in the words *Revolution Française* : for, if (as was said in 1800, after Marengo) from those two words, involving nineteen letters, you subtract the king's VETO (viz. exactly those four letters), in that case there will remain—*Un Corse la finira*.

inform the reader by means of an old Latin couplet amongst
my schoolboy recollections—

> "Smyrna, Chios, Colophon, Salamis, Rhodos, Argos, Athenæ,
>   Orbis de patriâ certat, Homere, tuâ."

> "Smyrna, &c., nay the whole world, contends for the honour of thy
>   nativity, O Homer."

Among these, the two first, Smyrna and Chios, have very
superior pretensions. Had Homer been passed to his parish
as a vagrant, or had Colophon (finding a settlement likely to
be obtained by his widow) resolved upon trying the question,
she might probably have quashed any attempt to make the
family chargeable upon herself. But Smyrna lies under
strong suspicion : the two rivers from which Homer's
immediate progenitors were named — the *Mæon* and the
Meles—bound the plains close to Smyrna. And Wood
insists much upon the perfect correspondence of the climate
in that region of the Levant with each and all of Homer's
atmospherical indications. I suspect Smyrna myself, and
quite as much as Mr. Wood ; but still I hesitate to charge
any local idiosyncrasy upon the Smyrniote climate that could
nail it in an action of damages. Gay and sunny, pellucid in
air and water, I am sure that Smyrna is ; in short, everything that could be wished by the public in general, or by
currant-dealers in particular. But really that any city whatever, in that genial quarter of the Mediterranean, should pretend to a sort of patent for sunshine, looks very much like
an extract from a private letter to the marines.

Meantime those seven places are far from being all the
competitors that have entered their names with the clerk of
the course. Homer has been pronounced a Syrian,—which
name in early Greece of course included the Hebrew, the
Syrian proper, the Arab, and the Idumean ; and so the
"Iliad" may belong to the synagogue. Babylon, also, dusky
Babylon, has put in her claim to Homer ; so has Egypt.
And thus, if the poet were really derived from an oriental
race, his name (sinking the aspiration) may have been *Omar*.
But these oriental pretensions are mere bubbles, exhaling
from national vanity. The place which, to my thinking, lies
under the heaviest weight of suspicion as the seat of Homer's

connexions, and very often of his own residence, is the island of Crete. Smyrna, I doubt not, was his birthplace. But in those summer seas, quiet as lakes, and basking in everlasting sunshine, it would be inevitable for a stirring animated mind to float up and down the Ægean. " Home-keeping youths had ever homely wits," says a great poet of our own,[1] and I doubt not that Homer (if able to afford it) had a yacht, in which he visited all the festivals of the Ægean Islands. Thus he acquired that learned eye which he manifests for female beauty. *Rhododactylus*, "rosy-fingered"; *arguropeza*, "silver-footed"; *bathukolpos*, "full-bosomed"; *boopis*, "ox-eyed,"—with a large vocabulary of similar notices,—show how widely Homer had surveyed the different chambers of Grecian beauty; for it has happened, through accidents of migration and consequent modifications of origin, combined with varieties of diet and customs, that the Greek Islands still differ greatly in the style of their female beauty.[2] Now, the time for seeing the young women of a Grecian city all congregated under the happiest circumstances of display was in their local festivals. Many were the fair Phidiacan[3] forms which Homer had beheld moving like goddesses through the mazes of religious choral dances. But at the islands of Ios, of Chios, and of Crete, in particular, I am satisfied that he had a standing invitation. To this hour, the Cretan life presents us with the very echo of the Homeric delineations. Take four several cases :—

1. The old Homeric superstition, for instance, which connects horses by the closest sympathy, and even by prescience, with their masters — that superstition which Virgil has borrowed from Homer in his beautiful episode of Mezentius (*Rhœbe, diu, res si qua diu mortalibus ulla est, Viximus*)—still lingers unbroken in Crete. Horses foresee the fates of riders who are doomed, and express their prescience by weeping in

---

[1] Shakespeare, *Two Gentlemen of Verona.*—M.

[2] For instance, the Athenian females, even when mature women, seemed still girls in their graceful slenderness : they were, in modern French phrase, *sveltes*. But the Bœotian, even whilst yet young girls, seemed already mature women, fully developed.

[3] From the expression of *Phidiaca manu*—used by Horace—we learn that the adjective, derived from Phidias, the immortal architect and sculptor, was *Phidiacus*.

a human fashion. The horses of Achilles weep, in "Iliad" xvii, on seeing Automedon, their beloved driver, prostrate on the ground. With this view of the horse's capacity, it is singular that in Crete this animal by preference should be called το αλογον, the brute, or irrational creature. But the word ἱππος has, by some accident, been lost in the modern Greek. As an instance both of the disparaging name, and of the ennobling superstition, take the following stanza from a Cretan ballad of 1825, written in the modern Greek :—

" Ωντεν εκαβαλλικευε,
Εκλαιε τ᾽ αλογο του.
Και τοτεσα το εγνωρισε
Πως ειναι ὁ θανατος του."

"Upon which he mounted, and his horse wept ; and then he saw clearly how this should bode his death."

Under the same old Cretan faith, Homer, in "Iliad" xvii. 437, says—

" Δακρυα δε σφι
Θερμα κατα βλεφαρων χαμαδις ῥεε μυρομενοιϊν
Ἡνιοχοιο ποθῃ."

"Tears, scalding tears, trickled to the ground down the eyelids of them (the horses), fretting through grief for the loss of their charioteer."

2. Another almost decisive record of Homer's familiarity with Cretan life lies in his notice of the *agrimi*, a peculiar wild goat, or ibex, found in no part of the Mediterranean world, whether island or mainland, except in Crete. And it is a case almost without a parallel in literature, that Homer should have sent down to all posterity, in sounding Greek, the most minute measurement of this animal's horns; which measurement corresponds with all those recently examined by English travellers, and in particular with three separate pairs of these horns brought to England about the year 1836 by Mr. Pashley, the learned Mediterranean traveller of Trinity College, Cambridge. Mr. Pashley, at present (viz. in 1857) a barrister of philosophic as well as high forensic pretensions, has since published his travels, and from him I extract the following description of these shy but

powerful animals, furnished to Mr. Pashley by a Cretan mountaineer:—"The *agrimia* are so active that they will
" leap *up* a perpendicular rock of ten to fourteen feet high.
" They spring from precipice to precipice, and bound along
" with such speed that no dog would be able to keep up
" with them, even on better ground than that where they
" are found. The sportsman must never be to windward of
" them, or they will perceive his approach long before he
" comes within musket-shot. They often carry off a ball ;
" and, unless they fall immediately on being struck, are mostly
" lost to the sportsman, although they may have received
" a mortal wound. They are commonly found two, three, or
" four together ; sometimes a herd of eight, and even nine,
" is seen. They are always larger than the common goat.
" In the winter time they may be tracked by the sportsman
" in the snow. It is common for men to perish in the chase
" of them [in that respect resembling the chamois-hunter
" of the Alps]. They are of a reddish colour, and never
" black or parti-coloured like the common goat. The num-
" ber of prominences on each horn indicates the years of the
" animal's age."

Now, Homer, in "Iliad" iv. 105, on occasion of Pandarus drawing out his bow, notices it as an interesting fact that this bow, so beautifully polished, was derived from (the horns of) a wild goat, αιγος αγριου; and the epithet by which he describes this wild creature is ιξαλος—preternaturally agile. In his Homeric manner he adds a short digressional history of the fortunate shot from a secret ambush by which Pandarus had himself killed the creature. From this it appears that, before the invention of gunpowder, men did not think of chasing the Cretan ibex, so hopeless was the prospect of success ; and from the circumstantiality of the account it is evident that special honour attached to the sportsman who had succeeded in such a capture. He closes with the measurement of the horns in this memorable line (memorable as preserving such a fact for three thousand years)—

"Του κερα εκ κεφαλης ἑκκαιδεκα δωρα πεφυκει."

"The horns from this creature's head measured sixteen *dora* in
    length."

Ay ; but what is a *doron ?* In the Venetian "Scholia" some annotator had hit the truth, but had inadvertently used a wrong word. This word, an oversight, was viewed as such by Heyne ; who corrected it accordingly before any scholar had seen the animal. The *doron* is now ascertained to be a Homeric expression for the *palm,* or sixth part of a Grecian foot ; and thus the extent of the horns, in that specimen which Pandarus had shot, would be two feet eight inches. Now, the casual specimens sent to Cambridge by Mr. Pashley (not likely to be quite so select as that which formed a personal weapon for a man of rank) were all two feet seven and a-half inches on the outer margin, and two feet one and a-half inches on the inner. And thus the accuracy of Homer's account (which, as Heyne observes, had been greatly doubted in past ages) was not only remarkably confirmed, but confirmed in a way which at once identifies, beyond all question, the Homeric wild-goat ($\alpha\iota\xi\ \alpha\gamma\rho\iota\text{os}$) with the present *agrimi* of Crete—viz. by the unrivalled size of the animal's horns, and by the unrivalled agility of the animal's movements, which rendered it necessary, in days before the discovery of powder, to shoot it from an ambush.

But this result becomes still more conclusive for my present purpose—viz. for identifying Homer himself as in some measure a Cretan by his habits of life—when I mention the scientific report from Mr. Rothman of Trinity College, Cambridge, on the classification and *habitat* of the animal :—
"It is not," he says, "the *bouquetin* [of the Alps], to
" which, however, it bears considerable resemblance, but the
" real wild-goat, the *capra ægagrus* [Pallas], the supposed
" origin of all our domestic varieties. The horns present the
" anterior trenchant edge characteristic of this species. The
" discovery of the *ægagrus* in Crete is perhaps a fact of some
" zoological interest, *as it is the first well-authenticated Euro-*
" *pean locality of this animal."*
Here is about as rigorous a demonstration, emanating from Mr. Pashley, the Greek archæologist, that the sporting adventure of Pandarus must have been a Cretan adventure, as would be required by the same Mr. Pashley, barrister (and by this time I hope Q.C.) in the Court of Queen's Bench ; whilst the spirited delineation of the capture, in which every

word is emphatic, and picturesquely true to the very life of 1841,[1] indicates pretty strongly that Homer had participated in such modes of sporting himself.

3. Another argument for the Cretan habitudes of Homer is derived from his allusion to the Cretan tumblers—the $\kappa \upsilon \beta \iota \sigma \tau \eta \tau \eta \rho \epsilon s$—the most whimsical, perhaps, in the world; and to this hour the practice continues unaltered as in pre-Homeric days. The description is easily understood. Two men place themselves side by side; one stands upright in his natural posture; the other stands on his head. Of course, this latter would be unable to keep his feet aloft and in the place belonging to his head, were it not that his comrade throws his arms round his ankles, so as to sustain his legs inverted in the air. Thus placed, they begin to roll forward, head over heels, and heels over head; every tumble inverts their positions; but always there is one man, after each roll, standing upright on his pins, and another whose lower extremities are presented to the clouds. And thus they go on for hours. The performance obviously requires two associates; or, if the number were increased, it must still be by pairs; and, accordingly, Homer describes *his* tumblers as in the dual number.

4. A fourth, and most remarkable, among the Homeric mementoes of Cretan life, is the $\tau \eta \lambda \epsilon \lambda a \lambda \iota a$—or conversation from a distance. This it is, and must have been, which suggested to Homer his preternatural male voices: Stentor's, for instance, who spoke as loud "as other fifty men"; and that of Achilles, whom Antilochus roused up with a long pole, like a lion couchant in his lair, to come out and roar at the Trojans—simply by which roar he scares the whole Trojan army. Now, in Crete (and from Colonel Leake, it appears, in Albania, where I believe that all the emigrant settlers are Cretan), shepherds and others are found with voices so resonant,—aided, perhaps, by the quality of a Grecian atmosphere,—that they are able to challenge a person "out of sight," and will actually conduct a ceremonious conversation (for all Cretan mountaineers are as ceremonious as the Homeric heroes) at distances which to us seem incredible.

---

[1] 1841—viz. the date of publication for this little essay in its earliest form.

What distances? demands the litigious reader. Why, our own countrymen, modest and veracious, decline to state in punctilious arithmetical terms what they have not measured, or even had full means of computing. They content themselves with saying that sometimes their guide, from the midst of a solitary valley, would shout aloud to the European public in general—taking his chance of any strollers from that great body, though quite out of sight, chancing to be within mouth-shot. But the French are not so scrupulous. M. Zallony, in his "Voyage à l'Archipel," says that some of the Greek islanders "ont la voix forte et animée ; et deux habitans, à une distance d'une demi-lieue, même plus, peuvent très facilement s'entendre, et quelquefois s'entretenir." Now, a royal league is hard upon three English miles, and a sea league, I believe, is two and a-half ; so that half-a-league *et même plus* would bring us near to a mile and a-half, or twelve furlongs,—which seems a long interval at which to conduct a courtship. Yet possibly not. Some forty years back, a witness, under examination at the York Assizes, being asked by the presiding judge how he came to think that the defendant was making love to a lady concerned in the action, replied, because he talked to her *in italics.* Now, the hint in this precedent would suggest to any of us, when making love at Cretan distances, the propriety of talking to the lady *in capitals.* In Crete, meantime, and again, no doubt, from atmospheric advantages, the τηλεσκοπια, or power of descrying remote objects by the eye, is carried to an extent that, were it not countenanced by modern experience, would seem drawn from a fairy tale. This faculty also may be called Homeric ; for Homer repeatedly alludes to it.

5. But the legends and mythology of Crete are what most detect the intercourse of Homer with that island. A volume would be requisite for the full illustration of this truth. It will be sufficient here to remind the reader of the early civilisation, long anterior to that of Greece continental, which Crete had received. That premature refinement of itself furnishes an *a priori* argument for supposing that Homer would resort to Crete ; and, inversely, the elaborate Homeric use of Cretan traditions

furnishes an *a posteriori* argument that Homer *did* seek this island.

Let me not be thought by the courteous and malicious reader to be travelling into extrajudicial questions. It is of great use towards any full Homeric investigation that we should fix Homer's locality and trace his haunts; for locality, connected with the internal indications of the "Iliad," is the best means of approximating to Homer's true era; as, on the other hand, Homer's era, if otherwise deduced, would assist the indications of the "Iliad" to determine his locality. And, if any reader demands, in a spirit of mistrust, how it is that Crete, so harassed by intestine wars from Turkish, Venetian, and recently from Egyptian tyranny, the bloodiest and most exterminating, has been able, through three thousand years, to keep up unbroken her inheritance of traditions, I reply that the same cause has protected the Cretan usages which (since the days of our friend Pandarus) has protected the Cretan ibex — viz. the physical conformation of the island : its mountains; its secret passes, where one resolute band of two hundred men is equal to an army; ledges of rock which a mule cannot tread with safety ; crags where even infantry must break and lose their cohesion ; and, above all, the blessedness of rustic poverty, which offers no temptation to the marauder. These have been the Cretan safeguards ; and a brave Sfakian population, by many degrees the finest of all Grecian races in their persons and their hearts.

The main point about Homer the man which now remains to be settled, amongst the many that are desirable, and the few that are hopeful, is this—*Could he write?* and, if he could, did he use that method for fixing his thoughts and images as they arose, or did he trust to his own memory for the rough sketch, and to the chanters for publishing the revised copies ?

This question, however, as it will again meet us under the head *Solon and the Pisistratidæ*, I will defer to that section ; and I will close this personal section on Homer by one remark borrowed from Plato. The reader will have noticed that, amongst the cities pretending to Homer as a native child, stands the city of Argos.   Now, Plato, by way of putting a summary end to all such windy pretensions from Dorian cities, introduces in one of his dialogues a stranger, who remarks, as a leading characteristic of Homer, that everywhere he keeps the reader moving amongst scenes, images, and usages, which reflect the forms and colouring of IONIAN life.   This remark is important.

PART II

THE " ILIAD "

What is the " Iliad " about?   What is the true and proper subject of the " Iliad "?   If that could be settled, it would facilitate our inquiry.   Now, everybody knows that, according to the ordinary notion, founded upon the opening lines of this poem, the subject is the *Wrath of Achilles.* Others, however, have thought, with some reason, that this idea was not sufficiently self-diffusive—was not all-pervasive : it seemed a ligament that passed through some parts of the poem, and connected them intimately, but missed others altogether.   It has, therefore, become a serious question— How much of the " Iliad " is really interveined, or at all modified, by the son of Peleus and his feud with Aga- memnon ?

Thus far, at any rate, we must concede to the *Chorizontes,* or breakers-up of the " Iliad," that the original stem on which the " Iliad " grew was probably an " Achilleis " ; for it is inconceivable that Homer himself could have expected such a rope of sand as the " Iliad " *now* presents to preserve its order and succession under the rough handling of posterity. Watch the fate of any intricate machine in any private family. All the loose or detached parts of such a machine are sure to be lost.   Ask for it at the end of a year, and, the more elaborate was the machine, so much the more certain is the destruction which will have overtaken it.   It is only when any compound whole, whether engine, poem, or tale, carries its several parts absolutely interlocked with its own substance, that it has a chance of maintaining its integrity.

Now, certainly it cannot be argued by the most idolatrous lover of the "Iliad" that the main central books exhibit that sort of natural intercohesion which *determines* their place and order. But, says the reader, here they are : they *have* held together : no use in asking whether it was natural for them to hold together. They *have* reached us : it is now past asking—Could Homer expect them to reach us ? Yes, they *have* reached us : but since when ? Not, probably, in their present arrangement, from an earlier period than that of Pisistratus. When manuscripts had once become general, it might be easy to preserve even the loosest succession of parts—especially where great veneration for the author, and the general notoriety of the poems, would secure the fidelity of copies. But what the sceptics require to be enlightened upon is the principle of cohesion which could carry these loose parts of the "Iliad" over that gulf of years between Homer and Pisistratus—the one a whole millennium before our Christian era, the other little more than half a millennium —and whilst traditionary transmission through singers and harpers constituted, perhaps, the sole means of preservation, and therefore of arrangement.

Let not the reader suppose German scepticism to be the sole reason for jealousy with regard to the present canon of the "Iliad." On the contrary, *some* interpolations are confessed by all parties. For instance, it is *certain*—and even Eustathius records it as a regular tradition in Greece—that the night adventure of Diomed and Ulysses against the Trojan camp, their capture of the beautiful horses brought by Rhesus, and of Dolon the Trojan spy, did not originally form a part of the "Iliad." At present this adventure forms the tenth book ; but previously it had been an independent *epos*, or epic narrative, perhaps locally circulated amongst the descendants of Diomed,[1] and known by the title of the

---

[1] *Descendants*, or, perhaps, amongst the worshippers ; for, though everybody is not aware of that fact, many of the Grecian heroes at Troy were deified. Ulysses and his wife, Idomeneus, &c., assume even a mystical place in the subsequent superstitions of Greece. But Diomed also became a god : and the occasion was remarkable. A peerage (*i.e.* a godship) had been promised by the gods to his father Tydeus ; but, when the patent came to be enrolled, a flaw was detected —it was found that Tydeus had once eaten part of a man ! What was

"Doloneia."   Now, if one such intercalation could pass, why not more ?   With respect to this particular night episode, it has been remarked that its place in the series is not asserted by any *internal* indication.   There is an allusion, indeed, to the wrath of Achilles ; but probably introduced, to harmonise it as a part of the "Iliad," by the same authority which introduced the poem itself : else, the whole book may be dropped out without any *hiatus*.   The battle, suggested by Diomed at the end of the ninth book, takes place in the eleventh ; and, as the critics remark, no allusion is made in that eleventh book, by any of the Grecian chiefs, to the remarkable plot of the intervening night.

But of all the incoherences which have been detected in the "Iliad," as arising out of arbitrary juxtapositions between parts not originally related, the most amusing is that brought to light by the late Wilhelm Mueller.   "It is a fact," says he, "that (as the arrangement now stands) Ulysses is not ashamed to attend three dinner parties on one evening."   First, he had a dinner engagement with Agamemnon,—which, of course, he keeps (B. ix. 90) ; so prudent a man could not possibly neglect an invitation from the commander of the forces.   Even in free and independent England the sovereign does not *ask* you to dinner, but *commands* your attendance.   Next, this gormandising Ulysses dines with Achilles (B. ix. 221) ; and finally with Diomed (B. xi. 578).   Now, Diomed was a swell of the first magnitude, a man of fashion and a dandy, as may be seen in the "Troilus and Cressida" of Shakspere (who took his character from tradition, and, in making him the Greek rival of Troilus, unavoidably makes him an accomplished man).   He, therefore, pushes his dinner as far towards "to-morrow" as was well possible ; so that it is near morning before that dinner is over.   And the sum of the Ithacan's enormities is thus truly stated by Mueller :—"Deny it who will, the son of Laertes

to be done ?   The objection was fatal ; no cannibal could be a god, though a god might be a cannibal.   Tydeus, therefore, requested Jove to settle the reversion on his son Diomed.   Which arrangement was finally adopted.   I would beg the reader to notice, by the way, that this very capacity of apotheosis presupposes a venerable antiquity in its subjects, receding far from the vulgarising approaches of familiarity.

accepts three distinct feeds between the sunset, suppose, of Monday and the dawn of Tuesday!"

This is intolerable. Yet, perhaps, apologists will say (for some people will varnish anything), "If the man had three dinners in one day, often, perhaps, in three days he had but one dinner!" For myself I frankly confess that, if there is one man in the Grecian camp whom I should have believed capable of such a thing, it is precisely this reptile Ulysses. Mueller insists on calling him the "noble" Ulysses; but, to my thinking, his nearest representative in modern times is "Sixteen-string Jack," whose life may be read in the "Newgate Calendar." What most amuses myself in the business is Mueller's steady pursuit of Ulysses through two books of the "Iliad," in order to watch how many dinner parties he attended! And there is a good moral in the whole discovery; for it shows all knaves that, though hidden for three thousand years, their tricks are sure to be found out at the last.

In general, it is undeniable that some of the German objections to the present arrangement, as a possible Homeric arrangement, are valid. For instance, the following, against the present position of the duel between Paris and Menelaus:—"This duel, together with the perfidious shot of Pandarus, " and the general engagement which follows, all belonging " to the same *epos*, wear the appearance of being perfectly " insulated where they now stand, and betray no sort of con- " nexion with any of the succeeding cantos. In the 'Αριστεια " Διομηδους, which forms the fifth canto, the whole incident " is forgotten, and is never revived. The Grecians make no " complaint of the treachery practised; nor do the gods (*ex* " *officio* the avengers of perjury) take any steps to punish it. " Not many hours after the duel, Hector comes to his brother's " residence; but neither of them utters one word about the " recent duel, and as little about what had happened since " the duel, though necessarily unknown to Paris. Hector's " reproaches, again, to Paris, for his *lâcheté*, are in manifest " contradiction to the trial of gallantry involved in the single " combat which he had so recently faced. Yet Paris takes " no notice whatever of the energy manifested by himself. " And, as to his final evasion, *that* was no matter of reproach

" to him, since it was the irresistible work of a goddess.
" Besides, when he announces his intention to Hector of
" going again to the field of battle, who would not anticipate
" from him a proposal for re-establishing the interrupted
" duel ? Yet not a syllable of all that. Now, with these
" broad indications to direct our eyes upon the truth, can we
" doubt that the duel, in connexion with the breach of truce,
" and all that now fills the third and fourth books " [in a
foot-note Mueller adds—" and also the former half of the
" second book "] " originally composed an independent *epos*,
" which belonged, very probably, to an earlier stage of the
" Trojan war, and was first thrust, by the authorised arrangers
" of the 'Iliad,' into the unhappy place it now occupies—
" viz. in the course of a day already far overcrowded with
" events ? "

In the notes, where Mueller replies to some objections, he
again insists upon the impossibility, under the supposition
that Homer had authorised the present arrangement, of his
never afterwards making the Greeks allude to the infraction
of the treaty ; especially when Hector proposes a second duel
between himself and some one of the Grecian chiefs. Yet,
perhaps, as regards this particular feature—viz. the treachery
—of the duel, it might be suggested that, as the interposition
of Venus is not to be interpreted in any foolish allegorical
way (for the battle interferences of the gods are visible and
undisguised), doubtless the Greeks, not less than the Trojans,
understood the interruption as in effect divine ; after which,
the act of Pandarus is covered by that general apology, no
matter in what light Pandarus might have meant it. Even
in the first "Iliad," it is most childish to understand the
whispering of Minerva to Achilles as an allegorical way of
expressing that his good sense or his prudence arrested his
hand. Nonsense ! that is not Homer's style of thinking,
nor the style of Homeric ages. Where Mars, upon being
wounded, howls, and, instead of licking the man who offered
him this insult, shows the white feather and limps off in
confusion, do these critics imagine an allegory ? What is an
allegoric howl ? or what does a cur sneaking from a fight
indicate symbolically ? The Homeric simplicity speaks
plainly enough. Venus finds that her man is likely to be

beaten ; which, by the way, surprises us ; for a stout young shepherd, like Paris, ought to have found no trouble in taking the "conceit"—or (speaking in fresher slang) the "bounce"—out of an elderly diner-out, such as Menelaus. And, perhaps, with his mauleys, he would ; but with the scimitar and spear a shepherd like Paris, trained upon Mount Ida, was naturally not familiar. Finding, however, how the affair was likely to go, Venus withdraws her man. Paris does not come to time ; the umpires quarrel ; the mob breaks the ring ; and a battle-royal ensues. But the interference of Venus must have been palpable ; and this is one of the circumstances in the " Iliad " which satisfy me that the age of Troy was removed by several generations from the age of Homer. To elder days, and to men fancied more heroic than those of his own day (a fancy which Homer expressly acknowledges—viz. in valuing the paving-stones interchanged between Telamonian Ajax and his antagonists), he might find himself inclined to ascribe a personal intercourse with the gods ; and he would meet everywhere an audience favouring this belief. A generation of men that often rose themselves to divine honours might readily be conceived to mix personally with the gods. But no man could think thus of his own contemporaries, of whom he must know that the very best were liable to indigestion, and suspected often to have scirrhous livers. Really no : a dyspeptic demigod it makes one dyspeptic to think of !

Meantime, the duel of Paris is simply overlooked and neglected in the subsequent books of the "Iliad": it is nowhere absolutely contradicted by implication : but other cases have been noticed in the "Iliad" which involve direct contradictions : these, therefore, argue either that Homer in those "naps" which Horace imputes to him slumbered too profoundly, or that counterfeits got mixed up with the true bullion of the "Iliad." Amongst other examples pointed out by Heyne or by Franceson, the following deserve notice :—

1. Pylæmenes the Paphlagonian is killed by Menelaus (IL. v. 579-590); but further on (IL. xiii. 643-658) we find the poor man pretty well in his health, and chief mourner at the funeral of his son Harpalion.

2. Sarpedon is wounded in the leg by Tlepolemus (IL. v. 628, &c.) ; and an ugly wound it is, for the bone is touched, so that an operation might be looked for.   Operation indeed! Two days after, he is stumping about upon the wounded pin, and "operating" upon other people (IL. xii. 290, &c.)   The contradiction, if it really is one, was not found out until the approved chronology of the "Iliad" had been settled.   My reason for doubting about the contradiction is simply this :— Sarpedon was a son of Jupiter ; and Jupiter might have a salve for wounded legs ; or else the leg (as in Dean Swift's problem offered to the consideration of the Royal Society) might have been a wooden one, and thus liable to a sudden cure of its very worst fracture by a preparation of hemp.

3. Teucer, however, was an undeniable mortal.   Yet he (IL. viii. 323) is wounded desperately in the arm by Hector. His *neuré* is smashed,—which generally is taken to mean his bowstring ; but some surgical critics understand it as the sinew of his arm.   At all events it was no trifle ; his brother, Telamonian Ajax, and two other men, carry off the patient, groaning heavily, probably upon a shutter, to the hospital. He, at least, is booked for the doctor, you think.   Not at all.   Next morning he is abroad on the field of battle, and at his old trade of thumping respectable men (IL. xii. 387).

4. The history of Vulcan, and his long day's tumble from the sky, in IL. i. 586, does not harmonise with the account of the same accident in IL. xix. 394.

5. As an inconsistency, not in the "Iliad" internally, but between the "Iliad" and the "Odyssey," it has often been noticed that in the former this same Vulcan is married to Venus, whilst in the "Odyssey" his wife is one of the Graces.

"As upon earth," says Mueller, "so in Olympus, the " fable of the 'Iliad' is but loosely put together ; and we " are not to look for any very severe succession of motives " and results, of promises and performances, even amongst " the gods.   In the first 'Iliad,' Thetis receives a Jovian " guarantee — viz. Jove's authentic nod — on behalf of her " offended son Achilles, that he will glorify him in a par- " ticular way ; and the way was by making the Trojans " victorious, until the Grecians should see their error, and

" propitiate the irritated hero. Mindful of his promise,
" Jove disposes Agamemnon, by a delusive dream, to lead
" out the Grecian host to battle. At this point, however,
" Thetis, Achilles, and the ratifying nod, appear at once to
" be blown entirely out of the Jovian remembrance. The
" duel between Paris and Menelaus takes place, and the
" abrupt close of that duel by Venus, apparently with equal
" indifference on Jove's part to either incident. Even at
" the general meeting of the gods in the fourth book, there
" is no renewal of the proposal for the glorifying of Achilles.
" It is true that Jove, from old attachments, would willingly
" deliver the stronghold of Priam from ruin, and lead the
" whole feud to some pacific issue. But the passionate
" female divinities, Juno and Minerva, triumph over his
" moderation ; and the destruction of Troy is finally deter-
" mined. Now, grant that Jove wanted firmness for meet-
" ing the furious demands of the goddesses by a candid
" confession of his previous promise to Thetis, still we might
" have looked for some intimation that this degradation of
" himself in the eyes of a confiding suppliant had cost him
" a struggle. But no ; nothing of the kind. In the next
" great battle the Trojans are severely pressed, and the
" Greeks are far enough from feeling any regret for the
" absence of Achilles. Nay, as if expressly to show that
" Achilles was *not* wanted, Diomed turns out a trump of the
" first magnitude ; and a son of Priam describes him point-
" edly as more terrific than Pelides, the goddess-born !
" And, indeed, it was time to retreat before the man who
" had wounded Mars, making him yell with pain, and howl
" like ' ten thousand mortals.' This Mars, however—he at
" least must have given some check to the advancing Greeks ?
" True, he had so ; but not as fulfilling any Jovian counsels,
" which, on the contrary, tend rather to the issue of this
" god's being driven out of the Trojan ranks. First of all
" in the eighth book Jove steps forward to guide the course
" of war ; and, with remembrance of his promise to Thetis, he
" forbids peremptorily both gods and goddesses to interfere
" on either side ; and he seats himself on Mount Ida to over-
" look the field of battle, threatening to the Greeks, by his
" impartial scales, a preponderance of calamity. From this

" review, it appears tolerably certain that the third to the
" seventh book belong to no *epos* that could have been dedi-
" cated to the glory of Achilles. The wrath of that hero,
" his reconciliation, and his return to battle, having been
" announced in the opening as the theme of the poem, are
" used as a connecting link for holding together all the
" cantos about other heroes which had been intercalated
" between itself and the close ; but this tie is far too slack ;
" and one rude shake makes all the alien parts tumble out."

TIME OF THE "ILIAD"

Next let us ask, as a point very important towards investigating the true succession and possible *nexus* of the
events, what is the duration—the compass of time—through
which the action of the poem revolves ? This has been of
old a disputed point, and many are the different "diaries"
which have been abstracted by able men during the last two
centuries. Bossu made the period of the whole to be forty-
seven days ; Wood (in his earliest edition) forty ; and a
calculation in the "Memoirs de Trevoux" (May 1708)
carries it up to forty-nine. But the *computus* now finally
adopted, amended, and ruled irreversibly, is that of Heyne
(as given in a separate "Excursus"), countersigned by Wolf.
This makes the number to be fifty-two ; but, with a subsequent correction for an obvious oversight of Heyne's, fifty-
one :—

"Book i.—Nine days the plague rages (v. 53). On the
" tenth Achilles calls a meeting of the staff-officers. What
" occurs in that meeting subsequently occasions his mother's
" visit. She tells him (v. 422) that Jove had set off the day
" before to a festival of the Ethiopians, and is not expected
" back in less than twelve days. From this we gather that
" the visit of Thetis to Jove (v. 493) must be transplanted
" to the twenty-first day. With this day terminates the first
" book ; which contains, therefore, twenty-one days.

"Book ii, up to v. 293 of Book vii, comprehends a single
" day—viz. the twenty-second.

"Book vii (v. 381, 421, and 432), the twenty-third day.

"Book vii (v. 433-465), the twenty-fourth day.

"Book viii, up to the close of Book x, the twenty-fifth
" day and the succeeding night.

"Book xi, up to the close of Book xviii, the twenty-sixth
" day.

"Book xix, to v. 201 of Book xxiii, the twenty-seventh
" day, with the succeeding night.

"Book xxiii (v. 109-225), the twenty-eighth day.

"Book xxiii (v. 226 to the end), the twenty-ninth day.

" Book xxiv.—Eleven days long Achilles trails the corpse
" of Hector round the sepulchre of Patroclus.   On the
" twelfth day a meeting is called of the gods ; consequently
" on the thirty-ninth day of the general action; for this
" indignity to the dead body of Hector must be dated from
" the day of his death, which is the twenty-seventh of the
" entire poem.   On the same thirty-ninth day, towards
" evening, the body is ransomed by Priam, and during the
" night is conveyed to Troy.   With the morning of the
" following day — viz. the fortieth — the venerable king
" returns to Troy ; and the armistice of eleven days, which
" had been concluded with Achilles, is employed in mourn-
" ing for Hector during nine days, and in preparing his
" funeral.   On the tenth of these days takes place the burn-
" ing of the body and the funeral banquet.   On the eleventh
" is celebrated the solemn interment of the remains and the
" raising of the sepulchral mound.   With the twelfth recom-
" mences the war.

"Upon this deduction, the entire 'Iliad' is found to
" revolve within the space of fifty-one days.   Heyne's mis-
" reckoning is obvious : he had summed up the eleven days
" of the corpse-trailing as a clear addition, by just so much,
" to the twenty-seven previous days; whereas the twenty-
" seventh of those days coincides with the first of the trail-
" ing, and is thus counted twice over in effect."

This *computus*, in the circumstantial detail here presented,
is due to Wilhelm Mueller.   But substantially it is guaranteed by numerous scholars.   And, as to Heyne's little
blunder, corrected by Wolf, it is nothing ; for I have myself
known a Quaker, and a celebrated bank, the two select
models of accuracy, to make an error of the same amount,
in computing the number of days to run upon a bill at six

weeks. But I soon "*wolfed*" them into better arithmetic, upon finding that the error was against myself.

Name of the "Iliad"

What follows I offer as useful towards the final judgment. When first arose the great word, that ever memorable amongst human names—"Ilias," if Greek it is that we are expected to speak; the "Iliad," if English? This is past determination; but so much we know, that the eldest author now surviving, in whom that designation occurs as a regular familiar word, is Herodotus, and he was contemporary with Pericles. Herodotus must be considered as the senior author in that great stage of Athenian literary splendour, as Plato and Xenophon were the junior. Herodotus, therefore, might have seen Hipparchus, the son of Pisistratus, if that prince had not been cut off prematurely by Jacobinical daggers. It is, therefore, probable in a high degree that the name "Iliad" was already familiar to Pisistratus: first, because it is so used by Herodotus as to imply that it was no novelty to *him* at that time; secondly, because he, who first gathered the entire series of Trojan legends into artificial unity, would be the first to require an expression for that unity. The collector would be the first to want a collective title. Solon, therefore, or Pisistratus, no matter which, did (as I fully believe) first gather the whole cycle of Iliac romances into one body. And to this aggregate whole he gave the name of "Ilias." But why? in what sense? Not for any purpose of deception, small or great. Were that notion once admitted, then we open a door to all sorts of licentious conjectures. Consciously authorising one falsehood, there is no saying where he would have stopped. But there was no falsehood. Pisistratus, whose original motive for stirring in such an affair could have been only love and admiration, was not the author, but the sworn foe, of adulteration. It was to prevent changes, not to sanction them—to bar all frauds, not to promote them—that he could ever have interposed with the state authority. And what, then, did he mean by calling these collected poems "the Iliad"? He meant precisely what a man would now mean, who should publish a body of ancient romances relating to the Round Table of King Arthur, or to Charlemagne, or to the Crusades; not implying, by any unity in the title, that these romances were all one man's work, or several parts of one individual whole, but that they had a common reference to one terminal object. The unity implied would lie not in the mind conceiving, nor in the *nexus* of the several divisions, but in the community of subject,—as, when we call the five books of Moses by the name of the Pentateuch, we do not assert any unity running through these books, as though one took up the subject where another left it; for, in reality, some parts are purely historical, some purely legislative, some purely ceremonial. But we mean that all, whether record of fact or record of institution and precept, bear upon one object—viz. the founding a separate nation as the depository of theologic truth, and elaborately, therefore, kept, by countless distinctions in matters originally trivial, from ever blending with Pagans. On the one hand, therefore, I concede to the sceptics that several independent poems (though still by possibility from the same author) were united by Pisistratus. But, on the other hand, I deny any purpose of fraud in this —I deny that the name " Iliad " was framed to disguise and mask this independence. Some had a closer *nexus* than others. But what Pisistratus says is this :—Behold a series of poems, all ancient; all from Homeric days; and (whether Homer's or not) all relating to the great crusade against *Ilium*.

Solon and Pisistratus

What was it, service or injury, that these men did to Homer? No one question, in the whole series of Homeric questions, is more perplexing. Homer did a great service to *them;* if tradition is right, to *both* of them—viz. by settling a legal dispute for each; so that it was a knavish return for such national benefits, if they—if these two Athenian statesmen—went about to undermine that text from which they had reaped such singular fruits in their own administration. But I am sure that they did no such thing: they were both gentlemen, both scholars. Yet something, certainly, they must have done to Homer ; in that point all are agreed ; but what it was remains a mystery to this hour. Every man is entitled to his opinion ; I to mine ; which in some corner or other I shall whisper into the private ear of the public, and into the public ear of my private friends.

The first thing which puzzles every man of reflection, when he hears of this anecdote, is—the extraordinary co-incidence that two great lawgivers, at different eras, should both interest themselves in a poet ; and not only so, but the particular two who faced and confronted each other in the same way that any leader of English civilisation (Alfred, suppose) might be imagined as facing and confronting any leader (Charlemagne, suppose) of French civilisation. For Christian Europe, the names and tutelary powers of France and England are by analogy that same guiding constellation which for Pagan Greece were the names Sparta and Athens ; I mean, as respects the two great features of permanent rivalship and permanent leadership. From the moment when they were regularly organised by law and institutions, Athens and Sparta became the two counterforces—attracting and repelling—of Greece. About 800 B.C., Lycurgus draws up a system of laws for Sparta ; more than two centuries later, Solon draws up a correspondent system of laws for Athens. And, most unaccountably, each of these political leaders takes upon him, not passively, as a private literary citizen, to admire the Homeric poems—*that* might be natural in men of high birth enjoying the selectest advantages of education—but actually to privilege Homer, to place him on the *matricula* of denizens, to consecrate his name, and to set in motion the whole machinery of government on behalf of his poems. Wherefore, and for what purpose ? On the part of Lycurgus, for a purpose well known and appreciated —viz. to use the " Iliad " as the basis of a public education, and thus mediately as the basis of a warlike morality ; but, on the part of Solon, for no purpose ever yet ascertained. Strangely enough, from the literary land, and from the later period, we do *not* learn the " how " and the " why " ; from the gross illiterate land and the earlier period, we *do.*

What Lycurgus did was rather for an interest of Greece than for any interest of Homer. The order of his thoughts was not, as has been supposed, "I love Homer; and I will show my love by making Sparta co-operate in extending his influence": not at all; but this—"I love Sparta; and I will show my love by making Homer co-operate with the martial foundations of the land; I will introduce a martial poem, like the 'Iliad,' to operate through public education, through national training, and through hereditary festivals." For Solon, on the other hand, Homer must have been a final object; no means towards something else, but an end *per se.* Doubtless, Solon as little as Lycurgus could be indifferent to the value of this popular poem for his own professional objects. But, practically, it is not likely that Solon could find any opening for Homeric services in that direction. Precisely those two causes which would insure to Solon a vast superiority to Lycurgus in all modes of intellectual liberality—viz. his chronologic period and his country—must have also caused that the whole ground would be pre-occupied. For education, for popular influence, Athens would have already settled upon Homer all that dowry of distinction which Solon might wish to settle. Polished Athens surely in the sixth century B.C., if brutal Sparta in the ninth!

At this point our suspicions revolve upon us. That the two vanward potentates of Greece—Athens and Sparta—should each severally ascribe to her own greatest lawgiver a separate Homeric labour, looks too much like the Papal heraldries of European sovereigns; amongst whom all the great ones are presumed to have rendered some characteristic service to the Church. "Are you ruler of France, and therefore the *Most Christian?* Be it so; but I again, as King of Spain, am the *Most Catholic;* and my brother here, King of Portugal, is the *Most Faithful;* and this Britannic sovereign is *Defender of the Faith.*" Was Homer, do you say, an Ionian? "Well, be it so," the Spartan replies, "with all my heart: and we Dorians might seem to have no part in that inheritance, being rather asinine in our literary character; but, for all that, Dorian as he was, you cannot deny that my countryman, Lycurgus, first introduced Homer upon the continent of Greece." Indeed the Spartans had a craze about the "Iliad," as though it bore some special relation to themselves : for Plutarch mentions it as a current doctrine in Sparta that Hesiod was the poet for Helots (and, in a lower key, perhaps they added—for some other people beside), since, according to his poetry, the end of man's existence is to plough and to harrow; but Homer, said they, is the Spartan poet, since the moral of the " Iliad " proclaims that the whole duty of man lies in fighting.

Meantime, though it cannot be denied that these attempts in Greek statesmen to connect themselves with Homer by some capital service certainly *do* look too much like the conse quent attempts of western nations (Rome, Britain, &c.) to connect their ancestries with Troy, still there seems to be good historic authority for each of the cases separately. Or, if any case were suspicious, it would be that of Lycurgus. Solon, the legislatorial founder of Athens—the Pisistratidæ, or final princes of Athens—these great men, it is undeniable, *did* link their names with Homer : each and all by specific services. What services ? what could be the service of Solon ? Or, after Solon, what service *could* remain for Pisistratus ?

A fantastic Frenchman pretended to think that History, to be read beneficially, ought to be read backwards—*i.e.* in an order inverse to the chronological succession of events. This absurd rule might, in the present case, be applied with benefit. Pisistratus and his son Hipparchus stand last in the order of Homeric modifiers. Now, if we ascertain what it was that they *did*, this may show us what it was that their predecessors did *not* do ; and to that extent it will narrow the range from which we have to select the probable functions of those predecessors.

What, then, was the particular service to Homer by which Pisistratus and his son made themselves so famous ? The best account of this is contained in an obscure *grammaticus* or *littérateur*, one Diomedes, no small fool, who thus tells his tale :—" The poems of Homer, in process of time, were it by " fire, by flood, by earthquake, had come near to extinction ; " they had not absolutely perished, but they were continu- " ally coming nearer to that catastrophe, through wide " dispersion. From this dispersion it arose naturally that " one place possessed a hundred Homeric books ; some second " place a thousand ; some third place a couple of hundreds ;

" and the Homeric poetry was fast tending to a fractionary
" state.   In that conjuncture there occurred to Pisistratus,
" who ruled at Athens about 555 years B.C., the following
" scheme :—With the double purpose of gaining glory for
" himself and preservation for Homer, he dispersed a notifica-
" tion through Greece that every man who possessed any
" Homeric fragments was summoned, or was requested, to
" deliver them into Athenian hands at a fixed rate of com-
" pensation.   The possessors naturally hastened to remit
" their *quotas*, and were honestly paid.   Indeed, Pisistratus
" did not reject even those contributors who presented verses
" already sent in by another ; to these also he paid the
" stipulated price without any discount at all.   And by this
" means it happened that oftentimes he recovered, amongst a
" heap of repetitions, one, two, or more verses that were
" new.   At length this stage of the labour was completed ;
" all the returns from every quarter had come in.   Then it
" was that Pisistratus summoned seventy men of letters, at
" salaries suitable to their pretensions, as critical assessors
" upon these poems ; giving to each man separately a copy
" of the lines collected, with the commission of arranging
" them according to his individual judgment.   When, at
" last, the commissioners had closed their labours, Pisistratus
" assembled them, and called upon each man separately to
" exhibit his own result.   This having been done, the general
" voice, in mere homage to merit and the truth, unanimously
" pronounced the revisions of Aristarchus and Zenodotus to
" be the best ; and, after a second collation between these
" two, the edition of Aristarchus was found entitled to the
" palm."

Now, the reader must not allow himself to be repelled by
the absurd anachronisms of this account, which brings Pisistratus of the sixth century B.C. face to face with Aristarchus
of the third ; nor must he allow too much weight to the
obvious plagiarism from the old marvellous legend of the
seventy-two Jewish translators working upon the Mosaic
Pentateuch.   That very legend shows him how possible it is
for a heap of falsehoods, and even miracles, to be embroidered
upon a story which, after all, is true in its main texture.
We all know it to be true, in spite of the fables engrafted

upon this truth, that, under the patronage of a Macedonian prince, seventy-two learned Jews really *were* assembled at Alexandria, and *did* make that Greek translation of the Hebrew Scriptures which, from the number (*septuaginta*) of the translators, we still call the *Septuagint*. And so we must suppose this ignorant Diomedes, though embellishing the story according to his slender means, still to have built upon old traditions. Even the rate of payment has been elsewhere recorded; by which it appears that " penny-a-liners " (of whom we hear so much in our day) existed also for early Athens.

If this legend were accurate even in its commencement, it would put down Plato's story that the Homeric poems were first brought to Athens by Hipparchus, the son of Pisistratus ; and it would put down the mere possibility that Solon, thirty or forty years earlier than either, had ever intermeddled with those poems. But, if we adopt the tradition about Lycurgus, or even if we reject it, we must believe that copies of the " Iliad " and " Odyssey " (that is, *quoad* the substance, not *quoad* the present arrangement) existed in Athens long before the Pisistratidæ, or even before Solon. Were it only through the *rhapsodoi*, or continuous reciters of the Homeric poems, both "Iliad " and "Odyssey " must have been known many a long year before Pisistratus ; or else I undertake to say they would never have been known at all. For, in a maritime city like Athens, communicating so freely with Ionia and with all insular Greece,—so constitutionally gay besides,—how is it possible to suppose that the fine old poetic romances, chanted to the accompaniment of harps, about those ancestral Greek heroes whom we may style the *paladins* of Greece, could be unknown or unwelcomed, unless by supposing them non-existent ? If they lurked anywhere, they would assuredly float across those sunny seas of the Ægean to Athens ; that city which, in every age (according to Milton : " Paradise Regained "), was equally "*native* to famous wits " and " *hospitable* "—that is, equally fertile in giving *birth* to men of genius itself, and forward to welcome those of foreign birth.

Throughout this story of Diomedes, disfigured as it is, we may read that the labours of Pisistratus were applied to *written* copies. That is a great step in advance. And

instantly this step reacts upon Solon, as a means of approximating to the nature of *his* labours. If (as one German
writer holds) Solon was the very first person to take down the
" Iliad " in writing from the recitations of the *rhapsodoi*, then
it would seem that this step had suggested to Pisistratus the
further improvement of collating Solon's written copy with
such partial copies, or memorials, or fractional recollections
of reciters, or local and enchorial legends, as would be likely
to exist in many different parts of Greece, amongst families
or cities tracing their descent from particular heroes of the
" Iliad." If, on the other hand, Pisistratus was the first man
who matured a written copy, what will then remain open to
Solon for *his* share in the play ? This :—viz. that he applied
some useful check to the exorbitancies of the musical re-
hearsers. The famous Greek words still surviving in Plato,
and long after in Diogenes Laertius, support this notion.
The words must be true, though they may be obscure. They
must involve the fact, though they may conceal it. What
are these words ? Let us review them. To chant ἐξ
ὑπολήψεως—and to chant ἐξ ὑποβολης—these were the new
regulations introduced by Solon and his successor. Now,
what is the meaning of ὑπολήψις ? The commonest sense of
the word is *opinion*. Thus, on the title-page of Lord Shaftes-
bury's " Characteristics " stands, as a general motto, Παντα
ὑπολήψις—" All things are in effect opinion " ; *i.e.* nothing
really *is ;* but imperfectly it *is*, or it ıs *not*, according to the
hold which it has obtained over the general opinion of men.
This, however, is a sense which will not answer. Another and
rarer sense is—*succession*. And the way in which the preposi-
tions ὑπο and *sub* are used by the ancients to construct the idea
of succession (a problem which Dr. Parr failed to solve) is by
supposing such a case as the slated roof of a house. Were
the slates simply contiguous by their edges, the rain would
soon show that their succession was not perfect. But, by
making each to underlap the other, the series is made virtually perfect. In this way, the word came to be used for
succession. And, applied to the chanters, it must have meant
that, upon some great occasion periodically recurring, they
were obliged by the new law to pursue the entire series of
the several rhapsodies composing the " Iliad," and not to

pick and choose, as heretofore, with a view to their own convenience, or to local purposes. But what was the use of this? I presume that it had the same object in view as the rubric of the English Church (I believe also of the Jewish Synagogue) in arranging the succession of lessons appointed for each day's service—viz. to secure the certainty that, within a known period of time, the *whole* of the canonical books should be read once through from beginning to end. The particular purpose is of my own suggestion; but the fact itself is placed beyond all doubt. Plato says that the chanters were obliged, at the great Panathenaic festival, to recite the "Iliad" ἐξ ὑπολήψεως ἐφεξῆς; where the one expression applies to the succession of parts recited, and the other to the succession of persons reciting.

The popular translation would be that they were obliged, by relieving each other, or by regular relays of chanters, to recite the whole poem, in its order, by succession of parts from beginning to end. This very story is repeated by an orator still extant not long after Plato. And in his case there is no opening to doubt; for he does not affirm the story,—he assumes it, and recalls it to the people's attention as a thing notorious to them all. The other expression, ἐξ ὑποβολῆς or ὑποβλήδην, has occasioned some disputing; but why, I cannot conjecture. If ever there was a word whose meaning is certain in a position like this, that word is ὑποβάλλω, with its derivatives. And I am confounded at hearing that less than a Boeckh would not suffice to prove that the ἐξ ὑποβολῆς means "by way of suggestion," "under the condition of being prompted." The meaning of which is evident: a state copy of the "Iliad," however it had been obtained by Solon, a canon of the Homeric text, was confided to a prompter, whose duty was to check the slightest deviation from this authorised standard, to allow of no shortenings, omissions, or *sycophantic* [1] alterations.

---

[1] "*Sycophantic*":—The reader must remember that the danger was imminent: there was always a body ready to be bribed into forgery —viz. the mercenary *rhapsodoi:* there was always a body having a deep interest of family ostentation in bribing them into flattering interpolations. And standing by was a public the most uncritical and the most servile to literary forgeries (such as the Letters of Phalaris, of Themistocles, &c.) that ever can have existed.

In this sense the two regulations support and check each other.   One provides for quantity, the other for quality. One secures that the whole shall be recited—the "Iliad," the whole "Iliad," and nothing *but* the "Iliad"; the other secures the fidelity of this whole.   And here again comes in the story of Salamis to give us the "why" and the "wherefore" of these new regulations.   If a legal or international question about Salamis had just been decided by the mere authority of a passage in the "Iliad," it was high time for statesmen to look about them, and to see that a poem which was thus solemnly adjudged to be good evidence in the supreme courts of law, not only as between man and man, but also as between state and state, should have its text authenticated.   And, in fact, several new cases (see Eustathius on the second "Iliad") were decided not long after on the very same Homeric evidence.

But does not this prompter's copy presuppose a complete manuscript of the "Iliad"?   Most certainly it does; and the question is left to the reader : whether this in fact was the service by which Pisistratus followed up and completed the service of Solon (as to going through the whole "Iliad"); or whether both services were due to Solon,—in which case it will become necessary to look out for some idea of a new service that could remain open to Pisistratus.

Towards that idea, let us ask universally what services *could* be rendered by a statesman in that age to a poem situated as the "Iliad"?   Such a man might restore; might authenticate ; might assemble ; might arrange.

1. He might restore—as from incipient decay or corruption.

2. He might authenticate—as between readings that were doubtful.

3. He might assemble the scattered—as from local dispersion of parts.

4. He might arrange—as from confusion into self-justifying order—supplying links, healing dislocations, and revivifying the vestiges of more natural successions.

All these services, I have little doubt, were, in fact, rendered by Pisistratus.   The three first are already involved in the story of our foolish friend Diomedes.   Pisistratus would do justice to the wise enactment of Solon, by which the "Iliad" was raised into a liturgy periodically rehearsed by law at the greatest of the Athenian festivals: he would ratify the regulation as to the prompter's (or state) copy. But this latter ordinance was rather the outline of a useful idea than one which the first proposer could execute satisfactorily. Solon probably engrossed upon brazen tablets such a text as any one man could obtain. But it would be a work of time, of labour, of collation, and fine taste, to complete a sound edition. Even the work of Pisistratus was liable, as we know, to severe maltreatment by the Alexandrine critics. And, by the way, those very Alexandrine revisals presuppose a received and orthodox text; for how could Zenodotus or Aristarchus breathe their mildewing breath upon the received readings,—how could they pronounce X or Y, for instance, spurious,—unless by reference to some standard text in which X or Y had been adopted for legitimate? However, there is one single argument upon which the reader may safely allow himself to suspect the suspicions of Aristarchus, and to amend his emendations. It is this: Valkenaer, that exquisite Grecian, points out to merited reprobation a correction applied by Aristarchus to the autobiographical sketch of himself which Phœnix gives to Achilles in "Iliad" x. Phœnix, in his old age, goes back to his youthful errors in a spirit of amiable candour. Out of affection to his mother, whose unmerited ill treatment he witnessed with filial sympathy, he had offered, at her request, an affront to his father's *harem* for which he could obtain no forgiveness. Τῇ πιθομην, says Phœnix: her I obeyed. Which passage one villain alters into Τῇ οὐ πιθομην: her I did *not* obey; and thus the whole story is ruined. But Aristarchus goes further: he cancels and stilettoes [1] the whole passage. But why? Upon what conceivable objection? Simply, in both cases, upon the ridiculous allegation that this confession, so frank, and even pathetic, was immoral, and might put bad thoughts into the minds of "our young men." O, you two old vagabonds! And thus, it seems, we have had a Bowdler's "Iliad" long before our own Bowdler's Shakspere. It is fit, however,

---

[1] "*Stilettoes*":—*i.e.* obelises, or places his autocratic *obelus* before the passage.

that this anecdote should be known, as it shows the sort of principles that governed the revisal of Aristarchus. An editor who could castrate a text upon any plea of disliking the sentiment is not trustworthy ; such a man is ripe for the forgery of bank-notes. And, for my part, I should far prefer the authorised edition of Pisistratus to all the remodelled copies that issued from the Alexandrian Library.

So far with reference to the three superior functions of Pisistratus. As to the fourth, his labour of arrangement, there is an important explanation to be made. Had the question been simply this—given four-and-twenty cantos of the "Iliad," to place them in the most natural order— the trouble would have been trivial for the arranger, and the range of objections narrower for us. Some books determine their own place in the series ; and those which leave it doubtful are precisely the least important. But the case is supposed to have been very different. The existing distribution of the poem into twenty-four tolerably equal sections, designated by the twenty-four capitals of the Greek alphabet, is ascribed to Aristarchus, though one incomparable donkey, a Greek scholiast, actually denies this upon the following ground :—Do you know, reader (says he), why Homer began the "Iliad" with the word *menin* ($\mu\eta\nu\iota\nu$ [1]) ? Look this way and I will tell you : it is a great mystery. What does the little μ of the Greek alphabet signify numerically ? Why, forty. Good : and what does the η mean ? Why, eight. Now, put both together, you have a prophecy or a promise on the part of Homer that he meant to write forty-eight books, which proves that the "Iliad" must have had originally twenty-four ; because, if you take twenty-four from forty-eight, there remain just twenty-four books for the "Odyssey." *Quod erat demonstrandum.* Is not this a man for looking through milestones ?

The Aoidoi, Rhapsodoi, Homeridæ

The Germans are exceedingly offended that any man in ancient days should presume to call himself a *rhapsodos*

------

[1] The first words of the "Iliad" are, M$\eta\nu\iota\nu$ $\alpha\epsilon\iota\delta\epsilon$ $\Theta\epsilon\alpha$—*i.e.* Wrath sing, Goddess.

without sending down a sealed letter to posterity stating all the reasons which had induced him to take so unaccountable a step. And the uproar is inconceivable which they have raised about the office or function indicated by the word, as well as about the word itself considered etymologically. I for my part honestly confess that, instead of finding that perplexity in the *rhapsodos* which my German brothers find, I am chiefly perplexed in accounting for *their* perplexity. However, I had been seduced into writing a very long essay on the several classes named in my title, until I came to this discovery—that, however curious in itself, the whole inquiry *could* not be, and *was* not, by the Germans themselves, connected with any one point at issue about Homer or the "Iliad." After all the fighting on the question, it remains past denial, that the one sole proposition by which the *rhapsodoi* have been brought even into any semblance of connexion with Homer is the following :—Every narrative poem of any length was called a *rhapsodia ;* and hence it is that the several subordinate narratives of the "Iliad,"—such as that called the Αριστεια Αγαμεμνονος, The Prowess of Agamemnon, the Αριστεια Αιαντος, The Prowess of Ajax, Περιποταμιος μαχη, The Battle by the River-side, Ὁπλοποιια, The Fabric of the Arms, Νεων καταλογος, The Muster of the Ships, Δολωνεια, The Adventure of Dolon, and many others which are now united into the composite structure called the "Iliad,"—were always introduced by the chanter with a proemial address to some divinity. And the Hymns which we have now under the name of Homer are supposed by some to have been occasional preludes of that sort, detached subsequently from their original station by some forgotten accident. The single fact which we know about these preludes is that they were pure detached generalities, applicable to all cases indifferently ; ἀπαδοντα, irrelevant, as an old Greek author calls them ; and, to prevent any misconstruction of his meaning, as if that musical metaphor might have been applied by him to the mere music of the chanter, he adds—και ουδεν προς το πραγμα δηλοι: "and they foreshow nothing at all that relates to the matter." Now, from this little notice of their character, it is clear that, like doxologies, or choral burdens, or *refrains* to songs, they were not improvised ; not *impromptus;* they were stereotyped forms, ready for all occasions. *A Jove principium,* says Horace : with this opening a man could never go wrong, let the coming narrative point which way it would. And Pindar observes that all the Homeric *rhapsodoi* did in fact draw their openings from Jove. Or, by way of variety, the Muses might be a good inauguration, or Apollo ; and in a great city, like Athens or Ephesus, the local divinity—viz. the maiden goddess *Athene,* in the one case, or Artemis, in the other.

But the Germans, who will not leave this bone, after all its fruitless mumbling, want to pick a quarrel about the time when these *rhapsodoi* began to exist. What does *that* signify ? I will quarrel with no man "about the age of Sir Archy's great-grandmother" ; and yet, on consideration, I *will.* They say that their *rhapsodoi* were, comparatively with Homer, young people. I say that they were *not.* I cannot say that I know this "of my own knowledge" ; but I have better evidence *for* it than any which they can have *against* it. In a certain old scholiast on Aristophanes there is a couplet quoted from Hesiod in the following terms :—

"'Εν Δηλῳ τοτε πρωτον ἐγω και 'Ομηρος ἀοιδοι
    Μελπομεν, ἐν νεαροις ὑμνοις ῥαψαντες ἀοιδην."

"Then first in Delos did I and Homer, two bards, perform as musical reciters, laying the *nexus* of our poetry in original hymns."

Plato, again, who stood nearer to Homer than any one of us by the little difference of two thousand two hundred and sixty years, swears that he knows Homer to have been a *rhapsodos.*

But what does the word mean ? Strabo, in a passage which deserves closer attention than it has received, explains why it is that poetry in general was called ἀοιδη, or song. This name having been established, then afterwards each special kind of poetry bore this appellation—viz. *aoidé,* or *odé,* or *odia,* as a common or generic element in its designation, whilst its differential element was prefixed.   Thus, goat-song, or *tragodia*, revel-song, or *komodia*, were designations (derived from their occasional origins) of tragedy and comedy, both being chanted.   On the same principle, *rhapsodia* shows by its ending that it is poetry, some kind or other: but what kind ?   Why, that secret is confided to the keeping of *rhaps*.   And what may *rhaps* mean ?   Why, *rhapto* means *to sew with a needle*, consequently to *connect*. But, say you, all poetry must have some connexion, internally at least.   True; but this circumstance is more noticeable and emphatic with regard to long *narrative* poems. The more were the parts to be connected, the more was the connexion : more also depended upon it; and it caught the attention more forcibly.   An ode, a song, a hymn, might contain a single ebullition of feeling.   The connexion might lie in the very rapture and passion, without asking for any effort on the poet's part.   But, in any *epos* or epic romance, the several adventures, and parts of adventures, had a connecting link running through them, such as bespoke design and effort in the composer—viz. the agency of a single hero, or of a predominant hero.   And thus *rhapsodia*, or linked song, indicated, by an inevitable accident of all narrations, that it was narrative poetry.   And a *rhapsodos* was the personal correlate of such poetry; he was the man that chanted it.

Scarcely is one row over before another commences. Pindar, it seems, has noticed the *rhapsodoi;* and, as if it were not enough to fight furiously about the explanation of that word, a second course of fights is undertaken, by German critics, about Pindar's explanation of the explanation.   The Pindaric passages are two : one in the 3d Isthmian, where, speaking of Homer, Pindar says that he established (*i.e.* raised into life and celebrity) all modes of excellence, κατα ῥαβδον.   It is a poet's way of saying that Homer did this as a *rhapsodos*.   *Rhabdos*, therefore, is used as the symbol of a *rhapsodos;* it is, or it may be conceived to be, his instrument for connecting the narrative poem which gives him his designation.   But what instrument ? Is it a large darning-needle for sewing the parts together ? If so, Homer will want a thimble.   No, says one solemn critic, *not* a needle : none but a blockhead would think of such a thing.   Well, what is it, then ?   It is, says he, a cane —a wand—a rattan.   And what is Homer to do with a cane ?   Why, understand that, when his singing robes were on (for it is an undoubted fact that the ancient *rhapsodos* not only chanted in full pontificals, but had two sets of robes, *crimson* when he chanted the " Iliad," *violet-coloured* when he chanted the " Odyssey "), in that case the *rhapsodos* held his stick in his right hand.   But what sort of a stick ?   *Stick* is a large genus, running up from switch to cudgel, from rod to bludgeon.   And my own persuasion is that this stick, whether cylinder or pencil of wood, had something to do with the roll of remembrances (not perhaps written copies, but mechanical suggestions for recovering the main succession of paragraphs) which the *rhapsodos* used as shorthand notes for aiding his performance.   Perhaps it was a Lacedemonian *scytale.*

The other passage of Pindar is in the second Nemean— ‘Οθεν περ και ‘Ομηριδαι ῥαπτων ἐπεων τα πολλ’ ἀοιδοι ἀρχονται.[1]   Of a certain conqueror at the games, Pindar says that he took his beginning from that point—viz. Jove—whence the Homeridæ take theirs ; alluding to the prelusive hymns. Now, what seems most remarkable in this passage is the art with which Pindar identifies the three classes of — 1. *Homeridæ ;* 2. *Aoidoi ;* 3. *Rhapsodoi.*   The words ῥαπτων ἐπεων ἀοιδοι are an ingenious way of expressing that the *aoidoi* were the same as the *rhapsodoi.*   But, where Pindar saw no essential difference, except as a species differs from a genus, it is not likely that we of this day shall detect one. At all events, it is certain that no discussion connected with any one of these three classes has thrown any light upon the main question as to the integrity of the " Iliad."   The *aoidoi,* and perhaps the *rhapsodoi,* certainly existed in the days of Homer.   The *Homeridæ* must have arisen after him ; but when, or under what circumstances, no record remains to say. Only the place of the *Homeridæ* is known : it was Crete ; and this again brings us round to the *personal* connexion of

---

[1] Literally—*Whence also the Homeridæ, who are in effect the singers* (αοιδοι) *of continuous metrical narratives* (*i.e.* ραπτων επεων), *do for the most part* (τα πολλ') *derive their openings* (αρχονται).

Homer with that famous island. But all is too obscure to penetrate, and in fact has not been penetrated.

PART III

VERDICT ON THE HOMERIC QUESTION

I will now, reader, endeavour to give you the heads of a judgment, or verdict, on this intricate question, drawn up with extreme care by myself.

1. Rightly was it said by Voss that all arguments worth a straw in this matter must be derived from the internal structure of the " Iliad." Let us, therefore, hold an inquest upon the very body of this memorable poem ; and first of all let us consider its outside characteristics, its style, language, metrical structure.

One of the arguments on which the sceptics rely is this : a thousand years, say they, make a severe trial of a man's style. What is very good Greek at one end of that period will sometimes be unintelligible Greek at the other. And throughout this period it will have been the duty of the *rhapsodoi*, or public reciters, to court the public interest, to sustain it, to humour it, by adapting their own forms of delivery to the existing state of language. Well, what of that ? Why, this—that, under so many repeated alterations, the " Iliad," as we now have it, must resemble Sir Francis Drake's ship—repaired so often that not a spar of the original vessel can have remained.

In answer to this, I demand—why a thousand years ? Doubtless there was that space between Homer and the Christian era. But why particularly connect the Greek language with the Christian era ? In this artifice, reader, though it sounds natural to bring forward our Christian era in a question that is partly chronological, already there is bad faith. The Greek language had nothing to do with the Christian era. Mark this, and note well—that already in the era of Pericles, whose chronological *locus* is 444 years B.C., the Greek language had reached its consummation. And by that word I mean its state of rigid settlement. Will any man deny that the Greek of Thucydides, Sophocles, Euripides, who were, in the fullest sense, contemporaries with Pericles —that the Greek of Plato or Xenophon, who were at least children of some growth before Pericles died—continued through all after ages (in the etymological sense of the word) *standard* Greek? That is, it was standing Greek—Greek which *stood* still, and never afterwards shifted its ground; so that eighteen hundred and ninety years later, at the final capture of Constantinople by the Ottomans, it remained the true familiar Greek of educated people, such Greek as all educated people talked, and removed even from the vulgar Greek of the mob only as the written language of books always differs from the spoken dialect of the uneducated. The time, therefore, for which we have to account is, *not* a thousand years, but a little more than one-half of that space. The range, therefore—the compass of time within which Homer had to struggle with the agencies of change, viz. down to Pericles—was about five centuries and a-half.

Now, the tendency to change is different in different languages, both from internal causes (mechanism, &c.), and from causes external to the language, laid in the varying velocities of social progress. Secondly, besides this varying liability to change in one language as compared with another, there is also a varying rate of change in the same language compared with itself. Change in language is not, as in many natural products, continuous: it is not equable, but eminently moves by fits and starts. Probably one hundred and fifty years at stagnant periods of history do less to modify a language than forty years amidst great struggles of intellect. And one thing I must insist on; which is that between Homer and Pisistratus the changes in Grecian society likely to affect the language were not to be compared, for power, with those acting upon English society ever since the Reformation.

This being premised, I request attention to the following case. Precisely on this very summer day, so bright and brilliant, of 1841,[1] are the five hundred years completed (less by forty-five years than the interspace between Homer and Pisistratus) since Chaucer was a stout boy, "alive," and

---

[1] About which time this paper was first published.

probably "kicking," for he was fined, about 1341, for kicking a Franciscan friar in Fleet Street,—though Ritson erroneously asserts that the story was a "hum," invented by Chatterton. Now, what was the character of Chaucer's diction ?   A great delusion exists on that point.   Some ninety or one hundred words that are now obsolete, certainly not many more, vein the whole surface of Chaucer; and thus a *primâ facie* impression is conveyed that Chaucer is difficult to understand, whereas a very slight practice· familiarises his language. The "Canterbury Tales" were not made public until 1380 ; but the composition was certainly proceeding between 1350 and 1380,[1] and before 1360 some considerable parts were *published*—yes, *published.*   Here we have a space greater by thirty-five years than that between Homer and Pisistratus. And observe : had Chaucer's Tales enjoyed the benefit of an oral recitation,—were they assisted to the understanding by the pauses in one place, the hurrying and crowding of unimportant words at another, and by the proper distribution of emphasis everywhere (all which, though impracticable in regular singing, is well enough accomplished in a chant, or λογος μεμελισμενος),—there is no man, however unfamiliar with old English, but might be made to go along with the movement of his admirable tales, as regards the sense and the passion, though he might still remain at a loss for the meaning of insulated words.

Not Chaucer himself, however, but that model of language which Chaucer ridicules and parodies, as becoming obsolete in his days, the rhyme of Sir Thopas—a model which may be safely held to represent the language of the two centuries previous—is the point of appeal.   Sir Thopas is clearly a parody of the Metrical Romances.   Some of those hitherto published by Ritson, &c., are not older than Chaucer ; but some ascend much higher, and may be referred to 1200, or perhaps earlier.   Date them from 1240, and *that* places a period of six centuries complete between ourselves and them. Notwithstanding which, the greater part of the Metrical Romances, when aided by the connexion of events narrated,

---

[1] De Quincey's Chaucer datings have been superseded by recent research ; but the small discrepancy does not in the least affect his argument.—M.

or when impassioned, remain perfectly intelligible to this
hour.

> "What for labour, and what for faint,
> Sir Bevis was well nigh attaint."

This is a couplet in Bevis of Southampton ; and another I
will quote from memory in the romance of "Sir Gawaine
and Sir Ywaine."   In a vast forest, Sir Gawaine, by striking
a magical shield suspended to a tree, had caused a dreadful
storm to succeed ; which, subsiding, is followed by the
gloomy apparition of a mailed knight, who claims the forest
for his own, taxes Sir Gawaine with having intruded on his
domain, and concludes a tissue of complaints with saying
that he (Sir Gawaine) had

> "With weathers wakened him of rest,
> And done him wrong in his forést."

Now, these two casual recollections well and fairly represent
the general current of the language ; not certainly what
would now be written, but what is luminously intelligible
from the context.   At present, for instance, *faint* is an
adjective ; but the context, and the corresponding word *labour*,
easily teach the reader that it here means *faintness*.   So,
again, "weather" is not now used for storms ; but it is so
used by a writer as late as Lord Bacon, and yet survives in
such words as "weather-beaten," "weather-stained."
    Now, I say that the interval of time between these
romances and ourselves is greater than between Homer and
the age of Pericles.   I say, also, that the constant succession
of metrical writers connecting the time of Homer with that
of Pericles,—such as the authors of the "Nostoi" (or Memorable Returns homeward from Troy), of the "Cypria," of the
many Cyclical poems, next of the Lyric poets, a list closing
with Pindar, in immediate succession to whom, and through
most of his life strictly a contemporary with Pindar, comes
Æschylus, close upon whose heels follow the whole cluster of
dramatic poets who glorified the life of Pericles—this
apparently *continuous* series of verse-writers, without the
interposition of a single prose-writer, would inevitably have
the effect of keeping alive the poetic forms and choice of

words, in a degree not so reasonably to be expected under any interrupted succession. Our Chaucer died an old man, about seventy, in the year 1400; that is, in the *closing* year of the fourteenth century. The next century—that is, the fifteenth—was occupied in much of its latter half by the Civil Wars of the two Roses, which threw back the development of the English Literature, and tended to disturb the fluent transmission of Chaucer's and Gower's diction. The tumultuous century which came next—viz. the sixteenth, the former half of which was filled with the Reformation—caused a prodigious fermentation and expansion of the English intellect. But such convulsions are very unfavourable to the steady conservation of language, and of everything else depending upon usage. Now, in Grecian history, there are no corresponding agitations of society; the currents of tradition seem to flow downwards without meeting anything to ripple their surface. It is true that the great Persian War *did* agitate Greece profoundly; and, by combining the Greeks from every quarter in large masses, this memorable war must have given a powerful shock to the stagnant ideas inherited from antiquity. But, as this respects Homer, observe how thoroughly its operation is defeated: for the outrageous conflagration of Sardis by Grecian troops, which it was that provoked the invasion of Greece by the Persians under Darius, occurred about 500 B.C.; and the *final* events of the war under Xerxes — viz. Salamis, Platæa, &c. — occurred in 480 B.C. But already, by Pisistratus, whose *locus* is fifty years before the affair of Sardis, Homer had been revised and settled, and (as one might express it) stereotyped. Consequently, the chief political revolution affecting Greece collectively, if you except the Dorian migrations, &c., between Homer and Pericles, was intercepted from all possibility of affecting the Homeric diction, &c., through the seasonable authentication of the entire Homeric text under the seal and *imprimatur* of Pisistratus. Here is the old *physical* guarantee urged by Æsop's lamb *versus* wolf, that Homer's text could not have been reached by any influence, direct or oblique, from the greatest of post-Homeric political convulsions. It would be the old miracle of the Greek proverb ('Aνω ποταμων, &c.), which adopted the reflux of rivers towards their fountains as the liveliest type of the impossible.

There is also a philosophic reason why the range of diction in Chaucer should be much wider, and liable to greater changes, than that of Homer. Review those parts of Chaucer which at this day are most obscure, and it will uniformly be found that they are the *subjective* sections of his poetry; those, for instance, in which he is elaborately decomposing a character. A character is a subtle fugacious essence, which does, or does not, exist, according to the capacity of the eye which is applied to it. In Homer's age, no such meditative differences were perceived. All is *objective* in the descriptions, and external. And in those cases where the mind or its affections must be noticed, always it is by the broad distinctions of anger, fear, love, hatred, without any vestige of a sense for the more delicate interblendings or *nuances* of such qualities. But a language built upon these elementary distinctions is necessarily more durable than another, which, applying itself to the subtler phenomena of human nature, exactly in that proportion applies itself to what is capable of being variously viewed, or viewed in various combinations, as society shifts its aspects.

The result from all this is that, throughout the four hundred and forty-five years from Homer to Pisistratus, the diction even of real life would not have suffered so much alteration as in modern times it would be likely to do within some single centuries. But with respect to poetry the result is stronger.

The diction of poetry is everywhere a privileged diction; the antique or scriptural language is everywhere affected in serious or impassioned poetry. So that no call would arise for modern adaptations, until the language had grown unintelligible. Nor would *that* avail to raise such a call. The separate non-intelligibility of a word would cause no difficulty, whilst it would give the grace of antique colouring. For a word which is separately obscure is not so *in nexu*. Suppose, reader, we were to ask you the meaning of the English word *chode*, you might be a little puzzled. Yet it is an honest and once an industrious word, though now retired from business; and it stands in our authorised translation of the Bible;

where, if you had chanced to meet it *in loco*, you would easily have collected from the context that it was the past tense of *chide*.   Again, what southern reader of Sir Walter Scott's novels has failed to gather the full sense of the Scottish dialect? or what Scotchman to gather the sense of the Irish dialect, so plentifully strewed in modern tales? or what landsman to gather the sense of the marine dialect in our nautical novels?   Or—which is a case often of more trying effort—which of us Britishers has been repelled by the anomalous dialect of Mrs. Beecher Stowe (with its *sorter, kinder*, &c.) from working through the jungles of " Uncle Tom " ?   In all such cases, the passion, the animation and movement of the feeling, very often the logic, as they arise from the context, carry you fluently along with the meaning, though many of the words, taken separately and detached from this context, might have been unintelligible.

Equating, therefore, the sleeping state of early Greece with the stirring progress of modern Christian lands, I come to this conclusion : that Homer, the genuine unaltered Homer, would not, by all likelihood, be more archaic in his colouring of style to the age of Solon, or even of Pericles, than the " Froissart " of Lord Berners is to ourselves.   That is, I equate four hundred and forty-five early Greek years with the last three hundred and twenty English years.   But I will concede something more.   The common English translation of the long prose romance called " Mort d'Arthur " was composed, I believe, about the year 1480.[1]   This will, therefore, be three hundred and sixty years old.   Now, both Lord Berners[2] and the " Mort d'Arthur " are as intelligible as this morning's newspaper in June 1841.   And one proof that they are so is that both works have been reprinted *verbatim et literatim* in this generation for popular use.   Something venerable and solemn there is in both these works,—as again in the " Paston Letters," [3] which are hard upon four hundred

---

[1] Sir Thomas Malory completed his compilation or composition of the *Morte d'Arthur* in 1470, and it was published by Caxton in 1485.—M.

[2] Lord Berners, the translator of Froissart, 1474-1582.—M.

[3] The *Paston Letters*, a collection of letters, ranging in date from about 1450 to 1509, preserved among the papers of an old Norfolkshire family, were published in successive volumes between 1787 and 1823,

years old,—but no shadow of retarding difficulty to the least practised of modern readers.

B.—HOMER'S LEXIS

Now, reader, having stated, by known English examples, what effect was reasonably to have been anticipated from age, let us next inquire what effect has in fact taken place. Observe the monstrous dishonesty of these German critics. What if a man should argue thus : "This helmet never can have descended from Mambrino ; for, if it had, there would have been weather-stains, cracks, dents of swords," &c. To which it is replied :—"Doubtless ; but have you looked to see if there are *not* such marks of antiquity ?" Would you not think the disparager of the helmet worthy of the tread-mill, if it should turn out that he had never troubled himself to examine it ? These Germans argue *a priori* that, upon certain natural causes, there would arise a temptation to the Homeric chanters for adapting the diction to their audience. Conditionally I grant this—that is, if a deep night of darkness fell suddenly upon the language. But my answer is that this condition never would be realised ; and that a solemnising twilight is the very utmost which could ever steal over Homer's diction. Meantime, where is the sense of calculating *a priori* what would be *likely* to happen, when, by simply opening a book, we can see what *has* happened ? These Germans talk as if the Homer we now have spoke exactly such Greek as Euripides and Sophocles, or, if some slight differences are admitted, as though these were really too inconsiderable to meet the known operation of chance and change through four and a-half centuries. To hear *them*, you must suppose that Homer differed little more from the golden writers of Greece than as Pope's diction differs from that of 1841. Who now says *writ* for *wrote* and for *written?* Who says *'tis* and *'twas* since Queen Anne's reign ? There are not twelve consecutive lines in Pope, Swift, Addison, which will not be found marked by such slight peculiarities of their age. Yet their general agreement

and are now most completely accessible, to the number of over 500, in Mr. James Gairdner's edition of 1872-5.—M.

with ourselves is so striking that the difficulty is to detect the differences. Now, if Homer were in that condition relatively to the age of Pericles—were it even that he exhibited no more sombre hues than those which Æschylus exhibits, as compared with his younger brothers of the drama —I should grant at once that a case is made out, calling for some explanation. There has been a change ; there is something to account for. Somebody has been "doctoring" this man, would be the inference. But how stands the truth ? Why, reader, the Homeric *lexis* is so thoroughly peculiar and individual that it requires a separate lexicon ; and, if all men do not use a separate lexicon, it is only because that particular vocabulary has been digested into the series of general vocabularies. Pierce Plowman [1] is not more unlike in diction to Sir Walter Scott than is Homer to Euripides. And, instead of simply accounting for the time elapsed, and fairly answering to the reasonable attrition of that time, the Homeric diction is sufficient to account for three such spaces. What would the infidels have ? Homer, they say, is an old —old—very old man, whose trembling limbs have borne him to your door ; and, therefore—what ? Why, he ought to look very old indeed. Well, good men, he *does* look very old indeed. He ought, they say, to be covered with lichens and ivy. Well, he *is* covered with lichens and ivy. And sure I am that few people will undertake to know how a man looks when he is five hundred years old by comparison with himself at four hundred. Suffice it here to say, for the benefit of the unlearned, that not one of our own earliest writers, hardly Thomas of Ercildoune, [2] has more of peculiar antique words in his vocabulary than Homer.

C.—Homer's Metre

In this case the Germans themselves admit the extraordinary character of the Homeric *rhythmus*. "How free, how spirited in its motion !" they all exclaim ; "how charac-

---

[1] William Langland, the author of the *Piers Plowman* visions, lived from about 1332 to about 1400.—M.

[2] Thomas of Ercildoune, alias Thomas the Rhymer, reputed author of the metrical romance *Sir Tristrem*, died about 1299.—M.

teristically his own !" Well, now, did the father of sophisms ever hear of such stuff as this, when you connect it with what these Germans say elsewhere ? As well might a woman say that you had broken her china cups, but that you had artfully contrived to preserve the original Chinese designs. How could you preserve the form or surface, if you destroy the substance ? And, if these imaginary adapters of Homer, according to the German pretence, modernised his whole diction, how could they preserve his metrical effects ? With the peculiar word or idiom would vanish the peculiar prosody. Even a single word is not easily replaced by another having the same sense, the same number of syllables, and in each syllable the same metrical quantity ; but how immeasurably more difficult is this when the requisition is for a whole sentence or clause having the same sense in the same number of syllables and the same prosody ? Why, a man would not doctor three lines in a century under such intolerable conditions. And, at the end of his labour, like Addison's small poet, who worked for years upon the name of " Mary Bohun," whom he was courting, in order to bind its stubborn letters within the hoop-ring of an anagram, he would fail, and would go mad into the bargain, upon finding that the colloquial pronunciation of the name (viz. *Boon*) had misled him in his spelling. If the metre is characteristically Homeric, as say these infidels, then is the present text (so inextricably coadunated with the metre), upon their own showing, the good old Homeric text—and no mistake.

But, reader, the Homeric metre is not truly described by these men. It is certainly *kenspeck*, to use a good old English word—that is to say, recognisable ; you challenge it for Homer's whenever you meet it. Characteristic it is, but not exactly for the reason they assign. The fact is, though flowing and lively, it betrays the immaturity of the metrical art. Those constraints from which the Germans praise its freedom are the constraints of exquisite art—art of a kind unknown to the simple Homer. This is a difficult subject ; for, in our own literature, the true science of metrical effects has not belonged to our later poets, but to the elder. Spenser, Shakspere, Milton, are the great masters of exquisite versification. And Waller, who was idly reputed to have refined our metre, was a mere trickster, having a single tune moving in his imagination, without compass and without variety. Chaucer, also, whom Dryden in this point so thoroughly misunderstood, was undoubtedly a most elaborate master of metre, as will appear when we have a *really* good edition of him. But in the Pagan literature this was otherwise. We see in the Roman poets that, precisely as they were antique, they were careless, or at least very inartificial in the management of their metre. Thus Lucilius, Ennius, even Lucretius, leave a class of faults in their verse from which Virgil would have revolted.[1] And the very same class of faults is found in Homer. But, though faults as regards severe art, they are in the very spirit of *naiveté* or picturesque naturalness, and wear the stamp of a primitive age—artless and inexperienced.

This article would require a volume. But I will content myself with one illustration. Every scholar is aware of the miserable effect produced where there is no *cæsura*, in that sense of the word *cæsura* which means the interlocking of the several feet into the several words. Thus, imagine a line like this :—

"Urbem Romam primo condit Romulus anno.'

Here the six feet of the hexameter are separately made out by six several words. Each word is a foot ; and no foot interlocks into another. So that there is no *cæsura*. Yet even *that* is not the worst fault of the line. The other and more destructive is—the coincidence of the *ictus*, or emphasis, with the first syllable of every foot. Now, in Homer we see both faults repeatedly. Thus, to express the thundering pace with which a heavy stone comes trundling back from a hill-top, he says,

"Autis epeita pedónde kulindeto laäs anaides."

Here there is the shocking fault, to any metrical ear, of making the emphasis fall regularly on the first syllable, which in effect obliterates all the benefit of the cæsura. Now, Virgil, in an age of refinement, has not one such line, nor

---

[1] Ennius, B.C. 239-169 ; Lucilius, B.C. 148-103 ; Lucretius, B.C 95-55 ; Virgil, B.C. 70-19.—M.

could have endured such a line. In that verse, expressing the gallop of a horse, he also has five dactyles :

"Quadrupedante putrem sonitu quatit ungula campum."

But he takes care to distribute the accents properly,—on which so much even of the ancient versification depended : except in the two last feet, the emphasis of Virgil's line never coincides with the first syllable of the foot. Homer, it will be said, wished to express mimetically the rolling, thundering, leaping motion of the stone. True ; but so did Virgil wish to express the thundering gallop of the horse, in which the beats of the hoofs return with regular intervals. Each sought for a picturesque effect ; each adopted a dactylic structure : but to any man who has studied this subject I need not say that picturesqueness, like any other effect, must be subordinated to a higher law of beauty. Whence, indeed, it is that the very limits of imitation arise from every art,— sculpture, painting, &c.,—indicating what it ought to imitate, and what it ought not to imitate. And, unless regard is had to such higher restraints, metrical effects become as silly and childish as the musical effects in Kotzwarra's " Battle of Prague," with its ridiculous attempts to mimic the firing of cannon, groans of the wounded, &c., instead of involving the passion of a battle in the agitation of the music.

These rudenesses of art, however, are generally found in its early stages. And I am satisfied that, as art advanced, these defects must have been felt for such ; so that, had any licence of improvement existed,—which is what the Germans pretend,—they would have been removed. That they were left untouched in the ages of the great lyrical masters, when metre was so scientifically understood, is a strong argument that Homer was sacred from all tampering. Over the whole field of the Homeric versification, both for its quality of faults and its quality of merits, lies diffused this capital truth—that no opening existed for the correction of any fault in any age after the perception of that fault—(that is, no opening to correction when the temptation to correct could first have arisen).

D.—The Homeric Formulæ

Here is another countersign for the validity of our present Homeric text. In our own metrical romances, or wherever a poem is meant not for readers but for chanters and oral reciters, these *formulæ*, to meet the same recurring cases, exist by scores. Thus every woman in these metrical romances who happens to be young, is described as "so bright of blé," or complexion; always a man goes "the mountenance of a mile" before he overtakes or is overtaken. And so on through a vast bead-roll of cases. In the same spirit Homer has his eternal τον δ' αρ' ὑποδρα ιδων, or επεα πτεροεντα προσηυδα, or τον δ' απαμειβομενος προσεφη, &c. Now, these again, under any refining spirit of criticism at liberty to act freely, are characteristics that would have disappeared. Not that they are faults: on the contrary, to a reader of sensibility, such recurrences wear an aspect of childlike simplicity, beautifully recalling the features of Homer's primitive age. But they would have appeared faults to all commonplace critics in literary ages.

I say, therefore, that, first, the Diction of the "Iliad" (B); secondly, the Metre of the "Iliad" (C); thirdly, the Formulæ and recurring Clauses of the "Iliad" (D)—all present us with so many separate guarantees for good faith—so many separate attestations to the purity of the Homeric text from any considerable interference. For every one of these would have given way to the "Adapters," had any such people operated upon Homer.

2. The first class of arguments, therefore, for the sanity of the existing Homer is derived from language. A second argument I derive from THE IDEALITY OF ACHILLES. This I owe to a suggestion of Wordsworth's. Once, when I observed to him that of imagination, in his own sense, I saw no instance in the "Iliad," he replied, "Yes; there is the character of Achilles; this is imaginative, in the same sense as Ariosto's Angelica." *Character* is not properly the word, nor was it what Wordsworth meant. It is an idealised conception. The excessive beauty of Angelica, for instance, in the "Orlando Furioso," robs the paladins of their wits; draws

anchorites into guilt ; tempts the baptized into mortal feud ; summons the unbaptized to war ; brings nations together from the ends of the earth. And so, with different but analogous effects, the very perfection of courage, beauty, strength, speed, skill of eye, of voice, and all personal accomplishments, are embodied in the son of Peleus. He has the same supremacy in modes of courtesy, and doubtless, according to the poet's conception, in virtue. In fact, the astonishing blunder which Horace made in deciphering this Homeric portrait gives the best memorandum for recalling the real points of his most self-commanding character :

> "Impiger, iracundus, inexorabilis, acer,
> Jura negat sibi nata, nihil non arrogat armis."

Was that man "iracundus" who, in the very opening of the "Iliad," makes his anger, under the most brutal insult, bend to the public welfare? When two people quarrel, it is too commonly the unfair award of careless bystanders that "one is as bad as the other" ; whilst generally it happens that one of the parties is but the respondent in a quarrel originated by the other. I never witnessed a quarrel in my life where the fault was equally divided between the parties. Homer says of the two chiefs, διαστητην ερισαντε, they stood aloof in feud ; but what was the nature of the feud? Agamemnon had inflicted upon Achilles, himself a king, and the most brilliant chieftain of the confederate army, the very foulest outrage (matter and manner) that can be imagined. Because his own brutality to a priest of Apollo had caused a pestilence, and he finds that he must resign this priest's daughter, he declares that he will indemnify himself by seizing a female captive from the tents of Achilles. Why of Achilles more than of any other man? Colour of right, or any relation between his loss and his redress, this brutal Agamemnon does not offer by pretence. But he actually executes his threat. Nor does he *ever* atone for it ; since his returning Briseis, without disavowing his right to have seized her, is wide of the whole point at issue. Now, under what show of common sense can that man be called *iracundus* who calmly submits to such an indignity as this? Or is that man *inexorabilis* who sacrifices to the tears and grey hairs of Priam his own meditated revenge, giving back the body of the enemy who had robbed him of his dearest friend ?   Or is there any gleam of truth in saying that *jura negat sibi nata* when, of all the heroes in the "Iliad," he is the most punctiliously courteous, the most ceremonious in his religious observances, and the one who most cultivated the arts of peace ?   Or is that man the violent defier of all law and religion who submits with so pathetic a resignation to the doom of early death ?

> "Enough, I know my fate—to die ; to see no more
> My much-loved parents, or my native shore."

Charles XII of Sweden threatened to tickle that man who had libelled his hero Alexander.   But Alexander himself would have tickled Master Horace for this infernal libel on Achilles, if they had happened to be contemporaries.   I have a love for Horace ; but my wrath has always burned furiously against him for his horrible perversion of the truth in this well-known tissue of calumnies.

The character, in short, of the matchless Pelides has an ideal finish and a divinity about it which argue that it never could have been a fiction or a gradual accumulation from successive touches.   It was raised by a single flash of creative imagination ; it was a reality seen through the harmonising abstractions of two centuries[1] ; and it is in itself a great unity, which penetrates every section where it comes forward with an identification of these several parts as the work of one man.

3. Another powerful guarantee of the absolute integrity which belongs to the "Iliad" lies in the Ionic forms of language, combined everywhere (as Plato remarks) with Ionic forms of life.   Homer had seen the modes of Dorian life, as in many cities of Crete.   But his heart turned habitually to the Ionian life of his infancy.   Here the man who builds on pretences of recasting, &c., will find himself in this dilemma. If, in order to account for the poem still retaining its Ionic dress, which must have been affected by any serious attempts

---

[1] "*Two centuries*" :—*i.e* the supposed interval between Troy and Homer.

at modernising it, he should argue that the Ionic dialect, though not used on the continent, continued to be perfectly intelligible, then, my good sir, what call for recasting it? Nobody supposes that an antique form of language would be objectionable *per se*, or that it would be other than solemn and religious in its effect, so long as it continued to be intelligible. On the other hand, if he argues that it must gradually have grown unintelligible or less intelligible (for that the Ionic of Herodotus, in the age of Pericles, was very different from the Homeric), in that case to *whom* would it be unintelligible? Why, to the Athenians, for example, or to some people of continental Greece. But, on that supposition, it would have been exchanged for some form of Attic or other continental Greek. To be Ionian by descent did not imply the use of a dialect formed in Asia Minor. And not only would heterogeneous forms of language have thus crept into the "Iliad," but inevitably, in making these changes, other heterogeneities in the substance would have crept in concurrently. That purity and sincerity of Ionic life which arrested the eye of Plato would have melted away under such modern adulterations.

4. But another argument against the possibility of such recasts is founded upon a known remarkable fact. It is a fact of history, coming down to us from several quarters, that the people of Athens were exceedingly discontented with the slight notice taken of themselves in the "Iliad." Now, observe, already this slight notice is in itself one argument of Homer's antiquity; and the Athenians did wrong to murmur at so many petty towns of the Peloponnesus being glorified while in *their* case Homer only gives one line or so to Menestheus their chief. Let them be thankful for getting anything. Homer knew what Athens was in those days much better than any of us; and surely Glasgow or Liverpool could not complain of being left out of the play in a poem on the Crusades. But there was another case that annoyed the Athenians equally. Theseus, it is well known, was a great scamp; in fact, a very bad fellow indeed. You need go no further than Ariadne (who, by most traditions, hanged herself in her garters at Naxos) to prove *that*. Now, Homer, who was determined to tell no

lies in the matter, roundly blurts out the motive of Theseus for his base desertion of Ariadne, which had the double guilt of cruelty and of ingratitude, as in Jason's conduct towards Medea. It was, says the honest bard, because he was desperately in love with Ægle. This line in Homer was like a coroner's verdict on Ariadne—*died by the visitation of Theseus.* It was impossible to hide this act of the national hero, if the line were suffered to stand. An attempt was therefore made to eject it. Pisistratus is charged, in this one instance, with having smuggled in a single forged line. But, even in his own lifetime, it was dismally suspected ; and, when Pisistratus saw men looking askance at it, he would say, " Well, sir, what's in the wind now ? What are you squinting at ? " Upon which the man would answer, " Oh, nothing, sir ; I was only looking at things in general." But Pisistratus knew better : it was no go—*that* he saw ; and the line is obelised to this day. Now, where Athens failed, is it conceivable that anybody else would succeed ?

5. A fifth argument, upon which we rely much, is the CIRCUMSTANTIALITY of the " Iliad." Let the reader pause to consider what *that* means in this particular case. The invention of little personal circumstances and details is now a well-known artifice of novelists. We see, even in our oldest metrical romances, a tendency to this mode of giving a lively expression to the characters, as well as of giving a colourable reality to the tale. Yet, even with us, it is an art that has never but once been successfully applied to regular history. De Foe is the only author known who has so plausibly circumstantiated his false historical records as to make them pass for genuine, even with literary men and critics. In his " Memoirs of a Cavalier," one of his poorest forgeries, he assumes the character of a soldier who had fought under Gustavus Adolphus (1628-31), and afterwards (1642-45) in our own Parliamentary War ; in fact, he corresponds chronologically to Captain Dalgetty. In other works he personates a sea - captain, a hosier, a runaway apprentice, an officer under Lord Peterborough in his Catalonian expedition. In this last character he imposed upon Dr. Johnson ; and, by men better read in History than Dr. Johnson, he has actually been quoted as a regular historical

authority. How did he accomplish so difficult an end? Simply by inventing such little circumstantiations of any character or incident as seem, by their apparent inertness of effect, to verify themselves; for, where the reader is told that such a person was the posthumous son of a tanner, that his mother married afterwards a Presbyterian schoolmaster, who gave him a smattering of Latin, but, the schoolmaster dying of the plague, that he was compelled at sixteen to enlist for bread — in all this, as there is nothing at all amusing, we conclude that the author could have no reason to detain us with such particulars but simply because they were true. To invent, when nothing at all is gained by inventing, there seems no imaginable temptation. It never occurs to us that this very construction of the case, this very inference from such neutral details, was precisely the object which De Foe had in view—was the very thing which he counted on, and by which he meant to profit. He thus gains the opportunity of impressing upon his tales a double character: he makes them so amusing that girls read them for novels; and he gives them such an air of verisimilitude that men read them for histories.

Now, this is one amongst the many arts by which, in comparison of the ancients, we have so prodigiously extended the compass of literature. In Grecian, or even in Roman literature, no dream ever arose of interweaving a fictitious interest with a true one. Nor was the possibility then recognised of any interest founded in fiction, even though kept apart from historic records. Look at Statius; look at Virgil; look at Valerius Flaccus; or look at the entire Greek drama: not one incident beyond the mere descriptive circumstances of a battle, or a storm, or a funeral solemnity, with the ordinary turns of skill or chance in the games which succeed, can be looked upon as matter of invention. All rested upon actual tradition:—in the "Æneid," for instance, upon ancient Italian traditions still lingering amongst a most ignorant people; in the "Thebaid," where the antiquity of the story is too great to allow of this explanation, doubtless they were found in Grecian poems. Four centuries after the Christian era,—if the "Satyricon" of Petronius Arbiter is excepted, and a few sketches of

Lucian,[1]—we find the first feeble tentative development of
the romance interest. The "Cyropædia" was not so much
a romance as simply one-sided in its information. But in
the "Iliad" we meet with many of these little individual
circumstances, which can be explained (consistently with the
remark here made) upon no principle whatever except that
of downright notorious truth. Homer could not have
wandered so far astray from the universal sympathies of
his country as ever to think of fictions so useless ; and,
if he had, he would soon have been recalled to the truth by
disagreeable experiences ; for the construction would have
been that he was a person very ill informed, and not trustworthy through ignorance.

Thus, in speaking of Polydamas, Homer says ("Iliad"
xviii. 250) that he and Hector were old cronies ; which might
strike the reader as odd, since Polydamas was no fighting
man at all, but cultivated the arts of peace. Partly, therefore,
by way of explaining their connexion—partly for the simple
reason that doubtless it was a fact—Homer adds that they
were both born in the same night ; a circumstance which is
known to have had considerable weight upon early friendships
in the houses of oriental princes.

" Ἑκτορι δ' ην ἑταιρος, ιη δ' εν νυκτι γενοντο."

"To Hector he was a bosom friend,
For in one night they were born."

I argue, therefore, that, had Homer not lived within a reasonable number of generations after Troy, he never would have
learned a little fact of this kind. He heard it perhaps from
his nurse, good old creature, who again had heard it from
her grandfather when talking with emotion of Troy and its
glorious palaces, and of the noble line of princes that perished
in its final catastrophe. A ray of that great sunset had still
lingered in the old man's imagination ; and the deep impression of so memorable a tragedy had carried into popular
remembrance vast numbers of specialties and circumstanti-
alities, such as might now be picked out of the "Iliad," that
could have no attraction for the mind but simply under the
one condition that they were true. An interval as great as

<hr>

[1] Petronius Arbiter. d. A.D. 66 ; Lucian, about A.D. 200.—M.

four centuries, when all relation between the house of Priam
and the surrounding population must have been obliterated,
would cause such petty anecdotes to lose their entire interest;
and, in that case, they would never have reached Homer.
Here, therefore, is a collateral indication that Homer lived
probably within two centuries of Troy.   On the other hand,
if the "Iliad" had ever become so obsolete in its diction
that popular feeling called for a *diaskeué*, or thorough recast,
in that case I argue that all such trivial circumstances
(interesting only to those who happened to know them for
facts) would have dropped out of the composition.

6. That argument is of a nature to yield me an extensive
field, if I had space to pursue its cultivation.   The following
argument is negative, but far from unimportant.   It lies in
the absence of all anachronisms, which would most certainly
have arisen in any modern remodelling, and which do in fact
disfigure all the Greek forgeries of letters, &c., in Alexandrian
ages.   How inevitable, amongst a people so thoroughly uncritical as the Greeks, would have been the introduction of
anachronisms by wholesale, had a more modern hand been
allowed to tamper with the texture of the poem!   But, on
the contrary, all inventions, rights, usages, known to have
been of later origin than the Homeric ages are absent from
the "Iliad."   For instance, in any recast subsequent to the
era of 700 B.C., how natural it would have been (as has been
more than once remarked) to introduce the trumpet!   Yet
this is absent from the "Iliad."   Cavalry, again, how
excellent a resource for varying and inspiriting the battles;
yet Homer introduces horses only as attached to the chariots,
and the chariots as used only by a few leading heroes, whose
heavy mail made it impossible for *them* to go on foot, as the
mass of the army did.   Why, then, did Homer himself forbear
to introduce cavalry?   Was he blind to the variety he would
have gained for his descriptive scenes?   No; but simply
upon the principle (so absolute for *him*) of adhering to the
facts.   But what caused the fact?   Why was there no
cavalry?   Evidently from the enormous difficulty of carrying
any number of horses by sea, under the universal non-adapta-
tion to such a purpose of the Greek shipping.   To form a
cavalry, a man must begin by horse-stealing.   The "horse

marines" had not begun to show out ; and a proper "troop-ship" must have been as little known to Agamemnon as Havanna cigars, or as duelling pistols to Menelaus.

7. A seventh argument for the integrity of our present "Iliad," in its main section, lies in the *nexus* of its subordinate parts. Every canto in this main section implies every other. Thus the funeral of Hector implies that his body had been ransomed. That fact implies the whole journey of Priam to the tents of Achilles. This journey, so fatiguing to the aged king, and in the compulsory absence of his body-guards so alarming to a feeble old prince, implies the death and capture of Hector. For no calamity less than *that* could have prompted such an extreme step as a suppliant and perilous pilgrimage to the capital enemy of his house and throne. But how should Hector and Achilles have met in battle after the wrathful vow of Achilles ? That argues the death of Patroclus as furnishing the sufficient motive. But the death of Patroclus argues the death of Sarpedon, the Trojan ally, which it was that roused the vindictive fury of Hector. These events in their turn argue the previous success of the Trojans, which had moved Patroclus to interfere. And this success of the Trojans argues the absence of Achilles, which again argues the feud with Agamemnon. The whole of this story unfolds like a process of vegetation. And the close intertexture of the several parts is as strong a proof of unity in the design and execution as the intense life and consistency in the conception of Achilles.

8. By an eighth argument, I meet the objection sometimes made to the transmission of the "Iliad" through the *rhapsodoi* from the burden which so long a poem would have imposed upon the memory. Some years ago I published a paper on the Flight of the Kalmuck Tartars from Russia. Bergmann, the German from whom that account was chiefly drawn, resided for a long time amongst the Kalmucks, and had frequent opportunities of hearing musical recitations selected from the "Dschangæriade." This is the great Tartar epic ; and it extends to three hundred and sixty cantos, each averaging the length of a Homeric book. Now, it was an ordinary effort for a Tartar minstrel to master a score of these cantos ; which amounts pretty nearly to the length of

the "Iliad." But a case more entirely in point is found in a minor work of Xenophon's. A young man is there introduced as boasting that he could repeat by heart the whole of the "Iliad" and the "Odyssey"—a feat, by the way, which has been more than once accomplished by English schoolboys.[1] But the answer made to this young man is that there is nothing at all extraordinary in that; for that every common *rhapsodos* could do as much. To me, indeed, the whole objection seems idle. The human memory is capable of far greater efforts; and the music would prodigiously lighten the effort. But, as it is an objection often started, we may consider it fortunate that we have such a passage as this in Xenophon, which not only illustrates the kind of qualification looked for in a *rhapsodos*, but shows also that such a class of people continued to practise in the generation subsequent to that of Pericles.

Upon these eight arguments I build. This is my case. They are amply sufficient for the purpose. Homer is not a person known to us separately and previously, concerning whom we are inquiring whether, in addition to what else we know of him, he did not also write the "Iliad." "Homer" means nothing else but the man who wrote the "Iliad." Somebody, you will say, must have written it. True; but, if that somebody should appear, by any probable argument, to have been a multitude of persons, there goes to wreck the unity which is essential to the idea of a Homer. Now, this unity is sufficiently secured if it should appear that a considerable section of the "Iliad"—and that section by far the most full of motion, of human interest, of tragical catastrophe, and through which runs, as the connecting principle, a character the most brilliant, magnanimous, and noble that Pagan morality could conceive—was, and must have been, the work and conception of a single mind. Achilles revolves through that section of the "Iliad" in a series of phases, each of which looks forward and backward to all the rest. He travels like the sun through his diurnal course. We see him first of all rising upon us as a princely councillor for the

<hr>

[1] In particular, by an Eton boy about the beginning of this century, known extensively as *Homeric Wright.*

welfare of the Grecian host. We see him atrociously insulted in this office ; yet still, though a king, and unused to opposition, and boiling with youthful blood, nevertheless controlling his passion, and retiring in clouded majesty. Even thus, though having now so excellent a plea for leaving the army, and though aware of the early death that awaited him if he staid, he disdains to profit by the evasion. We see him still living in the tented field, and generously unable to desert those who had so insultingly deserted *him*. We see him in a dignified retirement, fulfilling all the duties of religion, friendship, hospitality ; and, like an accomplished man of taste, cultivating the arts of peace. We see him so far surrendering his wrath to the earnest persuasion of friendship that he comes forth at a critical moment for the Greeks to save them from ruin. What are his arms ? He has none at all. Simply by his voice he changes the face of the battle. He shouts and nations fly from the sound. Never but once again is such a shout recorded by a poet—

> "He called so loud that all the hollow deep
> Of Hell resounded."

Who called ? *That* shout was the shout of an archangel. Next we see him reluctantly allowing his dearest friend to assume his own arms ; the kindness and the modesty of his nature forbidding him to suggest that not the divine weapons, but the immortal arm of the wielder, had made them invincible. His friend perishes. Then we see him rise in his noontide wrath, before which no life could stand. The frenzy of his grief makes him for a time cruel and implacable. He sweeps the field of battle like a monsoon. His revenge descends perfect, sudden, like a curse from heaven. We now recognise the goddess-born. This is his avatar—the incarnate descent of his wrath. Had he moved to battle under the ordinary impulses of Ajax, Diomed, and the other heroes, we never could have sympathised or gone along with so withering a course. We should have viewed him as a "scourge of God," or fiend, born for the tears of wives and the maledictions of mothers. But the poet, before he would let him loose upon men, creates for him a sufficient, or at least palliating, motive. In the sternest of his acts we read only the anguish of his grief. This is surely the perfection of art. At length the work of destruction is finished ; but, if the poet leaves him at this point, there would be a want of repose, and we should be left with a painful impression of his hero as forgetting the earlier humanities of his nature, and brought forward only for final exhibition in his terrific phases. Now, therefore, by machinery the most natural, we see this paramount hero travelling back within our gentler sympathies, and revolving to his rest like the vesper sun disrobed of his blazing terrors. We see him settling down to that humane and princely character in which he had been first exhibited ; we see him relenting at the sight of Priam's grey hairs, touched with the sense of human calamity, and once again mastering his passion (grief now), as formerly he had mastered his wrath. He consents that his feud shall sleep ; he surrenders the corpse of his capital enemy ; and the last farewell chords of the poem rise with a solemn intonation from the grave of " Hector, the tamer of horses " —that noble soldier who had so long been the column of his country, and to whom, in his dying moments, the stern Achilles had declared (but then in the middle career of his grief) that no honourable burial should ever be granted.

Such is the outline of an Achilleis, as it might be gathered from the " Iliad "; and, for the use of schools, I am surprised that such a beautiful whole has not long since been extracted. A tale more affecting by its story and vicissitudes does not exist ; and, after this, who cares in what order the *non-essential* parts of the poem may be arranged, or whether Homer was their author ? It is sufficient that one mind must have executed this Achilleis, in consequence of its intense unity. Every part implies every other part. With such a model before him as this poem on the wrath of Achilles, Aristotle could not carry his notions of unity too high. And the unifying mind which could conceive and execute this Achilleis—that is what we mean by Homer. As well might it be said that the parabola described by a cannon-ball was in one half due to a first discharge, and in the other half to a second, as that one poet could lay the preparations for the passion and sweep of such a poem, whilst another conducted it to a close. Creation does not proceed by instalments : the steps of its revolution are not successive, but simultaneous ; and the last book of the Achilleis was undoubtedly conceived in the same moment as the first.

What effect such an Achilleis, abstracted from the " Iliad," would probably leave upon the mind, it happens that I can measure by my own childish experience. In Russell's " Ancient Europe," a book much used in the last century, there is an abstract of the " Iliad," which presents very nearly the outline of an Achilleis such as I have sketched. The heroes are made to speak in a sort of stilted, or at least buskined language, not unsuited to a youthful taste ; and, from the close convergement of the separate parts, the interest is condensed. This book in my eighth year I read. It was my first introduction to the " Tale of Troy divine " ; and I do not deceive myself in saying that this memorable experience drew from me the first tears that ever I owed to a book, and, by the stings of grief which it left behind, demonstrated its own natural pathos.

Whether the same mind conceived also the " Odyssey " is a separate question. I am myself strongly inclined to believe that the " Odyssey " belongs to a post-Homeric generation—to the generation of the *Nostoi*, or homeward voyages of the several Grecian chiefs. And, with respect to all the burlesque or satiric poems ascribed to Homer, such as the " Batrachomyo-machia," the " Margites," &c., the whole fiction seems to have arisen out of an uncritical blunder : they had been classed as Homeric poems—meaning by the word " Homeric," simply that they had a relation or reference to objects in which Homer was interested ; which they certainly have. At least we may say this of the " Batrachomyomachia," which still survives, —that it undoubtedly points to the " Iliad," as a mock-heroic parody upon its majestic forms and diction. In that sense it is Homeric—*i.e.* it relates to Homer's poetry ; it presupposes it as the basis of its own fun. But subsequent generations, careless and uncritical, understood the word Homeric to mean actually composed by Homer. How impossible this was the reader may easily imagine to himself by the parallel case of our own parodies on Scripture. What opening for a parody could have arisen in the same age as that scriptural translation ? " Howbeit," " peradventure," "lifted up his voice and wept," "found favour in thy sight"—phrases such as these have, to our modern feelings, a deep colouring of antiquity; placed, therefore, in juxtaposition with modern words or modern ideas, they produce a sense of contrast which is strongly connected with the ludicrous. But nothing of this result could possibly exist for those who first used these phrases in translation. The words were such as, in their own age, ranked as classical and proper. These were no more liable to associations of the ludicrous than the serious style of our own age is at this moment. And on the same principle, in order to suppose the language of the "Iliad,"—as, for example, the solemn *formulæ* which introduce all the replies and rejoinders,—open to the ludicrous, they must, first of all, have had time to assume the sombre hues of antiquity. But even that is not enough: the "Iliad" must previously have become so popular that a man might count with certainty upon his own ludicrous travesties as applying themselves at once to a serious model radicated in the universal feeling. Otherwise, to express the case mechanically, there is no resistance, and consequently no possibility of a rebound. Hence it is certain that the burlesques of the "Iliad" could not be Homeric, in the sense which an unlearned Grecian public imagined; and, as to the satiric poem of the "Margites," it is contrary to all the tendencies of human nature that a public sensibility to satire should exist until the simple age of Homer had been supplanted by an age of large cities, and a complex state of social refinement. Thus far I abjure, as monstrous moral anachronisms, the parodies and lampoons attributed to Homer. But, finally, as regards the "Iliad," I hold that its noblest section has a perfect and separate unity; that so far, therefore, it was written by one man; that it was also written a thousand years before our Christian era; and that it has not been essentially altered. These are the elements which make up my compound meaning when I assert the existence of Homer in any sense interesting to modern ages. And for the affirmation of that question in that interesting sense I presume myself to have offered perhaps more and weightier arguments than all which any German army of infidels has yet been able to muster against it.

In the paper *On Homer and the Homeridæ* it will be observed that I have uniformly assumed the chronologic date of Homer as 1000 years B.C. Among the reasons for this some are so transcendent that it would not have been worth while to detain the reader upon minute grounds of approximation to that date. One ground is sufficient: Lycurgus, the Spartan lawgiver, seems accurately placed about 800 years B.C. Now, if at that era Lycurgus naturalises the "Iliad" as a great educational power in Sparta (led to this, no doubt, by gratitude for Homer's glorification of so many cities in the Peloponnesus), then—because one main reason for this must have been the venerable antiquity of Homer—it is impossible to assign him less *at that time* than 200 years of duration. An antiquity that was already venerable in the year 800 B.C. would argue, at the very least, a natal origin for the poet (if not for the poem) of 1000 B.C.

A second explanation is due to the reader upon another point: I have repeatedly spoken of "*publication*" as an incident to which literary works were, or might be, liable in the times of Solon and Pisistratus; that is, in times that ranged between 500 and 600 years B.C. But, as very many readers — especially female readers — make no distinction between the act of *printing* and the act of *publication*, there are few who will not be perplexed by this form of expres-

[1] What is here printed as a postscript was part of De Quincey's "Preface" to the volume of his collected writings containing his reprint of the Homeric Essay.—M.

sion, as supposing that neither one nor the other was an advantage physically open in those days to any author whatever. Printing, it is true, was not; but for a very different reason from that ordinarily assigned—viz. that it had not been discovered. It *had* been discovered many times over; and many times forgotten. Paper it was, cheap paper (as many writers have noticed), that had not been discovered; which failing, the other discovery fell back constantly into oblivion. This want forced the art of printing to slumber for pretty nearly the *exact* period of 2000 years from the era of Pisistratus. But that want did not affect the power of publication. Æschylus, Sophocles, Euripides, Aristophanes, Menander, were all published, to the extent of many modern editions, on the majestic stage of Athens; published to myriads in one day; published with advantages of life-like action, noble enunciation, and impassioned music. No modern author, except Thomas à Kempis, has ever been half so well published. The Greek orators on the *Bema* were published to more than all the citizens of Athens. And, some 2000 and odd years later, in regal London, at Whitehall, the dramas of Shakspere were published effectually to two consecutive Princes of Wales, Henry and Charles, with royal apparatus of scenery and music.

PHILOSOPHY OF HERODOTUS [1]

FEW, even amongst literary people, are aware of the true
place occupied, *de facto* or *de jure*, by Herodotus in universal
literature ; scarce here and there a scholar up and down a
century is led to reflect upon the *multiplicity* of his relations
to the whole range of civilisation. We endeavour in these
words to catch, as in a net, the gross prominent faults of his
appreciation. On which account, first, we say pointedly
universal literature, not Grecian—since the primary error is
to regard Herodotus merely in relation to the literature of
Greece ; secondly, on which account we notice the circuit,
the numerical amount, of his collisions with science—because
the second and greater error is to regard him exclusively as
an historian. But now, under a juster allocation of his
rank, as the general father of prose composition, Herodotus
is nearly related to all literature whatsoever, modern not
less than ancient ; and, as the father of what may be called
ethnographical geography, as a man who speculated most
ably on all the *humanities* of science—that is, on all the
scientific questions which naturally interest our human
sensibilities in this great temple which we look up to, the
pavilion of the sky, the sun, the moon, the atmosphere, with
its climates and its winds, or in this home which we inherit,
the earth, with its hills and rivers—Herodotus ought least
of all to be classed amongst historians. *That* is but a
secondary title for *him ;* he deserves to be rated as the

---

[1] From *Blackwood's Magazine* for January 1842 : reprinted by De
Quincey, revised and with added footnotes, in 1858, in the ninth
volume of his Collected Writings.—M.

leader amongst philosophical "polyhistors"; which is the nearest designation to that of "encyclopædist" current in the Greek literature.

And yet is not this word *encyclopædist* much lower than his ancient name—*father of history?* Doubtless it is no great distinction *at present* to be an encyclopædist; which is often but another name for bookmaker, craftsman, mechanic, journeyman, in his meanest degeneration. Yet in those early days, when the timid muse of science had scarcely ventured sandal-deep into waters so unfathomable, it seems to us a great thing indeed that one solitary man should have founded an entire encyclopædia for his countrymen upon those difficult problems which challenged their primary attention, because starting forward from the very roof— the walls—the floor of that beautiful theatre which they tenanted. The habitable world, ἡ οἰκουμενη, was now daily becoming better known to the human race; but how? Chiefly through Herodotus. There are amusing evidences extant of the profound ignorance in which nations the most enlightened had hitherto lived as to all lands beyond their own and its frontier adjacencies. But within the single generation (or the single half century) previous to the birth of Herodotus vast changes had taken place. The mere revolutions consequent upon the foundation of the Persian Empire had approximated the whole world of civilisation. First came the conquest of Egypt by the second of the new emperors. This event, had it stood alone, was immeasurable in its effects for meeting curiosity, and in its immediate excitement for prompting it. It brought the whole vast chain of Persian dependencies, from the river Indus eastwards to the Nile westwards, or even through Cyrene to the gates of Carthage, under the unity of a single sceptre. The world was open. Jealous interdicts, inhospitable laws, national hostilities, always *in procinctu*, no longer fettered the feet of the merchant, or neutralized the exploring instincts of the philosophic traveller. Next came the restoration of the Jewish people. Judea, no longer weeping by the Euphrates, was again sitting for another half millennium of divine probation under her ancient palm-tree. Next after that came the convulsions of Greece,

earthquake upon earthquake; the trampling myriads of
Darius, but six years before the birth of Herodotus; the
river-draining millions of Xerxes in the fifth year of his
wandering infancy. Whilst the swell from this great storm
was yet angry and hardly subsiding (a metaphor used by
Herodotus himself, ἔτι οἰδεόντων πρηγματων), whilst the
scars of Greece were yet raw from the Persian scimitar, her
towns and temples to the east of the Corinthian isthmus
smouldering ruins yet reeking from the Persian torch, the
young Herodotus had wandered forth in a rapture of impassioned curiosity to see, to touch, to measure, all those
great objects, whose names had been recently so rife in men's
mouths. The luxurious Sardis, the nation of Babylon, the
Nile, that oldest of rivers, Memphis and Thebes the hundred-
gated, that were but amongst Nile's youngest daughters,
with the pyramids inscrutable as the heavens—all these he
had visited. As far up the Nile as Elephantine he had
personally pushed his inquiries; and far beyond *that* by his
obstinate questions from all men presumably equal to the
answers. Tyre, even, he made a separate voyage to explore.
Palestine he had trodden with Grecian feet; the mysterious
Jerusalem he had visited, and had computed her proportions.
Finally, as to Greece continental, though not otherwise connected with it himself than by the bond of language, and as
the home of his Ionian ancestors (in which view he often
calls by the great moral name of *Hellas* regions that geographically belong to Asia and even to Africa), he seems, by
mere casual notices, now prompted by an historical incident,
now for the purpose of an illustrative comparison, to have
known it so familiarly that Pausanias in after ages does not
describe more minutely the local features to which he had
dedicated a life than this extraordinary traveller, for whom
they did but point a period or circumstantiate a parenthesis.
As a geographer, often as a hydrographer — witness his
soundings thirty miles off the mouths of the Nile—Herodotus was the first great parent of discovery; as between
nation and nation he was the author of mutual revelation;
whatsoever any one nation knew of its own little ringfence
through daily use and experience, or had received by ancestral tradition, *that* he published to all other nations. He

was the first central interpreter, the common dragoman to the general college of civilisation that now belted the Mediterranean, holding up, in a language already laying the foundations of universality, one comprehensive mirror, reflecting to them all the separate chorography, habits, institutions, and religious systems of each. Nor was it in the facts merely that he retraced the portraits of all leading states : whatsoever in these facts was mysterious, for that he had a self-originated solution ; whatsoever was perplexing by equiponderant counter-assumptions, for that he brought a determining impulse to the one side or the other ; whatsoever seemed contradictory, for that he brought a reconciling hypothesis. Were it the annual rise of a river, were it the formation of a famous kingdom by alluvial depositions, were it the unexpected event of a battle, or the apparently capricious migration of a people—for all alike Herodotus had such resources of knowledge as took the sting out of the marvellous, or such resources of ability as at least suggested the plausible. Antiquities or mythology, martial institutions or pastoral, the secret motives to a falsehood which he exposes, or the hidden nature of some truth which he deciphers : all alike lay within the searching dissection of this astonishing intellect, the most powerful lens by far that has ever been brought to bear upon the mixed objects of a speculative traveller.

To have classed this man as a mere fabling annalist,—or even if it should be said on better thoughts, "No, not as a fabling annalist, but as a great scenical historian,"—is so monstrous an oversight, so mere a neglect of the proportions maintained amongst the topics treated by Herodotus, that we do not conceive any apology requisite for revising, in this place or at this time, the general estimate on a subject *always* interesting. What is everybody's business the proverb instructs us to view as nobody's by duty ; but under the same rule it is *any*body's by right ; and what belongs to all hours alike may, for that reason, belong without blame to January of the year 1842. Yet, if any man, obstinate in demanding for all acts a "sufficient reason" (to speak *Leibnitice*), demurs to our revision, as having no special invitation at this immediate moment, then we are happy to tell him that Mr. Hermann Bobrik has furnished us with such an invitation by a recent review of Herodotus as a geographer,[1] and thus furnished even a technical plea for calling up the great man before our bar.

We have already said something towards reconsidering the thoughtless classification of a writer whose works do actually, in their major proportion, not essentially concern that subject to which by their *translated* title they are exclusively referred ; or even that part which *is* historical often moves by mere anecdotes or personal sketches.   And the uniform object of these is not the history, but the political condition, of the particular state or province.   But we now feel disposed to press this rectification a little more keenly by asking—What was the reason for this apparently wilful error ?   The reason is palpable : it was the ignorance of irreflectiveness.

I. For with respect to the first oversight on the claim of Herodotus as an earliest archetype of composition so much is evident : that, if prose were simply the negation of verse, were it the fact that prose had no separate laws of its own, but that to be a composer in prose meant only his privilege of being inartificial, his dispensation from the restraints of metre, then, indeed, it would be a slight nominal honour to have been the Father of Prose.   But this is ignorance, though a pretty common ignorance.   To walk well, it is not enough that a man abstains from dancing.   Walking has rules of its own the more difficult to perceive or to practise as they are less broadly *prononcés*.   To forbear singing is not, therefore, to speak well or to read well : each of which offices rests upon a separate art of its own.   Numerous laws of transition, connexion, preparation, are different for a writer in verse and a writer in prose.   Each mode of composition is a great art ; well executed, is the highest and most difficult of arts.   And we are satisfied that, one century before the age of Herodotus, the effort must have been greater to wean the feelings from a key of poetic composition to which all minds had long been attuned and prepared than

---

[1] Geographie des Herodot, dargestellt von Hermann Bobrik. Konigsberg, 1838.

at present it would be for any paragraphist in the newspapers to make the inverse revolution by *suddenly* renouncing the modesty of prose for the impassioned forms of lyrical poetry. It was a great thing to be the leader of prose composition ; great even, as we all can see at other times, to be absolutely first in any one subdivision of composition : how much more in one whole bisection of literature ! And, if it is objected that Herodotus was *not* the eldest of prose writers, doubtless, in an absolute sense, no man was. There must always have been short public inscriptions, not admitting of metre, as where numbers, quantities, dimensions, were concerned. It is enough that all feeble tentative explorers of the art had been too meagre in matter, too rude in manner, like Fabius Pictor amongst the Romans, to captivate the ears of men, and *thus* to insure their own propagation. Without annoying the reader by the cheap erudition of parading defunct names before him, it is certain that Scylax, an author still surviving, was nearly contemporary with Herodotus ; and not very wide of him by his subject.[1] In *his* case it is probable that the mere practical benefits of his book to the navigators of the Mediterranean in that early period, had multiplied his book so as eventually to preserve it. Yet, as Major Rennel remarks, " Geog. Syst. of Herod.," p. 610—" Scylax must be regarded as a seaman or pilot, and the author of a coasting directory " ; as a mechanic artisan, ranking with Hamilton Moore or Gunter,—not as a great liberal artist, an *intellectual* potentate, like Herodotus. Such now upon the scale of intellectual claims as was this geographical rival by comparison with Herodotus, such doubtless were his rivals or predecessors in history, in antiquities, and in the other provinces which he occupied. And, generally, the fragments of these authors, surviving in Pagan as well as Christian collections, show that they were such. So that, in a high, virtual sense,

---

[1] Scylax, a Carian, was sent by Darius Hystaspes, King of Persia (B.C. 521-485), on a voyage down the Indus. He returned by the Indian Ocean and the Red Sea, completing the voyage in thirty months. The Greek book bearing his name, and giving an account of the voyage is generally attributed now to a later compiler ; but De Quincey keeps to the old opinion. In that case Scylax *was* an author nearly contemporary with Herodotus (B.C. 484-408), who mentions him and describes his voyage.—M.

Herodotus was to prose composition what Homer, six hundred years earlier, had been to Verse.

II. But whence arose the other mistake about Herodotus —the fancy that his great work was exclusively (or even chiefly) a history? It arose simply from a mistranslation, which subsists everywhere to this day. We remember that Kant, in one of his miscellaneous essays, finding a necessity for explaining the term *Historie* (why we cannot say, since the Germans have the self-grown word *Geschichte* for that idea), deduces it, of course, from the Greek Ἱστορια. This brings him to an occasion for defining the term. And how? It is laughable to imagine the anxious reader bending his ear to catch the Kantean whisper, and finally solemnly hearing that Ἱστορια means—History. Really, Professor Kant, we should almost have guessed as much. But such derivations teach no more than the ample circuit of Bardolph's definition —" *accommodated*: that whereby a man is, or may be thought to be "—what ? " *accommodated*." Kant was a masterly *Latin* scholar,—in fact, a fellow-pupil with the admirable D. Ruhnken,—but an indifferent Grecian. And, spite of the old traditional " Historiarum Libri Novem," which stands upon all Latin title-pages of Herodotus, we need scarcely remind a Greek scholar, that the verb ἱστορεω or the noun ἱστορια *never* bears, in this writer, the latter sense of recording and memorializing. The substantive is a word frequently employed by Herodotus, often in the plural number, and uniformly it means *inquiries* or *investigations*; so that the proper English version of the title-page would be—" Of the *Researches* made by Herodotus, Nine Books " And, in reality, that is the very meaning, and the secret drift of the consecration (running overhead through these nine sections) to the nine Muses. Had the work been designed as chiefly historical, it would have been placed under the patronage of the one sole muse presiding over History. But, because the very opening sentence tells us that it is *not* chiefly historical, that it is so partially, that it rehearses the acts of men (τα γενομενα) together with the monumental structures of human labour (τα ἐργα)—for the true sense of which word, in this position, see the first sentence in section thirty-five of *Euterpe*,—and other things beside (τα τε ἀλλα); because, in

short, not any limited annals, because the mighty revelation
of the world to its scattered inhabitants, because

> "Quicquid agunt homines, votum, timor, ira, voluptas,
>   Gaudia, discursus, nostri est farrago libelli" :

therefore it was that a running title, or superscription, so
extensive and so aspiring had at some time been adopted.
Every muse, and not one only, is presumed to be interested
in the work ; and, in simple truth, this legend of dedication
is but an expansion of variety more impressively conveyed of
what had been already notified in the inaugural sentence ;
whilst both this sentence and that dedication were designed
to meet that very misconception which has since, notwithstanding, prevailed.[1]

These rectifications ought to have some effect in elevating
— first, the rank of Herodotus ; secondly, his present
attractions.   Most certain we are that few readers are aware
of the *various* amusement conveyed from all sources then
existing by this most splendid of travellers.   Dr. Johnson
has expressed in print (and not merely in the strife of conversation) the following extravagant idea—that to Homer, as
its original author, may be traced back, at least in outline,
every tale or complication of incidents now moving in modern poems, romances, or novels.   Now, it is not necessary to
denounce such an assertion as false, because, upon two separate
reasons, it shows itself to be impossible.   In the first place,
the motive to such an assertion was to emblazon the inventive
faculty of Homer ; but it happens that Homer could not
invent anything, small or great, under the very principles
of Grecian art.   To be a fiction as to matters of *action* (for

---

[1] But—"*How* has it prevailed," some will ask, "if an error?
Have not great scholars sate upon Herodotus?"   Doubtless, many.
There is none greater, for instance, merely as a Grecian scholar, than
Valckenaer.   Whence we conclude that inevitably this error has been
remarked somewhere.   And, as to the erroneous Latin version still
keeping its ground, partly that may be due to the sort of superstition
which everywhere protects old usages in formal situations like a title-
page, partly to the fact that there is no happy Latin word to express
"Researches."   But, however that may be, all the scholars in the
world cannot get rid of the evidence involved in the general use of
the word ἱστορία (*investigation*) by Herodotus.

in embellishments the rule might be otherwise) was to be ridiculous and unmeaning in Grecian eyes We may illustrate the Grecian feeling on this point (however little known to modern readers) by our own dolorous disappointment when we opened the *Alhambra* of Mr. Washington Irving. We had supposed it to be some real Spanish or Moorish legend connected with that grand architectural romance ; and, behold ! it was a mere Sadler's Wells travesty (we speak of its plan, not of its execution) applied to some slender fragments from past days. Such, but far stronger, would have been the disappointment to Grecian feelings in finding any poetic (*a fortiori*, any prose) legend to be a fiction of the writer's : words cannot measure the reaction of disgust. And thence it was that no tragic poet of Athens ever took for his theme any tale or fable not already pre-existing in *some* known version of it, though now and then it might be the least popular version. It was *capital* as an offence of the intellect, it was lunatic, to do otherwise. This is a most important characteristic of ancient taste, and most interesting in its philosophic value for any comparative estimate of modern art as against ancient. In particular, no just commentary can ever be written on the Poetics of Aristotle which leaves this out of sight. Secondly, as against Dr. Johnson, it is evident that the whole character, the very principle of movement, in many modern stories, depends upon sentiments derived remotely from Christianity, and others upon usages or manners peculiar to modern civilisation ; so as in either case to involve a moral anachronism if viewed as Homeric, consequently as Pagan. Not the colouring only of the fable, but the very incidents, one and all, and the situations, and the perplexities, are constantly the product of something characteristically modern in the circumstances, —sometimes, for instance, in the climate ; *for the ancients had no experimental knowledge of severe climates.* With these double impossibilities before us of any absolute fictions in a Pagan author that could be generally fitted to anticipate modern tales, we shall not transfer to Herodotus the impracticable compliment paid by Dr. Johnson to Homer. But it is certain that the very best collection of stories furnished by Pagan funds lies dispersed through his great

work. One of the best of the *Arabian Nights*, the *very* best
as regards the structure of the plot—viz. the tale of *Ali Baba
and the Forty Thieves*—is evidently derived from an incident
in that remarkable Egyptian legend connected with the
treasury-house of Rhampsinitus. This, except two of his
Persian legends (Cyrus and Darius), is the longest tale in
Herodotus, and by much the best in an artist's sense ;
indeed, its own remarkable merit, as a fable in which the
incidents *successively generate each other*, caused it to be
transplanted by the Greeks to their own country. Vossius,
in his work on the Greek historians, and, a hundred years
later, Valckenaer, with many other scholars, had pointed out
the singular conformity of this memorable Egyptian story
with several that afterwards circulated in Greece. The
eldest of these transfers was undoubtedly the Bœotian tale (but
in days before the name Bœotia existed) of Agamedes and
Trophonius, architects, and sons to the King of Orchomenos,
who built a treasure-house at Hyria (noticed by Homer in
his ship catalogue), followed by tragical circumstances, the
very same as those recorded by Herodotus. It is true that
the latter incidents, according to the Egyptian version—the
monstrous device of Rhampsinitus for discovering the robber
at the price of his daughter's honour, and the final reward of
the robber for his petty ingenuity (which, after all, belonged
chiefly to the deceased architect)—ruin the tale as a whole.
But these latter incidents are obviously forgeries of another
age ; "*angeschlossen*," fastened on by fraud, "*an den ersten
aelteren theil*," to the first and elder part, as Mueller rightly
observes, p. 97 of his *Orchomenos*. And even here it is
pleasing to notice the incredulity of Herodotus ; who was
not, like so many of his Christian commentators, sceptical
upon previous system and by wholesale, but equally prone
to believe wherever his heart (naturally reverential) suggested
an interference of superior natures, and ready to doubt where-
ever his excellent judgment detected marks of incoherency.
He records the entire series of incidents as τα λεγομενα
ἀκοη, reports of events which had reached him by hearsay,
ἐμοι δε οὐ πιστα—"but to me," he says pointedly, "not
credible."

In this view, as a *thesaurus fabularum*, a great repository of anecdotes and legends, tragic or romantic, Herodotus is so far beyond all Pagan competition that we are thrown upon Christian literatures for any corresponding form of merit. The case has often been imagined playfully that a man were restricted to one book, and in that case what ought to be his choice ; and, supposing all books so solemn as those of a religious interest to be laid out of the question, many are the answers which have been pronounced, according to the difference of men's minds. Rousseau, as is well known, on such an assumption made his election for Plutarch. But shall we tell the reader *why?* It was not altogether his taste, or his judicious choice, which decided him ; for choice there can be none amongst elements unexamined—it was his limited reading. Rousseau, like William Wordsworth, had read at the outside twelve volumes 8vo in his whole life-time. Except a few papers in the French *Encyclopédie* during his maturer years, and some dozen of works presented to him by their authors where they happened to be his own friends, Rousseau had read little (if anything at all) beyond Plutarch's Lives in a bad French translation, and Montaigne. Though not a Frenchman, having had an education (if such one can call it) thoroughly French, he had the usual puerile French craze about Roman virtue, and republican simplicity, and Cato, and " all that." So that *his* decision goes for little. And even he, had he read Herodotus, would have thought twice before he made up his mind. The truth is that in such a case,—suppose, for example, Robinson Crusoe empowered to import one book and no more into his insular hermitage,— the most powerful of human books must be unavoidably excluded, and for the following reason : that in the direct ratio of its profundity will be the unity of any fictitious interest ; a *Paradise Lost,* or a *King Lear,* could not agitate or possess the mind in the degree that they do if they were at leisure to " amuse " us. So far from relying on its unity, the work which should aim at the *maximum* of amusement ought to rely on the *maximum* of variety. And in that view it is that we urge the paramount pretensions of Herodotus : since not only are his topics separately of primary interest, each for itself, but they are collectively the most varied in the quality of that interest, and they are touched with the most flying and least lingering pen ; for, of all writers, Herodotus is the most cautious not to trespass on his reader's patience : his transitions are the most fluent whilst they are the most endless, justifying themselves to the understanding as much as they recommend themselves to the spirit of hurrying curiosity ; and his narrations or descriptions are the most animated by the generality of their abstractions, whilst they are the most faithfully individual by the felicity of their selection amongst circumstances.

Once, and in a public situation, I myself denominated Herodotus the Froissart of antiquity. But I was then speaking of him exclusively in his character of historian ; and, even so, I did him injustice. Thus far it is true the two men agree, that both are less political, or reflecting, or moralizing, as historians, than they are scenical and splendidly picturesque. But Froissart is little else than an annalist, whereas Herodotus is the counterpart of some ideal Pandora by the universality of his accomplishments. He is a traveller of discovery, like Captain Cook or Park. He is a naturalist, the earliest that existed. He is a mythologist, and a speculator on the origin, as well as value, of religious rites. He is a political economist by instinct of genius, before the science of economy had a name or a conscious function ; and, by two great records, he has put us up to the level of *all* that can excite our curiosity at that great era of moving civilisation : first, as respects Persia, by the elaborate review of the various satrapies or great lieutenancies of the empire—that vast empire which had absorbed the Assyrian, Median, Babylonian, Little Syrian, and Egyptian kingdoms—registering against each separate viceroyalty, from Algiers to Lahore beyond the Indus, what was the amount of its annual tribute to the gorgeous exchequer of Susa ; and, secondly, as respects Greece, by his review of the numerous little Grecian states, and their several contingents in ships, or in soldiers, or in both (according as their position happened to be inland or maritime), towards the universal armament against the second and greatest of the Persian invasions. Two such documents, two such archives of political economy, two monuments of corresponding value, do not exist elsewhere in history. Egypt had now ceased, and we may say that (according to the scriptural prophecy) it had ceased for ever, to be an independent realm. Persia had now for seventy years had her foot upon the neck of this unhappy land ; and, in one century beyond the death of Herodotus, the two-horned [1] he-goat of Macedon was destined to butt it down into hopeless prostration. But, so far as Egypt, from her vast antiquity, or from her great resources, was entitled to a more circumstantial notice than any other satrapy of the great empire, such a notice she has ; and I do not scruple to say, though it may seem a bold word, that from the many scattered features of Egyptian habits or usages incidentally indicated by Herodotus a better portrait of Egyptian life, and a better abstract of Egyptian political economy, might even yet be gathered than from all the writers of Greece for the cities of their native land.

But take him as an exploratory traveller and as a naturalist, who had to break ground for the earliest entrenchments in these new functions of knowledge : it may be said without exaggeration that, *mutatis mutandis* and *concessis concedendis*, Herodotus has the separate qualifications of the two men whom we would select by preference as the most distinguished amongst Christian traveller-naturalists. He has the universality of the Prussian Humboldt ; and he has the picturesque fidelity to nature of the English Dampier—of whom the last was a simple self-educated seaman, but strong-minded by nature, austerely accurate through his moral reverence for truth, and zealous in pursuit of knowledge to an excess which raises him to a level with the noble Greek. Dampier, when in the last stage of exhaustion from a malignant dysentery, unable to stand upright, and surrounded by perils in a land of infidel fanatics, crawled on his hands

---

[1] " *Two-horned* " :—In one view, as having no successor, Alexander was called the *one-horned.* But it is very singular that all Oriental nations, without knowing anything of the scriptural symbols under which Alexander is described by Daniel as the strong he-goat who butted against the ram of Persia, have always called him the "two-horned," with a covert allusion to his European and his Asiatic kingdom. And it is equally singular that unintentionally this symbol falls in with Alexander's own assumption of a descent from Libyan Jupiter-Ammon, to whom the double horns were an indispensable and characteristic symbol.

and feet to verify a question in natural history, under the blazing forenoon of the tropics ; and Herodotus, having no motive but his own inexhaustible thirst of knowledge, embarked on a separate voyage, fraught with hardships, towards a chance of clearing up what seemed a difficulty of some importance in deducing the religious mythology of his country.

But it is in those characters by which he is best known to the world—viz. as a historian and a geographer—that Herodotus levies the heaviest tribute on our reverence ; and precisely in those characters it is that he now claims the amplest atonement, having formerly sustained the grossest outrages of insult and slander on the peculiar merits attached to each of those characters. Credulous he was supposed to be, in a degree transcending the privilege of old garrulous nurses ; hyperbolically extravagant beyond Sir John Mandeville ; and lastly, as if he had been a Mendez Pinto or a Munchausen, he was saluted as the " father of lies." [1] Now, on these calumnies, it is pleasant to know that his most fervent admirer no longer feels it requisite to utter one word in the way of complaint or vindication. Time has carried him round to the diametrical counterpole of estimation. Examination and more learned study have justified every iota of those statements *to which he pledged his own private authority.* His chronology is better to this day than any single system opposed to it. His dimensions and distances are so far superior to those of later travellers, whose hands were strengthened by all the powers of military command and regal autocracy, that Major Rennel, upon a deliberate retrospect of his works, preferred his authority to that of those who came after him as conquerors and rulers of the kingdoms which he had described as a simple traveller ; nay, to the later authority of those who had conquered those conquerors. It is gratifying that a judge so just and thoughtful as the Major should declare the reports of Alexander's officers on the distances and stations in the Asiatic part of his empire less trustworthy by much than the reports of

---

[1] Viz. (as I believe) by Vicesimus Knox—a writer now entirely forgotten. "*Father of History* you call him ? Much rather the *Father of Lies.*"

Herodotus : yet, who was more liberally devoted to science than Alexander ? or what were the humble powers of the foot traveller in comparison with those of the mighty earth-shaker, for whom prophecy had been on the watch for centuries ? It is gratifying that a judge like the Major should find the same advantage on the side of Herodotus, as to the distances in the Egyptian and Libyan part of this empire, on a comparison with the most accomplished of Romans,—Pliny, Strabo, Ptolemy (for all are Romans who benefited by any Roman machinery),—coming five and six centuries later.   I, for my part, hold the accuracy of Herodotus to be all but marvellous, considering the wretched apparatus which he could then command in the popular measures.   The *stadium*, it is true, was more accurate, because less equivocal, in those Grecian days than afterwards, when it inter-oscillated with the Roman *stadium ;* but all the multiples of that stadium, such as the *schœnus*, the Persian *parasang*, or the military *stathmus*, were only less vague than the *coss* of Hindostan in their ideal standards, and as fluctuating *practically* as are all computed distances at all times and places.   The close approximations of Herodotus to the returns of distances upon caravan routes of five hundred miles by the most vigilant of modern travellers, checked by the caravan controllers, is a bitter retort upon his calumniators.   And, as to the consummation of the insults against him in the charge of wilful falsehood, I explain it out of hasty reading and slight acquaintance with Greek.   The sensibility of Herodotus to his own future character in this respect, under a deep consciousness of his upright forbearance on the one side, and of the extreme liability on the other side to uncharitable construction for any man moving amongst Egyptian thaumaturgical traditions, comes forward continually in his anxious distinctions between what he gives on his own ocular experience (ὄψις)—what upon his own inquiries, or combination of inquiries with previous knowledge (ἱστοριη) —what upon hearsay (ἀκοη)—what upon current tradition (λογος).   And the evidences are multiplied, over and above these distinctions, of the irritation which besieged his mind as to the future wrongs he might sustain from the careless and the unprincipled.   Had truth been less precious in his eyes, was it tolerable to be supposed a liar for so vulgar an object as that of creating a stare by wonder-making? The high-minded Grecian, justly proud of his superb intellectual resources for taking captive the imaginations of his half-polished countrymen, disdained such base artifices, which belong more properly to an effeminate and over-stimulated stage of civilisation. And, once for all, he had announced at an early point as the *principle* of his work, as what ran along the whole line of his statements by way of basis or subsumption (παρα παντα τον λογον ὑποκειται)—that he wrote upon the faith of hearsay from the Egyptians severally : meaning by "severally" (ἑκαστων) that he did not adopt any chance hearsay, but such as was guaranteed by the men who presided over each several department of Egyptian official or ceremonial life.

Having thus said something towards revindicating for Herodotus his proper station—first, as a *power* in literature ; next, as a geographer, economist, mythologist, antiquary, historian—I shall draw the reader's attention to the remarkable "set of the current" towards that very consummation and result of justice amongst the learned within the last two generations. There is no similar case extant of truth slowly righting itself. Seventy years ago the reputation of Herodotus for veracity was at the lowest ebb. That prejudice still survives popularly. But amongst the learned it has gradually given way to better scholarship, and to two generations of travellers, starting with far superior preparation for their difficult labours. Accordingly, at this day, each successive commentator, better able to read Greek, and better provided with solutions for the inevitable errors of a *reporter*, drawing upon others for his facts, with only an occasional interposition of his own opinion, comes with increasing reverence to his author. The *laudator temporis acti* takes for granted in his sweeping ignorance that we of the present generation are less learned than our immediate predecessors. It happens that all over Europe the course of learning has been precisely in the inverse direction. Poor was the condition of Greek learning in England when Dr. Cooke (one of the five wretched old boys who operated upon Gray's *Elegy* in the character of Greek translators) presided at Cambridge as their Greek professor.   See, or rather touch with the tongs, his edition of Aristotle's *Poetics*.[1]   Equally poor was its condition in Germany ; for, if one swallow could make a summer, we had that in England.   Poorer by far was its condition (as generally it is) in France, where a great Don in Greek letters, an Abbé who passed for unfathomably learned, having occasion to translate a Greek sentence, saying that "Herodotus, even whilst Ionicizing (using the Ionic dialect), had yet spelt a particular name with the *alpha* and not with the *eta*," rendered the passage "Herodote et aussi Jazon."   The Greek words were these three—Ἡρόδοτος καὶ ἰαζων—*i.e.* Herodotus even whilst Ionicizing.   He had never heard that καὶ means *even* almost as often as it means *and :* thus he introduced to the world a fine new author,—one Jazon, Esquire ; and the squire holds his place in the learned Abbé's book to this day. Good Greek scholars are now in the proportion of perhaps sixty to one by comparison with the penultimate generation : and this proportion holds equally for Germany and for England.   So that the restoration of Herodotus to his place in literature, his *Palingenesia*, has been no caprice, but is due to the vast depositions of knowledge, equal for the last seventy or eighty years to the accumulated product of the entire previous interval from Herodotus himself down to 1760, in every one of those particular fields which this author was led by his situation to cultivate.

Meantime, the work of cleansing this great tank or depository of archæology (the one sole reservoir so placed in point of time as to collect and draw all the contributions from the frontier ground between the *mythical* and the *historical* period) is still proceeding.   Every fresh labourer, by new accessions of direct aid, or by new combinations of old suggestions, finds himself able to purify the interpretation of Herodotus by wider analogies, or to account for his mistakes

---

[1] Which edition the arrogant Mathias in his *Pursuits of Literature* (by far the most popular of books from 1797 to 1802) highly praised ; though otherwise amusing himself with the folly of the other greyheaded men contending for a school-boy's prize.   It was the loss of dignity, however, in the reverend translator, not their worthless Greek, which he saw cause to ridicule ; for Mathias, though reading ordinary Greek with facility, and citing it with a needless and a pedantic profusion, was not in any exquisite sense a Grecian.

by more accurately developing the situation of the speaker.
We also bring our own unborrowed contributions. We also
would wish to promote this great labour,—which, be it remembered, concerns no secondary section of human progress,
searches no blind corners or nooks of history, but traverses
the very crests and summits of human annals, with a solitary
exception for the Hebrew Scriptures, so far as opening
civilisation is concerned. The commencement—the solemn
inauguration—of History is placed no doubt in the commencement of the Olympiads, 777 years before Christ. The doors
of the great theatre were then thrown open. That is undeniable. But the performance did not actually commence
till 555 B.C. (the *locus* of Cyrus). Then began the great
tumult of nations—the *termashaw*, to speak *Bengalicè*. Then
began the procession, the pomp, the interweaving of the
western tribes, not always by bodily presence, but by the
actio in distans of politics. And the birth of Herodotus was
precisely in the seventy-first year from that period. It is
the greatest of periods that is concerned. And we also, as
willingly we repeat, would offer our contingent. What we
propose to do is to bring forward two or three important
suggestions of others not yet popularly known—shaping and
pointing, if possible, their application—brightening their
justice, or strengthening their outlines. And with these we
propose to intermingle one or two suggestions more exclusively our own.

I.—*The Non-Planetary Earth of Herodotus in its relation to
the Planetary Sun.*

Mr. Hermann Bobrik is the first torch-bearer to Herodotus
who has thrown a strong light on his theory of the earth's
relation to the solar system. This is one of the *præcognita*
literally indispensable to the comprehension of the geographical
basis assumed by Herodotus. And it is really interesting to see
how one original error had drawn after it a train of others—
how one restoration of light has now illuminated a whole
hemisphere of objects. We suppose it the very next thing to
a fatal impossibility that any man should at once rid his
mind so profoundly of all natural biases from education, or

almost from human instinct, as barely to suspect the physical theory of Herodotus—barely to imagine the idea of a divorce occurring in *any* theory between the solar orb and the great phenomena of summer and winter. Prejudications, having the force of a necessity, had blinded generation after generation of students to the very admission *in limine* of such a theory as could go the length of dethroning the sun himself from all influence over the great vicissitudes of heat and cold —seed-time and harvest—for man. They did not see what actually *was*, what lay broadly below their eyes, in Herodotus, because it seemed too fantastic a dream to suppose that it *could* be. The case is far more common than feeble psychologists imagine. Numerous are the instances in which we actually see—not that which is really there to be seen, but that which we believe *a priori* ought to be there. And in cases so palpable as that of an external sense it is not difficult to set the student on his guard. But in cases more intellectural or moral, like several in Herodotus, it is difficult for the teacher himself to be effectually vigilant. It was not anything actually seen by Herodotus which led him into denying the solar functions; it was his own independent speculation. This suggested to him a plausible hypothesis : plausible it was for that age of the world ; and afterwards, on applying it to the actual difficulties of the case, this hypothesis seemed so far good that it did really unlock them. The case stood thus :—Herodotus contemplated Cold not as a mere privation of Heat, but as a positive quality ; quite as much entitled to " high consideration," in the language of ambassadors, as its rival Heat ; and quite as much to a " retiring pension," in case of being superannuated. Thus we all know, from Addison's fine raillery, that a certain philosopher regarded darkness not at all as any result from the absence of light, but fancied that, as some heavenly bodies are luminaries, so others (which he called *tenebrific stars*) might have the office of " raying out positive darkness." In the infancy of science the idea is natural to the human mind ; and we remember hearing a great man of our own times declare that no sense of conscious power had ever so vividly dilated his mind, nothing so like a revelation, as when one day in broad sunshine, whilst yet a child, he dis-

covered that his own shadow, which he had often angrily
hunted, was no real existence, but a mere *hindering* of the
sun's light from filling up the space screened by his own
body.   The old grudge, which he cherished against this coy
fugitive shadow, melted away in the rapture of this great
discovery.   To him the discovery had doubtless been originally half suggested by explanations of his elders imperfectly
comprehended.   But in itself the distinction between the
affirmative and the *negative* is a step perhaps the most costly
in *effort* of any that the human mind is summoned to take ;
and the greatest indulgence is due to those early stages of
civilisation when this step had *not* been taken.   For Herodotus there existed two great counter-forces in absolute hostility—heat and cold ; and these forces were incarnated in the
WINDS.   It was the north and north-east wind, not any distance of the sun, which radiated cold and frost ; it was the
southern wind from Ethiopia, not at all the sun, which radiated
heat.   But could a man so sagacious as Herodotus stand with
his ample Grecian forehead exposed to the noonday sun, and
suspect no part of the calorific agency to be seated in the
sun ?   Certainly he could not.   But this partial agency is
no more than what we of this day allow to secondary or tertiary
causes apart from the principal.   We, that regard the sun as
upon the whole our planetary fountain of light, yet recognise
an electrical *aurora*, a zodiacal light, &c., as substitutes not
palpably dependent.   We, that regard the sun as upon the
whole our fountain of heat, yet recognise many co-operative,
many modifying, forces having the same office—such as the
local configuration of ground—such as sea neighbourhoods or
land neighbourhoods, marshes or none, forests or none, strata
of soil fitted to retain heat and fund it, or to disperse it and
cool it.   Precisely in the same way Herodotus did allow an
agency to the sun upon the *daily* range of heat, though he
allowed none to the same luminary in regulating the *annual*
range.   What caused the spring and autumn, the summer
and winter (though generally in those ages there were but
two seasons recognised), was the action of the winds.   The
diurnal arch of heat (as we may call it) ascending from sun-
rise to some hour (say two P.M.) when the sum of the two
heats (the funded annual heat and the fresh increments of

daily heat) reaches its *maximum*, and the descending limb of the same arch from this hour to sunset—this he explained entirely out of the sun's *daily* revolution, which to him was, of course, no apparent motion, but a real one in the sun. It is truly amusing to hear the great man's infantine simplicity in describing the effects of the solar journey. The sun rises, it seems, in India[1]; and these poor Indians, roasted by whole nations at breakfast-time, are then up to their chins in water, whilst we thankless Westerns are taking " tea and toast " at our ease. However, it is a long lane which has no turning ; and by noon the sun has driven so many stages away from India that the poor creatures begin to come out of their rivers, and really find things tolerably comfortable. India is now cooled down to a balmy Grecian temperature. " All right behind ! " as the mail-coach guards proclaim ; but not quite right ahead, when the sun is racing away over the boiling brains of the Ethiopians, Libyans, &c., and driving Jupiter-Ammon perfectly distracted with his furnace. But, when things are at the worst, the proverb assures us that they will mend. And, for an early five o'clock dinner, Ethiopia finds that she has no great reason to complain. All civilized people are now cool and happy for the rest of the day. But, as to the woolly-headed rascals on the west coast of Africa, they " catch it " towards sunset, and " no mistake." Yet why trouble our heads about inconsiderable black fellows like them, who have been cool all day whilst better men were melting away by pailfuls ? And such is the history of a summer's day in the heavens above and on the earth beneath. As to little Greece, she is but skirted by the sun,

---

[1] Which word *India*, it must be remembered, was liable to no such equivocation as it is now. India meant simply the land of the river Indus, *i.e.* all the territory lying eastward of that river down to the mouths of the Ganges ; and the Indians meant simply the Hindoos, or natives of Hindostan. Whereas, at present, we give a secondary sense to the word *Indian*, applying it to a race of savages in the New World, *viz.* to all the *aboriginal* natives of the American continent, and also to the aboriginal natives of all the islands scattered over the Pacific Ocean to the west of that continent, and all the islands in the Gulf of Mexico to the east of it. Standing confusion has thus been introduced into the acceptation of the word *Indian ;* a confusion corresponding to that which besieged the ancient use of the term *Scythian,* and, in a minor degree, the term *Ethiopian.*

who keeps away far to the south ; thus she is maintained in a charming state of equilibrium by her fortunate position on the very frontier line of the fierce *Boreas* and the too voluptuous *Notos.*

Meantime one effect follows from this transfer of the solar functions to the winds, which has not been remarked, —viz. that Herodotus has a double north ; one governed by the old noisy Boreas, another by the silent constellation Arktos. And the consequence of this fluctuating north, as might be guessed, is the want of any true north at all : for the two points of the wind and the constellation do not coincide, in the first place ; and, secondly, the wind does not coincide with itself, but naturally traverses through a few points right and left. Next, the east also will be indeterminate from a separate cause. Had Herodotus lived in a high northern latitude, there is no doubt that the ample range of difference between the northerly points of rising in the summer and the southerly in winter would have forced his attention upon the fact that only at the equinox, vernal or autumnal, does the sun's rising accurately coincide with the east. But in his Ionian climate the deflections either way, to the north or to the south, were too inconsiderable to *force* themselves upon the eye ; and thus a more indeterminate east would arise—never rigorously corrected, because requiring so moderate a correction. Now, a vague unsettled east would support a vague unsettled north. And, of course, through whatever arch of variations either of these points vibrated, precisely upon that scale the west and the south would follow them.

Thus arises, upon a simple and easy genesis, that condition of the compass (to use the word by anticipation) which must have tended to confuse the geographical system of Herodotus, and which does, in fact, account for the else unaccountable obscurities in some of its leading features. These anomalous features would, on their own account, have deserved notice ; but now, after this explanation, they will have a separate value of illustrated proofs in relation to the present article, No. I.

II.—*The Danube of Herodotus considered as a*
counterpole to the Nile.

There is nothing more perplexing to some of the many
commentators on Herodotus than all which he says of the
river Danube : nor anything easier, under the preparation of
the preceding article.   The Danube, or, in the nomenclature
of Herodotus, the *Istros*, is described as being in all respects
ἐκ παραλλήλου ; by which we must understand corresponding rigorously, yet antistrophically (as the Greeks express it),
—similar angles, similar dimensions, but in an inverse
order,—to the Egyptian Nile.   The Nile, in its most easterly
section, flows from south to north.   Consequently the Danube,
by the rule of *parallelism*, ought to flow through a corresponding section from north to south.   But, say the commentators, it does *not*.   Now, verbally they might seem
wrong ; but substantially, as regards the justification of
Herodotus, they are right.   Our business, however, is not to
justify Herodotus, but to explain him.   Undoubtedly there
is a point, about one hundred and fifty miles east of Vienna,
where the Danube descends almost due south for a space of
three hundred miles ; and this is a very memorable reach of
the river ; for somewhere within that long corridor of land
which lies between itself (this Danube section) and a direct
parallel section, equally long, of the Hungarian river Theiss,
once lay, in the fifth century, the royal city or encampment
of Attila.   Gibbon placed the city in the northern part of
this corridor (or, strictly speaking, this Mesopotamia), consequently about two hundred miles to the east of Vienna ; but
others, and especially Hungarian writers, better acquainted
by personal examination with the ground, remove it to one
hundred and fifty miles more to the south,—that is, to the
centre of the corridor (or gallery of land margined by the two
rivers).   Now, undoubtedly, except along the margin of this
Attila's corridor, there is no considerable section of the Danube
which flows southward : and this will not answer the
postulates of Herodotus.   Generally speaking, the Danube
holds a headlong course to the east.   Undoubtedly this must
be granted : and so far it might seem hopeless to seek for

that kind of parallelism to the Nile which Herodotus asserts. But the question for us does not concern what *is* or then *was* —the question is solely about what Herodotus can be shown to have meant. And here comes in, seasonably and serviceably, that vagueness as to the points of the compass which we have explained in the preceding article. This, connected with the positive assertion of Herodotus as to an inverse correspondency with the Nile (north and south, therefore, as the antistrophe to south and north), would place beyond a doubt the creed of Herodotus—which is the question that concerns *us*. And, *vice versâ*, this creed of Herodotus as to the course of the Danube, in its main latter section when approaching the Euxine Sea, reacts to confirm all we have said, *proprio marte*, on the indeterminate articulation of the Ionian compass then current. Here we have at once the *a priori* reasons making it probable that Herodotus would have a vagrant compass ; secondly, many separate instances confirming this probability ; thirdly, the particular instance of the Danube, as antistrophizing with the Nile, not reconcilable with any other principle ; and, fourthly, the following independent demonstration that the Ionian compass must have been confused in its leading divisions. Mark, reader. Herodotus terminates his account of the Danube and its course by affirming that this mighty river enters the Euxine —at what point ? Opposite, says he, to Sinope. Could that have been imagined ? Sinope, being a Greek settlement in a region where such settlements were rare, was notorious to all the world as the flourishing emporium, on the south shore of the Black Sea, for a civilized people, literally *hustled* by barbarians. Consequently—and this is a point to which all commentators alike are blind—the Danube of Herodotus descends upon the Euxine in a line running due south. Else, we demand, how could it antistrophize with the Nile ? Else, we demand, how could it lie right over against Sinope ? Else, we demand, how could it make that right-angle bend to the west in the earlier section of its course which is presupposed in its perfect analogy to the Nile of Herodotus ? If already it were lying east and west in that lower part of its course which approaches the Euxine, what occasion could it offer for a right-angle turn, or for any turn at all—what possibility for any *angle* whatever between this lower reach and that superior reach so confessedly running eastward, according to *all* accounts of its derivation ?

For, as respects the Nile, by way of close to this article, it remains to inform the reader that Herodotus had evidently met in Upper Egypt slaves or captives in war from the regions of Soudan, Tombuctoo, &c. This is the opinion of Rennel, of Browne, the visitor of the Ammonian Oasis, and many other principal authorities ; and for a *reason* which we always regard with more respect, though it were the weakest of reasons, than all the authorities of this world clubbed together. And this reason was the coincidence of what Herodotus reports with the truth of facts first ascertained thousands of years later. These slaves, or some people from those quarters, had told him of a vast river lying east and west,— of course the Niger, but (as he and they supposed) a superior section of the Nile ; and, therefore, by geometrical necessity, falling at right angles upon that other section of the Nile, so familiar to himself, lying south and north. Hence arose a faith (that is to say, not primarily hence, but hence in combination with a previous construction existing in his mind for the geometry of the Danube) that the two rivers Danube and Nile had a mystic relation as arctic and antarctic powers over man. Herodotus had been taught to figure the Danube as a stream of two main inclinations—an upper section rising in the extreme west of Europe, whence he travelled with the arrow's flight due east in search of his wife the Euxine ; but, somewhere in the middle of his course, hearing that her dwelling lay far to the south, and having then completed his distance in longitude, afterwards he ran down his latitude with the headlong precipitation of a lover, and surprised the bride due north from Sinope. This construction it was of the Danube's course which subsequently, upon his hearing of a corresponding western limb for the Nile, led him to perceive the completion of that analogy between the two rivers, its absolute perfection, which already he had partially suspected. Their very figurations now appeared to reflect and repeat each other in solemn mimicry, as previously he had discovered the mimical correspondence of their functions ; for this latter doctrine had been revealed to him by the

Egyptian priests, the then chief depositaries of the Egyptian learning. They had informed him, and evidently had persuaded him, that already more than once the sun had gone round to the region of Europe ; pursuing his diurnal arch as far to the north of Greece as now he did to the south, and carrying in his equipage all the changes of every kind which were required to make Scythia an Egypt, and consequently to make the Istros a Nile. The same annual swelling then filled the channel of the Danube which at present gladdens the Nile. The same luxuriance of vegetation succeeded as a dowry to the gay summer-land of Trans-Euxine and Para-Danubian Europe which for thousands of years had seemed the peculiar heritage of Egypt. Old Boreas — we are glad of that — was required to pack up " his alls," and be off ; his new business was to plague the black rascals, and to bake them with hoar-frost ; which must have caused them to shake their ears in some astonishment for a few centuries, until they got used to it. Whereas " the sweet south wind " of the Ancient Mariner, leaving Africa, pursued the " mariner's holloa " all over the Euxine and the *Palus Mœotis*. The Danube, in short, became the Nile in another zone ; and the same deadly curiosity haunted its fountains. But all in vain : nobody would reach the fountains ; particularly as there would be another arm, El-Abiad or White River.

We are sorry that Herodotus should have been so vague and uncircumstantial in his account of these vicissitudes ; since it is pretty evident to any man who reflects on the case that, had he pursued the train of changes inevitable to Egypt under the one single revolution affecting the Nile itself as a slime-depositing river, his judicious intellect would soon have descried the obliteration of the whole Egyptian valley (elsewhere he himself calls that valley δωρον του Νειλου—a gift of the Nile), consequently the obliteration of the people, consequently the immemorial extinction of all those records—or, if they were posterior to the last revolution in favour of Egypt, at any rate of the one record —which could have transmitted the memory of such an astonishing transfer. Meantime the reader is now in possession of the whole theory contemplated by Herodotus.

It was no mere *lusus naturæ* that the one river repeated the other, and, as it were, mocked the other in form and geographical relations. It was no joke that lurked under that mask of resemblance. Each *was* the other alternately. It was the case of Castor and Pollux, one brother rising as the other set. The Danube could always comfort himself with the idea that he was the Nile "elect"; the other, or provisional Nile, only "continuing to hold the seals until his successor should be installed in office." The Nile, in fact, appears to have the best of it in our time; but then there is "a braw time coming," and, after all, swelling as he is with annual conceit, Father Nile, in parliamentary phrase, is but the "warming-pan" for the Danube, keeping the office warm for him. A new administration is formed, and out he goes, bag and baggage.

It is less important, however, for us, though far more so for the two rivers, to speculate on the reversion of their final prospects than upon the present symbols of this reversion in the unity of their forms. That is, it less concerns us to deduce the harmony of their functions from the harmony of their geographical courses than to abide by the inverse argument—that, where the former harmony was so loudly inferred from the latter, at any rate that fact will demonstrate the existence of the latter harmony in the judgment and faith of Herodotus. He could not possibly have insisted on the analogy between the two channels geographically, as good in logic for authenticating a secret and prophetic analogy between their alternating offices, but that at least he must firmly have believed in the first of these analogies—as already existing and open to the verification of the human eye. The second or ulterior analogy might be false, and yet affect only its own separate credit, whilst the falsehood of the first was ruinous to the credit of both. Whence it is evident that, of the two resemblances in form and function, the resemblance in form was the least disputable of the two for Herodotus.

This argument, and the others which we have indicated, and, amongst those others, above all, the position of the Danube's mouths right over against a city situated as was Sinope—*i.e.* not doubtfully emerging from either flank of the Euxine, west or east, but broadly and almost centrally planted on the southern basis of that sea—we offer as a body of demonstrative proof that, to the mature faith of Herodotus, the Danube or Istros ran north and south in its Euxine section, and that its right angled section ran west and east: a very important element towards the true Europe of Herodotus, which, as we contend, has not yet been justly conceived or figured by his geographical commentators.

III.—*On the Africa of Herodotus.*

There is an amusing blunder on this subject committed by Major Rennel. How often do we hear people commenting on the Scriptures, and raising up aerial edifices of argument, in which every iota of the logic rests, unconsciously to themselves, upon the accidental words of the English version, and melts away when applied to the original text; so that, in fact, the whole has no more strength than if it were built upon a pun or an *équivoque*. Such is the blunder of the excellent Major. And it is not timidly expressed. At p. 410, *Geog. Hist. of Herodotus*, he thus delivers himself:—"Although the term Lybia" (thus does Rennel always spell it, instead of *Libya*—a most unscholarlike blunder, but most pardonable in one so honestly professing to be no Greek scholar) "is occasionally used by Herodotus as synonymous to Africa (especially in *Melpom.*, &c. &c.), yet it is almost exclusively applied to that part bordering on the Mediterranean Sea between the Greater Syrtis and Egypt"; and he concludes the paragraph thus:—"So that Africa, and not Lybia, is the term generally employed by Herodotus." We stared on reading these words, as Aladdin stared when he found his palace missing, and the old thief, who had bought his lamp, trotting off with it on his back far beyond the bills of mortality. Naturally we concluded that it was ourselves who must be dreaming, and not the Major; so, taking a bed-candle, off we marched to bed. But, the next morning, air clear and frosty, ourselves as sagacious as a greyhound, we pounced at first sight on the self-same words. Thus, after all, it was the conceit mantling in our brain (of being in that instance a cut above the Major) which turned out to be the sober truth ; and our modesty, our sobriety of mind, it was which turned out a windy tympany. Certainly, said we, if this be so, and that the word Africa is really standing in Herodotus, then it must be like that secret island called Ἐλβω, lying in some Egyptian lake, which was reported to Herodotus as having concealed itself from human eyes for five hundred and four years: a capital place it must have been against duns and the sheriff ; for it was an English mile in diameter, and yet no man could see it until a fugitive king, happening to be hard pressed in the rear, dived into the water, and came up to the light in the good little island ; where he lived happily for fifty years, and every day got bousy as a piper, in spite of all his enemies, who were roaming about the lake night and day to catch his most gracious majesty He was king, at least, of Elbo, if he had no particular subjects but himself, as Nap was in our days of Elba ; and perhaps both were less plagued with rebels than when sitting on the ampler thrones of Egypt and France.   But surely the good Major must have dreamed a dream about this word *Africa;* for how would it look in Ionic Greek—Ἀφρικη ? Did any man ever see such a word ?   However, let not the reader believe that we are triumphing meanly in the advantage of our Greek.   Milton, in one of his controversial works, exposing an insolent antagonist who pretended to a knowledge of Hebrew, which, in fact, he had not, remarks that the man must be ignoble, whoever he were, that would catch at a spurious credit, though it were but from a language which really he did not understand.[1] But so far was Major Rennel from doing this that, when no call upon him existed for saying one word upon the subject, frankly he volunteered a confession to all the world—that Greek he had none. The marvel is the greater that, as Saunderson, blind from his infancy, was the best lecturer on colours early in the eighteenth century, so by far the best commentator on the Greek Herodotus has proved to be a military man who knew nothing at all of Greek. Yet mark the excellence of upright dealing. Had Major Rennel pretended to Greek, were it but as much as

---

[1] The passage occurs in *Colasterion,* one of Milton's Divorce Pamphlets.—M.

went to the spelling of the word Africa, here was he a lost
man. *Blackwood's Magazine* would now have exposed him.
Whereas, things being as they are, we respect him and admire
him sincerely.   And, as to his wanting this one accomplishment, every man wants some.   We ourselves can neither
dance a hornpipe nor whistle Jim Crow [1] without driving the
whole musical world into black despair.

Africa, meantime, is a word imported into Herodotus by
Mr. Beloe ; whose name, we have been given to understand,
was pronounced like that of our old domesticated friend
the *bellows*, shorn of the *s* ; and whose translation, judging
from such extracts as we have seen in books, may be better
than Littlebury's ; but, if so, we should be driven into a
mournful opinion of Mr. Littlebury.[2]   Strange that nearly
all the classics, Roman as well as Greek, should be so meanly
represented by their English reproducers.   The French
translators, it is true, are worse as a body.   But in this
particular instance of Herodotus they have a respectable translator.   Larcher read Greek sufficiently ; and was as much
master of his author's peculiar learning as any one *general*
commentator that can be mentioned.

But Africa the thing, not Africa the name, is that which
puzzles all· students of Herodotus, as, indeed, no little it
puzzled Herodotus himself.   Rennel makes one difficulty
where, in fact, there is none ; viz. that sometimes Herodotus refers Egypt to Libya, and sometimes refuses to do so.
But in this there is no inconsistency, and no forgetfulness.
Herodotus wisely adopted the excellent rule of " thinking
with the learned, and talking with the people."   Having
once firmly explained his reasons for holding Egypt to be
neither an Asiatic nor an African region, but the neutral
frontier artificially created by the Nile,—as, in short, a long
corridor of separation between Asia and Africa,—thus having,
once for all, borne witness to the truth, afterwards, and
generally, he is too little of a pedant to make war upon
current forms of speech.   What is the use of drawing off

---

[1] *Jim Crow*, — which political air, at the time when this was
written, every other man did (or could) whistle.

[2] The translation of Herodotus by Isaac Littlebury was published
in 1709 ; that by the Rev. William Beloe, in 1791.—M.

men's attention, in questions about *things*, by impertinent revisions of diction or by alien theories ?   Some people have made it a question whether Great Britain were not extra - European ; and the island of Candia is generally assumed to be so.   Some lawyers also (nay, some courts of justice) have entertained the question whether a man could be held related to his own mother ?   Not as though too remotely related, but as too nearly, and, in fact, absorbed within the lunar beams.   Permit us to improve upon this by asking—Is a man related to himself ?   Yet, in all such cases, the publicist, the geographer, the lawyer, continue to talk as other people do ; and, assuredly, the lawyer would regard a witness as perjured who should say, in speaking of a woman notoriously his mother, "Oh ! I do assure you, sir, the woman is no relation of mine."   The world of that day (and, indeed, it is not much more candid even now) would have it that Libya comprehended Egypt ; and Herodotus, like the wise man that he was, having once or twice lodged his protest against that idea, then replies to the world—"Very well, if you say so, it *is* so " ; precisely as Petruchio's wife, to soothe her mad husband, agrees that the sun is the moon, and, back again, that it is *not* the moon.

Here there is no real difficulty ; for the arguments of Herodotus are of two separate classes, and both too strong to leave any doubt that his private opinion never varied by a hair's-breadth on this question.   And it was a question far from verbal ; of which any man may convince himself by reflecting on the disputes, at different periods, with regard to Macedon (both *Macedon* the original germ, and *Macedonia* the expanded kingdom) as a claimant of co-membership in the household of Greece, or on the disputes, more angry if less scornful, between Carthage and Cyrene as to the true limits between this dissyllabic daughter of Tyre and the trisyllabic daughter of Greece.[1]   The very colour of the soil in Egypt—the rich black loam, precipitated by the creative river—already symbolized to Herodotus the deep repulsion lying between Egypt, on the one side, and Libya, where all

---

[1] Καρχηδων, the Greek name for Carthage, is certainly more than dissyllabic ; but we speak of the English names.

was red ; between Egypt, on the one side, and Asia, where all was calcined into white sand. And, as to the name, does not the reader catch *us* still using the word "Africa" instead of Libya, after all our sparring against that word as scarcely known by possibility to Herodotus ?

But, beyond this controversy as to the true marches or frontier lines of the two great continents in common—Asia and Africa—there was another and a more grave one as to the size, shape, and limitations of Africa in particular. It is true that both Europe and Asia were imperfectly defined for Herodotus. But he fancied otherwise ; for them he could trace a vague,· rambling outline. Not so for Africa, unless a great event in Egyptian records were adopted for true. This was the voyage of circumnavigation accomplished under the orders of Pharaoh Necho.[1] Disallowing this earliest recorded *Periplus*, then no man could say of Africa whether it were a large island or a boundless continent having no outline traceable by man, or (which, doubtless, would have been the favourite creed) whether it were not a technical *akté* such as Asia Minor ; that is, not a peninsula like the Peloponnesus, or the tongues of land near mount Athos—because in that case the idea required a narrow neck or isthmus at the point of junction with the adjacent continent—but a square, tabular plate of ground, " a block of ground " (as the Americans say), having three sides washed by some sea, but a fourth side absolutely untouched by any sea whatever. On this word *akté*, as a term but recently drawn out of obscurity, we may say a word or two elsewhere ;. at present we proceed with the great African *Periplus*. We, like the rest of this world, held *that* to be a pure fable, so long as we had never anxiously studied the ancient geography, and consequently had never meditated on the circumstances of this story under the light of that geography, or of the current astronomy. But we have since greatly changed our opinion. And, though it would not have shaken that opinion to find Rennel dissenting,

---

[1] The reference is to the amazing circumnavigation of Africa, in the fifty or sixth century B.C., by the Carthaginian Hanno. The Greek *Periplus*, or account of this circumnavigation, of which De Quincey goes on to speak, is supposed to be a version or tradition of a Carthaginian original.—M.

undoubtedly it much strengthened our opinion to find so
cautious a judge concurring.   Perhaps the very strongest
argument in favour of the voyage, if we speak of any *single*
argument, is that which Rennel insists on—namely, the sole
circumstance reported by the voyagers which Herodotus pronounced incredible, viz. the assertion that in one part of it
they had the sun on the right hand.   And, as we have
always found young students at a loss for the meaning of
that expression, since naturally it struck them that a man
might bring the sun at any place on either hand, or on
neither, we will stop for one moment to explain, for the use
of such youthful readers, that,—as in military descriptions
you are always presumed to look *down* the current of a river,
so that the "right" bank of the Rhine, for instance, is *always*
to a soldier the German bank, the "left" *always* in a military
sense the French bank, in contempt of the traveller's position,
—so, in speaking of the sun, you are presumed to place your
back to the east, and to accompany him on his daily route.
In that position it will be impossible for a man in our latitudes
to bring the sun on his *right* shoulder, since the sun never
even rises to be vertically over his head.   First when the
man goes south so far as to enter the northern tropic would
such a phenomenon be possible ; and, if he persisted in going
beyond the equator and southern tropic, then he would find
all things inverted as regards our hemisphere.   Then he
would find it as impossible, when moving concurrently with
the sun, *not* to have the sun on his right hand as with us to
realize that phenomenon.   Now, it is very clear that, if the
Egyptian voyagers did actually double the Cape of Good
Hope so far to the south of the equator, then, by mere
necessity, this inexplicable phenomenon (for to them it *was*
inexplicable) would pursue them for months in succession.
Here is the point in this argument which we would press on
the reader's consideration ; and, inadvertently, Rennel has
omitted this aspect of the argument altogether.   To Herodotus,
as we have seen, it was so absolutely incredible a romance
that he rejected it summarily.   And why not, therefore, go
the entire length, and reject the total voyage, when thus in
his view partially discredited ?   That question recalls us to
the certainty that there must have been *other* proofs, inde-

pendent of this striking allegation, too strong to allow of scepticism in this wise man's mind. He fancied (and, with *his* theory of the heavens, in which there was no equator, no central limit, no province of equal tropics on either hand of that limit, could he have done otherwise than fancy?) that Jack, after his long voyage, having then no tobacco for his recreation, and no grog, took out his allowance in the shape of wonder-making. He "bounced" a little, he "Cretized"[1]; and who could be angry? And laughable it is to reflect that, — like the poor credulous mother who listened complacently to her seafaring son whilst using a Sinbad's licence of romancing, but gravely reproved him for the sin of untruth when he told her of flying fish or some other simple zoological fact,—so Herodotus would have made careful memoranda of this Egyptian voyage had it told of men "whose heads do grow beneath their shoulders" (since, if he himself doubted about the one-eyed Arimaspians, he yet thought the legend entitled to a report), but scouted with all his energy the one great truth of the *Periplus*, and eternal monument of its reality, as a fable too monstrous for toleration. On the other hand, for us, who know its truth, and how *inevadibly* it must have haunted for months the Egyptians in the face of all their previous impressions, it ought to stand for an argument, strong "as proofs of holy writ," that the voyage did really take place. There is exactly one possibility, but a very slight one, that this truth might have been otherwise learned—learned independently ; and *that* is from the chance that those same Africans of the interior who had truly reported the Niger to Herodotus (though erroneously as a section of the Nile) might simultaneously have reported the phenomena of the sun's course. But we reply to that possible suggestion—that, in fact, it could scarcely have happened. Many other remarkable phenomena of Nigritia had *not* been reported, or had been dropped out of the record as idle or worthless. Secondly, as slaves they would have obtained little credit, except when *falling in with a previous idea or belief.* Thirdly, none of these men would be derived from any place to the south of the line, still less south of the

---

[1] "All the Cretans are liars" : old Mediterranean proverb—Κρητες δει ψευσται.

southern tropic. Generally they would belong to the northern tropic: and (that being premised) what would have been the true form of the report? Not that they had the sun on the right hand, but that sometimes he was directly vertical, sometimes on the left hand, sometimes on the right. "What, ye black villains! The sun, that never was known to change, unless when he reeled a little at seeing the anthropophagous banquet of Thyestes, — *he* to dance cotillons in this absurd way up and down the heavens, —why, crucifixion is too light a punishment for such insults to Apollo": so would a Greek have spoken. And, at least, if the report had survived at all, it would have been in this shape—as the report of an *uncertain* movement in the African sun.

But, as a regular nautical report made to the Pharaoh of the day, as an extract from the log-book, for this reason it must be received as unanswerable evidence, as an argument that *never* can be surmounted on behalf of the voyage, that it contradicted all theories whatsoever—Greek no less than Egyptian—and was irreconcilable with all systems that the wit of men had *yet* devised (viz. two centuries before Herodotus) for explaining the solar motions. Upon this logic we will take our stand. Here is the stronghold, the citadel, of the truth. Many a thing has been fabled, many a thing carefully passed down by tradition as a fact of absolute experience, simply because it fell in with some previous fancy or prejudice of men. And even Baron Munchausen's amusing falsehoods,[1] if examined by a logician, will uniformly be found squared or adjusted—not, indeed, to a belief, but to a whimsical sort of plausibility, that reconciles the mind to the extravagance for the single instant that is required. If he drives up a hill of snow, and next morning finds his horse and gig hanging from the top of a church steeple, the monstrous fiction is still countenanced by the sudden thaw that had taken place in the night-time, and so far physically possible as to be removed beyond the limits of magic. And the very disgust which revolts us in a *supplement* to the

---

[1] Lowndes gives 1786 as the date of the third edition of the famous *Travels, Campaigns, Voyages, and Adventures of Baron Munckhousen, commonly called Munchhausen.*—M.

Baron that we remember to have seen arises from the neglect of those smooth plausibilities.[1] We are there summoned to believe blank impossibilities, without a particle of the Baron's most ingenious and winning speciousness of preparation. The Baron candidly admits the impossibility; faces it; regrets it for the sake of truth: but a *fact* is a *fact;* and he puts it to our equity whether we also have not met with strange events. And never in a single instance does the Baron build upwards without a massy foundation of specious physical plausibility. Whereas the fiction, if it had been a fiction, recorded by Herodotus, is precisely of that order which must have roused the *incredulus odi* in the fulness of perfection. Neither in the wisdom of man, nor in his follies, was there one resource for mitigating the disgust which would have pursued it. This powerful reason for believing the main fact of the circumnavigation let the reader, courteous or not, if he is but the logical reader, condescend to balance in his judgment.

Other arguments, only less strong, on behalf of the voyage we will not here notice—except this one, most reasonably urged by Rennel, from his peculiar familiarity, even in that day (1799), with the currents and the prevalent winds of the Indian ocean: viz. that such a circumnavigation of Africa was almost sure to prosper if commenced from the Red Sea (as it was) along the *east* coast of Africa, and even more sure to fail if taken in the inverse order,—that is to say, through the Straits of Gibraltar, and so down the western shore of Africa. In that order, which was peculiarly tempting for two reasons to the Carthaginian sailor or Phœnician, Rennel has shown how all the currents, the *monsoons*, &c., would baffle the navigator; whilst, taken in the opposite series, they might easily co-operate with the bold enterpriser, so as to waft him, if once starting at a proper season, almost to the Cape, before (to use Sir Bingo Binks's phrase) he could say dumpling. Accordingly, a Persian nobleman of high rank, having been allowed to commute his sentence of capital

[1] De Quincey may refer to a *Sequel to the Adventures of Baron Munchausen* published in 1792 by way of jest upon Bruce, the African traveller, and sometimes bound up with the original and genuine *Munchausen.*—M.

punishment for that of sailing round Africa, did actually fail from the cause developed by Rennel. Naturally he had a Phœnician crew, as the king's best nautical subjects. Naturally they preferred the false route by Gibraltar. Naturally they failed. And the nobleman, returning from transportation before his time, as well as *re infectâ*, was executed.

But (ah, villainous word!) some ugly objector puts in his oar, and demands to know—why, if so vast an event had actually occurred, it could have ever been forgotten, or at all have faded? To this we answer briefly what properly ought to form a separate section in our notice of Herodotus. The event was *not* so vast as we, with our present knowledge of Africa, should regard it.

This is a very interesting aspect of the subject. We laugh long and loud when we hear Des Cartes (great man as he was) laying it down amongst the golden rules for guiding his studies that he would guard himself against all "prejudices"; because we know that, when a prejudice of any class whatever is seen *as* such, when it is recognised *for* a prejudice, from that moment it ceases to *be* a prejudice. Those are the true baffling prejudices for man which he never suspects for prejudices. How widely, from the truisms of experience, could we illustrate this truth! But we abstain. We content ourselves with this case. Even Major Rennel, starting semi-consciously from his own previous knowledge (the fruit of researches pursued through many centuries after Herodotus), lays down an Africa at least ten times too great for meeting the Greek idea. Unavoidably Herodotus knew the Mediterranean dimensions of Africa; else he would have figured it to himself as an island, equal perhaps to Greece, Macedon, and Thrace. As it was, there is no doubt to us, from many indications, that the Libya of Herodotus, after all, did not exceed the total bulk of Asia Minor carried eastwards to the Tigris. But there is not such an awful corrupter of truth in the whole world,—there is not such an unconquerable enslaver of men's minds,—as the blind instinct by which they yield to the ancient root-bound trebly-anchored prejudications of their childhood and original belief. Misconceive us not, reader. We do not mean that, having learned such and such doctrines, afterwards they cling to them by affection. Not at all. We mean that, duped by a word and the associations clinging to it, they cleave to certain notions, not from any partiality to them, but because this pre-occupation intercepts the very earliest dawn of a possible conception or conjecture in the opposite direction. The most tremendous error in human annals is of that order. It has existed for seventeen centuries in strength; and is not extinct, though public in its action, as upon another occasion we shall show. In this case of Africa, it was not that men resisted the truth according to the ordinary notion of a "prejudice"; it was that every commentator in succession upon Herodotus, coming to the case with the fullest knowledge that Africa was a vast continent, ranging far and wide in both hemispheres, unconsciously slipped into the feeling that this had always been the belief of men,—possibly some might a little fall short of the true estimate, some a little exceed it,—but that, on the whole, it was at least as truly figured to men's minds as either of the two other continents. Accordingly, one and all have presumed a bulk for the Libya of Herodotus absolutely at war with the whole indications. And, if they had once again read Herodotus under the guiding light furnished by a blank denial of this notion, they would have found a meaning in many a word of Herodotus, such as they never suspected whilst trying it only from one side. In this blind submission to a prejudice of words and clustering associations Rennel also shares.

It will be retorted, however, that the long *time* allowed by Herodotus for the voyage argues a corresponding amplitude of dimensions. Doubtless a time upwards of two years is long for a modern *Periplus*, even of that vast continent. But Herodotus knew nothing of monsoons, or trade-winds, or currents: he allowed nothing for these accelerating forces, which were enormous, though allowing fully (could any Greek have neglected to allow?) for all the retarding forces. Daily advances of thirty-three miles at most; nightly reposes, of necessity to men without the compass; above all, a *coasting* navigation, searching (if it were only for water) every nook and inlet, bay, and river's mouth, except only where the winds or currents might violently sweep them past these objects. Then we are to allow for a long stay on the shore of Western Africa, for the sake of reaping, or getting reaped by natives, a wheat harvest—a fact which strengthens the probability of the voyage, but diminishes the disposable time which Herodotus would use as the exponent of the space. We must remember the *want of sails aloft* in ancient vessels, the awkwardness of their build for fast sailing, and, above all, their cautious policy of never tempting the deep, unless when the wind would not be denied. And, in the meantime, all the compensatory forces of air and water, so utterly unsuspected by Herodotus, we must subtract from *his* final summation of the effective motion, leaving for the actual measure of the sailing, as inferred by Herodotus — consequently for the measure of the *virtual* time, consequently of the African space, as only to be collected from the time so corrected—a very small proportion indeed, compared with the results of a similar voyage, even by the Portuguese, about A.D. 1500. To Herodotus we are satisfied that Libya (disarming it of its power over the world's mind in the pompous name of Africa) was not bigger than the true Arabia, or even Spain, as known to ourselves.

And hence, also, by a natural result, the obliteration of this *Periplus* from the minds of men. It accomplished no great service, as men judged. It put a zone about a large region undoubtedly ; but what sort of a region ? A mere worthless wilderness,—here θηριωδης, dedicated by the gods to wild beasts, there ἀμμωδης, trackless from sands, and everywhere fountainless, arid, scorched (as they believed) in the interior. Subtract Egypt, as not being part, and to the world of civilisation at that time Africa must have seemed a worthless desert, except for Cyrene and Carthage, its two choice gardens, already occupied by Phœnicians and Greeks. This, by the way, suggests a new consideration, viz. that even the Mediterranean extent of Africa must have been unknown to Herodotus — since all beyond Carthage, as Mauritania, &c., would wind up into a small inconsiderable tract, as being *dispuncted* by no great states or colonies.

Therefore it was that this most interesting of all circumnavigations at the present day did virtually and could not but perish as a vivid record. It measured a region which

touched no man's prosperity. It recorded a discovery for
which there was no permanent appreciator. A case exists
at this moment, in London, precisely parallel. There is a
chart of New Holland still preserved among the κειμηλια
of the British Museum, which exhibits a *Periplus* of that
vast region from some navigator almost by three centuries
prior to Captain Cook. A rude outline of Cook's labours in
that section had been anticipated at a time when it was not
wanted. Nobody cared about it : value it had none, or
interest ; and it was utterly forgotten. That it did not also
perish in the literal sense, as well as in spirit, was owing to
an accident.

IV.—*The Geographical* Akté *of Greece.*

We had intended to transfer, for the use of our readers,
the diagram imagined by Niebuhr in illustration of this
idea. But our growing exorbitance from our limits warns
us to desist. Two points only we shall notice :—1. That
Niebuhr—not the traveller, as might have been expected,
but his son, the philosophic historian [1]—first threw light on
this idea, which had puzzled multitudes of honest men.
Here we see the same singularity as in the case of Rennel.
In that instance a man without a particle of Greek
"whipped" (to speak *Kentuckicè*) whole crowds of drones
who had more Greek than they could turn to any good
account ; and in the other instance we see a sedentary
scholar, travelling chiefly between his study and his bedroom, doing the work that properly belonged to active travellers. 2. Though we have already given one illustration
of an *Akté* in Asia Minor, it may be well to mention as
another the vast region of Arabia. In fact, to Herodotus
the tract of Arabia and Syria, on the one hand, made up
one akté (the southern) for the Persian Empire ; Asia Minor,
with part of Armenia, made up another akté (the western)
for the same empire : the two being at right angles, and
both abutting on imaginary lines drawn from different points
of the Euphrates.

---

[1] Carsten Niebuhr, the traveller, 1733-1815 ; Berthold G. Niebuhr,
the historian, 1776-1831.—M.

V.—*Chronology of Herodotus.*

The commentator of Herodotus who enjoys the reputation of having best unfolded his chronology is the French President Bouhier.[1] We cannot say that this opinion coincides with our own. There is a lamentable imbecility in all the chronological commentators, of two opposite tendencies. Either they fall into that folly of drivelling infidelity which shivers at every fresh revelation of geology, and every fresh romance of fabulous chronology, as fatal to religious truths ; or, with wiser feelings, but equal silliness, they seek to protect Christianity, by feeble parryings, from a danger which exists only for those who never had any rational principles of faith ; as if the mighty *spiritual* power of Christianity were to be thrown upon her defence as often as any old woman's legend from Hindostan (see Bailly's *Astronomie*), or from Egypt (see · the whole series of chronological commentators on Herodotus), became immeasurably extravagant, and exactly in proportion to that extravagance. Amongst these latter chronologers, perhaps Larcher[2] is the most false and treacherous. He affects a tragical start as often as he rehearses the traditions of the Egyptian priests, and assumes a holy shuddering. "Eh quoi ! Ce seroit donc ces gens-là qui auroient osé insulter à notre sainte religion !" But, all the while, beneath his mask the reader can perceive, not obscurely, a perfidious smile ; as on the face of some indulgent mother, who affects to menace with her hand some favourite child at a distance whilst the present subject of a stranger's complaint, but in fact ill disguises her foolish applause to its petulance.

Two remarks only we shall allow ourselves upon this extensive theme ; which, if once entered in good earnest, would go on to a length more than commensurate with all the rest of our discussion.

1. The three hundred and thirty kings of Egypt who were interposed by the Egyptian priests between the endless dynasty of the gods and the pretty long dynasty of real

---

[1] Bouhier, 1673-1746.—M.
[2] P. H. Larcher, 1726-1812.—M.

kings (the Shepherds, the Pharaohs, &c.) are upon this argument to be objected as mere unmeaning fictions : viz. *that they did nothing.* This argument is reported as a fact (*not as* an argument of rejection) by Herodotus himself, and reported from the volunteer testimony of the priests themselves ; so that the authority for the number of kings is also the authority for their inertia. Can there be better proof needed that they were men of straw, got up to colour the legend of a prodigious antiquity ? The reign of the gods was felt to be somewhat equivocal, as susceptible of allegoric explanations. So this long human dynasty is invented to furnish a substantial basis for the chronology. Meantime, the whole three hundred and thirty are such absolute *fainéans* that confessedly not one act—not one monument of art or labour—is ascribed to their auspices ; whilst *every one* of the real unquestionable sovereigns, coinciding with known periods in the tradition of Greece, or with undeniable events in the divine simplicity of the Hebrew Scriptures, is memorable for some warlike act, some munificent institution, or some almost imperishable monument of architectural power.

2. But weaker even than the fabling spirit of these genealogical inanities is the idle attempt to explode them by turning the years into days. In this way, it is true, we get rid of pretensions to a cloudy antiquity by wholesale clusters. The moonshine and the fairy tales vanish—but how ? To leave us all in a moonless quagmire of substantial difficulties, from which (as has been suggested more than once) there is no extrication at all ; for, if the diurnal years are to reconcile us to the three hundred and thirty kings, what becomes of the incomprehensibly short reigns (not averaging above two or three months for each) on the long basis of time assumed by the priests ; and this in the most peaceful of realms, and in fatal contradiction to another estimate of the priests, by which the kings are made to tally with as many γενεαι, or generations of men ? Herodotus, and doubtless the priests, understood a generation in the sense then universally current ; agreeably to which three generations were equated to a century.

But the questions are endless which grow out of Herodotus. Pliny's Natural History has been usually thought

the greatest Encyclopædia of ancient learning.   But we hold
that Herodotus furnishes by much the largest basis for vast
commentaries revealing the archæologics of the human race ;
whilst, as the eldest of prose writers, he justifies his majestic
station as a brotherly assessor on the same throne with
Homer.

THE THEBAN SPHINX [1]

THE most ancient [2] story in the Pagan records, older by two generations than the story of Troy, is that of Œdipus and his mysterious fate, which wrapt in ruin both himself and all his kindred. No story whatever continued so long to impress the Greek sensibilities with religious awe, or was felt by the great tragic poets to be so supremely fitted for scenical representation. In one of its stages, this story is clothed with the majesty of darkness; in another stage, it is radiant with burning lights of female love, the most faithful and heroic, offering a beautiful relief to the preternatural malice dividing the two sons of Œdipus. This malice was so intense that, when the corpses of both brothers were burned together on the same funeral pyre (as by one tradition they were), the flames from each parted asunder, and refused to mingle.

---

[1] Appeared in one of the numbers for 1849 of the Edinburgh periodical called *Hogg's Instructor*; and reprinted by De Quincey in 1859, in vol. x of his Collected Writings.—M.

[2] That is, amongst stories not wearing a *mythologic* character, such as those of Prometheus, Hercules, &c. The era ot Troy and its siege is doubtless by some centuries older than its usual chronologic date of nine centuries before Christ. And, considering the mature age of Eteocles and Polynices, the two sons of Œdipus, at the period of the "*Seven against Thebes*,"—which seven were contemporary with the *fathers* of the heroes engaged in the Trojan War,—it becomes necessary to add sixty or seventy years to the Trojan date, in order to obtain that of Œdipus and the Sphinx. Out of the Hebrew Scriptures, there is nothing purely historic so old as this. [Œdipus is mentioned both in the Iliad and in the Odyssey; but the legend of his life comes to us most fully and grandly in two of the tragedies of Sophocles—*Œdipus Tyrannus* and *Œdipus Coloneus*.—M.]

This female love was so intense that it survived the death of its object, cared not for human praise or blame, and laughed at the grave which waited in the rear for itself, yawning visibly for immediate retribution.   There are four separate movements through which this impassioned tale devolves; all are of commanding interest, and all wear a character of portentous solemnity, which fits them for harmonizing with the dusky shadows of that deep antiquity into which they ascend.

One only feature there is in the story,—and this belongs to its second stage (which is also its sublimest stage),—where a pure taste is likely to pause, and to revolt from something not perfectly reconciled with the general depth of the colouring.   This lies in the Sphinx's Riddle, which, as hitherto explained, seems to us deplorably below the grandeur of the occasion.   Three thousand years, at the least, have passed away since that riddle was propounded; and it seems odd enough that the proper solution should not present itself till November of 1849.   That is true: it seems odd, but still it is possible that we, in *anno domini* 1849, may see further through a milestone than Œdipus, the king, in the year B.C. twelve or thirteen hundred.   The long interval between the enigma and its answer may remind the reader of an old story in Joe Miller, where a traveller, apparently an inquisitive person, in passing through a toll-bar, said to the keeper, "How do you like your eggs dressed?"   Without waiting for the answer, he rode off; but twenty-five years later, riding through the same bar, kept by the same man, the traveller looked steadfastly at him, and received the monosyllabic answer, "*Poached.*"   A long parenthesis is twenty-five years; and we, gazing back over a far wider gulf of time, shall endeavour to look hard at the Sphinx, and to convince that mysterious young lady—if our voice can reach her—that she was too easily satisfied with the answer given; that the true answer is yet to come; and that, in fact, Œdipus shouted before he was out of the wood.

But, first of all, let us rehearse the circumstances of this old Grecian story.   For in a popular journal it is always a duty to assume that perhaps three readers out of four may have had no opportunity, by the course of their education, for making themselves acquainted with classical legends. And in this present case, besides the indispensableness of the story to the proper comprehension of our own improved answer to the Sphinx, the story has a separate and independent value of its own; for it illustrates a profound but obscure idea of pagan ages, which is connected with the elementary glimpses of man into the abysses of his higher relations, and lurks mysteriously amongst what Milton so finely calls "the dark foundations" of our human nature. This notion it is hard to express in modern phrase, for we have no idea exactly corresponding to it; but in Latin it was called *piacularity*. The reader must understand upon our authority, *nostro periculo*, and in defiance of all the false translations spread through books, that the ancients (meaning the Greeks and Romans before the time of Christianity) had no idea, not by the faintest vestige, of what in the scriptural system is called *sin*. The Latin word *peccatum*, the Greek word *amartia*, are translated continually by the word *sin*; but neither one word nor the other has any such meaning in writers belonging to the pure classical period. When baptized into new meanings through their adoption by Christianity, these words, in common with many others, transmigrated into new and philosophic functions. But originally they tended towards no such acceptations; nor *could* have done so, —seeing that the ancients had no avenue opened to them through which the profound idea of *sin* would have been even dimly intelligible. Plato, 400 years before Christ, or Cicero, more than 300 years later, was fully equal to the idea of *guilt* through all its gamut; but no more equal to the idea of *sin* than a sagacious hound to the idea of gravitation, or of central forces. It is the tremendous postulate upon which this idea reposes that constitutes the initial moment of that revelation which is common to Judaism and to Christianity. We have no intention of wandering into any discussion upon this question. It will suffice for the service of the occasion if we say that guilt, in all its modifications, implies only a defect or a wound in the individual. Sin, on the other hand, the most mysterious, and the most sorrowful of all ideas, implies a taint not in the individual but in the race, —*that* is the distinction; or a taint in the individual, not through any local disease of his own, but through a scrofula equally diffused through the infinite family of man. We are not speaking controversially, either as teachers of theology or of philosophy ; and we are careless of the particular construction by which the reader interprets to himself this profound idea. What we affirm is, that this idea was utterly and exquisitely inappreciable by Pagan Greece and Rome ; that various translations from Pindar,[1] from Aristophanes, and from the Greek tragedians, embodying at intervals this word *sin*, are more extravagant than would be the word *category*, or the *synthetic unity of consciousness*, introduced into the harangue of an Indian sachem amongst the Cherokees ; and, finally, that the very nearest approach to the abysmal idea which we Christians attach to the word sin (an approach, but to that which never can be touched ; a writing as of palmistry upon each man's hand, but a writing which "no man can read ") lies in the pagan idea of *piacularity ;* which is an idea thus far like hereditary sin, that it expresses an evil to which the party affected has not consciously concurred ; which is thus far *not* like hereditary sin, that it expresses an evil personal to the individual, and not extending itself to the race.

This was the evil exemplified in Œdipus. He was loaded with an insupportable burthen of pariah participation in pollution and misery, to which his will had never consented. He seemed to have committed the most atrocious crimes ; he was a murderer, he was a parricide, he was persistently incestuous ; and yet how ? In the case where he might be thought a murderer, he had stood upon his self-defence, not

---

[1] And, when we are speaking of this subject, it may be proper to mention (as the very extreme anachronism which the case admits of), that Mr. Archdeacon W. has absolutely introduced the idea of sin into the *Iliad*, and, in a regular octavo volume, has represented it as the key to the whole movement of the fable. It was once made a reproach to Southey that his Don Roderick spoke, in his penitential moods, a language too much resembling that of Methodism : yet, after all, that prince was a Christian, and a Christian amongst Mussulmans. But what are we to think of Achilles and Ajax, when described as being (or *not* being) "under convictions of sin " ? [The " Mr. Archdeacon W." of this note was Archdeacon Williams, a learned and eccentric Welshman, and a familiar figure in Edinburgh from 1824 onwards, when he was Rector of the Edinburgh Academy.—M.]

benefiting by any superior resources, but, on the contrary,
fighting as one man against three, and under the provocation
of insufferable insolence. Had he been a parricide? What
matter, as regarded the moral guilt, if his father (and by the
fault of that father) were utterly unknown to him? Incestuous had he been? but how, if the very oracles of fate, as
expounded by events, and by mysterious creatures such as
the Sphinx, had stranded him, like a ship left by the tide,
upon this dark unknown shore of a criminality unsuspected
by himself? All these treasons against the sanctities of
nature had Œdipus committed; and yet was this Œdipus a
thoroughly good man, no more dreaming of the horrors in
which he was entangled than the eye at noon-day in mid-
summer is conscious of the stars that lie far behind the daylight. Let us review rapidly the incidents of his life.

Laius, king of Thebes, the descendant of Labdacus, and
representing the illustrious house of the Labdacidæ, about the
time when his wife, Jocasta, promised to present him with a
child, had learned from various prophetic voices that this
unborn child was destined to be his murderer. It is singular
that in all such cases, which are many, spread through classical
literature, the parties menaced by fate believe the menace,—
else why do they seek to evade it; and yet believe it not,—
else why do they fancy themselves able to evade it? This
fatal child, who was the Œdipus of tragedy, being at length
born, Laius committed the infant to a slave, with orders to
expose it on Mount Cithæron. This was done: the infant
was suspended, by thongs running through the fleshy parts
of his feet, to the branches of a tree, and he was supposed to
have perished by wild beasts. But a shepherd, who found
him in this perishing state, pitied his helplessness, and carried
him to his master and mistress, king and queen of Corinth,
who adopted and educated him as their own child. That he
was *not* their own child, and that in fact he was a foundling
of unknown parentage, Œdipus was not slow of finding from
the taunts of his schoolfellows; and, at length, with the
determination of learning his origin and his fate, being now
a full-grown young man, he strode off from Corinth to Delphi.
The oracle at Delphi, being as usual in collusion with his
evil destiny, sent him off to seek his parents at Thebes. On

his journey thither, he met, in a narrow part of the road, a chariot proceeding in the counter direction from Thebes to Delphi. The charioteer, relying upon the grandeur of his master, insolently ordered the young stranger to clear the road ; upon which, under the impulse of his youthful blood, Œdipus slew him on the spot. The haughty grandee who occupied the chariot rose up in fury to avenge this outrage, fought with the younger stranger, and was himself killed. One attendant upon the chariot remained ; but he, warned by the fate of his master and his fellow-servant, withdrew quietly into the forest that skirted the road, revealing no word of what had happened, but reserved by the dark destiny of Œdipus to that evil day on which *his* evidence, concurring with other circumstantial exposures, should convict the young Corinthian emigrant of parricide. For the present, Œdipus viewed himself as no criminal, but much rather as an injured man, who had simply used his natural powers of self-defence against an insolent aggressor. This aggressor, as the reader will suppose, was Laius. The throne therefore was empty on the arrival of Œdipus in Thebes : the king's death was known indeed, but not the mode of it ; and that Œdipus was the murderer could not reasonably be suspected either by the people of Thebes, or by Œdipus himself. The whole affair would have had no interest for the young stranger, but through the accident of a public calamity then desolating the land. A mysterious monster, called the Sphinx, half woman and half brute, was at that time on the coast of Bœotia, and levying a daily tribute of human lives from the Bœotian territory. This tribute, it was understood, would continue to be levied from the territories attached to Thebes, until a riddle proposed by the monster should have been satisfactorily solved. By way of encouragement to all who might feel prompted to undertake so dangerous an adventure, the authorities of Thebes offered the throne and the hand of the widowed Jocasta as the prize of success ; and Œdipus, either on public or on selfish motives, entered the lists as a competitor.

The riddle proposed by the Sphinx ran in these terms : " What creature is that which moves on four feet in the " morning, on two feet at noon-day, and on three towards the

" going down of the sun ? " Œdipus, after some consideration, answered that the creature was MAN, who creeps on the ground with hands and feet when an infant, walks upright in the vigour of manhood, and leans upon a staff in old age. Immediately the dreadful Sphinx confessed the truth of his solution by throwing herself headlong from a point of rock into the sea ; her power being overthrown as soon as her secret had been detected. Thus was the Sphinx destroyed ; and, according to the promise of the proclamation, for this great service to the state Œdipus was immediately recompensed. He was saluted King of Thebes, and married to the royal widow Jocasta. In this way it happened, but without suspicion either in himself or others pointing to the truth, that Œdipus had slain his father, had ascended his father's throne, and had married his own mother.

Through a course of years all these dreadful events lay hushed in darkness ; but at length a pestilence arose, and an embassy was despatched to Delphi, in order to ascertain the cause of the heavenly wrath, and the proper means of propitiating that wrath. The embassy returned to Thebes armed with a knowledge of the fatal secrets connected with Œdipus, but under some restraints of prudence in making a publication of what so dreadfully affected the most powerful personage in the state. Perhaps in the whole history of human art as applied to the evolution of a poetic fable there is nothing more exquisite than the management of this crisis by Sophocles. A natural discovery, first of all, connects Œdipus with the death of Laius. That discovery comes upon him with some surprise, but with no shock of fear or remorse. That he had killed a man of rank in a sudden quarrel, he had always known ; that this man was now discovered to be Laius added nothing to the reasons for regret. The affair remained as it was. It was simply a case of personal strife on the highroad, and one which had really grown out of aristocratic violence in the adverse party. Œdipus had asserted his own rights and dignity only as all brave men would have done in an age that knew nothing of civic police.

It was true that this first discovery—the identification of himself as the slayer of Laius—drew after it two others : viz. that it was the throne of his victim on which he had seated himself, and that it was *his* widow whom he married. But these were no offences : and, on the contrary, they were distinctions won at great risk to himself, and by a great service to the country. Suddenly, however, the reappearance and disclosures of the shepherd who had saved his life during infancy in one moment threw a dazzling but funereal light upon the previous discoveries that else had seemed so trivial. In an instant everything was read in another sense. The death of Laius, the marriage with his widow, the appropriation of his throne, the incest with his mother, which had called into life four children (two daughters Ismene and Antigone, with two fierce rival sons Eteocles and Polynices), all towered into colossal crimes, illimitable, and opening no avenues to atonement. Œdipus, in the agonies of his horror, inflicts blindness upon himself ; Jocasta commits suicide ; the two sons fall into fiery feuds for the assertion of their separate claims on the throne, but previously unite for the expulsion of Œdipus, as one who had become a curse to Thebes. And thus the poor heart-shattered king would have been turned out upon the public roads, aged, blind, and a helpless vagrant, but for the sublime piety of his two daughters, but especially of Antigone, the elder. They share with their unhappy father the hardships and perils of the road, and do not leave him until the moment of his mysterious summons to some ineffable death in the woods of Colonus, not far from Athens. The expulsion of Polynices, the younger son, from Thebes ; his return with a confederate band of princes for the recovery of his rights ; the death of the two brothers in single combat ; the public prohibition of funeral rites to Polynices, as one who had levied war against his native land ; and the final reappearance of Antigone, who defies the law, and secures a grave to her brother at the certain price of a grave to herself :—these are the sequels and arrears of the family overthrow accomplished through the dark destiny of Œdipus.

And now, having reviewed the incidents of the story, in what respect is it that we object to the solution of the Sphinx's Riddle ? We do not object to it as *a* solution of the riddle, and the only one possible at the moment. It is really *a* solution ; and for the moment a satisfactory solution ;

but what we contend is that it is not *the* solution.   All great prophecies, all great mysteries, are likely to involve double, triple, or even quadruple interpretations ; each rising in dignity, each cryptically involving another.   Even amongst natural agencies, precisely as they rise in grandeur, they multiply their final purposes.   Rivers and seas, for instance, are useful, not merely as means of separating nations from each other, but also as means of uniting them ; not merely as baths, and for all purposes of washing and cleansing, but also as reservoirs of fish, as highroads for the conveyance of commodities, as permanent sources of agricultural fertility, &c.   In like manner, a mystery of any sort having a public reference may be presumed to couch within it a secondary and a profounder interpretation.   The reader may think that the Sphinx ought to have understood her own riddle best ; and that, if *she* were satisfied with the answer of Œdipus, it must be impertinent in us at this time of day to censure it. To censure, indeed, is more than we propose.   The solution of Œdipus was a true one ; and it was all that he *could* have given in that early period of his life.   But perhaps, at the moment of his death amongst the gloomy thickets of Attica, he might have been able to suggest another and a better.   If not, then we have the satisfaction of thinking ourselves somewhat less dense than Œdipus.   The slave in Terence, viz. Davus, though otherwise a clever fellow, when puzzled by a secret, or (as in America they say) *teetotaciously exfluncticated*, excuses himself by saying—" Davus sum, non Œdipus " ; but we make no such excuse.   We hold ourselves a cut above Œdipus and the Sphinx together.   Exfluncticated we certainly were : but not teetotaciously ; for a few years' meditation whispered to us that revelation, that second vision of truth, which not Davus, nor even Œdipus, in moments when it might have saved him, could guess ; for, in our opinion, the full and *final* answer to the Sphinx's riddle lay in the word ŒDIPUS.   Œdipus himself it was that fulfilled the conditions of the enigma.   He it was, in the most pathetic sense, that went upon four feet when an infant ; for the general condition of helplessness attached to all mankind in the period of infancy, and which is expressed symbolically by this image of creeping, applied to Œdipus in a far more significant manner, as one abandoned by all his natural protectors, thrown upon the chances of a wilderness, and upon the mercies of a slave. The allusion to this general helplessness had, besides, a special propriety in the case of Œdipus, who drew his very name (viz. *Swollen Foot*) from the injury done to his infant feet. He again it was that, in a more emphatic sense than usual, asserted that majestic self-sufficingness and independence of all alien aid which is typified by the act of walking upright at noonday upon his own natural basis. Throwing off all the power and splendour borrowed from his royal protectors at Corinth, trusting exclusively to his native powers as a man, he had fought his way through insult and outrage to the presence of the dreadful Sphinx ; her he had confounded and vanquished ; he had leaped into a throne, the throne of him who had insulted him, without other resources than such as he drew from himself; and he had in the same way obtained a royal bride. With good right, therefore, he was foreshadowed in the riddle as one who walked upright by his own masculine vigour, and relied upon no gifts but those of nature. Lastly, but by a sad and a pitying image, Œdipus is described as supporting himself at nightfall on three feet : for Œdipus it was that by his cruel sons would have been rejected from Thebes with no auxiliary means of motion or support beyond his own languishing powers : blind and broken-hearted, he must have wandered into snares and ruin ; his own feet must have been supplanted immediately ; but then came to his aid another foot, the holy Antigone. She it was that guided and cheered him when all the world had forsaken him ; she it was that already, in the vision of the cruel Sphinx, had been prefigured dimly as the staff upon which Œdipus should lean, as the *third* foot that should support his steps when the deep shadows of his sunset were gathering and settling about his grave.

In this way we obtain a solution of the Sphinx's Riddle more commensurate and symmetrical with the other features of the story, which are all clothed with the grandeur of mystery. This Sphinx herself is a mystery. Whence came her monstrous nature, that so often renewed its remembrance amongst men of distant lands in Egyptian or Ethiopian marble ?   Whence came her wrath against Thebes ?   This wrath, how durst it tower so high as to measure itself against the enmity of a nation ?   This wrath, how came it to sink so low as to collapse at the echo of a word from a friendless stranger ?   Mysterious again is the blind collusion of this unhappy stranger with the dark decrees of fate.   The very misfortunes of his infancy had given into his hands one chance more for escape : these misfortunes had transferred him to Corinth ; and, staying *there*, he was safe.   But the headstrong haughtiness of youthful blood causes him to recoil unknowingly upon the one sole spot of all the earth where the co-efficients for ratifying his destruction are all lying in ambush.   Heaven and earth are silent for a generation ; one might fancy that they are *treacherously* silent, in order that Œdipus may have time for building up to the clouds the pyramid of his mysterious offences.   His four children, incestuously born—sons that are his brothers, daughters that are his sisters—have grown up to be men and women before the first mutterings are becoming audible of that great tide, slowly coming up from the sea, which is to sweep away himself and the foundations of his house.   Heaven and earth must now bear joint witness against him.   Heaven speaks first : the pestilence that walketh in darkness is made the earliest minister of the discovery ; the pestilence it is, scourging the seven-gated Thebes, as very soon the Sphinx also will scourge her, that is appointed to usher in, like some great ceremonial herald, that sad drama of Nemesis, that vast procession of revelation and retribution which the earth, and the graves of the earth, must finish.   Mysterious also is the pomp of ruin with which this revelation of the past descends upon that ancient house of Thebes.   Like a shell from modern artillery, it leaves no time for prayer or evasion, but shatters by the same explosion all that stand within its circle of fury.   Every member of that devoted household, as if they had been sitting not around a sacred domestic hearth, but around the crater of some surging volcano,—all alike, father and mother, sons and daughters, are wrapt at once in fiery whirlwinds of ruin.   And, amidst this general agony of destroying wrath, one central mystery, as a darkness within a darkness, withdraws itself into a secrecy unapproachable by eyesight, or by filial love, or by guesses of the brain,—and *that* is the death of Œdipus. *Did* he die? Even *that* is more than we can say. How dreadful does the sound fall upon the heart of some poor, horror-stricken criminal, pirate or murderer, that has offended by a mere human offence, when, at nightfall, tempted by the sweet spectacle of a peaceful hearth, he creeps stealthily into some village inn, and hopes for one night's respite from his terror, but suddenly feels the touch and hears the voice of the stern officer, saying, "Sir, you are wanted." Yet that summons is but too intelligible: it shocks, but it bewilders not; and the utmost of its malice is bounded by the scaffold. "Deep," says the unhappy man, "is the downward path of anguish which I am called to tread; but it has been trodden by others." For Œdipus there was no such comfort. What language of earth or trumpet of heaven could decipher the woe of that unfathomable call, when, from the depth of ancient woods, a voice that drew like gravitation, that sucked in like a vortex, far off yet near,—in some distant world, yet close at hand,—cried, "Hark, Œdipus! King Œdipus! come hither! thou art wanted!" *Wanted!* for what? Was it for death? was it for judgment? was it for some wilderness of pariah eternities? No man ever knew. Chasms opened in the earth; dark gigantic arms stretched out to receive the king; clouds and vapour settled over the penal abyss; and of him only, though the neighbourhood of his disappearance was known, no trace or visible record survived,—neither bones, nor grave, nor dust, nor epitaph.

Did the Sphinx follow with her cruel eye this fatal tissue of calamity to its shadowy crisis at Colonus? As the billows closed over her head, did she perhaps attempt to sting with her dying words? Did she say, "I, the daughter of mystery, am *called*; I am *wanted*. But, amidst the uproar of the sea, and the clangour of sea-birds, high over all I hear another though a distant summons. I can hear that thou, Œdipus, son of mystery, art *called* from afar; thou also wilt be *wanted*." Did the wicked Sphinx labour in vain, amidst her parting convulsions, to breathe this freezing whisper into the heart of him that had overthrown her?

Who can say? Both of these enemies were pariah

mysteries, and may have faced each other again with blazing malice in some pariah world. But all things in this dreadful story ought to be harmonized. Already in itself it is an ennobling and an idealizing of the riddle that it is made a double riddle : that it contains an exoteric sense obvious to all the world, but also an esoteric sense— now suggested conjecturally after thousands of years—*possibly* unknown to the Sphinx, and *certainly* unknown to Œdipus ; that this second riddle is hid within the first ; that the one riddle is the secret commentary upon the other ; and that the earliest is the hieroglyphic of the last. Thus far as regards the riddle itself ; and, as regards Œdipus in particular, it exalts the mystery around him, that, in reading this riddle, and in tracing the vicissitudes from infancy to old age attached to the general destiny of his race, unconsciously he was tracing the dreadful vicissitudes attached specially and separately to his own.

TOILETTE OF THE HEBREW LADY

EXHIBITED IN SIX SCENES[1]

To the Editor of a great Literary Journal[2]

SIR,—Some years ago you published a translation of
Bottiger's *Sabina*, a learned account of the Roman toilette.
I here send you a companion to that work,—not a direct
translation, but a very minute abstract (weeded of that wordi-
ness which has made the original unreadable, and therefore
unread) from a similar dissertation by Hartmann on the
toilette and the wardrobe of the ladies of ancient Palestine.
Hartmann was a respectable Oriental scholar, and he published his researches, which occupy three thick octavos,
making in all one thousand four hundred and eighty-eight
pages, under the title of *Die Hebräerin am Putztische und als
Braut*, Amsterdam, 1809 (*The Hebrew Woman at her Toilette,
and in her Bridal Character*). I understand that the poor
man is now gone to Hades; where, let us hope that it is
considered by Minos or Rhadamanthus no crime in a learned
man to be exceedingly tedious, and to repeat the same thing
ten times over, or even, upon occasion, fifteen times, provided that his own upright heart should incline him to think
that course the most advisable. Certainly Mr. Hartmann
has the most excellent gifts at verbal expansion, and talents
the most splendid for tautology, that ever came within my

---

[1] In *Blackwood's Magazine* for March 1828; reprinted by De
Quincey in 1859 in the twelfth volume of his Collected Writings.—M.

[2] Originally "To the Editor of *Blackwood's Magazine*," and one
hardly sees why De Quincey made the change.—M.

knowledge ; and I have found no particular difficulty in compressing every tittle of what relates to his subject into a compass which, I imagine, will fill about one twenty-eighth part at the utmost of the original work.

It was not to be expected, with the scanty materials before him, that an illustrator of the Hebrew costume should be as full and explicit as Böttiger, with the advantage of writing upon a theme more familiar to us Europeans of this day than any parallel theme even in our own national archæologies of two centuries back. United, however, with his great reading, this barrenness of the subject is so far an advantage for Hartmann, as it yields a strong presumption that he has exhausted it. The male costume of ancient Palestine is yet to be illustrated ; but, for the female, it is probable that little could be added to what Hartmann has collected,[1] and that any clever dressmaker would, with the indications here given, enable any lady at the next great masquerade in London to support the part of one of the ancient daughters of Palestine, and to call ˙ back, after eighteen centuries of sleep, the buried pomps of Jerusalem. As to the *talking*, there would be no difficulty at all in that point : bishops and other " sacred " people, if they ever go a-masquing, for their own sakes will not be likely to betray themselves by putting impertinent questions in Hebrew ; and, for " profane " people like myself, who might like the impertinence, they would very much dislike the Hebrew ; indeed, of uncircumcised Hebrews, barring always the clergy, it is not thought that any are extant. In other respects, and as a *spectacle*, the Hebrew masque would infallibly eclipse every other in the room. The upper and under

---

[1] It is one great advantage to the illustrator of ancient costume that,—when almost everything in this sort of usages was fixed and determined either by religion and state policy (as with the Jews), or by state policy alone (as with the Romans), or by superstition and by settled climate (as with both) ; and when there was no stimulation to vanity in the love of change from an inventive condition of art and manufacturing skill ; and where the system and interests of the government relied for no part of its power on such a condition,—dress was stationary for ages, both as to materials and fashion. Rebecca, the Bedouin, was dressed pretty nearly as Mariamne, the wife of Herod, in the age of the Cæsars. And thus the labours of a learned investigator for one age are valid for many which follow and precede.

chemise, if managed properly (and either you or I, Mr. Editor, will be most proud to communicate our private advice on that subject, without fee or *pot-de-vin*, as the French style a bribe), would transcend, in gorgeous display, the coronation robes of queens ; nose-pendants would cause the masque to be immediately and unerringly recognised ; or, if those were not thought advisable, the silver ankle-bells, with their melodious chimes—the sandals, with their jewelled network—and the golden diadem, binding the fore-head, and dropping from each extremity of the polished temples a rouleau of pearls, which, after traversing the cheeks, unite below the chin,—are all so unique and exclusively Hebraic that each and all would have the same advantageous effect ; proclaiming and notifying the character, without putting the fair supporter to any disagreeable expense of Hebrew or Chaldee. The silver bells alone would " bear the bell " from every competitor in the room ; and she might, besides, carry a cymbal, a dulcimer, or a timbrel in her hands.

In conclusion, my dear Sir, let me congratulate you that Mr. Hartmann is now in Hades (as I said before) rather than in ——— ; for, had he been in this latter place, he would have been the ruin of you. It was his intention, as I am well assured, just about the time that he took his flight for Elysium, to have commenced regular contributor to your journal ; so great was his admiration of you, and also of the terms which you offer to the literary world. As a learned Orientalist, you could not decorously have rejected him ; and yet, once admitted, he would have beggared you before any means could have been discovered by the learned for putting a stop to him. Ἀπεραντολογια, or what may be translated literally *world-without-ending-ness*, was his forte ; upon this he piqued himself, and most justly, since for covering the ground rapidly, and yet not advancing an inch, those who knew and valued him as he deserved would have backed him against the whole field of the *gens de plume* now in Europe. Had he lived, and fortunately for himself com-municated his *Hebrew Toilette* to the world through you, instead of foundering (as he did) at Amsterdam, he would have flourished upon your exchequer ; and you would not have heard the last of him or his Toilette for the next twenty years. He dates, you see, from Amsterdam ; and, had you been weak enough to take him on board, he would have proved that "Flying Dutchman" that would infallibly have sunk your vessel.

The more is your obligation to me, I think, for sweating him down to such slender dimensions. And, speaking seriously, both of us perhaps will rejoice that, even with *his* talents for telling everything, he was obliged on this subject to leave many things untold. For, though it might be gratifying to a mere interest of curiosity, yet I believe that we should both be grieved if anything were to unsettle in our feelings the mysterious sanctities of Jerusalem, or to disturb that awful twilight which will for ever brood over Judea, by letting in upon it the "common light of day" ; and this effect would infallibly take place, if any one department of daily life as it existed in Judea were brought, with all the degrading minutiæ of its details, within the petty finishing of a domestic portrait.

Farewell, my dear Sir, and believe me always your devoted servant and admirer, Ω. Φ.[1]

Scene the First

I. That simple body-cloth, framed of leaves, skins, flax, wool, &c., which modesty had first introduced, for many centuries perhaps sufficed as the common attire of both sexes amongst the Hebrew Bedouins. It extended downwards to the knees, and upwards to the hips, about which it was fastened. Such a dress is seen upon many of the figures in the sculptures of Persepolis ; even in modern times, Niebuhr found it the ordinary costume of the lower Arabians in Hedsjas ; and Shaw assures us that, from its commodious shape, it is still a favourite dishabille of the Arabian women when they are behind the curtains of the tent.

From this early rudiment was derived, by gradual elon-

---

[1] In the original of this letter in *Blackwood* the ending had been in this form, "Farewell, my dear North, and believe me your old friend and admirer, Ω. Φ." So in the preceding sentences "Mr. North" or "dear North," had stood for "Sir" or "dear Sir."—M.

gation, that well-known under-habiliment which in Hebrew is called *Ch'tonet*, and in Greek and Latin by words of similar sound.[1]   In this stage of its progress, when extended to the neck and the shoulders, it represents pretty accurately the modern shirt, *camisa* or *chemise*—except that the sleeves are wanting ; and during the first period of Jewish history it was probably worn as the sole under-garment by women of all ranks, both amongst the Bedouin-Hebrews and those who lived in cities.   A very little further extension to the elbows and the calves of the legs, and it takes a shape which survives even to this day in Asia.   Now, as then, the female habiliment was distinguished from the corresponding male one by its greater length ; and through all antiquity we find long clothes a subject of reproach to men, as an argument of effeminacy.

According to the rank or vanity of the wearer, this tunic was made of more or less costly materials ; for wool and flax was often substituted the finest byssus, or other silky substance ; and perhaps, in the latter periods, amongst families of distinction in Jerusalem, even silk itself.   Splendour of colouring was not neglected ; and the opening at the throat was eagerly turned to account as an occasion for displaying fringe or rich embroidery.

Bottiger remarks that, even in the age of Augustus, the morning dress of Roman ladies when at home was nothing more than this very tunic, which, if it sate close, did not even require a girdle.   The same remark applies to the Hebrew women, who, during the nomadic period of their history, had been accustomed to wear no night chemises at all, but slept quite naked,[2] or, at the utmost, with a cestus or zone : by way of bed-clothes, however, it must be observed that they swathed their person in the folds of a robe or

---

[1] *Chiton* (Χιτων), in Greek, and, by inversion of the syllables, *Tunica* in Latin ; that is (1.) *Chi-ton ;* then (2.) *Ton-chi.*   But, if so, (3.) Why not *Ton-cha ;* and (4.) Why not *Tun-cha ;* as also (5.) Why not *Tun-i-ca ?*—Q. E. D.   Such, I believe, is the received derivation.

[2] When the little Scottish King, about 1566, was taken ill in the night at Holyrood, Pinkerton mentions that all his attendants, male and female, rushed out into the adjacent gallery, naked as they were born ; and thence comes the phrase so often used in the contemporary ballads—"Even as I left my naked bed."

shawl. Up to the time of Solomon this practice obtained through all ranks, and so long the universal household dress of a Hebrew lady in her harem was the tunic as here described ; and in this she dressed herself the very moment that she rose from bed. Indeed, so long as the Hebrew women were content with a single tunic, it flowed loose in liberal folds about the body, and was fastened by a belt or a clasp, just as we find it at this day amongst all Asiatic nations. But, when a second under-garment was introduced, the inner one fitted close to the shape, whilst the outer one remained full and free as before.

II. No fashion of the female toilet is of higher antiquity than that of dyeing the margin of the eyelids and the eye-brows with a black pigment. It is mentioned or alluded to, 2 Kings ix. 30, Jeremiah iv. 30, Ezekiel xxiii. 40 ; to which may be added Isaiah iii. 16. The practice had its origin in a discovery made accidentally in Egypt. For it happens that the substance used for this purpose in ancient times is a powerful remedy in cases of ophthalmia and inflammation of the eyes,—complaints to which Egypt is, from local causes, peculiarly exposed. This endemic infirmity, in connexion with the medical science for which Egypt was so distinguished, easily accounts for their discovering the uses of antimony, which is the principal ingredient in the pigments of this class. Egypt was famous for the fashion of painting the face from an early period ; and in some remarkable curiosities illustrating the Egyptian toilette, which were discovered in the catacombs of Sahara in Middle Egypt, there was a single joint of a common reed containing an ounce or more of the colouring powder, and one of the needles for applying it. The entire process was as follows :—The mineral powder, finely prepared, was mixed up with a preparation of vinegar and gall-apples—sometimes with oil of almonds or other oils —sometimes, by very luxurious women, with costly gums and balsams.[1] And perhaps, as Sonnini describes the practice

---

[1] Cheaper materials were used by the poorer Hebrews, especially of the Bedouin tribes—burnt almonds, lamp-black, soot, the ashes of particular woods, the gall-apple boiled and pulverised, or any dark powder made into an unguent by suitable liquors. The modern Grecian women, in some districts, as Sonnini tells us, use the spine of

among the Mussulman women at present, the whole mass thus compounded was dried and again reduced to an impalpable powder, and consistency then given to it by the vapours of some odorous and unctuous substance.   Thus prepared, the pigment was applied to the tip or pointed ferule of a little metallic pencil, called in Hebrew *Makachol*, and made of silver, gold, or ivory ; the eyelids were then closed, and the little pencil, or probe, held horizontally, was inserted between them, a process which is briefly and picturesquely described in the Bible.   The effect of the black rim which the pigment traced about the eyelid was to throw a dark and majestic shadow over the eye ; to give it a languishing and yet a lustrous expression ; to increase its apparent size, and to apply the force of contrast to the white of the eye.   Together with the eyelids, the Hebrew women coloured the eyebrows . the point aimed at being twofold—to curve them into a beautiful arch of brilliant ebony, and, at the same time, to make the inner ends meet or flow into each other.

III. EAR-RINGS of gold, silver, inferior metals, or even horn, were worn by the Hebrew women in all ages ; and, in the flourishing period of the Jewish kingdom, probably by men ; and so essential an ornament were they deemed that in the idolatrous times even the images of their false gods were not considered becomingly attired without them.   Their ear-rings were larger, according to the Asiatic taste, but whether quite large enough to admit the hand is doubtful. In a later age, as we collect from the Thalmud, Part vi. 43, the Jewish ladies wore gold or silver pendants, of which the upper part was shaped like a lentil, and the lower hollowed like a little cup or pipkin.   It is probable also that, even in the oldest ages, it was a practice amongst them to suspend gold and silver rings, not merely from the lower but also from the upper end of the ear, which was perforated like a sieve.   The tinkling sound with which, upon the slightest motion, two or three tiers of rings would be set a-dancing about the cheeks, was very agreeable to the baby taste of the Asiatics.

the sea-polypus, calcined and finally pulverised, for this purpose. Boxes of horn were used for keeping the pigment by the poorer Hebrews,—of onyx or alabaster by the richer.

From a very early age the ears of Hebrew women were prepared for this load of trinketry; for, according to the Thalmud (ii. 23), they kept open the little holes after they were pierced by threads or slips of wood, a fact which may show the importance they attached to this ornament.

IV. NOSE-RINGS at an early period became a universal ornament in Palestine. We learn, from Biblical and from Arabic authority, that it was a practice of Patriarchal descent, amongst both the African and Asiatic Bedouins, to suspend rings of iron, wood, or braided hair, from the nostrils of camels, oxen, &c.—the rope by which the animal was guided being attached to these rings. It is probable, therefore, that the early Hebrews, who dwelt in tents, and who in the barrenness of desert scenery drew most of their hints for improving their personal embellishment from the objects immediately about them, were indebted for their nose-rings to this precedent of their camels. Sometimes a ring depended from both nostrils; and the size of it was equal to that of the ear-ring; so that, at times, its compass included both upper and under lip, as in the frame of a picture; and, in the age succeeding to Solomon's reign, we hear of rings which were not less than three inches in diameter. Hebrew ladies of distinction had sometimes a cluster of nose-rings, as well for the tinkling sound which they were contrived to emit, as for the shining light which they threw off upon the face.

That the nose-ring possessed no unimportant place in the Jewish toilette is evident from its being ranked, during the nomadic state of the Israelites, as one of the most valuable presents that a young Hebrew woman could receive from her lover. Amongst the Midianites, who were enriched by the caravan commerce, even men adopted this ornament: and this appears to have been the case in the family to which Job belonged (chap. xli. 2). Under these circumstances, we should naturally presume that the Jewish courtezans, in the cities of Palestine, would not omit so conspicuous a trinket, with its glancing lights, and its tinkling sound: this we might presume, even without the authority of the Bible; but, in fact, both Isaiah and

Ezekiel expressly mention it amongst their artifices of attraction.

Judith, when she appeared before the tent of Holofernes in the whole pomp of her charms, and apparelled with the most elaborate attention to splendour of effect, for the purpose of captivating the hostile general, did not omit this ornament. Even the Jewish proverbs show how highly it was valued ; and that it continued to be valued in later times appears from the ordinances of the Thalmud (ii. 21) in respect to the parts of the female wardrobe which were allowed to be worn on the Sabbath.

V. The Hebrew women of high rank, in the flourishing period of their state, wore NECKLACES, composed of multiple rows of pearls. The thread on which the pearls were strung was of flax or woollen,—and sometimes coloured, as we learn from the Thalmud (vi. 43) ; and the different rows were not exactly concentric ; but, whilst some invested the throat, others descended to the bosom, and in many cases even to the zone. On this part of the dress was lavished the greatest expense ; and the Roman reproach was sometimes true of a Hebrew family, that its whole estate was locked up in a necklace. Tertullian complains heavily of a particular pearl necklace, which had cost about ten thousand pounds of English money, as of an enormity of extravagance. But, after making every allowance for greater proximity to the pearl fisheries, and for other advantages enjoyed by the people of Palestine, there is reason to believe that some Hebrew ladies possessed pearls which had cost at least five times that sum.[1] So much may be affirmed, without meaning to compare the most lavish of the ladies of Jerusalem with those of Rome, where it is recorded of some *élégantes* that they actually slept with little bags of pearls suspended from their necks, that, even when sleeping, they might have mementoes of their pomp.

But the Hebrew necklaces were not always composed

---

[1] Cleopatra had a couple at that value ; and Julius Cæsar had one, which he gave to Servilia, the beautiful mother of Brutus, valued by knaves who wished to buy (*empturiebant*) at forty-eight thousand pounds English, but by the envious female world of Rome at sixty-three thousand.

of pearls, or of pearls only : sometimes it was the custom to interchange the pearls with little golden bulbs or berries : sometimes they were blended with the precious stones ; and at other times the pearls were strung two and two, and their beautiful whiteness relieved by the interposition of red coral.

VI. Next came the BRACELETS, of gold or ivory, and fitted up at the open side with a buckle or enamelled clasp of elaborate workmanship. These bracelets were also occasionally composed of gold or silver thread ; and it was not unusual for a series of them to ascend from the wrist to the elbow. From the clasp, or other fastening of the bracelet, depended a delicate chain-work or netting of gold, and in some instances miniature festoons of pearls. Sometimes the gold chain-work was exchanged for little silver bells, which could be used, upon occasion, as signals of warning or invitation to a lover.

VII. This *bijouterie* for the arms naturally reminded the Hebrew lady of the ANKLE BELLS, and other similar ornaments for the feet and legs. These ornaments consisted partly in golden belts, or rings, which, descending from above the ankle, compressed the foot in various parts, and partly in shells and little jingling chains, which depended so as to strike against clappers fixed into the metallic belts. The pleasant tinkle of the golden belts in collision, the chains rattling, and the melodious chime of little silver ankle-bells, keeping time with the motions of the foot, made an accompaniment so agreeable to female vanity that the stately daughters of Jerusalem, with their sweeping trains flowing after them, appear to have adopted a sort of measured tread, by way of impressing a regular cadence upon the music of their feet. The chains of gold were exchanged, as luxury advanced, for strings of pearls and jewels, which swept in snaky folds about the feet and ankles.

This, like many other peculiarities in the Hebrew dress, had its origin in a circumstance of their early nomadic life. It is usual with the Bedouins to lead the camel, when disposed to be restive, by a rope or a belt fastened to one of the fore-feet, sometimes to both ; and it is also a familiar practice to soothe and to cheer the long-suffering animal with the sound of little bells, attached either to the neck or to one of the fore legs. Girls are commonly employed to lead the camels to water ; and it naturally happened that, with their lively fancies, some Hebrew or Arabian girl should be prompted to repeat, on her own person, what had so often been connected with an agreeable impression in her mute companions to the well.

It is probable, however, that afterwards, having once been introduced, this fashion was supported and extended by Oriental jealousy. For it rendered all clandestine movements very difficult in women ; and, by giving notice of their approach, it had the effect of preparing men for their presence, and keeping the road free from all spectacles that could be offensive to female delicacy.

From the Hebrew Bedouins this custom passed to all the nations of Asia,—Medes, Persians, Lydians, Arabs, &c.,—and is dwelt on with peculiar delight by the elder Arabic poets. That it had spread to the westernmost parts of Africa early in the Christian times we learn from Tertullian, who (foolish man) cannot suppress his astonishment that the foolish women of his time should bear to inflict such compression upon their tender feet. Even as early as the times of Herodotus, we find, from his account of a Libyan nation, that the women and girls universally wore copper rings about their ankles. And at an after period these ornaments were so much cherished by the Egyptian ladies that, sooner than appear in public without their tinkling ankle-chimes, they preferred to bury themselves in the loneliest apartments of the harem.

Finally, the fashion spread partially into Europe,—to Greece even, and to polished Rome,—in so far as regarded the ankle-belts, and the other ornamental appendages, with the single exception of the silver bells : these were too entirely in the barbaresque taste to support themselves under the frown of European culture.

VIII. The first rude sketch of the Hebrew SANDAL may be traced in that little tablet of undrest hide which the Arabs are in the habit of tying beneath the feet of their camels. This primitive form, after all the modifications and improvements it has received, still betrays itself to an attentive observer in the very latest fashions of the sandal which Palestine has adopted.

To raw hides succeeded tanned leather, made of goat-skin, deer-skin, &c. : this, after being accurately cut out to the shape of the sole, was fastened on the bare upper surface of the foot by two thongs, of which one was usually carried within the great toe, and the other in many circumvolutions round about the ankles, so that both finally met and tied just above the instep.

The laced sole or sandal of this form continued in Palestine to be the universal out-of-doors protection for the foot, up to the Christian era ; and it served for both sexes alike. It was not, however, worn within doors. At the threshold of the inner apartments the sandals were laid aside, and visitors from a distance were presented with a vessel of water to cleanse the feet from the soiling of dust and perspiration.[1]

With this extreme simplicity in the form of the foot-apparel, there was no great field for improvement. The article contained two parts—the sole and the fastening. The first, as a subject for decoration, was absolutely desperate ; coarse leather being exchanged for fine, all was done that could be done ; and the wit of man was able to devise no further improvement. Hence it happened that the whole power of the inventive faculty was accumulated upon the fastenings, as the only subject that remained. These were infinitely varied. Belts of bright yellow, of purple, and of crimson, were adopted by ladies of distinction—especially those of Palestine ; and it was a trial of art to throw these into the greatest possible varieties of convolution, and to carry them on to a nexus of the happiest form, by which means a reticulation, or trellis-work, was accomplished, of the most brilliant colouring, which brought into powerful relief the dazzling colour of the skin.

It is possible that, in the general rage for ornaments of

---

[1] Washing the feet was a ceremony of ancient times, adopted not merely with a view, 1*st*, to personal comfort in hotter climates, or, 2*d*, to decorum of appearance, where people walked about barefooted ; but also, 3*d*, to the reclining posture in use at meals, which necessarily brought the feet into immediate contact with the snowy swan-down cushions, squabs, &c., of couches.

gold which possessed the people of Palestine during the ages of excessive luxury, the beauties of Jerusalem may have adopted gilt sandals with gilt fastenings, as the ladies of Egypt did. It is possible also that the Hebrew ladies adopted at one time, in exchange for the sandal, slippers that covered the entire foot, such as were once worn at Babylon, and are still to be seen on many of the principal figures on the monuments of Persepolis; and, if this were really so, ample scope would in that case have been obtained for inventive art : variations without end might then have been devised on the fashion or the materials of the subject; and, by means of colour, embroidery, and infinite combinations of jewellery and pearls, an unceasing stimulation of novelty applied to the taste of the gorgeous, but still sensual and barbaresque, Asiatic.

IX. The VEIL, of various texture—coarse or fine, according to circumstances—was thrown over the head by the Hebrew lady, when she was unexpectedly surprised, or when a sudden noise gave reason to expect the approach of a stranger. This beautiful piece of drapery, which flowed back in massy folds over the shoulders, is particularly noticed by Isaiah, as holding an indispensable place in the wardrobe of his haughty countrywomen; and in this it was that the enamoured Hebrew woman sought the beloved of her heart.

ADDENDA TO SCENE THE FIRST

I. Of the Hebrew ornaments for the throat, some were true necklaces, in the modern sense, of several rows, the outermost of which descended to the breast, and had little pendulous cylinders of gold (in the poorer classes, of copper), so contrived as to make a jingling sound on the least motion of the person; others were more properly golden stocks, or throat-bands, fitted so close as to produce in the spectator an unpleasant imagination, and in the wearer, as we learn from the Thalmud (vi. 43), until reconciled by use, to produce an actual feeling of constriction approaching to suffocation. Necklaces were, from the earliest times, a favourite ornament of the male sex in the East, and expressed the dignity of the wearer, as we see in the instances of Joseph, of Daniel, &c. ; indeed the gold chain of office, still the badge of civic (and, until lately, of military) dignities, is no more than the outermost row of the Oriental necklace. Philo of Alexandria, and many other writers, both Persic and Arabian, give us some idea of the importance attached by the women of Asia to this beautiful ornament, and of the extraordinary money value which it sometimes bore : and, from the case of the necklace of gold and amber in the 15th Odyssey (v. 458), combined with many other instances of the same kind, there can be no doubt that it was the neighbouring land of Phœnicia from which the Hebrew women obtained their necklaces and the practice of wearing them.

II. The fashion, however, of adorning the necklace with golden *Suns* and *Moons*, so agreeable to the Hebrew ladies of Isaiah's time (chap. iii. 18), was not derived from Phœnicia, but from Arabia. At an earlier period (Judges viii. 21) the camels of the Midianites were adorned with golden moons, which also decorated the necks of the emirs of that nomadic tribe These appendages were not used merely by way of ornament, but originally as talismans, or amulets, against sickness, danger, and every species of calamity to which the desert was liable. The particular form of the amulet is to be explained out of the primitive religion which prevailed in Arabia up to the rise of Mohammedanism in the seventh century of Christianity, viz. the *Sabean* religion, or worship of the heavenly host—sun, moon, and stars—the most natural of all idolatries, and especially to a nomadic people in flat and pathless deserts, without a single way-mark or guidance for their wanderings, except what they drew from the silent heavens above them. It is certain, therefore, that long before their emigration into Palestine the Israelites had received the practice of wearing suns and moons from the Midianites ; even after their settlement in Palestine, it is certain that the worship of the starry host struck root pretty deeply at different periods, and that to the sun and moon, in particular, were offered incense and libations.

From Arabia, this fashion diffused itself over many countries ; and it was not without great displeasure that, in a remote age, Jerome and Tertullian discovered this idolatrous ornament upon the bosoms of their country-women.

The crescents, or *half*-moons of silver, in connexion with the golden suns,[1] were sometimes set in a brilliant frame that represented a halo, and still kept their ground on the Persian and Turkish toilette, as a favourite ornament.

III. The GOLDEN SNAKES, worn as one of the Hebrew appendages to the necklace, had the same idolatrous derivation, and originally were applied to the same superstitious use—as an amulet, or prophylactic ornament. For minds predisposed to this sort of superstition, the serpent had a special attraction under the circumstances of the Hebrews, from the conspicuous part which this reptile sustains in the mythologies of the East. From the earliest periods to which tradition ascends, serpents of various species were consecrated to the religious feelings of Egypt by temples, sacrifices, and formal rites of worship. This mode of idolatry had at various periods infected Palestine. According to 2 Kings xviii. 4, at the accession of King Hezekiah, the Israelites had raised peculiar altars to a great brazen serpent, and burned incense upon them. Even at this day the Abyssinians have an unlimited reverence for serpents ; and the blacks in general regard them as fit subjects for divine honours. Sonnini (ii. 388) tells us that a serpent's skin is still looked upon in Egypt as a prophylactic against complaints of the head, and also as a certain cure for them. And of the same origin, no doubt, was the general belief of antiquity (according to Pliny, 30, 12) that the serpent's skin was a remedy for spasms. That the golden serpent kept its place as an ornament of the throat and bosom after the Christian era we learn from Clement of Alexandria. That zealous father, so intolerant of superstitious mummery under every shape, directs his efforts against this fashion, as against a device of the devil.

IV. To the lowest of the several concentric circles which composed the necklace was attached a little box, exquisitely wrought in silver or gold, sometimes an onyx phial of

---

[1] Chemistry had its first origin in Arabia ; and it is not impossible that the chemical nomenclature for gold and silver, viz. *sol* and *luna*, was derived from this early superstition of the Bedouin dress.

dazzling whiteness, depending to the bosom or even to the cincture, and filled with the rarest aromas and odorous spices of the East. What were the favourite essences preserved in this beautiful appendage to the female costume of Palestine it is not possible at this distance of time to determine with certainty—Isaiah having altogether neglected the case, and Hosea, who appears to allude to it (ii. 14), having only once distinctly mentioned it (ii. 20). However, the Thalmud particularizes musk, and the delightful oil distilled from the leaf of the aromatic *malabathrum* of Hindostan. To these we may venture to add oil of spikenard, myrrh, balsams, attar of roses, and rose-water, as the perfumes usually contained in the Hebrew scent-pendants.

Rose-water, which I am the first to mention as a Hebrew perfume, had, as I presume, a foremost place on the toilette of a Hebrew *belle*. Express scriptural authority for it undoubtedly there is none ; but it is notorious that Palestine availed itself of *all* the advantages of Egypt, amongst which the rose in every variety was one. *Fium*, a province of Central Egypt, which the ancients call the Garden of Egypt, was distinguished for innumerable species of the rose, and especially for those of the most balsamic order, and for the most costly preparations from it. The Thalmud not only speaks generally of the mixtures made by tempering it with oil (i. 135), but expressly cites (ii. 41) a peculiar rose-water as so costly an essence that from its high price alone it became impossible to introduce the use of it into the ordinary medical practice. Indeed this last consideration, and the fact that the highly-prized *quintessence* cannot be obtained except from an extraordinary multitude of the rarest roses, forbid us to suppose that even women of the first rank in Jerusalem could have made a very liberal use of rose-water. In our times Savary found a single phial of it in the place of its manufacture valued at four francs. As to the *oil of roses*, properly so called, which floats in a very inconsiderable quantity upon the surface of distilled rose-water, it is certain that the Hebrew ladies were *not* acquainted with it. This preparation can be obtained only from the balsamic roses of Fium, of Shiras, of Kerman, and of Kashmire, which surpass all the roses of the earth in power and delicacy of odour ;

and it is matter of absolute certainty, and incontrovertibly established by the celebrated Langlés, that this oil, which even in the four Asiatic countries just mentioned ranks with the greatest rarities, and in Shiras itself is valued at its weight in gold, was discovered by mere accident, on occasion of some festival solemnity in the year 1612.

V. To what I said in the first scene of my exhibition about the Hebrew ear-ornaments, I may add :—

1. That sometimes, as Best remarked of the Hindoo dancing girls, their ears were swollen from the innumerable perforations drilled into them to support their loads of trinketry.

2. That in the large pendants of coral which the Hebrew ladies were accustomed to attach to their ears, either in preference to jewels, or in alternation with jewels, they particularly delighted in that configuration which imitated a cluster of grapes.

3. That, in ear-rings made of gold, they preferred the form of drops, or of globes and bulbs.

4. That of all varieties, however, of this appendage, pearls maintained the preference amongst the ladies of Palestine, and were either strung upon a thread, or attached by little hooks—singly, or in groups, according to their size. This taste was very early established amongst the Jews, and chiefly, perhaps, through their intercourse with the Midianites, amongst whom we find the great emirs wearing pearl ornaments of this class.

Mutatis mutandis, these four remarks apply also and equally to the case of the nose ornaments.

SCENE THE SECOND

I. THE HAIR.—This section I omit altogether, though with more room at my disposal it would be well worth translating as a curiosity. It is the essay of a finished and perfect knave, who, not merely being rather bare of facts, but having literally not one solitary fact of any kind or degree, small or great, sits down to write a treatise on the mode of dressing hair amongst Hebrew ladies. Samson's hair, and the dressing it got from the Philistines, is the nearest approach that he ever makes to his subject ; and, being conscious that this case of Samson and the Philistines is the one sole allusion to the subject of Hebrew hair that he is possessed of—for he altogether overlooks (which surely in *him* is criminal and indictable inadvertence) the hair of Absalom — he brings it round upon the reader as often perhaps as it will bear, viz. not oftener than once every sixth page. The rest is one continued shuffle to avoid coming upon the ground ; and, upon the whole, though too barefaced, yet really not without ingenuity. Take, by way of specimen, his very satisfactory dissertation on the particular sort of combs which the Hebrew ladies were pleased to patronise :—

" *Combs.*—Whether the ladies of Palestine had upon their toilette a peculiar comb for parting the hair, another for turning it up, &c. ; as likewise whether these combs were, as in ancient Rome, made of box-wood or of ivory, or other costly and appropriate material, all these are questions upon which I——am not able, upon my honour, to communicate the least information. But from the general silence of antiquity, prophets and all,[1] upon the subject of Hebrew combs, my own private opinion is that the ladies used their fingers for this purpose, in which case there needs no more to be said on the subject of Hebrew combs." Certainly not. All questions are translated from the visionary combs to the palpable and fleshly fingers: the combs, being usually of ivory in the Roman establishments, were costly, and might breed disputes ; but the fingers were a dowry of nature, and cost nothing.

II. PERFUMES.—Before, however, the hair received its final arrangement from the hands of the waiting-maid, it was held open and dishevelled to receive the fumes of frankincense, aloeswood, cassia, costmary, and other odorous woods, gums, balsams, and spices of India, Arabia, or Palestine—placed upon glowing embers, in vessels of golden

---

[1] The Thalmud is the only Jewish authority which mentions such a utensil of the toilette as a comb (vi. 39), but without any particular description. Hartmann adds two remarks worth quoting. 1. That the Hebrew style of the *coiffure* may probably be collected from the Syrian coins ; and 2. That, black hair being admired in Palestine, and the Jewish hair being naturally black, it is probable that the Jewish ladies did not colour their hair, as the Romans did.

fretwork. It is probable also that the Hebrew ladies used amber, bisam, and the musk of Thibet; and, when fully arranged, the hair was sprinkled with oil of nard, myrrh, oil of cinnamon, &c. The importance attached to this part of the Hebrew toilette may be collected indeed from an ordinance of the Thalmud (iii. 80), which directs that the bridegroom shall set apart one-tenth of the income which the bride brings him for the purchase of perfumes, essences, precious ointments, &c. All these articles were preserved either in golden boxes or in little oval narrow-necked phials of dazzling white alabaster, which bore the name of onyx, from its resemblance to the precious stone of that name, but was in fact a very costly sort of marble, obtained in the quarries of Upper Egypt or those of the Libanus in Syria. Indeed, long before the birth of Christ, alabaster was in such general use for purposes of this kind in Palestine that it became the generic name for valuable boxes, no matter of what material. To prevent the evaporation of the contents, the narrow neck of the phial was re-sealed every time that it was opened. It is probable also that the *myrrhine* cups, about which there has been so much disputing, were no strangers to the Jewish toilette.

III. The MIRROR was not made of glass (for glass mirrors cannot be shown to have existed before the thirteenth century), but of polished metals; and amongst these silver was in the greatest esteem, as being capable of a higher burnish than other metals, and less liable to tarnish. Metallic mirrors are alluded to by Job (xxxvii. 18). But it appears from the Second Book of Moses (xxxviii. 8) that in that age copper must have been the metal employed throughout the harems of Palestine. For, a general contribution of mirrors being made upon one occasion by the Israelitish women, they were melted down and re-cast into washing vessels for the priestly service. Now, the sacred utensils, as we know from other sources, were undeniably of copper. There is reason to think, however, that the copper was alloyed, according to the prevailing practice in that age, with some proportions of lead or tin. In after ages, when silver was chiefly employed, it gave place occasionally to gold. Mines of this metal were well known in Palestine; but there is no evidence that precious stones, which were used for this purpose in the ages of European luxury, were ever so used in Palestine, or in any part of Asia.

As to shape, the Hebrew mirrors were always either circular or oval, and cast indifferently flat or concave. They were framed in superb settings, often of pearls and jewels, and, when tarnished, were cleaned with a sponge full of hyssop, the universal cleansing material in Palestine.

Scene the Third

Head-Dresses.

The head-dresses of the Hebrew ladies may be brought under three principal classes :—

The first was a NETWORK CAP, made of fine wool or cotton, and worked with purple or crimson flowers. Sometimes the meshes of the net were of gold thread. The rim or border of the cap, generally of variegated colouring, was often studded with jewellery or pearls, and at the back was ornamented with a bow, having a few ends or tassels flying loose.

Secondly, a TURBAN, managed in the following way :— First of all, one or more caps in the form of a half oval, such as are still to be seen upon the monuments of Egyptian and Persepolitan art, was fastened round the head by a ribbon or fillet tied behind. This cap was of linen, sometimes perhaps of cotton, and in the inferior ranks oftentimes of leather, or, according to the prevailing fashion, of some kind of metal ; and, in any case, it had ornaments worked into its substance. Round this white or glittering ground were carried, in snaky windings, ribbons of the finest tiffany, or of lawn resembling our cambric ; and, to conceal the joinings, a silky substance was carried in folds, which pursued the opposite direction, and crossed the tiffany at right angles. For the purpose of calling out and relieving the dazzling whiteness of the ground, colours of the most brilliant class were chosen for the ribbons ; and these ribbons were either embroidered with flowers in gold thread, or had ornaments of that description interwoven with their texture.

Thirdly, the HELMET, adorned pretty nearly as the turban, and, in imitation of the helmets worn by Chaldean generals, having long tails or tassels depending from the hinder part, and flowing loosely between the shoulders. According to the Oriental taste for perfumes, all the ribbons or fillets used in these helmets and turbans were previously steeped in perfumes.

Finally, in connexion with the turban, and often with the veil, was a beautiful ornament for the forehead and the face, which the ladies of this day would do well to recall. Round the brow ran a bandeau or tiara of gold or silver, three fingers'-breadth, and usually set with jewels or pearls: from this, at each of the temples, depended a chain of pearls or of coral, which, following the margin of the cheeks, either hung loose or united below the chin.

SCENE THE FOURTH

I. The reader has been already made acquainted with the *chemise*, or innermost under-dress. The Hebrew ladies, however, usually wore two under-dresses, the upper of which it now remains to describe. In substance it was generally of a fine transparent texture, like the muslins (if we may so call them) of Cos ; in the later ages it was no doubt of silk.

The chemise sate close up to the throat ; and we have already mentioned the elaborate work which adorned it about the opening. But the opening of the robe which we are now describing was of much larger compass, being cut down to the bosom ; and the embroidery, &c., which enriched it was still more magnificent. The *chemise* reached down only to the calf of the leg, and the sleeve of it to the elbow : but the upper chemise or tunic, if we may so call it, descended in ample draperies to the feet, scarcely allowing the point of the foot to discover itself ; and the sleeves enveloped the hands to their middle. Great pomp was lavished on the folds of the sleeves ; but still greater on the hem of the robe and the fringe attached to it. The hem was formed by a broad border of purple, shaded and relieved according to patterns, and sometimes embroidered in gold thread with the most elegant objects from the animal or vegetable kingdoms. To that part which fell immediately behind the heels there were attached thin plates of gold ; or, by way of variety, it was studded with golden stars and filigree-work, sometimes with jewels and pearls interchangeably.

II. On this upper tunic, to confine the exorbitance of its draperies, and to prevent their interfering with the free motions of the limbs, a suberb GIRDLE was bound about the hips. Here, if anywhere, the Hebrew ladies endeavoured to pour out the whole pomp of their splendour, both as to materials and workmanship. Belts from three to four inches broad, and of the most delicate cottony substance, were chosen as the ground of this important part of female attire. The finest flowers of Palestine were here exhibited in rich relief, and in their native colours, either woven in the loom, or by the needle of the embroiderer. The belts being thirty or forty feet long, and carried round and round the person, it was in the power of the wearer to exhibit an infinite variety of forms, by allowing any fold or number of folds at pleasure to rise up more or less to view, just as fans or the coloured edges of books with us are made to exhibit land-scapes, &c., capable of great varieties of expansion as they are more or less unfolded. The fastening was by a knot below the bosom, and the two ends descended below the fringe ; which, if not the only fashion in use, was, however, the prevailing one, as we learn both from the sculptures at Persepolis and from the costume of the high priest.

Great as the cost was of these girdles, it would have been far greater had the knot been exchanged for a clasp ; and in fact at a later period, when this fashion did really take place, there was no limit to the profusion with which pearls of the largest size and jewellery were accumulated upon this conspicuous centre of the dress. Latterly the girdles were fitted up with beautiful chains, by means of which they could be contracted or enlarged, and with gold buckles, and large bosses and clasps, that gradually became the basis for a ruinous display of expenditure.

In conclusion, I must remark that in Palestine, as else-where, the girdle was sometimes used as a purse ; whether it were that the girdle itself was made hollow (as is expressly affirmed of the high priest's girdle), or that, without being hollow, its numerous foldings afforded a secure depository for articles of small size. Even in our days it is the custom to conceal the dagger, the handkerchief for wiping the face, and other bagatelles of personal convenience, in the folds of the girdle. However, the richer and more distinguished classes in Palestine appear to have had a peculiar and separate article of that kind. And this was—

III. A PURSE, made either of metal (usually gold or silver) or of the softest leather, &c., which was attached by a lace to the girdle, or kept amongst its folds, and which, even in the eyes of Isaiah, was important enough to merit a distinct mention. It was of a conical shape, and at the broader end was usually enriched with ornaments of the most elaborate and exquisite workmanship. No long time after the Christian era, the cost of these purses had risen to such a height that Tertullian complains, with great displeasure, of the ladies of his time, that in the mere purse, apart from its contents, they carried about with them the price of a considerable estate.

The girdle, however, still continued to be the appropriate depository for the napkin (to use the old English word) or sudatory—*i.e.* handkerchief for clearing the forehead of perspiration. As to pocket-handkerchiefs, in our northern use of them, it has been satisfactorily shown by Bottiger, in a German Journal, that the Greek and Roman ladies knew nothing of that modern appendage to the pocket,[1] however indispensable it may appear to us ; and the same arguments apply with equal force to the climate of Palestine.

IV. The glittering RINGS with which (according to Isaiah iii. 21) the Hebrew ladies adorned their hands seem to me

---

[1] Or rather it was required only in a catarrh, or other case of checked perspiration, which in those climates was a case of very rare occurrence. It has often struck me that, without needing the elaborate aid of Bottiger's researches, simply from one clause in Juvenal's picture of old age and its infirmities we might deduce the Roman habit of dispensing with a pocket-handkerchief. Amongst these infirmities he notices the *madidi infantia nasi*—the second childhood of a nose that needs wiping. But, if this kind of defluxion was peculiar to infancy and extreme old age, it was obviously no affection of middle age.

originally to have been derived from the seal-rings which,
whether suspended from the neck, or worn upon the finger,
have in all ages been the most favourite ornament of Asiatics.
These splendid baubles were naturally in the highest degree
attractive to women, both from the beauty of the stones which
were usually selected for this purpose, and from the richness
of the setting—to say nothing of the exquisite art which the
ancient lapidaries displayed in cutting them. The stones
chiefly valued by the ladies of Palestine were rubies, emeralds,
and chrysolites ; and these, set in gold, sparkled on the
middle or little finger of the right hand, and in luxurious
times upon *all* the fingers, even the thumb,—nay, in some
cases, upon the great toe.

Scene the Fifth

Upper Garment

The upper or outer garments, which, for both sexes, under
all varieties and modifications, the Hebrews expressed by the
comprehensive denomination of SIMLAH, have in every age,
and through all parts of the hot climates, in Asia and Africa
alike, been of such voluminous compass as not only to envelope
the whole person, but to be fitted for a wide range of miscellaneous purposes. Sometimes (as in the triumphal entry of
Christ into Jerusalem) they were used as carpets ; sometimes
as coverings for the backs of camels, horses, or asses, to render
the rider's seat less incommodious ; sometimes as a bed cover-
lid or counterpane ; at other times as sacks for carrying
articles of value ; or, finally, as curtains, hangings of parlours,
occasional tapestry, or even as sails for boats.

From these illustrations of the uses to which it was applicable, we may collect the form of this robe : that it was
nothing more than a shawl of large dimensions, or long
square of cloth, just as it came from the weaver's loom, which
was immediately thrown round the person, without receiving
any artificial adjustment to the human shape.

So much for the *form :* with regard to the *material* there
was less uniformity ; originally it was of goats' or camels'
hair ; but, as civilization and the luxury of cities increased,

these coarse substances were rejected for the finest wool and Indian cotton. Indeed, through all antiquity, we find that pure unsullied white was the festal colour, and more especially in Palestine, where the indigenous soaps, and other cleaning materials, gave them peculiar advantages for adopting a dress of that delicate and perishable lustre.

With the advance of luxury, however, came a love of variety ; and this, added to the desire for more stimulating impressions than could be derived from blank unadorned white, gradually introduced all sorts of innovations, both in form and colour ; though, with respect to the first, amidst all the changes through which it travelled, the old original outline still manifestly predominated. An account of the leading varieties we find in the celebrated third chapter of Isaiah.

The most opulent women of Palestine, beyond all other colours for the upper robe, preferred purple ; or, if not purple throughout the entire robe, at any rate purple flowers upon a white ground. The winter clothing of the very richest families in Palestine was manufactured in their own houses ; and, for winter clothing more especially, the Hebrew taste, no less than the Grecian and the Roman, preferred the warm and sunny scarlet, the puce colour, the violet, and the regal purple.[1]

Very probable it is that the Hebrew ladies, like those of Greece, were no strangers to the half-mantle—fastened by a clasp in front of each shoulder, and suffered to flow in free draperies down the back : this was an occasional and supernumerary garment, flung over the regular upper robe, properly so called.

There was also a longer mantle, reaching to the ankles, usually of a violet colour, which, having no sleeves, was meant to expose to view the beauty not only of the upper robe, but even of the outer tunic formerly described.

By the way, it should be mentioned that, in order to steep them in fine odour, all parts of the wardrobe were stretched on a reticulated or grated vessel—called by the Thalmud (vi. 77) *Kanklin*—from which the steams of rich perfumes were made to ascend.

---

[1] By which was probably meant a colour nearer to crimson than to the blue or violet class of purples.

In what way the upper robe was worn and fastened may be collected perhaps with sufficient probability from the modern Oriental practice, as described by travellers ; but, as we have no *direct* authority on the subject, I shall not detain the reader with any conjectural speculations

Scene the Sixth

Dress of Ceremony

One magnificent dress remains yet to be mentioned, viz. the dress of honour or festival dress, which answers in every respect to the modern CAFTAN. This was used on all occasions of ceremony, as splendid weddings, presentations at the courts of kings, sumptuous entertainments, &c. ; and all persons who stood in close connexion with the throne, as favourites, crown-officers, distinguished military commanders, &c., received such a dress as a gift from the royal treasury, in order to prepare them at all times for the royal presence. According to the universal custom of Asia, the trains were proportioned in length to the rank of the wearer ; whence it is that the robes of the high-priest were adorned with a train of superb dimensions ; and even Jehovah is represented (Isaiah vi. 1) as filling the heavenly palace with the length of his train.[1] Another distinction of this festival robe was the extraordinary fulness and length of the sleeves : these descended to the knee, and often ran to the ankle or to the ground. In the sleeves and in the trains, but especially in the latter, lay the chief pride of a Hebrew *belle*, when dressed for any great solemnity or occasion of public display.

Final Notes

I. The *Syndon*, mentioned by Isaiah, &c., was a delicate and transparent substance, like our tiffany, and in point of money value was

---

[1] It has been doubted whether these trains were supported by train-bearers ; but one argument makes it probable that they were not,—viz. that they were particularly favourable to the peacock walk or strut which was an express object of imitation in the gait of the Hebrew women.

fully on a level with the Caftan ; but whether imported from Egypt
or imitated in the looms of the Hebrews and Phœnicians is doubtful.
It was worn next to the skin, and consequently, in the harems of the
great, occupied the place of the under tunic (or *chemise*) previously
described ; and, as luxury advanced, there is reason to think that it
was used as a night *chemise*.

II. The *Caftan* is the *Kalaat* of the East, or *Kelaat*, so often
mentioned by modern travellers ; thus, for example, Thevenot (tom.
iii. p. 352) says—"Le Roi fait assez souvent des présens à ses Khans,
&c., L'on appelle ces présens *Kalaat*." Chardin. (iii. 101), "On
appelle *Calaat* les habits que le Roi donne par honneur." And lately,
in Lord Amherst's progress through the northern provinces of our
Indian Empire, &c., we read continually of the *Khelawt*, or robe of
state, as a present made by the native princes to distinguished officers.

The Caftan, or festival robe of the Hebrews, was, in my opinion,
the Πεπλος of the Greeks, or *palla* of the Romans. Among the points
of resemblance are these :—

1. The *palla* was flung like a cloak or mantle over the *stola* or
uppermost robe, "Ad talos stola demissa et *circumdata* pallâ."

2. The *palla* not only descended in flowing draperies to the feet
(thus Tibullus, i. vii. C, "Fusa sed ad teneros lutea palla pedes"),
but absolutely swept the ground. "Verrit humum Tyrio saturatâ
murice pallâ."

3. The *palla* was one of the same wide compass, and equally distinguished for its splendour.

4. Like the Hebrew festival garment, the *palla* was a *vestis seposita*,
and reserved for rare solemnities.

With respect to the Πεπλος, Eustathius describes it as μεγαν και
περικαλλεα και ποικιλον περιβολαιον, a large and very beautiful and
variegated enveloping mantle ; and it would be easy in other respects
to prove its identity with the *Palla*.

Salmasius, by the way, in commenting upon Tertullian *de Pallio*,
is quite wrong where he says—"Palla nunquam de virili pallio
dicitur." Tibullus (tom. iii. iv. 35) sufficiently contradicts that
opinion.

CICERO [1]

In drawing attention to a great question of whatsoever
nature connected with Cicero, there is no danger of missing my purpose through any want of reputed interest in
the subject. *Nominally*, it is not easy to assign a period
more eventful, a revolution more important, or a personal
career more dramatic, than that period — that revolution
— that career which, with almost equal right, we may
describe as all essentially *Ciceronian* by the quality of the
interest which they excite. For the age, it was fruitful in
great men ; but, amongst them all, if we except the sublime
Julian leader, none as regards splendour of endowments
stood upon the same level as Cicero. For the revolution,
it was that unique event which brought ancient civilisation
into contact and commerce with modern ; since, if we figure
the two worlds of Paganism and Christianity under the idea
of two great continents, it is through the isthmus of Rome
imperialised that the one was able virtually to communicate
with the other. Civil Law and Christianity, the two central
forces of modern civilisation, were upon that isthmus of time
ripened into potent establishments. And through those two
establishments, combined with the antique literature, as
through so many organs of metempsychosis, did the Pagan
world send onwards whatever portion of its own life was
fitted for surviving its own peculiar forms. Yet, in a revolu-

---

[1] From *Blackwood's Magazine* for July 1842 : reprinted by De
Quincey in 1858 in the seventh volume of his Collected Writings,
with only such slight changes as the substitution of "I" for "we"
when the author speaks directly.—M.

tion thus unexampled for grandeur of results, the only great
actor who stood upon the authority of his character was
Cicero. All others, from Pompey, Curio, Domitius, Cato,
down to the final partisans at Actium, moved by the
authority of arms: "*tantum auctoritate valebant quantum
milite*"; and they could have moved by no other. Lastly,
as regards the personal biography, although the same series
of trials, perils, and calamities, would have been in any case
interesting for themselves, yet undeniably they derive a
separate power of affecting the mind from the peculiar merits
of the individual concerned. Cicero is one of the very few
Pagan statesmen who can be described as a thoughtfully
conscientious man.

It is not, therefore, any want of splendid attraction in
my subject from which I am likely to suffer. It is of this
very splendour that I complain, as having long ago defeated
the simplicities of truth, and preoccupied the minds of all
readers with ideas politically romantic. All tutors, school-
masters, academic authorities, together with the collective
corps of editors, critics, commentators, have a natural bias in
behalf of a literary man who did so much honour to literature,
and who, in all the storms of this difficult life, manifested so
much attachment to the pure literary interest. Readers of
sensibility acknowledge the effect from any large influence of
deep halcyon repose, when relieving the agitations of history ;
as, for example, that which arises in our domestic annals
from interposing between two bloody reigns, like those of
Henry VIII and his daughter Mary, the serene morning of a
child-like king, destined to an early grave, yet in the meantime occupied with benign counsels for propagating religion,
for teaching the young, or for protecting the poor. Such a
repose, the same luxury of rest for the mind, is felt, by all
who traverse the great circumstantial records of those
tumultuous Roman times, in the Ciceronian epistolary
correspondence. In this we come suddenly into deep lulls
of angry passions : here, upon some scheme for the extension
of literature by a domestic history, or by a comparison of
Greek with Roman jurisprudence ; there, again, upon some
ancient problem from the quiet fields of philosophy. And
all men are already prejudiced in favour of one who, in the

midst of belligerent partisans, was the patron of a deep *pacific* interest. But amongst Christian nations this unfair *personal* bias has struck deeper : Cicero was not merely a philosopher ; he was one who cultivated ethics ; he was himself the author of an ethical system, composed with the pious purpose of training to what he thought just moral views his only son. This system survives, is studied to this day, is honoured perhaps extravagantly, and has repeatedly been pronounced the best practical theory to which Pagan principles were equal. Were it only upon this impulse, it was natural that men should receive a *clinamen,* or silent bias, towards Cicero, as a *moral* authority amongst disputants whose arguments were legions. The author of a moral code cannot be supposed indifferent to the moral relations of his own party views. If he erred, it could not be through want of meditation upon the ground of judgment, or want of interest in the results. So far Cicero has an advantage. But he has more lively advantage in the comparison by which he benefits, at *every* stage of his life, with antagonists whom the reader is taught to believe dissolute, incendiary, and almost desperate citizens. Verres in the youth of Cicero, Catiline and Clodius in his middle age, Mark Antony in Cicero's old age, have all been left to operate on the modern reader's feelings precisely through that masquerade of misrepresentation which invariably accompanied the political eloquence of Rome. The monstrous caricatures from the forum, or the senate, or the democratic rostrum, which were so *confessedly* distortions, by original design, for attaining the ends of faction, have imposed upon scholars pretty generally as faithful portraits. Recluse scholars are rarely politicians ; and in the timid horror of German literati, at this day, when they read of real brickbats or of paving-stones not metaphorical, used as figures of speech by a Clodian mob, we British understand the little comprehension of that rough horse-play, proper to the hustings, which can as yet be available for the rectification of any continental judgment. "*Play,* do you call it ?" says a German commentator ; "why, that brickbat might break a man's leg ; and this paving-stone would be sufficient to fracture a skull." Too true : they certainly might do so. But, for all that, our British experience of electioneering

" rough-and-tumbling " has long blunted the edge of our
moral anger.   Contested elections are unknown to the
Continent—hitherto even to those nations of the Continent
which boast of representative governments.   And, with no
experience of their inconveniences, they have as yet none of
the popular forces in which such contests originate.   We, on
the other hand, are familiar with such scenes.   What Rome
saw upon one sole hustings, we see repeated upon hundreds.
And we all know that the bark of electioneering mobs is
worse than their bite.   Their fury is without malice, and
their insurrectionary violence is without system.   Most undoubtedly the mobs and seditions of Clodius are entitled to
the same benefits of construction.   And, with regard to the
graver charges against Catiline or Clodius, as men sunk
irredeemably into sensual debaucheries, these are exag-
gerations which have told only from want of attention to
Roman habits.   Such charges were the standing material,
the stock-in-trade, of every orator against every antagonist.
Cicero, with the same levity as every other public speaker,
tossed about such atrocious libels at random. ' And with
little blame where they were known and allowed for as
tricks.   Not *are they true ?* but *will they tell ?* was the question.
Insolvency and monstrous debauchery were the two ordi-
nary reproaches on the Roman hustings.   No man escaped
them who was rich enough, or had expectations notorious
enough, to win for such charges any colourable plausibility.
Those only were unmolested in this way who stood in no
man's path of ambition ; or who had been obscure (that is to
say, poor) in youth ; or who, being splendid by birth or connexions, had been notoriously occupied in distant campaigns.
The object in such calumnies was to produce a momentary
effect upon the populace : and sometimes, as happened to
Cæsar, the merest falsehoods of a partisan orator were adopted
subsequently for truths by the simple-minded soldiery.   But
the misapprehension of these libels in modern times origin-
ates in erroneous appreciation of Roman oratory.   Scandal
was its proper element.   Senate or law-tribunal, forum or
mob rostrum, made no difference in the licentious practice
of Roman eloquence.   And, unfortunately, the calumnies
survive; whilst the state of things which made it needless

to notice them in reply has entirely perished. During the transitional period between the old Roman frugality and the luxury succeeding to foreign conquest, a reproach of this nature would have stung with some severity ; and it was not without danger to a candidate. But the age of growing voluptuousness weakened the effect of such imputations ; and this age may be taken to have commenced in the youth of the Gracchi, about one hundred years before Pharsalia. The change in the direction of men's sensibilities since then was as marked as the change in their habits. Both changes had matured themselves in Cicero's days ; and one natural result was that few men of sense valued such reproaches (incapable, from their generality, of specific refutation), whether directed against friends or enemies. Cæsar, when assailed for the thousandth time by the old fable about Nicomedes the sovereign of Bithynia, no more troubled himself to expose its falsehood in the senate than when previously dispersed over Rome through the libellous *facetiæ* of Catullus. He knew that the object of such petty malice was simply to tease him ; and for himself to lose any temper, or to manifest anxiety, by a labour so hope-less as any effort towards the refutation of an unlimited scandal, was childishly to collude with his enemies. He treated the story, therefore, as if it had been true ; and showed that, even under that assumption, it would not avail for the purpose before the house. Subsequently, Suetonius, as an express collector of anecdotage and pointed personalities against great men, has revived many of these scurrilous jests ; but *his* authority, at the distance of two generations, can add nothing to the credit of calumnies originally founded on plebeian envy, or the jealousy of rivals. I may possibly find myself obliged to come back upon this subject. And at this point, therefore, I will not further pursue it than by remarking that no one snare has proved so fatal to the sound judgment of posterity upon public men in Rome as this blind credulity towards the oratorical billingsgate of ancient forensic licence. Libels, whose very point and jest lay in their extravagance, have been received for historical truth with respect to many amongst Cicero's enemies. And the reaction upon Cicero's own character has been naturally to exaggerate that imputed purity of morals which has availed to raise him into what is called a " pattern man."

The injurious effect upon biographic literature of all such wrenches to the truth is diffused everywhere. Fenelon, or Howard the philanthropist, may serve to illustrate the effect I mean, when viewed in relation to the stern simplicities of truth. Both these men have long been treated with such uniformity of dissimulation, —" petted " (so to speak) with such honeyed falsehoods as beings too bright and seraphic for human inquisition,—that now their real circumstantial merits, quite as much as their human frailties, have faded away in this blaze of fabling idolatry. Sir Isaac Newton, again, for about one entire century since his death in 1727, was painted by all biographers as a man so saintly in temper, so meek, so detached from worldly interests, that, by mere strength of potent falsehood, the portrait had ceased to be human, and a great man's life furnished no moral lessons to posterity. At length came the odious truth, exhibiting Sir Isaac in a character painful to contemplate,— as a fretful, peevish, and sometimes even malicious, intriguer; traits, however, in Sir Isaac already traceable in the sort of chicanery attending his subornation of managers in the Leibnitz controversy, and in the publication of the " Commercium Epistolicum." For the present, the effect has been purely to shock and to perplex. As regards moral instruction, the lesson comes too late ; it is now defeated by its inconsistency with our previous training in steady theatrical delusion.

I do not make it a reproach to Cicero that his reputation with posterity has been affected by these or similar arts of falsification. Eventually this had been his misfortune. Adhering to the truth, his indiscreet eulogists would have presented to the world a much more interesting picture ; not so much the representation of " *vir bonus cum malâ fortunâ compositus*," which is, after all, an ordinary spectacle for so much of the conflict as can ever be made public ; but that of a man generally upright, matched as in single duel with a standing temptation to error, growing out of his public position ; often seduced into false principles by the

necessities of ambition, or by the coercion of self-consistency ;
and often, as he himself admits, biassed fatally in a public
question by the partialities of friendship.   The violence of
that crisis was overwhelming to all moral sensibilities ; no
sense, no organ, remained true to the obligations of political
justice ; principles and feelings were alike darkened by the
extremities of the political quarrel ; the feelings obeyed the
personal engagements ; and the principles indicated only the
position of the individual—as between a senate clinging
desperately to oligarchic privileges and a Julian patriot
under a mask of partial self-interest fighting in effect for
extensions of popular influence.

So far nothing has happened to Cicero which does not
happen to all men entangled in political feuds.   There are
few cases of large party dispute which do not admit of contradictory delineations, as the mind is previously swayed
to this extreme or to that.   But the peculiarity in the case
of Cicero is—not that he has benefited by the mixed quality
of that cause which he adopted, but that the very dubious
character of the cause has benefited by *him*.   Usually it
happens that the individual partisan is sheltered under the
authority of his cause.   But here the whole merits of the
case have been predetermined and adjudged by the authority
of the partisan.   Had Cicero been absent, or had Cicero
practised that neutrality to which he often inclined, the
general verdict of posterity on the great Roman Civil War
would have been essentially different from that which we
find in History.   At present the error is an extreme one ;
and I call it such without hesitation, because it has maintained itself by imperfect reading even of such documents
as survive, and by too general an oblivion of the important
fact that these surviving documents (meaning the *contemporary*
documents) are pretty nearly all *ex parte*.[1]

[1] Even here there is a risk of being misunderstood. Some will
read this term *ex parte* in the sense that now there are no neutral
statements surviving.   But such statements there never were.   The
controversy moving for a whole century in Rome before Pharsalia was
not about facts, but about constitutional principles ; and as to that
question there could be no neutrality.   From the nature of the case,
the truth must have lain with one of the parties ; compromise, or
intermediate temperament, was inapplicable.   What I complain of as

To judge of the general equity in the treatment of Cicero, considered as a political partisan, let us turn to the most current of the regular biographies. Amongst the infinity of slighter sketches, which naturally draw for their materials upon those which are more elaborate, it would be useless to confer a special notice upon any. I will cite the two which at this moment stand foremost in European literature : that of Conyers Middleton, now about one century old, as the memoir most generally read[1]; that of Bernhard Abeken[2] (amongst that limited class of memoirs which build upon any political principles), as accidentally the latest.

Conyers Middleton is a name that cannot be mentioned without an expression of disgust. I sit down in perfect charity at the same table with deists or atheists alike. To me, simply in his *social* character, and supposing him sincere, a sceptic is as agreeable as another. Anyhow he is better than a craniologist, than a punster, than a St. Simonian, than a Jeremy-Benthamite, or an anti-corn-law lecturer. What signifies a name ? Free-thinker he calls himself ? Good—let him " free-think " as fast as he can ; but let him obey the ordinary laws of good faith. No sneering in the first place ; because, though it is untrue that "a sneer cannot be answered," the answer too often imposes circumlocution. And, upon a subject which makes wise men grave, a sneer argues so much perversion of heart that it cannot be thought uncandid to infer some corresponding perversion of intellect : perfect sincerity never existed in a professional sneerer. Secondly, no treachery, no betrayal of the cause which the man is sworn and paid to support ! Conyers Middleton held considerable preferment in the Church of England. Long after he had become an enemy to that Church (not separately for itself, but generally as a strong

overlooked is, not that the surviving records of the quarrel are partisan records (that being a mere necessity), but, in the forensic use of the term *ex parte*, that they are such without benefit of equilibrium or modification from the partisan statements in the opposite interest.

[1] *The History of the Life of Marcus Tullius Cicero*, by Conyers Middleton, D.D., was originally published in 1741, and was long the standard English Life of Cicero.—M.

[2] " Cicero in Seinen Briefen. VON BERNHARD RUDOLF ABEKEN, Professor am Raths-Gymnasium zu Osnabrück. Hanover, 1835."

form of Christianity), he continued to receive large quarterly cheques upon a bank in Lombard Street, of which the original condition had been that he should defend Christianity "with all his soul and with all his strength." Yet such was his perfidy to this sacred engagement that even his private or personal feuds grew out of his capital feud with the Christian faith. From the Church he drew his bread ; and the labour of his life was to bring the Church into contempt. He hated Bentley, he hated Warburton, he hated Waterland ; and why ? All alike as powerful champions of that religion which he himself daily betrayed ; and Waterland, as the strongest of these champions, he hated most. But all these by-currents of malignity emptied themselves into one vast *cloaca maxima* of rancorous animosity to the mere spirit, temper, and tendencies, of Christianity. Even in treason there is room for courage ; but Middleton, in the manner, was as cowardly as he was treacherous in the matter. He wished to have it whispered about that he was worse than he seemed, and that he would be a *fort esprit* of a high caste but for the bigotry of his Church. It was a fine thing, he fancied, to have the credit of infidelity without paying for a licence ; to sport over those manors without a qualification. As a scholar, meantime, he was trivial and incapable of labour. Even the Roman antiquities, political or juristic, he had studied neither by research and erudition, nor by meditation on their value and analogies. Lastly, his English style, for which at one time he obtained some credit through the caprice of a fashionable critic, is such that, by weeding away from it whatever is colloquial, you would strip it of all that is characteristic ; and, if you should remove its slang vulgarisms, you would remove its whole principle of vitality.

That man misapprehends the case who fancies that the infidelity of Middleton can have but a limited operation upon a memoir of Cicero. On the contrary, because this prepossession was rather a passion of hatred [1] than any non-

---

[1] "*Hatred*" :—It exemplifies the pertinacity of this hatred to mention that Middleton was one of the men who sought, for twenty years, some historical fact that might conform to Leslie's four conditions ("Short Method with the Deists"), and yet evade Leslie's logic I think little of Leslie's argument, which never could have been valued

conformity of the intellect, it operated as a false bias universally ; and, in default of any sufficient analogy between
Roman politics and the politics of England at Middleton's
time of publication, there was no other popular bias derived
from modern ages which could have been available. It was
the object of Middleton to paint, in the person of Cicero, a
pure Pagan model of scrupulous morality, and to show that,
in most difficult times, he had acted with a self-restraint and
a considerate integrity to which Christian ethics could have
added no element of value. Now, this object had the effect
of, already in the preconception, laying a restraint over all
freedom in the execution. No man could start from the
assumption of Cicero's uniform uprightness and afterwards
retain any latitude of free judgment upon the most momentous
transactions of Cicero's life ; because, unless some plausible
hypothesis could be framed for giving body and consistency
to the pretences of the Pompeian cause, it must, upon any
examination, turn out to have been as merely a selfish cabal,
for the benefit of a few lordly families, as ever yet has
prompted a conspiracy. The slang words "*respublica*" and
"*causa*" are caught up by Middleton from the letters of
Cicero ; but never, in any one instance, has either Cicero or
a modern commentator been able to explain what general
interest of the Roman people was represented by these vague
abstractions as then paraded. The strife was not then
between the conservative instinct, as organised in the upper
classes, and the destroying instinct, as concentrated in the
lowest. The strife was not between the property of the
nation and its rapacious pauperism — the strife was not
between the honours, titles, institutions, created by the state,
and the plebeian malice of levellers, seeking for a commencement *de novo*, with the benefits of a general scramble :—it
was a strife between a small fraction of confederated oligarchs
upon the one hand and the nation upon the other. Or,
looking still more narrowly into the nature of the separate
purposes at issue, it was, on the Julian side, an attempt to
make such a re-distribution of constitutional functions as
should harmonise the necessities of the public service with

by a sincerely religious man. But the rage of Middleton, and his
perseverance, illustrate the *temper* of his warfare.

the working of the republican machinery : whereas, under
the existing condition of Rome, through the silent changes
of time operating upon the relations of property and upon
the character of the populace, it had been long evident that
armed supporters—now legionary soldiers, now gladiators,
—enormous bribery, and the constant reserve of anarchy in
the rear, were become the *regular* counters for conducting the
desperate game of the mere ordinary civil administration.
Not the demagogue only, but the peaceful or patriotic citizen,
and the constitutional magistrate, could now move and
exercise their public functions only through the deadliest
combinations of violence and fraud.   This dreadful condition
of things, which no longer acted through that salutary
opposition of parties essential to the energy of free countries,
but involved all Rome in a permanent panic, was acceptable
to the senate only ; and of the senate, in sincerity, to a very
small section.   Some score of great houses there was, that,
by vigilance of intrigues, by far-sighted arrangements for
armed force or for critical retreat, and by overwhelming command of money, could always guarantee their own denomination.   For this purpose all that they needed was a secret
understanding with each other, and the interchange of mutual
pledges by means of marriage alliances.   Any revolution
which should put an end to this anarchy of selfishness must
reduce the exorbitant power of the paramount grandees.
They naturally confederated against a result so shocking to
their pride.   Cicero, as a new member of this faction, himself rich [1] in a degree sufficient for the indefinite aggrandise-
ment of his son, and sure of support from all the interior
cabal of the senators, had adopted their selfish sympathies.
And it is probable enough that all changes in a system which
worked so well for himself, to which also he had always
looked up from his youngest days as the reward and haven of
his toils, did seriously strike him as dreadful innovations.
Names were now to be altered for the sake of things ; forms

[1] *"Rich"* :—We may consider Cicero as worth, in a case of necessity,
at least £400,000.   Upon that part of this property which lay in
money there was always a very high interest to be obtained ; but not so
readily a good security for the principal.   The means of increasing
this fortune by marriage was continually offering to a leading senator,
such as Cicero ; and the facility of divorce aided this resource.

for the sake of substances : this already gave some *verbal* power of delusion to the senatorial faction.   And a prospect still more startling to them all was the necessity towards any restoration of the old republic that some one eminent grandee should hold provisionally a dictatorial power during the period of transition.

Abeken—and it is honourable to him as a scholar of a section not conversant with politics—saw enough into the situation of Rome at that time to be sure that Cicero was profoundly in error upon the capital point of the dispute ; that is, in mistaking a cabal for the commonwealth, and the narrowest of intrigues for a public "cause."   Abeken, like an honest man, had sought for any national interest cloaked by the wordy pretences of Pompey, and he had found none. He had seen the necessity, towards any regeneration of Rome, that Cæsar, or some leader pursuing the same objects, should be armed for a time with extraordinary power.   In that way only had both Marius and Sylla, each in the same *general* circumstances, though with different feelings, been enabled to preserve Rome from total anarchy.   I give Abeken's express words, that I may not seem to tax him with any responsi- bility beyond what he courted.   At p. 342 (8th sect.) he owns it as a rule of the sole conservative policy possible for Rome :—" Dass Cæsar der einzige war der ohne weitere " stuerme Rom zu dem ziele zu fuehren vermochte welchem " es seit einem jahrhundert sich zuwendete "—(" that Cæsar " was the sole man who had it in his power, without farther " convulsions, to lead Rome onwards to that final mark to- " wards which, in tendency, she had been travelling through- " out one whole century ").   Neither could it be of much consequence whether Cæsar should personally find it safe to imitate the example of Sylla in laying down his authority, provided he so matured the safeguards of the reformed con- stitution that, on the withdrawal of this temporary scaffolding, the great arch was found capable of self-support.   Thus far, as an ingenuous student of Cicero's correspondence, Abeken gains a glimpse of the truth which has been so constantly obscured by historians.   But, with the natural incapacity for practical politics which besieges all Germans, he fails in most of the subordinate cases to decipher the intrigues at

work, and oftentimes finds special palliation for Cicero's
conduct where, in reality, it was but a reiteration of
that selfish policy in which he had united himself with
Pompey.

By way of slightly reviewing this policy, as it expressed
itself in the acts or opinions of Pompey, I will pursue it
through the chief stages of the contest. Where was it that
Cicero first heard of the appalling news of a civil war as
inevitable? It was at Ephesus, at the moment of reaching
that city on his return homewards from his proconsular
government in Cilicia; and the circumstances of his position
were these :—On the last day of July 703 *Ab Urb. Cond.*,
he had formally entered on that office. On the last day but
one of the same month in 704 he laid it down. The conduct of Cicero in this command was meritorious. And, if
my purpose had been generally to examine his merits, I could
show cause for making a higher estimate of those merits than
has been offered by his professional eulogists. The circumstances, however, in the opposite scale ought not to be overlooked. He knew himself to be under a jealous supervision
from the friends of Verres, or all who might have the same
interest. This is one of the two facts which may be pleaded
in abatement of his disinterested merit. The other is that,
after all, he did undeniably pocket a large sum of money
(more than twenty thousand pounds) upon his year's administration; whilst, in the counter scale, the utmost extent
of that sum by which he refused to profit was *not* large.
This at least we are entitled to say with regard to the only
specific sum brought under our notice as one *certainly* awaiting his private disposal.

Here occurs a very important error of Middleton's. In
a question of money very much will turn upon the specific
amount. An abstinence which is exemplary may be shown
in resisting an enormous gain; whereas under a slight
temptation the abstinence may be little or none. Middleton
makes the extravagant, almost maniacal, assertion, that the
sum available by custom as a perquisite to Cicero's suite was
"eight hundred thousand pounds sterling." Not long after
the period in which Middleton wrote, newspapers, and the
increased facilities for travelling in England, had begun to

operate powerfully upon the character of our English univer-
sities. Rectors and students, childishly ignorant of the
world (such as Parson Adams and the Vicar of Wakefield) became a rare class. Possibly Middleton was the last clergyman
of that order—though, in any amiable sense, having little
enough of guileless simplicity. In my own experience I have
met with but one similar case of heroic ignorance. This
occurred near Caernarvon. A poor Welshwoman, leaving
home to attend an annual meeting of the Methodists, replied
to me, who had questioned her as to the numerical amount
of the probable assemblage, "that perhaps there would be a
matter of four millions!" This in little Caernarvon, that
by no possibility could accommodate as many thousands!
Yet, in justice to the poor cottager, it should be said that she
spoke doubtingly, and with an anxious look, whereas Middleton announces this little *bonus* of eight hundred thousand
pounds with a glib fluency that demonstrates him to have
seen nothing in the amount worth a comment. Let the
reader take along with him these little adjuncts of the case.
First of all, the money was a mere *surplus* arising on the
public expenditure, and resigned in any case to the suite of
the governor only under the presumption that it must be
too trivial to call for any more deliberate appropriation.
Secondly, it was the surplus of a *single* year's expenditure.
Thirdly, the province itself was chiefly Grecian in the composition of its population,—that is, poor in a degree not
understood by most Englishmen, frugally penurious in its
habits. Fourthly, the public service was of the very simplest
nature. The administration of justice, and the military application of about eight thousand regular troops to the local
seditions of the Isaurian freebooters, or to the occasional
sallies from the Parthian frontier—these functions of the proconsul summed up his public duties. To me the marvel is
how there could arise a surplus even equal to eight thousand
pounds, which some copies countenance. Eight pounds I
should have surmised. But, to justify Middleton, he ought
to have found in the text "*millies*"—a reading which exists
nowhere. Figures, in such cases, are always so suspicious as
scarcely to warrant more than a slight bias to the sense which
they establish : and words are little better, since they may

always have been derived from a previous authority in figures. Meantime, simply as a blunder in accurate scholarship, I should think it unfair to have pressed it. But it is in the light of an evidence against Middleton's good sense and thoughtfulness that I regard it as capital. The man who *could* believe that a sum not far from a million sterling had arisen in the course of twelve months from a province sown chiefly with paving-stones, as a little bagatelle of office, a *pot-de-vin*, mere customary fees, payable to the discretional appropriation of one who held the most fleeting relation to the province, is not entitled to an opinion upon any question of doubtful tenor. Had this been the scale of regular profits upon a poor province, why should any Verres create risk for himself by an arbitrary scale ?

In cases, therefore, where the merit turns upon money, unavoidably the ultimate question will turn upon the amount. And the very terms of the transaction, as they are reported by Cicero, indicating that the sum was entirely at his own disposal, argue its trivial value. Another argument implies the same construction. Former magistrates, most of whom took such offices with an express view to the creation of a fortune by embezzlement and by bribes, had established the precedent of relinquishing this surplus to their official "family." This fact of itself shows that the amount must have been uniformly trifling : being at all subject to fluctuations in the amount, most certainly it would have been made to depend for its appropriation upon the separate merits of each annual case as it came to be known. In this particular case Cicero's suite grumbled a little at his decision : he ordered that the money should be carried to the credit of the public. But, had a sum so vast as Middleton's been at his disposal in mere perquisites, *proh deum atque hominum fidem!* the honourable gentlemen of the suite would have taken unpleasant liberties with the proconsular throat. They would have been entitled to divide on the average forty thousand pounds a-man ; and they would have married into senatorian houses. Because a score or so of monstrous fortunes existed in Rome, we must not forget that in any age of the Republic a sum of twenty-five thousand pounds would have constituted a most respectable fortune for a man not embarked upon a

public career ; and with sufficient connexions it would furnish the early costs even for such a career.

I have noticed this affair with some minuteness, both
from its importance to the accuser of Verres, and because I
shall here have occasion to insist on this very case, as amongst
those which illustrate the call for political revolution at
Rome.   Returning from Cicero the governor to Cicero the
man, I may remark that, although his whole life had been
adapted to purposes of ostentation, and *a fortiori* this
particular provincial interlude was sure to challenge from
his enemies a vindictive scrutiny, still I find cause to think
Cicero very sincere in his purity as a magistrate.   Many of
his acts were not mere showy renunciations of doubtful
privileges, but were connected with painful circumstances of
offence to intimate friends.   Indirectly we may find in these
cases a pretty ample revelation of the Roman morals.   Pretended philosophers in Rome, who prated in set books about
" virtue " and the " summum bonum," made no scruple, in
the character of magistrates, to pursue the most extensive
plans of extortion, through the worst abuses of military
licence ; some, as the " virtuous " Marcus Brutus, not stop-
ping short of murder.   A foul case of this description had
occurred in the previous year under the sanction of Brutus ;
and Cicero had to stand his friend, by seeming to be his
enemy, in nobly refusing to abet the further prosecution of
the very same atrocity.   Even in the case of the perquisites,
as stated above, Cicero had a more painful duty than that of
merely sacrificing a small sum of money : he was summoned
by his conscience to offend those men with whom he lived
as a modern prince or ambassador lives amongst the members of his official " family."   Naturally it could be no trifle
to a gentle-hearted man that he was creating for himself a
necessity of encountering frowns from those who surrounded
him, and who might think, with some reason, that, in bringing them to a distant land, he had authorised them to look
for all such remunerations as precedent had established.
Right or wrong in the casuistical point—I believe him to
have been wrong—Cicero was eminently right, when once
satisfied by arguments, sound or not sound, as to the point of
duty, in pursuing that duty through all the vexations which

it entailed. This justice I owe him pointedly in a review which has for its general object the condemnation of his political conduct.

Never was a child, torn from its mother's arms to an odious school, more homesick at this moment than was Cicero. He languished for Rome ; and, when he stood before the gates of Rome, about five months later, not at liberty to enter them, he sighed profoundly after that vanished peace of mind which he had enjoyed in his wild mountainous province. " Quæsivit lucem — ingemuitque repertâ." Vainly he flattered himself that he could compose, by his single mediation, the mighty conflict which had now opened. As he pursued his voyage homewards, through the months of August, September, October, and November, he was met, at every port where he touched for a few days' repose, by reports, more and more gloomy, of the impending rupture between the great partisan leaders. These reports ran along, like the undulations of an earthquake, to the last recesses of the east. Every king and every people had been canvassed for the coming conflict ; and many had been already associated by pledges to the one side or the other. The fancy faded away from Cicero's thoughts as he drew nearer to Italy that any effect could now be anticipated for media-torial counsels. The controversy, indeed, was still pursued through diplomacy ; and the negotiations had not reached an *ultimatum* from either side. But Cicero was still distant from the parties ; and, before it was possible that any general congress representing both interests could assemble, it was certain that reciprocal distrust would have coerced them into irrevocable measures of hostility. Cicero landed at Otranto. He went forward by land to Brundusium, where, on the 25th of November, his wife and daughter, who had come from Rome to meet him, entered the public square of that town at the same moment with himself. Without delay he moved towards Rome ; but he could not gratify his ardour for a personal interference in the great crisis of the hour without entering Rome ; and *that* he was not at liberty to do without surrendering his pretensions to the honour of a triumph.

Many writers have amused themselves with the idle vanity of Cicero in standing upon a claim so windy under circumstances so awful.   But, on the one hand, it should be remembered how eloquent a monument it was of civil grandeur for a *novus homo* to have established his own amongst the few surviving triumphal families of Rome ; and, on the other hand, he could have effected nothing by his presence in the senate.   No man could at this moment · Cicero least of all ; because his policy had been thus arranged—ultimately to support Pompey, but in the mean-time, as strengthening the chances against war, to exhibit a perfect neutrality.   Bringing, therefore, nothing in his counsels, he could hope for nothing influential in the result.   Cæsar was now at Ravenna, as the city nearest to Rome of all which he could make his military head-quarters within the Italian (*i.e.* the Cisalpine) province of Gaul.   But he held his forces well in hand, and ready for a start, with his eyes almost fastened on the walls of Rome, so near had he approached.   Cicero warned his friend Atticus that a dreadful and perfectly unexampled war—a struggle " of life and death " — was awaiting them ; and that in his opinion nothing could avert it, short of a great Parthian invasion, deluging the eastern provinces—Greece, Asia Minor, Syria —such as might force the two chieftains into an instant dis-traction of their efforts.   Out of that would grow the absence of one or other ; and upon that separation, for the present, might hang an incalculable series of changes.   Else, and but for this one contingency, he announced the fate of Rome to be sealed.

The new year came, the year 705, and with it new consuls.   One of these, C. Marcellus, was distinguished amongst the enemies of Cæsar by his personal rancour—a feeling which he shared with his twin-brother Marcus.   On the first day of this month, the Senate was to decide upon Cæsar's proposals, as a basis for future arrangement.   They did so ; they voted the proposals, by a large majority, un-satisfactory—instantly assumed a fierce martial attitude— fulminated the most hostile of all decrees, and authorised shocking outrages upon those who, in official situations, represented Cæsar's interest.   These men fled for their lives. Cæsar, on receiving their report, gave the signal for advance ; and in forty-eight hours had crossed the little brook, called the Rubicon, which determined the marches or frontier line of his province. Earlier by a month than this great event, Cicero had travelled southwards. Thus his object was to place himself in personal communication with Pompey, whose vast Neapolitan estates drew him often into that quarter. But, to his great consternation, he found himself soon followed by the whole stream of Roman grandees, flying before Cæsar through the first two months of the year. A majority of the senators had chosen, together with the consuls, to become emigrants from Rome, rather than abide any compromise with Cæsar. And, as these were chiefly the rich and potent in the aristocracy, naturally they drew along with themselves many humble dependants, both in a pecuniary and a political sense. A strange rumour prevailed at this moment, to which even Cicero showed himself maliciously credulous, that Cæsar's natural temper was cruel, and that his policy also had taken that direction. But the brilliant result within the next six or seven weeks changed the face of politics, disabused everybody of their delusions, and showed how large a portion of the panic had been due to monstrous misconceptions. For already in March multitudes of refugees had returned to Cæsar. By the first week of April, that "monster of energy," that τερας of superhuman despatch, as Cicero repeatedly styles Cæsar, had marched through Italy—had received the submission of every strong fortress—had driven Pompey into his last Calabrian retreat of Brundusium (at which point it was that this unhappy man unconsciously took his last farewell of Italian ground)— had summarily kicked him out of Brundusium—and, having thus cleared all Italy of enemies, was on his road back to Rome. From this city, within the first ten days of April, he moved onwards to the Spanish War, where, in reality, the true strength of Pompey's cause—strong legions of soldiers, chiefly Italian—awaited him in strong positions, chosen at leisure, under Afranius and Petreius. For the rest of this year (705) Pompey was unmolested. In 706, Cæsar, victorious from Spain, addressed himself to the task of overthrowing Pompey in person; and on the 9th of August in that year took place the ever-memorable battle on the river Pharsalus in Thessaly.

During all this period of about one year and a-half Cicero's letters, at intermitting periods, hold the same language. They fluctuate, indeed, strangely in temper ; for they run through all the changes incident to hoping, trusting, and disappointed friendship. Nothing can equal the expression of his scorn for Pompey's *inertia*, when contrasted with energy so astonishing on the part of his antagonist. Cicero had also been deceived as to facts. The plan of the campaign had, to him in particular, not been communicated ; he had been allowed to calculate on a final resistance in Italy. This was certainly impossible. But the policy of maintaining a show of opposition which it was intended to abandon at *every* point, or of procuring for Cæsar the credit of so many successive triumphs which might all have been evaded, has never received any explanation.

Towards the middle of February, Cicero acknowledges the receipt of letters from Rome, which in one sense are valuable, as exposing the system of self-delusion prevailing. Domitius, it seems, who soon after laid down his arms *at* Corfinium and *with* Corfinium, parading his forces only to make a more solemn surrender, had, as the despatches from Rome asserted, an army on which he could rely ; as to Cæsar, that nothing was easier than to intercept him ; that such was Cæsar's own impression ; that honest men were recovering their spirits ; and that the rogues at Rome (*Romæ improbos*) were one and all in consternation. It tells powerfully for Cicero's sagacity that now, amidst this general explosion of childish hopes, he only was sternly incredulous. " *Hæc metuo, equidem, ne sint somnia.*" Yes, he had learned by this time to appreciate the windy reliances of his party. He had an argument from experience for slighting their vain demonstrations ; and he had a better argument from the future, as that future was *really* contemplated in the very counsels of the leader. Pompey, though nominally controlled by other men of consular rank, was at present an autocrat for the management of the war. What was his policy ? Cicero had now discovered, not so much through confidential interviews, as by the mute tendencies of all the measures adopted : Cicero was satisfied that his total policy had been, from the first, a policy of despair.

The position of Pompey, as an old invalid, from whom his party exacted the services of youth, is worthy of separate notice. There is not, perhaps, a more pitiable situation than that of a veteran reposing upon his past laurels who is summoned from beds of down, and from the elaborate system of comforts engrafted upon a princely establishment, suddenly to re-assume his armour—to prepare for personal hardships of every kind—to renew his youthful anxieties, without support from youthful energies—once again to dispute sword in hand the title to his own honours—to pay back into the chancery of war, as into some fund of abeyance, all his own prizes, and palms of every kind—to re-open every decision or award by which he had ever benefited—and to view his own national distinctions of name, trophy, laurel crown,[1] as all but so many stakes provisionally resumed, which must be redeemed by services tenfold more difficult than those by which originally they had been earned.

Here was a trial, painful, unexpected, sudden ; such as any man, at any age, might have honourably declined. The very best contingency in such a struggle was that nothing might be lost; whilst along with this doubtful hope ran the certainty that nothing could be gained. More glorious in the popular estimate of his countrymen Pompey could not become, for his honours were already historical, and touched with the autumnal hues of antiquity, having been won in a generation now gone by ; but, on the other hand, he might lose everything: for, in a contest with so dreadful an antagonist as Cæsar, he could not hope to come off un-scorched ; and, whatever might be the final event, one result must have struck him as inevitable—viz. that a new genera-tion of men, who had come forward into the arena of life within the last twenty years, would watch the approaching collision with Cæsar as putting to the test a question much canvassed of late with regard to the soundness and legitimacy

---

[1] "*Laurel crown*" :—Amongst the honours granted to Pompey at a very early period was the liberty to wear a diadem or *corona* on ceremonial occasions. The common reading was "*auream coronam*," until Lipsius suggested *lauream ;* which correction has since been generally adopted into the text. This idstinction is remarkable when contrasted with the same trophy as afterwards conceded to Cæsar, in relation to the popular feelings, so different in the two cases.

of Pompey's military exploits.   As a commander-in-chief,
Pompey was known to have been inequitably fortunate.   The
bloody contests of Marius, Cinna, Sylla, and their vindictive,
but perhaps unavoidable, proscription, had thinned the ranks
of natural competitors at the very opening of Pompey's career.
That interval of about eight years by which he was senior to
Cæsar happened to make the whole difference between a
crowded list of candidates for offices of trust and no list at
all.   Even more lucky had Pompey found himself in the
character of his appointments, and in the quality of his
antagonists.   All his wars had been of that class which yield
great splendour of external show, but impose small exertion
and less risk.   In the war with Mithridates he succeeded to
great captains who had sapped the whole stamina and resistance of the contest; besides that, after all the varnishings
of Cicero, when speaking for the Manilian law, the enemy
was too notoriously effeminate.   The by - battle with the
Cilician pirates is more obscure; but it is certain that the
extraordinary powers conferred on Pompey by the Gabinian
law gave to *him*, as compared with his predecessors in the
same effort at cleansing the Levant from a nuisance, something like the unfair superiority above their brethren enjoyed
by some of Charlemagne's paladins in the possession of en-
chanted weapons.   The success was already insured by the
great armament placed at Pompey's disposal ; and still more
by his unlimited commission, which enabled him to force
these water-rats out of their holes, and to bring them all
into one focus; whilst the pompous name of *Bellum Piraticum*
exaggerated to all after years a success which had been at the
moment too partially facilitated.   Finally, in his triumph
over Sertorius, where only he would have found a great
Roman enemy capable of applying some measure of power
to himself by the energies of resistance, although the transaction is circumstantially involved in much darkness, enough
remains to show that Pompey shrank from open contest :
passively, how far co-operatively it is hard to say, Pompey
owed his triumph to mere acts of decoy and subsequent
assassination.

Upon this sketch of Pompey's military life, it is evident
that he must have been regarded, after the enthusiasm of

the moment had gone by, as a hollow scenical pageant.
But what had produced this enthusiasm at the moment?
It was the remoteness of the scenes. The pirates had been
a troublesome enemy, precisely in that sense which made the
Pindarrees of India such to ourselves; because, as flying
marauders, lurking and watching their opportunities, they
could seldom be brought to action; so that not their power,
but their want of power, made them formidable, indisposing
themselves to concentration, and consequently weakening the
motive to a combined effort against them. Then, as to
Mithridates, a great error prevailed in Rome with regard to
the quality of his power. The spaciousness of his kingdom,
its remoteness, his power of retreat into Armenia—all enabled
him to draw out the war into a lingering struggle. These
local advantages were misinterpreted. A man who could
resist Sylla, Lucullus, and others, approved himself to the
raw judgments of the multitude as a dangerous enemy.
Whence a very disproportionate appreciation of Pompey—
as of a second Scipio who had destroyed a second Hannibal.
If Hannibal had transferred the war to the gates of Rome,
why not Mithridates, who had come westwards as far as
Greece? And, upon that argument, the panicstruck people
of Rome fancied that Mithridates might repeat the experiment. They overlooked the changes which nearly one
hundred and fifty years since Hannibal had wrought. As
possible it would have been for Scindia and Holkar fifty
years ago, as possible for Tharawaddie at this moment,[1] to
conduct an expedition into England, as for Mithridates to
have invaded Italy at the era of 670-80 of Rome. There is
a wild romantic legend, surviving in old Scandinavian literature, that Mithridates did not die by suicide, but that he
passed over the Black Sea from Pontus on the south-east of
that sea to the Baltic, crossed the Baltic, and became that
Odin whose fierce vindictive spirit reacted upon Rome, in
after centuries, through the Goths and Vandals, his supposed
descendants,—just as the blood of Dido, the Carthaginian
queen, after mounting to the heavens, under her dying
imprecation,

[1] "*Tharawaddie*" : — The Burmese Emperor then [1842] invaded
by us.

" Exoriare aliquis nostro de sanguine vindex,"

came round in a vast arch of bloodshed upon Rome, under the retaliation of Hannibal, four or five centuries later. This Scandinavian legend might answer for a grand romance, carrying with it, like the Punic legend, a semblance of mighty retribution ; but, as a historical possibility, any Mithridatic invasion of Italy would be extravagant.   Having been swallowed, however, by Roman credulity as a danger always *in procinctu* so long as the old Pontic lion should be unchained, naturally it had happened that this groundless panic, from its very indistinctness and shadowy outline, became more available for Pompey's immoderate glorification than any service so much nearer to home as to be more rationally appreciable.   With the same unexampled luck, Pompey, as the last man in the series against Mithridates, stepped into the inheritance of merit belonging to the entire succession in that service, and, as the labourer who without effort and without merit reaped the harvest, practically threw into oblivion all those who had so painfully sown it.

But a special Nemesis haunts the steps of men who become great and illustrious by appropriating the trophies of their brothers. Pompey, more strikingly than any man in history, illustrates this moral in his catastrophe.   It is perilous to be dishonourably prosperous ; and equally so, as the ancients imagined, whether by direct perfidies (of which Pompey is deeply suspected) or by silent acquiescence in unjust advantages.   Seared as Pompey's sensibilities might be through long self-indulgence, and latterly by annual fits of illness, founded on dyspepsy, — which again probably founded on gluttony, — he must have had, at this great era, a dim misgiving that his good genius was forsaking him.   No Shakspere had then proclaimed the dark retribution which awaited his final year : but the sentiment of Shakspere (see his Sonnets) is eternal, and must have whispered itself to Pompey's heart, as he saw the billowy war advancing upon him in his old age—

" The painful warrior famousèd for fight,
After a thousand victories once foiled,
Is from the book of honour razèd quite,
And all the rest forgot for which he toiled."

To say the truth, in this instance as in so many others, the great moral of the retribution escapes us because we do not connect the scattered phenomena into their rigorous unity. Most readers pursue the early steps of this mightiest amongst all civil wars with the hopes and shifting sympathies natural to those who *accompanied* its motions. Cicero must ever be the great authority for the daily fluctuations of public opinion and confidence in the one party, as Cæsar, with a few later authors, for those in the other. But inevitably these coeval authorities, shifting their own positions as events advanced, break the uniformity of the lesson. They did not see, as we may if we will, to the end. Sometimes the Pompeian partisans are cheerful; sometimes even they are sanguine; once or twice there is absolutely a slight success to colour their vaunts. But much of this is mere political dissimulation. We now find, from the confidential parts of Cicero's correspondence, that he had never heartily hoped from the hour when he first ascertained Pompey's drooping spirits and his desponding policy. And, in a subsequent stage of the contest, when the war had crossed the Adriatic, we now know, by a remarkable passage in his "De Divinatione," that, whatever he might think it prudent to say, never from the moment when he personally attached himself to Pompey's camp had he felt any reliance whatever on the composition of the army. Even to Pompey's misgiving ear in solitude a fatal summons must have been sometimes audible, to resign his quiet life and his showy prosperity. The call was in effect "Leave your palaces; come back to camps—never more to know a quiet hour!" What if he could have heard the ultimate moral of the silent call! "Live through a brief season of calamity; live long enough for total ruin; live for a morning on which it will be said, *All is lost;* as a panicstricken fugitive, sue to the mercies of slaves; and in return, as a headless trunk, lie like a poor mutilated mariner, rejected by the sea, a wreck from a wreck—owing even the last rites of burial to the pity of a solitary exile." This doom, and thus circumstantially, no man could know. But, in features that were even gloomier than these, Pompey might, through his long experience of men, have foreseen the bitter course which he had to traverse. It did not require any extraordinary self-knowledge to guess that continued opposition upon the plan of the campaign would breed fretfulness in himself; that the irritation of frequent failure, inseparable from a war so widely spread, would cause blame and decaying confidence; that his coming experience would be a mere chaos of obstinacy in council, loud remonstrance in action, crimination and recrimination, insolent dictation from rivals, treachery on the part of friends, flight and desertion on the part of confidants. Yet even this fell short of the shocking consummation into which the frenzy of faction ripened itself within a few months. I know of but one case which resembles it in a single remarkable feature. Those readers who are acquainted with Lord Clarendon's "History" will remember the very striking portrait which he draws of the king's small army of reserve in Devonshire and the adjacent districts, subsequently to the great parliamentary triumph of Naseby in June 1645. The ground was now cleared; no work remained for Fairfax but to advance, and to sweep away the last relics of opposition. In every case this would have proved no trying task. But what was the condition of the hostile forces? Lord Clarendon, who had personally presided at their head-quarters whilst in attendance upon the Prince of Wales, describes them in these emphatic terms—"a wicked beaten army." Rarely does History present us with such a picture of utter debasement in an army—coming from no enemy, but from one who, at the very moment of painting the portrait, knew this army to be the king's final resource. Reluctant as a wise man must feel to reject as irredeemable in vileness that which he knows to be indispensable to hope, this solemn opinion of Lord Clarendon's upon his royal master's last stake had been in earlier ages prefigured by Cicero, under the very same circumstances, with regard to the analogous ultimate resource. The army which Pompey had concentrated in the regions of northern Greece *was* the ultimate resource of that party; because, though a strong *nucleus* for other armies existed in other provinces, these remoter dependencies were in all likelihood contingent upon the result from this: were Pompey prosperous, *they* would be prosperous; if not, not. Knowing, therefore, the fatal emphasis which belonged to his words, not blind to the inference which they involved, Cicero did, notwithstanding, pronounce confidentially that same judgment of despair upon the army soon to perish at Pharsalia which, from its strange identity of tenor and circumstances, I have quoted from Lord Clarendon. Both statesmen spoke confessedly of a last sheet-anchor ; both spoke of an army vicious in its military composition : but also,—which is the peculiarity of the case, — both charged the *onus* of their own despair upon the non-professional qualities of the soldiers, upon their licentious uncivic temper, upon their open anticipations of plunder, and upon their tiger-training towards a great festival of coming revenge.

Lord Clarendon, however, it may be said, did not include in *his* denunciation the commander of the Devonshire army. No : and *there* it is that the two reports differ. Cicero *did*. It was the commander whom he had chiefly in his eye. Others, indeed, were parties to the horrid conspiracy against the country which he charged upon Pompey : for *non datur conjuratio aliter quam per plures ;* but these "others" were not the private soldiers—they were the leading officers, the staff, the council at Pompey's head-quarters, and generally the men of senatorial rank. Yet still, to complete the dismal unity of the prospect, these conspirators had an army of ruffians under their orders, such as formed an appropriate engine for their horrid purposes.

This is a most important point for clearing up the true character of the war ; and it has been neglected by historians. It is notorious that Cicero, on first joining the faction of Pompey after the declaration of hostilities, had for some months justified his conduct on the doctrine that the "causa," the constitutional merits of the dispute, lay with Pompey. He could not deny that Cæsar had grievances to plead ; but he insisted on two things :—1, that the mode of redress by which Cæsar made his appeal was radically illegal ; 2, that the certain tendency of this redress was to a civil revolution. Such had been the consistent representation of Cicero, until the course of events made him better acquainted with Pompey's real temper and policy. It is also notorious—and here lies the key to the error of all biographers—that about two years later, when the miserable death of Pompey had indisposed Cicero to remember his wicked unaccomplished pur-

poses, and when the assassination of Cæsar had made it safe
to resume his ancient mysterious animosity to the very name
of that great man, Cicero did undoubtedly go back to his
early way of distinguishing between them. As an orator,
and as a philosopher, he brought back his original distortions
of the case. Pompey, it was again pleaded, had been a
champion of the state (sometimes he ventured upon saying,
of liberty); Cæsar had been a traitor and a tyrant. The
two extreme terms of his own politics, the earliest and the
last, do in fact meet and blend. But the proper object of
scrutiny for the sincere inquirer is this parenthesis of time,
that intermediate experience which placed him in daily com-
munion with the real Pompey of the year *Ab Urbe Cond.*
705, and which extorted from his indignant patriotism
revelations to his friend Atticus so atrocious that nothing in
history approaches them.

This is the period to examine ; for the logic of the case is
urgent. Were Cicero now alive, he could make no resistance
to a construction and a personal appeal such as this. Easily
(we should say to him)—easily you might have a motive,
subsequently to your friend's death, for dissembling the evil
you had once imputed to him. But it is impossible that, as
an unwilling witness, you could have had any motive at all
for counterfeiting or exaggerating on your friend an evil
purpose that did not exist. The dissimulation might be
natural—the simulation was inconceivable. To suppress a
true scandal was the office of a sorrowing friend—to propagate a false one was the office of a knave : not, therefore,
that later testimony which to have garbled was amiable, but
that coeval testimony which to have invented would have
been insanity,—this it is which we must abide by. Besides
that, there is another explanation of Cicero's later language
than simple piety to the memory of a friend. His discovery
of Pompey's execrable plan was limited to a few months ; so
that, equally from its brief duration, its suddenness, and its
astonishing contradiction to all he had previously believed of
Pompey, such a painful secret was likely enough to fade from
his recollection after it had ceased to have any practical
importance for the world. On the other hand, Cicero had a
deep vindictive policy in keeping back any evil that he knew

of Pompey.   It was a mere necessity of logic that, if Pompey had meditated the utter destruction of his country by fire and sword—if, more atrociously still, he had cherished a resolution of unchaining upon Italy the most ferocious barbarians he could gather about his eagles, Getæ for instance, Colchians, Armenians—if he had ransacked the ports of the whole Mediterranean world, and had mustered all the shipping from fourteen separate states enumerated by Cicero, with an express purpose of intercepting all supplies for Rome, and of inflicting the slow torments of famine upon that vast yet non-belligerent city—then, in opposing such a monster, Cæsar was undeniably a public benefactor.   Cicero could not hide from himself that result.   He felt also that not only would the magnanimity and the gracious spirit of forgiveness in Cæsar be recalled with advantage into men's thoughts by any confession of this hideous malignity in his antagonist ; but that it really became impossible to sustain any theory of ambitious violence in Cæsar, when regarded under his relations to such a body of parricidal conspirators. Fighting for public objects that are difficult of explaining to a mob, easily may any chieftain of a party be misrepresented as a child of selfish ambition.   But, once emblazoned as the sole barrier between his native land and a merciless avenger by fire and famine, he would take a tutelary character in the minds of all men.   To confess one solitary council—such as Cicero had attended repeatedly at Pompey's head-quarters in Epirus—was, by acclamation from every house in Rome, to evoke a hymn of gratitude towards that great Julian deliverer whose Pharsalia had turned aside from Italy a deeper woe than any which Paganism records.

I insist inexorably upon this state of relations as existing between Cicero and the two combatants.   I refuse to quit this position.   I affirm that, at a time when Cicero argued upon the purposes of Cæsar in a manner confessedly conjectural, on the other hand, with regard to Pompey, from confidential communications, he reported it as a dreadful discovery that mere destruction to Rome was, upon Pompey's policy, the catastrophe of the war.   Cæsar, he might persuade himself, would revolutionise Rome ; but Pompey, he knew in confidence, meant to leave no Rome to revolutionise.   Does any reader fail to condemn the selfishness of the Constable Bourbon—ranging himself at Pavia in a pitched battle against his sovereign on an argument of private wrong?   Yet the Constable's treason had perhaps identified itself with his self-preservation ; and he had no reason to anticipate a lasting calamity to his country from any act possible to an individual.   If we look into Ancient History, the case of Hippias, the son of Pisistratus, scarcely approaches to this. He indeed returned to Athens in company with the invading hosts of Darius.   But he had probably been expelled from Athens by violent injustice ; and, though attending a hostile invasion, he could not have caused it.   Hardly a second case can be found in all History as a parallel to the dreadful design of Pompey, unless it be that of Count Julian calling in the Saracens to ravage Spain, and to overthrow the altars of Christianity, on the provocation of one outrage to his own house,—early in the eighth century invoking a scourge that was not entirely to be withdrawn until the sixteenth.

But then for Count Julian it may be pleaded—that the whole tradition is doubtful ; that, if true to the letter, his own provocation was enormous ; and that we must not take the measure of what he meditated by the frightful consequences which actually ensued.   Count Julian might have relied on the weakness of Don Roderick for giving a present effect to his vengeance, but might still rely consistently enough on the natural strength of his country, when once coerced into union, for ultimately confounding the enemy, and perhaps for confounding the Mahometan fanaticism itself. For the worst traitor whom History has recorded there remains some plea of mitigation, something in aggravation of the wrongs which he had sustained, something in abatement of the retaliation which he designed.   Only for Pompey there is none.   Rome had given him no subject of complaint. It was true that the strength of Cæsar lay there ; because immediate hopes from revolution belonged to the democracy, to the oppressed, to the multitudes in debt, for whom the law had neglected to provide any prospect or degree of relief ; and these were exactly the class of persons that could not find funds for emigrating.   But still there was no overt act, no official act, no representative act, by which Rome had declared herself for either party.

Cicero was now aghast at the discoveries he made with regard to Pompey. Imbecility of purpose, distraction of counsels, feebleness in their dilatory execution, all tended to one dilemma: either that Pompey, as a mere favourite of luck, never had possessed any military talents, or that, by age and conscious inequality to his enemy, these talents were now in a state of collapse. Having first, therefore, made the discovery that his too celebrated friend was anything but a statesman (ἀπολιτικωτατος), Cicero came at length to pronounce him ἀστρατηγικωτατον—anything but a general. But all this was nothing in the way of degradation to Pompey's character, by comparison with the final discovery of the horrid retaliation which he meditated upon all Italy by coming back with barbarous troops to make a wilderness of the opulent land, and upon Rome in particular by so posting his blockading fleets and his cruisers as to intercept all supplies of corn from Sicily, from the province of Africa, and from Egypt. The great moral, therefore, from Cicero's confidential confessions is that he abandoned the cause as untenable; that he abandoned the supposed party of "good men," as found upon trial to be odious intriguers; and that he abandoned Pompey in any privileged character of a patriotic leader. If he still adhered to Pompey as an individual, it was in memory of his personal obligations to that oligarch; but, secondly, for the very generous reason that Pompey's fortunes were declining, and because Cicero would not be thought to have shunned that man in his misfortunes whom in reality he had felt tempted to despise only for his enormous errors.

After these distinct and reiterated acknowledgments, it is impossible to find the smallest justification for the great harmony of historians in representing Cicero as having abided by those opinions with which he first entered upon the party strife. Even at that time it is probable that Cicero's deep sense of gratitude to Pompey secretly had entered more largely into his decision than he had ever acknowledged to himself. For he had at first exerted himself anxiously to mediate between the two parties. Now, if he really fancied the views of Cæsar to proceed on principles of destruction to the Roman constitution, all mediation was a hopeless attempt. Compromise between extremes lying so widely apart, and in fact as between the affirmation and the negation of the same propositions, must have been too plainly impossible to have justified any countenance to so impracticable a speculation.

But was not such a compromise impossible in practice, even upon our own theory of the opposite requisitions?   No. And a closer statement of the true principles concerned will show it was not.   The great object of the Julian party was to heal the permanent collision between the supposed functions of the people, in their electoral capacity, in their powers of patronage, and in their vast appellate jurisdiction, with the assumed privileges of the Senate.   We all know how dreadful have been the disputes in our own country as to the limits of the constitutional forces composing the total state. Between the privileges of the Commons and the prerogative of the Crown, how long a time, and how severe a struggle, was required to adjust the true temperament !   To say nothing of the fermenting disaffection towards the government throughout the reign of James I and the first fifteen years of his son, the great Civil War grew out of the sheer contradictions arising between the necessities of the public service and the *letter* of superannuated prerogatives.   The simple history of that great strife was that the democracy, the popular element, in the commonwealth, had outgrown the provisions of old usages and statutes.   The King, a man wishing to be conscientious, believed that the efforts of the Commons, which represented only the instincts of rapid growth in all popular interests, cloaked a secret plan of encroachment on the essential rights of the sovereign.   In this view he was confirmed by lawyers, the most dangerous of all advisers in political struggles ; for they naturally seek the solution of all contested claims either in the positive determination of ancient usage or in the constructive view of its analogies. Whereas here the very question was concerning a body of usage and precedent not denied in many cases as facts,— whether that condition of policy, not unreasonable as adapted to a community having but two dominant interests, were any longer safely tenable under the rise and expansion of a third.

For instance, the whole management of our foreign policy had always been reserved to the crown, as one of its most sacred mysteries, or ἀπορρητα ; yet, if the people could obtain no indirect control of this policy through the amplest control of the public purse, even their domestic rights might easily be made nugatory. Again, it was indispensable that the crown, free from all direct responsibility, should be checked by some responsibility operating in a way to preserve the sovereign in his constitutional sanctity. This was finally effected by the admirable compromise of lodging the responsibility in the persons of all servants by or through whom the sovereign could act. But this was so little understood by Charles I as any constitutional privilege of the people that he resented the proposal as much more insulting to himself than that of fixing the responsibility in his own person. The latter proposal he viewed as a violation of his own prerogative, founded upon open wrong. There was an injury, but no insult. On the other hand, to require of him the sacrifice of a servant, whose only offence had been in his fidelity to himself, was to expect that he should act collusively with those who sought to dishonour him. The absolute *Io el Rey* of Spanish kings, in the last resort, seemed in Charles's eye indispensable to the dignity of his crown. And his legal counsellors assured him that, in conceding this point, he would degrade himself into a sort of upper constable, having some disagreeable functions, but none which could surround him with majestic attributes in the eyes of his subjects. Feeling thus, and thus advised, and religiously persuaded that he held his powers for the benefit of his people, so as to be under a deep moral incapacity to surrender " one dowle "[1] from his royal plumage, he did right to struggle with that energy and that cost of blood which marked his own personal war from 1642 to 1645. Now, on the other hand, we know that nearly all the concessions sought from the king, and refused as mere treasonable demands, were subsequently reaffirmed, assumed into our constitutional law, and solemnly established for ever, about forty years later, by the Revolution of 1688-89. And this great event was in the nature of a compromise. For the patriots of 1642 had been betrayed

---

[1] "*One dowle*" :—Shakspere [*Tempest*, III. 3].

into some capital errors, claims both irreconcilable with the dignity of the crown, and useless to the people. This ought not to surprise us, and does not extinguish our debt of gratitude to those great men. Where has been the man, much less the party of men, that did not, in a first essay upon so difficult an adjustment as that of an equilibration between the limits of political forces, travel into some excesses ? But forty years' experience, the restoration of a party familiar with the invaluable uses of royalty, and the harmonious co-operation of a new sovereign, already trained to a system of restraints, made this final settlement as near to a perfect adjustment and compromise between all conflicting rights as perhaps human wisdom could attain.

Now, from this English analogy, we may explain something of what is most essential in the Roman conflict. This great feature was common to the two cases—that the change sought by the revolutionary party was not an arbitrary change, but in the way of a natural *nisus*, working secretly throughout two or three generations. It was a tendency that would not be denied,—just as, in the England of 1640, it is impossible to imagine that, under any immediate result whatever, ultimately the mere necessities of expansion in a people ebullient with juvenile energies, and passing, at every decennium, into new stages of development, could have been gainsaid or much retarded. Had the nation embodied less of that stern political temperament which leads eventually to extremities in action, it is possible that the upright and thoughtful character of the sovereign might have reconciled the Commons to expedients of present redress, and for thirty years the crisis might have been evaded. But the licentious character of Charles II would inevitably have challenged the resumption of the struggle in a more embittered shape ; for, in the actual war of 1642, the *separate* resources of the crown were soon exhausted, and a deep sentiment of respect towards the king kept alive the principle of fidelity to the crown through all the oscillations of the public mind. Under a stronger reaction against the personal sovereign, it is not absolutely impossible that the aristocracy might have come into the project of a republic. Whenever this body stood aloof, and by alliance with the Church, as well as with a very large section of the Democracy, their non-adhesion to republican plans finally brought them to extinction. But the principle cannot be refused—that the conflict was inevitable ; that the collision could in no way have been evaded, and for the same reason as spoke out so loudly in Rome— because the grievances to be redressed, and the incapacities to be removed, and the organs to be renewed, were absolute and urgent ; that the evil grew out of the political system ; that this system had generally been the silent product of time ; and that, as the sovereign in the English case most conscientiously, so, on the other hand, in Rome, the Pompeian faction, with no conscience at all, stood upon the letter of usage and precedent, where the secret truth was that nature herself,—that nature which works in political things by change, by growth, by destruction, not less certainly than in physical organisations,—had long been silently superannuating these precedents, and preparing the transition into forms more in harmony with public safety, with public wants, and with public intelligence.

The capital fault in the operative constitution of Rome had long been in the *antinomies*, if I may be pardoned for so learned a term, of the public service. It is not so true an expression that anarchy was always to be apprehended as, in fact, that anarchy always subsisted. What made this anarchy more and less dangerous was the personal character of the particular man militant for the moment ; next, the variable interest which such a party might have staked upon the contest ; and, lastly, the variable means at his disposal towards public agitation. Fortunately for the public safety, these forces, like all forces in this world of compensations and of fluctuations, obeying steady laws, rose but seldom into the excess which menaced the framework of the state. Even in disorder, when long continued, there is an order that can be calculated : dangers were foreseen ; remedies were put into an early state of preparation. But, because the evil had not been so ruinous as might have been predicted, it was not the less an evil, and it was not the less enormously increasing. The democracy retained a large class of functions, for which the original uses had been long extinct. Powers which had utterly ceased to be available for interests of their own were now used purely as the tenures by which they held a vested interest in bribery. The sums requisite for bribery were rising as the great estates rose. No man, even in a gentlemanly rank, no *equcs*, no ancient noble even, unless his income were hyperbolically vast, or unless as the creature of some party in the background, could at length face the ruin of a political career. I do not speak of men anticipating a special resistance, but of those who stood in ordinary circumstances. Atticus is not a man whom I should cite for any authority in a question of principle, for I believe him to have been a dissembling knave, and the most perfect vicar of Bray extant ; but in a question of prudence his example is decisive. Latterly he was worth a hundred thousand pounds. Four-fifths of this sum, it is true, had been derived from a casual bequest ; however, he had been rich enough, even in early life, to present all the poor citizens of Athens—probably twelve thousand families—with a year's consumption for two individuals of excellent wheat ; and he had been distinguished for other ostentatious largesses : yet this man held it to be ridiculous, in common prudence, that he should embark upon any political career. Merely the costs of an ædileship, to which he might have arrived in early life, would have swallowed up the entire hundred thousand pounds of his mature good luck. " Honores non petiit, quod neque peti more majorum, neque capi possent, conservatis legibus, in tam effusis largitionibus, neque geri sine periculo, corruptis civitatis moribus "—(*"For public honours he was no candidate; because, under a system of bribery so unlimited, such distinctions could neither be sought after in the old ancestral mode, nor won without violation of the laws ; nor administered satisfactorily, as regarded the duties which they imposed, without personal risk in a condition of civic morals so generally relaxed "*). But this argument on the part of Atticus pointed to a modest and pacific career. When the politics of a man, or his special purpose, happened to be polemic, the costs, and the personal risk, and the risk to the public peace, were on a scale prodigiously greater. No man with such views could think of coming forward without a princely fortune, and the courage of a martyr. Milo, Curio, Decimus Brutus, and many persons besides, in a lapse of twenty-five years, spent fortunes of four

and five hundred thousand pounds, and without accomplishing, after all, much of what they proposed. In other shapes,
the evil was still more malignant : and, as these circumstantial cases are the most impressive, I will bring forward
a few.

1. *Provisional administrations.*—The Romans were not
characteristically a rapacious or dishonest people—the
Greeks were ; and it is a fact strongly illustrative of that
infirmity in principle and levity which made the Greek so
contemptible to the graver judgments of Rome that hardly a
trustworthy man could be found for the receipt of taxes.
The regular course of business was that the Greeks absconded
with the money, unless narrowly watched. Whatever else
they might be—sculptors, buffoons, dancers, tumblers—they
were a nation of swindlers. For the art of fidelity in peculation you might depend upon them to any amount. Now,
amongst the Romans, these petty knaveries were generally
unknown. Even as knaves they had aspiring minds ; and
the original key to their spoliations in the provinces was
undoubtedly the vast scale of their domestic corruption. A
man who had to begin by bribing one nation must end by
fleecing another. Almost the only open channels through
which a Roman nobleman could create a fortune (always
allowing for a large means of marrying to advantage, since a
man might shoot a whole series of divorces, still refunding
the last dowry, but still replacing it with a better) were
these two : lending money on sea risks, or to embarrassed
municipal corporations on good landed or personal security,
with the gain of twenty, thirty, or even forty per cent ; and,
secondly, the grand resource of a provincial government.
The abuses I need not state : the prolongation of these lieutenancies beyond the legitimate year was one source of
enormous evil ; and it was the more rooted an abuse because
very often it was undeniable that other evils arose in the
opposite scale from too hasty a succession of governors, upon
which principle no consistency of local improvements could
be insured, nor any harmony even in the administration of
justice, since each successive governor brought his own
system of legal rules. As to the other and more flagrant

abuses, in extortion from the province, in garbling the accounts and defeating all scrutiny at Rome, in embezzlement of military pay, and in selling every kind of private advantage for bribes, these have been made notorious by the very circumstantial exposure of Verres. But some of the worst evils are still unpublished, and must be looked for in the indirect revelations of Cicero when himself a governor, as well as the incidental relations by special facts and cases. I, on my part, will venture to raise a doubt whether Verres ought really to be considered that exorbitant criminal whose guilt has been so profoundly impressed upon us all by the forensic artifices of Cicero. The true reasons for his condemnation must be sought, first, in the proximity to Rome of that Sicilian province where many of his alleged oppressions had occurred. The fluent intercourse with this island, and the multiplied interconnexions of individual towns with Roman grandees, aggravated the facilities of making charges; whilst the proofs were anything but satisfactory in the Roman judicature. Here lay one disadvantage of Verres; but another was that the ordinary system of bribes—viz. the sacrifice of one portion from the spoils in the shape of bribes to the jury (*judices*) in order to redeem the other portions— in this case could not be applied. The spoils were chiefly works of art. Verres was the very first man who formed a gallery of art in Rome ; and a French writer in the " Académie des Inscriptions " has written a most elaborate *catalogue raisonné* to this gallery—drawn from the materials left by Cicero and Pliny. But this was obviously a sort of treasure that did not admit of partition. And the object of Verres would equally have been defeated by selling a part for the costs of " salvage " on the rest. In this sad dilemma, Verres, upon the whole, resolved to take his chance ; or, if bribery were applied to some extent, it must have stopped far short of that excess to which it would have proceeded under a more disposable form of his gains. But I will not conceal the truth which Cicero indirectly reveals. The capital abuse in the provincial system was, not that the guilty governor might escape, but that the innocent governor might be ruined. It is evident that, in a majority of cases, this magistrate was thrown upon his own discretion. Nothing could be so indefinite and uncircumstantial as the Roman laws on this head. The most upright administrator was almost as cruelly laid open to the fury of calumnious persecution as the worst ; both were often cited to answer upon parts of their administration altogether blameless ; but, when the original rule had been so wide and lax, the final resource must be in the mercy of the particular tribunal.

2. *The Roman judicial system.*—This would require a separate volume, and chiefly upon this ground—that in no country upon earth, except Rome, has the ordinary administration of justice been applied as a great political engine. Men who could not otherwise be removed were constantly assailed by impeachments, and oftentimes for acts done forty or fifty years before the time of trial. But this dreadful aggravation of the injustice was not generally needed. The system of trial was the most corrupt that has ever prevailed under European civilisation. The composition of their courts, as to the *rank* of the numerous jury, was continually changed : but no change availed to raise them above bribery. The rules of evidence were simply none at all. Every hearsay, erroneous rumour, or atrocious libel, was allowed to be offered as evidence. Much of this never could be repelled, as it had not been anticipated. And, even in those cases where no bribery was attempted, the issue was dependent, almost in a desperate extent, upon the impression made by the advocate. And, finally, it must be borne in mind that there was no presiding *judge*, in our sense of the word, to sum up, to mitigate the effect of arts or falsehood in the advocate, to point the true bearing of the evidence, still less to state and to restrict the law. Law there very seldom was any, in a precise circumstantial shape. The verdict might be looked for accordingly. And I do not scruple to say that so triumphant a machinery of oppression has never existed—no, not in the dungeons of the Inquisition.

3. *The licence of public libelling.*—Upon this I had proposed to enlarge. But I must forbear. One only caution I must impress upon the reader : he may fancy that Cicero

would not practise or defend in others the absolute abuse of confidence on the part of the jury and audience by employing direct falsehoods. But this is a mistake. Cicero, in his justification of the artifices used at the bar, evidently goes the whole length of advising the employment of all mis-statements whatsoever which wear a plausible air. His own practice leads to the same inference. Not the falsehood, but the defect of probability, is what in his eyes degrades any possible assertion or insinuation. And he holds, also, that a barrister is not accountable for the frequent self-contradictions in which he must be thus involved at different periods of time. The immediate purpose is paramount to all extrajudicial consequences whatever, and to all subsequent exposures of the very grossest inconsistency in the most calumnious falsehoods.

4. *The morality of expediency employed by Roman statesmen.* —The regular relief furnished to Rome under the system of anarchy which Cæsar proposed to set aside lay in seasonable murders. When a man grew potent in political annoyance, somebody was employed to murder him. Never was there a viler or better established murder than that of Claudius by Milo, or that of Carbo and others by Pompey when a young man, acting as the tool of Sylla. Yet these, and the murders of the two Gracchi, nearly a century before, Cicero justifies as necessary. So little progress had law and sound political wisdom then made that Cicero was not aware of anything monstrous in pleading for a most villainous act that circum-stances had made it expedient. Such a man is massacred, and Cicero appeals to all your natural feelings of honour against the murderers. Such another is massacred, on the opposite side, and Cicero thinks it quite sufficient to reply, "Oh, but I assure you he was a bad man—I knew him to be a bad man. And it was his duty to be murdered, as the sole service he could render the commonwealth." So again, in common with all his professional brethren, Cicero never scruples to ascribe the foulest lust and abominable propen-sities to any public antagonist ; never asking himself any question but this, Will it look plausible ? He personally escaped such slanders, because, as a young man, he was

known to be rather poor, and very studious. But in later life a horrible calumny of that very class settled upon himself, and one peculiarly shocking to his parental grief; for he was then sorrowing in extremity for the departed lady who had been associated in the slander. Do I lend a moment's credit to the foul insinuation? No. But I see the equity of this retribution revolving upon one who had so often slandered others in the same malicious way. At last the poisoned chalice came round to his own lips, and at a moment when its venom reached his heart of hearts.

5. *The continued repetition of convulsions in the state.*— Under the last head I have noticed a consequence of the long Roman Anarchy dreadful enough to contemplate—viz. the necessity of murder as a sole relief to the extremities continually recurring, and as a permànent temptation to the vitiation of all moral ideas in the necessity of defending it imposed often upon such men as Cicero. This was an evil which cannot be exaggerated : but a more extensive evil lay in the recurrence of those conspiracies which the public anarchy promoted. We have all been deluded upon this point. The conspiracy of Catiline, to those who weigh well the mystery still enveloping the names of Cæsar, of the Consul C. Antonius, and others suspected as partial accomplices in this plot, and who consider also what parties were the exposers or merciless avengers of this plot, was but a reiteration of the attempts made within the previous fifty years by Marius, Cinna, Sylla, and finally by Cæsar and by his heir Octavius, to raise a reformed government, safe and stable, upon this hideous oligarchy that annually almost brought the people of Rome into the necessity of a war and the danger of a merciless proscription. That the usual system of fraudulent falsehoods was offered by way of evidence against Catiline, is pretty obvious. Indeed, why should it have been spared ? The evidence, in a lawyer's sense, is after all none at all. The pretended revelations of foreign envoys go for nothing. These could have been suborned most easily. And the shocking defect of the case is that the accused parties were never put on their defence, never confronted with the base tools of the accusers, and the senators

amongst them were overwhelmed with clamours if they attempted their defence in the senate. The motive to this dreadful injustice is manifest. There *was* a conspiracy; that I do not doubt; and of the same nature as Cæsar's. Else why should eminent men, too dangerous for Cicero to touch, have been implicated in the obscurer charges? How had they any interest in the ruin of Rome? How had Catiline any interest in such a tragedy? But all the grandees, who were too much embarrassed in debt to bear the means of profiting by the machinery of bribes applied to so vast a populace, naturally wished to place the administration of public affairs on another footing; many from merely selfish purposes, like Cethegus or Lentulus—some, I doubt not, from purer motives of enlarged patriotism. One charge against Catiline I may quote from many, as having tainted the most plausible part of the pretended evidence with damnatory suspicions. The reader may not have remarked —but the fact is such—that one of the standing artifices for injuring a man with the populace of Rome, when all other arts had failed, was to say that amongst his plots was one for burning the city. This cured that indifference with which otherwise the mob listened to stories of mere political conspiracy against a system which they hated. Now, this most senseless charge was renewed against Catiline. It is hardly worthy of notice. Of what value to him could be a heap of ruins? Or how could he hope to found an influence amongst those who were yet reeking from such a calamity?

But, in reality, this conspiracy was that effort continually moving underground, and which would have continually exploded in shocks dreadful to the quiet of the nation, which mere necessity, and the instincts of position, prompted to the parties interested. Let the reader only remember the long and really ludicrous succession of men sent out against Antony at Mutina by the Senate, viz. Octavius, Plancus, Asinius Pollio, Lepidus, every one of whom fell away almost instantly to the anti-senatorial cause, to say nothing of the consuls, Hirtius and Pansa, who would undoubtedly have followed the general precedent, had they not been killed prematurely: and it will become apparent how irresistible this popular cause was, as the sole introduction to a patriotic reformation, ranged too notoriously against a narrow scheme of selfishness, which interested hardly forty families. It does not follow that all men, simply as enemies of an oligarchy, would have afterwards exhibited a pure patriotism. Cæsar, however, did. His reforms, even before his Pompeian struggle, were the greatest ever made by an individual; and those which he carried through after that struggle, and during that brief term which his murderers allowed him, transcended by much all that in any one century had been accomplished by the collective patriotism of Rome.

POSTSCRIPT [1]

THE late Dr. Arnold of Rugby mentions that, when he was meditating a work on some section (I forget what) of Ancient History, there reached him from one of the Napiers (either Sir William, it must have been, or the late General Sir Charles) an admonitory caution to beware of treating Pompey with any harshness or undervaluation under the common notion that he had been spoiled in youth by unmerited success, had been petted by a most ignorant populace through half-a-century, and, finally, coming into collision with the greatest of men, had naturally made a total shipwreck; for that, on the contrary, he was a very great strategist; yes, in spite of Pharsalia (and in spite, I presume, of his previous Italian campaign). Now, the Napiers, a distinguished family, "*multum nostræ quæ proderat urbi*," and qualified to offer suit and service "*tam Marti quam Mercurio*," have a right to legislate on such a subject,—have a limited right even to dogmatise, and to rivet their conclusions (if at any odd corner shaky) by what Germans term a *macht-spruch*. But the general impression is likely to prevail, until his annals are re-written, that, in the fullest sense of that modern sneer, Pompey (if any man on the rolls of History) was "a Sepoy General": he earned his reputation too surely by building on other men's foundations; and he prospered in any brilliant degree only so long as he contended with Asiatic antagonists. That famous sneer came round with

---

[1] What is here printed as a Postscript appeared originally as part of a "Preface" prefixed by De Quincey in 1858 to the volume of his Collected Writings containing his paper on Cicero.—M.

killing recoil before the play was over upon those that launched it, like the *boomerang* of the poor Australian savage in unskilful hands : but it is a sneer that still tells retrospectively upon the Pompey that in his morning hours was the pet of ill-distinguishing Rome. A Sepoy General is one to whom the praise of the martinet is the breath of his nostrils,—who thinks it a bagatelle in a soldier to have the trick of running away, provided he runs with grace and a stately air ; and, above all, a Sepoy General is one that reaps a perpetual consolation under calamities from the luxury of " prospecting " malice. " I may be beaten," says the gallant man, " on the open field of battle. But what then ? My secret consolations remain : 'my mind to me a kingdom is.' And this mind suggests that, if unable to face my enemy in the daylight, I may yet find the means to murder him at night." Such as these were the habits and the reversionary consolations of Pompey. And I should have suggested to Dr. Arnold that, after all, since there is no State Paper Office in Rome surviving from classical days that might contribute new materials when the old had failed, and since Pompeii itself, though built on the Neapolitan landed estate of this very Pharsalian Pompey, has hitherto furnished, amongst all her unrolled *papyri*, nothing at all towards the military vindication of her ground landlord, even the Napiers must be content for the present with the old documents that have failed to whitewash the pompous old torso, now lying without a head, somewhere on the coast of Aboukir, at the bottom of the sea. Meantime all this relates to Pompey as a military captain and tactician ; upon which aspect of his pretensions I have said nothing at all. It is Pompey as a man, and as a citizen more deeply indebted to Rome than any other amongst his contemporaries, that I am reviewing. A bad man he was,—a vile man ; and upon the evidence of one who would have been (and long *had* been) his friend for purposes that could be decently avowed, and his horrorstruck confidant for such as could not. On the impulse of mere vindictive fury against Cæsar and the supporters of Cæsar, he would have visited Rome with famine and the sword. All the absurd designs against Rome that ever were *mendaciously* imputed to Catiline Pompey in

his secret purposes entertained steadily and inexorably. Cicero
was far from being a good man : too ambitious he was by
much ; and the enjoyment of his patrician honours was too
incompatible with the general welfare for any true civic
patriotism.   But he was too moderate and decent a man to
harmonise with the faction that had formed itself in Pompey's camp.   But this subject I will not pursue ; it would
be *actum agere,*—as it is already sketched, though rapidly
and insufficiently, in the paper entitled " Cicero."

THE CÆSARS[1]

INTRODUCTION[2]

THE majesty of the Roman Cæsar Semper Augustus has never yet been fully appreciated ; nor has any man yet explained sufficiently in what respects this title and this office were absolutely unique. There was but one Rome : no other city, as we are satisfied by the collation of many facts, has ever rivalled this astonishing metropolis in the grandeur of magnitude ; and not many—perhaps, if we except the cities built under Grecian auspices along the line of three thousand miles from Western Capua or Syracuse to the Euphrates and oriental Palmyra, none at all—in the grandeur of architectural display. Speaking even of London, we ought in all reason to say the *Nation of London*, and not the City of London ; but of Rome in her meridian hours nothing else could be said in the naked rigour of logic. A million and a half of souls—that population, apart from any other distinctions, is *per se* for London a justifying ground for such a classification ; *a fortiori*, then, will it belong to a city which counted from one horn to the other of its mighty suburbs not less than four millions of inhabitants at the very least,—as we resolutely maintain after reviewing all that has

[1] The series of papers with this title appeared originally in *Blackwood's Magazine* for October and November 1832, January 1833, and June, July, and August 1834. They were reprinted by De Quincey in 1859 in the tenth volume of his Collected Writings, with slight changes of phraseology here and there, and some added footnotes.—M.

[2] This was the first portion of the first Paper on "The Cæsars" as it stood in *Blackwood* for October 1832.—M.

been written on that much-vexed theme,—and not impossibly half as many more.[1] Republican Rome had her *prerogative* Tribe ; the Earth has its *prerogative* City ; and that City was Rome.

As was the City, such was its Prince—mysterious, solitary, unique. Each was to the other an adequate counterpart, each reciprocally that perfect mirror which reflected, as *in alia materia*, those incommunicable attributes of grandeur that under the same shape and denomination never upon this earth were destined to be revived. Rome has not been repeated ; neither has Cæsar. *Ubi Cæsar, ibi Roma*, was a

---

[1] "*A million and a half*," which was the true numerical return of population from the English capital about twenty years back [1832], when this paper was written. At present [1859], and for some time, it has stood at two millions *plus* as many thousands as express the days of a solar year. But, if adjusted to meet the corrections due upon the annual growths of the people, in that case the true return must *now* (viz. January of the year 1859) show a considerable excess beyond two and a half millions. Do we mean to assert, then, that the ancient Rome of the Cæsars, that mighty ancestral forerunner of the *Papal* Rome,—which, in this year 1859, counts about 180,000 citizens (or, in fact, above Edinburgh by a trifle, by 200,000 below Glasgow, by 150,000 below Manchester),—did in reality ever surmount numerically the now awful London ? Is that what we mean ? Yes ; that is what we mean. We must remember the prodigious *area* which Rome stretched over. We must remember that feature in the Roman domestic architecture (so impressively insisted on by the rhetorician Aristides) in which the ancient Rome resembled the ancient Edinburgh, and so far greatly eclipsed London, viz. the vast ascending series of storeys, laying stratum upon stratum, tier upon tier, of men and women, as in some mighty theatre of human hives. Not that London is deficient in thousands of lofty streets ; but the storeys rarely ascend beyond the fourth, or, at most, the fifth ; whereas the old Rome and the old Edinburgh counted at intervals by sevens or even tens. This element in the calculation being allowed for, perhaps the four millions of Lipsius may seem a reasonable population for the flourishing days of *Cæsarian* Rome, which ran far ahead of Republican Rome. On this assumption, Rome will take the *first* place, London (as it now is) the *second*, Paris (of to-day) the *third*, New York (800,000) and probably the ancient Alexandria the *fourth* places, on the world's register of mighty metropolitan cities. Babylon and Nineveh are too entirely within the exaggerating influences of misty traditions and nursery fables, like the vapoury exhalations of the *Fata Morgana*—a species of delusion resting upon a primary basis of reality, but repeating this reality so often, through endless self-multiplication, by means of optical reflexion and refraction, that the final result is little better

maxim of Roman jurisprudence. And the same maxim may be translated into a wider meaning; in which it becomes true also for our historical experience. Cæsar and Rome have flourished and expired together. Each reciprocally was essential to the other. Even the Olympian Pantheon needed Rome for its full glorification; and Jove himself first knew his own grandeur when robed and shrined as Jupiter Capitolinus. The illimitable attributes of the Roman Prince, boundless and comprehensive as the universal air—like that also bright and apprehensible to the most vagrant eye, yet in parts (and those not far removed) unfathomable as outer

than absolute fiction. And, universally, with regard to Asiatic cities (above all, with regard to Chinese cities), the reader must carry with him these cautions :—

1*st*, That Asiatics, with rare exceptions, have little regard for truth : by habit and policy they are even more mendacious than they are perfidious. Fidelity to engagements, sincerity, and disinterested veracity, rank, in Oriental estimates, as the perfection of idiocy.

2*d*, That, having no *liberal* curiosity, the Chinese man never troubles his head about the statistical circumstances of his own city, province, or natal territory. Such researches he would regard as ploughing the sands of the sea-shore, or counting the waves.

3*d*, That, two grounds of falsification being thus laid, in (A) the ostentatious mendacity, and (B), which glories in its own blindness, the ignorance of all those who ought to be authorities upon such questions, a third ground arises naturally from the peculiar and special character of Eastern cities, which, for all European ears, too readily aids in misleading. Too often such cities are improvised by means of mud, turf, light spars, canvas, &c. Hibernian cabins, Scotch bothies (which word is radically the same as the *booth* of English fairs), hovels for sheltering cattle from the weather,—or buildings of a similar style and fugitive make-shift character, under the hurried workmanship of three or four hundred thousand men,—run up within a single forenoon a perishable town that meets the necessities of a southern climate. Schiller, in his "Wallenstein," sketches such a light canvas town as the hurried *extempore* creation of soldiers. Schiller's description is a sketch ; and such a military creation is itself but a sketch of a regular and finished town. Military by its first outline and suggestion, such a frail scenical town always retains its military make-shift character ; and is, in fact, to the very last, an encampment of gipsies or migrating travellers, rather than an architectural residence of settlers who have ceased from vagrancy. Even as an *improvised* home, such a stage mimicry of a city could find toleration only in a warm climate. But such a climate, and such slender masquerading abodes, are found throughout the Northern Tropic in the southern regions of Asia.

darkness (for no chamber in a dungeon could shroud in more impenetrable concealment a deed of murder than the upper chambers of the air) : these attributes, so impressive to the imagination, and which all the subtlety of the Roman [1] wit could as little fathom as the fleets of Cæsar could traverse the Polar basin or unlock the gates of the Pacific, are best symbolized, and find their most appropriate exponent, in the illimitable City itself—that Rome, whose centre, the Capitol, was immovable as Teneriffe or Atlas, but whose circumference was shadowy, uncertain, restless, and advancing as the frontiers of her all-conquering empire.   It is false to say that with Cæsar came the destruction of Roman greatness. Peace, hollow rhetoricians ! until Cæsar came, Rome was a minor ; by him she attained her majority, and fulfilled her destiny. Caius Julius, you say, deflowered the virgin purity of her civil liberties.   Doubtless, then, Rome had risen immaculate from the arms of Sylla and of Marius.   But, if it were Caius Julius that deflowered Rome, if under him she forfeited her dowry of civic purity, if to him she first unloosed her maiden zone, then be it affirmed boldly that she reserved her greatest favours for the noblest of her wooers ; and we may plead the justification of Falconbridge for his mother's transgression with the lion-hearted king—such a sin was self-ennobled. Did Julius deflower Rome ? Then, by that consummation, he caused her to fulfil the functions of her nature ; he compelled her to exchange the imperfect and inchoate condition of a mere *fœmina* for the perfections of a *mulier*. And, metaphor apart, we maintain that Rome lost no liberties by the mighty Julius.   That which in tendency and by the spirit of her institutions, that which by her very corruptions and abuses co-operating with her laws, Rome promised and involved in the germ—even that, and nothing less or different, did Rome unfold and accomplish under this Julian violence. The rape (if such it were) of Cæsar, her final Romulus, completed for Rome that which the rape under Romulus, her initial or in-augurating Cæsar, had prosperously begun. And thus by one

---

[1] Or even of modern wit ; witness the vain attempt of so many eminent JCTI (*i.e.* jurisconsulti), and illustrious *Antecessors* (*i.e.* doctors of law), to explain in self-consistency the differing functions of the Roman Cæsar, and in what sense he was *legibus solutus*.

supreme man was a nation-city matured ; and from the ever-lasting and nameless [1] city was a man produced capable of taming her indomitable nature, and of forcing her to immolate her wild virginity to the state best fitted for the destined "Mother of Empires." Peace, then, rhetoricians, false threnodists of false liberty! hollow chanters over the ashes of a hollow republic! Without Cæsar we affirm a thousand times that there would have been no perfect Rome ; and, but for Rome, there could have been no such man as Cæsar.

Both then were immortal ; each worthy of each. And the *Cui viget nihil simile aut secundum* of the poet was as true of one as of the other. For, if by comparison with Rome other cities were but villages, with even more propriety it may be asserted that after the Roman Cæsars all modern kings, kesars, or emperors are mere phantoms of royalty. The Cæsar of Western Rome—he only of all earthly potentates, past or to come, could be said to reign as a *monarch*, that is, as a solitary king. He was not the greatest of princes, simply because there was no other but himself. There were doubtless a few outlying rulers, of unknown names and titles, upon the margins of his empire ; there were tributary lieutenants and barbarous *reguli*, the obscure vassals of his sceptre, whose homage was offered on the lowest step of his throne, and scarcely known to him but as objects of disdain. But these feudatories could no more break the unity of his empire, which embraced the whole οἰκουμενή—the total habitable world as then known to geography or recognised by the muse of history—than at this day the British Empire on the sea can be brought into question or made conditional because some chief of Owyhee or Tongataboo should proclaim a momentary independence of the British trident, or should even offer a transient outrage to her sovereign flag. Such a *tempestas in matulâ* might raise a brief uproar in his little native archipelago, but too feeble to reach the shores of Europe by an echo, or to ascend by so much as an infantine *susurrus* to the ears of the British Neptune. Parthia, it is true, might pretend to the dignity of an empire. But her sovereigns, though sitting in the seat of the great king

[1] "*Nameless* city" :—The true name of Rome it was a point of religion to conceal ; and, in fact, it was never revealed.

(ὁ βασιλεύς), were no longer the rulers of a vast and polished nation.   They were regarded as barbarians—potent only by their standing army, not upon the larger basis of civic strength ; and, even under this limitation, they were supposed to owe more to the circumstances of their position—their climate, their remoteness, and their inaccessibility except through arid and sultry deserts—than to intrinsic resources, such as could be permanently relied on in a serious trial of strength between the two powers.   The kings of Parthia, therefore, were far enough from being regarded in the light of antagonist forces to the majesty of Rome.   And, these withdrawn from the comparison, who else was there—what prince, what king, what potentate of any denomination—to break the universal calm that through centuries continued to lave, as with the quiet undulations of summer lakes, the sacred footsteps of the Cæsarean throne ?

The Byzantine Court, which, merely as the inheritor of some fragments from that august throne, was drunk with excess of pride, surrounded itself with elaborate expressions of a grandeur beyond what mortal eyes were supposed able to sustain.   These fastidious, and sometimes fantastic, ceremonies, originally devised as the very extremities of anti-barbarism, were often themselves but too nearly allied in spirit to the barbaresque in taste.   In reality, some parts of the Byzantine court ritual were arranged in the same spirit as that of China or the Burman Empire ; or fashioned by anticipation, as one might think, on the practice of that Oriental Cham (the progenitor, by the way, of the present Chinese Emperor) who used daily to proclaim by sound of trumpet to the kings in the four corners of the earth that they, having dutifully awaited the close of *his* dinner, might now with his royal licence go to their own.

From such vestiges of *derivative* grandeur, propagated to ages so remote from itself, and sustained by manners so different from the spirit of her own, we may faintly measure the strength of the original impulse given to the feelings of men by the *sacred* majesty of the Roman throne.   How potent must that splendour have been whose mere reflection shot rays upon a distant crown, under another heaven, and across the wilderness of fourteen centuries !   Splendour thus transmitted, thus sustained, and thus imperishable, argues a transcendent vigour in the basis of radical power. Broad and deep must those foundations have been laid which could support an "arch of empire" rising to that giddy altitude— an altitude which sufficed to bring it within the ken of posterity to the sixtieth generation.

Power is measured by resistance. Upon such a scale, if it were applied with skill, the *relations* of greatness in Rome to the greatest of all that has gone before her, and hitherto has come after her, would first be adequately revealed. The youngest reader will know that the grandest forms in which the *collective* might of the human race has manifested itself are the Four Monarchies. Four times have the distributive forces of nations gathered themselves, under the strong compression of the sword, into mighty aggregates—denominated *Universal Empires* or Monarchies. These are noticed in the Holy Scriptures ; and it is upon *their* warrant that men have supposed no Fifth Monarchy or Universal Empire possible in an earthly sense, but that, whenever such an empire arises, it will have Christ for its head,—in other words, that no fifth *monarchia* can take place until Christianity shall have swallowed up all other forms of religion, and shall have gathered the whole family of man into one fold under one all-conquering Shepherd. Hence the fanatics of 1650, who proclaimed Jesus for their king, and who did sincerely anticipate his near advent in great power, and under some personal manifestation, were usually styled *Fifth-Monarchists.*[1]

However, waiving the question (interesting enough in itself) whether upon earthly principles a fifth universal empire could by possibility arise in the present condition of knowledge for man individually and of organization for man in general—this question waived, and confining ourselves to the comparison of those four monarchies which actually have existed,—of the Assyrian, or earliest, we may remark that it

[1] This we mention because a great error has been sometimes committed in exposing *their* error ; which consisted, not in supposing that for a fifth time men were to be gathered under one sceptre, and that sceptre wielded by Jesus Christ, but in supposing that this great era had then arrived, or that with no deeper moral revolution men could be fitted for that yoke.

found men in no state of cohesion. This cause, which came in aid of its first foundation, would probably continue, and would diminish the *intensity* of the power in the same proportion as it promoted its *extension.* This monarchy would be absolute only by the personal presence of the monarch ; elsewhere, from mere defect of organization, it would and must betray the total imperfections of an elementary state, and of a first experiment. More by the weakness inherent in its enemy than by its own strength, did the Persian spear of Cyrus prevail against the Assyrian. Two centuries revolved, seven or eight generations, when Alexander found himself in the same position as Cyrus for building a third monarchy, and aided by the self-same vices of luxurious effeminacy in his enemy, confronted with the self-same virtues of enterprise and hardihood in his compatriot soldiers. The native Persians, in the earliest and very limited import of that name, were a poor and hardy race of mountaineers. So were the men of Macedon ; and neither one tribe nor the other found any adequate resistance in the luxurious occupants of Babylonia. We may add, with respect to these two earliest monarchies, that the Assyrian was undefined with regard to space, and the Persian fugitive with regard to time. But, for the third—the Grecian or Macedonian—we know that the arts of civility and of civil organization had made great progress before the Roman strength was measured against it. In Macedon, in Achaia, in Syria, in Asia Minor, in Egypt,—everywhere the members of this empire had begun to knit ; the cohesion was far closer, the development of their resources more complete ; the resistance, therefore, by many hundred degrees more formidable : consequently, by the fairest inference, the power in that proportion greater which laid the foundations of this last great monarchy. It is probable, indeed, both *a priori* and upon the evidence of various facts which have survived, that each of the four great empires successively triumphed over an antagonist barbarous in comparison of itself, and each *by* and through that very superiority in the arts and policy of civilisation.

Rome, therefore, which came last in the succession, and swallowed up the three great powers that had *seriatim* cast the human race into one mould, and had brought them under the unity of a single will, entered by inheritance upon all that its predecessors in that career had appropriated, but in a condition of far ampler development. Estimated merely by longitude and latitude, the territory of the Roman Empire was the finest by much that has ever fallen under a single sceptre. Amongst modern empires, doubtless, the Spanish of the sixteenth century, and the British of the present, cannot but be admired as prodigious growths out of so small a stem. In that view, they will be endless monuments in attestation of the marvels which are lodged in civilisation. But, considered in and for itself, and with no reference to the proportion of the creating forces, each of these empires has the great defect of being disjointed, and even insusceptible of perfect union. It is in fact no *vinculum* of social organization which held them together, but the ideal *vinculum* of a common fealty, and of submission to the same sceptre. This is not like the tie of manners, operative even where it is not perceived, but like the distinctions of geography—existing to-day, forgotten to-morrow, and abolished by a stroke of the pen, or a trick of diplomacy. Russia, again, a mighty empire as respects the simple grandeur of magnitude, builds her power upon sterility. She has it in her power to seduce an invading foe into vast circles of starvation, of which the radii measure a thousand leagues. Frost and snow are confederates of her strength. She is strong by her very weakness. But Rome laid a belt about the Mediterranean of a thousand miles in breadth—of more than two thousand in length ; and within that zone she comprehended not only all the great cities of the ancient world, but so perfectly did she lay the garden of the world in every climate, and for every mode of natural wealth, within her own ring-fence, that since that era no land, *not* having been part and parcel of the Roman Empire, has ever risen into strength and opulence, except where unusual artificial industry has availed to counteract the tendencies of nature. So entirely had Rome engrossed whatsoever was rich by the mere bounty of native endowment.

Vast, therefore, unexampled, immeasurable, was the basis of natural power upon which the Roman throne reposed. The military force which put Rome in possession of this inordinate power was certainly in some respects artificial ; but the power itself was natural, and not subject to the ebbs and flows which attend the commercial empires of our days ; and, in fact, to be commercial is the very laurel-crown of man's development as civilisation slowly ascends to its supreme stages, for all are in part commercial. The depression, the reverses, of Rome, were confined to one shape— famine ; a terrific shape, doubtless, but one which levies its penalty of suffering not by elaborate processes that do not exhaust their total cycle in less than long periods of years. Fortunately for those who survive, no arrears of misery are allowed by this scourge of ancient days[1] ; the total penalty is paid down at once. As respected the hand of man, Rome slept for ages in absolute security. She could suffer only by the wrath of Providence ; and, so long as she continued to be Rome, for many a generation she only of all the monarchies has feared no mortal hand :[2]

> ———— "God and his Son except,
> Created thing nought valued she nor shunned."

---

[1] "*Of ancient days*" :—For it is remarkable, and it serves to mark an indubitable progress of mankind, that before the Christian era famines were of frequent occurrence in countries the most civilised ; afterwards they became rare, and latterly have entirely altered their character into occasional dearths.

[2] Unless that hand were her own armed against herself ; upon which topic there is a burst of noble eloquence in one of the ancient Panegyrici, when haranguing the Emperor Theodosius : "Thou, Rome ! " that, having once suffered by the madness of Cinna, and of the cruel " Marius raging from banishment, and of Sylla, that won his wreath " of prosperity from thy disasters, and of Cæsar, compassionate to the " dead, didst shudder at every blast of the trumpet filled by the " breath of civil commotion,—thou, that, besides the wreck of thy " soldiery perishing on either side, didst bewail, amongst thy spec- " tacles of domestic woe, the luminaries of thy senate extinguished, " the heads of thy consuls fixed upon a halberd, weeping for ages over " thy self-slaughtered Catos, thy headless Ciceros (*truncosque Cicer- " ones*) and unburied Pompeys ;—to whom the party madness of thy " own children had wrought in every age heavier woe than the Car- " thaginian thundering at thy gates, or the Gaul admitted within thy " walls ; on whom Œmathia, more fatal than the day of Allia,— " Collina, more dismal than Cannæ,—had inflicted such deep memorials " of wounds that, from bitter experience of thy own valour, no enemy " was to thee so formidable as thyself ;—thou, Rome ! didst now for " the first time behold a civil war issuing in a hallowed prosperity, a

That the possessor and wielder of such enormous power—power alike admirable for its extent, for its intensity, and for its consecration from all counter-forces which could restrain it, or endanger it—should be regarded as sharing in the attributes of supernatural beings, is no more than might naturally be expected. All other known power in human hands has either been extensive, but wanting in intensity—or intense, but wanting in extent—or, thirdly, liable to permanent control and hazard from some antagonist power commensurate with itself. But the Roman power, in its centuries of grandeur, involved every mode of strength, with absolute immunity from all kinds and degrees of weakness. It ought not, therefore, to surprise us that the Emperor, as the depositary of this charmed power, should have been looked upon as a *sacred* person, and the imperial family considered a "*divina* domus." It is an error to regard this as excess of adulation, or as built *originally* upon hypocrisy. Undoubtedly the expressions of this feeling are sometimes gross and overcharged, as we find them in the very greatest of the Roman poets ; for example, it shocks us to find a fine writer, in anticipating the future canonization of his patron, and his instalment amongst the heavenly hosts, begging him to keep his distance warily from this or that constellation, and to be cautious of throwing his weight into either hemisphere, until the scale of proportions were accurately adjusted. These, doubtless, are passages degrading alike to the poet and his subject. But why ? Not because they ascribe to the Emperor a sanctity which he had not in the minds of men universally, or which even to the writer's feeling was exaggerated, but because it was expressed coarsely, and as a *physical* power. Now, everything physical is measurable by weight, motion, and resistance, and is therefore definite. But the very essence of whatsoever is supernatural lies in the indefinite. That power, therefore, with which the minds of men invested the Emperor was vulgarized (in Roman phrase *obsolefiebat*) by this coarse translation into the region

---

" soldiery appeased, recovered Italy, and for thyself liberty established.
" Now first in thy long annals thou didst rest from a civil war in such
" a peace that righteously, and with maternal tenderness, thou mightst
" claim for it the honours of a civic triumph.

of physics.   Else it is evident that any power which, by standing above all human control, occupies the next station to superhuman modes of authority, must be invested by all minds alike with some dim and undefined relation to the sanctities of the unseen world.   Thus, for instance, the Pope, as the father of Catholic Christendom, could not *but* be viewed with awe by any Christian of deep feeling, as standing in some relation to the true and unseen Father of the spiritual body.   Nay, considering that even false religions, as those of Pagan mythology, have probably never been utterly stripped of all truth, but that every such mode of error has perhaps been designed as a process, and adapted by Providence to the case of those who were capable of admitting no more perfect shape of truth—even the heads of such superstitions (the Dalai Lama, for instance) may not unreasonably be presumed as within the cognisance and special protection of Heaven.   Much more may this be supposed of him to whose care was confided the weightier part of the human race ; who had it in his power to promote or to suspend the progress of human improvement ; and of whom, and the motions of whose will, the very prophets of Judea took cognisance.   No nation, and no king, was utterly divorced from the councils of God.   Palestine, as a central chamber of God's administration, stood in some relation to all.   It has been remarked, as a mysterious and significant fact, that the founders of the great empires all had some connexion, more or less, with the temple of Jerusalem. Melanchthon even observes it, in his Sketch of Universal History, as worthy of notice that Pompey died, as it were, within sight of that very temple which he had polluted. Let us not suppose that Paganism, or Pagan nations, were therefore excluded from the concern and tender interest of Heaven.   They also had their place allowed.   And we may be sure that, amongst them, the Roman Emperor, as the great steward and factor for the happiness of more men, and men more cultivated, than ever before were intrusted to the motions of a single will, had a special, singular, and mysterious relation to the secret counsels of Heaven.

Even we, therefore, may lawfully attribute some sanctity to the Roman Emperor.   That the Romans did so with absolute sincerity is certain. The altars of the Emperor had a twofold consecration; to violate them was the double crime of treason and sacrilege. In his appearances of state and ceremony, the fire, the sacred fire, ἐπόμπευε, moved pompously in ceremonial solemnity before him; and every other circumstance of divine worship attended the Emperor in his lifetime.[1]

To this view of the imperial character and relations must be added one single circumstance, which in some measure altered the whole for the individual who happened to fill the office. The Emperor *de facto* might be viewed under two aspects; there was the man, and there was the office. In his office he was immortal and sacred: but, as a question might still be raised, by means of a mercenary army, as to the claims of the particular individual who at any time filled the office, the very sanctity and privilege of the character with which he was clothed might actually be turned against himself; and here it is, at this point, that the character of Roman Emperor became truly and mysteriously awful. Gibbon has taken notice of the extraordinary situation of a *subject* in the Roman Empire who should attempt to fly from the wrath of the Cæsar. Such was the ubiquity of the Emperor that this was metaphysically hopeless. Except across pathless deserts or amongst barbarous nomads, it was impossible to find even a transient sanctuary from the imperial pursuit. If the fugitive went down to the sea, there he met the Emperor: if he took the wings of the morning, and fled to the uttermost parts of the earth, there also was Cæsar in the person of his lieutenants. But, by a dreadful counter-charm, the same omnipresence of imperial anger and retribution which withered the hopes of the poor humble prisoner met and confounded the Emperor himself, when hurled from his elevation by some fortunate rival. All the kingdoms of the earth, to one in that situation, became but so many wards of the same infinite prison. Flight, if it were even successful for the moment, did but a

---

[1] The fact is that the Emperor was more of a sacred and divine creature in his lifetime than after his death. His consecrated character as a living ruler was a truth; his canonization, a fiction of tenderness to his memory.

little retard his inevitable doom. And so evident was this that hardly in one instance did the fallen prince *attempt* to fly; passively he met the death which was inevitable, in the very spot where ruin had overtaken him. Neither was it possible even for a merciful conqueror to show mercy; for, in the presence of an army so mercenary and factious, his own safety was but too deeply involved in the extermination of rival pretenders to the crown.

Such, amidst the sacred security and inviolability of the office, was the hazardous tenure of the individual. Nor did his danger always arise from persons in the rank of competitors and rivals. Sometimes it menaced him in quarters which his eye had never penetrated, and from enemies too obscure to have reached his ear. By way of illustration we will cite a case from the life of the Emperor Commodus, which is wild enough to have furnished the plot of a romance, though as well authenticated as any other passage in that reign. The story is narrated by Herodian, and the outline was this :—A slave of noble qualities, and of magnificent person, having liberated himself from the degradation of bondage, determined to avenge his own wrongs by inflicting continual terror upon the town and neighbourhood which had witnessed his humiliation. For this purpose he resorted to the woody recesses of the province (somewhere in the modern Transsylvania), and, attracting to his wild encampment as many fugitives as he could, by degrees he succeeded in training a very formidable troop of freebooters. Partly from the energy of his own nature, and partly from the neglect and remissness of the provincial magistrates, the robber captain rose from less to more, until he had formed a little army, equal to the task of assaulting fortified cities. In this stage of his adventures, he encountered and defeated several of the imperial officers commanding large detachments of troops; and at length grew of consequence sufficient to draw upon himself the Emperor's eye, and the honour of his personal displeasure. In high wrath and disdain at the insults offered to his eagles by this fugitive slave, Commodus fulminated against him such an edict as left him no hope of much longer escaping with impunity.

Public vengeance was now awakened ; the imperial troops were marching from every quarter upon the same centre ; and the slave became sensible that in a very short space of time he must be surrounded and destroyed. In this desperate situation he took a desperate resolution : he assembled his troops, laid before them his plan, concerted the various steps for carrying it into effect, and then dismissed them as independent wanderers. So ends the first chapter of the tale.

The next opens in the passes of the Alps, whither, by various routes, of seven or eight hundred miles in extent, these men had threaded their way in manifold disguises through the very midst of the Emperor's camps. According to this man's gigantic enterprise, in which the means were as audacious as the purpose, the conspirators were to rendezvous, and first to recognise each other, at the gates of Rome. From the Danube to the Tiber did this band of robbers severally pursue their perilous routes through all the difficulties of the road and the jealousies of the military stations, sustained by the mere thirst of vengeance—vengeance against that mighty foe whom they knew only by his proclamations against themselves. Everything continued to prosper ; the conspirators met under the walls of Rome ; the final details were arranged ; and those also would have prospered but for a trifling accident. The season was one of general carnival at Rome ; and, by the help of those disguises which the licence of this festival time allowed, the murderers were to have penetrated as maskers to the Emperor's retirement, when a casual word or two awoke the suspicions of a sentinel. One of the conspirators was arrested ; under the terror and uncertainty of the moment, he made much ampler discoveries than were expected of him ; the other accomplices were secured ; and Commodus was delivered from the uplifted daggers of those who had sought him by months of patient wanderings, pursued through all the depths of the Illyrian forests, and the difficulties of the Alpine passes. It is not easy to find words of admiration commensurate to the energetic hardihood of a slave who, by way of answer and reprisal to an edict summarily consigning him to persecution and death, determines to cross Europe in quest of its author, though no less a person than the master of the world—to seek him out in the inmost recesses of his capital city, of his private palace, of his consecrated bed-chamber—and there to lodge a dagger in his heart, as the adequate reply to the imperial sentence of proscription against himself.

Such, amidst the superhuman grandeur and hallowed privileges of the Roman Emperor's office, were the extraordinary perils which menaced the individual officer. The office rose by its grandeur to a region above the clouds and vapours of earth : the officer might find his personal security as unsubstantial as those wandering vapours. Nor is it possible that these circumstances of violent opposition can be better illustrated than in this tale of Herodian. Whilst the Emperor's mighty arms were stretched out to arrest some potentate in the heart of Asia, a poor slave is silently and stealthily creeping round the base of the Alps, with the purpose of winning his way as a murderer to the imperial bed-chamber ; Cæsar is watching some potent rebel of the Orient at a distance of two thousand leagues, and he overlooks the dagger which is within three stealthy steps, and one tiger's leap, of his own heart. All the heights and the depths which belong to man's frailty, all the contrasts of glory and meanness, the extremities of what is highest and lowest in human casualties, meeting in the station of the Roman Cæsar Semper Augustus, have combined to call him into high marble relief, and to make him the most interesting study of all whom History has emblazoned with colours of fire and blood, or has crowned most lavishly with diadems of cypress and laurel.

This, as a general proposition, will be readily admitted. But, meantime, it is remarkable that no field has been less trodden than the private memorials of those very Cæsars ; whilst, at the same time, it is equally remarkable that precisely with the first of the Cæsars commences the first page of what, in modern times, we understand by Anecdotes. Suetonius is the earliest writer in that department of Biography ; so far as we know, he may be held first to have devised it as a mode of History, for he came a little before Plutarch. The six writers whose sketches are collected under the general title of the *Augustan History* followed in the same track.[1] Though full of entertainment and of the

---

[1] Suetonius, the author of *The Lives of the Cæsars,* was born about

most curious researches, they are all of them entirely unknown, except to a few elaborate scholars. We purpose to collect from these obscure but most interesting memorialists a few sketches and biographical portraits of those great princes, whose public life is sometimes known, but very rarely any part of their private and personal memoirs. We must, of course, commence with the mighty founder of the Cæsars. In his case we cannot expect so much of absolute novelty as in that of those who succeed. But, if, in this first instance, we are forced to touch a little upon old things, we shall confine ourselves as much as possible to those which are susceptible of new aspects. For the whole gallery of those who follow, we can undertake that the memorials which we shall bring forward may be looked upon as belonging pretty much to what has hitherto been a sealed book.

A.D. 70, and died about A.D. 130. This book contains anecdotes respecting the first twelve of the Emperors,—viz. Julius Cæsar, Augustus, Tiberius, Caligula, Claudius, Nero, Galba, Otho, Vitellius, Vespasian, Titus, and Domitian. The so-called *Augustan History*, which may be regarded as a continuation of the work of Suetonius, consists of a collection of similar biographies of the long series of the later Emperors (Trajan and Hadrian skipped) down to Diocletian, written by six independent authors of the fourth century,—to wit, Aelius Spartianus, Julius Capitolinus, Aelius Lampridius, Vulcatius Gallicanus, Trebellius Pollio, and Flavius Vopiscus.—M.

CHAPTER I

JULIUS CÆSAR [1]

(B.C. 100—B.C. 44)

THE character of the First Cæsar has perhaps never been worse appreciated than by him who in one sense described it best; that is, with most force and eloquence wherever he really *did* comprehend it. This was Lucan,[2] who has nowhere exhibited more brilliant rhetoric, nor wandered more from the truth, than in the contrasted portraits of Cæsar and Pompey. The famous line, "*Nil actum reputans si quid superesset agendum*," is a fine feature of the real character, finely expressed. But, if it had been Lucan's purpose (as possibly, with a view to Pompey's benefit, in some respects it was) utterly and extravagantly to falsify the character of the great Dictator, by no single trait could he more effectually have fulfilled that purpose, nor in fewer words, than by this expressive passage, "*Gaudensque viam fecisse ruinâ.*" Such a trait would be almost extravagant applied even to Marius, who (though in many respects a perfect model of Roman grandeur, massy, columnar, imperturbable, and more perhaps than any one man recorded in History capable of justifying the bold illustration of that character in Horace, "*Si fractus illabatur orbis, impavidum ferient ruinæ*") had, however, a ferocity in his character, and a touch of the devil in him,

---

[1] In *Blackwood* for October 1832, as continuation of the preceding Introduction on the Cæsars generally —M.

[2] M. Annæus Lucanus, A.D. 38—A.D. 65. His *Pharsalia* is an epic poem on the Civil War between Cæsar and Pompey.—M.

very rarely united with the same tranquil intrepidity.   But, for Cæsar, the all-accomplished statesman, the splendid orator, the man of elegant habits and polished taste, the patron of the fine arts in a degree transcending all example of his own or the previous age, and as a man of general literature so much beyond his contemporaries, except Cicero, that he looked down even upon the brilliant Sylla as an illiterate person—to class such a man with the race of furious destroyers exulting in the desolations they spread is to err not by an individual trait, but by the whole genus.   The Attilas and the Tamerlanes, who rejoice in avowing themselves the scourges of God, and the special instruments of his wrath, have no one feature of affinity to the polished and humane Cæsar, and would as little have comprehended his character as he could have respected theirs.   Even Cato, the unworthy hero of Lucan, might have suggested to him a little more truth in this instance, by a celebrated remark which he made on the characteristic distinction of Cæsar, in comparison with other revolutionary disturbers ; for, said he, whereas others had attempted the overthrow of the state in a continued paroxysm of fury, and in a state of mind resembling the lunacy of intoxication, Cæsar, on the contrary, among that whole class of civil disturbers, was the only one who had come to the task in a temper of sobriety and moderation (*unum accessisse sobrium ad rempublicam delendam*).

In reality, Lucan did not think as he wrote.   He had a purpose to serve ; and, in an age when to act like a freeman was no longer safe, he determined at least to write in that character.   It is probable, also, that he wrote with a vindictive or a malicious feeling towards Nero, and, as the single means he had for gratifying such impulses, resolved upon sacrificing the grandeur of Cæsar's character wherever it should be found possible.   Meantime, in spite of himself, Lucan for ever betrays his lurking consciousness of the truth. Nor are there any testimonies to Cæsar's vast superiority more memorably pointed than those which are indirectly and involuntarily extorted from this Catonic poet by the course of his narration.   Never, for example, was there within the same compass of words a more emphatic expression of Cæsar's essential and inseparable grandeur of thought, which could not be disguised or be laid aside for an instant, could not be taught or trained to run in the harness of ordinary unaspiring life, than is found in the three casual words— *Indocilis privata loqui.* The very mould, it seems, by Lucan's confession, of his trivial conversation was regal ; nor could he abjure it for so much as a casual purpose. The acts of Cæsar speak also the same language ; and, as these are less susceptible of a false colouring than the features of a general character, we find this poet of liberty, in the midst of one continuous effort to distort the truth, and to dress up two scenical heroes, nevertheless forced by the mere necessities of history into a reluctant homage to Cæsar's supremacy of moral grandeur.

Of so great a man it must be interesting to know all the well-attested opinions which bear upon topics of universal interest to human nature ; as indeed no others stood much chance of preservation, unless it were from so minute and curious a collector of *anecdotage* as Suetonius. And, first, it would be gratifying to know the opinion of Cæsar, if he had any peculiar to himself, on the great theme of Religion. It has been held, indeed, that the constitution of his mind, and the general cast of his character, indisposed him to religious thoughts. Nay, it has been common to class him amongst deliberate atheists ; and some well-known anecdotes are current in books, which illustrate his contempt for the vulgar class of religious credulities. In this, however, he went no farther than Cicero, and other great contemporaries, who assuredly were no atheists. One mark perhaps of the wide interval which, in Cæsar's age, had begun to separate the Roman nobility from the hungry and venal populace who were daily put up to sale, and bought in crowds by the highest bidder, manifested itself in the increasing disdain for the tastes and ruling sympathies of the mere rude Quirites. No mob could be more abjectly servile than was that of Rome to the superstition of portents, prodigies, and omens. Thus far, in common with his order, and in this sense, Julius Cæsar was naturally a despiser of superstition. Mere strength of understanding would, perhaps, have made him such in any age, and apart from the circumstances of his personal history. But this natural tendency in him would doubtless receive a further bias in the same direction from the office of Pontifex Maximus, which he held at an early stage of his public career. This office, by letting him too much behind the curtain, and exposing too entirely the base machinery of ropes and pulleys which sustained the miserable jugglery played off upon the popular credulity, impressed him perhaps even unduly with contempt for those who *could* be its dupes. And we may add that Cæsar was constitutionally, as well as by accident of position, too much a man of the world, had too powerful a leaning to the virtues of *active* life, was governed by too partial a sympathy with the whole class of *active* forces in human nature, as contradistinguished from those which tend to contemplative purposes, under any circumstances to have become a profound believer, or a stead-fast reposer of his fears and anxieties, in religious influences. A man of the world is but another designation for a man indisposed to religious awe or to spiritual enthusiasm. Still it is a doctrine which we cherish that grandeur of mind in any one department whatsoever, supposing only that it exists in excess, disposes a man to some degree of sympathy with all other grandeur, however alien in its quality or different in its form. And upon this ground we presume the great Dictator to have had an interest in religious themes by mere compulsion of his own extraordinary elevation of mind, after making the fullest allowance for the special quality of that mind, which did certainly, to the whole extent of its characteristics, tend entirely to estrange him from such themes. We find, accordingly, that, though sincerely a despiser of superstition, and with a frankness which must sometimes have been hazardous in that age, Cæsar was himself also superstitious. No man could have been otherwise who lived and conversed with that generation and people. But, if superstitious, he was so after a mode of his own. In his very infirmities Cæsar manifested his greatness : his very littlenesses were noble.

" Nec licuit populis parvum te, Nile, videre."

That he placed some confidence in dreams, for instance, is certain : because, had he slighted them unreservedly, he would not have dwelt upon them afterwards, or have troubled himself to recall their circumstances.   Here we trace his human weakness.   Yet again we are reminded that it was the weakness of Cæsar ; for the dreams were noble in their imagery, and Cæsarean (so to speak) in their tone of moral feeling. Thus, for example, the night before he was assassinated, he dreamt at intervals that he was soaring above the clouds on wings, and that he placed his hand within the right hand of Jove.   It would seem that perhaps some obscure and half-formed image floated in his mind, of the eagle, as the king of birds ; secondly, as the tutelary emblem under which his conquering legions had so often obeyed his voice ; and, thirdly, as the bird of Jove.   To this triple relation of the bird his dream covertly appears to point.   And a singular coincidence appears between this dream and a little anecdote brought down to us, as having actually occurred in Rome about twenty-four hours before his death.   A little bird, which by some is represented as a very small kind of sparrow, but which, both to the Greeks and the Romans, was known by a name implying a regal station (probably from the ambitious courage which at times prompted it to attack the hawk), was observed to direct its flight towards the senate-house consecrated by Pompey, whilst a crowd of other birds were seen to hang upon its flight in close pursuit.   What might be the object of the chase, whether the little king himself, or a sprig of laurel which he bore in his mouth, could not be determined.   The whole train, pursuers and pursued, continued their flight towards Pompey's hall.   Flight and pursuit were there alike arrested ; the little king was overtaken by his enemies, who fell upon him as so many conspirators, and tore him limb from limb.

If this anecdote were reported to Cæsar,—which is not at all improbable, considering the earnestness with which his friends laboured to dissuade him from his purpose of meeting the Senate on the approaching Ides of March,—it is very little to be doubted that it had a considerable effect upon his feelings, and that, in fact, his own dream grew out of the impression which it had made.   This way of linking the two anecdotes, as cause and effect, would also bring a third anecdote under the same *nexus*.   We are told that Calpurnia, the last wife of Cæsar, dreamed on the same night, and to the same ominous result. The circumstances of *her* dream are less striking, because less figurative ; but on that account its import was less open to doubt : she dreamed, in fact, that, after the roof of their mansion had fallen in, her husband was stabbed in her bosom. Laying all these omens together, Cæsar would have been more or less than human had he continued utterly undepressed by them. And, if so much superstition as even this implies must be taken to argue some little weakness, on the other hand let it not be forgotten that this very weakness does but the more illustrate the unusual force of mind, and the heroic will, which obstinately laid aside these *concurring* prefigurations of impending destruction ; concurring, we say, amongst themselves—and concurring also with a prophecy of older date, which was totally independent of them all.

There is another and somewhat sublime story of the same class, which belongs to the most interesting moment of Cæsar's life ; and those who are disposed to explain all such tales upon physiological principles will find an easy solution of this, in particular, in the exhaustion of body and the intense anxiety which must have debilitated even Cæsar under the whole circumstances of the case. On the ever memorable night when he had resolved to take the first step (and in such a case the first step, as regarded the power of retreating, was also the final step) which placed him in arms against the state, it happened that his head-quarters were at some distance from the little river Rubicon, which formed the boundary of his province. With his usual caution, that no news of his motions might run before himself, on this night Cæsar gave an entertainment to his friends, in the midst of which he slipped away unobserved, and with a small retinue proceeded through the woods to the point of the river at which he designed to cross. The night[1] was stormy, and by the

---

[1] It is an interesting circumstance in the habits of the ancient Romans that their journeys were pursued very much in the night-time, and by torchlight. Cicero, in one of his letters, speaks of passing through the towns of Italy by night as a serviceable scheme for some political purpose, either of avoiding too much to publish his motions, or of evading the necessity (else perhaps not avoidable) of drawing out the party sentiments of the magistrates in the circumstances of honour or neglect with which they might choose to receive

violence of the wind all the torches of his escort were blown out, so that the whole party lost their road, having probably at first intentionally deviated from the main route, and wandered about through the whole night, until the early dawn enabled them to recover their true course. The light was still grey and uncertain as Cæsar and his retinue rode down upon the banks of the fatal river—to cross which with arms in his hands, since the further bank lay within the territory of the Republic, *ipso facto* proclaimed any Roman a rebel and a traitor. No man, the firmest or the most obtuse, could be otherwise than deeply agitated when looking down upon this little brook—so insignificant in itself, but invested by law with a sanctity so awful, and so dire a consecration.

him. His words, however, imply that the practice was by no means an uncommon one. And, indeed, from some passages in writers of the Augustan era, it would seem that this custom was not confined to people of distinction, but was familiar to a class of travellers so low in rank as to be capable of abusing their opportunities of concealment for the infliction of wanton injury upon the woods and fences which bounded the margin of the high-road. Under the cloud of night and solitude, the mischief-loving traveller was often in the habit of applying his torch to the withered boughs of woods, or to artificial hedges; and extensive ravages by fire, such as now happen not unfrequently in the American woods (but generally from carelessness in scattering the glowing embers of a fire, or even the ashes of a pipe), were then occasionally the result of mere wantonness of mischief. Ovid accordingly notices, as one amongst the familiar images of daybreak, the half-burnt torch of the traveller; and, apparently, from the position which it holds in his description, where it is ranked with the most familiar of all circumstances in all countries — that of the rural labourer going out to his morning tasks—it must have been common indeed:

> " Semiustamque facem vigilatâ nocte viator
> Ponet ; et ad solitum rusticus ibit opus."

This occurs in the *Fasti* :—elsewhere he notices it for its danger :

> " Ut facibus sepes ardent, cum forte viator
> Vel nimis admovit, vel jam sub luce reliquit."

He, however, we see, good-naturedly ascribes the danger to mere carelessness, in bringing the torch too near to the hedge, or tossing it away at daybreak. But Varro, a more matter-of-fact observer, does not disguise the plain truth, that these disasters were often the product of pure malicious frolic. For instance, in recommending a certain kind of quickset fence, he insists upon it, as one of its advan-

The whole course of future history, and the fate of every nation, would necessarily be determined by the irretrievable act of the next half hour.

In these moments, and with this spectacle before him, and contemplating these immeasurable consequences consciously for the last time that could allow him a retreat,—impressed also by the solemnity and deep tranquillity of the silent dawn, whilst the exhaustion of his night wanderings predisposed him to nervous irritation,—Cæsar, we may be sure, was profoundly agitated. The whole elements of the scene were almost scenically disposed ; the law of antagonism having perhaps never been employed with so much effect : the little quiet brook presenting a direct antithesis to its grand political character ; and the innocent dawn, with its pure, un-

tages, that it will not readily ignite under the torch of the mischievous wayfarer : " Naturale sepimentum," says he, " quod obseri solet virgultis aut spinis, *prœtereuntis lascivi non metuet facem.*" It is not easy to see the origin or advantage of this practice of nocturnal travelling (which must have considerably increased the hazards of a journey), excepting only in the heats of summer. It is probable, however, that men of high rank and public station may have introduced the practice by way of releasing corporate bodies in large towns from the burdensome ceremonies of public receptions ; thus making a compromise between their own dignity and the convenience of the provincial public. Once introduced, and the arrangements upon the road for meeting the wants of travellers once adapted to such a practice, it would easily become universal. It is, however, very possible that mere horror of the heats of day-time may have been the original ground for it. The ancients appear to have shrunk from no hardship so trying and insufferable as that of heat. And, in relation to that subject, it is interesting to observe the way in which the ordinary use of language has accommodated itself to that feeling. Our northern way of expressing effeminacy is derived chiefly from the hardships of cold. He that shrinks from the trials and rough experience of real life in any department is described by the contemptuous prefix of *chimney-corner*, as if shrinking from the cold which he would meet on coming out into the open air amongst his fellow-men. Thus, a *chimney-corner* politician, for a mere speculator or unpractical dreamer. But the very same indolent habit of aërial speculation, which courts no test of real life and practice, is described by the ancients under the term *umbraticus*, or seeking the cool shade, and shrinking from the heat. Thus, an *umbraticus doctor* is one who has no practical solidity in his teaching. The fatigue and hardship of real life, in short, are represented by the ancients under the uniform image of heat, and by the moderns under that of cold.

troubled repose, contrasting potently, to a man of any intellectual sensibility, with the long chaos of bloodshed, darkness, and anarchy, which was to take its rise from the apparently trifling acts of this one morning. So prepared, we need not much wonder at what followed. Cæsar was yet lingering on the hither bank, when suddenly, at a point not far distant from himself, an apparition was descried in a sitting posture, and holding in its hand what seemed a flute. This phantom was of unusual size, and of beauty more than human, so far as its lineaments could be traced in the early dawn. What is singular, however, in the story, on any hypothesis which would explain it out of Cæsar's individual condition, is that others saw it as well as he; both pastoral labourers (who were present, probably, in the character of guides) and some of the sentinels stationed at the passage of the river. These men fancied even that a strain of music issued from this aërial flute. And some, both of the shepherds and the Roman soldiers, who were bolder than the rest, advanced towards the figure. Amongst this party, it happened that there were a few Roman trumpeters. From one of these, the phantom, rising as they advanced nearer, suddenly caught a trumpet, and, blowing through it a blast of superhuman strength, plunged into the Rubicon, passed to the other bank, and disappeared in the dusky twilight of the dawn. Upon which Cæsar exclaimed :—" It is finished—the die is cast—let us follow whither the guiding portents from Heaven, and the malice of our enemy, alike summon us to go." So saying, he crossed the river with impetuosity ; and, in a sudden rapture of passionate and vindictive ambition, placed himself and his retinue upon the Italian soil ; and, as if by inspiration from Heaven, in one moment involved himself and his followers in treason, raised the standard of revolt, put his foot upon the neck of the invincible republic which had humbled all the kings of the earth, and founded an empire which was to last for a thousand and half a thousand years. In what manner this spectral appearance was managed— whether Cæsar were its author, or its dupe—will remain unknown for ever. But undoubtedly this was the first time that the advanced guard of a victorious army was headed by an apparition; and we may conjecture that it will be the last.[1]

In the mingled yarn of human life tragedy is never far asunder from farce; and it is amusing to trace in immediate succession to this incident of epic dignity,—which has its only parallel, by the way, in the case of Vasco de Gama (according to the narrative of Camoens) when met and confronted by a sea phantom whilst attempting to double the Cape of Storms (Cape of Good Hope),—a ludicrous passage, in which one felicitous blunder did Cæsar a better service than all the truths which Greece and Rome could have furnished. In our own experience, we once witnessed a blunder about as gross.—Lord Brougham, in his first electioneering contest with the Lowthers (A.D. 1818), upon some occasion where he was recriminating upon the other party, and complaining that stratagems which *they* might practise with impunity were denied to him and his, happened to point the moral of his complaint by alleging the old adage that one man might steal a horse with more hope of indulgence than another could look over the hedge. Whereupon, by benefit of the universal mishearing in the outermost ring of the audience, it became generally reported that Lord Lowther had once been engaged in an affair of horse-stealing, and that he, Henry Brougham, could (had he pleased) have lodged an information against him, seeing that he was then looking over the hedge. And this charge naturally won the more credit because it was notorious and past denying that his lordship

---

[1] According to Suetonius, the circumstances of this memorable night were as follows:—As soon as the decisive intelligence was received that the intrigues of his enemies had prevailed at Rome, and that the interposition of the popular magistrates (the tribunes) was set aside, Cæsar sent forward the troops, who were then at his headquarters, but in as private a manner as possible. He himself, by way of masque (*per dissimulationem*), attended a public spectacle, gave an audience to an architect who wished to lay before him a plan for a school of gladiators which Cæsar designed to build, and finally presented himself at a banquet, which was very numerously attended. From this, about sunset, he set forward in a carriage, drawn by mules, and with a small escort (*modico comitatu*). Losing his road, which was the most private he could find (*occultissimum*), he quitted his carriage and proceeded on foot. At dawn he met with a guide; after which followed the above incidents.

was a capital horseman, fond of horses, and much connected
with the turf.   To this hour, therefore, amongst some worthy
shepherds and other "dalesmen" of bonny Westmoreland,
it is a received article of their creed, and (as they justly
observe in northern pronunciation) a *sham*ful thing to be
told, that Lord Lowther was once a horse-stealer, and that
he escaped *lagging* by reason of Harry Brougham's pity
for his tender years and hopeful looks.—Not less was the
blunder which, on the banks of the Rubicon, befriended
Cæsar.   Immediately after crossing, he harangued the troops
whom he had sent forward, and others who there met him
from the neighbouring garrison of Ariminium.   The tribunes
of the people, those great officers of the democracy, corresponding by some of their functions to our House of Commons,—men personally, and by their position in the state,
entirely in Cæsar's interest, and who, for his sake, had fled
from home,—there and then he produced to the soldiery ;
thus identified his cause, and that of the soldiers, with the
cause of the people of Rome and of Roman liberty ; and,
perhaps with needless rhetoric, attempted to conciliate those
who were, by a thousand ties and by claims innumerable, his
own already ; for never yet has it been found that with the
soldier, who from youth upwards passes his life in camps,
could the duties or the interests of the citizen survive those
stronger and more personal relations connecting him with his
military superior.   In the course of this harangue, Cæsar
often raised his left hand with Demosthenic action, and once
or twice he drew off the ring which every Roman gentleman
—simply *as* such—wore as the inseparable adjunct and
symbol of his rank.   By this action he wished to give
emphasis to the accompanying words, in which he protested,
that, sooner than fail in satisfying and doing justice to any
the least of those who heard him and followed his fortunes,
he would be content to part with his own birthright, and to
forgo his dearest claims.   This was what he really said ;
but the outermost circle of his auditors, who rather saw
his gestures than distinctly heard his words, carried off the
notion (which they were careful everywhere to disperse
amongst the legions afterwards associated with them in the
same camps) that Cæsar had vowed never to lay down his

arms until he had obtained for every man, the very meanest of those who heard him, the rank, privileges, and appointments of a Roman knight. Here was a piece of sovereign good luck. Had he really made such a promise, Cæsar might have found that he had laid himself under very embarrassing obligations ; but, as the case stood, he had, through all his following campaigns, the total benefit of such a promise, and yet could always absolve himself from the embarrassing penalties of responsibility which it imposed by appealing to the evidence of those who happened to stand in the first ranks of his audience. The blunder was gross and palpable ; and yet, with the unreflecting and dull-witted soldier, it did him service greater than all the subtilities of all the schools could have accomplished, and a service which subsisted to the end of the war.

Great as Cæsar was by the benefit of his original nature, there can be no doubt that he, like others, owed something to circumstances ; and perhaps amongst those which were most favourable to the premature development of great self-dependence we must reckon the early death of his father. It is, or it is not, according to the nature of men, an advantage to be orphaned at an early age. Perhaps utter orphanage is rarely or never such : but to lose a father betimes may, under appropriate circumstances, profit a strong mind greatly. To Cæsar it was a prodigious benefit that he lost his father when not much more than fifteen. Perhaps it was an advantage also to his father that he died thus early. Had he stayed a year longer, he might have seen himself despised, baffled, and made ridiculous. For where, let us ask, in any age, was the father capable of adequately sustaining that relation to the unique Caius Julius —to him, in the appropriate language of Shakspere,

"The foremost man of all this world"?

And, in this fine and Cæsarean line, "this world" is to be understood not of the order of co-existences merely, but also of the order of successions ; he was the foremost man not only of his contemporaries, but also, within his own intellectual class, of men generally—of all that ever should come after him, or should sit on thrones under the denominations of Czars, Kesars, or Cæsars of the Bosphorus and the Danube ; of all in every age that should inherit his supremacy of mind, or should subject to themselves the generations of ordinary men by qualities analogous to his   Of this infinite superiority some part must be ascribed to his early emancipation from paternal control.   There are very many cases in which, simply from considerations of sex, a female cannot stand forward as the head of a family, or as its suitable representative.   If they are even ladies paramount, and in situations of command, they are also women.   The staff of authority does not annihilate their sex ; and scruples of female delicacy interfere for ever to unnerve and emasculate in their hands the sceptre however otherwise potent.   Hence we see, in noble families, the merest boys put forward to represent the family dignity, as fitter supporters of that burden than their mature mothers.   And of Cæsar's mother, though little is recorded, and that little incidentally, this much at least we learn—that, if she looked down upon him with maternal pride and delight, she looked up to him with female ambition as the re-edifier of her husband's honours,— looked with reverence as to a column of the Roman grandeur, and with fear and feminine anxieties as to one whose aspiring spirit carried him but too prematurely into the fields of adventurous strife.   One slight and evanescent sketch of the relations which subsisted between Cæsar and his mother, caught from the wrecks of time, is preserved both by Plutarch and Suetonius.   We see in the early dawn the young patrician standing upon the steps of his patrimonial portico, his mother with her arms wreathed about his neck, looking up to his noble countenance, sometimes drawing auguries of hope from features so fitted for command, sometimes boding an early blight to promises so dangerously magnificent.   That she had something of her son's aspiring character, or that he presumed so much in a mother of his, we learn from the few words which survive of their conversation.   He addressed to her no language that could tranquillize her fears.   On the contrary, to any but a Roman mother his valedictory words, taken in connexion with the known determination of his character, were of a nature to consummate her depression, as they tended to confirm the very worst of her fears.   He was then

going to stand his chance in a popular electioneering contest
for an office of the highest dignity, and to launch himself
upon the storms of the Campus Martius. At that period,
besides other and more ordinary dangers, the bands of
gladiators, kept in the pay of the more ambitious or turbulent
amongst the Roman nobles, gave a popular tone of ferocity
and of personal risk to the course of such contests ; and,
either to forestall the victory of an antagonist, or to avenge
their own defeat, it was not at all impossible that a body of
incensed competitors might intercept his final triumph by
assassination. For this danger, however, he had no leisure
in his thoughts of consolation ; the sole danger which *he*
contemplated, or supposed his mother to contemplate, was
the danger of defeat, and for that he reserved his consolations.
He bade her fear nothing ; for that his determination was to
return with victory, and with the ensigns of the dignity he
sought, or to return a corpse.

Early indeed did Cæsar's trials commence ; and it is probable, that, had not the death of his father, by throwing him
prematurely upon his own resources, prematurely developed
the masculine features of his character, forcing him whilst yet
a boy under the discipline of civil conflict and the yoke of
practical life, even *his* energies might have been insufficient
to sustain them.   His age is not exactly ascertained ; but it is
past a doubt that he had not reached his twentieth year when
he had the hardihood to engage in a struggle with Sylla, then
Dictator, and exercising the immoderate powers of that office
with the licence and the severity which History has made so
memorable. He had neither any distinct grounds of hope,
nor any eminent example at that time, to countenance him in
this struggle—which yet he pushed on in the most uncompromising style, and to the utmost verge of defiance. The
subject of the contrast gives it a further interest. It was the
youthful wife of the youthful Cæsar who stood under the
shadow of the great Dictator's displeasure ; not personally,
but politically, on account of her connexions : and her it was,
Cornelia, the daughter of a man who had been four times
consul, that Cæsar was required to divorce : but he spurned
the haughty mandate, and carried his determination to a
triumphant issue, notwithstanding his life was at stake,

and at one time saved only by shifting his place of concealment every night ; and this young lady it was who afterwards
became the mother of his only daughter. Both mother
and daughter, it is remarkable, perished prematurely,
and at critical periods of Cæsar's life ; for it is probable
enough that these irreparable wounds to Cæsar's domestic
affections threw him with more exclusiveness of devotion
upon the fascinations of glory and ambition than might have
happened under a happier condition of his private life.
That Cæsar should have escaped destruction in this unequal
contest with an enemy then wielding the whole thunders of
the state, is somewhat surprising ; and historians have sought
their solution of the mystery in the powerful intercessions of
the vestal virgins, and several others of high rank amongst
the connexions of his great house. These may have done
something ; but it is due to Sylla, who had a sympathy with
everything truly noble, to suppose him struck with powerful
admiration for the audacity of the young patrician, standing
out in such severe solitude among so many examples of timid
concession ; and that to this magnanimous feeling in the
Dictator much of the indulgence which he showed may have
been really due. In fact, according to some accounts, it was
not Sylla, but the creatures of Sylla (*adjutores*), who pursued
Cæsar. We know, at all events, that Sylla formed a right
estimate of Cæsar's character, and that, from the complexion
of his conduct in this one instance, he drew that famous
prophecy of his future destiny ; bidding his friends beware
of that slipshod boy, "for that in him lay couchant many a
Marius." A grander testimony to the awe which Cæsar
inspired, or from one who knew better the qualities of that
Cyclopean man by whose scale he measured the patrician boy,
cannot be imagined.

It is not our intention, or consistent with our plan, to
pursue this great man through the whole circumstances of his
romantic career ; though it is certain that many parts of his
life require investigation much keener than has ever been
applied to them, and that many might be placed in a new
light. Indeed, the whole of this most momentous section of
ancient history ought to be recomposed with the critical
scepticism of a Niebuhr, and the same comprehensive collation,

resting, if possible, on the felicitous interpretation of authorities. In reality it is the hinge upon which turned the future destiny of the whole earth, and, having therefore a common relation to all modern nations whatsoever, should naturally have been cultivated with the zeal which belongs to a personal concern. In general, the anecdotes which express most vividly the grandeur of character in the first Cæsar are those which illustrate his defiance of danger in extremity: the prodigious energy and rapidity of his decisions and motions in the field (looking to which it was that Cicero called him a τερας or portentous revelation); the skill with which he penetrated the designs of his enemies, and the electric speed with which he met disasters with remedy and reparation, or, where that was impossible, with relief; the extraordinary presence of mind which he showed in turning adverse omens to his own advantage, as when, upon stumbling in coming on shore (which was esteemed a capital omen of evil), he transfigured as it were in one instant its whole meaning by exclaiming, "Thus, and by this contact with the earth, do I take possession of thee, O Africa!" in that way giving to an accident the semblance of a symbolic purpose. Equally conspicuous was the grandeur of fortitude with which he faced the whole extent of a calamity when palliation could do no good, "non negando, minuendove, sed insuper amplificando, *ementicndoque*"; as when, upon finding his soldiery alarmed at the approach of Juba, with forces really great, but exaggerated by their terrors, he addressed them in a military harangue to the following effect :—" Know that within a few days the king will come up with us, bringing with him sixty thousand legionaries, thirty thousand cavalry, one hundred thousand light troops, besides three hundred elephants. Such being the case, let me hear no more of conjectures and opinions, for you have now my warrant for the fact, whose information is past doubting. Therefore, be satisfied; otherwise, I will put every man of you on board some crazy old fleet, and whistle you down the tide—no matter under what winds, no matter towards what shore." Finally, we might seek for *characteristic* anecdotes of Cæsar in his unexampled liberalities and contempt of money.[1]

[1] Middleton's Life of Cicero, which still continues to be the most

Upon this last topic it is the just remark of Casaubon that some instances of Cæsar's munificence have been thought apocryphal, or to rest upon false readings, simply from ignorance of the heroic scale upon which the Roman splendours of that age proceeded. A forum which Cæsar built out of the products of his last campaign, by way of a present to the Roman people, cost him—for the ground merely on which it stood—nearly eight hundred thousand pounds. To the *citizens* of Rome he presented, in one *congiary*, about two guineas and a half a head. To his army, in one *donation*, upon the termination of the Civil War, he gave a sum which allowed about two hundred pounds a man to the infantry, and four hundred to the cavalry. It is true that the legionary troops were then much reduced by the sword of the enemy, and by the tremendous hardships of their last campaigns. In this, however, he did perhaps no more than repay a debt. For it is an instance of military attachment, beyond all that Wallenstein or any commander, the most beloved amongst his troops, has ever experienced, that, on the breaking out of the Civil War, not only did the centurions of every legion severally maintain a horse soldier, but even the privates volunteered to serve without pay, and (what might seem impossible) without their daily rations. This was accomplished by subscriptions amongst themselves, the more opulent undertaking for the maintenance of the needy. Their disinterested love for Cæsar appeared in another and more difficult illustration : it was a traditionary anecdote in Rome that the majority of those amongst Cæsar's troops who had the misfortune to fall into the enemy's hands refused to accept their lives under the condition of serving against *him*.

In connexion with this subject of his extraordinary munificence, there is one aspect of Cæsar's life which has suffered much from the misrepresentations of historians, and that is— the vast pecuniary embarrassments under which he laboured, until the profits of war had turned the scale even more

readable digest of these affairs, is feeble and contradictory. He discovers that Cæsar was no general ! But the single merit which M.'s work was supposed to possess, viz. the better and more critical arrangement of Cicero's Letters in respect to their chronology, has of late years been detected as a robbery from the celebrated Bellenden, of James the First's time. [See *ante,* Vol. V. p. 140.]

prodigiously in his favour. At one time of his life, when appointed to a foreign office, so numerous and so clamorous were his creditors that he could not have left Rome on his public duties had not Crassus come forward with assistance in money, or by guarantees, to the amount of nearly two hundred thousand pounds. And at another he was accustomed to amuse himself with computing how much money it would require to make him worth exactly nothing (*i.e.* simply to clear him of debts); this, by one account, amounted to upwards of two millions sterling. Now, the error of historians has been to represent these debts as the original ground of his ambition and his revolutionary projects, as though the desperate condition of his private affairs had suggested a civil war to his calculations as the best or only mode of redressing it. Such a policy would have resembled the last desperate resource of an unprincipled gambler, who, on seeing his final game at chess, and the accumulated stakes depending upon it, all on the brink of irretrievable sacrifice, dexterously upsets the chess-board, or extinguishes the lights. But Julius, the one sole patriot of Rome, could find no advantage to his plans in darkness or in confusion. Honestly supported, he would have crushed the oligarchies of Rome by crushing in its lairs that venal and hunger-bitten democracy which made oligarchy and its machineries resistless. Cæsar's debts, far from being stimulants and exciting causes of his political ambition, stood in an inverse relation to the ambition; they were its results, and represented its natural costs, being contracted from first to last in the service of his political intrigues, for raising and maintaining a powerful body of partisans, both in Rome and elsewhere. Whosoever indeed will take the trouble to investigate the progress of Cæsar's ambition, from such materials as even yet remain, may satisfy himself that the scheme of revolutionizing the Republic, and placing himself at its head, was no growth of accident or circumstances; above all, that it did not arise upon any so petty and indirect a suggestion as that of his debts; but that his debts were in their very first origin purely ministerial to his wise, indispensable, and patriotic ambition; and that his revolutionary plans were at all periods of his life a direct and foremost object, but in no case bottomed upon casual impulses. In this there was not only patriotism, but in fact the one sole mode of patriotism which could have prospered, or could have found a field of action. Chatter not, sublime reader, commonplaces of scoundrel moralists against ambition. In some cases ambition is a hopeful virtue ; in others (as in the Rome of our resplendent Julius) ambition was the virtue by which any other could flourish. It had become evident to everybody that Rome, under its present constitution, must fall ; and the sole question was—by whom ? Even Pompey, not by nature of an aspiring turn, and prompted to his ambitious course undoubtedly by circumstances and the friends who besieged him, was in the habit of saying, "Sylla potuit : ego non potero ?" *Sylla found it possible : shall I find it not so ?* Possible to do what ? To overthrow the political system of the Republic. This had silently collapsed into an order of things so vicious, growing also so hopelessly worse, that all honest patriots invoked a purifying revolution, even though bought at the heavy price of a tyranny, rather than face the chaos of murderous distractions to which the tide of feuds and frenzies was violently tending. Such a revolution at such a price was not less Pompey's object than Cæsar's. In a case, therefore, where no benefit of choice was allowed to Rome as respected the thing, but only as respected the person, Cæsar had the same right to enter the arena in the character of combatant as could belong to any one of his rivals. And that he *did* enter that arena constructively, and by secret design, from his very earliest manhood, may be gathered from this—that he suffered no openings towards a revolution, provided they had any hope in them, to escape his participation. It is familiarly known that he was engaged pretty deeply in the conspiracy of Catiline,[1] and that he incurred considerable risk on that occasion ; but it is less known that he was a party to at least two other conspiracies. There was even a fourth, meditated by Crassus, which Cæsar so far

---

[1] Suetonius, speaking of this conspiracy, says that Cæsar was *nominatus inter socios Catilinæ;* which has been erroneously understood to mean that he was *talked of* as an accomplice ; but in fact, as Casaubon first pointed out, *nominatus* is a technical term of the Roman jurisprudence, and means that he was formally denounced.

encouraged as to undertake a journey to Rome from a very distant quarter merely with a view to such chances as it might offer to him ; but, as it did not, upon examination, seem to him a very promising scheme, he judged it best to look coldly upon it, or not to embark in it by any personal co-operation.   Upon these and other facts we build our inference—that the scheme of a revolution was the one great purpose of Cæsar from his first entrance upon public life. Nor does it appear that he cared much by whom it was undertaken, provided only there seemed to be any sufficient resources for carrying it through, and for sustaining the first collision with the regular forces of the existing oligarchies, taking or *not* taking the shape of triumvirates.   He relied, it seems, on his own personal superiority for raising him to the head of affairs eventually, let who would take the nominal lead at first.   To the same result, it will be found, tended the vast stream of Cæsar's liberalities.   From the senator downwards to the lowest *fæx Romuli*, he had a hired body of dependents, both in and out of Rome, equal in numbers to a nation.   In the provinces, and in distant kingdoms, he pursued the same schemes.   Everywhere he had a body of mercenary partisans ; kings even are known to have taken his pay.   And it is remarkable that even in his character of commander-in-chief, where the number of legions allowed to him for the accomplishment of his Gaulish mission raised him for a number of years above all fear of coercion or control, he persevered steadily in the same plan of providing for the distant day when he might need assistance, not *from* the state, but *against* the state.   For, amongst the private anecdotes which came to light under the researches made into his history after his death, was this—that, soon after his first entrance upon his government in Gaul, he had raised, equipped, disciplined, and maintained, from his own private funds, a legion amounting, possibly, to six or seven thousand men, who were bound by no sacrament of military obedience to the state, nor owed fealty to any auspices except those of Cæsar.   This legion, from the fashion of their crested helmets, which resembled the heads of a small aspiring bird, received the popular name of the *Alauda* (or Lark) legion.   And very singular it was that Cato, or

Marcellus, or some amongst those enemies of Cæsar who watched his conduct during the period of his Gaulish command with the vigilance of rancorous malice, should not have come to the knowledge of this fact ; in which case we may be sure that it would have been denounced to the Senate.

Such, then, for its purpose and its uniform motive, was the sagacious munificence of Cæsar. Apart from this motive, and considered in and for itself, and simply with a reference to the splendid forms which it often assumed, this munificence would furnish the materials for a volume. The public entertainments of Cæsar, his spectacles and shows, his naumachiæ, and the pomps of his unrivalled triumphs (the closing triumphs of the Republic), were severally the finest of their kind which had then been brought forward. Sea-fights were exhibited upon the grandest scale, according to every known variety of nautical equipment and mode of conflict, upon a vast lake formed artificially for that express purpose. Mimic land-fights were conducted, in which all the circumstances of real war were so faithfully rehearsed that even elephants "indorsed with towers,"[1] twenty on each side, took part in the combat. Dramas were represented in every known language (*per omnium linguarum histriones*). And hence (that is, from the conciliatory feeling thus expressed towards the various tribes of foreigners resident in Rome) some have derived an explanation of what is else a mysterious circumstance amongst the ceremonial observances at Cæsar's funeral—that all people of foreign nations then residing at Rome distinguished themselves by the conspicuous share which they took in the public mourning ; and that, beyond all other foreigners, the Jews for night after night kept watch and ward about the Emperor's grave. Never before, according to traditions which lasted through several generations in Rome, had there been so vast a conflux of the human race congregated to any one centre, on any one attraction of business or of pleasure, as to Rome on occasion of these triumphal spectacles exhibited by Cæsar.

In our days, the greatest occasional gatherings of the

---

[1] "*Elephants indorsed with towers*" :—See Milton's gorgeous description of the Parthian warfare in the *Paradise Regained.*

human race are in India, especially at the great fair of the *Hurdwar* on the Ganges in northern Hindustan : a confluence of some millions is sometimes seen at that spot, brought together under the mixed influences of devotion and commercial business, but very soon dispersed as rapidly as they had been convoked. Some such spectacle of nations crowding upon nations, and some such Babylonian confusion of dresses, complexions, languages, and jargons, was then witnessed at Rome. Accommodations within doors, and under roofs of houses, or roofs of temples, was altogether impossible. Myriads encamped along the streets, and along the high-roads, fields, or gardens. Myriads lay stretched on the ground, without even the slight protection of tents, in a vast circuit about the city. Multitudes of men, even senators, and others of the highest rank, were trampled to death in the crowds. And the whole family of man might seem at that time to be converged at the bidding of the dead Dictator. But these, or any other themes connected with the public life of Cæsar, we notice only in those circumstances which have been overlooked, or partially represented, by historians. Let us now, in conclusion, bring forward, from the obscurity in which they have hitherto lurked, the anecdotes which describe the habits of his private life, his tastes, and personal peculiarities.

In person, he was tall,[1] fair, gracile, and of limbs distinguished for their elegant proportions. His eyes were black and piercing. These circumstances continued to be long remembered, and no doubt were constantly recalled to the eyes of all persons in the imperial palaces by pictures, busts, and statues ; for we find the same description of his personal appearance three centuries afterwards in a work of

---

[1] "*Tall*" : — Whereas, to show the lawless caprices upon which French writers have endeavoured to found a brief notoriety, some contributor to the memoirs of *L'Académie des Inscriptions* expressly asserts, without a vestige of countenance from any authority whatsoever, that Cæsar was "several feet high," but, being "invited" to circumstantiate, replied "five feet nothing" ; but this, being French measure, would give him (if we rightly remember the French scale) about five times three-fourths of an inch more. Nonsense ! Suetonius, who stood so near to the Julian generation, is guarantee for his *proceritas.*

the Emperor Julian's.   He was a most accomplished horseman, and a master (*peritissimus*) in the use of arms.   But,
notwithstanding his skill and horsemanship, it seems that,
when he accompanied his army on marches, he walked oftener
than he rode ; no doubt, with a view to the benefit of his
example, and to express that sympathy with his soldiers
which gained him their hearts so entirely.   On other occasions,
when travelling apart from his army, he seems more frequently
to have ridden in a carriage than on horseback.   His purpose,
in this preference, must have been with a view to the transport of luggage.   The carriage which he generally used was
a *rheda*, a sort of gig, or rather curricle ; for it was a *four*-
wheeled carriage, and adapted (as we find from the imperial
regulations for the public carriages, &c.) to the conveyance of
about half a ton.   The mere personal baggage which Cæsar
carried with him was probably considerable ; for he was a
man of elegant habits, and in all parts of his life sedulously
attentive to elegance of personal appearance.   The length of
journeys which he accomplished within a given time appears
even to us at this day, and might well therefore appear to his
contemporaries, truly astonishing.   A distance of one hundred
miles was no extraordinary day's journey for him in a *rheda*,
such as we have described it.   So refined were his habits,
and so constant his demand for the luxurious accommodations
of polished life as it then existed in Rome, that he is said to
have carried with him, as indispensable parts of his personal
baggage, the little ivory lozenges, squares and circles or ovals,
with other costly materials, wanted for the tessellated flooring
of his tent.   Habits such as these will easily account for his
travelling in a carriage rather than on horseback.
The courtesy and obliging disposition of Cæsar were
notorious ; and both were illustrated in some anecdotes
which survived for generations in Rome.   Dining on one
occasion, as an invited guest, at a table where the servants
had inadvertently, for salad-oil, furnished some sort of coarse
lamp-oil, Cæsar would not allow the rest of the company to
point out the mistake to their host, for fear of shocking him
too much by exposing what might have been construed into
inhospitality.   At another time, whilst halting at a little
cabaret, when one of his retinue was suddenly taken ill,

Cæsar resigned to his use the sole bed which the house afforded.   Incidents as trifling as these express the urbanity of Cæsar's nature ; and hence one is the more surprised to find the alienation of the Senate charged, in no trifling degree, upon a gross and most culpable failure in point of courtesy.   Cæsar, it is alleged — but might we presume to call upon antiquity for its authority ?—neglected to rise from his seat, on their approaching him with an address of congratulation.   It is said, and we can believe it, that he gave deeper offence by this one defect in a matter of ceremonial observance than by all his substantial attacks upon their privileges.   What we find it difficult to believe is not that result from that offence—this is no more than we should all anticipate—not *that*, but the possibility of the offence itself, from one so little arrogant as Cæsar, and so entirely a man of the world.   He was told of the disgust which he had given ; and we are bound to believe his apology, in which he charged it upon sickness, that would not at the moment allow him to maintain a standing attitude.   Certainly the whole tenor of his life was not courteous only, but kind, and to his enemies merciful in a degree which implied so much more magnanimity than men in general could understand that by many it was put down to the account of weakness.

Weakness, however, there was none in Caius Cæsar ; and, that there might be none, it was fortunate that conspiracy should have cut him off in the full vigour of his faculties, in the very meridian of his glory, and on the brink of completing a series of gigantic achievements.   Amongst these are numbered :—a digest of the entire body of laws, even then become unwieldy and oppressive ; the establishment of vast and comprehensive public libraries, Greek as well as Latin ; the chastisement of Dacia (that needed a cow-hiding for insolence as much as Affghanistan from us in 1840) ; the conquest of Parthia ; and the cutting a ship canal through the Isthmus of Corinth.   The reformation of the Calendar he had already accomplished.   And of all his projects it may be said that they were equally patriotic in their purpose and colossal in their proportions.

As an orator, Cæsar's merit was so eminent that, according to the general belief, had he found time to cultivate this department of civil exertion, the received supremacy of Cicero would have been made questionable, or the honours would have been divided. Cicero himself was of that opinion, and on different occasions applied the epithet *splendidus* to Cæsar, as though in some exclusive sense, or with some peculiar emphasis, due to him. His taste was much simpler, chaster, and less inclined to the *florid* and Asiatic, than that of Cicero. So far he would, in that condition of the Roman culture and feeling, have been less acceptable to the public ; but, on the other hand, he would have compensated this disadvantage by much more of natural and Demosthenic fervour.

In literature, the merits of Cæsar are familiar to most readers. Under the modest title of *Commentaries*, he meant to offer the records of his Gallic and British campaigns, simply as notes, or memoranda, afterwards to be worked up by regular historians ; but, as Cicero observes, their merit was such in the eyes of the discerning that all judicious writers shrank from the attempt to alter them. In another instance of his literary labours he showed a very just sense of true dignity. Rightly conceiving that everything patriotic was dignified, and that to illustrate or polish his native language was a service of real and paramount patriotism, he composed a work on the grammar and orthoepy of the Latin language. Cicero and himself were the only Romans of distinction in that age who applied themselves with true patriotism to the task of purifying and ennobling their mother tongue. Both were aware of a transcendent value in the Grecian literature as it then stood ; but that splendour did not depress their hopes of raising their own to something of the same level. As respected the natural wealth of the two languages, it was the private opinion of Cicero that the Latin had the advantage ; and, if Cæsar did not accompany him to that length,—which, perhaps, under some limitations he ought to have done,—he yet felt that it was but the more necessary to draw forth any special or exceptional advantage which it really had.[1]

---

[1] Cæsar had the merit of being the first person to propose the daily publication of the acts and votes of the Senate. So far, *i.e.* to the extent of laying a large foundation, Cæsar was the *Father of*

Was Cæsar, upon the whole, the greatest of men? We restrict the question, of course, to the classes of men great in *action:* great by the extent of their influence over their social contemporaries ; great by throwing open avenues to extended powers that previously had been closed ; great by making obstacles once vast to become trivial, or prizes that once were trivial to be glorified by expansion. I (said Augustus Cæsar) found Rome built of brick ; but I left it built of marble. Well, my man, we reply, for a wondrously little chap, you did what in Westmoreland they call a good *darroch* (day's work) ; and, if *navvies* had been wanted in those days, you should have had our vote to a certainty. But Caius Julius, even under such a limitation of the comparison, did a thing as much transcending this as it was greater to project Rome across the Alps and the Pyrenees, — expanding the grand Republic into crowning provinces of 1. France (*Gallia*), 2. Belgium, 3. Holland (*Batavia*), 4. England (*Britannia*), 5. Savoy (*Allobroges*), 6. Switzerland (*Helvetia*), 7. Spain (*Hispania*),—than to decorate a street or to found an amphitheatre. Dr. Beattie once observed that, if that question as to the greatest man in action upon the rolls of History were left to be collected from the suffrages already expressed in books and scattered throughout the literature of all nations, the scale would be found to have turned prodigiously in Cæsar's favour as against any single competitor ; and there is no doubt whatsoever that even amongst his own countrymen, and his own contemporaries, the same verdict would have been returned, had it been collected upon the famous principle of Themistocles, that *he* should be reputed the first whom the greatest number of rival voices had pronounced to be the second.

Newspapers. In the form of public and official despatches he made also some useful innovations ; and it may be mentioned, for the curiosity of the incident, that the cipher which he used in his correspondence was the following very simple one :—For every letter of the alphabet he substituted that which stood third removed from it in the order of succession. Thus, for A, he used D ; for D, G ; and so on.

CHAPTER II

AUGUSTUS CÆSAR [1]

(B.C. 31—A.D. 14)

THE situation of the Second Cæsar at the crisis of the great Dictator's assassination was so hazardous and delicate as to confer interest upon a character not otherwise attractive. To many, we know, it was positively repulsive, and in the very highest degree. In particular, it is recorded of Sir William Jones that he regarded this Emperor with feelings of abhorrence so *personal* and deadly as to refuse him his customary titular honours whenever he had occasion to mention him by name. Yet it was the whole Roman people that conferred upon him his title of *Augustus*. But Sir William, ascribing no force to the acts of a people who had sunk so low as to exult in their chains, and to decorate with honours the very instruments of their own vassalage, would not recognise this popular creation, and spoke of him always by his family name of Octavius.[2] The flattery of the populace, by the way, must, in this instance, have been doubly acceptable to the Emperor, — first, for what it gave, and, secondly, for what it concealed. Of his grand-uncle, the first Cæsar, a tradition survives—that of all the distinctions created in his favour, either by the Senate or the People, he put most value upon the laurel crown which was voted to him after his last campaigns, a beautiful and conspicuous

---

[1] From *Blackwood* for December 1832.—M.

[2] His original name was Caius Octavius, after his father; his mother was a niece (daughter of a sister) of Julius Cæsar.—M.

memorial to every eye of his great public acts, and at the same time an overshadowing veil of his one sole personal defect. This laurel diadem at once proclaimed his grand career of victory and concealed his baldness—a defect which was more mortifying to a Roman than it would be to ourselves, from the peculiar theory which then prevailed as to its probable origin. A gratitude of the same mixed quality must naturally have been felt by the Second Cæsar for his title of *Augustus;* which, whilst it illustrated his public character by the highest expression of majesty,[1] set apart and sequestrated to public functions, had also the agreeable effect of withdrawing from the general remembrance his obscure descent. For the Octavian house (*gens*) had in neither of its branches risen to any great splendour of civic distinction ; and in his own branch to little or none. But for their alliance with a Julian family (by intermarriage with the niece of Cæsar), the Octavian family was a cipher in Rome. The same titular decoration, therefore, so offensive to the celebrated English Whig, was, in the eyes of Augustus, at once a trophy of public merit, a monument of public gratitude, and an effectual obliteration of his own natal obscurity.

But, if merely odious to men of Sir William's principles, to others the character of Augustus, in relation to the circumstances which surrounded him, was not without its appropriate interest. He was summoned in early youth, and without warning, to face a crisis of tremendous hazard, being at the same time himself a man of no very great constitutional courage ; perhaps he was even a coward. And this we say without meaning to adopt as gospel truths all the party reproaches of Antony. Certainly he was utterly unfurnished by nature with those endowments which *seemed* to be indispensable in a successor to the power of the great Dictator. But exactly in these deficiencies, and in certain accidents unfavourable to his ambition, lay his security. He had been adopted by his grand-uncle, Julius. That adoption made him, to all intents and purposes of law, the son[2]

---

[1] Yes, of majesty, but majesty combined with sanctity.

[2] "*The son*" :—This is a fact which we should do well to remember more seriously than we have ever done in the cases of Indian princes claiming under this title. The miscreant Nana Sahib to all

of his great patron ; and doubtless, in a short time, this adoption would have been applied to more extensive uses, and as a station of vantage for introducing him to the public favour. From the inheritance of the Julian estates and family honours, he would have been trained to mount, as from a stepping-stone, to the inheritance of the Julian power and political station ; and the Roman People would have been familiarized to regard him in that character. But, luckily for himself, the finishing or ceremonial acts were yet wanting in this process — the political heirship was inchoate and imperfect. Tacitly understood, indeed, it was ; but, had it been formally proposed and ratified, there cannot be a doubt that the young Octavius would have been pointed out to the vengeance of the patriots, and included in the scheme of the conspirators, as a fellow-victim with his nominal father, and would have been cut off too suddenly to benefit by that reaction of popular feeling which saved the partisans of the Dictator by separating the conspirators, and obliging them, without loss of time, to look to their own safety. It was by this fortunate accident that the young heir and adopted son of the first Cæsar not only escaped assassination, but was enabled to postpone indefinitely the final and military struggle for the vacant seat of empire, and in the meantime to maintain a coequal rank with the leaders in the state by those arts and resources in which he was superior to his competitors. His place in the favour of Caius Julius was of power sufficient to give him a share in any triumvirate which could be formed ; but, wanting the formality of a regular introduction to the people, and the ratification of their acceptance, that place was not sufficient to raise him permanently into the perilous and invidious station of absolute supremacy which he afterwards occupied. The *felicity* of Augustus was often vaunted by antiquity (with whom success was not so much a test of merit as itself a merit of the highest quality), and in no instance was this felicity more conspicuous than in the first act of his entrance

appearance was really ill-used originally by us: was he not really and truly the child by *adoption* of the Peishwah ? Let us recollect that one of the Scipios, received for such by the whole Roman world, was really an *Emilian*, and a Scipio only by adoption.

upon the political scene. No doubt his friends and enemies alike thought of him, at the moment of Cæsar's assassination, as we now think of a young man heir-elect to some person of immense wealth, cut off by a sudden death before he has had time to ratify a will in execution of his purposes. Yet in fact the case was far otherwise. Brought forward distinctly as the successor of Cæsar's power, had he even, by some favourable accident of absence from Rome, or otherwise, escaped being involved in that great man's fate, he would at all events have been thrown upon the instant necessity of defending his supreme station by arms. To have left it unasserted, when once solemnly created in his favour by a reversionary title, would have been deliberately to resign it. This would have been a confession of weakness liable to no disguise, and ruinous to any subsequent pretensions. Yet, without preparation of means, with no development of resources nor growth of circumstances, an appeal to arms would, in his case, have been of very doubtful issue. His true weapons, for a long period, were the arts of vigilance and dissimulation. Cultivating these, he was enabled to prepare for a contest which, undertaken prematurely, must have ruined him, and to raise himself to a station of even military pre-eminence to those who naturally, and by circumstances, were originally every way superior to himself.

The qualities in which he really excelled, the gifts of intrigue, patience, long-suffering, dissimulation, and tortuous fraud, were thus brought into play, and allowed their full value. Such qualities had every chance of prevailing in the long-run against the noble carelessness and the impetuosity of the passionate Antony—and they *did* prevail. Always on the watch to lay hold of those opportunities which the generous negligence of his rival was but too frequently throwing in his way—unless by the sudden reverses of war and the accidents of battle, which as much as possible, and as long as possible, he declined—there could be little question in any man's mind that eventually He would win his way to a solitary throne by a policy so full of caution and subtlety. He was sure to risk nothing which could be had on easier terms, and nothing unless for a great overbalance of gain in prospect ; to lose nothing which he had once gained, and in no case to miss an advantage, or sacrifice an opportunity, by any consideration of generosity. No modern insurance office but would have guaranteed an event depending upon the final success of Augustus on terms far below those which they must in prudence have exacted from the fiery and adventurous Antony. Each was an ideal in his own class. But Augustus, having finally triumphed, has met with more than justice from succeeding ages. Even Lord Bacon says that, by comparison with Julius Cæsar, he was "*non tam impar quam dispar*"—surely a most extravagant encomium, applied to whomsoever. On the other hand, Antony, amongst the most signal misfortunes of his life, might number it that Cicero, the great dispenser of immortality, in whose hands (more perhaps than in any one man's of any age) were the vials of good and evil fame, should happen to have been his bitter and persevering enemy. It is, however, some balance to this that Shakspere had a just conception of the original grandeur which lay beneath that wild tempestuous nature presented by Antony to the eye of the undiscriminating world. It is to the honour of Shakspere that he should have been able to discern the true colouring of this most original character under the smoke and tarnish of antiquity. It is no less to the honour of the great triumvir that a strength of colouring should survive in his character, capable of baffling the wrongs and ravages of time; capable of forcing its way by mere weight of metal through a tract of sixteen hundred and odd years to the notice of one immortal eye that could read its true lineaments and proportions. Neither is it to be thought strange that a character should have been misunderstood and falsely appreciated for nearly two thousand years. It happens not uncommonly, especially amongst an unimaginative people like the Romans, that the characters of men are ciphers and enigmas to their own age, and are first read and interpreted by a far-distant posterity. Stars are supposed to exist whose light has been travelling for many thousands of years without having yet reached our system; and the eyes are yet unborn upon which their earliest rays will fall. Men like Mark Antony, with minds of chaotic composition—light conflicting with darkness, proportions of colossal grandeur disfigured by unsymmetrical arrangement, the angelic in close neighbourhood with the brutal—are first read in their true meaning by an age learned in the philosophy of the human heart. Of this philosophy the Romans had, by the necessities of education and domestic discipline, not less than by original constitution of mind, the very narrowest visual range. In no literature whatsoever are so few tolerable notices to be found of any great truths in Psychology. Nor could this have been otherwise amongst a people who tried everything by the standard of *social* value; never seeking for a canon of excellence in man considered abstractedly in and for himself, and as having an independent value, but always and exclusively in man as a gregarious being, and designed for social uses and functions. Not man in his own separate nature, but man in his relations to other men, was the station from which the Roman speculators took up their philosophy of human nature. Tried by such standard, Mark Antony would be found wanting. As a citizen, he was irretrievably licentious, and therefore there needed not the bitter personal feud which circumstances had generated between them to account for the *acharnement* with which Cicero pursued him. Had Antony been his friend even, or his near kinsman, Cicero must still have been his public enemy. And not merely for his vices; for even the grander features of his character, his towering ambition, his magnanimity, and the fascinations of his popular qualities, were all, in the circumstances of those times, and in *his* position, of a tendency dangerously uncivic.

So remarkable was the opposition, at all points, between the Second Cæsar and his rival that, whereas Antony even in his virtues seemed dangerous to the state, Octavius gave a civic colouring to his most indifferent actions, and, with a Machiavelian policy, observed a scrupulous regard to the forms of the Republic, after every fragment of the republican institutions, the privileges of the republican magistrates, and the functions of the great popular officers, had been absorbed into his own autocracy. Even in the most prosperous days of the Roman State, when the democratic forces balanced, and were balanced by, those of the aristocracy, it was far from being a general or common praise that a man was of

a civic turn of mind, *animo civili*.   Yet this praise did
Augustus affect, and in reality attain, at a time when the
very object of all civic feeling was absolutely extinct; so
much are men governed by words.   Suetonius assures us
that many evidences were current even to his times of this
popular disposition (*civilitas*) in the emperor, and that it
survived every experience of servile adulation in the Roman
populace, and all the effects of long familiarity with irresponsible power in himself.   Such a moderation of feeling
we are almost obliged to consider as a genuine and unaffected
expression of his real nature; for, as an artifice of policy, it
had soon lost its uses.   And it is worthy of notice that with
the army he laid aside those popular manners as soon as
possible, addressing them haughtily as *milites*, not (according
to his earlier practice) by the conciliatory title of *commili-
tones*.   It concerned his own security to be jealous of encroachments on his power.   But of his rank, and the honours
which accompanied it, he seems to have been uniformly
careless.   Thus, he would never leave a town or enter it by
daylight, unless some higher rule of policy obliged him to do
so; by which means he evaded a ceremonial of public
honour which was burdensome to all the parties concerned
in it.   Sometimes, however, we find that men careless of
honours in their own persons are glad to see them settling
upon their family and immediate connexion.   But here
again Augustus showed the sincerity of his moderation.
For, upon one occasion, when the whole audience in the
Roman theatre had risen upon the entrance of his two
adopted sons, at that time not seventeen years old, he was
highly displeased, and even thought it necessary to publish
his displeasure in a separate edict.   It is another, and a
striking, illustration of his humility that he willingly
accepted of public appointments, and sedulously discharged
the duties attached to them, in conjunction with colleagues
who had been chosen with little regard to his personal
partialities.   In the debates of the Senate he showed the
same equanimity,—suffering himself patiently to be contradicted, and even with circumstances of studied incivility.   In
the public elections he gave his vote like any private citizen;
and, when he happened to be a candidate himself, he can-

vassed the electors with the same earnestness of personal
application as any other candidate with the least possible
title to public favour from present power or past services.
But perhaps by no expressions of his civic spirit did Augustus
so much conciliate men's minds as by the readiness with
which he participated in their social pleasures, and by the
uniform severity with which he refused to apply his influence
in any way that could disturb the pure administration of
justice. The Roman juries (*judices* they were called) were
very corrupt, and easily swayed to an unconscientious verdict
by the appearance in court of any great man on behalf of one
of the parties interested : nor was such an interference with
the course of private justice anyways injurious to the great
man's character. The wrong which he promoted did but
the more forcibly proclaim the warmth and fidelity of his
friendships. So much the more generally was the uprightness of the Emperor appreciated, who would neither tamper
with justice himself, nor countenance any motion in that
direction, though it were to serve his very dearest friend,
either by his personal presence, or by the use of his name.
And, as if it had been a trifle merely to forbear, and to show
his regard to justice in this negative way, he even allowed
himself to be summoned as a witness on trials, and showed
no anger when his own evidence was overborne by stronger
on the other side. This disinterested love of justice, and an
integrity so rare in the great men of Rome, could not but
command the reverence of the people. But their affection,
doubtless, was more conciliated by the freedom with which
the Emperor accepted invitations from all quarters, and
shared continually in the festal pleasures of his subjects.
This practice, however, he discontinued, or narrowed, as he
advanced in years. Suetonius, who, as a true anecdote-
monger, would solve everything and account for every change
by some definite incident, charges this alteration in the
Emperor's condescensions upon one particular party at a
wedding feast, where the crowd incommoded him much by
their pressure and heat. But, doubtless, it happened to
Augustus as to other men : his spirits failed, and his powers
of supporting fatigue or bustle, as years stole upon him.
Changes coming by insensible steps, and not willingly

acknowledged, for some time escape notice; until some sudden shock reminds a man forcibly to do that which he has long meditated in an irresolute way. The marriage banquet may have been the particular occasion from which Augustus stepped into the habits of old age, but certainly not the cause of so entire a revolution in his mode of living.

It might seem to throw some doubt, if not upon the fact, yet at least upon the sincerity, of his *civism*, that undoubtedly Augustus cultivated his kingly connexions with considerable anxiety. It may have been upon motives merely political that he kept at Rome the children of nearly all the kings then known as allies or vassals of the Roman power: a curious fact, and not generally known. In his own palace were reared a number of youthful princes; and they were educated jointly with his own children. It is also upon record that in many instances the fathers of these princes spontaneously repaired to Rome, and there, assuming the Roman dress—as an expression of reverence to the majesty of the omnipotent state—did personal "suit and service" (*more clientum*) to Augustus. It is an anecdote of not less curiosity that a whole "college" of kings subscribed money for a temple at Athens, to be dedicated in the name of Augustus. Throughout his life, indeed, this Emperor paid a marked attention to all royal houses then known to Rome as occupying the thrones upon the vast margin of the empire. It is true that in part this attention might be interpreted as given politically to so many lieutenants, wielding a remote or inaccessible power for the benefit of Rome. And the children of these kings might be regarded as hostages, ostensibly entertained for the sake of education, but really as pledges for their parents' fidelity, and also with a view to the large reversionary advantages which might be expected to arise upon the basis of so early and affectionate a connexion. But it is not the less true that, at one period of his life, Augustus did certainly meditate some closer personal connexion with the royal families of the earth. He speculated, undoubtedly, on a marriage for himself with some barbarous princess, and at one time designed his daughter Julia as a wife for Cotiso, the king of the Getæ. Superstition perhaps disturbed the one scheme, and policy the other. He married,

as is well known, for his final wife, and the partner of his
life through its whole triumphant stage, Livia Drusilla ;
compelling her husband, Tiberius Nero, to divorce her, notwithstanding she was then six months advanced in pregnancy.
With this lady, who was distinguished for her beauty, it is
certain that he was deeply in love ; and that might be
sufficient to account for the marriage.   It is equally certain,
however, upon the concurring evidence of independent writers,
that this connexion had an oracular sanction—not to say,
suggestion ; a circumstance *which was long remembered*, and
was afterwards noticed by the Christian poet Prudentius :—

> " Idque Deûm sortes et Apollinis antra dederunt
> Consilium : nunquam meliùs nam cædere tædas
> Responsum est quàm cum prægnans nova nupta jugatur."

His daughter Julia had been promised by turns, and
always upon reasons of state, to a whole muster-roll of suitors :
first of all, to a son of Mark Antony ; secondly, to a
barbarous king ; thirdly, to her first cousin—that Marcellus,
the son of Octavia, only sister to Augustus, whose early
death, in the midst of great expectations, Virgil has introduced into the vision of Roman grandeurs as yet unborn
which Æneas beholds in the shades : fourthly, she was promised
(and this time the promise was kept) to the fortunate soldier
Agrippa, whose low birth was not permitted to obscure his
military merits.   By him she had a family of children, upon
whom, if upon any in this world, the wrath of Providence
seems to have rested ; for, excepting one, and in spite of all
the favours that earth and heaven could unite to shower
upon them, all came to an early, a violent, and an infamous
end.   Fifthly, upon the death of Agrippa, and again upon
motives of policy, and in atrocious contempt of all the ties
that nature and the human heart and human laws have
hallowed, she was promised (if that word may be applied to
the violent obtrusion upon a man's bed of one who was
doubly a curse—first, for what she brought, and, secondly,
for what she took away) and given to Tiberius, the future
Emperor.   Upon the whole, as far as we can at this day
make out the connexion of a man's acts and purposes, which
even to his own age were never entirely cleared up, it is

probable that, so long as the triumvirate survived, and so long as the condition of Roman power or intrigues, and the distribution of Roman influence, were such as to leave a possibility that any new triumvirate should arise—so long Augustus was secretly meditating a retreat for himself at some barbarous court, against any sudden reverse of fortune, by means of a domestic connexion which should give him the claim of a kinsman. Such a court, as against a sudden emergency, might prove a tower of strength, however unable to make head against the collective power of Rome : such a court might offer a momentary front of resistance to any single partisan who should attain a brief ascendency ; or, at the worst, as a merely defensive power, might offer a retreat, strong by its distance, or by its difficult access ; or might be available as a means of delay for recovering from some else fatal defeat.   It is certain that Augustus viewed Egypt with jealousy as a province which might be turned to account in some such way by any aspiring insurgent.   And it must have often struck him as a remarkable circumstance, which by good luck had turned out entirely to the advantage of his own family, but which might as readily have had an opposite result, that the three decisive battles of Pharsalia, of Thapsus, and of Munda, in which the empire of the world was three times over staked on the issue, had severally brought upon the defeated leaders a ruin which was total, absolute, and final.   One hour had seen the whole fabric of their aspiring fortunes fuming away in smoke ; and no resource was left to them but either in suicide (which, accordingly, even Cæsar had meditated at one crisis in the battle of Munda, when it seemed to be going against him) or in the mercy of the victor.

That a victor in a hundred fights should in his hundred-and-first,[1] as in his first, risk the loss of that particular battle, is inseparable from the condition of man, and the uncertainty of human means ; but that the loss of this one battle should be equally fatal and irrecoverable with the loss of his first,

---

[1] " The painful warrior famousèd for fight,
         After a thousand victories once foiled,
     Is from the book of honour razèd quite,
         And all the rest forgot for which he toiled."
                                        SHAKSPERE'S *Sonnets.*

that it should leave him with means no more cemented, and resources no better matured for retarding his fall, and throwing a long succession of hindrances in the way of his conqueror, argues some essential defect of system. Under our modern policy, military power—though it may be the growth of one man's life—soon takes root ; a succession of campaigns is required for its extirpation; and it revolves backwards to its final extinction through all the stages by which originally it grew. On the Roman system this was mainly impossible from the solitariness of the Roman power : co-rival nations who might balance the victorious party there were absolutely none ; and all the underlings hastened to make their peace, whilst peace was yet open to them, on the known terms of absolute treachery to their former master, and instant surrender to the victor of the hour. For this capital defect in the tenure of Roman power, no matter in whose hands deposited, there was no absolute remedy. Many a sleepless night, during the perilous game which he played with Antony, must have familiarized Octavius with that view of the risk which to some extent was inseparable from his position as the leader in such a struggle carried on in such an empire. In this dilemma, struck with the extreme necessity of applying some palliation to the case, we have no doubt that Augustus would devise the scheme of laying some distant king under such obligations to fidelity as would suffice to stand the first shock of misfortune. Such a person would have power enough, of a direct military kind, to face the storm at its outbreak. He would have power of another kind in his distance. He would be sustained by the courage of hope, as a kinsman having a contingent interest in a kinsman's prosperity. And, finally, he would be sustained by the courage of despair, as one who never could expect to be trusted by the opposite party. In the worst case, such a prince would always offer a breathing time and a respite to his friends, were it only by his remoteness, and if not the *means* of rallying, yet at least the *time* for rallying, more especially as the escape to his frontier would be easy to one who had long forecast it. We can hardly doubt that Augustus meditated such schemes ; that he laid them aside only as his power began to cement and to knit together after the battle of

Actium ; and that the memory and the prudential tradition of this plan survived in the imperial family so long as itself survived.   Amongst other anecdotes of the same tendency, two are recorded of Nero, the emperor in whom expired the line of the original Cæsars, which strengthen us in a belief of what is otherwise in itself so probable.   Nero, in his first distractions, upon receiving the fatal tidings of the revolt in Gaul, when reviewing all possible plans of escape from the impending danger, thought at intervals of throwing himself on the protection of the barbarous King Vologesus.   And, twenty years afterwards, when the Pseudo-Nero appeared, he found a strenuous champion and protector in the King of the Parthians.   Possibly, had an opportunity offered for searching the Parthian chancery, some treaty would have been found binding the Kings of Parthia, from the age of Augustus through some generations downwards, in requital of services there specified, or of treasures lodged, to secure a perpetual asylum to the posterity of the Julian family.

The cruelties of Augustus were perhaps equal in atrocity to any which are recorded ; and the equivocal apology for those acts (one which might as well be used to aggravate as to palliate the case) is that they were not prompted by a ferocious nature, but by calculating policy.   He once actually slaughtered upon an altar a large body of his prisoners ; and such was the contempt with which he was regarded by some of that number that, when led out to death, they saluted their other proscriber, Antony, with military honours, acknowledging merit even in an enemy,—in words beautiful and memorable they paid their homage, *Morituri te salutamus*,— but Augustus they passed with scornful silence, or with loud reproaches.   Too certainly no man has ever contended for empire with unsullied conscience, or laid pure hands upon the ark of so magnificent a prize.   Every friend to Augustus must have wished that the twelve years of his struggle might for ever be blotted out from human remembrance.   During the forty-two years of his prosperity and his triumph, being above fear, he showed his natural or prudential lenity.

That prosperity, in a public sense, has been rarely equalled ; but far different was his fate, and memorable was the con- trast, within the circuit of his own family.   This lord of the universe groaned as often as the ladies of his house, his daughter and grand-daughter, were mentioned. The shame which he felt on their account led him even to unnatural designs, and to wishes not less so : for at one time he entertained a plan for putting the elder Julia to death ; and at another, upon hearing that Phœbe (one of the female slaves in his household) had hanged herself, he exclaimed audibly, —"Would that I had been the father of a Phœbe !" It must, however, be granted that in this dark episode or parenthesis of his public life he behaved with very little of his usual discretion. In the first paroxysms of his rage, on discovering his daughter's criminal conduct, he made a communication of the whole to the Senate. That body could do nothing in such a matter, either by act or by suggestion ; and in a short time, as everybody could have foreseen, he himself repented of his own deficient self-command. Upon the whole, it cannot be denied that, according to the remark of Jeremy Taylor, of all the men signally decorated by History, Augustus Cæsar is that one who exemplifies, in the most emphatic forms, the mixed tenor of human life, and the equitable distribution, even on this earth, of good and evil fortune. He made himself master of the world, and against the most formidable competitors ; his power was absolute, from the rising to the setting sun ; and yet in his own house, where the peasant who does the humblest chares claims an undisputed authority, he was baffled, dishonoured, and made ridiculous. He was loved by nobody ; and, if at the moment of his death he desired his friends to dismiss him from this world by the common expression of scenical applause (*vos plaudite !*), in that valedictory injunction he expressed inadvertently the true value of his own long life : which, in strict candour, may be pronounced one continued series of histrionic efforts ; of dissimulation, therefore, even if usefully directed ; yes, little man ! one huge *étalage* of excellent acting, adapted to ends essentially selfish.

CHAPTER III

CALIGULA, NERO, AND OTHERS [1]

(A.D. 37—A.D. 117)

THE three next Emperors,—Caligula, Claudius, and Nero,[2]—
were the last princes who had any connexion by blood [3] with
the Julian house. In Nero, the sixth emperor, expired the
last of the Cæsars who was such in reality. These three
were also the first in that long line of monsters who, at
different times, under the title of Cæsars, dishonoured humanity

---

[1] From *Blackwood* for January 1833. The heading of the chapter
is not De Quincey's own ; but it fairly describes the matter.—M.

[2] The opening phrase of this chapter, "The three next Emperors,
—Caligula, Claudius, and Nero," coming immediately after the chapter
devoted to Augustus, makes one inquire what had become of Augustus's
successor, Tiberius. As De Quincey cannot have forgotten an Emperor
so important, and who would have been such an interesting theme for
his pen, one wonders whether a paper on Tiberius dropped out of the
series by some mishap. At all events, in *Blackwood* for January 1833
it is this paper on Caligula, &c., that follows that on Augustus in the
number for December 1832.—M.

[3] And this was entirely by the female side. The family descent of
the first six Cæsars is so intricate that it is rarely understood accurately ; so that it may be well to state it briefly. Augustus was
grand-nephew to Julius Cæsar, being the son of Cæsar's sister's
daughter. Augustus was also, by adoption, the *son* of Julius. He
himself had one child only, viz. the infamous Julia, who was brought
him by his second wife Scribonia ; and through this Julia it was that
the three princes who succeeded to Tiberius claimed relationship to
Augustus. On that emperor's third and last marriage, viz. with
Livia, he adopted the two sons whom she had borne to her divorced
husband. These two noblemen, who stood in no degree of consanguinity whatever to Augustus, were Tiberius and Drusus. Tiberius,

more memorably than was possible except in the cases of those (if any such can be named) who have abused the same enormous powers in times of the same civility and in defiance of the same general illumination. But for them, it is a fact that some crimes which now stain the page of History would have been accounted fabulous dreams of impure romancers, taxing their extravagant imaginations to create combinations of wickedness more hideous than civilized men would tolerate, and more unnatural than the human heart could conceive. Let us, by way of example, take a short chapter from the diabolic life of Caligula.

In what way did he treat his nearest and tenderest female connexions? His mother had been tortured and murdered by another tyrant almost as fiendish as himself. She was happily removed from his cruelty. Disdaining, however, to acknowledge any connexion with the blood of so obscure a man as Agrippa, he publicly gave out that his mother was indeed the daughter of Julia, but by an incestuous commerce with her father Augustus. His three sisters he debauched. One died, and her he canonized ; the other two he prostituted to the basest of his own attendants. Of his wives, it would be hard to say whether they were first sought and won with

who succeeded his adopted father, Augustus, as emperor, left no children ; but Drusus, the younger of the two brothers, by his marriage with the younger Antonia (daughter of Mark Antony), had the celebrated Germanicus, and Claudius, afterwards emperor. Germanicus, though adopted by his uncle Tiberius, and destined to the empire, died prematurely. But, like Banquo, though he wore no crown, he left descendants who did. For, by his marriage with Agrippina, a daughter of Julia's by Agrippa (and therefore grand-daughter of Augustus), he had a large family ; of whom one son became the Emperor Caligula, and one of the daughters, Agrippina the younger, by her marriage with a Roman nobleman, became the mother of the Emperor Nero. Hence it appears that Tiberius was uncle to Claudius, Claudius was uncle to Caligula, Caligula was uncle to Nero : a worshipful succession of uncles. But it is observable that Nero and Caligula stood in another degree of consanguinity to each other through their grandmothers, who were both daughters of Mark Antony the triumvir ; for the elder Antonia married the grandfather of Nero ; the younger Antonia (as we have stated above) married Drusus, the grandfather of Caligula ; and again, by these two ladies, they were connected not only with each other, but also with the Julian house, for the two Antonias were daughters of Mark Antony by Octavia, sister to Augustus.

more circumstances of injury and outrage, or dismissed with more insult and levity. The one whom he treated best, and with most profession of love, and who commonly rode by his side, equipped with spear and shield, to his military inspections and reviews of the soldiery, though not particularly beautiful, was exhibited to his friends at banquets in a state of absolute nudity. His motive for treating her with so much kindness was probably that she brought him a daughter; and her he acknowledged as his own child, from the early brutality with which she attacked the eyes and cheeks of other infants who were presented to her as play-fellows. Hence it would appear that he was aware of his own ferocity, and treated it as a jest. The levity, indeed, which he mingled with his worst and most inhuman acts, and the slightness of the occasions upon which he delighted to hang his most memorable atrocities, aggravated their impression at the time, and must have contributed greatly to sharpen the sword of vengeance. His palace happened to be contiguous to the circus. Some seats, it seems, were open indiscriminately to the public; consequently, the only way in which they could be appropriated was by taking possession of them as early as the midnight preceding any great exhibitions. Once, when it happened that his sleep was disturbed by such an occasion, he sent in soldiers to eject them, and with orders so rigorous, as it appeared by the event, that in this singular tumult twenty Roman knights, and as many mothers of families, were cudgelled to death upon the spot, to say nothing of what the reporter calls "innumeram turbam ceteram."

But this is a trifle to another anecdote reported by the same authority:—On some occasion it happened that a dearth prevailed, either generally of cattle, or of such cattle as were used for feeding the wild beasts reserved for the bloody exhibitions of the amphitheatre. Food could be had, and perhaps at no very exorbitant price, but on terms somewhat higher than the ordinary market price. A slight excuse served with Caligula for acts the most monstrous. Instantly repairing to the public jails, he caused all the prisoners to pass in review before him (*custodiarum seriem recognovit*), and then, pointing to two bald-headed men, he ordered that the whole file of intermediate persons should be marched off to the dens of the wild beasts : "Tell them off," said he, "from the bald man to the bald man." Yet these were prisoners committed, not for punishment, but trial. Nor, had it been otherwise, were the charges against them equal, but running through every graduation of guilt. But the *elogia*, or records of their commitment, he would not so much as look at. With such inordinate capacities for cruelty, we cannot wonder that he should in his common conversation have deplored the tameness and insipidity of his own times and reign, as likely to be marked by no wide-spreading calamity. "Augustus," said he, "was happy ; ah, yes, he was fortunate, for in his reign occurred the slaughter of Varus and his legions. Tiberius was happy ; for in his occurred that glorious fall of the great amphi-theatre at Fidenæ. But for me—alas ! alas !" And then he would pray earnestly for fire or slaughter, pestilence or famine. Famine, indeed, was to some extent in his own power ; and, accordingly, as far as his courage would carry him, he did occasionally try that mode of tragedy upon the people of Rome, by shutting up the public granaries against them. As he blended his mirth and a truculent sense of the humorous with his cruelties, we cannot wonder that he should soon blend his cruelties with his ordinary festivities, and that his daily banquets would soon become insipid without them. Hence he required a daily supply of exe-cutions in his own halls and banqueting-rooms ; nor was a dinner held to be complete without such a dessert. Artists were sought out who had dexterity and strength enough to do what Lucan somewhere calls *ensem rotare*, that is to cut off a human head with one whirl of the sword. Even this became insipid, as wanting one main element of misery to the sufferer and an indispensable condiment to the jaded palate of the connoisseur, viz. a lingering duration. As a pleasant variety, therefore, the tormentors were introduced with their various instruments of torture ; and many a dismal tragedy in that mode of human suffering was con-ducted in the sacred presence during the Emperor's hours of amiable relaxation.

The result of these horrid indulgences was exactly what

we might suppose,—that even such scenes ceased to irritate the languid appetite, and yet that without them life was not endurable.   Jaded and exhausted as the sense of pleasure had become in Caligula, still it could be roused into any activity by nothing short of these murderous luxuries. Hence it seems that he was continually tampering and dallying with the thought of murder; and, like the old Parisian jeweller Cardillac, in Louis XIV's time, who was stung with a perpetual lust for murdering the possessors of fine diamonds—not so much for the value of the prize (of which he never hoped to make any use) as from an unconquerable desire for precipitating himself into the difficulties and hazards of the murder—Caligula never failed to experience (and sometimes even to acknowledge) a secret temptation to any murder which seemed either more than usually abominable, or more than usually difficult.   Thus, when the two consuls were seated at his table, he burst out into sudden and profuse laughter; and, upon their courteously requesting to know what witty and admirable conceit might be the occasion of the imperial mirth, he frankly owned to them, and doubtless he did not improve their appetites by this confession, that in fact he was laughing, and that he could not *but* laugh (and then the monster laughed immoderately again), at the pleasant thought of seeing them both headless, and that with so little trouble to himself (*uno suo nutu*) he could have both their throats cut.   No doubt he was continually balancing the arguments for and against such little *escapades;* nor had any person a reason for security in the extraordinary obligations, whether of hospitality or of religious vows, which seemed to lay him under some peculiar restraints in that case above all others; for such circumstances of peculiarity, by which the murder would be stamped with unusual atrocity, were but the more likely to make its fascinations irresistible.   Hence he dallied with the thoughts of murdering her whom he loved best, and indeed exclusively —his wife Cæsonia; and, whilst fondling her, and toying playfully with her polished throat, he was distracted (as he half insinuated to her) between the desire of caressing it, which might be often repeated, and that of cutting it, which could be gratified but once.

Nero (for, as to Claudius, he came too late to the throne to indulge any propensities of this nature with so little discretion) was but a variety of the same species. He also was an amateur, and an enthusiastic amateur, of murder. But, as this taste, in the most ingenious hands, is limited and monotonous in its modes of manifestation, it would be tedious to run through the long Suetonian roll-call of his peccadilloes in this way. One only we shall cite, to illustrate the amorous delight with which he pursued any murder which happened to be seasoned highly to his taste by enormous atrocity, and by almost unconquerable difficulty. It would really be pleasant, were it not for the revolting consideration of the persons concerned, and their relation to each other, to watch the tortuous pursuit of the hunter, and the doubles of the game, in this obstinate chase. For certain reasons of state, as Nero attempted to persuade himself, but in reality because no other crime had the same attractions of unnatural horror about it, he resolved to murder his mother Agrippina. This being settled, the next thing was to arrange the mode and the tools. Naturally enough, according to the custom then prevalent in Rome, he first attempted the thing by poison. The poison failed : for Agrippina, anticipating tricks of this kind, had armed her constitution against them, like Mithridates, and daily took potent antidotes and prophylactics. Or else (which is more probable) the Emperor's agent in such purposes, fearing his sudden repentance and remorse on first hearing of his mother's death, or possibly even witnessing her agonies, had composed a poison of inferior strength. This had certainly occurred in the case of Britannicus, who had thrown off with ease the first dose administered to him by Nero. Upon which he had summoned to his presence the woman employed in the affair, and, compelling her by threats to mingle a more powerful potion in his own presence, had tried it successively upon different animals, until he was satisfied with its effects ; after which, immediately inviting Britannicus to a banquet, he had finally despatched him. On Agrippina, however, no changes in the poison, whether of kind or strength, had any effect ; so that, after various trials, this mode of murder was abandoned, and the Emperor addressed himself to other plans.

The first of these was some curious mechanical device by which a false ceiling was to have been suspended by bolts above her bed, and in the middle of the night, the bolt being suddenly drawn, a vast weight would have descended with a ruinous destruction to all below. This scheme, however, taking air from the indiscretion of some amongst the accomplices, reached the ears of Agrippina; upon which the old lady looked about her too sharply to leave much hope in that scheme: so *that* also was abandoned. Next, he conceived the idea of an artificial ship, which, at the touch of a few springs, might fall to pieces in deep water. Such a ship was prepared, and stationed at a suitable point. But the main difficulty remained; which was to persuade the old lady to go on board. Not that she knew in this case *who* had been the ship-builder, for that would have ruined all; but it seems that she took it ill to be hunted in this murderous spirit, and was out of humour with her son; besides that any proposal coming from him, though previously indifferent to her, would have instantly become suspected. To meet this difficulty, a sort of reconciliation was proposed, and a very affectionate message sent, which had the effect of throwing Agrippina off her guard, and seduced her to Baiæ for the purpose of joining the Emperor's party at a grand banquet held in commemoration of a solemn festival. She came by water in a sort of light frigate, and was to return in the same way. Meantime Nero tampered with the commander of her vessel, and prevailed upon him to wreck it. What was to be done? The great lady was anxious to return to Rome, and no proper conveyance was at hand. Suddenly it was suggested, as if by chance, that a ship of the Emperor's, new and properly equipped, was moored at a neighbouring station. This was readily accepted by Agrippina: the Emperor accompanied her to the place of embarkation, took a most tender leave of her, and saw her set sail. It was necessary that the vessel should get into deep water before the experiment could be made; and with the utmost agitation this pious son awaited news of the result. Suddenly a messenger rushed breathless into his presence, and horrified him by the joyful information that his august mother had met with an alarming accident, but,

by the blessing of Heaven, had escaped safe and sound, and
was now on her road to mingle congratulations with her
affectionate son. The ship, it seems, had done its office ; the
mechanism had played admirably ; but who can provide for
everything ? The old lady, it turned out, could swim like a
duck ; and the whole result had been to refresh her with a
little sea-bathing. Here was worshipful intelligence. Could
any man's temper be expected to stand such continued
sieges ? Money, and trouble, and infinite contrivance, wasted
upon one old woman, who absolutely would not, upon any
terms, be murdered ! Provoking it certainly was ; and of a
man like Nero it could not be expected that he should any
longer dissemble his disgust, or put up with such repeated
affronts. He rushed upon his simple congratulating friend,
swore that he had come to murder him ; and, as nobody
could have suborned him but Agrippina, he ordered her off
to instant execution. And, unquestionably, if people will
not be murdered quietly and in a civil way, they must expect
that such forbearance is not to continue for ever, and obviously
have themselves only to blame for any harshness or violence
which they may have rendered necessary.

It is singular, and shocking at the same time, to mention
that, for this atrocity, Nero did absolutely receive solemn
congratulations from all orders of men. With such evidences
of base servility in the public mind, and of the utter corruption which they had sustained in their elementary feelings,
it is the less astonishing that he should have made other
experiments upon the public patience, which seem expressly
designed to try how much it would support. Whether he
were really the author of the desolating fire which consumed
Rome for six days and seven nights,[1] and drove the mass
of the people into the tombs and sepulchres for shelter, is
yet a matter of some doubt. But one great presumption
against it, founded on its desperate imprudence, as attacking
the people in their primary comforts, is considerably weakened
by the enormous servility of the Romans in the case just
stated : they who could volunteer congratulations to a son
for butchering his mother (no matter on what pretended

---

[1] But a memorial stone, in its inscription, makes the time longer :
"Quando urbs per novem dies arsit Neronianis temporibus."

suspicions) might reasonably be supposed incapable of any resistance which required courage even in a case of self-defence or of just revenge.   The direct reasons, however, for implicating him in this affair seem at present insufficient. He was displeased, it seems, with the irregularity and un-sightliness of the antique buildings, and also with the streets, as too narrow and winding (*angustiis flexurisque vicorum*). But in this he did but express what was no doubt the common judgment of all his contemporaries who had seen the beautiful cities of Greece and Asia Minor.   The Rome of that time was in many parts built of wood ; and there is much prob-ability that it must have been a *picturesque* city, and in parts almost grotesque.   But it is remarkable, and a fact which we have nowhere seen noticed, that the ancients, whether Greeks or Romans, had no eye for the picturesque ; nay, that it was a sense utterly unawakened amongst them, and that the very conception of the picturesque, as of a thing distinct from the beautiful, is not once alluded to through the whole course of ancient literature, nor would it have been intelligible to any ancient critic ; so that, whatever attraction for the eye might exist in the Rome of that day, there is little doubt that it was of a kind to be felt only by modern spectators.   Mere dissatisfaction with its external appearance, which must have been a pretty general senti-ment, argued, therefore, no necessary purpose of destroying it.   Certainly it would be a weightier ground of suspicion, if it were really true, that some of his agents were detected on the premises of different senators in the act of applying combustibles to their mansions.   But this story wears a very fabulous air.   For why resort to the private dwellings of great men, where any intruder was sure of attracting notice, when the same effect, and with the same deadly results, might have been attained quietly and secretly in so many of the humble Roman *cœnacula*, *i.e.* garrets ?

The great loss on this memorable occasion was in the heraldic and ancestral honours of the city.   Historic Rome then went to wreck for ever.   Then perished the *domus priscorum ducum hostilibus adhuc spoliis adornatæ* : the "rostral" palace ; the mansion of the Pompeys ; the Blen-heims and the Strathfieldsayes of the Scipios, the Marcelli.

the Paulli, and the Cæsars; then perished the aged trophies from Carthage and from Gaul; and, in short, as the historian sums up the lamentable desolation, "*quidquid visendum atque memorabile ex antiquitate duraverat.*" And this of itself might lead one to suspect the Emperor's hand as the original agent; for by no one act was it possible so entirely and so suddenly to wean the people from their old republican recollections, and in one week to obliterate the memorials of their popular forces, and their trophies of many ages. The old people of Rome were gone; their characteristic dress even was gone; for already in the time of Augustus they had laid aside the *toga*, and assumed the cheaper and scantier *pœnula*, so that the eye sought in vain for Virgil's

"Romanos rerum dominos gentemque *togatam* "

Why, then, after all the constituents of Roman grandeur had passed away, should their historical trophies survive, recalling to them the scenes of departed heroism in which they had no personal property, and suggesting to them vain hopes, which for them were never to be other than chimeras? Even in that sense, therefore, and as a great depository of heart-stirring historical remembrances, Rome was profitably destroyed; and in any other sense, whether for health or for the conveniences of polished life, or for architectural magnificence, there never was a doubt that the Roman people gained infinitely by this conflagration. For, like London, it arose from its ashes with a splendour proportioned to its vast expansion of wealth and population; and marble took the place of wood. For the moment, however, this event must have been felt by the people as an overwhelming calamity. And it serves to illustrate the passive endurance and timidity of the popular temper, and to what extent it might be provoked with impunity, that in this state of general irritation and effervescence Nero absolutely forbade them to meddle with the ruins of their own dwellings— taking that charge upon himself, with a view to the vast wealth which he anticipated from sifting the rubbish. And, as if that mode of plunder were not sufficient, he exacted compulsory contributions to the rebuilding of the city so indiscriminately as to press heavily upon all men's finances;

and thus, in the public account which universally imputed the fire to him, he was viewed as a twofold robber, who sought to heal one calamity by the infliction of another and a greater.

The monotony of wickedness and outrage becomes at length fatiguing to the coarsest and most callous senses ; and the historian even who caters professedly for the taste which feeds upon the monstrous and the hyperbolical is glad at length to escape from the long evolution of his insane atrocities, to the striking and truly scenical catastrophe of retribution which overtook them, and avenged the wrongs of an insulted world.   Perhaps History contains no more impressive scenes than those in which the justice of Providence at length arrested the monstrous career of Nero.

It was at Naples, and, by a remarkable fatality, on the very anniversary of his mother's murder, that he received the first intelligence of the revolt in Gaul under the Proprætor Vindex.   This news for about a week he treated with levity ; and,—like Henry VII of England, who was nettled not so much at being proclaimed a rebel as because he was described under the slighting denomination of "one Henry Tidder or Tudor,"—he complained bitterly that Vindex hád mentioned him by his family name of Ænobarbus, rather than his assumed one of Nero.   But much more keenly he resented the insulting description of himself as a "miserable harper," appealing to all about him whether they had ever known a better, and offering to stake the truth of all the other charges against himself upon the accuracy of this in particular.   So little even in this instance was he alive to the true point of the insult ; not thinking it any disgrace that a Roman Emperor should be chiefly known to the world in the character of a harper, but only if he should happen to be a bad one.   Even in those days, however, imperfect as were the means of travelling, rebellion moved somewhat too rapidly to allow any long interval of security so light-minded as this.   One courier followed upon the heels of another, until he felt the necessity for leaving Naples ; and he returned to Rome, as the historian says, *prætrepidus* : by which word, however, according to its genuine classical acceptation, we apprehend, is not meant that he was highly alarmed, but only that he was in a great hurry. That he was not yet under any real alarm (for he trusted in certain prophecies, which, like those made to the Scottish tyrant, "kept the promise to the ear, but broke it to the sense") is pretty evident from his conduct on reaching the capital. For, without any appeal to the Senate or the People, but sending out a few summonses to some men of rank, he held a hasty council, which he speedily dismissed, and occupied the rest of the day with experiments on certain musical instruments of recent invention, in which the keys were moved by hydraulic machineries. He had come to Rome, it appeared, merely from a sense of decorum.

Suddenly, however, arrived news, which fell upon him with the shock of a thunderbolt, that the revolt had extended to the Spanish provinces, and was headed by Galba. He fainted upon hearing this; and, falling to the ground, lay for a long time lifeless, as it seemed, and speechless. Upon coming to himself again, he tore his robe, struck his forehead, and exclaimed aloud that for him all was over. In this agony of mind, it strikes across the utter darkness of the scene with the sense of a sudden and cheering flash, recalling to us the possible goodness and fidelity of human nature, when we read that one humble creature adhered to him, and, according to her slender means, gave him consolation during these trying moments: this was the woman who had tended his infant years; and she now recalled to his remembrance such instances of former princes in adversity as appeared fitted to sustain his drooping spirits. It seems, however, that, according to the general course of violent emotions, the rebound of high spirits was in proportion to his first despondency. He omitted nothing of his usual luxury or self-indulgence, and even found spirits for going *incognito* to the theatre, where he took sufficient interest in the public performances to send a message to a favourite actor. At times, even in this hopeless situation, his native ferocity returned upon him, and he was believed to have framed plans for removing all his enemies at once: the leaders of the rebellion, by appointing successors to their offices, and secretly sending assassins to despatch their persons; the senate, by poison at a great banquet; the Gaulish provinces, by delivering them up for pillage to the army ; the city, by again setting it on fire, whilst, at the same time, a vast number of wild beasts was to have been turned loose upon the unarmed populace, for the double purpose of destroying them and of distracting their attention from the fire. But, as the mood of his frenzy changed, these sanguinary schemes were abandoned (not, however, under any feelings of remorse, but from mere despair of effecting them), and on the same day, *but after a luxurious dinner*, the imperial monster grew bland and pathetic in his ideas: he would proceed to the rebellious army ; he would present himself unarmed to their view, and would recall them to their duty by the mere spectacle of his tears. Upon the pathos with which he would weep he was resolved to rely entirely. And, having received the guilty to his mercy without distinction, upon the following day he would unite *his* joy with *their* joy, and would chant hymns of victory (*epinicia*) ; "which, by the way," said he, suddenly, breaking off to his favourite pursuits, "it is necessary that I should immediately compose." This caprice vanished like the rest ; and he made an effort to enlist the slaves and citizens into his service, and to raise by extortion a large military chest. But in the midst of these vacillating purposes fresh tidings surprised him ; other armies had revolted, and the rebellion was spreading contagiously. This consummation of his alarms reached him at dinner ; and the expressions of his angry fears took even a scenical air: he tore the despatches, upset the table, and dashed to pieces upon the ground two crystal beakers, which, from the sculptures that adorned them, had a high value as works of art even in the *Aurea Domus*.

He now took steps for flight ; and, sending forward commissioners to prepare the fleet at Ostia for his reception, he tampered with such officers of the army as were at hand, to prevail upon them to accompany his retreat. But all showed themselves indisposed to such schemes, and some flatly refused. Upon which he turned to other counsels ; sometimes meditating a flight to the King of Parthia, or even to throw himself on the mercy of Galba ; sometimes inclining rather to the plan of venturing into the forum in mourning apparel, begging pardon for all past offences, and, as a last resource, entreating that he might receive the appointment of Egyptian prefect. This plan, however, he hesitated to adopt, from some apprehension that he should be torn to pieces on his road to the forum . and, at all events, he concluded to postpone it to the following day. Meantime events were now hurrying to their catastrophe, which for ever anticipated that intention. His hours were numbered, and the closing scene was at hand.

Record there is not amongst libraries of man, libraries that stretch into infinity like the armies of Xerxes, of a human agony distilling itself through moments and pulses of intermitting misery so cruel, and into such depths of darkness descending from such glittering heights. In the middle of the night he was aroused from slumber with the intelligence that the military guard who did duty at the palace had all quitted their posts. Upon this the unhappy prince leaped from his couch, never again to taste the luxury of sleep, and despatched messengers to his friends. No answers were returned; and upon that he went personally with a small retinue to their hotels. But he found their doors everywhere closed; and all his importunities could not avail to extort an answer. Sadly and slowly he returned to his own bed-chamber; but there again he found fresh instances of desertion, which had occurred during his short absence. The pages of his bed-chamber had fled, carrying with them the coverlids of the imperial bed, which were probably inwrought with gold thread, and even a golden box, in which Nero had on the preceding day deposited poison prepared against the last extremity. Wounded to the heart by this general perfidy, and by some special case, no doubt, of ingratitude, such as would probably enough be signalized in the flight of his personal favourites, he called for a gladiator of the household to come and despatch him But, none appearing—"What!" said he, "have I neither friend nor foe?" This pretty little epigrammatic query we suspect to be the manufacture of the rhetorician in after days, embroidering the case at his leisure. For the honour of human nature, we rejoice that one *man* in Rome was capable of gratitude and stern fidelity. Else the poor nurse would have placed our rascally sex at a discount. And, so saying, or perhaps *not* saying, he ran towards the Tiber, with the purpose of drowning himself. But that paroxysm, like all the rest, proved transient ; and he expressed a wish for some hiding-place, or momentary asylum, in which he might collect his unsettled spirits, and fortify his wandering resolution. Such a retreat was offered to him by his *libertus* Phaon, in his own rural villa, about four miles distant from Rome. This offer was accepted ; and the Emperor, without further preparation than that of throwing over his person a short mantle of a dusky hue, and enveloping his head and face in a handker-chief, mounted his horse, and left Rome with four attendants. It was still night, but probably verging towards the early dawn ; and even at that hour the imperial party met some travellers on their way to Rome (coming up, no doubt,[1] on law business), who said, as they passed, " These men, doubt-less, are in chase of Nero." Two other incidents, of an interesting nature, are recorded of this short but memorable ride. At one point of the road the shouts of the soldiery assailed their ears from the neighbouring encampment of Galba. They were probably then getting under arms for their final march to take possession of the palace. At another point an accident occurred of a more ominous kind, but so natural and so well circumstantiated that it serves to verify the whole narrative. A dead body was lying on the road, at which the Emperor's horse started so violently as nearly to dismount his rider ; the difficulty of the moment compelled the Emperor to drop the hand which held up the handkerchief, so that with the suddenness of a theatrical surprise his features were exposed. Only for a moment was this exposure ; but a moment was sufficient. Precisely at this critical moment it happened that an old half-pay officer passed, recognised the Emperor, and saluted him. Perhaps it was with some purpose of applying a remedy to this unfortunate rencontre that the party dismounted at a point where several roads met, and turned their horses adrift, to graze at will amongst the furze and brambles. Their own

---

[1] At this early hour witnesses, sureties, &c., and all concerned in the law courts, came up to Rome from villas, country towns, &c. But no ordinary call existed to summon travellers in the opposite direction ; which accounts for the comment of the travellers on the errand of Nero and his attendants.

purpose was to make their way to the back of the villa ; but, to accomplish *that*, it was necessary that they should first cross a plantation of reeds, from the peculiar marshy state of which they found themselves obliged to cover successively each space upon which they trode with parts of their dress, in order to gain any supportable footing. In this way, and contending with such hardships, they reached at length the postern side of the villa. Here we must suppose that there was no regular ingress ; for, after waiting until an entrance was pierced, it seems that the Emperor could avail himself of this entrance in no more dignified posture than by creeping through the hole on his hands and feet (*quadrupes per angustias receptus*).

Now, then, after such anxiety, alarm, and hardship, Nero had reached a quiet rural asylum. But for the unfortunate concurrence of his horse's alarm with the passing of the soldier, he might perhaps have counted on the respite of a day or two in this noiseless and obscure abode. But what a habitation for him who was yet ruler of the world in the eye of law, and even *de facto* was so had any fatal accident befallen his aged competitor ! The room in which (as the one most removed from notice and suspicion) he had secreted himself was a cella, or little sleeping-closet of a slave, furnished only with a miserable pallet and a coarse rug. Here lay the founder and possessor of the Golden House, too happy if he might hope for the peaceable possession even of this miserable crypt. But that, he knew too well, was impossible. Could he ever have believed it possible ? A rival pretender to the empire was like the plague of fire—as dangerous in the shape of a single spark left unextinguished as in that of a prosperous conflagration. But a few brief sands yet remained to run in the Emperor's hour-glass ; much variety of degradation or suffering seemed scarcely within the possibilities of his situation, or within the compass of the time. Yet, as though Providence had decreed that his humiliation should pass through every shape and stage, and speak by every expression which came home to his understanding, or was intelligible to his senses, even in those few moments he was attacked by hunger and thirst. No other bread could be obtained (or, perhaps, if the Emperor's

presence were concealed from the household, it was not safe
to raise suspicion by calling for better) than that which was
ordinarily given to slaves,—coarse, black, and, to a palate so
luxurious, doubtless disgusting. This accordingly he rejected;
but a little tepid water he drank. After which, with the
haste of one who fears that he may be prematurely interrupted, but otherwise with all the reluctance which we may
imagine, and which his streaming tears proclaimed, he
addressed himself to the last labour in which he supposed
himself to have any interest on this earth,—that of digging
a grave. Measuring a space adjusted to the proportions of
his person, he inquired anxiously for any loose fragments of
marble, such as might suffice to line it. He requested also
to be furnished with wood and water, as the materials for
the last sepulchral rites. And these labours were accompanied, or continually interrupted, by tears and lamentations,
or by passionate ejaculations on the blindness of fortune, in
suffering so divine a musical artist to be thus violently
snatched away, and on the calamitous fate of musical science,
which then stood on the brink of so dire an eclipse. In
these moments he was most truly in an *agony*, according to
the original meaning of that word; for the *conflict* was great
between two master principles of his nature : on the one
hand, he clung with the weakness of a girl to life, even in
that miserable shape to which it had now sunk ; and, like
the poor malefactor with whose last struggles Prior had so
atrociously amused himself, "he often took leave, but was
loth to depart." Yet, on the other hand, to resign his life
very speedily seemed his only chance for escaping the con-
tumelies, perhaps the tortures, of his enemies, and, above all
other considerations, for making sure of a burial, and possibly
of burial rites ; to want which, in the judgment of the
ancients, was the last consummation of misery. Thus
occupied and thus distracted—sternly attracted to the grave
by his creed, hideously repelled by infirmity of nature—he
was suddenly interrupted by a courier with letters for the
master of the house : letters, and from Rome ! What was
their import ? That was soon told : briefly that Nero was
adjudged to be a public enemy by the base sycophantic
Senate, and that official orders were issued for apprehending

him, in order that he might be brought to condign punishment according to the method of ancient precedent.   Ancient
precedent! *more majorum!*   And how was that? eagerly
demanded the Emperor.   He was answered that the state
criminal in such cases was first stripped naked, then impaled
as it were between the prongs of a pitchfork, and in that
condition scourged to death.   Horror-struck with this account,
he drew forth two poniards, or short swords, tried their edges,
and then, in utter imbecility of purpose, returned them to
their scabbards, alleging that the destined moment had not
yet arrived.   Then he called upon Sporus, the infamous
partner in his former excesses, to commence the funeral
anthem.   Others, again, he besought to lead the way in
dying, and to sustain him by the spectacle of their example.
But this purpose also he dismissed in the very moment of
utterance; and, turning away despairingly, he apostrophized
himself in words reproachful or animating, now taxing his
nature with infirmity of purpose, now calling on himself by
name, with abjurations to remember his dignity, and to act
worthily of his station: οὐ πρέπει Νερωνι, cried he; οὐ
πρέπει· νήφειν δεῖ ἐν τοῖς τοιούτοις· ἄγε, ἔγειρε σεαυτον—
i.e. "Fie, fie, then, Nero! this is not becoming to Nero.   In
such extremities a man should be wide awake.   Up, then,
and rouse thyself to action."
    Thus, and in similar efforts to master the weakness of his
reluctant nature—weakness which would extort pity from
the severest minds, were it not from the odious connexion
which in him it had with cruelty the most merciless—did
this unhappy prince, *jam non salutis spem sed exitii solatium
quærens,* no longer looking for any hope of deliverance, but
simply for consolation in his ruin, consume the flying
moments, until at length his ears caught the fatal sounds or
echoes from a body of horsemen riding up to the villa.
These were the officers charged with his arrest; and, if he
should fall into their hands alive, he knew that his last
chance was over for liberating himself, by a Roman death,
from the burden of ignominious life, and from a lingering
torture.   He paused from his restless motions, listened
attentively, then repeated a line from Homer—

    Ἵππων μ' ὠκυπόδων ἀμφὶ κτύπος οὔατα βάλλει·

("The resounding tread of swift-footed horses reverberates upon my ears"); then, under some momentary impulse of courage, gained perhaps by figuring to himself the bloody populace rioting upon his mangled body, yet even then needing the auxiliary hand and vicarious courage of his private secretary, the feeble-hearted prince stabbed himself in the throat.   The wound, however, was not such as to cause instant death.   He was still breathing, and not quite speechless, when the centurion who commanded the party entered the closet; and to this officer, who uttered a few hollow words of encouragement, he was still able to make a brief reply.   But in the very effort of speaking he expired, and with an expression of horror impressed upon his stiffened features which communicated a sympathetic horror to all beholders.

Such was the too memorable tragedy which closed for ever the brilliant line of the Julian family, and translated the august title of Cæsar from its original purpose as a proper name to that of an official designation.   It is the most striking instance upon record of a dramatic and extreme vengeance overtaking extreme guilt; for, as Nero had exhausted the utmost possibilities of crime, so it may be affirmed that he drank off the cup of suffering to the very extremity of what his peculiar nature allowed.   And in no life of so short a duration have ever been crowded equal extremities of gorgeous prosperity and abject infamy.   It may be added, as another striking illustration of the rapid mutability and revolutionary excesses which belonged to what has been properly called the *stratocracy* or martial despotism then disposing of the world, that within no very great succession of weeks that same victorious rebel, the Emperor Galba, at whose feet Nero had been self-immolated, was laid a murdered corpse in the same identical cell which had witnessed the lingering agonies of his unhappy victim.   This was the act of an emancipated slave, anxious, by a vindictive insult to the remains of one prince, to place on record his gratitude to another.   "So runs the world away!"   And in this striking way is retribution sometimes dispensed.

In the sixth Cæsar terminated the Julian line.   The

three next princes in the succession were personally unin-
teresting, and, with a slight reserve in favour of Otho, whose
motives for committing suicide (if truly reported) argue great
nobility of mind,[1] were even brutal in the tenor of their
lives and monstrous ; besides that the extreme brevity of their
several reigns (all three, taken conjunctly, having held the
supreme power for no more than twelve months and twenty
days) dismisses them from all effectual station or right to a
separate notice in the line of Cæsars. Coming to the tenth
in the succession, Vespasian, and his two sons, Titus and
Domitian, who make up the list of the Twelve Cæsars, as they
are usually called, we find matter for deeper political meditation
and subjects of curious research. But these Emperors would
be more properly classed with the five who succeed them—
Nerva, Trajan, Hadrian, and the two Antonines ; after whom
comes the young ruffian, Commodus, another Caligula or
Nero, from whose short and infamous reign Gibbon takes up
his tale of the Decline of the Empire. And this classification
would probably have prevailed, had not a very curious work
of Suetonius, whose own life and period of observation
determined the series and cycle of his subjects, led to a
different distribution. But, as it is evident that, in the
succession of the first twelve Cæsars, the six latter have no
connexion whatever by descent, collaterally, or otherwise,
with the six first, it would be a more logical distribution to
combine them according to the fortunes of the state itself,
and the succession of its prosperity through the several stages
of splendour, declension, revival, and final decay. Under
this arrangement, the first seventeen would belong to the
first stage ; Commodus would open the second ; Aurelian
down to Constantine or Julian would fill the third ; and
Jovian to Augustulus would bring up the melancholy rear.
Meantime it will be proper, after thus briefly throwing our
eyes over the monstrous atrocities of the early Cæsars, to
spend a few lines in examining their origin, and the circum-

---

[1] We may add that the unexampled public grief which followed the
death of Otho, exceeding even that which followed the death of
Germanicus, and causing several officers to commit suicide, implies
some remarkable goodness in this prince, and a very unusual power of
conciliating attachment.

stances which favoured their growth. For a mere hunter after hidden or forgotten singularities, a lover on their own account of all strange perversities and freaks of nature, whether in action, taste, or opinion, for a collector and amateur of misgrowths and abortions—for a Suetonius, in short—it may be quite enough to state and to arrange his cabinet of specimens from the marvellous in human nature. But certainly in modern times any historian, however little affecting the praise of a philosophic investigator, would feel himself called upon to remove a little the taint of the strange and preternatural which adheres to such anecdotes by entering into the psychological grounds of their possibility,—whether lying in any peculiarly vicious education, early familiarity with bad models, corrupting associations, or other plausible key to effects which, taken separately, and out of their natural connexion with their explanatory causes, are apt rather to startle and revolt the feelings of sober thinkers. Except, perhaps, in some chapters of Italian history,—as, for example, among the most profligate of the Papal houses, and amongst some of the Florentine princes,—we find hardly any parallel to the atrocities of Caligula and Nero ; nor indeed was Tiberius much (if at all) behind them, though otherwise so wary and cautious in his conduct. The same tenor of licentiousness beyond the needs of the individual, the same craving after the monstrous and the stupendous in guilt, is continually emerging in succeeding Emperors—in Vitellius, in Domitian, in Commodus, in Caracalla—everywhere, in short, where it was not overruled by one of two causes : either by original goodness of nature too powerful to be mastered by ordinary seductions (and in some cases removed from their influence by an early apprenticeship to camps), or by the terrors of an exemplary ruin immediately preceding. For such a determinate tendency to the enormous and the anomalous sufficient causes must exist. What were they ?

In the first place, we may observe that the people of Rome in that age were generally more corrupt by many degrees than has been usually supposed possible. The effect of revolutionary times to relax all modes of moral obligation, and to unsettle the moral sense, has been well and philosophically stated by Coleridge ; but that would hardly account for the utter licentiousness and depravity of Imperial Rome. Looking back to Republican Rome, and considering the state of public morals but fifty years before the Emperors, we can with difficulty believe that the descendants of a people so severe in their habits could thus rapidly degenerate, and that a populace once so hard and masculine should assume the manners which we might expect in the debauchees of Daphne (the infamous suburb of Antioch), or of Canopus, into which settled the very lees and dregs of the vicious Alexandria. Such extreme changes would falsify all that we know of human nature : we might *a priori* pronounce them impossible ; and in fact, upon searching history, we find other modes of solving the difficulty. In reality, the citizens of Rome were at this time a new race, brought together from every quarter of the world, but especially from Asia. So vast a proportion of the ancient citizens had been cut off by the sword, and, partly to conceal this waste of population, but much more by way of cheaply requiting services, or of showing favour, or of acquiring influence, slaves had been emancipated in such great multitudes, and afterwards invested with all the rights of citizens, that, in a single generation, Rome became almost transmuted into a baser metal, the progeny of those whom the last generation had purchased from the slave merchants. These people derived their stock from Cappadocia, Pontus, &c., and the other populous regions of Asia Minor ; and hence the taint of Asiatic luxury and depravity which was so conspicuous to all the Romans of the old republican austerity. Juvenal is to be understood more literally than is sometimes supposed when he complains that long before his time the Orontes (that river which washed the infamous capital of Syria) had mingled his impure waters with those of the Tiber. And, a little before him, Lucan speaks with more historic gravity when he says—

> " Vivant Galatæque Syrique,
> Cappadoces, Gallique, extremique orbis Iberi,
> Armenii, Cilices : *nam post civilia bella*
> *Hic Populus Romanus erit.*" [1]

---

[1] Blackwell, in his *Court of Augustus*, vol. i. p. 382, when noticing

Probably in the time of Nero not one man in six was of pure Roman descent.[1]   And the consequences were answerable. Scarcely a family has come down to our knowledge that could not in one generation enumerate a long catalogue of divorces within its own contracted circle.   Every man had married a series of wives ; every woman a series of husbands. Even in the palace of Augustus, who wished to be viewed as an *exemplar* or ideal model of domestic purity, every principal member of his family was tainted in that way ; himself in a manner and a degree infamous even at that time.[2]   For the first four hundred years of Rome not one

these lines, upon occasion of the murder of Cicero in the final proscription under the last triumvirate, comments thus : " Those of the greatest and truly Roman spirit had been murdered in the field by Julius Cæsar ; the rest were now massacred in the city by his son and successors , in their room came Syrians, Cappadocians, Phrygians, and other enfranchised slaves from the conquered nations."—"These in half a century had sunk so low that Tiberius pronounced her very senators to be *homines ad servitutem natos*—men born to be slaves."

[1] Suetonius indeed pretends that Augustus, personally at least, struggled against this ruinous practice—thinking it a matter of the highest moment "sincerum atque ab omni colluvione peregrini et servilis sanguinis incorruptum servare populum."   And Horace is ready with his flatteries on the same topic, lib. 3, Od 6.   But the facts are against them ; for the question is not what Augustus did in his own person (which at most could not operate very widely except by the example), but what he permitted to be done.   Now, there was a practice familiar to those times : that, when a congiary or any other popular liberality was announced, multitudes were enfranchised by avaricious masters in order to make them capable of the bounty (as citizens) and yet under the condition of transferring to their emancipators whatsoever they should receive ; ἵνα τὸν δημοσίως διδομένον σιτὸν λαμβάνοντες κατὰ μῆνα φέρωσι τοῖς δεδώκασι τὴν ἐλευθερίαν, says Dionysius of Halicarnassus, in order that, after receiving the corn given publicly in every month, they might carry it to those who had bestowed upon them their freedom.   In a case, then, where an extensive practice of this kind was exposed to Augustus, and publicly reproved by him, how did he proceed ?   Did he reject the new-made citizens ?   No ; he contented himself with diminishing the proportion originally destined for each, so that, the same absolute sum being distributed among a number increased by the whole amount of the new enrolments, of necessity the relative sum for each separately was so much less.   But this was a remedy applied only to the pecuniary fraud as it would have affected himself.   The permanent mischief to the state went unredressed.

[2] Part of the story is well known, but not the whole.   Tiberius

divorce had been granted or asked, although the statute
which allowed of this indulgence had always been in force.
But in the age succeeding to the Civil Wars men and women
"married," says one author, "with a view to divorce, and
divorced in order to marry. Many of these changes happened
within the year, especially if the lady had a large fortune,
which always went back with her, and procured her choice
of transient husbands." And, "Can one imagine," asks the
same writer, "that the fair one who changed her husband
every quarter strictly kept her matrimonial faith all the
three months?" Thus the very fountain of all the "household charities" and household virtues was polluted. And
after that we need little wonder at the assassinations, poison-
ings, and forging of wills, which then laid waste the domestic
life of the Romans.

2. A second source of the universal depravity was the
growing inefficacy of the public religion; and this arose
from its disproportion and inadequacy to the intellectual
advances of the nation. *Religion*, in its very etymology, has
been held to imply a *religatio*, that is a reiterated or secondary

Nero, a promising young nobleman, had recently married a very
splendid beauty. Unfortunately for him, at the marriage of Octavia
(sister to Augustus) with Mark Antony, he allowed his young wife,
then about eighteen, to attend upon the bride. Augustus was deeply
and suddenly fascinated by her charms, and without further scruple
sent a message to Nero, intimating that he was in love with his wife,
and would thank him to resign her. The other, thinking it vain, in
those days of lawless proscription, to contest a point of this nature
with one who commanded thirty legions, obeyed the requisition.
Upon some motive, now unknown, he was persuaded even to degrade
himself further; for he actually officiated at the marriage in character
of father, and gave away to his insolent rival the insolent beauty, at
that time six months advanced in pregnancy by himself. These
humiliating concessions were extorted from him, and yielded (probably
at the instigation of friends) in order to save his life. In the sequel
they had the very opposite result; for he died soon after, and it is
reasonably supposed of grief and mortification. At the marriage feast
an incident occurred which threw the whole company into confusion.
A little boy, roving from couch to couch among the guests, came at
length to that in which Livia (the bride) was reclining by the side
of Augustus; whereupon he cried out aloud,—"Lady, what are you
doing here? You are mistaken; this is not your husband; he is
there" (pointing to Tiberius): "go, go; arise, lady, and recline beside
him."

obligation of morals ; a sanction supplementary to that of the conscience.   Now, for a rude and uncultivated people, the Pagan mythology might not be too gross to discharge the main functions of such a religious sanction.   So long as the understanding could submit to the fables of the Pagan creed, so long it was possible that the hopes and fears built upon that creed might be practically efficient on men's lives and intentions.   But, when the foundation gave way, the whole superstructure of necessity fell to the ground.   Those who were obliged to reject the ridiculous legends which invested the whole of their Pantheon, together with the fabulous adjudgers of future punishments, could not but dismiss the punishments, which were, in fact, as laughable, and as obviously the fictions of human ingenuity, as their dispensers. In short, the civilized part of the world in those days lay in this dreadful condition : their intellect had far outgrown their religion ; the disproportions between the two were at length become monstrous ; and as yet no purer or more elevated faith was prepared for their acceptance.   The case was as shocking as if, with our present intellectual needs, we should be unhappy enough to have no creed on which to rest the burden of our final hopes and fears, of our moral obligations, and of our consolations in misery, except the fairy mythology of our nurses.   The condition of a people so situated, of a people under the calamity of having outgrown its religious faith, has never been sufficiently considered.   It is probable that such a condition has never existed before or since that era of the world.   The consequences to Rome were that the reasoning and disputatious part of her population took refuge from the painful state of doubt in Atheism ; amongst the thoughtless and irreflective the consequences were chiefly felt in their morals, which were thus sapped in their foundation.

3. A third cause, which from the first had exercised a most baleful influence upon the arts and upon literature in Rome, had by this time matured its disastrous tendencies towards the extinction of the moral sensibilities.   This was the circus, and the whole machinery, form and substance, of the circensian shows, but, far more than the simply brutal circus, the human amphitheatre.   Why had tragedy no existence as a part of the Roman literature ?   Because—and *that*

was a reason which would have sufficed to stifle all the dramatic genius of Greece and England—there was too much tragedy in the shape of gross reality almost daily before their eyes. The amphitheatre extinguished the theatre. How was it possible that the fine and intellectual griefs of the drama should win their way to hearts seared and rendered callous by the continual exhibition of scenes the most hideous, in which human blood was poured out like water, and a human life sacrificed at any moment either to caprice in the populace, or to a strife of rivalry between the *ays* and the *noes*, or as the penalty for any trifling instance of awkwardness in the gladiator himself ? Even the more innocent exhibitions, in which brutes only were the sufferers, could not but be mortal to all the finer sensibilities. Five thousand wild animals, torn from their native abodes in the wilderness or forest, were often turned out to be hunted, or for mutual slaughter, in the course of a single exhibition of this nature ; and it sometimes happened (a fact which of itself proclaims the course of the public propensities) that the person at whose expense the shows were exhibited, by way of paying special court to the people and meriting their favour in the way most conspicuously open to him, issued orders that all, without a solitary exception, should be slaughtered. He made it known, as the very highest gratification which the case allowed, that (in the language of our modern auctioneers) the whole, " without reserve," should perish before their eyes. Even such spectacles must have hardened the heart, and blunted the more delicate sensibilities ; but these would soon cease to stimulate the pampered and exhausted sense. From the combats of tigers or leopards, in which the passions of the contending brutes could only be gathered indirectly, and by way of inference from the motions, the transition must have been almost inevitable to those of men, whose nobler and more varied passions spoke directly, and by the intelligible language of the eye, to human spectators ; and from the frequent contemplation of these authorized murders,—in which a whole people, women [1] as much as men, and children

---

[1] Augustus, indeed, strove to exclude the women from one part of the circensian spectacles ; and what was that ? Simply from the sight of the *Athletæ*, as being naked. But that they should witness the

intermingled with both, looked on with leisurely indifference, with anxious expectation, or with rapturous delight, whilst below them were passing the direct revelations of human agony, and not seldom its dying pangs,—it was impossible to expect a result different from that which did in fact take place : universal hardness of heart, obdurate depravity, and a twofold degradation of human nature, which acted simultaneously upon the two pillars of morality (otherwise not often assailed together),—of natural sensibility in the first place, and, in the second, of conscientious principle.

4. But these were circumstances which applied to the whole population indiscriminately. Superadded to these, in the case of the Emperor, and affecting *him* exclusively, was this prodigious disadvantage—that all ancient reverence for the immediate witnesses of his actions, and for the People and Senate, who would under other circumstances have exercised the old functions of the Censor, was, as to the Emperor, pretty nearly obliterated. The very title of *imperator*, from which we have derived our modern one of *emperor*, proclaims the nature of the government, and the tenure of that office. It was a merely *military* title, not popular or democratic by the smallest trace, but exclusively *castrensian ;* and, if born in camps, necessarily the gift of a rude and perhaps wicked soldiery, trained in licentious habits, and often, by the coercion of their situation, robbers and ruffians. The government of an Imperator was therefore purely a government by the sword, or permanent *Stratocracy* having a moveable head. Never was there a people who inquired so impertinently as the Romans into the domestic conduct of each private citizen. No rank escaped this jealous vigilance; and private liberty, even in the most indifferent circumstances of taste or expense,

pangs of the dying gladiators he deemed quite allowable. The smooth barbarian considered that a licence of the first sort offended against decorum, whilst the other violated only the sanctities of the human heart, and the whole sexual character of women. It is our opinion that to the brutalizing effect of these exhibitions we are to ascribe not only the early extinction of the Roman Drama, but generally the inferiority of Rome to Greece in every department of the fine arts. The fine temper of Roman sensibility, which no culture could have brought to the level of the Grecian, was thus dulled for *every* application.

was sacrificed to this inquisitorial rigour of *surveillance*
exercised on behalf of the State, sometimes by erroneous
patriotism, too often by malice in disguise. To this spirit
the highest public officers were obliged to bow; the Consuls,
not less than others. And even the occasional Dictator, if
by law irresponsible, acted nevertheless as one who knew
that any change which depressed his party might eventually
abrogate his privilege. For the first time in the person of
an Imperator was seen a supreme autocrat, who had virtually
and effectively all the irresponsibility which the law assigned
and the origin of his office presumed. Satisfied to know
that he possessed such power, Augustus, as much from natural
taste as policy, was glad to dissemble it, and by every means
to withdraw it from public notice. But *he* had passed his
youth as citizen of a Republic, and in the state of transition
to autocracy, in his office of triumvir, had experimentally
known the perils of rivalship, and the pains of alien control,
too feelingly to provoke unnecessarily any sleeping embers of
the Republican spirit. Tiberius, though familiar from his
infancy with the servile homage of a court, was yet modified
by the popular temper of Augustus ; and he came late to the
throne. Caligula was the first prince on whom the entire
effect of his political situation was allowed to operate ; and
the natural results were seen,—he was the first absolute
monster. He must early have seen the realities of his position, and from what quarter it was that any cloud could arise
to menace his security. To the Senate or People any respect
which he might think proper to pay must have been imputed
by all parties to the lingering superstitions of custom, to
involuntary habit, to court dissimulation, or to the decencies
of external form, and the prescriptive reverence for ancient
names. But neither Senate nor People could enforce their
claims, whatever they might happen to be. Their sanction
and ratifying vote might be worth having, as consecrating
what was already secure, and conciliating the scruples of the
weak to the absolute decision of the strong. But their resistance, as an original movement, was so wholly without hope
that they were seldom weak enough to threaten it.

The Army was the true successor to their places, being
the *ultimate* depository of power. Yet, as the Army was

necessarily subdivided, as the shifting circumstances upon every frontier were continually varying the strength of the several divisions as to numbers and state of discipline, one part might be balanced against any other by an Imperator standing in the centre of the whole. The rigour of the military *sacramentum*, or oath of allegiance, made it dangerous to offer the first overtures to rebellion ; and the money which the soldiers were continually depositing in the bank placed at the foot of their military standards, if sometimes turned against the Emperor, was also liable to be sequestrated in his favour. There were then, in fact, two great forces in the government acting in and by each other—the Stratocracy and the Autocracy. Each needed the other ; each stood in awe of each. But, as regarded all other forces in the empire, constitutional or irregular, popular or senatorial, neither had anything to fear. Under any ordinary circumstances, therefore, considering the hazards of a rebellion, the Emperor was substantially liberated from all control. Vexations or outrages upon the populace were not such to the army. It was but rarely that the soldier participated in the emotions of the citizen. And thus, being effectually without check, the most vicious of the Cæsars went on without fear, presuming upon the weakness in one part of his subjects, and the indifference in the other, until he was tempted onwards to atrocities which armed against him the common feelings of human nature ; so that all mankind, as it were, rose in a body with one voice, and apparently with one heart, united by mere force of indignant sympathy, to put him down, and "abate" him as a monster. But, until he brought matters to this extremity, Cæsar had no cause to fear. Nor was it at all certain, in any one instance where this exemplary chastisement overtook him, that the apparent unanimity of the actors went further than the *practical* conclusion of "abating" the imperial nuisance, or that their indignation had settled upon the same offences. In general, the Army measured the guilt by the public scandal rather than by its moral atrocity, and Cæsar suffered perhaps in every case not so much because he had violated his duties as because he had dishonoured his office.

It is, therefore, in the total absence of the checks which

have almost universally existed to control other despots under
some indirect shape, even where none was provided by the
laws, that we must seek for the main peculiarity affecting the
condition of the Roman Cæsar; which peculiarity it was,
superadded to the other three, that finally made those three
operative in their fullest extent. It is in the perfection of
the Stratocracy that we must look for the key to the excesses
of the Autocrat. Even in the bloody despotisms of the
Barbary States there has always existed, in the religious
prejudices of the people, which could not be violated with
safety, one check more upon the caprices of the despot than
was found at Rome. Upon the whole, therefore, what affects
us on the first reading as a prodigy or anomaly in the frantic
outrages of the early Cæsars falls within the natural bounds
of intelligible human nature when we state the case consider-
ately. Surrounded by a population which had not only
gone through a most vicious and corrupting discipline, and
had been utterly ruined by the licence of revolutionary times
and the bloodiest proscriptions, but had even been extensively
changed in its very elements, and from the descendants of
Romulus had been transmuted into an Asiatic mob; starting
from this point, and considering, as the second feature of the
case, that this transfigured people, *morally* so degenerate, were
carried; however, by the progress of civilisation to a certain
intellectual altitude,—which the popular religion had not
strength to ascend, but from inherent disproportion remained
at the base of the general civilisation, incapable of accompanying the other elements in their advance,—thirdly, that
this polished condition of society, which should naturally
with the evils of a luxurious repose have counted upon its
pacific benefits, had yet, by means of its circus and its gladiatorial contests, applied a constant irritation and a system of
provocations to the appetites for blood, such as in all other
nations are connected with the rudest stages of society, and
with the most barbarous modes of warfare, nor even in
such circumstances without many palliatives wanting to the
spectators of the amphitheatre : combining these considerations, we have already a key to the enormities and hideous
excesses of the Roman Imperator. The hot blood which
excites, and the adventurous courage which accompanies, the

excesses of sanguinary warfare, presuppose a condition of the moral nature not to be compared for malignity and baleful tendency to the cool and cowardly spirit of amateurship in which the Roman (who might after all be an effeminate Asiatic) sat looking down upon the bravest of men (Thracians, or other Europeans) mangling each other for his recreation. When, lastly, from such a population, and thus disciplined from his nursery days, we suppose the case of one individual selected, privileged, and raised to a conscious irresponsibility, except at the bar of one extrajudicial tribunal, not easily irritated, and notoriously to be propitiated by other means than those of upright or impartial conduct, we lay together the elements of a situation too trying for human nature, and fitted only to the faculties of an angel or a demon : of an angel, if he should resist its temptations; of a demon, if he should revel in its opportunities. Thus interpreted and solved, Caligula and Nero become ordinary and almost natural men.

But, finally, what if, after all, the worst of the Cæsars, and these in particular, were entitled to the benefit of a still more summary and conclusive apology ? What if, in a true medical sense, they were insane ? It is certain that a vein of madness ran in the family ; and anecdotes are recorded of the three worst which go far to establish it as a fact, and others which would imply it as symptoms preceding or accompanying. As belonging to the former class, take the following story :—At midnight, an elderly gentleman suddenly sends round a message to a select party of noblemen, rouses them out of bed, and summons them instantly to his palace. Trembling for their lives from the suddenness of the summons, and from the unseasonable hour, and scarcely doubting that by some anonymous *delator* they have been denounced as parties to a conspiracy, they hurry to the palace, are received in portentous silence by the ushers and pages in attendance, are conducted to a saloon, where (as everywhere else) the silence of night prevails, united with the silence of fear and whispering expectation. All are seated ; all look at each other in ominous anxiety. Which is accuser ? Which is the accused ? On whom shall their suspicion settle ; on whom their pity ? All are silent, almost speechless ; and even the current of their thoughts is frost-bound by fear. Suddenly the sound of a fiddle is caught from a distance; it swells upon the ear; steps approach; and in another moment in rushes the elderly gentleman, grave and gloomy as his audience, but capering about in a frenzy of excitement. For half an hour he continues to perform all possible evolutions of caprioles, pirouettes, and other extravagant feats of activity, accompanying himself on the fiddle; and, at length, not having once looked at his guests, the elderly gentleman whirls out of the room in the same transport of emotion with which he entered it. The panic-struck visitors are requested by a slave to consider themselves dismissed; they retire; resume their couches; the nocturnal pageant has "dislimned" and vanished; and on the following morning, were it not for their concurring testimonies, all would be disposed to take this interruption of their sleep for one of its most fantastic dreams. The elderly gentleman that figured in this delirious *pas seul*— who was he? He was Tiberius Cæsar, king of kings, and lord of the terraqueous globe.[1] Would a British jury demand better evidence than this of a disturbed intellect in any formal process *de lunatico inquirendo?* For Caligula, again, the evidence of symptoms is still plainer. He knew his own defect, and proposed going through a course of hellebore, —white hellebore, we believe, cultivated in the Mediterranean island of Anticyra expressly as a remedy for insanity. Sleep-lessness, one among the commonest indications of lunacy, haunted him in an excess rarely recorded.[2] The same or

[1] See footnote, *ante*, p. 282.—M.

[2] No fiction of romance presents so awful a picture of the ideal tyrant as that of Caligula by Suetonius. His palace radiant with purple and gold, but murder everywhere lurking beneath flowers; his smiles and echoing laughter, masking (yet hardly meant to mask) his foul treachery of heart; his hideous and tumultuous dreams, his baffled sleep, and his sleepless nights: compose the picture of an Æschylus. What a master's sketch lies in these few lines · "Incita-batur insomnio maxime; neque enim plus tribus horis nocturnis quiescebat; ac ne his placidâ quiete, at pavidâ miris rerum imagini-bus: ut qui inter ceteras pelagi quondam speciem colloquentem secum videre visus sit. Ideoque magna parte noctis, vigiliæ cubandique tædio, nunc toro residens, nunc per longissimas porticus vagus, invo-care identidem atque exspectare lucem consueverat": *i.e.* "But, above all, he was tormented with nervous irritation, by sleeplessness;

similar facts might be brought forward on behalf of Nero. And thus these unfortunate princes, who have so long (and with so little investigation of their cases) passed for monsters or for demoniac counterfeits of men, would at length be brought back within the fold of humanity, as objects rather of pity than of abhorrence, and, when thus reconciled at last to our human charities, would first of all be made intelligible to our understandings.

for he enjoyed not more than three hours of nocturnal repose ; nor even these in pure untroubled rest, but agitated by phantasmata of portentous augury ; as, for example, upon one occasion among other spectral visions he fancied that he saw the Sea, under some definite impersonation, conversing with himself.   Hence it was, and from this incapacity of sleeping, and from weariness of lying awake, that he had fallen into habits of ranging all the night long through the palace, sometimes throwing himself on a couch, sometimes wandering along the vast corridors, watching for the earliest dawn, and anxiously invoking its approach."

CHAPTER IV

HADRIAN, ANTONINUS PIUS, MARCUS AURELIUS, AND OTHERS [1]

(A.D. 117—A.D. 180)

THE five Cæsars—viz. Nerva, Trajan, Hadrian, and the two
Antonines, Pius, and his adopted son, Marcus Aurelius,—
who succeeded immediately to the first twelve, were, in as
high a sense as their office allowed, patriots. Hadrian is
perhaps the first of all whom circumstances permitted to
show his patriotism without fear. It illustrates at one and
the same moment a trait in this Emperor's character, and in
the Roman habits, that he acquired much reputation for
hardiness by walking bareheaded. "Never, on any occasion," says one of his memorialists (Dio), "neither in summer heat nor in winter's cold, did he cover his head ; but,
as well in the Celtic snows as in Egyptian heats, he went
about bareheaded." This anecdote could not fail to win the
especial admiration of Isaac Casaubon, who lived in an age
when men believed a hat no less indispensable to the head,
even within doors, than shoes or stockings to the feet. At
the time when Isaac Casaubon was writing his commentary
on the six authors of the *Augustan History*,—viz., in all
likelihood, during the seven last years of Queen Elizabeth
(1595-1602),—no man, gentle or simple, *doffed* his night-cap
without *donning* his hat ; which he wore all day long at home
or abroad. His astonishment on the occasion is thus expressed:
"Tantum est ἡ ἄσκησις " : such and so mighty is the force

---

[1] From *Blackwood* for June 1834 ; where it was printed under the
title "The Patriot Emperors."—M.

of habit and daily use. And then he goes on to ask : "Quis hodie nudum caput radiis solis, aut omnia perurenti frigori, ausit exponere ?—Who is it that now-a-days would dare to expose his uncovered head to the solar beams, or to the all-scorching and withering frost ?" Who is it ? dost thou ask, Isaac ? why, pretty nearly everybody ; and, amongst others, we ourselves that are writing this book. Yes, we and our illustrious friend, Christopher North, did for three-and-twenty years walk amongst our British lakes and mountains hatless, and amidst both snow and rain, such as Romans did not often experience. We were naked, but were not ashamed. Nor in this are we altogether singular. But, says Casaubon, the Romans went farther ; for they walked about the streets of Rome bareheaded,[1] and never assumed a hat or a cap, a *petasus* or a *galerus*, a Macedonian *causia*, or a *pileus*, whether Thessalian, Arcadian, or Laconic, unless when they entered upon a journey. Nay, some there were, as Massinissa and Julius Cæsar, who declined even on such an occasion to cover their heads. Perhaps in imitation of these celebrated leaders it might be that Hadrian adopted the same practice, but not with the same result ; for to him, either from age or constitution, this very custom proved the original occasion of his last illness.

Imitation, indeed, was a general principle of action with Hadrian, and the key to much of his public conduct ; and allowably enough, considering the exemplary lives (in a public sense) of some who had preceded him, and the singular anxiety with which he distinguished between the lights and shadows of their examples. He imitated the great Dictator, Julius, in his vigilance of inspection into the civil, not less than the martial police of his times, shaping his new regulations to meet abuses as they arose, and strenuously maintaining the old ones in vigorous operation. As respected the Army, this was matter of peculiar praise, because peculiarly disinterested ; for his foreign policy was pacific[2] ; he made no new conquests ; and he retired from

---

[1] And hence we may the better estimate the trial to a Roman's feelings in the personal deformity of baldness, connected with the Roman theory of its cause ; for the exposure of it was perpetual.

[2] "Expeditiones sub eo," says Spartian, "graves nullæ fuerunt.

the old ones of Trajan, where they could not have been maintained without disproportionate bloodshed, or a jealousy beyond the value of the stake. In this point of his administration he took Augustus for his model; as again in his care of the Army, in his occasional bounties, and in his paternal solicitude for their comforts, he looked rather to the example of Julius. Him also he imitated in his affability and in his ambitious courtesies; one instance of which, as blending an artifice of political subtlety and simulation with a remarkable exertion of memory, it may be well to mention. The custom was, in canvassing the citizens of Rome, that the candidate should address every voter by his name; it being a fiction of republican etiquette that every man participating in the political privileges of the State, every man who prided himself on possessing the *jus suffragii*, must be personally known to public aspirants. But, as this was impossible, in any literal sense, to men with the ordinary endowments of memory, in order to reconcile the pretensions of republican hauteur with the necessities of human weakness, a custom had grown up of relying upon a class of men, called *nomenclators*, whose express business and profession it was to make themselves acquainted with the person and name of each individual citizen. One of these people accompanied every candidate, and quietly whispered into his ear the name of each voter as he came in sight. Few, indeed, were they who could dispense with the services of such an assessor; for the office imposed a twofold memory, that of names and of persons; and, to estimate the immensity of the effort, we must recollect that the number of voters often far exceeded one quarter of a million. Hadrian, however, relied upon his own unprompted powers for the discharge of this duty. The very same trial of memory he undertook with respect to his own army,—in this instance recalling the well-known feat, or pretended feat, of Mithridates. And throughout his life he did not once forget the face or name of any veteran soldier whom he had ever occasion to notice, no matter under what remote climate, or under what difference of circumstances. Wonderful is the effect upon soldiers

Bella etiam silentio pene transacta." But he does not the less add, " A militibus, propter curam exercitus nimiam, multum amatus est."

of such enduring and separate remembrance ; which operates always as the most touching kind of personal flattery, and which, in every age of the world since the social sensibilities of men have been much developed, military commanders are found to have played upon as the most effectual chord in the great system which they modulated · some few by a rare endowment of nature . others, as Napoleon Bonaparte, by elaborate mimicries of pantomimic art [1]

Other modes he had of winning affection from the Army ; in particular that, so often practised before and since, of accommodating himself to the strictest ritual of martial discipline and castrensian life.   He slept in the open air ; or, if he used a tent (papilio), it was open at the sides.   He ate the ordinary rations of cheese, bacon, &c. ; he used no other drink than that composition of vinegar and water, known by the name of *posca*, which formed the sole beverage allowed through a thousand years in the Roman camps.   He joined personally in the periodical exercises of the army—those even which were trying to the most vigorous youth and health : marching, for example, on stated occasions, twenty English miles without intermission, in full armour and completely accoutred.   Luxury of every kind he not only interdicted to the soldier by severe ordinances, himself enforcing their execution, but discountenanced it (though elsewhere splendid and even gorgeous in his personal habits) by his own continual example.   In dress, for instance, he sternly banished the purple and gold embroideries, the jewelled arms, and the floating draperies, so little in accordance with the severe character of "*war in procinct*."[2] Hardly would he

---

[1] In the true spirit of Parisian mummery, Bonaparte caused letters to be written from the War Office, in his own name, to particular soldiers of high military reputation in every brigade (whose private history he had previously caused to be investigated), alluding circumstantially to the leading facts in their personal or family career. A furlough accompanied this letter ; and they were requested to repair to Paris, where the Emperor anxiously desired to see them Thus was the paternal interest expressed which their leader took in each man's fortunes ; and the effect of every such letter, it was not doubted, would diffuse itself through ten thousand other men.

[2] " *War in procinct* " :—A phrase of Milton's in *Paradise Regained* which strikingly illustrates his love of Latin phraseology ; for, unless to a scholar, previously acquainted with the Latin phrase of *in pro-*

allow himself an ivory hilt to his sabre. The same severe proscription he extended to every sort of furniture, or decorations of art, which sheltered even in the bosom of camps those habits of effeminate luxury—so apt in all great empires to steal by imperceptible steps from the voluptuous palace to the soldier's tent—following in the equipage of great leading officers, or of subalterns highly connected. There was at that time a practice prevailing, in the great standing camps on the several frontiers, and at all the military stations, of renewing as much as possible the image of distant Rome by the erection of long colonnades and piazzas —single, double, or triple; of crypts, or subterranean saloons[1] (and sometimes subterranean galleries and corridors), for evading the sultry noontides of July and August; of verdant cloisters or arcades, with roofs high over-arched, constructed entirely out of flexile shrubs, box, myrtle, and others, trained and trimmed in regular forms; besides endless other applications of the *topiary* art,[2] which in those days (like the needlework of Miss Linwood[3] in our

cinctu, it is so absolutely unintelligible as to interrupt the current of the feeling.

[1] "*Crypts*":—These, which Spartian, in his life of Hadrian, denominates simply *cryptæ*, are the same which, in the Roman jurisprudence, and in the architectural works of the Romans yet surviving, are termed *hypogææ deambulationes*, *i.e.* subterranean parades. Vitruvius treats of this luxurious class of apartments in connexion with the *Apothecæ*, and other repositories or store-rooms, which were also in many cases under ground, for the same reason as our ice-houses, wine-cellars, &c. He (and from him Pliny and Apollinaris Sidonius) calls them *crypto-porticus* (cloistral colonnades); and Ulpian calls them *refugia* (sanctuaries, or places of refuge). St. Ambrose notices them, under the name of *hypogæa* and *umbrosa penetralia*, as the resorts of voluptuaries: *Luxuriosorum est*, says he, *hypogæa quærere captantium frigus æstivum;* and again he speaks of *desidiosi qui ignava sub terris agant otia.*

[2] "*The topiary art*":—So called, as Salmasius thinks, from τοπ-ηίον, *a rope;* because the process of construction was conducted chiefly by means of cords and strings. This art was much practised in the 17th century; and Casaubon describes one which existed in his early days, somewhere in the suburbs of Paris, on so elaborate a scale that it represented Troy besieged, with the two hosts, their several leaders, and all other objects in their full proportion.

[3] "*Miss Linwood*":—Alas! *Fuit Ilium;* and it has actually become necessary, in a generation that knew not Joseph, that we should

own), though no more than a mechanic craft, in some measure realized the effects of a fine art by the perfect skill of its execution.   All these modes of luxury, with a policy that had the more merit as it thwarted his own private inclinations, did Hadrian peremptorily abolish ; perhaps, amongst other more obvious purposes, seeking to intercept the earliest buddings of those local attachments which are as injurious to the martial character (for the soldier's vocation obliges him to consider himself eternally under marching orders) as they are propitious to all the best interests of society in connexion with the feelings of civic life.

We dwell upon this prince not without reason in connexion with this particular distinction, *i.e.* the discipline of the Army.   This, which since the period of Augustus had been drooping through the neglect of preceding Emperors, Hadrian by personal efforts re-established ; for, amongst the Cæsars, Hadrian stands forward in high relief as a reformer of the Army.   Well and truly it might be said of him that *post Cæsarem Octavianum labantem disciplinam incuriâ superiorum principum ipse retinuit.*   Not content with the cleansings and purgations we have mentioned, he placed upon a new footing the whole tenure, duties, and pledges, of military offices.[1]   It cannot much surprise us that this department of the public service should gradually have gone to ruin or decay.   Under the Senate and People,—under the auspices of those awful symbols (letters more significant and ominous than ever before had troubled the eyes of man, except upon Belshazzar's wall) " S. P. Q. R.,"—the officers of the Roman army had been kept true to their duties by

tell the reader who was Miss Linwood.   For many a long year between 1800 and perhaps 1835 or 1840, she had in Leicester Square, London, a most gorgeous exhibition of needlework—arras that by its exquisite effects rivalled the works of the mighty painters.

[1] Very remarkable it is, and a fact which speaks volumes as to the democratic constitution of the Roman Army, in the midst of that aristocracy which enveloped its parent state in a civil sense, that, although there was a name for a *common soldier* (or *sentinel*, as he was termed by our ancestors)—viz. *miles gregarius*, or *miles manipularis* —there was none for an *officer :* that is to say, each several rank of officers had a name ; but there was no generalization to express the idea of an officer abstracted from its several species or classes : a fact almost incredible !

emulation and a healthy ambition. But, when the ripeness of corruption had, by dissolving the body of the State, brought out of its ashes a new mode of life, and had recast the Aristocratic Republic, by aid of its democratic elements then suddenly victorious, into a pure Autocracy, whatever might be the advantages in other respects of this great change, in one point it had certainly injured the public service, by throwing the higher military appointments, all in fact which conferred any authority, into the channels of court favour, and by consequence into a mercenary disposal. Each successive Emperor had been too anxious for his own immediate security to find leisure for the remoter interests of the Empire ; the *Imperium* was lost sight of in the *Imperator ;* all looked to the Army, as it were, for their own immediate security against competitors, without venturing to tamper with its constitution, to risk popularity by reforming abuses, to balance present interest against a remote one, or to cultivate the public welfare at the hazard of their own : contented with obtaining this last, they left the internal arrangements of so formidable a body in that condition to which circumstances had brought it, and to which naturally the views of all existing beneficiaries had gradually adjusted themselves. What these might be, and to what further results they might tend, was a matter of moment doubtless to the Empire. But the Empire was strong ; if its motive energy for going ahead was decaying, its *vis inertiæ* for resistance was for ages enormous : whilst the Emperor was always in the beginning of his authority weak, and pledged by instant interest, no less than by express promises, to the support of that body whose favour had substantially supported himself. Hadrian was the first who turned his· attention effectually in the counter direction : whether it were that he first was struck with the tendency of the abuses, or that he valued the hazard less which he incurred in correcting them, or that, having no successor of his own blood, he had a less personal and affecting interest at stake in setting this hazard at defiance. Hitherto, the highest regimental rank, that of tribune, had been disposed of in two ways,—either civilly upon popular favour and election, or upon the express recommendation of the soldiery. This custom had prevailed under the Republic, and the force of habit had availed to propagate that practice under a new mode of government. But now were introduced new regulations: the tribune (or colonel commandant) was selected for his military qualities and experience : none was appointed to this important office " *nisi barbâ plenâ.*" The centurion's truncheon (his *vitis* or vine-tree cane or cudgel with which he cudgelled the five or six hundred men under his command [1]), again, was given to no man " *nisi robusto et bonæ famæ.*" The arms and military appointments (*supellectilis*) were revised ; the register of names was duly called over ; and none suffered to remain in the camps who was either above or below the military age. The same vigilance and jealousy were extended to the great stationary stores and repositories of biscuit, vinegar, and other equipments for the soldiery. All things were in constant readiness in the capital and the provinces, in the garrisons and camps, abroad and at home, to meet the outbreak of a foreign war or a domestic sedition. Whatever were the service, it could by no possibility find Hadrian unprepared. And he first, in fact, of all the Cæsars, restored to its ancient Republican standard, as reformed and perfected by Marius, the old martial discipline of the Scipios and the Paulli— that discipline to which, more than to any physical superiority of her soldiery, Rome had been indebted for her conquest of the earth, and which had inevitably decayed in the long series of wars growing out of personal ambition. From the days of Marius, every great leader had sacrificed to the necessities of courting favour from the troops as much as was possible of the hardships incident to actual service, and as

---

[1] *Vitis* : and it deserves to be mentioned that this staff, or cudgel, which was the official engine and cognizance of the centurion's dignity, was meant expressly to be used in caning or cudgelling the inferior soldiers : "*propterea* vitis in manum data," says Salmasius, " *verberando scilicet militi qui deliquisset*"—"For that very reason a vine-tree cane or wand was furnished to the head, viz. for the purpose of cudgelling any soldier trespassing." We are no patrons of corporal chastisement ; which, on the contrary, as the vilest of degradations to all nobility of feeling, we abominate more vehemently, as the Homeric Achilles says of lying, than the gates of hell. The soldier who does not feel himself dishonoured by it is already dishonoured beyond hope or redemption. But still let this degradation not be mendaciously imputed to the English Army exclusively.

much as he dared of the once rigorous discipline. Hadrian first found himself in circumstances, or was the first who had courage enough, to decline a momentary interest in favour of a greater in reversion, and a personal object which was but transient in exchange for a State one that was continually revolving.

For a prince with no children of his own it is in any case a task of peculiar delicacy to select a successor. In the Roman Empire the difficulties were much aggravated. The interests of the State were, in the first place, to be consulted ; for a mighty burthen of responsibility rested upon the Emperor in the most personal sense. Duties of every kind fell to his station which, from the peculiar constitution of the government, and from circumstances rooted in the very origin of the imperatorial office, could not be devolved upon a council. Council there was none that could be recognised as such in the State machinery. The Emperor, himself a sacred and sequestered creature, might be supposed to enjoy the secret tutelage of the Supreme Deity ; but a Council, composed of subordinate and responsible agents, could *not*. Again, the auspices of the Emperor, and his edicts, apart even from any celestial or supernatural inspiration, simply as emanations of his own consecrated character, had a value and a sanctity which could never belong to those of a Council, or to those even which had been sullied by the breath of any less august reviser. The Emperor, therefore, or (as with a view to his solitary and unique character we ought to call him), in the original irrepresentable term, the Imperator, could not delegate his duties, or execute them in any avowed form by proxies or representatives. He was himself the great fountain of law, of honour, of preferment, of civil and political regulations. He was the fountain also of good and evil fame. He was the great chancellor, or supreme dispenser of equity to all climates, nations, and languages of his mighty dominions ; which connected the turbaned races of the Orient, and those who sat in the gates of the rising sun, with the islands of the West and the unfathomed depths of the mysterious Scandinavia. He was the universal guardian of the public and private interests which composed the great edifice of the social system as then existing amongst his subjects. Above all, and out of his own private purse, he supported the heraldries of his dominions—the peerage, Senatorial or Prætorian, and the great gentry or chivalry of the Equites. These were classes who would have been dishonoured by the censorship of a less august comptroller. And, for the classes below these, by how much they were lower and more remote from his ocular superintendence, by so much the more were they linked to him in a connexion of absolute dependence. Cæsar it was who provided their daily food, Cæsar who provided their pleasures and relaxations. He chartered the fleets which brought grain to the Tiber; he bespoke the Sardinian granaries whilst yet unformed, and the harvests of the Nile whilst yet unsown. Not the connexion between a mother and her unborn infant is more intimate and vital than that which subsisted between the mighty populace of the Roman capital and their paternal Emperor. They drew their nutriment from him; they lived and were happy by sympathy with the motions of his will; to him also the arts, the knowledge, and the literature of the Empire looked for support, and stood frozen like ice-bound rivers until Cæsar's hand had indicated the channels in which they should flow. To him the armies looked for their laurels, and the eagles in every clime turned their aspiring eyes, waiting to bend their flight according to the signal of his Jovian nod. And all these vast functions and ministrations arose partly as a natural effect, but partly also they were a cause of the Emperor's own divinity. He was capable of services so exalted because he also, even whilst yet on earth, was held a god, and had his own altars, his own incense, his own worship, and his separate priests. Such was the cause, and such was the result, of his bearing on his own shoulders a burthen so mighty and Atlantean.

Yet, if in this view it was needful to have a man of talent, on the other hand there was reason to dread a man of talents too adventurous, too aspiring, or too intriguing. His situation, not as Augustus, but as Cæsar or Crown Prince after the title of Cæsar had come to denote the secondary office, flung into his hands a power of fomenting conspiracies, and of concealing them until the very moment of explosion, which made him an object of almost exclusive terror to his principal, the Cæsar Augustus. His situation, again, as an heir voluntarily adopted made him the proper object of public affection and caresses, which became peculiarly embarrassing to one who had, perhaps, soon found reasons for suspecting, fearing, and hating him beyond all other men.

The young nobleman whom Hadrian adopted by his earliest choice was Lucius Aurelius Verus, the son of Ceionius Commodus. These names were borne also by the son ; but, after his adoption into the Ælian family, he was generally known by the appellation of Ælius Verus. The scandal of those times imputed his adoption to the worst motives. "*Adriano,*" says one author, ("*ut malevoli loquunter*), *acceptior formâ quam moribus.*" And thus much undoubtedly there is to countenance so shocking an insinuation that very little is recorded of the young prince but such anecdotes as illustrate his excessive luxury and effeminate dedication to pleasure. Still, it is our private opinion that Hadrian's real motives have been misrepresented ; that he sought in the young man's extraordinary beauty—for he was, says Spartian, *pulchritudinis regiæ*—a plausible pretext that should be sufficient to explain and to countenance his preference, whilst under this provisional adoption he was enabled to postpone the definitive choice of an imperator elect until his own more advanced age might diminish the motives for intriguing against himself. It was, therefore, a mere *ad interim* adoption ; for it is certain, however we may choose to explain the fact, that Hadrian foresaw and calculated on the early death of Ælius. This prophetic knowledge may have been grounded on a private familiarity with some constitutional infirmity affecting his daily health, or with some habits of life incompatible with longevity, or with both combined. It is pretended that this distinguished mark of favour was conferred in fulfilment of a direct contract on the Emperor's part, as the price of favours such as the Latin reader will easily understand from the strong expression of Spartian above cited. But it is far more probable that Hadrian relied on this admirable beauty, and allowed it so much weight, as being for the multitude the most intelligible explanation of his choice, and for the nobility the least invidious solution of a preference which raised one of their own number so far above the level of his natural peers. The necessities of the moment were thus satisfied without present or future danger ;—as respected the future, he knew or believed that Verus was marked out for early death, and would often say, in a strain of compliment somewhat disproportionate, applying to him the Virgilian lines on the hopeful and lamented Marcellus,

> "Ostendent terris hunc tantum fata, neque ultra
>   Esse sinent."

And, at the same time, to countenance the belief that he had been disappointed, he would affect to sigh, exclaiming— "Ah ! that I should thus fruitlessly have squandered a sum of three millions sterling [1] !" for so much had been distributed in largesses to the people and the army on the occasion of his inauguration. Meantime, as respected the present, the qualities of the young man were amply fitted to sustain a Roman popularity : for, in addition to his extreme and statuesque beauty of person, already, as a military officer, he had a respectable character [2] ; as an orator he was more than respectable ; and in other qualifications that might be less interesting to the populace he had that happy mediocrity of merit which was best fitted for his delicate and difficult situation,—sufficient to do credit to the Emperor's preference, sufficient to sustain the popular regard, but not brilliant enough to throw his patron into the shade. For the rest, his vices were of a nature not greatly or necessarily to interfere with his public duties, and emphatically such as met with the readiest indulgence from the Roman laxity of morals. Some few instances, indeed, are noticed of cruelty ; but there is reason to think that it was merely by accident, and as an indirect result of other purposes, that he ever allowed him-

---

[1] In the original *ter millies*, which is not much above two millions and one hundred and fifty thousand pounds sterling ; but it must be remembered that one-third as much, in addition to this popular largess, had been given to the Army.

[2] —— "Nam bene gestis rebus, vel potius feliciter, etsi non summi, medii tamen obtinuit ducis famam "—"For by the able, or rather by the fortunate, conduct of affairs, he won the reputation—though not of a supreme—yet of a tolerable or second-class strategist."

self in such manifestations of irresponsible power—not as gratifying any harsh impulses of his native character. The most remarkable neglect of humanity with which he has been taxed occurred in the treatment of his couriers. These were the bearers of news and official despatches, at that time fulfilling the functions of the modern post ; and it must be borne in mind that as yet they were not slaves (as afterwards by the reformation of Alexander Severus), but free citizens. They had been already dressed in a particular livery or uniform, and possibly they might wear some symbolical badges of their profession ; but the new Cæsar chose to dress them altogether in character as winged Cupids, affixing literal wings to their shoulders, and facetiously distinguishing them by the names of the cardinal winds (Boreas, Notus, &c.), and others as levanters or hurricanes (Circius, &c.) Thus far he did no more than indulge a blameless fancy, and such, in fact, as our own solemn Admiralty indulge allowably in christening their little saucy gun-boats—for instance, the Spitfire, the Boxer, the Blazer, the Vixen [1] ; but in his anxiety that his runners should emulate their patron winds, and do credit to the names which he had assigned them, he is said to have exacted a degree of speed inconsistent with any merciful regard for their bodily powers.[2] But these were, after all, perhaps, mere improvements of malice upon some solitary incident. The true stain upon his memory, and one which is open to no doubt whatever, is excessive and extravagant luxury—excessive in degree, extravagant and even ludicrous in its forms. For example, he constructed a sort of

[1] And, as it is not absolutely impossible that we may see Mr. Roebuck a Lord of the Admiralty, in that case we shall, of course, have a *Tear'em.*—See his famous speech on Cherbourg, &c.

[2] This, however, is a point in which royal personages claim an old prescriptive right to be unreasonable in their exactions ; and some even amongst the most humane of Christian princes have erred as flagrantly as Ælius Verus. George IV, we have understood, was generally escorted from Dalkeith to Holyrood at a rate of twenty-two miles an hour. And of his father, the truly kind and paternal king, it is recorded by Miss Hawkins (daughter of Sir J. Hawkins, the biographer of Johnson, &c.) that families who happened to have a son, brother, lover, &c., in the particular regiment of cavalry which furnished the escort to Windsor for the day used to suffer as much anxiety for the result as on the eve of a great battle.

bed or sofa, protected from insects by an awning of network composed of lilies, delicately fabricated into the proper meshes, &c., and the couches composed wholly of rose-leaves, but even of these not without an exquisite preparation ; for the white parts of the leaves, as coarser and harsher to the touch (possibly, also, as less odorous), were scrupulously rejected. Here he lay indolently stretched amongst favourite ladies,

> "And like a naked Indian slept himself away."

He had also tables composed of the same delicate material—prepared and purified in the same elaborate way ; and to these were adapted seats in the fashion of sofas (*accubationes*), corresponding in their material, and in their mode of preparation. He was also an expert performer, and even an original inventor, in the art of cookery ; and one dish of his discovery, which, from its four component parts, obtained the name of *tetrapharmacum*, was so far from owing its celebrity to its royal birth that it maintained its place on Hadrian's table to the time of his death. These, however, were mere fopperies or pardonable extravagancies in one so young and so exalted, traits not becoming to the state character with which he had been clothed, yet still noways tending to public mischief ; "quæ, etsi non decora," as the historian observes, "non tamen ad perniciem publicam prompta sunt." A graver mode of licentiousness appeared in his connexions with women. He made no secret of his lawless amours ; and to his own wife, on her expostulating with him on his aberrations in this respect, he replied that "*wife*" was a designation of rank and official dignity, not of tenderness and affection, or implying any claim of love on either side ; upon which distinction he begged that she would mind her own affairs, and leave him to pursue such as he might himself be involved in by his sensibility to female charms.

However, he and all his errors, his "regal beauty," his princely pomps, and his authorized hopes, were suddenly swallowed up by the inexorable grave ; and he would have passed away like an exhalation, and leaving no remembrance of himself more durable than his own beds of rose-leaves

and his reticulated canopies of lilies, had it not been that
Hadrian filled the world with images of his perfect fawn-
like beauty in the shape of colossal statues, and raised
temples even to his memory in various cities. This Cæsar,
therefore, dying thus prematurely, never tasted of empire ;
and his name would have had but a doubtful title to a place
in the imperatorial roll, had it not been recalled to a second
chance for the sacred honours in the person of his son—
whom it was the pleasure of Hadrian, by way of testifying
his affection for the father, to associate in the order of
succession with the philosophic Marcus Aurelius Antoninus.
This fact, and the certainty that to the second Ælius Verus
he gave his own daughter in marriage, rather than to his
associate Cæsar Marcus Aurelius, make it evident that his
regret for the elder Verus was unaffected and deep ; and
they overthrow effectually the common report of historians,
that he repented of his earliest choice, as of one that had
been disappointed not by the decrees of fate, but by the
violent defect of merits in its object. On the contrary, he
prefaced his inauguration of this junior Cæsar by the following tender words : " Let us confound the rapine of the grave,
and let the Empire possess amongst her rulers a second
Ælius Verus. Rise again, therefore, departed Ælius, incarnation of heavenly beauty ; rise a second time for the homage
of Rome and of her subject Earth ! "

"*Diis aliter visum est*" : the blood of the Ælian family
was not privileged to ascend or aspire : it gravitated violently
to extinction ; and this junior Verus is supposed to have
been as much indebted to his assessor on the throne for
shielding his obscure vices, and drawing over his defects the
ample draperies of the imperatorial robe, as he was to Hadrian,
his grandfather by fiction of law, for his adoption into the
reigning family, and his consecration as one of the Cæsars.
He, says one historian, shed no ray of light or illustration
upon the imperial house, except by one solitary quality.
This bears a harsh sound : but it has the effect of a sudden
redemption for his memory when we learn that this solitary
quality, in virtue of which he claimed a natural affinity to
the sacred house, and challenged a natural interest in the
purple, was the very princely one of a merciful disposition.

The two Antonines fix an era in the Imperial History ; for they were both eminent models of wise and good rulers : and some would say that they fixed a crisis ; for with their successor commenced, in the popular belief, the decline of the Empire.   That at least is the doctrine of Gibbon ; but perhaps it would not be found altogether able to sustain itself against a closer and philosophic examination of the true elements involved in the idea of declension as applied to political bodies.   Be that as it may, however, and waiving any interest which might happen to invest the Antonines as the last princes who kept up the Empire to its original level, both of them had enough of merit to challenge a separate notice in their personal characters, and apart from the accidents of their great official station.

The elder of the two, who is usually distinguished by the title of *Pius*, is thus described by one of his biographers : " He was externally of remarkable beauty ; eminent for his " moral character, full of benign dispositions, noble, with " a countenance of a most gentle expression, intellectually of " singularendowments, possessing an elegant style of eloquence, " distinguished for his literature, generally temperate, an " earnest lover of agricultural pursuits, mild in his deport- " ment, bountiful in the use of his own, but a stern respecter " of the rights of others ; and, finally, he was all this without " ostentation, and with a constant regard to the proportions " of cases, and to the demands of time and place."   His bounty displayed itself in a way which may be worth mentioning, as at once illustrating the age, and the prudence with which he controlled the most generous of his impulses : " *Fœnus trientarium*,"[1] says the historian, " *hoc et minimis usuris exercuit, ut patrimonio suo plurimos adjuvaret.*"   The meaning of which is this :—In Rome the customary interest for money was technically called *centesimæ usuræ* ; that is, the hundredth part, or one per cent.   But, as this expressed not the annual, but the *monthly*, interest, the true rate was, in fact, twelve per cent ; and that is the meaning of *centesimæ*

---

[1] " He practised a mode of usury at the very lowest rates, viz. under a discount of two-thirds from the ordinary terms, so as that, from his own private patrimonial funds, he might thus relieve the greatest number possible of clients."

usuræ. Nor could money be obtained anywhere on better terms than these ; and, moreover, this one per cent was exacted rigorously as the monthly day came round, no arrears being suffered to lie over. Under these circumstances, it was a prodigious service to lend money at a diminished rate, and one which furnished many men with the means of saving themselves from ruin. Pius, then, by way of extending his aid as far as possible, reduced the monthly rate of his loans to one-third per cent, which made the annual interest the very moderate one of four per cent. The channels which public spirit had as yet opened to the beneficence of the opulent were few indeed ; charity and munificence languished, or they were abused, or they were inefficiently directed, simply through defects in the structure of society. Social organization, for its large development, demanded the agency of newspapers (together with many other forms of assistance from the press), of banks, of public carriages on an extensive scale, besides infinite other inventions or establishments not yet created—which support and powerfully react upon that same progress of society which originally gave birth to themselves. All things considered, in the Rome of that day, where the utmost munificence confined itself to direct largesses of a few leading viands or condiments, a great step was taken, and the best step, in this lending of money at a low interest, towards a more refined and beneficial mode of charity.

In his public character, he was perhaps the most patriotic of Roman Emperors, and the purest from all taint of corrupt or indirect ends. Peculation, embezzlement, or misapplication of the public funds, were universally corrected ; provincial oppressors were exposed and defeated : the taxes and tributes were diminished ; and the public expenses were thrown as much as possible upon the public estates, and in some instances upon private estates. So far, indeed, did Pius stretch his sympathy with the poorer classes of his subjects that on this account chiefly he resided permanently in the capital , alleging in excuse partly that he thus stationed himself in the very centre of his mighty empire, to which all couriers could come by the shortest radii, but chiefly that he thus spared the provincialists those burthens which must else have alighted upon them : "For," said he, "even the slenderest retinue of a Roman Emperor is burthensome to the whole line of its progress."   His tenderness and consideration, indeed, were extended to all classes, and all relations of his subjects, even to those who stood within the shadow of his public displeasure as State delinquents, or as the most atrocious criminals.   To the children of great treasury defaulters he returned the confiscated estates of their fathers, deducting only what might indemnify the exchequer. And so resolutely did he refuse to shed the blood of any in the senatorial order, to whom he conceived himself more especially bound in paternal ties, that even a parricide, whom the laws would not suffer to live, was simply exposed upon a desert island.

Little indeed did Pius want of being a perfect Christian in heart and in practice.   Yet all this display of goodness and merciful indulgence,—nay, all his munificence,—would have availed him little with the people at large, had he neglected to furnish on the arena shows and exhibitions of suitable magnificence.   Luckily for his reputation, he exceeded the general standard of imperial splendour not less as the patron of the amphitheatre than as the benign *Pater Patriæ*. It is recorded of him that in one *missio* he sent forward on the arena a hundred lions.   Nor was he less distinguished by the rarity of the wild animals which he exhibited than by their number.   There were elephants, there were crocodiles, there were hippopotami, at one time upon the stage : there was also the rhinoceros, and the still rarer *crocuta* or *corocotta*, with a few *strepsikerotes*.   Some of these were matched in duels, some in general battles with tigers ; in fact, there was no species of wild animal throughout the deserts and sandy Zaarras of Africa, the infinite *steppes* of Asia, or the lawny recesses and dim forests of then sylvan Europe,[1]—no species known to natural history (and some even of which naturalists

[1] And not impossibly of America ; for it must be remembered that, when we speak of America as a quarter of the earth yet unknown, we mean unknown to ourselves of the western climates ; since, as respects the eastern quarters of Asia, doubtless America was known there familiarly enough before Christ, or even before Romulus ; and the high bounties of imperial Rome on rare animals would sometimes perhaps propagate their influence even to those regions.

have lost sight),—which the Emperor Pius did not produce to his Roman subjects on his ceremonious pomps. And in another point he carried his splendours to a point which set the seal to his liberality. In the phrase of modern auctioneers, he gave up the wild beasts to slaughter "without reserve." It was the custom, in ordinary cases, so far to consider the enormous cost of these far-fetched rarities as to preserve for future occasions those which escaped the arrows of the populace, or survived the bloody combats in which they were engaged. Thus, out of the overflowings of one great exhibition, would be found materials for another. But Pius would not allow of these reservations. All were given up unreservedly to the savage purposes of the spectators; land and sea were ransacked; the sanctuaries of the torrid zone were violated; columns of the army were put in motion: and all for the transient effect of crowning an extra hour with hecatombs of forest blood, each separate minute of which hour had cost a king's ransom.

Yet these displays were alien to the nature of Pius; and even through the tyranny of custom he had been so little changed that to the last he continued to turn aside, as often as the public ritual of his duty allowed him, from these fierce spectacles to the gentler amusements of fishing and hunting. His taste and his affections naturally carried him to all domestic pleasures of a quiet nature. A walk in a shrubbery or along a piazza, enlivened with the conversation of a literary friend, pleased him better than all the court festivals; and among festivals, or anniversary celebrations, he preferred those which, like the harvest-home or like the feast of the vintagers, whilst they sanctioned a total carelessness and dismissal of public anxieties, were at the same time coloured by the innocent gaiety which belongs to rural and to patriarchal manners.

In person this Emperor was tall and dignified (*statura elevata decorus*); but latterly he stooped; to remedy which defect, that he might discharge his public part with the more decorum, he wore stays.[1] Of his other personal habits

---

[1] In default of whalebone, one is curious to know of what these stays were made: thin tablets of the linden-tree, it appears, were the best materials which the Augustus of that day could command.

little is recorded, except that, early in the morning, and just before receiving the compliments of his friends and dependants (*salutatores*), or what in modern phrase would be called his *levée*, he ate a little plain bread (*panem siccum comedit*),—that is, bread without condiments or accompaniments of any kind, —by way of breakfast.   In no meal has rational luxury improved more upon the model of the ancients than in this : the dinners (*cœnæ*) of the Romans were even more luxurious, and a thousand times more costly, than our own ; but their breakfasts were scandalously meagre, and with many men breakfast was no acknowledged meal at all.   Galen tells us that a little bread, and at most a little seasoning of oil, honey, or dried fruits, was the utmost breakfast which men generally allowed themselves : some indeed drank wine after it, but this was an unusual practice.[1]

The Emperor Pius died in his seventieth year.   The immediate occasion of his death was—not breakfast nor *cœna*, but something of the kind.   He had received a present of Alpine cheese, and he ordered some for supper.   The trap for his life was baited with toasted cheese.   There is no reason to think that he ate immoderately ; but that night he was seized with indigestion.   Delirium followed ; during which it is singular that his mind teemed with a class of imagery and of passions the most remote (as it might have been thought) from the voluntary occupations of his thoughts. He raved about the State, and about those Kings with whom he was displeased; nor were his thoughts one moment removed from the public service.   Yet he was the least ambitious of princes, and his reign was emphatically said to be bloodless. Finding his fever increase, he became sensible that he was dying ; and he ordered the golden statue of Prosperity, a household symbol of Empire, to be transferred from his own bedroom to that of his successor.   Once, again, however, for

---

[1] There is, however, a good deal of delusion prevalent on such subjects.   In some English cavalry regiments, the custom is [1825] for the privates to take only one meal a day, which of course is dinner ; and by some curious experiments it has appeared that such a mode of life is the healthiest.   But, at the same time, we have ascertained that the quantity of porter or substantial ale drunk in these regiments does virtually allow several meals by comparison with the washy tea breakfasts of most Englishmen.

the last time, he gave the word to the officer of the guard ; and, soon after, turning away his face to the wall against which his bed was placed, he passed out of life in the very gentlest sleep : *" quasi dormiret, spiritum reddidit "* ; or, as a Greek author expresses it, κατ᾽ ἰσὸν ὕπνῳ τῷ μαλακωτάτῳ, showing an exact conformity in all respects to sleep the very gentlest. He was one of those few Roman Emperors whom posterity truly honoured with the title of ἀναίμακτος (or bloodless): *solusque omnium propè principum prorsus sine civili sanguine et hostili vixit.* In the whole tenor of his life and character he was thought to resemble Numa. And Pausanias, after remarking on his title of Εὐσεβής (or Pius), —upon the meaning and origin of which there are several different hypotheses, — closes with this memorable tribute to his paternal qualities : δοξῇ δὲ ἐμῇ καὶ τὸ ὄνομα τὸ τοῦ Κύρου φέροιτο ἀν τοῦ πρεσβυτέρου, Πατὴρ ᾽Ανθρώπων καλουμενος : *but, in my opinion, he should also bear the designation of Cyrus the Elder, being hailed as the Father of the Human Race.*

A thoughtful Roman would have been apt to exclaim *This is too good to last* upon finding so admirable a ruler succeeded by one still more admirable, in the person of Marcus Aurelius. From the first dawn of his infancy this prince indicated, by his grave deportment, the philosophic character of his mind ; and at eleven years of age he professed himself a formal devotee of philosophy in its strictest form,—assuming the garb, and submitting to its most ascetic ordinances. In particular, he slept upon the ground, and in other respects he practised a style of living the most simple and remote from the habits of rich men (or, in his own words, τὸ λιτὸν κατὰ τὴν δίαιταν, καὶ πόρρω τῆς πλουσιακῆς ἀγωγῆς : the simple as regards diet, and far removed from the training of opulence) ; though it is true that he himself ascribes this simplicity of life to the influence of his mother, and not to the premature assumption of the stoical character. He pushed his austerities indeed to excess ; for Dio mentions that in his boyish days he was reduced to great weakness by exercises too severe and a diet of too little nutriment. In fact, his whole heart was set upon philosophic attainments, and perhaps upon philosophic glory. All the great philosophers of his own time, whether Stoic or Peripatetic, and amongst them Sextus of Cheronæa, a nephew of Plutarch, were retained as his instructors. There was none whom he did not enrich; and as many as were fitted by birth and manners to fill important situations he raised to the highest offices in the State.[1] Philosophy, however, did not so much absorb his affections but that he found time to cultivate the fine arts (painting he both studied and practised) and such gymnastic exercises as he held consistent with his public dignity. Wrestling, hunting, fowling, playing at cricket (*pila*), he admired and patronized by personal participation. He tried his powers even as a runner. But, with these tasks, and entering critically, both as a connoisseur and as a practising amateur, into such trials of skill, so little did he relish the very same spectacles when connected with the cruel exhibitions of the circus and amphitheatre that it was not without some friendly violence on the part of those who could venture on such a liberty, nor even thus perhaps without the coercion of his official station, that he would be persuaded to visit either one or the other.[2] In this he

[1] We should all have been much indebted to the philosophic Emperor had he found it convenient to tell us with what result to the public interests, as also to the despatch of business. Napoleon made La Place a Secretary of State, but had reason to rue his appointment. Our own Addison suffered a kind of locked jaw in dictating despatches as Foreign Secretary. And about a hundred years earlier Lord Bacon played " H— and Tommy " when casually raised to the supreme seat in the Council by the brief absence in Edinburgh of the King and the Duke of Buckingham [in 1617, when King James revisited Scotland, after he had been fourteen years King of England.—M.]

[2] So much improvement had Christianity already accomplished in the feelings of men since the time of Augustus. That prince, in whose reign the Founder of this ennobling religion was born, had delighted so much and indulged so freely in the spectacles of the amphitheatre that Mecænas summoned him reproachfully to leave them by saying, " Surge tandem, carnifex ": " Rise, headsman ; rise, hangman, at last."—It is the remark of Capitoline [respecting Marcus Aurelius] that " gladiatoria spectacula omnifariam temperavit ; temperavit etiam scenicas donationes " ; — " he controlled in every possible way the gladiatorial spectacles ; he controlled also the rates of allowance to the stage performers." In these latter reforms, which simply restrained the exorbitant salaries of a class dedicated to the public pleasures, and unprofitable to the state, Marcus may have had no further view than that which is usually connected with sumptuary

meditated no reflection upon his father by adoption, the Emperor Pius (who also, for aught we know, might secretly revolt from a species of amusement which, as the prescriptive test of munificence in the popular estimate, he found it unavoidable to support): on the contrary, he obeyed him with the punctiliousness of a Roman obedience ; he watched the very motions of his countenance ; and he waited so continually upon his pleasure that, for three-and-twenty years

laws. But in the restraints upon the gladiators it is not impossible to believe that his highest purpose was that of elevating human nature, and preparing the way for still higher regulations. As little can it be believed that this lofty conception, and the sense of a degradation entailed upon human nature itself in the spectacle of human beings matched against each other like brute beasts, and pouring out their blood upon the arena as a libation to the caprices of a mob, could have been derived from any other source than the contagion of Christian standards and Christian sentiments, then beginning to pervade and ventilate the atmosphere of society in its higher and philosophic regions. Christianity, without expressly affirming, everywhere indirectly supposes and presumes the infinite value and dignity of man as a creature exclusively concerned in a vast and mysterious economy of restoration to a state of moral beauty and power in some former age mysteriously forfeited. Equally interested in its benefits, joint-heirs of its promises, all men, of every colour, language, and rank, Gentile or Jew, were here first represented as in one sense (and that the most important) equal ; in the eye of this religion, they were by necessity of logic equal, as equal participators in the ruin, equal in the restoration. Here first, in any available sense, was communicated to the standard of human nature a vast and sudden elevation ; and reasonable enough it is to suppose that some obscure sense of this, some sympathy with the great changes for man then beginning to operate, would first of all reach the inquisitive students of philosophy, and chiefly those in high stations who cultivated an intercourse with all the men of original genius throughout the civilized world. The Emperor Hadrian had taken one solitary step (already noticed) in the elevation of human nature, and not, we may believe, without some sub-conscious influence received directly or indirectly from Christianity. So again, with respect to Marcus, it is hardly conceivable that he, a prince so indulgent and popular, could have thwarted, and violently gainsaid, a passionate taste of the Roman populace without some adequate motive ; and none *could* be adequate which was not built upon some new and exalted views of human nature with which these gladiatorial sacrifices were altogether at war. The reforms which Marcus introduced into these "crudelissima spectacula," all having the common purpose of limiting their extent, were three. First, he set bounds to the extreme cost of these exhibitions : no man was any longer at liberty to lavish an *unlimited* sum upon the amphitheatre ; and this which they lived together, he is recorded to have slept out of his father's palace only for two nights. This rigour of filial duty illustrates a feature of Roman life ; for such was the sanctity of law that a father created by legal fiction was in all respects treated with the same veneration and affection as a father who claimed upon the most unquestioned footing of natural right. Such, however, is the universal baseness of courts that even this scrupulous and minute attention to

restriction of the cost covertly operated as a restriction of the practice. The limitation operated as a withdrawal of State *Bounties*, as refrigerations of enthusiasm, as curbs upon aristocratic rivalships. Secondly (and this ordinance took effect whenever he was personally present, if not oftener), he commanded, on great occasions, that these displays should be bloodless. Dion Cassius notices this fact in the following words :—"The Emperor Marcus was so far from taking "delight in spectacles of bloodshed that even the gladiators in Rome "could not obtain his inspection of their contests, unless, like the "wrestlers, they contended without imminent risk ; for he never "allowed them the use of sharpened weapons, but universally they "fought before him with weapons previously blunted" (or perhaps *buttoned*, fibulated, as in the case of our own *foils*). Thirdly, he repealed the old and uniform regulation which secured to the gladiators a perpetual immunity from military service. This necessarily diminished their available amount. Being now liable to serve their country usefully in the field of battle, whilst the concurrent limitation of the expenses in this direction prevented any commensurate increase of their numbers, they were so much the less disposable in aid of the public luxury. Thus, by the drains of the military service, when turning round to look for adequate supplementary accessions from abroad, they found the requisite supplies cut off by the action of the new sumptuary law. *Habet!* ejaculated the neutral philosophic looker-on, simply regarding the gladiatorial interest.[1] His fatherly care of all classes, and the universal benignity with which he attempted to raise the abject estimate and condition of even the lowest *pariahs* in his vast empire, appear in another little anecdote, relating to a class of men equally with the gladiators given up to the service of luxury in a haughty and cruel populace. Attending one day at an exhibition of rope-dancing, one of the performers (a boy) fell and hurt himself ; from which time the Paternal Emperor would never allow the rope-dancers to perform without mattresses or feather-beds spread below to mitigate the violence of their falls.

---

1 "*Habet*" :—He has it, he has got it—*i e.* has got his death-warrant,—was the cruel ejaculation of triumph from the Roman mob of spectators whenever a poor gladiator was (or seemed to be) reached by some mortal blow. The selfsame yell of triumph we are supposing to have ascended from the miso-gladiatorial party on witnessing the unparried blow of the philosophic Emperor

his duties did not protect Marcus from the injurious insinuations of whisperers. There were not wanting persons who endeavoured to turn to account the general circumstances in the situation of the Cæsar which pointed him out to the jealousy of the Emperor. But these, being no more than what adhere necessarily to the case of every heir *as* such, and meeting fortunately with as little of encouragement in the unsuspicious nature of the father as they did of countenance in the habitual conduct of the son, prospered so ill that, from pure defect of all natural root on either side, the very attempts of court malice died away.

The most interesting political crisis in the reign of Marcus was the war in Germany with the Marcomanni, concurrently with pestilence in Rome. The agitation of the public mind was intense ; and prophets arose, as since under corresponding circumstances in Christian countries, who announced the approaching dissolution of the world. The purse of Marcus was open, as usual, to the distresses of his subjects. But it was chiefly for the expense of funerals that his aid was claimed. In this way he alleviated the domestic calamities of his capital, or expressed his sympathy with the sufferers where alleviation was beyond his power ; whilst, by the energy of his movements and his personal presence on the Danube, he soon dissipated those anxieties of Rome which pointed in a foreign direction. The war, however, had been a dreadful one ; and it had excited such just fears in the most experienced heads of the State that, happening in its outbreak to coincide with a Parthian attack, it was skilfully protracted until the entire thunders of Rome, and the undivided energies of her supreme captains, could be concentrated upon this single point. Both Emperors [1] left Rome, and crossed the Alps ; the war was thrown back upon its native seats—Austria and the modern Hungary : great battles were fought and won ; and peace, with consequent relief and restoration to liberty, was reconquered for many friendly nations who had suffered under the ravages of the Marcomanni, the Sarmatians, the Quadi, and the Vandals ; whilst

[1] Marcus had been associated, as Cæsar and as Emperor, with the son of the late beautiful Verus, who is usually mentioned by the same name.

some of the hostile peoples were nearly obliterated from the map, and their names blotted out from the memory of men.

Since the days of Gaul as an independent power, no war had so much alarmed the people of Rome ; and their fear was justified by the difficulties and prodigious efforts which accompanied its suppression. The public treasury was exhausted ; loans were an engine of fiscal policy not then understood or perhaps practicable ; and great distress was at hand for the State. In these circumstances, Marcus adopted a wise (though it was then esteemed a violent or desperate) remedy. Time and excessive luxury had accumulated in the imperial palaces and villas vast repositories of apparel, furniture, jewels, pictures, and household utensils, valuable alike for the materials and the workmanship. Many of these articles were consecrated, by colour [1] or otherwise, to the use of the *sacred* household ; and to have been found in possession of them, or with the materials for making them, would have entailed the penalties of treason. All these stores were now brought out to open day, and put up to public sale by auction, — free license being first granted to the bidders, whoever they might be, to use, and otherwise to exercise the fullest rights of ownership upon all they bought. The auction lasted for two months. Every man was guaranteed in the peaceable possession of his purchases. And afterwards, when the public distress had passed over, a still further indulgence was extended to the purchasers. Notice was given that all who were dissatisfied with their purchases, or who for other reasons might wish to recover their cost, would receive back the purchase-money upon returning the

---

[1] "*By colour*" :—It must be remembered that the true *purple* (about which the controversy has been endless, and is yet unsettled : possibly it was our *crimson*, though this seems properly expressed by the word *puniceus ;* possibly it was our common *violet ;* but, of whatever tint, this colour of purple) was interdicted to the Roman people, and consecrated to the sole personal use of the imperatorial house. Recollecting the early "taboo" in this point amongst the children of Romulus, and that thus far it had not been suspended under the two gentlest and most philosophic princes of the *divina domus,* we feel that some injustice has perhaps been done to Dioclesian in representing *him* as the importer of oriental degradations.

articles. Dinner-services of gold and crystal, murrhine vases,[1] and even his wife's wardrobe of silken robes interwoven with gold, — all these, and countless other articles, were under this offer returned, and the full auction prices paid back ; or were *not* returned, and no displeasure shown to those who publicly displayed them as their own. Having gone so far, overruled by the necessities of the public service, in breaking down those legal barriers by which a peculiar dress, furniture, equipage, &c., were appropriated to the imperial house, as distinguished from the very highest of the noble houses, Marcus had a sufficient pretext for extending indefinitely the effect of the dispensation then granted. Articles purchased at the auction bore no characteristic marks to distinguish them from others of the same form and texture : so that a licence to use any one article of the *sacred* pattern became necessarily a general licence for all others which resembled them. And thus, without abrogating the prejudices which protected the imperial precedency, a body of sumptuary laws—the most ruinous to the progress of manufacturing skill which has ever been devised [2]—were silently suspended. One or two aspiring families might be offended by these innovations, which meantime gave the pleasures of enjoyment to thousands, and of hope to millions.

But these, though very noticeable relaxations of the exist-

---

[1] "*Murrhine vases*":—What might these Pagan articles be ? Unlearned reader, if any such is amongst the flock of our audience, the question you ask has been asked by four or five centuries that have fleeted away, and hitherto has had no answer. They were not porcelain from China , they could not be Venetian glass, into which, when poison was poured, suddenly the venom fermented, bubbled, boiled, and finally shivered the glass into fragments (so at least saith the pretty fable of our ancestors) ; this it *could* not be : why ? Because Venice herself did not arise until two and a half centuries after Marcus Aurelius. They were, however, like diaphanous china, but did not break on falling. The Japanese still possess a sort of porcelain much superior to any now produced in China. And, by Chinese confession, a far superior order of porcelain was long ago manufactured in China itself, of which the art is now wholly lost. Perhaps the murrhine vase might belong to this forgotten class of *vertu.*

[2] Because the most effectual extinguishers of all ambition applied in that direction ; since the very excellence of any particular fabric was the surest pledge of its virtual suppression by means of its legal restriction (which followed inevitably) to the use of the imperial house.

ing prerogative, were, as respected the temper which dictated them, no more than everyday manifestations of the Emperor's perpetual benignity. Fortunately for Marcus, the indestructible privilege of the *divina domus* exalted it so unapproachably beyond all competition that no possible remissions of aulic rigour could ever be misinterpreted ; fear there could be none lest such paternal indulgences should lose their effect and acceptation as pure condescensions. They could neither injure their author, who was otherwise charmed and consecrated from disrespect ; nor could they suffer injury themselves by misconstruction, or seem other than sincere, coming from a prince whose entire life was one long series of acts expressing the same affable spirit. Such, indeed, was the effect of this uninterrupted benevolence in the Emperor that at length all men, according to their several years, hailed him as their father, son, or brother. And, when he died, in the sixty-first year of his life (the eighteenth of his reign), he was lamented with a corresponding peculiarity in the public ceremonial,— such, for instance, as the studied interfusion of the senatorial body with the populace, expressive of the levelling power of a true and comprehensive grief ; a peculiarity for which no precedent was found, and which never afterwards became itself a precedent for similar honours to the best of his successors.

But malice has the divine privilege of ubiquity ; and therefore it was that even this great model of private and public virtue did not escape the foulest libels. He was twice accused of murder : once on the person of a gladiator with whom the Empress is said to have intrigued ; and, again, upon his associate in the empire, who died in reality of an apoplectic seizure on his return from the German campaign. Neither of these atrocious fictions ever gained the least hold of the public attention, so entirely were they put down by the *primâ facie* evidence of facts, and of the Emperor's notorious character. In fact, his faults, if he had any in his public life, were entirely those of too much indulgence. In a few cases of enormous guilt it is recorded that he showed himself inexorable. But, generally speaking, he was far otherwise ; and, in particular, he carried his indulgence to his wife's vices so far beyond the allowance of prudence or public decorum as to draw upon himself the satirical notice of the stage.

The gladiators, and still more the sailors of that age, were constantly to be seen plying naked ; and Faustina was shameless enough to take her station in places which gave her the advantages of a leisurely review, and she actually selected favourites from both classes on the ground of a personal inspection.   With others of greater rank she is said even to have been surprised by her husband ; in particular with one called Tertullus, at dinner.[1]   But to all remonstrances on this subject Marcus is reported to have replied "*Si uxorem dimittimus, reddamus et dotem*"; meaning that, having received his right of succession to the Empire simply by his adoption into the family of Pius, his wife's father, gratitude and filial duty obliged him to view any dishonours emanating from his wife's conduct as joint legacies with the splendours inherited from their common father ; in short, that he was not at liberty to separate the rose from its thorns.   Faustina had, in fact, brought him the empire as her bridal dowry ; and, according to the notorious law of divorce in Rome, the repudiated wife carried back all that she had brought.   However, the facts are not sufficiently known to warrant us in criticising very severely his behaviour on so trying an occasion.   It would be too much for human frailty that absolutely no stain should remain upon his memory.   The reflection upon this story by one of his biographers is this—"Such is " the force of daily life in a good ruler, so great the power of " his sanctity, gentleness, and piety, that no breath of slander " or invidious suggestion from an acquaintance can avail to " sully his memory.   In short, to Antonine, immutable as " the heavens in the tenor of his own life, and in the mani- " festations of his own moral temper, and who was not by " possibility liable to any impulse or movement of change on " any alien suggestion, it was not eventually an injury that " he was dishonoured by some of his connexions ; on him, " invulnerable in his own character, neither a harlot for his " wife, nor a gladiator for his son, could inflict a wound.

[1] Upon which some *mimographus* built an occasional notice of the scandal then floating on the public breath in the following terms : One of the actors having asked " *Who was the adulterous paramour ?* " receives for answer, " *Tullus.* "   " Who ? " he asks again ; and again for three times running he is answered, " *Tullus.* "   But, asking a fourth time, the rejoinder is, " Jam dixi *ter Tullus* (*i.e.* Tertullus).

" Then as now, O sacred Lord Dioclesian ! he was reputed a
" god ; not as others are reputed, but specially and in a
" separate sense, and with a privilege to such worship from
" all men as is addressed to his memory by yourself, who
" often breathe a wish to heaven that you were or could be
" such in life and merciful disposition as was Marcus Aurelius."

What this encomiast says in a rhetorical tone was literally
true.   Marcus was raised to divine honours, or canonized [1]
(as in Christian phrase we might express it).   That was a
matter of course for a Cæsar ; and, considering with whom
he shared such honours, they are of little account in expressing the grief and veneration which followed him.   A circumstance more characteristic in the record of those observances
which attested the public feeling is this ;—that he who at
that time had no bust, picture, or statue of Marcus in his
house, was looked upon as a profane and irreligious man.
Finally, to do him honour not by testimonies of men's opinions
in his favour, but by facts of his own life and conduct, one
memorable trophy there is amongst the moral distinctions of
the philosophic Cæsar, utterly unnoticed hitherto by historians,
but which will hereafter obtain a conspicuous place in any
perfect record of the steps by which civilisation has advanced
and human nature has been exalted.   It is this : Marcus
Aurelius was the first great military leader (and his civil
office as supreme interpreter and creator of law consecrated
his example) who allowed rights indefeasible, rights uncan-
celled by his misfortune in the field, to the prisoner of war.
Others had been merciful and variously indulgent, upon their
own discretion, and upon a random impulse to some, or
possibly to all of their prisoners ; but this was either in
submission to the usage of that particular war, or to special self-
interest, or at most to individual good feeling.   None had
allowed a prisoner to challenge any forbearance as of right.

---

[1] In reality, if by *divus* and *divine honours* we understand a saint
or spiritualized being having a right of intercession with the Supreme
Deity,—and by his temple, &c., if we understand a shrine attended by
a priest to direct the prayers of his devotees,—there is no such wide
chasm between this pagan superstition and the adoration of saints in
the Romish Church as at first sight appears.   The fault is purely in
the names : *divus* and *templum* are words too undistinguishing and
generic.

But Marcus Aurelius first resolutely maintained that certain indestructible rights adhered to every soldier, simply as a man ; which rights capture by the sword, or any other accident of war, could do nothing to shake or to diminish. We have noticed other instances in which Marcus Aurelius laboured, at the risk of his popularity, to elevate the condition of human nature. But those, though equally expressing the goodness and loftiness of his nature, were by accident directed to a perishable institution, which time has swept away, and along with it therefore his reformations. Here, however, is an immortal act of goodness built upon an immortal basis : so long as armies congregate, and the sword is the arbiter of international quarrels, so long it will deserve to be had in remembrance that the first man who set limits to the empire of wrong, and first translated within the jurisdiction of man's moral nature that state of war which had heretofore been consigned, by principle no less than by practice, to anarchy, animal violence, and brute force, was also the first philosopher who sat upon a throne.

In this, and in his universal spirit of forgiveness, we cannot but acknowledge a Christian by anticipation ; nor can we hesitate to believe that, through one or other of his many philosophic friends,[1] whose attention Christianity was by that

---

[1] Not long after this, Alexander Severus meditated a temple to Christ ; upon which design Lampridius observes,—*Quod et Hadrianus cogitâsse fertur ;* and, as Lampridius was himself a pagan, we believe him to have been right in his report, in spite of all which has been written by Casaubon and others, who maintain that these imperfect temples of Hadrian were left void of all images or idols,—not in respect to the Christian practice, but because he designed them eventually to be dedicated to himself. However, be this as it may, thus much appears on the face of the story,—that Christ and Christianity had by that time begun to challenge the imperial attention ; and of this there is an indirect indication, as it has been interpreted, even in the memoir of Marcus himself. The passage is this : "Fama fuit sanè quod sub philosophorum specie quidam rempublicam vexarent et privatos." The *philosophi* here mentioned by Capitoline are by some supposed to be the Christians ; and for many reasons we believe it ; and we understand the molestations of the public services and of private individuals, here charged upon them, as a very natural reference to the Christian doctrines falsely understood. There is, by the way, a fine remark upon Christianity, made by an infidel philosopher of Germany, which suggests a remarkable feature in the merits of Marcus Aurelius. There were, as this German philosopher used to observe, two schemes of thinking amongst the ancients, which severally fulfilled the two functions of a

time powerful to attract, some reflex images of Christian doctrines—some half-conscious perception of its perfect beauty —had flashed upon his mind.   And, when we view him from this distant age, as heading that shining array, the Howards and the Clarksons, who have since then in a practical sense hearkened to the sighs of "all prisoners and captives," we are ready to suppose him addressed by the great Founder of Christianity in the words of Scripture, "*Verily, I say unto thee, Thou art not far from the kingdom of heaven.*"

As a supplement to the reign of Marcus Aurelius, we ought to notice the rise of one great rebel, the sole civil disturber of his time, in Syria.   This was Avidius Cassius, whose descent from Cassius (the noted conspirator against the Dictator Julius) seems to have suggested to him a wandering idea, and at length a formal purpose, of restoring the ancient

sound philosophy, as respected the moral nature of man.   One of these schemes presented us with a just ideal of moral excellence, a standard sufficiently exalted : this was the Stoic philosophy ; and thus far its pretensions were unexceptionable and perfect.   But, unfortunately, whilst contemplating this pure ideal of man as he ought to be, the Stoic totally forgot the frail nature of man as he is ; and, by refusing all compromises and all condescensions to human infirmity, this philosophy of the Porch presented to us a brilliant prize and object for our efforts, but placed on an inaccessible height.   On the other hand, there was a very different philosophy at the very antagonist pole,—not binding itself by abstractions too elevated, submitting to what it finds, bending to the absolute facts and realities of man's nature, and affably adapting itself to human imperfections.   This was the philosophy of Epicurus ; and, undoubtedly, as a beginning, and for the elementary purpose of conciliating the affections of the pupil, it was well devised : but here the misfortune was that the ideal or *maximum perfectionis* attainable by human nature was pitched so low that the humility of its condescensions and the excellence of its means were all to no purpose, as leading to nothing further.   One mode presented a splendid end, but insulated, and with no means fitted to a human aspirant for communicating with its splendours ; the other, an excellent road, but leading to no worthy or proportionate end.   Yet these, as regarded models, were the best and ultimate achievements of the Pagan World. Now, Christianity, said he, is the synthesis of whatever is separately excellent in either.   It will abate as little as the haughtiest Stoicism of the ideal which it contemplates as the first postulate of true morality ; the absolute holiness and purity which it demands are as much raised above the poor performances of actual man as the absolute wisdom and impeccability of the Stoic.   Yet, unlike the Stoic scheme, Christianity is aware of the necessity, and provides for it, that the means of appro-

Republic.   Avidius was the commander-in-chief of the Oriental army, whose head-quarters were then fixed at Antioch.   His native disposition, which inclined him to cruelty, and his political views, made him, from his first entrance upon office, a severe disciplinarian.   The well-known enormities of the neighbouring Daphne gave him ample opportunities for the exercise of his harsh propensities in reforming the dissolute soldiery.   He amputated heads, arms, feet, and hands : he turned out his mutilated victims, as walking spectacles of warning ; he burned them ; he smoked them to death ; and, in one instance, he crucified a detachment of his army, together with their centurions, for having, unauthorized, gained a decisive victory, and captured a large booty on the Danube.   Upon this the soldiers mutinied against him, in mere indignation at his tyranny.

priating this ideal perfection should be such as are consistent with the nature of a most erring and imperfect creature.   Its motion is *towards* the divine, but *by* and *through* the human.   In fact, it offers the Stoic humanized in his scheme of means, and the Epicurean exalted in his final objects.   Nor is it possible to conceive a practicable scheme of morals which should not rest upon such a synthesis of the two elements as the Christian scheme presents : a mighty ideal ; nor any other mode of fulfilling that demand than such a one as is there first brought forward, viz. a double or Janus nature, which stands in an equivocal relation,—to the Divine nature by his actual perfections, to the human nature by his participation in the same animal frailties and capacities of fleshly temptation.   No other vinculum could bind the two postulates together, of an absolute perfection in the end proposed, and yet of utter imperfection in the means for attaining it.   Such was the outline of this famous tribute by an unbelieving philosopher to the merits of Christianity as a scheme of moral discipline.   Now, it must be remembered that Marcus Aurelius was by profession a Stoic, and that generally, as a theoretical philosopher, but still more as a Stoic philosopher, he might be supposed incapable of descending from these airy altitudes of speculation to the true needs, infirmities, and capacities of human nature.   Yet strange it is that he, of all the good Emperors, was the most thoroughly human and practical.   In evidence of which, one body of records is amply sufficient,—which is the very extensive and wise reforms which he, beyond all the Cæsars, executed in the existing laws.   To all the exigencies of the times, and to all the new necessities developed by the progress of society, he adjusted the old laws, or supplied new ones.   The same praise, therefore, belongs to him which the German philosopher conceded to Christianity, of reconciling the austerest ideal with the practical ; and hence another argument for presuming him half baptized into the new faith.

However, he prosecuted his purpose, and prevailed, by his bold contempt of the danger which menaced him. From the abuses in the Army, he proceeded to attack the abuses of the Civil Administration. But, as these were protected by the example of the great proconsular lieutenants and provincial governors, policy obliged him to confine himself to verbal expressions of anger ; until at length, sensible that this impotent railing did but expose him to contempt, he resolved to arm himself with the powers of radical reform by open rebellion. His ultimate purpose was the restoration of the ancient Republic, or (as he himself expresses it in an interesting letter, which yet survives) "*ut in antiquum statum publica forma reddatur*,"—*i.e.* that the constitution should be restored to its original condition. And this must be effected by military violence and the aid of the executioner, or, in his own words, *multis gladiis, multis elogiis* [1] (by innumerable sabres, by innumerable records of condemnation). Against this man Marcus was warned by his imperial colleague Lucius Verus, in a very remarkable letter. After expressing his suspicions of him generally, the writer goes on to say—"I " would you had him closely watched. For he is a general " disliker of us and of our doings ; he is gathering together " an enormous treasure, and he makes an open jest of our " literary pursuits. You, for instance, he calls a philosophiz- " ing old woman, and me a dissolute buffoon and scamp. " Consider what you would have done. For my part, I bear " the fellow no ill-will ; but again I say, Take care that he " does not do a mischief to yourself or your children."

The answer of Marcus is noble and characteristic : " I " have read your letter, and I will confess to you I think it " more scrupulously timid than becomes an Emperor, and " timid in a way unsuited to the spirit of our times. Con- " sider this : if the Empire is destined to Cassius by the " decrees of Providence, in that case it will not be in our " power to put him to death, however much we may " desire to do so. You know your great-grandfather's " saying, 'No prince ever killed his own heir' ; no man, " that is, ever yet prevailed against one whom Providence

[1] "*Elogiis*" :—The elogium was the public record or *titulus* of a malefactor's crime inscribed upon his cross or scaffold.

" had marked out as his successor. On the other hand, if
" Providence opposes him, then, without any cruelty on our
" part, he will spontaneously fall into some snare spread for
" him by destiny. Besides, we cannot treat a man as under
" impeachment whom nobody impeaches, and whom, by your
" own confession, the soldiers love. Then again, in cases of
" high treason, even those criminals who are convicted upon
" the clearest evidence, yet, as friendless and deserted per-
" sons contending against the powerful, and matched against
" men armed with the whole authority of the State, seem to
" suffer some wrong. You remember what your grandfather
" said—'Wretched, indeed, is the fate of princes, who then
" first obtain credit in any charges of conspiracy which they
" allege, when they happen to seal the validity of their
" charges against the plotters by falling martyrs to the plot.'
" Domitian it was, in fact, who first uttered this truth ; but
" I choose rather to place it under the authority of Hadrian,
" because the sayings of tyrants, even when they are true
" and happy, carry less weight with them than naturally
" they ought. For Cassius, then, let him keep his present
" temper and inclinations ; and the more so, being (as he is)
" a good general, austere in his discipline, brave, and one
" whom the State cannot afford to lose. For, as to what
" you insinuate, that I ought to provide for my children's
" interests by putting this man judicially out of the way,
" very frankly I say to you — 'Perish my children, if
" Avidius shall deserve more attachment than they, and
" if it shall prove salutary to the State that Cassius should
" triumph rather than the children of Marcus should sur-
" vive.' "

This letter affords a singular illustration of fatalism, such
certainly as we might expect in a Stoic, but carried even to
a Turkish excess ; and not theoretically professed only, but
practically acted upon in a case of capital hazard. *That no
prince ever killed his own successor,*—*i.e.* that it was vain for
a prince to put conspirators to death, because, by the very
possibility of doing so, a demonstration is obtained that such
conspirators had never been destined to prosper,—is as
pungent an expression of fatalism as ever has been devised.
The rest of the letter, where not imbecile, is noble, and

breathes the very soul of careless magnanimity reposing upon conscious innocence.

Meantime, Cassius increased in power and influence : his army had become a most formidable engine of his ambition through its restored discipline ; and his own authority was sevenfold greater because he had himself created that discipline in the face of unequalled temptations hourly renewed and rooted in the very centre of his head - quarters. " Daphne, by Orontes," a suburb of Antioch, was infamous for its seductions ; and *Daphnic luxury* had become proverbial for expressing an excess of voluptuousness, such as other places could not rival, by mere defect of means and preparations elaborate enough to sustain it in all its varieties of mode, or to conceal it from public notice. In the very purlieus of this great nest, or sty of sensuality, within sight and touch of its pollutions, did he keep his army fiercely reined up, daring and defying them, as it were, to taste of the banquet whose very odour they inhaled.

Thus provided with the means, and improved instruments for executing his purpose, he broke out into open rebellion ; and, though hostile to the *principatus*, or personal supremacy of one man, he did not feel his republican purism at all wounded by the style and title of *Imperator*,—that being a military term, and a mere titular honour, which had co-existed with the severest forms of Republicanism. *Imperator*, then, he was saluted and proclaimed ; and doubtless the writer of the warning letter from Syria would now declare that the sequel had justified the fears which Marcus had thought so unbecoming to a Roman Emperor. But again Marcus would have said, " Let us wait for the sequel of the sequel " ; and that would have justified him. It is often found by experience that men who have learned to reverence a person in authority chiefly by his offices of correction applied to their own aberrations—who have known and feared him, in short, in his character of reformer—will be more than usually inclined to desert him on his first movement in the direction of wrong. Their obedience being founded on fear, and fear being never wholly disconnected from hatred, they naturally seize with eagerness upon the first lawful pretext for disobedience ; the luxury of revenge is, in such a case, too potent—a meritorious disobedience too novel a temptation—to have a chance of being rejected. Never, indeed, does erring human nature look more abject than in the person of a severe exactor of duty, who has immolated thousands to the wrath of offended law, suddenly himself becoming a capital offender, a glózing tempter in search of accomplices, and in that character at once standing before the meanest of his own dependants as a self-deposed officer, liable to any man's arrest. The stern and haughty Cassius, who had so often tightened the cords of discipline until they threatened to snap asunder, now found, experimentally, the bitterness of these obvious truths. The trembling sentinel now looked insolently in his face; the cowering legionary, with whom "to hear was to obey," now mused or even bandied words upon his orders; the great lieutenants of his office, who stood next to his own person in authority, were preparing for revolt, open or secret, as circumstances should prescribe; not the accuser only, but the very avenger, was upon his steps; Nemesis, that Nemesis who once so closely adhered to the name and fortunes of the lawful Cæsar, turning against every one of his assassins[1] the edge of his own assassinating sword, was already at his heels; and, in the midst of a sudden prosperity and its accompanying shouts of gratulation, he heard the sullen knells of approaching death. Antioch, it was true, the great Roman capital of the Orient, bore him, for certain motives of self-interest, peculiar good-will. But there was no city of the world in which the Roman Cæsar did not reckon many liege-men and partisans. And the very hands which dressed his altars and crowned his Prætorian pavilion might not improbably in that same hour put an edge upon the sabre which was to avenge the injuries of the too indulgent and long-suffering Antoninus. Meantime, to give a colour of patriotism to his treason, Cassius alleged public motives. In a letter which he wrote after assuming the purple, he says: "Wretched Empire, "miserable state, which endures these hungry blood-suckers "battening on her vitals!—A worthy man, doubtless, is

---

[1] "*Turning against every one of his assassins*":—It was a general belief at the time that each individual among the murderers of Cæsar had died by his own sword.

" Marcus ; who, in his eagerness to be reputed clement,
" suffers those to live whose conduct he himself abhors.
" Where is that L. Cassius whose name I vainly inherit?
" Where is that Marcus—not Aurelius, mark you, but Cato
" Censorius ? Where the good old discipline of ancestral
" times, long since indeed disused, but now not so much as
" yearned for in our aspirations? Marcus Antoninus is a
" scholar; he enacts the philosopher; and he tries conclu-
" sions upon the four elements, and upon the nature of the
" soul; and he discourses learnedly upon the *Honestum;*
" and concerning the *Summum Bonum* he is unanswerable.
" Meanwhile, is he learned in the interests of the State?
" Can he argue a point upon the public economy? You see
" what a host of sabres is required, what a host of impeach-
" ments, sentences, executions, before the Commonwealth
" can reassume its ancient integrity![1] What! shall I
" esteem as proconsuls, as governors, those who for that end
" only deem themselves invested with lieutenancies or great
" senatorial appointments, that they may gorge themselves
" with the provincial luxuries and wealth? No doubt, you
" heard in what way our friend the philosopher gave the
" place of prætorian prefect to one who but three days
" before was a bankrupt—insolvent, by G— ! and a beggar.
" But be you content : that same gentleman is now as rich as
" a prefect should be ; and has been so, I tell you, any time
" these three days. And how, I pray you, how ; how, my
" good sir ? How but out of the bowels of the provinces,
" and the marrow of their bones ? But no matter : let them
" be rich ; let them be blood-suckers ; so much, God willing !
" shall they regorge into the treasury of the Empire. Let
" but Heaven smile upon our party, and the Cassiani shall
" restore to the Republic its old impersonal supremacy."

But Heaven did *not* smile; nor did man. Rome heard
with bitter indignation of this old traitor's ingratitude, and
his false mask of republican civism. Excepting Marcus
Aurelius himself, not one man but thirsted for revenge.
And that was soon obtained. He and all his supporters,
one after the other, rapidly fell (as Marcus had predicted)
into snares laid by the officers who continued true to their

---

[1] In these words we hear the very spirit of Robespierre.

allegiance. Except the family and household of Cassius, there remained in a short time none for the vengeance of the Senate, or for the mercy of the Emperor. In *them* centred the last arrears of hope and fear, of chastisement or pardon, depending upon this memorable revolt. And about the disposal of their persons arose the final question to which the case gave birth. The letters yet remain in which the several parties interested gave utterance to the passions which possessed them. Faustina, the Empress, urged her husband with feminine violence to adopt against his prisoners comprehensive acts of vengeance. "Noli parcere hominibus," says she, "qui tibi non pepercerunt ; et nec mihi nec filiis nostris parcerent[1] si vicissent." And elsewhere she irritates his wrath against the Army as accomplices for the time, and as a body of men "qui, nisi opprimuntur, opprimunt." We may be sure of the result. After commending her zeal for her own family, he says, " Ego vero et ejus liberis parcam, et genero, et uxori ; et ad senatum scribam ne aut proscriptio gravior sit aut poena crudelior" ; adding that, had his counsels prevailed, not even Cassius himself should have perished. As to his relatives, " Why," he asks, " should I speak of pardon to them, who indeed have done no wrong, and are blameless even in purpose ?" Accordingly, his letter of intercession to the Senate protests that, so far from asking for further victims to the crime of Avidius Cassius, would to God he could call back from the dead many of those who had fallen ! With immense applause, and with turbulent acclamations, the Senate granted all his requests " in consideration of his philosophy, of his long-suffering, of his learning and accomplishments, of his nobility, of his innocence." And, until a monster arose who delighted in the blood of the guiltless, it is recorded that the posterity of Avidius Cassius lived in security, and were admitted to honours and public distinctions by favour of him whose life and empire that memorable traitor had sought to undermine under the favour of his guileless master's too confiding magnanimity.

[1] " *Parcerent* " :—She means *pepercissent.* " Don't," she says, " show mercy to men that showed none to you, nor would have shown any to me or my sons in case they had gained the victory."

CHAPTER V

FROM COMMODUS TO PHILIP THE ARAB[1]

(A.D. 180—A.D. 249)

THE Roman Empire and the Roman Emperors, it might naturally be supposed by one who had not as yet traversed that tremendous chapter in the history of man, would be likely to present a separate and almost equal interest. The Empire, in the first place, as the most magnificent monument of human power which our planet has beheld, must for that single reason, even though its records were otherwise of little interest, fix upon itself the very keenest gaze from all succeeding ages to the end of time. To trace the fortunes and revolutions of that unrivalled monarchy over which the Roman eagle brooded ; to follow the dilapidations of that aërial arch which silently and steadily through seven centuries ascended under the colossal architecture of the children of Romulus ; to watch the collapse of the Cyclopean masonry, and step by step to see paralysis stealing over the once perfect cohesion of the republican creations : cannot but insure a severe, though melancholy delight. On its own separate account, the decline of this throne-shattering power must and will engage the foremost place amongst all historical reviews. The "dislimning" and unmoulding of some mighty pageantry in the heavens has its own appropriate grandeurs, no less than the gathering of its cloudy pomps. The going down of the sun is contemplated with no less awe than his rising. Nor is anything portentous in its growth

---

[1] In *Blackwood* for July 1834.

which is not also portentous in the steps and "moments" of its decay. Hence, in the second place, we might presume a commensurate interest in the characters and fortunes of the successive Emperors. If the Empire challenged our first survey, the next would seem due to the Cæsars who guided its course,—to the great ones who retarded, and to the bad ones who precipitated, its ruin.

Such might be the natural expectation of an inexperienced reader. But it is *not* so. The Cæsars, throughout their long line, are not interesting; neither personally in themselves, nor derivatively from the tragic events to which their history is attached. Their whole interest lies in their situation—in the unapproachable altitude of their thrones. But, considered with a reference to their human qualities, scarcely one in the whole series, except the first, can be viewed with a human interest apart from the circumstances of his position. "Come like shadows, so depart!" The reason for this defect of all personal variety of interest in these enormous potentates must be sought in the constitution of their power and the very necessities of their office. Even the greatest among them, those who by way of distinction were called *the Great*, as Constantine and Theodosius, were *not* great, for they were not magnanimous; nor could they be so under *their* tenure of power, which made it a duty to be suspicious, and, by fastening on all varieties of original temper one dire necessity of bloodshed, extinguished under this monotonous cloud of cruel jealousy and everlasting panic every characteristic feature of genial human nature that would else have emerged through so long a train of princes. There is a remarkable story told of Agrippina, that, upon some occasion, when a wizard announced to her, as truths which he had read in the heavens, the two fatal necessities impending over her son,—one that he should ascend to empire, the other that he should murder herself,—she replied in these stern and memorable words :—*Occidat dum imperet ;* let him murder me, provided he rises to empire. Upon which a continental writer comments thus :—" Never before or since " have three such words issued from the lips of woman ; " and in truth, one knows not which most to abominate or " to admire—the aspiring princess or the loving mother.

" Meantime, in these few words lies naked to the day, in its
" whole hideous deformity, the very essence of Romanism
" and the Imperatorial Power, and one might here consider
" the mother of Nero as the impersonation of that monstrous
" condition."

This is true : *Occidat dum imperet* was the watchword and
very cognisance of the Roman Imperator.   But almost
equally it was his watchword—*Occidatur dum imperet*.   Doing
or suffering, the Cæsars were almost equally involved in
bloodshed ; few indeed of the Cæsars were not murderers,
and nearly all were themselves murdered.

The Empire, then, must be regarded as the primary
object of our interest, and it is in this way only that any
secondary interest arises for the Emperors.   Now, with respect to the Empire, the first question which presents itself
is—Whence, that is from what causes and from what era,
are we to date its decline ?   Gibbon, as we all know, dates
it from the reign of Commodus, the son of that merciful
Marcus Aurelius Antoninus whom we have just quitted,—
but certainly upon no sufficient or even plausible grounds.
Our own opinion we shall state boldly : the Empire itself,
from the very era of its establishment, was one long decline
of the Roman Power.   A vast monarchy had been created
and consolidated by the all-conquering instincts of a Republic cradled and nursed in wars, and essentially warlike
by means of all its institutions[1] and by the habits of the

---

[1] Amongst these institutions none appear to us so remarkable, or
fitted to accomplish so prodigious a circle of purposes belonging to the
highest state policy, as the Roman method of COLONISATION.   Colonies were, in effect, the great engine of Roman conquest ; and the
following are among a few of the great ends to which they were
applied :—First of all, how came it that the early armies of Rome
served, and served cheerfully, without pay ?   Simply because all who
were victorious knew that they would receive their arrears in the
fullest and amplest form upon their final discharge, viz. in the shape
of a colonial estate—large enough to rear a family in comfort, and
seated in the midst of similar allotments distributed to their old comrades in arms.   These lands were already, perhaps, in high cultivation, being often taken from conquered tribes ; but, if not, the new
occupants could rely for aid of every sort, for social intercourse, and
for all the offices of good neighbourhood, upon the surrounding proprietors, who were sure to be persons in the same circumstances as
themselves, and draughted from the same legion.   For be it remem-

people. This monarchy had been of too slow a growth, too
gradual, and too much according to the regular stages of
nature herself in its development, to have any chance of
being other than well cemented. The cohesion of its parts
was intense ; seven centuries of growth demand one or two

bered that in the primitive ages of Rome, concerning which it is that
we are now speaking, entire legions — privates and officers — were
transferred in one body to the new colony. "Antiquitus," says the
learned Goesius, "deducebantur integræ legiones, quibus parta
victoria." Neither was there much waiting for this honorary gift. In
later ages, it is true, when such resources were less plentiful, and
when regular pay was given to the soldiery, it was the veteran only
who obtained this splendid provision ; but in the earlier times a single
fortunate campaign not seldom dismissed the young recruit to a life of
ease and honour. "Multis legionibus," says Hyginus, "contigit
bellum feliciter transigere, et ad laboriosam agriculturæ requiem
primo tyrocinii gradu pervenire. Nam cum signis et aquila et primis
ordinibus et tribunis deducebantur." Tacitus also notices this organization of the early colonies, and adds the reason of it and its happy
effect, when contrasting it with the vicious arrangements of the colonizing system in his own days. "Olim," says he, "universæ legiones
deducebantur cum tribunis et centurionibus, et sui cujusque ordinis
militibus, *ut consensu et charitate rempublicam efficerent."* *Secondly,*
not only were the troops in this way paid at a time when the public
purse was unequal to the expenditure of war, but this pay, being contingent on the successful issue of the war, added the strength of
self-interest to that of patriotism in stimulating the soldier to extraordinary efforts. *Thirdly,* not only did the soldier in this way reap
his pay, but also he reaped a reward (and that besides a trophy and
perpetual monument of his public services) so munificent as to con-
stitute a permanent provision for a family ; and, accordingly, he was
now encouraged, nay enjoined, to marry. For here was a hereditary
landed estate equal to the liberal maintenance of a family. And thus
did a simple people, obeying its instinct of conquest, not only discover, in its earliest days, the subtle principle of Machiavel — *Let war
support war ;* but (which is far more than Machiavel's view) they made
each present war support many future wars, by making it support a
new offset from the population, bound to the mother city by indis-
soluble ties of privilege and civic duties , and in many other ways
they made every war, by and through the colonizing system to which
it gave occasion, serviceable to future aggrandizement. War, managed
in this way, and with these results, became to Rome what commerce
or rural industry is to other countries, viz. the only hopeful and
general way for making a fortune. *Fourthly,* by means of colonies it
was that Rome delivered herself from her surplus population. Prosperous and well governed, the Roman citizens of each generation out-
numbered those of the generation preceding. But the colonies
provided outlets for these continual accessions of people, and absorbed

at least for palpable decay ; and it is only for harlequin empires like that of Napoleon, run up with the rapidity of pantomime, to fall asunder under the instant reaction of a few false moves in politics, or a single disastrous campaign. Hence it was, and from the prudence of Augustus acting through a very long reign, sustained at no very distant interval by the personal inspection and revisions of Hadrian, that for some time the Roman Power seemed to be stationary.

them faster than they could arise.[1] And thus the great original sin of modern states, that heel of Achilles in which they are all vulnerable, and which (generally speaking) becomes more oppressive to the public prosperity as that prosperity happens to be greater (for in poor states and under despotic governments this evil does not exist), that flagrant infirmity of our own country, for which no statesman has devised any commensurate remedy, was to ancient Rome a perpetual foundation and well-head of public strength and enlarged resources. With us of modern times, when population greatly outruns the demand for labour—whether it be under the stimulus of upright government, and just laws justly administered, in combination with the manufacturing system (as in England), or (as in Ireland) under the stimulus of idle habits, cheap subsistence, and a low standard of comfort—we think it much if we can keep down insurrection by the bayonet and the sabre. *Lucro ponamus* is our cry if we can effect even thus much ; whereas Rome, in her simplest and pastoral days, converted this menacing danger and standing opprobrium of modern statesmanship to her own immense benefit. Not satisfied merely to have neutralized it, she drew from it the vital resources of her martial aggrandizement. For, *Fifthly*, these colonies were in two ways made the corner-stones of her martial policy : 1st, They were looked to as nurseries of her armies. During one generation the original colonists, already trained to military habits, were themselves disposable for this purpose on any great emergency ; these men transmitted heroic traditions to their posterity ; and, at all events, a more robust population was always at hand in agricultural colonies than could be had in the metropolis. Cato the elder, and all the early writers, notice the quality of such levies as being far superior to those drawn from a population of sedentary habits. 2dly, The Italian colonies, one and all, performed the functions which in our day are assigned to garrisoned towns and frontier fortresses. In the earliest times they discharged a still more critical service, by sometimes entirely displacing a hostile population, and more often by dividing it and breaking its unity. In cases of desperate resistance to the Roman arms, marked

---

[1] And in this way we must explain the fact that, in the many successive numerations of the people continually noticed by Livy and others, we do not find that sort of multiplication which we might have looked for in a state so ably governed. The truth is that the continual surpluses had been carried off by the colonizing drain before they could become noticeable or troublesome.

What else could be expected ?   The mere strength of the impetus derived from the Republican institutions could not but propagate itself, and cause even a motion in advance, for some time after those institutions had themselves begun to give way.   And, besides, the military institutions survived all others ; and the Army continued very much the same in its discipline and composition long after Rome and all its civic institutions had bent before an utter revolution.   It

by frequent infraction of treaties, it was usual to remove the offending population to a safer situation, separated from Rome by the Tiber ; sometimes entirely to disperse and scatter it.   But, where these extremities were not called for by expediency or the Roman maxims of justice, it was judged sufficient to *interpolate*, as it were, the hostile people by colonizations from Rome, which were completely organized[1] for mutual aid, having officers of all ranks dispersed amongst them, and for overawing the growth of insurrectionary movements amongst their neighbours.   Acting on this system, the Roman colonies in some measure resembled the *English Pale* as existing at one era in Ireland. This mode of service, it is true, became obsolete in process of time, concurrently with the dangers which it was shaped to meet ; for the whole of Italy proper, together with that part of Italy called Cisalpine Gaul, was at length reduced to unity and obedience by the almighty Republic.   But, in forwarding that great end and indispensable condition towards all foreign warfare, no one military engine in the whole armory of Rome availed so much as her Italian colonies.   The other use of these colonies, as frontier garrisons, or, at any rate, as interposing between a foreign enemy and the gates of Rome, they continued to perform long after their earlier uses had passed away ; and Cicero himself notices their value in this view.   "Colonias," says he (*Orat. in Rullum*), "sic idoneis in locis contra suspicionem periculi collocarunt, ut esse non oppida Italiæ sed *propugnacula* Imperii viderentur."   *Finally*, the colonies were the best means of promoting tillage, and the culture of vineyards.   And, though this service, as regarded the Italian colonies, was greatly defeated in succeeding times by the ruinous largesses of corn (*frumentationes*) and other vices of the Roman policy after the vast revolution effected by universal luxury, it is not the less true that, left to themselves and their natural tendency, the Roman colonies would have yielded this last benefit as certainly as any other.   Large volumes exist, illustrated by the learning of Rigaltius, Salmasius, and Goesius, upon the mere technical arrangements of the Roman colonies ; and whole libraries might be written on these same colonies, considered as engines of exquisite state policy.

---

[1] That is indeed involved in the technical term of *deductio ;* for, unless the ceremonies, religious and political, of inauguration and organization, were duly complied with, the colony was not entitled to be considered as *deducta,*—that is, solemnly and ceremonially transplanted from the metropolis.

was very possible even that Emperors should have arisen with martial propensities, and talents capable of masking for many years, by specious but transitory conquests, the causes that were silently sapping the foundations of Roman supremacy ; and thus, by accidents of personal character and taste, an Empire might even have expanded itself in appearance which, by all its permanent and real tendencies, was even then shrinking within narrower limits, and travelling downwards to dissolution.   In reality, one such Emperor there was.   Trajan, whether by martial inclinations, or (as some suppose) by dissatisfaction with his own position at Rome, when brought into more immediate connexion with the Senate, was driven into needless war ; and he achieved conquests in the direction of Dacia as well as Parthia.   But that these conquests were not substantial,—that they were connected by no true cement of cohesion with the existing Empire,—is evident from the rapidity with which the Roman grasp was relaxed, and the provinces recoiled into the hands of their old masters.   In the next reign the Empire had already rolled back within its former limits ; and in two reigns further on, under Marcus Antoninus, though a prince of elevated character and warlike in his policy, we find such concessions of territory made to the Marcomanni and others as indicate too plainly the shrinking energies of a waning Empire.   In reality, if we consider the polar opposition, in point of interest and situation, between the great officers of the Republic and the Augustus or Cæsar of the Empire, we cannot fail to see the immense effect which that difference must have had upon the permanent spirit of conquest.   The Cæsar was either adopted or elected to a situation of infinite luxury and enjoyment.   He had no interests to secure by fighting in person : and he had a powerful interest in preventing others from fighting ; since in that way only he could raise up competitors to himself, and dangerous seducers of the Army.   A consul, on the other hand, or great lieutenant of the senate, had nothing to enjoy or to hope for when his term of office should have expired, unless according to his success in creating military fame and influence for himself. Those Cæsars who fought whilst the Empire was or seemed to be stationary, as Trajan, did so from personal taste ;

those who fought in after centuries, when the decay became apparent and dangers drew nearer, as Aurelian, did so from the necessities of fear ; and under neither impulse were they likely to make durable conquests. The spirit of conquest having therefore departed at the very time when conquest would have become more difficult even to the Republican energies, both from remoteness of ground and from the martial character of the chief nations which stood beyond the frontier, it was a matter of necessity that with the Republican institutions should expire the whole principle of territorial aggrandizement, and that, if the Empire seemed to be stationary for some time after its establishment by Julius and its final settlement by Augustus, this was through no strength of its own, or inherent in its own constitution, but through the continued action of that strength which it had inherited from the Republic. In a philosophical sense, therefore, it may be affirmed that the Empire of the Cæsars was *always* in decline : ceasing to go forward, it could not do other than retrograde ; and even the first *appearances* of decline can with no propriety be referred to the reign of Commodus. His vices exposed him to public contempt and assassination ; but neither one nor the other had any effect upon the strength of the Empire.

Here, therefore, is one just subject of complaint against Gibbon, that he has dated the declension of the Roman Power from a commencement arbitrarily assumed. Another, and a heavier, is, that he has failed to notice the steps and separate indications of decline as they arose—the moments (to speak in the language of dynamics) through which the decline travelled onwards to its consummation. It is also a grievous offence, as regards the true purposes of History—and one which, in a complete exposition of the Imperial History, all readers would have a right to denounce—that Gibbon brings forward only such facts as allow of a scenical treatment, and seems everywhere, by the glancing style of his allusions, to presuppose an acquaintance the most familiar with that very history which he undertakes to deliver. Our immediate purpose, however, is simply to characterize the office of Emperor, and to notice such events and changes as operated for evil, and for a final effect of decay, upon the

Cæsars or upon their Empire.   As the best means of realizing this purpose, we shall rapidly review the history of both, premising that we confine ourselves to the true Cæsars, and the true Empire,—of the West.

The first overt act of weakness—the first expression of conscious declension, as regarded the foreign enemies of Rome—occurred in the reign of Hadrian; for it is a very different thing to forbear making conquests and to renounce them when made.   It is possible, however, that the cession then made of Mesopotamia and Armenia, however sure to be interpreted into the language of fear by the enemy, did not imply any such principle in this Emperor.   He was of a civic and paternal spirit, and anxious for the substantial welfare of the Empire rather than its ostentatious glory.   But such a distinction in practice depends for its prudence altogether on the quality of your antagonist.   With a wretched Asiatic enemy to lose an atom of lustre is to lose the substance of victory.   The internal administration of affairs had very much gone into neglect since the times of Augustus; and Hadrian supposed that he could effect more public good by an extensive progress through the Empire, and by a personal correction of abuses, than by any military enterprise.   It is, besides, asserted that he received an indemnity in money for the provinces beyond the Euphrates.   But still it remains true that in his reign the God Terminus made his first retrograde motion; and this Emperor became naturally an object of public obloquy at Rome, and his name fell under the superstitious ban of a fatal tradition connected with the foundation of the capitol.   The two Antonines, Titus and Marcus, who came next in succession, were truly good and patriotic princes,—perhaps the only princes in the whole series who combined the virtues of private and of public life. In their reigns the frontier line was maintained in its integrity, and at the expense of some severe fighting under Marcus, who was a strenuous general at the same time that he was a severe student.   It is, however, true, as we observed above, that, by allowing a settlement within the Roman frontier to a barbarous people, Marcus Aurelius raised the first ominous precedent in favour of those Gothic, Vandal, and Frankish hives who were as yet hidden behind a cloud of years. Homes had been obtained by Trans-Danubian barbarians upon the Cis-Danubian territory of Rome : that fact remained upon tradition : whilst the terms upon which they had been obtained, how much or how little connected with fear, necessarily became liable to doubt and to oblivion.

Here we pause to remark that the first twelve Cæsars, together with Nerva, Trajan, Hadrian, and the two Antonines, making seventeen Emperors, compose the first of four nearly equal groups, who occupied the throne in succession until the extinction of the Western Empire. And at this point, be it observed—that is, at the termination of the first group—we take leave of all genuine virtue. In no one of the succeeding princes, if we except Alexander Severus, do we meet with any goodness of heart, or even amiableness of manners. The best, in a public sense, of the future Emperors were harsh and repulsive in private character.

The second group, as we have classed them, terminating with Philip the Arab, commences with Commodus. This unworthy prince, although the son of the excellent Marcus Antoninus, turned out a monster of debauchery. At the moment of his father's death, he was present in person at the head-quarters of the Army on the Danube, and of necessity partook in many of their hardships. This it was which furnished his evil counsellors with their sole argument for urging his departure to the capital. A council having been convened, the faction of court sycophants pressed upon his attention the inclemency of the climate, contrasting it with the genial skies and sunny fields of Italy ; and the season, which happened to be winter, gave strength to their representations. What ! would the Emperor be content for ever to hew out the frozen water with an axe before he could assuage his thirst ? And, again, the total want of fruit-trees—did that recommend their present station as a fit one for the Imperial Court ? Commodus, ashamed to found his objections to the station upon grounds so unsoldierly as these, affected to be moved by political reasons : some great senatorial house might take advantage of his distance from home, might seize the palace, fortify it, and raise levies in Italy capable of sustaining its pretensions to the throne. These arguments were combated by Pompeianus; who, besides his personal weight as an officer, had married the eldest sister of the young Emperor. Shame prevailed for the present with Commodus, and he dismissed the council with an assurance that he would think farther of it. The sequel was easy to foresee. Orders were soon issued for the departure of the court to Rome; and the task of managing the barbarians of Dacia was delegated to lieutenants. The system upon which these officers executed their commission was a mixed one of terror and persuasion. Some they defeated in battle; and these were the majority; for Herodian says, πλείστους τῶν βαρβαρῶν ὅπλοις ἐχειρώσαντο [1] : others they bribed into peace by large sums of money. And no doubt this last article in the policy of Commodus was that which led Gibbon to assign to *his* reign the first rudiments of the Roman declension. But it should be remembered that, virtually, this policy was but the further prosecution of that which had already been adopted by Marcus Aurelius. Concessions and temperaments of any sort or degree showed that the Pannonian frontier was in too formidable a condition to be treated with uncompromising rigour. Τὸ ἀμέριμνον ὠνούμενος, purchasing an immunity from all further anxiety, Commodus (as the historian expresses it) πάντα ἐδίδου τὰ αἰτούμενα— conceded all demands whatever. His journey to Rome was one continued festival : and the whole population of Rome turned out to welcome him. At this period he was undoubtedly the darling of the people : his personal beauty was splendid ; and he was connected by blood with some of the greatest nobility. Over this flattering scene of hope and triumph clouds soon gathered : with the mob, indeed, there is reason to think that he continued a favourite to the last; but the respectable part of the citizens were speedily disgusted with his self-degradation, and came to hate him even more than ever or by any class he had been loved.

The Roman pride never shows itself more conspicuously throughout all history than in the alienation of heart which inevitably followed any great and continued outrages upon his own majesty committed by their Emperor. Cruelties the most atrocious, acts of vengeance the most bloody, fratricide, parricide, all were viewed with more toleration than oblivion of his own

---

[1] *i.e.* " Most of the barbarians they subdued by arms."

THE CÆSARS 365

inviolable sanctity. Hence we imagine the wrath with which Rome would behold Commodus, under the eyes of four hundred thousand spectators, making himself a party to the contests of gladiators. In his earlier exhibitions as an archer, it is possible that his matchless dexterity, and his unerring eye, would avail to mitigate the censures : but, when the Roman Imperator actually descended to the arena in the garb and equipments of a servile prize-fighter, and personally engaged in combat with such antagonists, having previously submitted to their training and discipline, the public indignation rose to a height which spoke aloud the language of encouragement to conspiracy and treason. These were not wanting : three memorable plots against his life were defeated ; one of them (that of Maternus, the robber) accompanied with romantic circumstances,[1] which we have narrated in an earlier paper of this series. Another was set on foot by his eldest sister, Lucilla ; nor did her close relationship protect her from capital punishment. In that instance, the immediate agent of her purposes, Quintianus, a young man of signal resolution and daring, who had attempted to stab the Emperor at the entrance of the amphitheatre, though baffled in his purpose, uttered a word which rang continually in the ears of Commodus, and poisoned his peace of mind for ever. His vengeance, perhaps, was thus more effectually accomplished than if he had at once dismissed his victim from life. "The Senate," Quintianus had said, " sends thee this through me " : and henceforward the Senate was the object of unslumbering suspicions to the Emperor. Yet the public suspicions settled upon a different quarter ; and a very memorable scene must have pointed his own in the same direction, supposing that he had previously been blind to his danger.

On a day of great solemnity, when Rome had assembled her myriads in the amphitheatre, just at the very moment when the nobles, the magistrates, the priests,—all, in short, that was venerable or consecrated in the State, with the

---

[1] [*Ante*, pp. 238-240.] On this occasion we may notice that the final execution of the vengeance projected by Maternus was reserved for a public festival exactly corresponding to the modern *carnival* ; and, from an expression used by Herodian, it is plain that *masquerading*, under gay and dramatic disguises, had been an ancient practice in Rome.

Imperator in their centre,—had taken their seats, and were waiting for the opening of the shows, a stranger, in the robe of a philosopher, bearing a staff in his hand (which also was the professional ensign of a philosopher [1]), stepped forward, and, by the waving of his hand, challenged the attention of Commodus. Deep silence ensued : upon which, in a few words, ominous to the ear as the handwriting on the wall to the eye of Belshazzar, the stranger unfolded to Commodus the instant peril which menaced both his life and his throne from his great servant Perennius. What personal purpose of benefit to himself this stranger might have connected with his public warning, or by whom he might have been suborned, was never discovered ; for he was instantly arrested by the agents of the great officer whom he had denounced, dragged away to punishment, and put to a cruel death. Commodus dissembled his panic for the present : but soon after, having received undeniable proofs (as is alleged) of the treason imputed to Perennius, in the shape of a coin which had been struck by his son, he caused the father to be assassinated ; and, on the same day, by means of forged letters, before this news could reach the son, who commanded the Illyrian armies, he lured *him* also to destruction, under the belief that he was obeying the summons of his father to a private interview on the Italian frontier. So perished those enemies, if enemies they really were. But to these tragedies succeeded others far more comprehensive in their mischief, and in more continuous succession than is recorded upon any other page of Universal History. Rome was ravaged by a pestilence— by a famine—by riots amounting to a civil war—by a dreadful massacre of the unarmed mob—by shocks of earthquake —and, finally, by a fire which consumed the national bank,[2] and the most sumptuous buildings of the city. To these horrors, with a rapidity characteristic of the Roman depravity, and possible only under the most extensive demoralization of the public mind, succeeded festivals of gorgeous pomp, and

---

[1] See Casaubon's notes upon Theophrastus.

[2] Viz. the Temple of Peace, at that time the most magnificent edifice in Rome. Temples, it is well known, were the places used in ancient times as banks of deposit. For this function they were admirably fitted by their inviolable sanctity.

amphitheatrical exhibitions upon a scale of grandeur absolutely unparalleled by all former attempts.   Then were beheld, and familiarized to the eyes of the Roman mob, to children, and to women, animals as yet known to us, says Herodian, only in pictures.   Whatever strange or rare animal could be drawn from the depths of India, from Siam and Pegu, or from the unvisited nooks of Ethiopia, were now brought together as subjects for the archery of the universal lord.[1]   Invitations (and the invitations of kings are commands) had been scattered on this occasion profusely : not, as heretofore, to individuals or to families, but, as was in proportion to the occasion where an Emperor was the chief performer, to nations.   People were summoned by circles of longitude and latitude to come and see things that eye had not seen, nor ear heard of—the specious miracles of nature brought together from arctic and from tropic deserts, putting forth their strength, their speed, or their beauty, and glorifying by their deaths the matchless hand of the Roman King.   *There* was beheld the lion from Bilidulgerid, and the leopard from Hindustan—the reindeer from polar latitudes—the antelope from the Zaara—and the leigh, or gigantic stag, from Britain.   Thither came the buffalo and the bison, the white bull of Northumberland and Galloway, the unicorn from the regions of Nepaul or Thibet, the rhinoceros and the river-horse from Senegal, with the elephant of Ceylon or Siam.   The ostrich and the camelopard, the wild ass and the zebra, the chamois from Alpine

---

[1] What a prodigious opportunity for the zoologist !   And, considering that these shows prevailed for 500 years, during all which period the amphitheatre gave bounties, as it were, to the hunter and the fowler of every climate, and that, by means of a stimulus so constantly applied, scarcely any animal, the shyest, rarest, fiercest, escaped the demands of the arena,—no one fact so much illustrates the inertia of the public mind in those days, and the indifference to all scientific pursuits, as that no annotator should have risen to Pliny the Elder,[2] no rival to the immortal tutor of Alexander.

---

[2] Whose great work is the earliest prophetic sketch, descending from classic times, of an *encyclopædia*.   Yet had not Greece, three centuries and more before Pliny, shown us sketches the most magnificent of such an encyclopædia in the various essays of Aristotle?   Certainly.   But the result is unsatisfactory, and doubly so.   Known works of Aristotle are wanting; and, inversely, others which offer themselves as *his* are either spurious beyond all question, or, upon internal evidence, are doubtful.

peaks of ice, the wild goat from Crete, and the ibex from the eternal sunshine of Angora,—all brought their tributes of beauty or deformity to these vast aceldamas of Rome : their savage voices ascended in tumultuous uproar to the chambers of the capitol: a million of spectators sat round them : standing in the centre was a single statuesque figure—the Imperial Sagittary, beautiful as an Antinous and majestic as a Jupiter, whose hand was so steady and whose eye so true that he was never known to miss, and who, in this accomplishment at least, was so absolute in his excellence that, as we are assured by a writer not disposed to flatter him, the very foremost of the Parthian archers and of the Mauritanian lancers (Παρθναίων οἱ τοξικὴν ἀκριβοῦντες, καὶ Μαυρούσιων οἱ ἀκοντιζεῖν ἄριστοι) were not able to contend with him. Juvenal, in a well-known passage upon the disproportionate endings of illustrious careers, drawing one of his examples from Marius, says that he ought, for his own glory, and to make his end correspondent to his life, to have died at the moment when he descended from his triumphal chariot at the portals of the Capitol. And of Commodus, in like manner, it may be affirmed that, had he died in the exercise of his peculiar art,—with a hecatomb of victims rendering homage to his miraculous skill by the regularity of the files which they presented as they lay stretched out dying or dead upon the arena,—he would have left a splendid and a characteristic impression of himself upon that nation of spectators who had witnessed his performance. He was the noblest artist in his own profession that the world had ever seen—in archery he was the Robin Hood of Rome ; he was in the very meridian of his youth ; and he was the most beautiful man of his own times (τῶν καθ᾽ ἑαυτὸν ἀνθρώπων κάλλει εὐπρεπέστατος). He would therefore have looked the part admirably of the dying gladiator ; and he would have died in his natural vocation. But it was ordered otherwise ; his death was destined to private malice, and to an ignoble hand. And much obscurity still rests upon the motives of the assassins, though its circumstances are reported possibly with truth, and certainly with unusual minuteness of detail. One thing is evident, that the public and patriotic motives assigned by the perpetrators as the remote grounds of their conspiracy cannot have been the true ones.

The grave historian may sum up his character of Commodus by saying that, however richly endowed with natural gifts, he abused them all to bad purposes ; that he derogated from his noble ancestors, and disavowed the obligations of his illustrious name ; and, as the climax of his offences, that he dishonoured the purple αἰσχροῖς ἐπιτηδεύμασιν — by the baseness of his pursuits. All that is true, and more than that. But these considerations were not of a nature to affect his parasitical attendants very nearly or keenly. Yet the story runs that Marcia, his privileged mistress, deeply affected by the anticipation of some further outrages upon his high dignity which he was then meditating, had carried the importunity of her deprecations too far ; that the irritated Emperor had consequently inscribed her name, in company with others (whom he had reason to tax with the same offence, or whom he suspected of similar sentiments), in his little black book, or pocket souvenir of death ; that this book, being left under the cushion of a sofa, had been conveyed into the hands of Marcia by a little pet boy, called Philo-Commodus, who was caressed equally by the Emperor and by Marcia ; that she had immediately called to her aid, and to the participation of her plot, those who participated in her danger ; and that the proximity of their own intended fate had prescribed to them an immediate attempt, the circumstances of which were these :—At mid-day the Emperor was accustomed to bathe, and at the same time to take refreshments. On this occasion, Marcia, agreeably to her custom, presented him with a goblet of wine, medicated with poison. Of this wine, having just returned from the fatigues of the chase, Commodus drank freely, and almost immediately fell into heavy slumbers ; from which, however, he was soon aroused by deadly sickness. That was a case which the conspirators had not taken into their calculations ; and they now began to fear that the violent vomiting which succeeded might throw off the poison. There was no time to be lost ; and the barbarous Marcia, who had so often slept in the arms of the young Emperor, was the person to propose that he should now be strangled. A young gladiator named

Narcissus was therefore introduced into the room ; what passed is not known circumstantially ; but, as the Emperor was young and athletic, though off his guard at the moment, and under the disadvantage of sickness, and as he had himself been regularly trained in the gladiatorial discipline, there can be little doubt that the vile assassin would meet with a desperate resistance.   And thus, after all, there is good reason to think that the Emperor resigned his life in the character of a dying gladiator.[1]

So perished the eldest and sole surviving son of the great Marcus Aurelius Antoninus ; and the throne passed into the momentary possession of two old men, who reigned in succession each for a few weeks.   The first of these was Pertinax, an upright man, a good officer, and an unseasonable reformer : unseasonable for those times, and, therefore, more so for himself.   Lætus, the ringleader in the assassination of Commodus, had been at that time the prætorian prefect, an office which a German writer considers as best represented to modern ideas by the Turkish post of grand vizier.   Needing a protector at this moment, he naturally fixed his eyes upon Pertinax, as then holding the powerful command of city prefect (or governor of Rome).   Him therefore he recommended to the soldiery,—that is, to the prætorian cohorts.   The soldiery had no particular objection to the old general, if he and they could agree upon terms,—his age being doubtless appreciated as a first-rate recommendation in a case where it insured a speedy renewal of the lucrative bargain : the bargain was good in proportion as it promised a speedy repetition.

The only demur arose with Pertinax himself.   He had

<hr>

[1] It is worthy of notice that, under any suspension of the imperatorial power or office, the Senate was the body to whom the Roman mind even yet continued to turn.   In this case, both to colour their crime with a show of public motives, and to interest this great body in their own favour by associating them in their own dangers, the conspirators pretended to have found a long roll of senatorial names included in the same page of condemnation with their own.   Shallow fabrication !   The story of the little black memorandum book is childish.   Courtezans are not anxious for the maintenance of public dignity ; and princes who are meditating vindictive murders do not need any written mementoes of their angry purposes.

been leader of the troops in Britain, subsequently superintendent of the police in Rome, thirdly proconsul in Africa, and finally consul and governor of Rome. In these great official stations he stood so near to the throne as to observe the dangers with which it was surrounded ; and it is asserted that he declined the offered dignity. But it is added that, finding the choice allowed him lay between immediate death and acceptance,[1] he closed with the proposals of the prætorian cohorts, at the rate of about ninety-six pounds per man ; which largess he paid by bringing to sale the rich furniture of the last Emperor. The danger which usually threatened a Roman Cæsar in such cases was lest he should not be able to fulfil his contract. But in the case of Pertinax the danger began from the moment when he *had* fulfilled it. As a debtor he was safe ; but, when the bill against him had been *receipted*, he became ripe for death. Conceiving himself to be now released from his dependency, on the reasonable assumption that his official authority was at length settled upon a sure foundation when the last arrears of the purchase money had been paid down, he commenced his reforms, civil as well as military, with a zeal which alarmed all those who had an interest in maintaining old abuses. To two great factions he thus made himself especially obnoxious,—to the prætorian cohorts, and to the courtiers under the last reign. The connecting link between these two parties was Lætus, who belonged personally to the last, but still retained his influence with the first. Possibly his fears were alarmed ; but, at all events, his cupidity was dissatisfied. He conceived himself to have been ill rewarded ; and, immediately resorting to the same weapons which he had used against Commodus, he stimulated the prætorian guards to murder the Emperor. Three hundred of them pressed into the palace : Pertinax attempted to harangue them, and to vindicate himself ; but, not being able to obtain a hearing, he folded his robe about his head, called upon Jove the Avenger, and was immediately despatched.

---

[1] Historians have failed to remark the contradiction between this statement and the allegation that Lætus selected Pertinax for the throne on a consideration of his ability to protect the assassins of Commodus.

The throne was again empty after a reign of about eighty days ; and now came the memorable scandal of putting up the Empire to auction.   There were two bidders, Sulpicianus and Didius Julianus.   The first, however, at that time governor of Rome, lay under a weight of suspicion, being the father-in-law of Pertinax, and likely enough to exact vengeance for his murder.   He was besides outbid by Julianus.   Sulpician offered about one hundred and sixty pounds a man to the guards ; his rival offered two hundred, and assured them besides of immediate payment ; " for," said he, " I have the money at home, without needing to raise it from the possessions of the crown."   Upon this the empire was knocked down to Didius as the highest bidder.   So shocking, however, was this transaction to the Roman pride that the guards durst not leave their own creation without military protection.   The resentment of an unarmed mob, however, soon ceased to be of foremost importance ; for this resentment extended rapidly to all the frontiers of the Empire,—where the armies felt that the prætorian cohorts had no exclusive title to give away the throne, and their leaders felt that, in a contest of this nature, their own claims were incomparably superior to those of the present occupant.   Three great candidates therefore started forward : Septimius Severus, who commanded the armies in Illyria ; Pescennius Niger in Syria ; and Albinus in Britain.   Severus, as the nearest to Rome, marched and possessed himself of that city.   Vengeance followed upon all the accomplices in the late murder.   Julianus, unable to complete his bargain, had already been put to death, as a deprecatory offering to the approaching army.   Severus himself inflicted death upon Lætus, and dismissed the prætorian cohorts.   Thence marching against his Syrian rival, Niger, who had formerly been his friend, and who was not wanting in military skill, he overthrew him in three great battles.   Niger fled to Antioch, the seat of his late government, and was there decapitated.   Meantime Albinus, the British commander-in-chief, had already been won over by the title of Cæsar or adopted heir to the new Augustus.   But the hollowness of this bribe soon became apparent ; and the two competitors met to decide their pretensions at Lyons.   In the great battle which followed,

Severus fell from his horse, and was at first supposed to be dead. But, recovering, he defeated his rival, who immediately committed suicide. Severus displayed his ferocious temper sufficiently by sending the head of Albinus to Rome. Other expressions of his natural character soon followed : he suspected strongly that Albinus had been favoured by the Senate ; forty of that body, with their wives and children, were immediately sacrificed to his wrath (is this credible ?) ; but he never forgave the rest, nor endured to live upon terms of amity amongst them. Quitting Rome in disgust, he employed himself first in making war upon the Parthians, who had naturally, from situation, befriended his Syrian rival. Their capital cities he overthrew, and afterwards, by way of employing his armies, made war in Britain. At the city of York he died ; and to his two sons, Geta and Caracalla, he bequeathed, as his dying advice, a maxim of policy which sufficiently indicates the situation of the Empire at that period. It was this—"to enrich the soldiery at any price, and to regard the rest of their subjects as so many ciphers." But, as a critical historian remarks, this was a short-sighted and self-destroying policy ; since in no way is the subsistence of the soldier made more insecure than by diminishing the general security of rights and property to those who are not soldiers, from whom, after all, the funds must be sought upon which the soldier himself must draw for pay and for supplies.

The two sons of Severus, whose bitter enmity is so memorably put on record by their actions, travelled simultaneously from York to Rome, but so mistrustful of each other that at every stage the rancorous brothers took up their quarters at different houses. Geta has obtained the sympathy of historians, because he happened to be the victim ; but there is reason to think that each of the princes was laying murderous snares for the other. The weak credulity, rather than the conscious innocence, of Geta led to the catastrophe. He presented himself at a preconcerted meeting with his brother in the presence of their common mother, and was murdered by Caracalla in his mother's arms. He was, however, avenged : the horrors of that tragedy, and remorse for the twenty thousand murders which had followed, never forsook the guilty Caracalla. Quitting Rome, but pursued into every region by the bloody image of his brother, the Emperor henceforward led a wandering life at the head of his legions ; but never was there a better illustration of the poet's maxim that

"Remorse is as the mind in which it grows" :

gloomy, in short, and fretful in a nature of ferocious instincts, but softening into gentle penitential issues only under gracious affections of love and pity and self-renunciation. Certainly Caracalla's remorse put on no shape of repentance. On the contrary, he carried anger and oppression wherever he moved, and protected himself from plots only by living in the very centre of a nomadic camp. Six years had passed away in this manner, when a mere accident led to his assassination. For the sake of security, the office of prætorian prefect had been divided between two commissioners,—one for military affairs, the other for civil. The latter of these two officers was Opilius Macrinus. This man has, by some historians, been supposed to have harboured no bad intentions ; but, unfortunately, an astrologer had foretold that he was destined to the throne. The prophet was laid in irons at Rome, and letters were despatched to Caracalla, apprising him of the case. These letters, as yet unopened, were transferred by the Emperor, then occupied in witnessing a race, to Macrinus, who thus became acquainted with the whole grounds of suspicion against himself,—grounds which to the jealousy of the Emperor he well knew would appear substantial proofs. Upon this he resolved to anticipate the Emperor in the work of murder. The head-quarters were then at Edessa ; and, upon his instigation, a disappointed centurion, named Martialis, animated also by revenge for the death of his brother, undertook to assassinate Caracalla. An opportunity soon offered, on a visit which the prince made to the celebrated temple of the moon at Carrhæ. The attempt was successful : the Emperor perished ; but Martialis paid the penalty of his crime in the same hour, being shot by a Scythian archer of the body-guard.

Macrinus, after three days' interregnum, being elected Emperor, began his reign by purchasing a peace from the

Parthians. What the Empire chiefly needed at this moment is evident from the next step taken by the new Emperor. He laboured to restore the ancient discipline of the armies in all its rigour. He was aware of the risk he ran in this attempt ; and that he *was* so is the best evidence of the strong necessity which existed for reform. Perhaps, however, he might have surmounted his difficulties and dangers had he met with no competitor round whose person the military malcontents could rally. But such a competitor soon arose ; and, to the astonishment of all the world, in the person of a Syrian. The Emperor Severus, on losing his first wife, had resolved to strengthen the pretensions of his family by a second marriage with some lady having a regal " genesis,"— that is, whose horoscope promised a regal destiny. Julia Domna, a native of Syria, offered him this dowry, and she became the mother of Geta. A sister of this Julia, called Mœsa, had, through different daughters, two grandsons— Heliogabalus and Alexander Severus. The mutineers of the Army rallied round the first of these ; a battle was fought ; and Macrinus, with his son Diadumenianus, whom he had adopted to the succession, was captured and put to death. Heliogabalus succeeded, and reigned in the monstrous manner which has rendered his name infamous in History. In what way, however, he lost the affections of the Army, has never been explained.[1] His mother, Soœmias, the eldest daughter of Mœsa, had represented herself as the concubine of Caracalla ; and Heliogabalus, being thus accredited as the son of that Emperor, whose memory was dear to the soldiery, had enjoyed the full benefit of that descent ; nor can it be readily explained how he came to lose it.

Here, in fact, we meet with an eminent instance of that dilemma which is so constantly recurring in the history of the Cæsars. If a prince is by temperament disposed to severity of manners, and naturally seeks to impress his own spirit upon the composition and discipline of the Army, we are sure to find that he was cut off in his attempts by private assassination or by public rebellion. On the other hand, if

---

[1] Elsewhere we have explained that Heliogabalus was simply a foolish boy, perhaps a lunatic, and left too early without natural guardians.

he wallows in sensuality, and is careless about all discipline, civil or military, we then find as certainly that he loses the esteem and affections of the Army to some rival of severer habits.   That very defect of sternness, viz. defect of a quality which would assuredly have entailed a murderous fate, is pleaded as a reciprocating or alternate ground of violent death by those brawling scoundrels, who know not even their own minds for six days in succession.   And in the midst of such oscillations, and with examples of such contradictory interpretation, we cannot wonder that the Roman princes did not oftener take warning by the misfortunes of their predecessors.   In the present instance, Alexander, the cousin of Heliogabalus, without intrigues of his own, and simply (as it appears) by the purity and sobriety of his conduct, had alienated the affections of the Army from the reigning prince.   Either jealousy or prudence had led Heliogabalus to make an attempt upon his rival's life ; and this attempt had nearly cost him his own through the mutiny which it caused.   In a second uproar, produced by some fresh intrigues of the Emperor against his cousin, the soldiers became un-manageable.   They were maddened by reports, true or false ; and they refused to pause until they had massacred Helioga-balus, together with his mother, and had raised his cousin Alexander to the throne.

The reforms of this prince, who reigned under the name of Alexander Severus, were extensive and searching,—not only in his court, which he purged of all notorious abuses, but throughout the whole machinery and framework of the army.   He cashiered, upon one occasion, an entire legion : and the legion of Rome, it must be remembered, though fluctuating (as might be expected) through a course of one thousand years, never amounted to less than five modern battalions of the last 150 years, i.e. five times 600 men. Three thousand men you may count on at the least.   But at some periods the legion numbered as much as five, or even six, thousand men, and, in fact, with its complementary wings of auxiliar cavalry, was virtually what in France (and . since the Crimean War at home) is called a *Division*.   He restored, as far as he was able, the ancient discipline ; and, above all, he liberated the provinces from military spoliation.

" Let the soldier," said he, "be contented with his pay ; and
" whatever more he wants, let him obtain it by victory from
" the enemy, not by pillage from his fellow-subject." But,
whatever might be the value or extent of his reforms in the
marching regiments, Alexander could not succeed in bending
the prætorian guards to his yoke. Under the guardianship
of his mother Mammæa, the conduct of state affairs had been
submitted to a council of sixteen persons ; at the head of
which stood the celebrated lawyer Ulpian. To this minister
the prætorians imputed the reforms, and perhaps the whole
principle and inspiration which breathed throughout the
actual reforms ; for they pursued him with a vengeance
which is else hardly to be explained. Many days was Ulpian
protected by the citizens of Rome, until the whole city was
threatened with conflagration ; he then fled to the palace of
the young Emperor, who in vain attempted to save him from
his pursuers under the shelter of the imperial purple. Ulpian
was murdered before his eyes ; nor was it found possible to
punish the ringleader in this foul conspiracy until he had
been removed by something like treachery to a remote government. So dreadful is the empire of triumphant wrong : outrage breeds outrage ; treachery necessitates treachery ; and
crimes, or criminals, that tower up to licentious heights,
disowning all responsibility, are reached by secret acts of
vengeance that destroy all sense of honour. Even extra-legal
powers, such as the Roman Dictatorship, or our own Suspension of the *Habeas Corpus*, or Proclamation of Martial
law (where instant execution follows the most hurried of
trials), are viewed with grief and jealousy by those even that
resort to such fearful instruments of public wrath. But, in
cases like those so often arising in imperial Rome, where an
insolent soldiery intercepted all action of law, regular or
irregular, and in a manner forced the rulers into secret or
circuitous acts of retribution that too much wore an air
vindictive or even perfidious, the tendency lay not towards
ultra-legal, but absolutely towards anti-social, results ; not
towards extremities of rigour wounding to all human sensibilities, but towards mere anarchy that uprooted the basis of
all social security.

Meantime, a great revolution and change of dynasty had

been effected in Parthia. The line of the Arsacidæ was ter-minated ; the Parthian Empire was at an end ; and the sceptre of Persia was restored under the new race of the Sassanides. Artaxerxes, the first prince of this resurgent race, sent an embassy of four hundred select knights, enjoin-ing the Roman Emperor to content himself with Europe, and to leave Asia to the Persians. In the event of a refusal, the ambassadors were instructed to offer a defiance to the Roman Prince. Upon such an insult, Alexander could not do less, with either safety or dignity, than prepare for war. It is probable, indeed, that by this expedition, which drew off the minds of the soldiery from brooding upon the reforms which offended them, the life of Alexander was prolonged. But the expedition itself was mismanaged, or, from some cause, was unfortunate. This result, however, does not seem charge-able upon Alexander. All the preparations were admirable on the march, and up to the enemy's frontier. The invasion it was which, in a strategic sense, seems to have been ill combined. Three armies were to have entered Persia simultaneously. One of these, which was destined to act on a flank of the general line, entangled itself in the marshy grounds near Babylon, and was cut off by the archery of an enemy whom it could not reach. The other wing, acting upon ground impracticable for the manœuvres of the Persian cavalry, and supported by Chosroes the king of Armenia, gave great trouble to Artaxerxes, and, with adequate support from the other armies, would doubtless have been victorious. But the central army, under the conduct of Alexander in person, discouraged by the destruction of one entire wing, remained stationary in Mesopotamia throughout the summer, and, at the close of the campaign, was withdrawn to Antioch, *re infectâ*. It has been observed that great mystery hangs over the operations and issue of this short war. We, how-ever, would beg to ask what Roman campaign, in any quarter beyond the Euphrates, was other than mysterious in its means or ends, its manœuvres or its results, from the days of Crassus and of Antony to those of Julian or Valerian? Thus much, however, is evident, — that nothing but the previous exhaustion of the Persian king saved the Roman armies from signal discomfiture ; and even thus there is no ground for claiming a victory (as most historians do) to the Roman arms.

Any termination of the Persian war, however, advantageous or not, was likely to be personally injurious to Alexander, by allowing leisure to the soldiery for recurring to their grievances. Sensible, no doubt, of this, Alexander was gratified by the occasion which then arose for repressing the hostile movements of the Germans. He led his army off upon this expedition ; but their temper was gloomy and threatening ; and at length, after reaching the seat of war at Mentz, an open mutiny broke out under the guidance of Maximin, which terminated in the murder of the Emperor and his mother. By Herodian the discontents of the army are referred to the ill management of the Persian campaign, and the unpromising commencement of the new war in Germany. But it seems probable that a dissolute and wicked army, like that of Alexander, had not murmured under the too little, but the too much, of military service. Not the buying a truce with gold was so likely to have offended them as the having led them at all upon an enterprise of danger and hardship.

To the high-principled Alexander, the first of the Cæsars that expressed a nascent disposition to favour Christianity (a disposition, by the way, which may secretly have precipitated his destruction), succeeded the brutal Maximin, originally a big-boned peasant, whose feats of strength, when he first courted the notice of the Emperor Severus, have been described by Gibbon. He was at that period a Thracian rustic ; since then he had risen gradually to high offices ; but, according to historians, he retained his Thracian brutality to the last. That may have been true ; but one remark must be made upon this occasion,—Maximin was especially opposed to the Senate, and, wherever that was the case, no justice was done to an Emperor. Why it was that Maximin would not ask for the confirmation of his election from the Senate has never been explained ; it is said that he anticipated a rejection. But, on the other hand, it seems probable that the Senate supposed its sanction to be despised. Nothing, apparently, but this reciprocal reserve in making approaches to each other was the cause of all the bloodshed which followed. The two Gordians, who commanded in Africa, were set up by the Senate against the new Emperor; and the consternation of that body must have been great when these champions were immediately overthrown and killed. They did not, however, despair: substituting the two governors of Rome, Pupienus and Balbinus, and associating to them the younger Gordian, they resolved to make a stand; for the severities of Maximin had by this time manifested that it was a contest of extermination—a duel of life and death. Meantime Maximin had broken up from Sirmium, the capital of Pannonia, and had advanced to Aquileia,—that famous fortress on the Adriatic which in every invasion of Italy was the first object of attack. The Senate had set a price upon his head; but there was every probability that he would have triumphed had he not disgusted his army by immoderate severities. It was, however, but reasonable that those who would not support the strict though equitable discipline of the mild Alexander should suffer under the barbarous and capricious rigour of Maximin. That rigour was his ruin. Sunk and degraded as the Senate was, and now but the shadow of a mighty name, it was found on this occasion to have long arms and dreadful digits for grappling with monsters even now in its closing stages of decay. Whatever might be the real weakness of this body, the rude soldiers yet felt a blind traditionary veneration for its sanction, when prompting them as patriots to an act which their own multiplied provocations had but too much recommended to their passions. The gigantic ploughman, whom they were invited by their august Senate to kill, was now become hateful to themselves from many past severities, and no less dreadful than hateful in regard to the many similar favours in reversion which Big-Bones promised to pay at sight. Up to this time Thrace had been content to export gladiators for the use of Rome; but now she was beginning to export Emperors. Could there be a happier windfall of luck than that him whom beyond all men known it would be a luxury to kill suddenly by the Senate's order it had become a duty to kill? It was patriotism, it was virtue, by *Senatûs Consultum* or Act of Parliament, to kill this man. For the first time in their lives the soldiers found themselves on the highroad to be virtuous. They all agreed to be intensely virtuous, and for that purpose marched off in a body to the imperial tent. A select party, sword in hand, deputed themselves to wait upon the huge hulk within : their words were not many : but in two minutes they had settled the long arrear between the parties. A deputation entered the tent of Maximin, and despatched the big old ruffian with the same unpitying haste which he had shown under similar circumstances to the gentle-minded Alexander. Aquileia opened her gates immediately, and thus made it evident that the war had been personal to Maximin.

A scene followed within a short time which is in the highest degree interesting. The Senate, in creating two Emperors at once (for the boy Gordian was probably associated to them only by way of masking their experiment), had made it evident that their purpose was to restore the old defunct Republic and its two Consuls. This was their meaning ; and the experiment had now been twice repeated. The Army saw through it : as to the double number of Emperors, *that* was of little consequence, farther than as it expressed their intention, viz. by bringing back the consular government to restore the power of the Senate, and to abrogate that of the Army. The prætorian troops, who were the most deeply interested in preventing any such revolution, watched their opportunity, and attacked the two Emperors in the palace. The deadly feud which had already arisen between these rival Cæsars led each to suppose himself under assault from the other. The mistake was not of long duration. Carried into the streets of Rome, they were both put to death, and treated with monstrous indignities. The young Gordian was adopted by the soldiery. It seems odd that even thus far the guards should sanction the choice of the Senate, having the purposes which they had ; but perhaps Gordian had recommended himself to their favour in a degree which might outweigh what they considered the original vice of his appointment ; and his youth promised them at least an immediate impunity. This prince, however, like so many of his predecessors, soon came to an unhappy end. Under the guardianship of the upright Misitheus, for a time he prospered ; and preparations were made upon a grand scale for the energetic administration of a Persian War. But Misitheus died, perhaps by poison, in the course of the campaign ; and to him succeeded, as prætorian prefect, an Arabian officer called Philip. The innocent boy, left without friends, was soon removed by murder ; and a monument was afterwards erected to his memory at the junction of the Aboras and the Euphrates. Great obscurity, however, clouds this part of History ; nor is it so much as known in what way the Persian War was conducted or terminated.

Philip, having made himself Emperor, celebrated, upon his arrival in Rome, the secular games, in the year 247 of the Christian era,—that being the completion of a thousand years[1] from the foundation of Rome. But Nemesis was already on his steps. An insurrection had broken out amongst the legions stationed in Mœsia ; and they had raised to the purple some officer of low rank. Philip, having occasion to notice this affair in the Senate, received for answer from Decius that probably the pseudo - imperator would prove a mere evanescent phantom. This conjecture was confirmed ; and Philip in consequence conceived a high opinion of Decius, whom (as the insurrection still continued) he judged to be the fittest man for suppressing it. Decius accordingly went, armed with the proper authority. But, on his arrival, he found himself compelled by the insurgent army to choose between empire and death. Thus constrained, he yielded to the wishes of the troops ; and then, hastening with a veteran army into Italy, he fought the battle of Verona, where Philip was defeated and killed, whilst the son of Philip—need it be said ?—was murdered at Rome by the prætorian guards.

---

[1] "*The completion of a thousand years*":—*i.e.* of a thousand years since the foundation of Rome, and not (let the reader observe) since the birth of Romulus. Subtract from 1000 (as the total lapse of years since the natal day of Rome) the number 247, as representing that part of the 1000 which had accumulated since the era of Christ at the epoch of the Secular Games, and there will remain 753 for the sum of the years between Rome's nativity and the year of our Lord. But, as Romulus must have reached manhood when he founded the robber city, suppose him 23 years old at that era, and his birth will fall in the year 776 before Christ. And this is the year generally assigned. But it must be remembered that there are dissentient schemes of chronology.

With Philip ends, according to our distribution, the second series of the Cæsars, comprehending Commodus, Pertinax, Didius Julianus, Septimius Severus, Caracalla, and Geta, Macrinus, Heliogabalus, Alexander Severus, Maximin, the two Gordians, Pupienus and Balbinus, the third Gordian, and Philip the Arab.

In looking back at this series of Cæsars, we are horror-struck at the blood-stained picture. Well might a foreign writer, in reviewing the same succession, declare that it is like passing into a new world when the transition is made from this chapter of the human history to that of Modern Europe. From Commodus to Decius are sixteen names, which, spreading through a space of fifty-nine years, assign to each Cæsar a reign of less than four years. And Casaubon remarks that in one period of 160 years there were seventy persons who assumed the Roman purple; which gives to each not much more than two years. On the other hand, in the history of France we find that through a period of 1200 years there have been no more than sixty-four kings : upon an average, therefore, each king appears to have enjoyed a reign of nearly nineteen years. This vast difference in security is due to two great principles,—that of primogeniture as between son and son, and of hereditary succession as between a son and every other pretender. Well may we hail the principle of hereditary right as realizing the praise of Burke applied to chivalry, viz. that it is " the cheap defence of nations " ; for the security which is thus obtained, be it recollected, does not regard a small succession of princes, but the whole rights and interests of social man : since the con-tests for the rights of belligerent rivals do not respect them-selves only, but very often spread ruin and proscription amongst all orders of men. The principle of hereditary succession, says one writer, had it been a discovery of any one individual, would deserve to be considered as the very greatest ever made ; and he adds acutely, in answer to the obvious but shallow objection to it (viz. its apparent assumption of equal ability in father and son for ever), that it is like the Copernican system of the heavenly bodies, so contradictory to our sense and first impressions, but true notwithstanding.

CHAPTER VI

RETURNING to our sketch of the Cæsars, at the head of the
third series we place Decius. He came to the throne at a
moment of great public embarrassment. The Goths were now
beginning to press southwards upon the Empire. Dacia they
had ravaged for some time. "And here," says a German
writer, "observe the shortsightedness of the Emperor Trajan.
" Had he left the Dacians in possession of their independence,
" they would, under their native kings, have made head
" against the Goths. But, being compelled to assume the
" character of Roman citizens, they had lost their warlike
" qualities." From Dacia the Goths had descended upon
Mœsia ; and, passing the Danube, they laid siege to Marcian-
opolis, a city built by Trajan in honour of his sister. The
inhabitants paid a heavy ransom for their town ; and the
Goths were persuaded for the present to return home. But,
sooner than was expected, they returned to Mœsia, under
their king, Kniva ; and they were already engaged in the
siege of Nicopolis when Decius came in sight at the head of
the Roman Army. The Goths retired, but it was to Thrace ;
and, in the conquest of Philippopolis, they found an ample
indemnity for their forced retreat and disappointment.
Decius pursued, but the King of the Goths turned suddenly
upon him ; the Emperor was obliged to fly ; the Roman
camp was plundered ; Philippopolis was taken by storm, and

---

[1] In *Blackwood* for August 1834.

its whole population, reputed at more than a hundred thousand souls, perished.

Such was the first great irruption of the Barbarians into the Roman territory ; and panic was diffused on the wings of the wind over the whole Empire. Decius, however, was firm, and made prodigious efforts to restore the balance of power to its ancient settlement. For the moment he had some partial successes. He cut off several detachments of Goths, on their road to reinforce the enemy ; and he strengthened the fortresses and garrisons of the Danube. But his last success was the means of his total ruin. He came up with the Goths at Forum Terebronii ; and, having surrounded their position, he had good reason to think their destruction inevitable. A great battle ensued, and a mighty victory to the Goths. Nothing is now known of the circumstances, except that the third line of the Romans was entangled inextricably in a morass (as had happened in the Persian expedition of Alexander). Decius perished on this occasion ; nor was it possible to find his dead body.[1]

This great defeat naturally raised the authority of the Senate, in the same proportion as it depressed that of the Army ; and by the will of that body Hostilianus, a son of Decius, was raised to the Empire ; with Gallus, however, an experienced commander, for his associate. Ostensibly, the reason assigned for this measure was the youth of Hostilianus ; but, in reality, the whole arrangement was governed by the secret policy of the Senate for restoring the Consulate and the ancient machinery of the Republic. But no skill or experience could avail to retrieve the sinking power of Rome upon the Illyrian frontier. The Roman Army was disorganized, panic-stricken, reduced to skeleton battalions.

---

[1] It does not absolutely follow from the mere fact, uncircumstantiated, of Decius having been a persecuting anti-Christian, that he must have been a bad man. But this is an inference too probable from the rancorous fury of his persecution. To *his* reign belongs the legend of the Seven Sleepers, a septemvirate of Christian youths who sought an asylum from the imperial wrath in the recesses of a cavern ; fell asleep, and first of all awakened from their slumbers some four generations later ; found their persecutor utterly forgotten ; and themselves restored to an inheritance of hopes no longer irreconcilable with the demands of their religious conscience.

Without an army, what could be done ?   And thus it may really have been no blame to Gallus that he made a treaty with the Goths more degrading than any parallel act in the long annals of Rome.   By the terms of this infamous bargain, the enemy were allowed to carry off an immense booty, amongst which was a long roll of distinguished prisoners ; and Cæsar himself it was—not any lieutenant or agent that might have been afterwards disavowed—who volunteered to purchase their future absence by an annual tribute.   The very army which had brought their Emperor into the necessity of submitting to such abject concessions were the first to take offence at this natural result of their own failures.   Gallus was already ruined in public opinion when further revelations deepened the shadows of his disgrace.   It was now supposed to have been discovered that the late dreadful overthrow of Forum Terebronii was due to his individual false counsels, however much of the disaster must, according to rule and custom, be laid at the door of Decius, who could not be divested of his supreme responsibility ; and, as the young Hostilianus happened to die about this time of a contagious disorder, Gallus was charged with his murder.

Even a ray of prosperity which just now gleamed upon the Roman arms aggravated the disgrace of Gallus, and was instantly made the handle of his ruin.   Æmilianus, the governor of Mœsia and Pannonia, inflicted some loss, whether damage or disgrace, upon the Goths ; and, in the enthusiasm of sudden pride, upon an occasion which contrasted so advantageously for him with the military conduct of Decius and Gallus, the soldiers of his own legion raised Æmilianus to the purple.   No time was to be lost. Summoned by the troops, Æmilianus marched into Italy ; and no sooner had he made his appearance there than the prætorian guards murdered the Emperor Gallus and his son Volusianus, by way of confirming the election of Æmilianus.

The new Emperor offered to secure the frontiers, both on the east and on the Danube, from the incursions of the Barbarians.   This offer may be regarded as thrown out for the conciliation of all classes in the Empire.   But to the Senate, in particular, he addressed a message which forcibly illustrates the political position of that body in those times.

Æmilianus proposed to resign the whole civil administration into the hands of the Senate, reserving to himself only the unenviable burthen of the military interests. His hope was that, in this way making himself in part the creation of the Senate, he might strengthen his title against competitors at Rome, whilst the entire military administration, going on under his own eyes, exclusively directed to that one object, would give him some chance of defeating the hasty and tumultuary competitions so apt to arise amongst the legions upon the frontier. In these calculations of Æmilianus the reader will notice—as one most impressive and ominous phenomenon—that all his anxiety is directed to intrigues and the balancing of parties at home, and no particle of his care pointed to the enemy outside. Such a policy might really be required; but in this necessity lay the deepest argument and gloomiest pledge of public ruin. We notice the transaction chiefly as indicating the anomalous situation of the Senate. Without power in a proper sense, or no more, however, than the indirect power of wealth, that ancient body retained an immense *auctoritas:* that is, an influence built upon ancient reputation, which, in their case, had the strength of a religious superstition in all Italian minds. This influence the Senators exerted with effect whenever the course of events had happened to cripple the Army or to prostrate the momentary Cæsar. And never did they make a more continuous and sustained effort for retrieving their ancient power and place, together with the whole system of the Republic, than during the period at which we have now arrived. From the time of Maximin, in fact, to the accession of Aurelian, the Senate perpetually interposed their credit and authority, like some *Deus ex machinâ* in dramatic catastrophes. And, if this one fact were all that had survived of the public annals at this period, we might sufficiently collect the situation of the two other parties in the Empire—the Army and the Imperator; the weakness and precarious tenure of the one, and the anarchy of the other. And hence it is that we can explain the hatred borne to the Senate by vigorous Emperors, such as Aurelian, succeeding to a long course of weak and troubled reigns. Such an Emperor presumed in the Senate, and not without reason, that same spirit of domineering interference as ready to manifest itself, upon any opportunity offered, against himself, which in his earlier days he had witnessed so repeatedly in successful operation upon the fates and prospects of others.

The situation indeed of the World—meaning by "*the World*" (or, in the phrase then current, ἡ οἰκουμένη) that great centre of civilisation which, running round the Mediterranean in one continuous belt of great breadth, still composed the Roman Empire—was at this time profoundly interesting. The crisis had arrived. In the East a new dynasty (the Sassanides) had remoulded ancient elements into a new form, and breathed a new life into an empire which else was gradually becoming crazy, or even palsied, from age, and which, at any rate, by losing its unity, must have lost its vigour as an offending power. Parthia was languishing and drooping as an anti-Roman state when the last of the Arsacidæ expired. A perfect *palingenesis* was wrought by the restorer of the Persian Empire, which pretty nearly re-occupied (and gloried in re-occupying) the very area that had once composed the Empire of Cyrus. Even this *palingenesis* might have terminated in a divided Empire : vigour might have been restored, but in the shape of a polyarchy (such as the Saxons established in England), rather than a monarchy; and, in reality, at one moment, that appeared to be a probable event. Now, had this been the course of the revolution, an alliance with one of these kingdoms would have tended to balance the hostility of any other (as was in fact the case when Alexander Severus saved himself from the Persian power by a momentary alliance with Armenia). But all the elements of disorder had in that quarter re-combined themselves into severe unity; and thus was Rome, upon her eastern frontier, laid open to a new power ebullient with juvenile activity and vigour, just at the period when the languor of the decaying Parthian had allowed the Roman discipline to fall into a corresponding declension. Such was the condition of Rome upon her oriental frontier.[1] On the

---

[1] And it is a striking illustration of the extent to which the revolution had gone that, previously to the Persian expedition of the last Gordian, Antioch, the Roman capital of Syria, had been occupied by the enemy.

northern it was much worse.   Precisely at the crisis of a
great revolution in Asia, which demanded in that quarter
more than the total strength of the Empire, and threatened
to demand it for ages to come, did the Goths, under their
earliest denomination of *Getæ*, with many other associate
tribes, begin to push with their horns against the northern
gates of the Empire.   The whole line of the Danube, and,
pretty nearly about the same time, of rivers more western
(upon which tribes from Swabia and Franconia were beginning to gather in terrific masses), now became insecure ; and
the great rivers ceased in effect to be the barriers of Rome.
Taking a middle point of time between the Parthian revolution and the fatal overthrow of Forum Terebronii, we may
fix upon the reign of Philip the Arab (who naturalized himself in Rome by the appellation of Marcus Julius) as the
epoch from which the Roman Empire, already sapped and
undermined by changes from within, began steadily to give
way from without.   And this reign dates itself in the series
by those ever-memorable secular or jubilee games which celebrated the thousandth year from the foundation of Rome.[1]

Resuming our sketch of the Imperial History, we may
remark the natural embarrassment which must have possessed
the Senate when two candidates for the purple were equally
earnest in appealing to *them*, and their deliberate choice, as
the best foundation for a valid election.   Scarcely had the
ground been cleared for Æmilianus by the murder of Gallus
and his son (the invariable clearance of the stage in the
succession of Cæsars !) when Valerian, a Roman Senator (of
such eminent merit, and confessedly so much the foremost
noble in all the qualities essential to the very delicate and
comprehensive functions of a Censor,[2] that Decius had revived

---

[1] This Arab Emperor reigned about five years ; and the jubilee
celebration occurred in his second year.   Another circumstance gives
importance to the Arabian,—that, according to one tradition, he was
the first Christian Emperor.   If so, it is singular that one of the
bitterest persecutors of Christianity should have been his immediate
successor—viz. Decius.

[2] It has proved a most difficult problem, in the hands of all speculators upon the Imperial History, to throw any light upon the purposes
of the Emperor Decius in attempting the revival of the ancient but
necessarily obsolete office of a public censorship.   Either it was an act

that office expressly in his behalf), entered Italy at the head of the army from Gaul. He had been summoned to his aid by the late Emperor, Gallus ; but, arriving too late for his support, he determined to avenge him. Both Æmilianus

of pure verbal pedantry or a mere titular decoration of honour (as if a modern prince should create a person Arch-Grand-Elector, with no objects assigned to his electing faculty) ; or else, if it really meant to revive the old duties of the censorship, and to assign the very same field for the exercise of those duties, it must be viewed as the very grossest practical anachronism that has ever been committed. We mean by an anachronism, in common usage, that sort of blunder when a man ascribes to one age the habits, customs, or the inalienable characteristics of another. This, however, may be a mere lapse of memory as to a matter of fact, and implying nothing at all discreditable to the understanding, but only that a man has shifted the boundaries of chronology a little this way or that ; as if, for example, a writer should speak of printed books as existing at the day of Agincourt, whereas that battle [A.D. 1415] preceded the invention of printing by nearly thirty years, or of artillery as existing in the first Crusade. Here would be an error, but a very venial one. A far worse kind of anachronism, though rarely noticed as such, is where a writer ascribes sentiments and modes of thought incapable of co-existing with the sort or the degree of civilisation then attained, or otherwise incompatible with the structure of society in the age or the country assigned. For instance, in Southey's *Don Roderick* there is a cast of sentiment in the Gothic King's remorse and contrition of heart which has struck many readers as utterly unsuitable to the social and moral development of that age, and redolent of modern Methodism. This, however, we mention only as an illustration, without wishing to hazard an opinion upon the justice of that criticism. But even such an anachronism is less startling and extravagant when it is confined to an ideal representation of things than where it is practically embodied and brought into play amongst the realities of life. What would be thought of a man who should attempt, in 1833, to revive the ancient office of *Fool*, as it existed down to the reign of Henry VIII in England ? Yet the error of the Emperor Decius was far greater, if he did in sincerity and good faith believe that the Rome of his times was amenable to that licence of unlimited correction, and of interference with private affairs, which Republican freedom and simplicity had once conceded to the Censor. In reality the ancient Censor, in some parts of his office, was neither more nor less than a compendious legislator. Acts of attainder, divorce bills, &c., illustrate the case in England ; they are cases of law, modified to meet the case of an individual ; and the Censor, having a sort of equity jurisdiction, was intrusted with discretionary powers for reviewing, revising, and amending, *pro re nata*, whatever in the private life of a Roman citizen seemed, to his experienced eye, alien to the simplicity of an austere Republic ; whatever tended to excess in household expenditure, according to their rude notions of and Valerian recognised the authority of the Senate, and professed to act under that sanction ; but it was the soldiery that cut the knot, as usual, by the sword. Æmilianus was encamped at Spoleto ; but, as the enemy drew near, his

political economy ; and, generally, whatever touched the interests of the Commonwealth, though not falling within the general province of legislation, either because it might appear undignified in its circum-stances, or too narrow in its range of operation for a public anxiety, or because considerations of delicacy and prudence might render it unfit for a public scrutiny. Take one case, drawn from actual experi-ence, as an illustration :—A Roman nobleman, under one of the early Emperors, had thought fit, by way of increasing his income, to retire into rural lodgings, or into some small villa, whilst his splendid mansion in Rome was let to a rich tenant. That a man who wore the *laticlave* (which in practical effect of splendour we may consider equal to the ribbon and star of a modern order) should descend to such a degrading method of raising money, was felt as a scandal to the whole nobility.[1] Yet what could be done? To have interfered with his conduct by an express law would be to infringe the sacred rights of property, and to say, in effect, that a man should not do what he would with his own. This would have been a remedy far worse than the evil to which it was applied ; nor could it have been possible so to shape the principle of a law as not to make it far more comprehensive than the momentary occasion demanded. The Senator's trespass was in a matter of decorum : but the law would have trespassed on the

---

[1] This feeling still exists in France "One winter," says the author of *The English Army in France*, vol. ii. pp. 106-107, "our commanding officer's wife formed the project of [illegible] during the absence of the owner ; but a more profound [illegible] been offered to a Chevalier de St Louis. Hire his house! What could these people take him for ? A sordid wretch who would stoop to make money by such means? They ought to be ashamed of themselves. He could never respect an Englishman again." "And yet," adds the writer, "this gentleman (had an officer been billeted there) would have " *sold* him a bottle of wine out of his cellar, or a cwt. of wood from his stack, " or an egg from his hen-house, at a profit of fifty per cent, not only without " scruple, but upon no other terms. It was as common as ordering wine at a " tavern to call the servant of any man's establishment where we happened " to be quartered, and demand an account of the cellar, as well as the price of " the wine selected!" This feeling existed, and perhaps to the same extent, two centuries ago, in England. Not only did the aristocracy think it a degra-dation to act the part of landlord with respect to their own houses, but also, except in [illegible] of tenant. Thus, the first Lord Brooke (the famous [illegible])—[illegible] shed it to be inscribed on his tomb *Here lies the Frie[illegible]*, and left writings (both prose and verse), obscure, it is true, but often full of profound thinking,—writing to inform his next neighbour, a woman of rank, that the house she occupied had been pur-chased by a London citizen, confesses his fears that he shall in consequence lose so valuable a [illegible] ; for doubtless, he adds, your ladyship will not remain a tenant to [illegible]." And yet this "fellow," whom it would be infamy to accept for a landlord, had notoriously held the office of Lord Mayor; which made him for the time a privy councillor, and consequently *Right Honour-able*. The Italians of this day make no scruple to let off the whole, or even part, of their fine mansions to strangers.

soldiers, shrinking no doubt from a contest with veteran troops, made their peace by murdering the new Emperor, and Valerian was elected in his stead.   This prince was already an old man at the time of his election ; but he lived long enough to look back upon the day of his inauguration as the blackest in his life.   Memorable were the calamities which fell upon himself, and upon the Empire, during his reign.   He began by associating to himself his son Gallienus, —partly, perhaps, for his own relief in public business, partly to indulge the Senate in their steady plan of dividing the Imperial authority.   The two Emperors undertook the military defence of the Empire, —Gallienus proceeding to the northern frontier, Valerian to the eastern.   Under Gallienus, the Franks—otherwise *Franci*, who gave the name to France, otherwise Φράγγοι (in pronunciation Franghoi),

first principles of justice.   Here, then, was a case within the jurisdiction of the Censor: he took notice, in his public report, of the senator's error ; or probably, before coming to that extremity, he admonished him privately.   Just as, in England, had there been such an officer, he would have reproved those men of rank about the era of Waterloo who patronized the *Whip Club* or the pugilistic *Fancy*, or rode their own horses in a match on a public racecourse.   Such a reproof, however, unless practically operative, and powerfully supported by the whole body of the aristocracy, would recoil upon its author as a piece of impertinence, and would soon be resented as an unwarrantable liberty taken with private rights ; the Censor would be kicked, or challenged to private combat, according to the taste of the parties aggrieved.   The office is clearly in this dilemma : if the Censor is supported by the state, then he combines in his own person both legislative and executive functions, and possesses a power which is frightfully irresponsible ; if, on the other hand, he is left to such support as he can find in the prevailing spirit of manners, and the old traditionary veneration for his own official character, he stands very much in the situation of a priesthood, which has great power or none at all according to the condition of a country in moral and religious feeling, coupled with the more or less primitive state of manners. How, then, with any rational prospect of success, could Decius attempt the revival of an office depending so entirely on moral supports, in an age when all those supports were withdrawn ?   The prevailing spirit of manners was hardly fitted to sustain even a toleration of such an office, so far from promising to it a conniving indulgence ; and, as to the traditionary veneration for its sacred character, *that*, probably from long disuse of its practical functions, was altogether extinct.   If these considerations are plain and intelligible even to us, by the men of that day they must have been felt with a degree of force that could

otherwise (as in Persia and Hindostan) Feringhees, or, as by
the Ottoman Turks they were called, Varangians (see Sir
Walter Scott's *Count Robert of Paris*)—began first to make
themselves heard of. Breaking into Gaul, they passed
through that country into Spain; captured Tarragona in
their route; crossed over to Africa; and conquered Mauritania or Morocco. At the same time, the Alemanni, who
had been in motion since the time of Caracalla, broke into
Lombardy, across the Rhætian Alps. The Senate, left without aid from either Emperor, were obliged to make preparations for the common defence against this host of Barbarians.
Luckily, the very magnitude of the enemy's success, by
overloading him with booty, made it his interest to retire
without fighting; and the degraded Senate, hanging upon
the traces of their retiring footsteps, without fighting or daring

leave no room for doubt or speculation on the matter. How was it,
then, that the Emperor only should have been blind to such general
light? In the absence of all other, even conjectural, solutions of this
difficulty, we will state our own theory of the matter. Decius, as is
evident from his fierce persecution of the Christians, was not disposed
to treat Christianity with indifference, under any form which it might
assume, or however masked. Yet there were quarters in which it
lurked, not liable to the ordinary modes of attack. Christianity was
creeping up with inaudible steps into high places,—nay, into the very
highest. The immediate predecessor of Decius upon the throne, Philip
the Arab, was supposed (some said was *known*) to be a disciple of the
new faith; and amongst the nobles of Rome, through the females and
the slaves (two orders of society often far asunder in rank, but agree-
ing in this, that to *them* exclusively the *nurseries*, from cottage upwards
to the most superb of palaces, were unavoidably open), that faith had
spread its roots in every direction. Some secrecy, however, attached
to the profession of a religion so often proscribed. Who should presume to tear away the mask which prudence or timidity had taken
up? A *delator*, or professional informer, was an infamous character.
To deal with the noble and illustrious, the descendants of the Marcelli
and the Gracchi, there must be nothing less than a great state officer,
supported by the Imperator and the Senate, having an unlimited
privilege of scrutiny and censure, authorized to inflict the brand of
infamy for offences not challenged by the letter of the law—an office
emanating from an elder institution, familiar to the days of reputed
liberty. Such an officer was the Censor; and such, according to *our*
solution of the case, were the antichristian purposes of Decius in his
revival. Not the prestige, nor the *auctoritas*, of the Censor was what
Decius coveted, but his power of sneaking and wriggling into house-
holds. The Censor was a Right Hon. Sneak.

to fight, claimed the honours of a victory. Even then, however, they did more than was agreeable to the jealousies of Gallienus ; who by an edict publicly rebuked their presumption, and forbade them in future to appear amongst the legions, or to exercise any military functions : for, in the eternal conflict of Senate and Cæsar, this late apparition of the Senate formed a bad precedent. Gallienus himself, meanwhile, could devise no better way of providing for the public security than by marrying the daughter of his chief enemy, the king of the Marcomanni. On this side of Europe the Barbarians were thus quieted for the present ; but the Goths of the Ukraine, in three marauding expeditions of unprecedented violence, ravaged the wealthy regions of Asia Minor, as well as the islands of the Ægean Archipelago, and at length, under the guidance of deserters, landed in the port of the Peiræus, which bears the same maritime relation to Athens that Leith does to Edinburgh. Advancing from this point, after sacking Athens and the chief cities of Greece, they marched on Epirus, and began to threaten Italy. But the defection at this crisis of a conspicuous chieftain, and the burden of their booty, made these wild marauders anxious to provide for a safe retreat ; the Imperial commanders in Mœsia listened eagerly to their offers : and it set the seal to the public dishonours that, after having traversed so vast a territory almost without resistance, these ruffians were now suffered to retire under the very guardianship of those whom they had visited with military execution.

Such were the terms upon which the Emperor Gallienus purchased a brief respite from his haughty enemies. For the moment, however, he *did* enjoy security. Far otherwise was the destiny of his unhappy father. Sapor now ruled in Persia ; the throne of Armenia had vainly striven to maintain its independency against his armies, and the daggers of his hired assassins. This revolution, which so much enfeebled the Roman means of war, exactly in that proportion increased the necessity for it. War, and that instantly, seemed to offer the only chance for maintaining the Roman name or existence in Asia. Carrhæ and Nisibis, the two potent fortresses in Mesopotamia, had fallen ; and the Persian arms were now triumphant on the right bank, not less than on the left bank, of the Euphrates. Valerian was not of a character to look with indifference upon such a scene, terminated by such a prospect. Prudence and temerity, fear and confidence, all spoke a common language in this great emergency ; and Valerian marched toward the Euphrates with a fixed purpose of driving the enemy beyond that river. By whose mismanagement the records of history do not enable us to say,—some think of Macrianus, the prætorian prefect, some of Valerian himself, but doubtless by the treachery of guides co-operating with errors in the general, —the Roman army, according to a fate which had now become as periodically recurrent as any tertian or quartan fever, was entangled in marshy ground ; partial actions followed, and skirmishes of cavalry, in which the Romans suddenly awoke to a ghastly consciousness of their situation : retreat was cut off, advance was barred, and to fight was now found to be without hope. In these circumstances they offered to capitulate. But the haughty Sapor would listen to nothing short of unconditional surrender ; and to that course the unhappy Emperor submitted. Various traditions have been preserved by history concerning the fate of Valerian [1] : all agree that he died in misery and captivity ; but some have circumstantiated this general statement by features of excessive misery and special degradation. But these were perhaps added afterwards as picturesque improvements of the scenical interest, or by ethical writers, in order to point and strengthen the moral. Gallienus now ruled alone, except as regarded the restless efforts of insurgent pretenders to the purple, thirty of whom are said to have arisen in his single reign. This, however, is probably an exaggeration. Nineteen such ambitious rebels are mentioned by name : of whom the chief were Calpurnius Piso, a Roman senator ; Tetricus, a man of rank who claimed a descent from Pompey, from Crassus, and even from Numa Pompilius,

---

[1] Some of these traditions have been preserved, which represent Sapor as using his imperial captive for his *horse-block* or *anabathrum* in mounting his horse. Others,—which is irreconcilable with this tale,—allege that Sapor actually flayed his unhappy prisoner while yet alive. The temptation to these stories was perhaps found in the craving for the marvellous, and in the desire to make the contrast more striking between the two extremes in Valerian's life.

and maintained himself some time in Gaul and Spain ; Tre-bellianus, who founded a republic of robbers in Isauria which survived himself by centuries ; and Odenathus, the Syrian. Others were mere *Terræ filii*, or adventurers, who flourished and decayed in a few days or weeks ; and of these the most remarkable was a working armourer named Marius. Not one of the whole number eventually prospered, except Odena-thus ; and he, though originally a rebel, yet, in consideration of services against Persia, was suffered to retain, and to transmit his pretty kingdom of Palmyra[1] to his widow Zenobia. He was even complimented with the absurd title of Augustus (*i.e.* of *Sebastus*, as in a Greek city). All the rest perished. Their rise, however, and local prosperity at so many different points of the empire, showed the distracted condition of the state, and its internal weakness. That again proclaimed its external peril. No other cause had called forth this diffusive spirit of insurrection than the general consciousness, so fatally warranted, of the debility which had now emasculated the government, and its incompetency to deal vigorously with the public enemies.[2] The very granaries of Rome, Sicily and Egypt, were the seats of continued *émeutes*, or (in language more commensurate) of convulsions ; in Alexandria, the second city of the Empire, there was even a civil war which lasted for twelve years. Dissension, misery, and morbid symptoms and frenzied movements of ambition, expressed themselves by sullen mutterings or whispers over the whole face of the Empire.

[1] Palmyra, the Scriptural *Tadmor in the Wilderness*, to which in our days Lady Hester Stanhope (niece to the great minister Pitt, and seventy times seven more orientally proud, though daughter of the freeborn nation, than ever was Zenobia, that from infancy trode on the necks of slaves) made her way from Damascus, at some risk, amongst clouds of Arabs, she riding the whole way on horseback in the centre of robber tribes, and with a train such as that of Sultans or of Roman Proconsuls.

[2] And this incompetency was *permanently* increased by rebellions that might be brief and fugitive in all other effects. In this particular effect the most trivial and fleeting insurrections left durable scars, since each separate insurgent almost necessarily maintained himself for the moment by spoliations and robberies which left lasting effects behind them ; and too often he was tempted to ally himself with some foreign enemy amongst the Barbarians, who perhaps in this way gained an introduction into the heart of the Empire.

The last of the rebels who directed his rebellion personally against Gallienus was Aureolus. Passing the Rhætian Alps, this leader sought out and defied the Emperor. He was defeated, and retreated upon Milan; but Gallienus, in pursuing him, was lured into an ambuscade, and perished from the wound inflicted by an archer. With his dying breath he is said to have recommended Claudius to the favour of the Senate; and at all events Claudius it was who succeeded. Scarcely was the new Emperor installed before he was summoned to a trial not only arduous in itself, but terrific by the very name of the enemy. The Goths of the Ukraine, in a new armament of six thousand vessels, had again descended by the Bosporus into the south, and had sat down before Thessalonica, the capital at that time of Macedonia. Claudius marched against them with the determination to vindicate the Roman name and honour: "Know," said he, writing to the Senate, "that 320,000 Goths have set foot upon the " Roman soil. Should I conquer them, your gratitude will " be my reward. Should I fall, do not forget who it is that " I have succeeded, and that the commonwealth is exhausted." No sooner did the Goths hear of his approach than, with transports of ferocious joy, they gave up the siege, and hurried to annihilate the last pillar of the Empire. The mighty battle which ensued, neither party seeking to evade it, took place at Naissus. At one time the legions were giving way, when suddenly, by some happy manœuvre of the Emperor, a Roman corps found its way to the rear of the enemy. The Goths gave way in *their* turn, and their defeat was total. According to most accounts they left 50,000 dead upon the field: probably a plausible guess from some great arithmetician. The campaign still lingered, however, at other points, until at last the Emperor succeeded in driving back the relics of the Gothic host into the fastnesses of the Balkan [1]; and there the greater part of them died of hunger and pestilence.

---

[1] "*Balkan*":—A Russian general in our own day, for crossing this difficult range of mountains as a victor, was by the Czar Nicholas raised to the title of *Balkanski*. But it seems there should rightfully have been an elder creation. Claudius might have pre-occupied the ground as the original Balkanski.

These great services performed within two years from his accession to the throne, Claudius, by the rarest of fates, died in his bed at Sirmium, the capital of Pannonia. His brother Quintilius, who had a great command in Aquileia, immediately assumed the purple; but his usurpation lasted only seventeen days; for the last Emperor, with a single eye to the public good, had recommended Aurelian as his successor, guided by his personal knowledge of that general's strategic qualities. The army of the Danube confirmed the appointment; and Quintilius upon that decision committed suicide. Aurelian was of the same harsh and forbidding character, but with the same qualities of energy and decision, as the Emperor Severus: he had, however, the qualities demanded by the times; stern and resolute, not amiable princes, were needed by the exigencies of the state. The hydra-headed Goths were again in the field on the Illyrian quarter: Italy itself was invaded by the Alemanni; and Tetricus, the rebel, still survived as a monument exemplifying the weakness of Gallienus. All these enemies were speedily repressed or vanquished by Aurelian. But it marks the real declension of the Empire, a declension which no personal vigour in the Emperor was any longer sufficient to disguise, that, even in the midst of victory, Aurelian found it necessary to make a formal surrender, by treaty, of that Dacia which Trajan had united with so much ostentation to the Empire. Europe was now again in repose; and Aurelian found himself at liberty to apply his powers as a re-organizer and restorer to the East. In that quarter of the world a marvellous revolution had occurred. The little oasis of Palmyra, from a Roman colony, had grown into the leading province of a great empire. This verdant island of the desert, together with Syria and Egypt, formed an independent and most insolent monarchy under the sceptre of Zenobia.[1] After two battles lost in Syria, Zenobia retreated to Palmyra. With great difficulty[2]

---

[1] Zenobia is complimented by all historians for her magnanimity; but with no foundation in truth. Her first salutation to Aurelian was a specimen of abject flattery; and her last *public* words were evidences of the basest treachery in giving up her generals, and her chief counsellor Longinus, to the vengeance of the ungenerous enemy.

[2] "*Difficulty*"!—Difficulty from what? We presume from scarcity of provisions, and (as regarded the siege) scarcity of wood. But mark

Aurelian pursued her; and with still greater difficulty he pressed the siege of Palmyra. Zenobia looked for relief from Persia; but at that moment Sapor died, and the Queen of Palmyra fled upon a dromedary, but was pursued and captured. Palmyra surrendered and was spared; but, unfortunately, with a folly which marks the haughty spirit of the place, untrained to face the chances of ordinary experiences, scarcely had the conquering army retired when a tumult arose and the Roman garrison (of 600 men) was slaughtered. Little knowledge could those have had of Aurelian's character who tempted him to acts but too welcome to his cruel nature by such an outrage as this. The news overtook the Emperor on the Hellespont. Earth has witnessed no such jubilant explosion of vindictive hatred, unless it were in the retaliation (too probably just, as we *now*, 1859, can guess) by Nadir Shah [1] on the perfidious citizens of Delhi for a similar massacre of the garrison which he had left behind. Instantly, without pause, "like Até hot from hell," Aurelian retraced his steps, reached the guilty city, and consigned it, with all its population, to that utter destruction from which it has never since arisen.

The energetic administration of Aurelian had now restored the Empire, not to its lost vigour—that was impossible—but to a condition of repose. This was a condition more agreeable to the Empire than to the Emperor. Peace was hateful to Aurelian; and he sought for war, where it could seldom be sought in vain, upon the Persian frontier. But he was not destined to reach the Euphrates; and it is worthy of notice, as a providential ordinance, that his own unmerciful nature was the ultimate cause of his fate. Anticipating the Emperor's severity in punishing some errors of his own, Mucassor, a general officer in whom Aurelian placed especial confidence, assassinated him between Byzantium and Heraclea. An interregnum of eight months succeeded, during which there occurred a contest of a memorable nature. Some

how these vaunted and vaunting Romans, so often as they found themselves in our modern straits, sat down to cry. Heavier by far have been our British perplexities upon many an Oriental field; but did we sit down to cry?

[1] Otherwise known as Kouli Khan.

historians have described it as strange and surprising. To us, on the contrary, it seems that no contest could be more natural. Heretofore the great strife had been in what way to secure the reversion or possession of that great dignity ; whereas now the rivalship lay in declining it. But surely such a competition had in it, under the circumstances of the Empire, little that can justly surprise us. Always a post of danger, and so regularly closed by assassination that in a course of two centuries there are hardly to be found three or four cases of exception, the imperatorial dignity had now become burdened with a public responsibility which exacted great military talents, and imposed a perpetual and personal activity. Formerly, if the Emperor knew himself to be surrounded with assassins, he might at least make his throne, so long as he enjoyed it, the couch of a voluptuary. The "*Ave Imperator !*" was then the summons, if to the supremacy in passive danger, so also to the supremacy in power, and honour, and enjoyment. But now it was a summons to never-ending tumults and alarms, an injunction to that sort of vigilance without intermission which even from the poor sentinel is exacted only when on duty. Not Rome, but the frontier ; not the *aurea domus*, but a camp, was the imperial residence. Power and rank, whilst in that residence, could be had in no larger measure by Cæsar *as* Cæsar than by the same individual as a military commander-in-chief ; and, as to enjoyment, *that* for the Roman Imperator was now extinct. Rest there could be none for him. Battle was the tenure by which he held his office ; and beyond the range of his trumpet's blare his sceptre was a broken reed. The office of Cæsar at this time resembled the situation (as it is sometimes described in romances) of a knight who has achieved the favour of some capricious lady, with the present possession of her castle and ample domains, but which he holds under the known and accepted condition of meeting all challenges whatsoever offered at the gate by wandering strangers, and also of jousting at any moment with each and all amongst the inmates of the castle, as often as a wish might arise to benefit by the chances in disputing his supremacy.

It is a circumstance, moreover, to be noticed in the aspect of the Roman Monarchy at this period, that the pressure of the evils we are now considering applied to this particular age of the Empire beyond all others, as being an age of transition from a greater to an inferior power. Had the power been either greater or conspicuously less, in that proportion would the pressure have been easier, or none at all. Being greater, for example, the danger would have been repelled to a distance so great that mere remoteness would have disarmed its terrors, or otherwise it would have been violently overawed. Being less, on the other hand, and less in an eminent degree, it would have disposed all parties, as it did at an after period, to regular and formal compromises in the shape of fixed annual tributes. At present the policy of the Barbarians along the vast line of the northern frontier was to tease and irritate the provinces which they were not entirely able, or were prudentially unwilling, to dismember. Yet, as the almost annual irruptions were at every instant ready to be converted into *coup-de-mains* upon Aquileia, upon Verona, or even upon Rome herself, unless vigorously curbed at the outset, each Emperor at this period found himself under the necessity of standing in the attitude of a champion or *propugnator* on the frontier line of his territory, ready for all comers, and with a pretty certain prospect of having one pitched battle at the least to fight in every successive summer. There were nations abroad at this epoch in Europe who did not migrate occasionally, or occasionally project themselves upon the civilised portion of the globe, but who made it their steady, regular occupation to do so, and lived for no other purpose. Through seven hundred years the Roman Republic might be styled a Republic militant: for about one century further it was an Empire triumphant; and now, long retrograde, it had reached that point at which again, but in a different sense, it might be styled an Empire militant. Originally it had militated for glory and power; now its militancy was for a free movement of aspiring and hopeful existence. War was again the trade of Rome, as it had been once before; but in that earlier period war had been its highest ambition; now it was its dire necessity.

Under this analysis of the Roman condition, need we wonder, with the crowd of unreflecting historians, that the

Senate, at the era of Aurelian's death, should dispute amongst each other,—not, as once, for the possession of the sacred purple, but for the luxury and safety of declining it ?   The sad pre-eminence was finally imposed upon Tacitus, a senator who traced his descent from the historian of that name. He had reached an age of seventy-five years, and possessed a fortune of three millions sterling.[1]   Vainly did the agitated old senator open his lips to decline the perilous honour ; five hundred voices insisted upon the necessity of his compliance ; he was actually hustled into empire ; and thus, as a foreign writer observes, was the descendant of him whose glory it had been to signalize himself as the hater of despotism under the absolute necessity of becoming, in his own person, an unrelenting despot.

This aged senator was thus compelled to be Emperor, and to exchange the voluptuous repose of a palace, which he was never to revisit, for the hardships of a distant camp.   His first act was strikingly illustrative of the Roman condition, as we have just described it.   Aurelian had attempted to disarm one set of enemies by turning the current of their fury upon another.   The Alani were in search of plunder, and strongly disposed to obtain it from Roman provinces. "No, no," said Aurelian ; "if you do that, I shall unchain my legions upon you.   Be better advised : keep those excellent dispositions of mind, and that admirable taste for plunder, until you come whither I will conduct you.   Then discharge your fury, and welcome ; besides which, I will pay you wages for your immediate abstinence ; and on the other side the Euphrates you shall pay yourselves."   Such was the outline of the contract ; and the Alans had accordingly held themselves in readiness to accompany Aurelian from Europe to his meditated Persian campaign.   Meantime, that Emperor had perished by treason ; and the Alani were still

---

[1] "*A fortune of three millions sterling*" :—Whence came these enormous fortunes ?   Several sources might be indicated ; but amongst them perhaps the commonest was this : every citizen of marked distinction made it a practice, if circumstances favoured, to leave a legacy to others of the same class whom he happened to esteem, or wished to acknowledge as special friends.   A very good custom, more honoured in the observance than the breach, and particularly well suited to our own merits !

waiting for his successor on the throne to complete his
engagements with themselves : that successor—if inheriting
his throne—inheriting also in *their* judgment his total
responsibilities.   It happened, from the state of the Empire,
as we have sketched it above, that Tacitus really *did* succeed
to the military plans of Aurelian.   The Persian expedition
was ordained to go forward ; and Tacitus began, as a preliminary step in that expedition, to look about for his good
allies the Barbarians.   Where might they be, and—what
doing ?   Naturally, they had long been weary of waiting.
The Persian booty might be good after *its* kind ; but it was
far away ; and, *en attendant,* Roman booty was doubtless
good after *its* kind.   And so, throughout the provinces of
Cappadocia, Pontus, &c., far as the eye could stretch, nothing
was to be seen but cities and villages in flames.   The Roman
Army hungered and thirsted to be unmuzzled and slipped
upon these false friends.   But this, for the present, Tacitus
would not allow.   He began by punctually fulfilling to the
letter Aurelian's contract,—a measure which Barbarians
inevitably construed into the language of fear.   But then
came the retribution.   Once having satisfied public justice,
the Emperor was now free for vengeance : he unchained his
legions : a brief space of time sufficed for the settlement of a
long reckoning : and through every outlet of Asia Minor the
Alani fled from the wrath of the Roman soldier.   Here, however, terminated the military labours of Tacitus : he died at
Tyana in Cappadocia,[1] as some say, from the effects of the
climate, co-operating with irritations from the insolence of
the soldiery : but, as Zosimus and Zonaras expressly assure
us, under the murderous hands of his own troops.   It was
certainly disagreeable to be murdered ; but else the old
senator had not much to complain of, as seventy-five to
seventy-six years make a fair allowance of life.

His brother Florianus at first usurped the purple, by the
aid of the Illyrian army ; but the choice of other armies,
afterwards confirmed by the Senate, settled upon Probus, a

---

[1] "*Tyana*" :—A city rendered famous as the birthplace and residence of that Apollonius whose conjurings and magical exploits were
paraded, in the early stages of Christianity, as eclipsing the miracles
of the New Testament.

general already celebrated under Aurelian. The two competitors drew near to each other for the usual decision by the sword, when the dastardly supporters of Florian offered up their chosen prince as the purchase-money of a compromise with his antagonist. Probus, settled in his seat by the usual quantity of murder and perfidy, addressed himself to the regular business of those times,—to the reduction of insurgent provinces, and the liberation of others from hostile molestations. Isauria and Egypt he visited in the character of a conqueror ; Gaul in the character of a deliverer. From the Gaulish provinces he chased in succession the Franks, the Burgundians, and the Lygians. He pursued the intruders far into their German thickets ; and nine of the native German princes came spontaneously into his camp, subscribed such conditions as he thought fit to dictate, and complied with his requisitions of tribute in horses and provisions.   This, however, is a delusive gleam of Roman energy, little corresponding with the true prevailing condition of the Roman power, and entirely due to the *personal* qualities of Probus.   This prince himself put on record the sense which he entertained of the political prospects opening before them, by carrying a stone wall, of considerable height, from the Danube to the Neckar. Once this important gallery of land had been defended by human intrepidity ; now by brute Chinese arts of masonry. He made various attempts also to effect a better distribution of barbarous tribes, by dislocating their settlements, and making extensive translations of their clans, according to the circumstances of those times. These arrangements, however, suggested often by short-sighted views, and carried into effect by mere violence, were sometimes defeated visibly at the time ; and, doubtless, in very few cases accomplished the ends proposed. In one instance, where a party of Franks had been transported into the Asiatic province of Pontus, as a column of defence against the intrusive Alans, they, being determined to revisit their own country, swam the Hellespont, landed on the coasts of Asia Minor, of Greece, and Sicily, plundered Syracuse, steered for the Straits of Gibraltar, sailed along the shores of Spain and Gaul, passing finally through the English Channel and the German Ocean, right onwards to

the Frisic and Batavian coasts, where they exultingly
rejoined their exulting friends. Meantime, all the energy
and military skill of Probus could not save him from the
competition of various rivals. Indeed, it must then have
been felt, as by us who look back on those times it is now
felt, that, amidst so continued a series of brief reigns,
violently interrupted by murders, scarcely any idea could
arise answering to our modern ideas of treason and usurpation. For the ideas of fealty and of allegiance, as to an
anointed monarch, could have no time to take root. Candidates for the purple must have been viewed rather as military rivals than as traitors to the reigning Cæsar. And
hence one reason for the slight resistance which was often
experienced by the seducers of armies. Probus, however, as
accident in his case ordered it, subdued all his personal
opponents—Saturninus in the East, Proculus and Bonoses in
Gaul. For these victories he triumphed in the year 281.
But his last hour was even then at hand. One point of his
military discipline, which he called back from elder days,
was to suffer no idleness in his camps. He it was who, by
military labour, translated into Gaul and Hungary the
Italian vine, to the great indignation of the Italian monopo-
list. The culture of vineyards, the laying of military roads,
the draining of marshes, and similar labours, perpetually
employed the hands of his stubborn and contumacious troops.
On some work of this nature the Army happened to be
employed near Sirmium, and Probus was looking on from a
tower, when a sudden frenzy of disobedience seized upon the
men : a party of the mutineers ran up to the Emperor, and
with a hundred wounds laid him instantly dead. That they
laid him dead we do not at all doubt ; but the how and the
why remain, as usual, perfectly in the dark. The unmeaning tale serves only to remind us that in this, as in all other
imperial murders, we are left without any vestige of a
rational inquisition into the circumstances. Hardly one of
these many murders has received any solution. The man
was murdered : *that* we understand : it is all regular. But
to tell us that a party of soldiers ran up to the top of a
tower, and there murdered him, as though the altitude of the
building, or its toilsome ascent, furnished a sort of key to an

atrocity else inexplicable, is to insult us with sheer non-sense. We are told by some writers that the Army was immediately seized with remorse for its own act; which, if truly reported, rather tends to confirm the image otherwise impressed upon us of the relations between the Army and Cæsar as pretty closely corresponding with those between some fierce wild beast and its keeper : the keeper, if not uniformly vigilant as an Argus, is continually liable to fall a sacrifice to the wild instincts of the brute, mastering at inter-vals the reverence and fear under which it has been habitu-ally trained. In this case both the murdering impulse and the remorse seem alike the effects of a brute instinct, and to have arisen under no guidance of rational purpose or reflection.

The person who profited by this murder was Carus, the captain of the guard, a man of advanced years. He was proclaimed Emperor by the Army ; and on this occasion there was no further reference to the Senate than by a dry statement of the facts for its information. Troubling himself little about the approbation of a body not likely in any way to affect his purposes (which were purely martial, and adapted to the tumultuous state of the empire), Carus made immediate preparations for pursuing the Persian expedition, —so long promised and so often interrupted. Having pro-vided for the security of the Illyrian frontier by a bloody victory over the Sarmatians, of whom we now hear for the first time, Carus advanced towards the Euphrates ; and from the summit of a mountain he pointed the eyes of his eager army upon the rich provinces of the Persian Empire. Varanes, the successor of Artaxerxes, vainly endeavoured to negotiate a peace. From some unknown cause, the Persian armies were not at this juncture disposable against Carus: it has been conjectured by some writers that they were engaged in an Indian war. Carus, it is certain, met with little resistance. He insisted on having the Roman supremacy acknowledged as a preliminary to any treaty ; and, having threatened to make Persia as bare as his own skull—which, luckily for the effect of his rhetoric, happened to be bald,— he is supposed to have kept his word with regard to Mesopo-tamia. The great cities of Ctesiphon and Seleucia he took ;

and vast expectations were formed at Rome of the events which stood next in succession, when, on Christmas-day, 283, a sudden and mysterious end overtook Carus and his victorious advance. We are all prepared of course for the customary murder, and the customary lie for disguising its incidents. The story transmitted to Rome was that a great storm and a sudden darkness had surprised the camp of Carus ; that the Emperor, previously ill and reposing in his tent, was obscured from sight ; that at length a cry had arisen, "The Emperor is dead !" and that, at the same moment, the imperial tent had taken fire. The fire was traced to the confusion of his attendants ; and this confusion was imputed by themselves to grief for their master's death. In all this it is easy to read pretty circumstantially a murder committed on the Emperer by corrupted servants, and an attempt afterwards to conceal the traces of this murder by the ravages of fire. The report propagated through the army, and at that time received with credit, was that Carus had been struck by lightning ; and that omen, according to the Roman interpretation, implied a necessity of retiring from the expedition. So that, apparently, the whole was a bloody *Roman* intrigue, set on foot for the purpose of baffling the Emperor's resolution to prosecute the war ; or else it was a *Persian* intrigue, buying off with money the army which they had no means or preparations for meeting on the field of battle.

His son Numerian succeeded to the rank of Emperor by the choice of the Army. But the mysterious faction of murderers were still at work. After eight months' march from the Tigris to the Thracian Bosporus, the Army halted at Chalcedon. At this point of time a report arose suddenly that the Emperor Numerian was dead. The impatience of the soldiery would brook no uncertainty : they rushed to the spot ; satisfied themselves of the fact, and, loudly denouncing as the murderer Aper, the captain of the guard, committed him to custody, and assigned to Diocletian, whom at the same time they invested with the supreme power, the duty of investigating the case. Diocletian acquitted himself of this task in a very summary way, by passing his sword through Aper before he could say a word in his defence.

Let us all hope that the worthy captain *had* no defence, so that his having no time for words is an advantage on all sides ; *least said*, observes the respectable old proverb, *is soonest mended.* As to mending, however, poor Numerian was far past it ; so a new Cæsar is wanted, the old one being cracked,—and who better than Diocletian ? It seems that Diocletian, having been promised the Empire by a prophetess as soon as he should have killed a wild boar (Aper), was anxious to realize the omen. The whole proceeding has been taxed with injustice so manifest as not even to seek a disguise. Meantime, it should be remembered that, *first*, Aper, as the captain of the guard, was answerable for the Emperor's safety, *secondly*, that his anxiety to profit by the Emperor's murder was a sure sign that he had participated in that act, and, *thirdly*, that the assent of the soldiery to the open and public act of Diocletian implies a conviction on their part of Aper's guilt.

Here let us pause, having now arrived at the fourth and last group of the Cæsars, to notice the changes which had been wrought by time, co-operating with political events, in the very nature and constitution of the imperial office.

If it should unfortunately happen that the palace of the Vatican, with its thirteen thousand chambers,[1] were to take fire, for a considerable space of time the fire would be retarded by the mere enormity of extent which it would have to traverse. But there would come at length a critical moment at which, the *maximum* of the retarding effect having been attained, the bulk and volume of the flaming mass would thenceforward assist the flames in the rapidity of their progress. Such was the effect upon the declension of the Roman Empire from the vast extent of its territory. For a very long period that very extent, which finally became the overwhelming caues of its ruin, served to retard and to disguise it. A small encroachment, made at any one point upon the integrity of the Empire, was neither much

---

[1] " *Thirteen thousand chambers* " :—The number of the chambers in this prodigious palace is sometimes estimated at that amount. But Lady Miller, who made particular inquiries on this subject, supposed herself to have ascertained that the total amount, including cellars and closets capable of receiving a bed, was fifteen thousand.

regarded at Rome, nor perhaps in and for itself much deserved to be regarded. But a very narrow belt of encroachments, made upon almost *every* part of so enormous a circumference, was sufficient of itself to compose something of an antagonist force. And to these external dilapidations we must add the far more important dilapidations from within, affecting all the institutions of the State, and all the forces, whether moral or political, which had originally raised it or maintained it. Causes which had been latent in the public arrangements ever since the time of Augustus, and had been silently preying upon its vitals, had now reached a height which would no longer brook concealment. The fire which had smouldered through generations had broken out at length into an open conflagration. Uproar and disorder, and the anarchy of a superannuated Empire, strong only to punish and impotent to defend, were at this time convulsing the provinces in every point of the compass. Rome herself, the eternal city, had been menaced repeatedly; and a still more awful indication of the coming storm had been felt far to the south of Rome. One long wave of the great German Deluge had stretched beyond the Pyrenees and the Pillars of Hercules, to the very homesteads of ancient Carthage. Victorious banners were already floating on the margin of the Great Desert, and they were *not* the banners of Cæsar. Some vigorous hand was demanded at this moment, or else the funeral knell of Rome was on the point of sounding. Indeed, there is every reason to believe that, had the imbecile Carinus (the brother of Numerian) succeeded to the command of the Roman armies at this time, or any other leader than Diocletian, the Empire of the West would have fallen to pieces within the next ten years.

Diocletian was doubtless that man of iron whom the times demanded; and a foreign writer has gone so far as to class him *amongst* the greatest of men, if he were not even himself the greatest. But the position of Diocletian was remarkable beyond all precedent, and was alone sufficient to prevent his being the greatest of men, by making it necessary that he should be the most selfish. For the case stood thus :—If Rome were in danger, much more so was Cæsar. If the condition of the Empire were such that hardly any energy or any foresight was adequate to its defence, for the Emperor, on the other hand, there was scarcely a possibility that he should escape destruction. The chances were in an overbalance against the Empire; but for the Emperor, considered as the representative officer embodying the state, there was no chance at all. He shared in all the hazards of the Empire, and had others so peculiarly pointed at himself that his assassination was now become as much a matter of certain calculation as seed-time and harvest, summer and winter, or any other periodic revolution of nature. The problem, therefore, for Diocletian was a double one,—so to provide for the defence and maintenance of the Empire as simultaneously (and, if possible, through the very same institution) to provide for the personal security of Cæsar This problem he solved, in some imperfect degree, by the only expedient perhaps open to him in that despotism, and in those times. But it is remarkable that, by the revolution which he effected, the office of Roman Imperator was completely altered, and Cæsar became henceforwards an Oriental Sultan or Padishah. Augustus, when moulding for his future purposes the form and constitution of that supremacy which he had obtained by inheritance and by arms, proceeded with so much caution and prudence that even the style and title of his office was discussed in council as a matter of the first moment. The principle of his policy was to absorb into his own functions all those offices which conferred any real power to balance or to control his own. For this reason he appropriated the tribunitian power; because that was a popular and representative office, which, as occasions arose, would have given some opening to democratic influences. But the consular office he left untouched; because all its power was transferred to the Imperator, by the entire command of the army, and by the new organization of the provincial governments.[1]   And in all the rest of his arrange-

<hr>

[1] In no point of his policy was the cunning or the sagacity of Augustus so much displayed as in his treaty of partition with the Senate, which settled the distribution of the provinces and their future administration. Seeming to take upon himself all the trouble and hazard, he did in effect appropriate all the power, and left to the Senate little more than trophies of show and ornament. As a first step, all the greater provinces, Spain and Gaul, were subdivided into

ments Augustus had proceeded on the principle of leaving as many openings to civic influences, and impressing upon all his institutions as much of the old Roman character, as was compatible with the real and substantial supremacy established in the person of the Emperor. Neither is it at all certain, as regarded even this aspect of the imperatorial office, that Augustus had the purpose, or so much as the wish, to annihilate all collateral power, and to invest the chief magistrate with absolute irresponsibility. For himself individually, as called upon to restore a shattered government, and out of the anarchy of civil wars to recombine the elements of power into some shape better fitted for duration (and, by consequence, for insuring peace and protection to

many smaller ones. This done, Augustus proposed that the Senate should preside over the administration of those amongst them which were peaceably settled, and which paid a regular tribute ; whilst all those which were the seats of danger, either as being exposed to hostile inroads, or to internal commotions,—all, therefore, in fact, *which could justify the keeping up of a military force,*—he assigned to himself. In virtue of this arrangement, the Senate possessed in Africa those provinces which had been formed out of Carthage, Cyrene, and the kingdom of Numidia ; in Europe, the richest and most quiet part of Spain (*Hispania Bœtica*), with the large islands of Sicily, Sardinia, Corsica, and Crete, and some districts of Greece ; in Asia, the kingdoms of Pontus and Bithynia, with that part of Asia Minor technically called Asia ; whilst, for his own share, Augustus retained Gaul, Syria, the chief part of Spain, and Egypt, the granary of Rome ; finally, all the military posts on the Euphrates, on the Danube, or the Rhine.— Yet even the showy concessions here made to the Senate were defeated by another political institution, settled at the same time. It had been agreed that the governors of provinces should be appointed by the Emperor and the Senate jointly. But within the senatorian jurisdiction these governors, with the title of *Proconsuls*, were to have no military power whatsoever ; and the appointments were good only for a single year. Whereas, in the imperatorial provinces, where the governor bore the title of *Proprœtor*, there was provision made for a military establishment ; and, as to duration, the office was regulated entirely by the Emperor's pleasure. One other ordinance, on the same head, riveted the vassalage of the Senate. Hitherto, a great source of the Senate's power had been found in the uncontrolled management of the provincial revenues ; but, at this time, Augustus so arranged that branch of the administration that, throughout the senatorian or proconsular provinces, all taxes were immediately paid into the *ærarium*, or treasury of the state ; whilst the whole revenues of the proprœtorian (or imperatorial) provinces from this time forward flowed into the *fiscus*, or private treasure of the individual Emperor.

the world) than the extinct Republic, it might be reasonable to seek such irresponsibility.   But, as regarded his successors, considering the great pains he took to discourage all manifestations of princely arrogance, and to develop by education and example the civic virtues of patriotism and affability in their whole bearing towards the People of Rome, there is reason to presume that he wished to remove them from popular control, without therefore removing them from popular influence.

Hence it was, and from this original precedent of Augustus, aided by the constitution which he had given to the office of Imperator, that up to the era of Diocletian no prince had dared utterly to neglect the Senate or the People of Rome. He might hate the Senate, like Severus or Aurelian ; he might even meditate their extermination, like the brutal Maximin.   But this arose from any cause rather than from contempt.   He hated them precisely because he feared them, or because he paid them an involuntary tribute of superstitious reverence, or because the malice of a tyrant interpreted into a sort of treason the rival influence of the Senate over the minds of men.   But, before Diocletian, the undervaluing of the Senate, or the harshest treatment of that body, had arisen from views which were *personal* to the individual Cæsar.   It was now made to arise from the very constitution of the office and the mode of the appointment.   To defend the Empire, it was the opinion of Diocletian that a single Emperor was not sufficient.   And it struck him, at the same time, that by the very institution of a plurality of Emperors, which was now destined to secure the integrity of the Empire, ample provision might be made for the personal security of each Emperor.   He carried his plan into immediate execution by appointing an associate to his own rank of Augustus in the person of Maximian — an experienced general ; whilst each of them in effect multiplied his own office still farther by severally appointing a Cæsar, or hereditary prince.   And thus the very same partition of the public authority by means of a duality of Emperors, to which the Senate had often resorted of late as the best means of restoring their own Republican Aristocracy, was now adopted by Diocletian as the simplest engine for overthrowing finally the power of either Senate or Army to interfere with the elective privilege. This he endeavoured to centre in the existing Emperors, and at the same moment to discourage treason or usurpation generally, whether in the party choosing or the party chosen, by securing to each Emperor, in the case of his own assassination, an avenger in the person of his surviving associate, as also in the persons of the two Cæsars, or adopted heirs and lieutenants. The Associate Emperor, Maximian, together with the two Cæsars—Galerius appointed by himself, and Constantius Chlorus by Maximian—were all bound to himself by ties of gratitude : all owing their stations ultimately to his own favour. And these ties he endeavoured to strengthen by other ties of affinity, each of the Augusti having given his daughter in marriage to his own adopted Cæsar. And thus it seemed scarcely possible that a usurpation should be successful against so firm a league of friends and relatives.

The direct purposes of Diocletian were but imperfectly attained. The internal peace of the Empire lasted only during his own reign ; and with his abdication of the Empire commenced the bloodiest civil wars which had desolated the world since the contests of the great triumvirate. But the collateral blow which he meditated against the authority of the Senate was entirely successful. Never again had the Senate any real influence on the fate of the world. And with the power of the Senate expired concurrently the weight and influence of Rome. Diocletian is supposed never to have seen Rome, except on the single occasion when he entered it for the ceremonial purpose of a triumph. Even for that purpose it ceased to be a city of resort ; for Diocletian's was the final triumph. And, lastly, even as the chief city of the Empire for business or for pleasure, it ceased to claim the homage of mankind : the Cæsar was already born whose destiny it was to cashier the metropolis of the world, and to appoint her overshadowing substitute. This also may be regarded in effect as the ordinance of Diocletian ; for he, by his long residence in Nicomedia, expressed his opinion pretty plainly that Rome was not central enough to perform the functions of a capital to so vast an Empire, that this was one cause of the declension now become so visible in the forces of the State, and that some city not very far from the Hellespont or the Ægean Sea would be a capital better adapted by position to the exigencies of the times.

But the revolutions effected by Diocletian did not stop here. The simplicity of its Republican origin had so far affected the external character and *entourage* of the Imperial office that in the midst of luxury the most unbounded, and spite of all other corruptions, a majestic plainness of manners, deportment, and dress, had still continued from generation to generation characteristic of the Roman Imperator in his intercourse with his subjects. All this was now changed ; and for the Roman was substituted the Persian dress, the Persian style of household, a Persian court, and Persian manners. A diadem, or tiara beset with pearls, now encircled the temples of the Roman Augustus ; his sandals were studded with pearls, as in the Persian court ; and the other parts of his dress were in harmony with these. The prince was instructed no longer to make himself familiar to the eyes of men. He sequestered himself from his subjects in the recesses of his palace. None who sought him could any longer gain easy admission to his presence. It was a point of his new duties to be difficult of access ; and they who were at length admitted to an audience found him surrounded by eunuchs, and were expected to make their approaches by genuflexions, by servile "adorations," and by real acts of worship as to a visible god.

It is strange that a ritual of court ceremonies so elaborate and artificial as this should first have been introduced by a soldier, and a warlike soldier, like Diocletian. This, however, is in part explained by his education and long residence in Eastern countries. But the same eastern training fell to the lot of Constantine, who was in effect his successor [1] ; and

[1] On the abdication of Diocletian and of Maximian, Galerius and Constantius succeeded as the new Augusti. The terms of that original family compact under which either of the two had any rights at all were, doubtless, drawn up with precision enough for honest men. But, interpreted by ambitious knaves, no treaty that ever swindler dictated, or hair-splitting lawyer improved by interlineations, but is found to be sown with ambiguities as thickly as the heavens are sown with stars. Drive a coach-and-six through it ! why, ten legions could find a broad ingress through page 1. Galerius, as the more immediate representative of Diocletian, thought himself entitled to appoint both Cæsars,—Daza (Maximinus) in Syria, Severus in Italy. Meantime,

the Oriental tone and standard established by these two
Emperors, though disturbed a little by the plain and military
bearing of Julian, and one or two more Emperors of the
same breeding, finally re-established itself with undisputed
sway in the Court when finally it became Byzantine.

Meantime, the institutions of Diocletian, if they had
destroyed Rome and the Senate as influences upon the course
of public affairs, and if they had destroyed the Roman features
of the Cæsars, do, notwithstanding, appear to have attained
one of their purposes, in limiting the extent of imperial
murders. Travelling through the brief list of the remaining
Cæsars, we perceive a little more security for life ; and hence
the successions are less rapid. Constantine, who (like Aaron's
rod) had swallowed up all his competitors *seriatim*, left the
Empire to his three sons ; and the last of these most unwill-
ingly to Julian. That prince's Persian expedition, so much
resembling in rashness and presumption the Russian campaign
of Napoleon, though so much below it in the scale of its
tragic results, led to the short reign of Jovian (or Jovinian),
which lasted only seven months. Upon his death succeeded
the house of Valentinian [1] ; in whose descendant of the third

Constantine, the son of Constantius, with difficulty obtaining permission from Galerius, paid a visit to his father ; upon whose death,
which followed soon after, Constantine came forward as a Cæsar, under
the appointment of his father To this with a bad grace Galerius submitted ; but immediately, by way of retaliating counterpoise, Maxentius,
a reputed son of Maximian, was roused by emulation with Constantine
to assume the purple , and, being joined by his father, they jointly
attacked and destroyed Severus. Galerius, to revenge the death of his
own Cæsar, advanced towards Rome ; but, being compelled to a
disastrous retreat, he resorted to the measure of associating another
Emperor with himself, as a balance to his new enemies. This was
Licinius ; and thus, at one time, there were six Emperors in the field,
either as Augusti or (with a mere *titular* inferiority of rank) as Cæsars.
Galerius dying, however, all the rest were in succession destroyed by
Constantine.

[1] Valentinian the First, who admitted his brother Valens to a
partnership in the Empire, had. by his first wife, an elder son, Gratian,
who reigned and married himself Theodosius, commonly called
the Great. By his second wife this First Valentinian had Valentinian the Second ; who, upon the death of his brother Gratian, was
allowed to share the Empire by Theodosius. Theodosius, by his first
wife, had two sons : Arcadius, who afterwards reigned as the Eastern
or Byzantine Emperor, and Honorius, whose Western Reign was so much

generation the Empire, properly speaking, expired : for the seven shadows who succeeded, from Avitus and Majorian to Julius Nepos and Romulus Augustulus, were in no proper sense Roman Emperors : they were not even Emperors of the West, but had a limited kingdom in the Italian Peninsula. Valentinian the Third was, in any adequate sense, the last Emperor of the West.

But, in a fuller and ampler sense, recurring to what we have said of Diocletian and the tenor of his great revolution, we may affirm that Probus and Carus were the final representatives of the majesty of Rome ; for they reigned over the whole Empire, not yet incapable of sustaining its own unity ; and in them were still preserved, not yet obliterated by oriental effeminacy, those majestic features which reflected Republican Consuls, and, through them, the Senate and People of Rome.   That which had offended Diocletian in the condition of the Roman Emperors was the grandest feature of their dignity.   It is true that the peril of the office had become intolerable : each Cæsar submitted to his sad inauguration with a certainty, liable even to hardly any disguise from the delusions of youthful hope, that for him, within the boundless Empire which he governed, there was no coast of safety, no shelter from the storm, no retreat, except the grave, from the dagger of the assassin.   Gibbon has described the hopeless condition of one who should attempt to fly from the wrath of the almost omnipresent Imperator.   But this dire impossibility of escape was in the end dreadfully retaliated upon that Imperator.   Persecutors and traitors were found everywhere ; and the vindictive or the ambitious subject found himself as omnipresent as the jealous or the offended Emperor.   There was no escape open,

illustrated by Stilicho, and glorified by the poet Claudian in the farewell music of the Roman harp.   By a second wife, daughter to Valentinian the First, Theodosius had a daughter (half-sister, therefore, to Honorius), whose son was Valentinian the Third ; and through this alliance it was that the two last Emperors of conspicuous mark united their two houses, and entwined their separate ciphers, so that more gracefully, and with the commensurate grandeur of a double-headed eagle —looking east and west to the rising, but also, alas ! to the *setting* sun —the brother Cæsars might take leave of the children of Romulus in the pathetic but lofty words of the departing gladiators, " *Morituri*, we that are now to die, *vos salutamus*, make our farewell salutation to you " !

says Gibbon, *from* Cæsar : true ; but neither was there any escape *for* Cæsar.   The crown of the Cæsars was therefore a crown of thorns ; and it must be admitted that never in this world have rank and power been purchased at so awful a cost in tranquillity and peace of mind.   The steps of Cæsar's throne were absolutely saturated with the blood of those who had possessed it ; and so inexorable was that murderous fate which overhung that gloomy eminence that at length it demanded the spirit of martyrdom in him who ventured to ascend it.   In these circumstances some change was imperatively demanded.   Human nature was no longer equal to the terrors which it was summoned to face.   But the changes of Diocletian transmuted that golden sceptre into a base oriental alloy.   They left nothing behind of what had so much challenged the veneration of man : for it was in the union of republican simplicity with the irresponsibility of illimitable power, it was in the antagonism between the merely human and approachable condition of Cæsar as a man and his divine supremacy as a potentate and king of kings, that the secret lay of his unrivalled grandeur.   This perished utterly under the reforming hands of Diocletian.   Cæsar only it was that could be permitted to extinguish Cæsar : and a Roman Imperator it was who, by remodelling, did in effect abolish,— by exorcising from its foul terrors, did in effect disenchant of its sanctity,—that imperatorial dignity which, having once perished, could have no second existence, and which was undoubtedly the sublimest incarnation of power, and a monument the mightiest of greatness built by human hands, which upon this planet has been suffered to appear.

The Cæsars, it may be right to mention, was written in
a situation which denied me the use of books ; so that, with
the exception of a few pencilled extracts in a pocket-book
from the Augustan History, I was obliged to depend upon my
memory for materials, in so far as respected facts.   These
materials for the Western Empire are not more scanty than
meagre ; and in that proportion so much the greater is the
temptation which they offer to free and sceptical speculation.
To this temptation I have yielded intermittingly ; but, from
a fear (perhaps a cowardly fear) of being classed as a dealer
in licentious paradox, I checked myself exactly where the
largest licence might have been properly allowed to a bold
spirit of incredulity.   In particular, I cannot bring myself to
believe, nor ought therefore to have assumed the tone of a
believer, in the inhuman atrocities charged upon the earlier
Cæsars.   Guided by my own instincts of truth and probability, I should, for instance, have summarily exploded the
most revolting among the crimes imputed to Nero.   But too
often writers who have been compelled to deal in ghastly
horrors form a taste for such scenes, and sometimes, as may
be seen exemplified in those who record the French " Reign
of Terror," become angrily credulous, and impatient of the
slightest hesitation in going along with the maniacal excesses
recorded.   Apparently Suetonius suffered from that morbid

---

[1] This appeared originally as part of De Quincey's Preface to vol. x
of his Collected Writings ; which volume contained the reprint of his
Cæsars.—M.

appetite. Else would he have countenanced the hyperbolical extravagances current about the murder of Agrippina? What motive had Nero for murdering his mother? or, assuming the slightest motive, what difficulty in accomplishing this murder by secret agencies? What need for the elaborate contrivance (as in some costly pantomime) of self-dissolving ships? But, waiving all this superfluity of useless mechanism, which by requiring many hands in working it must have multiplied the accomplices in the crime, and have published his intentions to all Rome, how do these statements tally with the instant resort of the lady herself, upon reaching land, to the affectionate sympathy of her son? Upon this sympathy she counted : but how, if all Rome knew that, like a hunted hare, she was then running on the traces of her last double before receiving her death-blow? Such a crime, so causeless as regarded provocation, so objectless as regarded purpose, and so revolting to the primal impulses of nature, would, unless properly viewed as the crime of a maniac, have alienated from Nero even his poor simple nurse and other dependants, who showed for many years after his death the strength of their attachment by adorning his grave with flowers, and by inflicting such vindictive insults as they could upon the corpse of his antagonist, Galba.

Meantime, that he might be insane, and entitled to the excuse of insanity, is possible. If not, what a monstrous part in the drama is played by the Roman People, who, after this alleged crime, and believing in it, yet sat with tranquillity to hear his musical performances! But a taint of insanity certainly did prevail in the blood of the earlier Cæsars, *i.e.* down to Nero.

Over and above this taint of physical insanity, we should do well to allow for the preternatural tendency towards moral insanity generated and nursed by the anomalous situation of the *Imperator*,—a situation unknown before or since ; in which situation the licence allowed to the individual, after the popular *comitia* had virtually become extinct, hid too often from his eyes the perilous fact that in one solitary direction, —viz. in regard to the representative functions which he discharged as embodying the Roman Majesty,—he, the supreme of men upon Earth, had a narrower licence or discretionary power of action than any slave upon whose neck he trode.   Better for *him*, for his own comfort in living, and for his chance of quiet in dying, that he should violate the moral sense by every act of bloody violence or brutal appetite than that he should trifle with the heraldic sanctity of his Imperatorial robe.

AELIUS LAMIA[1]

FOR a period of centuries there has existed an enigma, dark and insoluble as that of the Sphinx, in the text of Suetonius. Isaac Casaubon, as modest as he was learned, had vainly besieged it ; then, in a mood of revolting arrogance, Joseph Scaliger ; Ernesti, Gronovius, many others ; and all without a gleam of success. Had the treadmill been awarded (as might have been wished) to failure of attempts at solution, under the construction of having traded in false hopes,—*in smoke-selling*, as the Roman law entitled it,—one and all of these big-wigs must have mounted that aspiring machine of Tantalus, *nolentes volentes*.

The passage in Suetonius which so excruciatingly (but so unprofitably) has tormented the wits of such scholars as have sat in judgment upon it through a period of three hundred and fifty years arises in the tenth section of his Domitian. That prince, it seems, had displayed in his outset considerable promise of moral excellence ; in particular, neither rapacity nor cruelty was then apparently any feature in his character. Both qualities, however, found a pretty large and early development in his advancing career, but cruelty the largest

---

[1] Date of original publication has eluded my search : reprinted by De Quincey in 1859 in vol. x of his Collected Writings.—In the Preface to that volume, after admitting that there might be room for doubt as to some of his other historical conjectures in the volume, he added :—" But no such licence extends to the case of *Ælius Lamia*. " In that case I acknowledge no shadow of doubt. I have a list of " conjectural decipherings applied by classical doctors to desperate " lesions and abscesses in the text of famous classic authors ; and I am " really ashamed to say that my own emendation stands *facile princeps* " among them all. I must repeat, however, that this pre-eminence " is only that of luck ; and I must remind the critic that, in judging " of this case, he must not do as one writer did on the first publication " of this little paper : viz. entirely lose sight of the main incident in " the legend of Orpheus and Eurydice Never perhaps on this earth " was so threatening a whisper, a whisper so portentously significant, " uttered between man and man in a single word, as in that secret " suggestion of an *Orpheutic voice* where a *wife* was concerned."—M.

and earliest.   By way of illustration, Suetonius rehearses a list of distinguished men, clothed with senatorian or even consular rank, whom he had put to death upon allegations the most frivolous; amongst them, Aelius Lamia, a nobleman whose wife he had torn from him by open and insulting violence.   It may be as well to cite the exact words of Suetonius[1]: " Aelium Lamiam (interemit) ob suspiciosos quidem, verum et veteres et innoxios, jocos; quòd post abductam uxorem laudanti vocem suam dixerat, *Heu taceo*, quòdque Tito hortanti se ad alterum matrimonium responderat μὴ καὶ σὺ γαμῆσαι θέλεις ":—*Anglicè*, " Aelius Lamia he put to death on account of certain jests; jests liable to some jealousy, but, on the other hand, of old standing, and that had in fact proved harmless as regarded practical consequences,—namely, that to one who praised his voice as a singer he had replied *Heu taceo*, and that, on another occasion, in reply to the Emperor Titus, when urging him to a second marriage, he had said, " What now, I suppose *you* are looking out for a wife?"

The latter jest is intelligible enough, stinging, and in a high degree witty.   As if the young men of the Flavian family could fancy no wives but such as they had won by violence from other men, he affects in a bitter sarcasm to take for granted that Titus, in counselling his friends to marry, was simply contemplating the first step towards creating a fund of eligible wives.   The primal qualification of any lady as a consort being in Flavian eyes that she had been torn away violently from a friend, it became evident that the preliminary step towards a Flavian wedding was to persuade some incautious friend into marrying, and thus putting himself into a capacity of being robbed.   Such, at least in the stinging jest of Lamia, was the Flavian rule of conduct.

[1] The original Latin seems singularly careless: every (even though inattentive) reader says—*Innoxios*, harmless? But, if these jests were harmless, how could he call them *suspiciosos*, calculated to rouse suspicion?   The way to justify the drift of Suetonius in reconcilement with his precise words is thus: on account of certain repartees which undeniably had borne a sense justifying some uneasiness and jealousy at the time of utterance, but which the event had shown to be practically harmless, whatever had been the intention, and which were now obsolete.

And his friend Titus, therefore, simply as the brother of
Domitian, simply as a Flavian, he affected to regard as indirectly and provisionally extending his own conjugal fund
whenever he prevailed on a friend to select a wife.

The latter jest, therefore, when once apprehended, speaks
broadly and bitingly for itself. But the other! what can
it possibly mean? For centuries has that question been
reiterated; and hitherto without advancing by one step
nearer to solution. Isaac Casaubon, who about 250 years
since was the leading oracle in this field of literature, writing
an elaborate and continuous commentary upon Suetonius,
found himself unable to suggest any real aids for dispersing
the thick darkness overhanging the passage. What he says
is this: " Parum satisfaciunt mihi interpretes in explicatione
hujus Lamiæ dicti. Nam, quod putant *Heu taceo* suspirium
esse ejus,—indicem doloris ob abductam uxorem magni sed
latentis,—nobis non ita videtur; sed notatam potius fuisse
tyrannidem principis, qui omnia in suo genere pulchra et
excellentia possessoribus eriperet, unde necessitas incumbebat
sua bona dissimulandi celandique." In English thus:—
" Not at all satisfactory to me are the commentators in the
explanation of the *dictum* (here equivalent to *dicterium*) of
Lamia. For, whereas they imagine *Heu taceo* to be a sigh
of his—the record and indication of a sorrow, great though
concealed, on behalf of the wife that had been violently torn
away from him—me, I confess, the case does not strike in
that light; but rather that a satiric blow was aimed at the
despotism of the sovereign prince, who tore away from their
possessors all objects whatsoever marked by beauty or distinguished merit in their own peculiar class: whence arose a
pressure of necessity for dissembling and hiding their own
advantages "— " *Sic esse exponendum*," that such is the true
interpretation (continues Casaubon), " *docent illa verba,*
LAUDANTI VOCEM SUAM:" (we are instructed by these words:
TO ONE WHO PRAISED HIS SINGING VOICE).

This commentary was obscure enough, and did no particular honour to the native good sense of Isaac Casaubon,
usually so conspicuous. For, whilst proclaiming a settlement, in reality it settled nothing. Naturally, it made but
a feeble impression upon the scholars of the day; and, not

long after the publication of the book, Casaubon received
from Joseph Scaliger a friendly but gasconading letter, in
which that great scholar brought forward a new reading—
namely, εὐτάκτω, to which he assigned a profound technical
value as a musical term.　No person even affected to understand Scaliger.　Casaubon himself, while treating so
celebrated a man with kind and considerate deference, yet
frankly owned that, in all his vast reading, he had never met
with this Greek word in such a sense.　But, without entering
into any dispute upon that verbal question, and conceding to
Scaliger the word and his own interpretation of the word, no
man could understand in what way this new resource was
meant to affect the ultimate question at issue : namely, the
extrication of the passage from that thick darkness which
overshadowed it.

" *As you were* " (to speak in the phraseology of military
drill) was in effect the word of command.　All things reverted
to their original condition.　And two centuries of darkness
again enveloped this unsolved or insoluble perplexity of Roman
Literature.　The darkness had for a few moments seemed to
be unsettling itself in preparation for flight : but immediately
it rolled back again ; and through seven generations of men
this darkness was heavier, because now loaded with disappointment, and in that degree less hopeful than before.

At length, then, I believe, all things are ready for the
explosion of a catastrophe.　"Which catastrophe," I hear
some malicious reader whispering, " is doubtless destined to
glorify himself" (meaning the unworthy writer of this little
paper). I cannot deny it. A truth *is* a truth. And, since no
medal, nor riband, nor cross of any known order, is disposable
for the most brilliant successes in dealing with desperate (or
what may be called *condemned*) passages in pagan literature,—
mere sloughs of despond that yawn across the pages of many
a heathen dog, poet and orator, that I could mention,—so
much the more reasonable it is that a large allowance should
be served out of boasting and self-glorification to all those
whose merits upon this field national governments have
neglected to proclaim.　The Scaligers, both father and son,
I believe, acted upon this doctrine ; and drew largely by
anticipation upon that reversionary bank which they con-

ceived to be answerable for such drafts. Joseph Scaliger, it strikes me, was drunk when he wrote his letter on the present occasion, and in that way failed to see (what Casaubon saw clearly enough) that he had commenced shouting before he was out of the wood. For my own part, if I go so far as to say that the result promises, in the Frenchman's phrase, " to cover me with glory," I beg the reader to remember that the idea of " covering " is of most variable extent: the glory may envelop one in a voluminous robe, a princely mantle that may require a long suite of train-bearers, or may pinch and vice one's arms into that succinct garment (now superannuated) which some eighty years ago drew its name from the distinguished Whig family in England of Spencer.

All being now ready, and the arena being cleared of competitors (for I suppose it is fully understood that everybody but myself has retired from the contest), let it be clearly understood what it is that the contest turns upon. Supposing that one had been called, like Œdipus of old, to a turn-up with that venerable girl the Sphinx, most essential it would have been that the clerk of the course (or however you designate the judge, the umpire, &c.) should have read the riddle propounded : how else judge of the solution ? At present the elements of the case to be decided stand thus :—

A Roman noble—a man, in fact, of senatorial rank,—has been robbed, robbed with violence, and with cruel scorn, of a lovely young wife, to whom he was most tenderly attached. But by whom ? the indignant reader demands. By a younger son [1] of the Roman Emperor Vespasian. For some

---

[1] But holding what rank, and what precise station, at the time of the outrage ? At this point I acknowledge a difficulty. The criminal was in this case Domitian, the younger son of the tenth Cæsar, viz. of Vespasian · 2*dly*, younger brother of Titus, the eleventh Cæsar ; and himself, 3*dly*, under the name of Domitian, the twelfth of the Cæsars. Now the difficulty lies here, which yet I have never seen noticed in any book : was this violence perpetrated before or after Domitian's assumption of the purple ? If *after*, how, then, could the injured husband have received that advice from Titus (as to repairing his loss by a second marriage) which suggested the earliest *bon-mot* between Titus and Lamia ? Yet, again, if not after but before, how was it that Lamia had not invoked the protection of Vespasian, or of Titus—the latter of whom enjoyed a theatrically fine reputation for equity and moderation ? By the way, another *bon-mot* arose out of this brutal

years the wrong has been borne in silence: the sufferer knew himself to be powerless as against such an oppressor; and that to show symptoms of impotent hatred was but to call down thunderbolts upon his own head. Generally, therefore, prudence had guided him. *Patience* had been the word; *silence*, and below all the deep, deep word, *watch and wait!* It is, however, an awful aggravation of such afflictions that the lady herself might have co-operated in the later stages of the tragedy with the purposes of the imperial ruffian. Lamia had been suffered to live, because as a living man he yielded up into the hands of his tormentor his whole capacity of suffering; no part of it escaped the hellish range of his enemy's eye. But this advantage for the torturer had also its weak and doubtful side. Use and monotony might secretly be wearing away the edge of the organs on and through which the corrosion of the inner heart proceeded. And, when that point was reached — a callousness which neutralized the further powers of the tormentor,—it then became the true policy of such a fiend (as being his one sole unexhausted resource) to inflict death. On the whole, therefore, putting together the facts of the case, it seems to have been resolved that he should die, but previously that he should drink off a final cup of anguish, the bitterest that had yet been offered. The lady herself, again, had she also suffered in sympathy with her martyred husband? That must have been known to a certainty in the outset of the case by him that knew too profoundly on what terms of love they had lived. Possibly to resist indefinitely might have menaced herself with ruin, whilst offering no benefit to her husband. There is besides this dreadful fact, placed ten thousand times

Domitian's evil reputation. He had a taste for petty cruelties; especially upon the common house-fly, which in the Syrian mythology enjoys the condescending patronage of the god Belzebub. Flies did Cæsar massacre in spite of Belzebub by bushels; and the carnage was the greater because this Apollyon of flies was always armed; since the metallic *stylus*, with which the Roman ploughed his waxen tablets in writing memoranda, was the best of weapons in a pitched battle with a fly; in fact, Cæsar had an unfair advantage. Meantime this habit of his had become notorious: and one day a man, wishing for a private audience, inquired in the antechambers if Cæsar were alone. *Quite alone*, was the reply. "Are you sure? Is nobody with him?" *Nobody: not so much as a fly (ne musca quidem).*

on record, that the very goodness of the human heart in such
a case ministers fuel to the moral degradation of a female
combatant. Any woman, and exactly in proportion to the
moral sensibility of her nature, finds it painful to live in the
same house with a man not odiously repulsive in manners or
in person on terms of eternal hostility. What it was circumstantially that passed long since has been overtaken and
swallowed up by the vast oblivions of time. This only
survives — namely, that what Lamia had said gave signal
offence in the highest quarter, was not forgotten, and that
his death followed eventually. But what was it that he *did*
say ? That is precisely the question, and the whole question,
which we have to answer. At present we know, and we do
not know, what it was that he said. We find bequeathed to
us by history the munificent legacy of two words, involving
eight letters, which in their present form,—with submission
to certain grandees of classic literature, more particularly to
the scoundrel Joe Scaliger (son of the old original ruffian
J. C. Scaliger),—mean exactly nothing. These two words
must be regarded as the raw material upon which we have
to work ; and out of these we are required to turn out a
rational, but also, be it observed, a memorably caustic, saying
for Aelius Lamia, under the following five conditions : First,
it must allude to his wife, as one that is lost to him irrecover-
ably ; secondly, it must glance at a gloomy tyrant who bars
him from rejoining her ; thirdly, it must reply to the compliment which had been paid to the sweetness of his own
voice ; fourthly, it should in strictness contain some allusion
calculated not only to irritate, but even to alarm or threaten
his jealous and vigilant enemy,—else how was it suspicious ?
fifthly, doing all these things, it ought also to absorb, as its
own main elements, the eight letters contained in the present
senseless words—" *Heu taceo.*"

Here is a monstrous quantity of work to throw upon any
two words in any possible language. Even Shakspere's
clown,[1] when challenged to furnish a catholic answer applicable to all conceivable occasions, cannot do it in less than
nine letters, namely, *Oh lord, sir !* I, for my part, satisfied
that the existing form of *Heu taceo* was mere indictable and

[1] See *All's Well that Ends Well*, Act ii. Scene 2.

punishable nonsense, but yet that this nonsense must enter as chief element into the stinging sense of Lamia, gazed for I cannot tell how many weeks (weeks, indeed! say years), at these impregnable letters, viewing them sometimes as a fortress that I was called upon to escalade, sometimes as an anagram that I was called upon to re-organize into the life which it had lost through some dislocation of arrangement. One day I looked at it through a microscope; next day I looked at it from a distance through a telescope.   Then I reconnoitred it downwards from the top round of a ladder; then upwards, in partnership with Truth, from the bottom of a well.   Finally, the result in which I landed, and which fulfilled all the conditions laid down, was this :—Let me premise, however, what *at any rate* the existing darkness attests, that some disturbance of the text must in some way have arisen; whether from the gnawing of a rat, or the spilling of some obliterating fluid at this point of some unique MS.   It is sufficient for us that the vital word has survived.   I suppose, therefore, that Lamia had replied to the friend who praised the sweetness of his voice, "Sweet, is it ?   Ah, would to Heaven it might prove *so* sweet *as* to be even Orpheutic !"   Ominous in this case would be the word Orpheutic to the ears of Domitian; for every schoolboy knows that this means a *wife-revoking voice*.   Let me remark that there is such a legitimate word as *Orpheutaceam ;* and in that case the Latin repartee of Lamia would stand thus : *Suavem dixisti ?   Quam vellem et Orpheutaceam.*   But, perhaps, reader, you fail to recognise in this form our old friend *Heu taceo.*   But here he is to a certainty, in spite of the rat : and in a different form of letters the compositor will show him to you as—*vellem et Orp* [HEU TACEAM].   Here, then, shines out at once—(1) Eurydice the lovely wife ; (2) detained by the gloomy tyrant Pluto ; (3) who, however, is forced into surrendering her to her husband, whose voice (the sweetest ever known) drew stocks and stones to follow him, and finally his wife ; (4) the word Orpheutic involves, therefore, an alarming threat, showing that the hope of recovering the lady still survived ; (5) we now find involved in the restoration all the eight, or perhaps nine, letters of the erroneous (and for so long a time unintelligible) form.

PHILOSOPHY OF ROMAN HISTORY [1]

It would be thought strange indeed if there should exist a large, a memorable, section of History, traversed by many a scholar with various objects, reviewed by many a reader in a spirit of anxious scrutiny, and yet to this hour misunderstood ; erroneously appreciated ; its tendencies mistaken, and its whole meaning, import, value, not so much inadequately as falsely, ignorantly, perversely, deciphered. *Primâ facie*, one would pronounce this impossible. Nevertheless it is a truth ; and it is a solemn truth ; and what gives to it this solemnity is the mysterious meaning, the obscure hint of a still profounder meaning in the background, which begins to dawn upon the eye when first piercing the darkness now resting on the subject.

Perhaps no one arc or segment detached from the total cycle of human records promises so much beforehand, so much instruction, so much gratification to curiosity, so much splendour, so much depth of interest, as the great period— the systole and diastole, flux and reflux—of the Western Roman Empire. Its parentage was magnificent and Titanic. It was a birth out of the death-struggles of the colossal Republic : its foundations were laid by that sublime dictator, "the foremost man of all this world," who was unquestionably for comprehensive talents the Lucifer, the Protagonist, of all

---

[1] In *Blackwood* for November 1839, with the sub-title "On the True Relations to Civilization and Barbarism of the Roman Western Empire" : *not* reprinted by De Quincey in his edition of his Collective Writings, probably because it was one of the papers he had not overtaken in his task of revision.—M.

Antiquity. Its range, the compass of its extent, was appalling to the imagination. Coming last amongst what are called the Great Monarchies of Prophecy, it was the only one which realized in perfection the idea of a *monarchia*, being (except for Parthia and the great fable of India beyond it) strictly coincident with ἡ οικουμενη, or the Civilized World. Civilization and this Empire were commensurate : they were interchangeable ideas, and co-extensive. Finally, the path of this great Empire, through its arch of progress, synchronized with that of Christianity : the ascending orbit of each was pretty nearly the same, and traversed the same series of generations. These elements, in combination, seemed to promise a succession of golden harvests : from the specular station of the Augustan age, the eye caught glimpses by anticipation of some glorious El Dorado for human hopes. What was the practical result for our historic experience ? Answer — A sterile Zaarrah. Prelibations, as of some heavenly vintage, were inhaled by the Virgils of the day, looking forward in the spirit of prophetic rapture ; whilst, in the very sadness of truth, from that age forwards the Roman World drank from stagnant marshes. A paradise of roses was prefigured : a wilderness of thorns was found.

Even this fact has been missed—even the bare fact has been overlooked ; much more the causes, the principles, the philosophy of this fact. The rapid barbarism which closed in behind Cæsar's chariot wheels has been hid by the pomp and equipage of the imperial court. The vast power and domination of the Roman Empire, for the three centuries which followed the battle of Actium, have dazzled the historic eye, and have had the usual reaction on the power of vision : a dazzled eye is always left in a condition of darkness. The Battle of Actium was followed by the final conquest of Egypt. That conquest rounded and integrated the glorious Empire ; it was now circular as a shield— orbicular as the disk of a planet : the great Julian arch was now locked into the cohesion of granite by its last key-stone. From that day forward, for three hundred years, there was silence in the world : no muttering was heard : no eye winked beneath the wing. Winds of hostility might still rave at intervals : but it was on the outside of the mighty

Empire : it was at a dream-like distance ; and, like the storms that beat against some monumental castle, "and at the doors and windows seem to call," they rather irritated and vivified the sense of security than at all disturbed its luxurious lull.

That seemed to all men the consummation of political wisdom, the ultimate object of all strife, the very euthanasy of war. Except on some fabulous frontier, armies seemed gay pageants of the Roman rank rather than necessary bulwarks of the Roman power : spear and shield were idle trophies of the past : the trumpet spoke not to the alarmed throng. "Hush, ye palpitations of Rome !" was the cry of the superb Aurelian,[1] from his far-off pavilion in the deserts of the Euphrates—"Hush, fluttering heart of the Eternal City ! Fall back into slumber, ye wars, and rumours of wars ! Turn upon your couches of down, ye Children of Romulus—sink back into your voluptuous repose ! We, your almighty Armies, have chased into darkness those phantoms that had broken your dreams. We have chased, we have besieged, we have crucified, we have slain."—"*Nihil est, Romulei Quirites, quod timere possitis. Ego efficiam ne sit aliqua solicitudo Romana. Vacate ludis, vacate circensibus. Nos publicæ necessitates teneant : vos occupent voluptates.*"— Did ever Siren warble so dulcet a song to ears already prepossessed and medicated with spells of Circean effeminacy ?

But in this world all things re-act ; and the very extremity of any force is the seed and nucleus of a counter-agency. You might have thought it as easy (in the words of Shakspere) to

> "Wound the loud winds, or with be-mock'd-at stabs
> Kill the still-closing waters,"

as to violate the majesty of the imperial eagle, or to ruffle

---

[1] "*Of the superb Aurelian*" :—The particular occasion was the insurrection in the East of which the ostensible leaders were the great lieutenants of Palmyra—Odenathus, and his widow, Zenobia. The alarm at Rome was out of all proportion to the danger, and well illustrated the force of the great historian's aphorism, *Omne ignotum pro magnifico.* In one sentence of his despatch, Aurelian aimed at a contest with the great Julian gasconade of *Veni, vidi, vici.* His words are—*Fugavimus, obsedimus, cruciavimus, occidimus.*

"one dowle that's in his plume." But luxurious ease is the surest harbinger of pain ; and the dead lulls of tropical seas are the immediate forerunners of tornadoes. The more absolute was the security obtained by Cæsar for his people, the more inevitable was his own ruin. Scarcely had Aurelian sung his requiem to the agitations of Rome before a requiem was sung by his assassins to his own warlike spirit. Scarcely had Probus, another Aurelian, proclaimed the eternity of peace, and, by way of attesting his own martial supremacy, had commanded "that the brazen throat of war should cease to roar," when the trumpets of the four winds proclaimed his own death by murder. Not as anything extraordinary ; for, in fact, violent death—death by assassination—was the regular portal (the *porta Libitina*, or funeral gate) through which the Cæsars passed out of this world ; and to die in their beds was the very rare exception to the stern rule of fate. Not, therefore, as in itself at all noticeable, but because this particular murder of Probus stands scenically contrasted with the great vision of *Peace* which he fancied as lying in clear revelation before him, permit us, before we proceed with our argument, to rehearse his golden promises. The sabres were already unsheathed, the shirt-sleeves were already pushed up from those murderous hands which were to lacerate his throat and to pierce his heart, when he ascended the Pisgah from which he descried the Saturnian ages to succeed :—"*Brevi*," said he, "*milites non necessarios habebimus. Romanus jam miles erit nullus. Omnia possidebimus. Respublica orbis terrarum, ubique secura, non arma fabricabit. Boves habebuntur aratro : equus nascetur ad pacem. Nulla erunt bella, nulla captivitas. Ubique pax : ubique Romanæ leges : ubique judices nostri.*" The historian himself, tame and creeping as he is in his ordinary style, warms in sympathy with the Emperor : his diction blazes up into a sudden explosion of prophetic grandeur : and he adopts all the views of Cæsar. "Nonne omnes barbaras nationes subjecerat pedibus ?" he demands with lyrical tumult, and then, while confessing the immediate disappointment of his hopes, thus repeats the great elements of the public felicity whenever they should be realized by a Cæsar equally martial for others, but more fortunate for himself :—" *Æternos thesauros haberet Romana Respublica.   Nihil expenderetur a principe : nihil a possessore redderetur.   Aureum profecto seculum promittebat.   Nulla futura erant castra : nusquam lituus audiendus : arma non erant fabricanda. Populus iste militantium, qui nunc bellis civilibus Rempublicam vexat*"—ay ! how was *that* to be absorbed ?   How would that vast crowd of half-pay *emeriti* employ itself ?   " *Araret : studiis incumberet : erudiretur artibus : navigaret.*"   And he closes his prophetic raptures thus : " *Adde quod nullus occideretur in bello.   Dii boni !   quid tandem vos offenderet Respublica Romana, cui talem principem sustulistis ?* "

Even in his lamentations, it is clear that he mourns as for a blessing delayed—not finally denied.   The land of promise still lay, as before, in steady vision below his feet ; only that it waited for some happier Augustus, who, in the great lottery of Cæsarian destinies, might happen to draw the rare prize of a prosperous reign not prematurely blighted by the assassin ; with whose purple *alourgis* might mingle no *fasciæ* of crape, with whose imperial laurels might entwine no ominous cypress.   The hope of a millennial armistice, of an eternal rest for the earth, was not dead : once again only, and for a time, it was sleeping in abeyance and expectation. That blessing, that millennial blessing, it seems, might be the gift of Imperial Rome.

II.—Well : and why not ? the reader demands.   What have we to say against it ?   This Cæsar, or that historian, may have carried his views a little too far, or too prematurely ; yet, after all, the very enormity of what they promised must be held to argue the enormity of what had been accomplished.   To give any plausibility to a scheme of perpetual peace, war must already have become rare, and must have been banished to a prodigious distance.   It was no longer the hearths and the altars, home and religious worship, which quaked under the tumults of war.   It was the purse which suffered : the exchequer of the state ; secondly, the exchequer of each individual ; thirdly, and in the end, the interests of agriculture, of commerce, of navigation.   This is what the historian indicates in promising his brother Romans that " *omnia possidebimus* " : by which, perhaps, he did not mean to lay the stress on "*omnia*," as if, in addition to their own property, they were to have that of alien or frontier nations, but (laying the stress on the word *possidebimus*) meant to say, with regard to property already their own—" We shall no longer hold it as joint proprietors with the state, and as liable to fluctuating taxation, but shall henceforwards *possess* it in absolute exclusive property." This is what he indicates in saying " *Boves habebuntur aratro* " : that is, the oxen, one and all available for the plough, shall no longer be open to the everlasting claims of the public *frumentarii* for conveying supplies to the frontier armies. This is what he indicates in saying, of the individual liable to military service, that he should no longer live to slay or to be slain, for barren bloodshed or violence, but that henceforth " *araret* " or " *navigaret*." All these passages, by pointing the expectations emphatically to benefits of purse exonerated, and industry emancipated, sufficiently argue the class of interests which then suffered by war : that it was the interests of private property, of agricultural improvement, of commercial industry, upon which exclusively fell the evils of a belligerent state under the Roman Empire : and there already lies a mighty blessing achieved for social existence when sleep is made sacred and thresholds secure, when the temple of human life is safe, and the temple of female honour is hallowed. These great interests, it is admitted, were sheltered under the mighty dome of the Roman Empire : that is already an advance made towards the highest civilization ; and this is not shaken because a particular Emperor should be extravagant, or a particular Historian romantic.

No, certainly : but stop a moment at this point ! Civilization, to the extent of security for life and the primal rights of man, necessarily grows out of every strong government. And it follows also that, as this government widens its sphere, as it pushes back its frontiers *ultra et Garamantas et Indos*, in that proportion will the danger diminish (for in fact the possibility diminishes) of foreign incursions. The sense of permanent security from conquest, or from the inroad of marauders, must of course have been prodigiously increased when the nearest standing army of Rome was beyond the

Tigris and the Inn, as compared with those times when Carthage, Spain, Gaul, Macedon, presented a ring-fence of venomous rivals, and when every little nook in the Eastern Mediterranean swarmed with pirates. Thus far, inevitably, the Roman police, planting one foot of his golden compasses in the same eternal centre, and with the other describing an arch continually wider, must have banished all idea of public enemies, and have deepened the sense of security beyond calculation. Thus far we have the benefits of police ; and those are amongst the earliest blessings of civilization ; and they are one indispensable condition—what in logic is called the *conditio sine qua non*—for all the other blessings. But that, in other words, is a *negative* cause,—a cause which being absent, the effect is absent ; but not the *positive* cause, or *causa sufficiens*, which being present, the effect will be present. The security of the Roman Empire was the indispensable condition, but not in itself a sufficient cause, of those other elements which compose a true civilization. Rome was the centre of a high police, which radiated to Parthia eastwards, to Britain westwards, but not of a high civilization.

On the contrary, what we maintain is that the Roman Civilization was imperfect *ab intra*—imperfect in its central principle ; was a piece of watchwork that began to go down —to lose its spring—and was slowly retrograding to a dead stop from the very moment that it had completed its task of foreign conquest : that it was kept going from the very first by strong reaction and antagonism ; that it fell into torpor from the moment when this antagonism ceased to operate ; that thenceforwards it oscillated backwards violently to barbarism : that, left to its own principles of civilization, the Roman Empire was barbarizing rapidly from the time of Trajan : that, abstracting from all alien agencies whatever, whether accelerating or retarding, and supposing Western Rome to have been thrown exclusively upon the resources and elasticity of her own proper civilization, she was crazy and superannuated by the time of Commodus—must soon have gone to pieces—must have foundered ; and, under any possible benefit from favourable accidents co-operating with alien forces, could not, by any great term, have retarded that doom which was written on her drooping energies, prescribed by internal decay, and not at all (as is universally imagined) by external assault.

III. — "Barbarizing rapidly!" the reader murmurs— "Barbarism! Oh yes, I remember the Barbarians broke in upon the Western Empire — the Ostrogoths, Visigoths, Vandals, Burgundians, Huns, Heruli, and swarms beside. These wretches had no taste—no literature, probably very few ideas; and naturally they barbarized and rebarbarized wherever they moved. But surely the writer errs: this influx of barbarism was not in Trajan's time, at the very opening of the second century from Christ, but throughout the fifth century." No, reader; it is not we who err, but you. These were not the barbarians of Rome. That is the miserable fiction of Italian vanity, always stigmatizing better men than themselves by the name of Barbarians; and in fact we all know, that to be an Ultramontane is with them to be a Barbarian. The horrible charge against the Greeks of old, viz. that *sua tantum mirantur*, a charge implying in its objects the last descent of narrow sensibility and of illiterate bigotry, in modern times has been true only of two nations; and those two are the French and the Italians. But, waiving the topic, we affirm—and it is the purpose of our essay to affirm—that the barbarism of Rome grew out of Rome herself; that those pretended barbarians—Gothic, Vandalish,[1] Lombard, or by whatever name known to Modern History— were in reality the restorers and regenerators of the effete Roman intellect; that, but for them, the indigenous Italian would probably have died out in scrofula, madness, leprosy; that the sixth or seventh century would have seen the utter

---

[1] "*Pretended barbarians, Gothic, Vandalish,*" &c.—Had it been true that these tramontane people were as ferocious in manners or appearance as was alleged, it would not therefore have followed that they were barbarous in their modes of thinking and feeling; or, if that also had been true, surely it became the Romans to recollect what very barbarians, both in mind, and manners, and appearance, were some of their own Cæsars. Meantime it appears that not only Alaric the Goth, but even Attila the Hun, in popular repute the most absolute Ogre of all the Transalpine invaders, turns out in more thoughtful representations to have been a prince of peculiarly mild demeanour, and apparently upright character.

extinction of these Italian *strulbrugs:* for which opinion, if it were important, we could show cause. But it is much less important to show cause in behalf of this negative proposition "that the Goths and Vandals were *not* the barbarians of the western empire," than in behalf of this affirmative proposition, "that the Romans *were.*" We do not wish to overlay the subject, but simply to indicate a few of the many evidences which it is in our power to adduce. We mean to rely, for the present, upon four arguments, as exponents of the barbarous and barbarizing tone of feeling which, like so much moss or lichens, had gradually overgrown the Roman mind, and by the third century had strangled all healthy vegetation of natural and manly thought. During this third century it was, in its latter half, that most of the *Augustan History* was probably composed. Laying aside the two Victors, Dion Cassius, Ammianus Marcellinus, and a few more indirect notices of History during this period, there is little other authority for the annals of the Western Empire than this *Augustan History;* and at all events, this is the chief well-head of that History. Hither we must resort for most of the personal biography and the portraiture of characters connected with that period; and here only we find the regular series of princes — the whole gallery of Cæsars, from Trajan to the immediate predecessor of Diocletian. The composition of this work has been usually distributed amongst six authors, viz. Spartian, Capitolinus, Lampridius, Volcatius Gallicanus, Trebellius Pollio, and Vopiscus.[1] Their several shares, it is true, have been much disputed to and fro; and other questions have been raised, affecting the very existence of some amongst them. But all this is irrelevant to our present purpose; which applies to the work, but not at all to the writers, excepting in so far as they (by whatever names known) were notoriously and demonstrably persons belonging to that era, trained in Roman habits of thinking, connected with the Court, intimate with the great Palatine officers, and therefore presumably men of rank and education. We rely, in so far as we rely at all upon this work, upon these two among its characteristic features: 1st, Upon the quality and style of its biographic

---

[1] See footnote, *ante*, p. 241.—M.

notices ; 2dly, Upon the remarkable uncertainty which hangs over all lives a little removed from the personal cognisance or immediate era of the writer. But, as respects, not the History, but the subjects of the History, we rely, 3dly, Upon the peculiar traits of feeling which gradually began to disfigure the ideal conception of the Roman Cæsar in the minds of his subjects ; 4thly, Without reference to the Augustan History, or to the subjects of that History, we rely generally, for establishing the growing barbarism of Rome, upon the condition of the Roman Literature after the period of the first twelve Cæsars.

IV.—First of all, we infer the increasing barbarism of the Roman mind from the quality of the personal notices and portraitures exhibited throughout these biographical records. The whole may be described by one word—*Anecdotage.*   It is impossible to conceive the dignity of History more degraded than by the petty nature of the anecdotes which compose the bulk of the communications about every Cæsar, good or bad, great or little.   They are not merely domestic and purely personal, when they ought to have been Cæsarian, Augustan, Imperatorial : they pursue Cæsar not only to his fireside, but into his bed-chamber, into his bath, into his cabinet, nay, even (*sit honor auribus !*) into his *cabinet d'aisance ;* not merely into the Palatine closet, but into the Palatine water-closet. Thus of Heliogabalus we are told—" *onus ventris auro excepit —minxit myrrhinis et onychinis* "; that is, Cæsar's *lasanum* was made of gold, and his *matula* was made of onyx, or of the undetermined *myrrhine* material.   And so on with respect to the dresses of Cæsar ;—how many of every kind he wore in a week—of what material they were made—with what ornaments. So, again, with respect to the meals of Cæsar ;—what dishes, what condiments, what fruits, what confection prevailed at each course ; what wines he preferred ; how many glasses (*cyathos*) he usually drank ; whether he drank more when he was angry ; whether he diluted his wine with water ; half-and-half, or how ?   Did he get drunk often ?   How many times a week ?   What did he generally do when he was drunk ?   How many chemises did he allow to his wife ?   How were they fringed ?   At what cost per chemise ?

In this strain — how truly worthy of the children of Romulus — how becoming to the descendants from Scipio Africanus, from Paulus Æmilius, from the colossal Marius and the godlike Julius — the whole of the Augustan History moves. There is a superb line in Lucan which represents the mighty phantom of Paulus standing at a banquet to reproach or to alarm —

> "Et Pauli ingentem stare miraberis umbram!"

What a horror would have seized this Augustan scribbler, this Roman Tims, if he could have seen this "mighty phantom" at his elbow looking over his inanities; and what a horror would have seized the phantom! Once, in the course of his aulic memorabilia, the writer is struck with a sudden glimpse of such an idea; and he reproaches himself for recording such infinite littleness. After reporting some anecdotes, in the usual Augustan style, about an Imperial rebel, — as, for instance, that he had ridden upon ostriches (which he says was the next thing to flying); that he had eaten a dish of boiled hippopotamus[1] ; and that, having a fancy for tickling the catastrophes of crocodiles, he had anointed himself with crocodile fat, by which means he humbugged the crocodiles, ceasing to be Cæsar, and passing for a crocodile, swimming and playing amongst them : these glorious facts being recorded, he goes on to say — "*Sed hæc scire quid prodest? cum et Livius et Sallustius taceant res leves de iis quorum vitas scribendas arripuerint. Non enim scimus quales mulos Clodius habuerit; nec utrum Tusco equo sederit Catilina an Sardo; vel quali chlamyde Pompeius usus fuerit, an purpurâ.*" No: we do *not* know. Livy would have died in the high Roman fashion before he would have degraded himself by such babble of nursery-maids or of palace pimps and eavesdroppers.

But it is too evident that babble of this kind grew up not by any accident, but as a natural growth, and by a sort of physical necessity, from the condition of the Roman mind

---

[1] "*Eaten a dish of boiled hippopotamus*" :—We once thought that some error might exist in the text—*edisse* for *edidisse*—and that a man exposed a hippopotamus at the games of the amphitheatre ; but we are now satisfied that he ate the hippopotamus.

after it had ceased to be excited by opposition in foreign nations.   It was not merely the extinction of Republican institutions which operated; that might operate as a co-cause; but, had these institutions even survived, the unresisted energies of the Roman mind, having no purchase, nothing to push against, would have collapsed.   The eagle, of all birds, would be the first to flutter and sink plumb down if the atmosphere should make no resistance to his wings.   The first Roman of note who began this system of anecdotage was Suetonius.   In him the poison of the degradation was much diluted by the strong remembrances, still surviving, of the mighty Republic.   The glorious sunset was still burning with gold and orange lights in the west.   True, the disease had commenced; but the habits of health were still strong for restraint and for conflict with its power.   Besides that, Suetonius graces his minutiæ, and embalms them in amber, by the exquisite finish of his rhetoric.   But his case, coming so early among the Cæsarian annals, is sufficient to show that the growth of such History was a spontaneous growth from the circumstances of the empire, viz. from the total collapse of all public antagonism.

The next Literature in which the spirit of anecdotage arose was that of France.   From the age of Louis Treize, or perhaps of Henri Quatre, to the Revolution, this species of chamber memoirs—this eavesdropping biography—prevailed so as to strangle authentic History.   The parasitical plant absolutely killed the supporting tree.   And one remark we will venture to make on that fact: the French Literature would have been killed, and the national mind reduced to the *strulbrug* condition, had it not been for the situation of France amongst other great kingdoms, making her liable to potent reactions from them.   The Memoirs of France,—that is, the *valet-de-chambre's* archives substituted for the statesman's, the ambassador's, the soldier's, the politician's,—would have extinguished all other historic composition, as in fact they nearly did, but for the insulation of France amongst nations with more masculine habits of thought.   That saved France.   Rome had no such advantage; and Rome gave way.   The props, the buttresses, of the Roman intellect were all cancered and honeycombed by this dry-rot in her political energies. One excuse there is: storms yield tragedies for the historian; the dead calms of a universal monarchy leave him little but personal memoranda. In such a case he is nothing if he is not anecdotical.

V.—Secondly, we infer the barbarism of Rome, and the increasing barbarism, from the inconceivable ignorance which prevailed throughout the Western Empire as to the most interesting public facts that were not taken down on the spot by a *tachygraphus* or short-hand reporter. Let a few years pass, and everything was forgotten about everybody. Within a few years after the death of Aurelian, though a kind of saint amongst the Armies and the Populace of Rome (for to the Senate he was odious), no person could tell who was the Emperor's mother, or where she lived; though she must have been a woman of station and notoriety in her lifetime, having been a high priestess at some temple unknown. Alexander Severus, a very interesting Cæsar, who recalls to an Englishman the idea of his own Edward the Sixth,—both as a prince equally amiable, equally disposed to piety, equally to reforms, and because, like Edward, he was so placed with respect to the succession and position of his reign, between unnatural monsters and bloody exterminators, as to reap all the benefit of contrast and soft relief;—this Alexander was assassinated. That was of course. But still, though the fact was of course, the motives often varied, and the circumstances varied; and the reader would be glad to know, in Shakspere's language, "for which of his virtues" it was deemed requisite to murder him; as also, if it would not be too much trouble to the historian, *who* might be the murderers, and what might be their rank, and their names, and their recompense—whether a halter or a palace. But nothing of all this can be learned. And why? All had been forgotten.[1] Lethe had sent all

1 " *All had been forgotten* ":—It is true that the Augustan writer, rather than appear to know nothing at all, tells a most idle fable about a *scurra* having intruded into Cæsar's tent, and, upon finding the young Emperor awake, excited his comrades to the murder for fear of being punished for his insolent intrusion. But the whole story is nonsense: a camp legend, or at the best a fable put forth by the real conspirators to mask the truth. The writer did not believe it himself

her waves over the whole transaction ; and the man who wrote within thirty years found no vestige recoverable of the imperial murder more than you or we, reader, would find at this day, if we should search for fragments of that imperial tent in which the murder happened. Again, with respect to the princes who succeeded immediately to their part of the Augustan History now surviving,—princes the most remarkable, and *cardinal* to the movement of History, viz. Diocletian and Constantine,—many of the weightiest transactions in their lives are washed out as by a sponge. Did Diocletian hang himself in his garters ? or did he die in his bed ? Nobody knows. And, if Diocletian hanged himself, why did Diocletian hang himself ? Nobody can guess. Did Constantine, again, marry a second wife ?—did this second wife fall in love with her step-son Crispus ?—did she, in resentment of his scorn, bear false witness against him to his father ?—did his father, in consequence, put him to death ? What an awful domestic tragedy !—was it true ? Nobody knows. On the one hand, Eusebius does not so much as allude to it ; but, on the other hand, Eusebius had his golden reasons for favouring Constantine, and this was a matter to be hushed up rather than blazoned. Tell it not in Gath ! Publish it not in Askelon ! Then again, on the one hand, the tale seems absolutely a leaf torn out of the Hippolytus of Euripides. It is the identical story, only the name is changed : Constantine is Theseus, his new wife is Phædra, Crispus is Hippolytus. So far it seems rank with forgery. Yet again, on the other hand, such a duplicate did *bonâ fide* occur in Modern History. Such a domestic tragedy was actually rehearsed, with one unimportant change ; such a leaf was positively torn out of Euripides. Philip II played the part of Theseus, Don Carlos the part of Hippolytus, and the Queen filled the situation (without the *animus*) of Phædra. Again, therefore, one is reduced to blank ignorance, and the world will never know the true history of the Cæsar who

—By the way, a *scurra* does not retain its classical sense of a buffoon in the Augustan History ; it means a σωματοφυλαξ, or body-guard ; but why, is yet undiscovered. Our own belief is that the word is a Thracian or a Gothic word ; the body-guards being derived from those nations.

first gave an establishment and an earthly throne to Christianity, because History had slept the sleep of death before that Cæsar's time, and because the great Muse of History had descended from Parnassus, and was running about Cæsar's palace in the bed-gown and slippers of a chambermaid.

Many hundreds of similar *lacunæ* we could assign with regard to facts the most indispensable to be known ; but we must hurry onwards. Meantime, let the reader contrast with this dearth of primary facts in the History of the Empire, and their utter extinction after even the lapse of twenty years, the extreme circumstantiality of the Republican History through many centuries back.

VI.—Thirdly, we infer the growing barbarism of Rome, that is, of the Roman people, as well as the Roman Armies, from the brutal, bloody, and Tartar style of their festal exultations after victory, and the Moloch sort of character and functions with which they gradually invested their great Sultan, the Cæsar. One of the *ballisteia*, that is, the *ballets* or dances carried through scenes and representative changes, which were performed by the soldiery and by the mobs of Rome upon occasion of any triumphal display, has been preserved, in so far as relates to the words which accompanied the performance ; for there was always a verbal accompaniment to the choral parts of the *ballisteia*. These words ran thus :—

"Mille, mille, mille, mille, mille, mille, [six times repeated] decolla-
   vimus.
      Unus homo mille, mille, mille, mille, [four times] decollavit :
      Mille, mille, mille, vivat annos, qui mille, mille occidit.
   Tantum vini habet nemo quantum Cæsar fudit sanguinis.'

And, again, a part of a *ballisteion* runs thus :—

   "Mille Francos, mille Sarmatas, semel occidimus :
      Mille, mille, mille, mille, mille, Persas quærimus."

But, in reality, the national mind was convulsed and revolutionized by many causes ; and we may be assured that it must have been so, both as a cause and as an effect, before that mind could have contemplated with steadiness the fearful scene of Turkish murder and bloodshed going on for ever in high places.   The palace floors in Rome actually rocked and quaked with assassination ; snakes were sleeping for ever beneath the flowers and palms of empire : the throne was built upon coffins : and any Christian who had read the Apocalypse, whenever he looked at the altar consecrated to Cæsar, on which the sacred fire was burning for ever in the Augustan halls, must have seen below them " the souls of those who had been martyred," and have fancied that he heard them crying out to the angel of retribution—" How long ? O Lord ! how long ? "

Gibbon has left us a description, not very powerful, of a case which is all-powerful of itself, and needs no expansion : the case of a state criminal vainly attempting to escape or hide himself from Cæsar—from the arm wrapped in clouds, and stretching over kingdoms alike, or oceans, that arrested and drew back the wretch to judgment—from the inevitable eye that slept not nor slumbered, and from which, neither Alps interposing, nor immeasurable deserts, nor trackless seas, nor a four months' flight, nor perfect innocence, could screen him.   The world, the world of civilization, was Cæsar's ; and he who fled from the wrath of Cæsar said to himself, of necessity—" If I go down to the sea, there is Cæsar on the shore ; if I go into the sands of Bilidulgerid, there is Cæsar waiting for me in the desert ; if I take the wings of the morning, and go to the utmost recesses of wild beasts, there is Cæsar before me."   All this makes the condition of a criminal under the Western Empire terrific, and the condition even of a subject perilous.   But how strange it is,—or would be so, had Gibbon been a man of more sensibility,—that he should have overlooked the converse of the case : viz. the terrific condition of Cæsar amidst the terror which he caused to others.   In fact, both conditions were full of despair.   But Cæsar's was the worst, by a great pre-eminence ; for the state criminal could not be made such without his own concurrence : for one moment, at least, it had been within his choice to be no criminal at all ; and then for him the thunderbolts of Cæsar slept.   But Cæsar had rarely any choice as to his own election ; and for him, therefore, the dagger of the assassin never *could* sleep. Other men's houses, other men's bedchambers, were generally asylums; but for Cæsar his own palace had not the privileges of a home. His own armies were no guards; his own pavilion, rising in the very centre of his armies sleeping around him, was no sanctuary. In all these places had Cæsar many times been murdered. All these pledges and sanctities—his household gods, the majesty of the empire, the "sacramentum militare,"—all had given way, all had yawned beneath his feet.

The imagination of man can frame nothing so awful—the experience of man has witnessed nothing so awful—as the situation and tenure of the Western Cæsar. The danger which threatened him was like the pestilence which walketh in darkness, but which also walketh in noon-day. Morning and evening, summer and winter, brought no change or shadow of turning to this particular evil. In that respect it enjoyed the immunities of God: it was the same yesterday, to-day, and forever. After three centuries it had lost nothing of its virulence; it was growing worse continually: the heart of man ached under the evil, and the necessity of the evil. Can any man measure the sickening fear which must have possessed the hearts of the ladies and the children composing the imperial family? To them the mere terror, entailed like an inheritance of leprosy upon their family above all others, must have made it a woe like one of the evils in the Revelations,—such in its infliction, such in its inevitability. It was what Pagan language denominated "a *sacred* danger," a danger charmed and consecrated against human alleviation.

At length, but not until about three hundred and twenty years of murder had elapsed from the inaugural murder of the great imperial founder, Diocletian rose, and, as a last resource of despair, said, Let us multiply our image, and try if that will discourage our murderers. Like Kehama, entering the eight gates of Padalon at once, and facing himself eight times over, he appointed an assessor for himself; and, each of these co-ordinate Augusti having a subordinate Cæsar, there were in fact four coeval Emperors. Cæsar enjoyed a perfect *alibi:* like the royal ghost in Hamlet, Cæsar was *hic et ubique.* And, unless treason enjoyed the same ubiquity, now, at least, one would have expected that

Cæsar might sleep in security.   But murder — imperial murder—is a Briareus.   There was a curse upon the throne of Western Rome : it rocked like the sea, and for some mysterious reason could not find rest ; and few princes were more memorably afflicted than the immediate successors to this arrangement.

A nation living in the bosom of these funereal convulsions, this endless billowy oscillation of prosperous murder and thrones overturned, could not have been moral ; and therefore could not have reached a high civilization, had other influences favoured.   No causes act so fatally on public morality as convulsions in the state.   And against Rome all other influences combined.   It was a period of awful transition.   It was a period of tremendous conflict between all false religions in the world (for thirty thousand gods were worshipped in Rome) and a religion too pure to be comprehended.   That light could not be comprehended by that darkness.   And, in strict philosophic truth, Christianity did not reach its mature period, even of infancy, until the days of the Protestant Reformation.   In Rome it has always blended with Paganism : it does so to this day.   But *then*, *i.e.* up to Diocletian (or the period of the *Augustan History*) even that sort of Christianity, even this foul adulteration of Christianity, had no national influence.   Even a pure and holy religion, therefore, by arraying demoniac passions on the side of Paganism, contributed to the barbarizing of Western Rome.

VII.—Finally, we infer the barbarism of Rome from the condition of her current Literature.   Anything more contemptible than the literature of Western (or indeed of Eastern) Rome after Trajan it is not possible to conceive. Claudian, and two or three others, about the times of Carinus, are the sole writers in verse through a period of four centuries.[1]   Writers in prose there are none after Tacitus and the younger Pliny.   Nor in Greek Literature is there one man of genius after Plutarch, excepting Lucian.   As to Libanius,[2] he would have been "a decent priest where

---

[1] Claudian, reputed the last of the Roman poets, lived about A.D. 380–420.—M.

[2] Libanius, from A.D. 314 to about A.D. 390.—M.

monkeys are the gods "; and he was worthy to fumigate with his leaden censer, and with incense from such dull weeds as root themselves in Lethe, that earthly idol of modern infidels, the shallow but at the same time stupid Julian. Upon this subject, however, we may have two summary observations to make :—1st, It is a fatal ignorance in disputing, and has lost many a good cause, not to perceive on which side rests the *onus* of proof. Here, because on our allegation the proposition to be proved would be negative, the *onus probandi* must lie with our opponents. For we peremptorily affirm that from Trajan downwards there was no literature in Rome. To prove a negative is impossible. But any opponent who takes the affirmative side and says there *was* will find it easy to refute us. Only be it remembered that one swallow does not make a summer. 2dly (which, if true, ought to make all writers on general literature ashamed), we maintain that in any one period of sixty years, in any one of those centuries which we call so familiarly the Dark Ages (yes, even in the 10th or 11th), we engage to name more and better books as the product of the period given than were produced in the whole three hundred and fifty years from Trajan to Honorius and Attila. Here, therefore, is at once a great cause, a great effect, and a great exponent of the barbarism which had overshadowed the Western Empire before either Goth or Vandal had gained a settlement in the land. The quality of their History, the tenure of the Cæsars, the total abolition of Literature, and the convulsion of public morals,—these were the true key to the Roman decay.

END OF VOL. VI

Printed by R. & R. CLARK, LIMITED, *Edinburgh*.

www.ingramcontent.com/pod-product-compliance
Lightning Source LLC
Chambersburg PA
CBHW031057110726
47900CB00003B/959